Ride the Storm

A CASSIE PALMER NOVEL

KAREN CHANCE

BERKLEY
New York

BERKLEY

An imprint of Penguin Random House LLC
375 Hudson Street, New York, New York 10014

Copyright © 2017 by Karen Chance

Penguin Random House supports copyright. Copyright fuels creativity, encourages
diverse voices, promotes free speech, and creates a vibrant culture. Thank you for buying
an authorized edition of this book and for complying with copyright laws by not
reproducing, scanning, or distributing any part of it in any form without permission.
You are supporting writers and allowing Penguin Random House to continue to
publish books for every reader.

BERKLEY is a registered trademark and the B colophon is a trademark
of Penguin Random House LLC.

ISBN 9781101989982

First Edition: August 2017

Printed in the United States of America
1   3   5   7   9   10   8   6   4   2

Cover art by Larry Rostant
Cover design by Adam Auerbach

This is a work of fiction. Names, characters, places, and incidents either are the product
of the author's imagination or are used fictitiously, and any resemblance to actual persons,
living or dead, business establishments, events, or locales is entirely coincidental.

If you purchased this book without a cover, you should be aware that this book is stolen
property. It was reported as "unsold and destroyed" to the publisher, and neither the author
nor the publisher has received any payment for this "stripped book."

*To all the readers who have
supported me from the beginning.
This is your book.*

Chapter One

The cherries were dancing.

They bounced around happily in front of my vision as I swam back to consciousness, plump and bright red and framed by rich green leaves. They covered almost everything in the old-fashioned bedroom, from the lamp on a nearby table, to the curtains at a tall, narrow window, to the washbasin and jug on another table across from the bed. The whole room was awash in a sea of red.

Up close, individual pieces were sort of cute. All together, and with my current blurry vision, it looked like a massacre had taken place. I stared at the hideously cheerful things for a moment, trying to remember why the sight was giving me hives. And then I groaned and dragged a pillow over my head.

My name is Cassie Palmer and, frankly, this wasn't the worst place I'd woken up. Since becoming Pythia, the supernatural world's chief seer and favorite punching bag, I'd opened my eyes on a vampire stronghold in Vegas, a torture-filled castle in France, a dank dungeon in Faerie, and a couch in hell. And, most recently, on a spine-contorting tree root in sixth-century Wales that I still hadn't recovered from.

So, it could be worse, I told myself grimly.

"Are you planning to just lie there all night?" a pissy voice demanded.

Oh, look. It was worse.

I poked an eye out from under the pillow and saw what I'd expected: greasy blond hair, narrowed green eyes, a nose made for looking down on people with, and an expression that matched the voice.

And an outfit that didn't.

As lord of the incubi, the demon race best known for suave seduction, Rosier should have been sporting a Hugh Hefner smoking jacket and silk lounge pants. Instead, he was wearing a mud-streaked homespun tunic and had dirty knees. But then, he shouldn't have been here at all, wherever here was, although I had a pretty good idea.

And that was before I tried moving my right arm.

Handcuffs.

I was cuffed to a bed.

A bed covered in cherries.

"What happened?" I croaked, because my voice didn't work any better than my eyes.

"Nothing," Rosier said, glancing around disparagingly. "Believe it or not, this is perfectly normal for the Victorian age."

"No." I sat up and immediately regretted it when the cherries started dancing a whole lot faster. I lay back down and watched the fruit-covered wallpaper do the boogaloo. "No, I mean, what *happened*?"

"You came to rescue me." The sarcasm was palpable.

I decided to stare at the ceiling for a while instead. It was white and plain, and gave my eyes a rest. And, slowly, things started coming back to me.

Rosier and I had been on a seemingly never-ending mission to save his son and my usual partner in crime, John Pritkin, from a demon curse. I didn't know what the thing was called, but it was basically a sadist's Benjamin Button: Pritkin's soul had been sent careening back through the years of his life, and when it reached the end—poof. No more Pritkin. It would literally erase him from existence.

It seemed like a damn complicated way to kill someone, but then, the demon council—the bastards who had laid it—knew me. Or, rather, they knew what I could do. Being Pythia has a lot of downsides, but it does come with a certain skill set, part of which is the ability to time-travel. So the council had to get inventive if they wanted Pritkin to stay dead.

And they did.

They'd ensured that I couldn't just go back to the moment he was cursed and save him, because his body might be there, but his soul wouldn't. It was on an epic journey into the past, riding a reverse, erratic time stream that I couldn't change or influence unless I caught up with it. Or got ahead of it, so Rosier could place the countercurse as soon as it showed up. Only that hadn't been going so well, either.

So far, we'd utterly failed.

Only no, I corrected grimly, we hadn't *failed*. We'd been *prevented*. Which also explained our current situation.

"We're at the Pythian Court?" I rasped.

"Yes."

"Under arrest?"

"Oh yes."

"And I feel like this because?"

"Drugs. To prevent you from twitching your nose, or whatever you do, and getting us out of this. They hit you with a dart as soon as you showed up. Don't you remember?"

"No."

I pulled the pillow back over my face.

As if the problem with the curse wasn't bad enough, there was an added complication. Namely, that I wasn't the only Pythia. Each age had one, tasked with preserving her little corner of the timeline from dark mages and crazed cultists and anybody else with the insanity and power to risk a time spell. Most of us ignored each other out of professional courtesy, whenever duty required a trip back in time. But Gertie, my nineteenth-century counterpart, had decided to make an exception for me.

And for the denizen of hell I was dragging back through time along with me.

I guessed good little Pythias didn't hang out with powerful demon lords.

Not that Rosier *was* powerful at the moment. Which was why he was just sitting there, frustrated, furious and, yes, about half-mad, because the demon council that had cursed his son had also put a block on his power.

Meaning that, other than for mumbling the countercurse, he was utterly useless.

Which was a problem since, right now, so was I.

"At least they didn't strip you," Rosier said, after a minute. "It wasn't bad enough that they ran me across half the countryside—they had to take my clothes, too! There I was, barely managing to hide from the damn fey, when I was set upon by two of those cursed acolytes."

He was talking about the white-robed Pythias-in-training every court but mine seemed to have a lot of. They received a small amount of the Pythian power, enough to allow them to learn the ropes of the office and to compete for the top spot one day. And in the meantime, they helped the boss screw over anyone who started joyriding through the centuries in bad company.

"I thought I was doing a fair job of passing myself off as a typical Celt," he added, "when hey, presto! No cloak! And a moment after that, no trousers! And no underwear! They used some spell to strip me butt naked, in the middle of the damn road, looking for weapons I didn't even have because of your constant nagging about the timeline. They even took my last shoe!"

"Those bitches."

"Yes! And afterward they had the temerity to act shocked, as if they'd never seen a naked man before! I thought they were Pythian acolytes, not vestal virgins. Of course, given the outfit, I suppose I should have known—"

"I'm working on the outfit."

"You're not going to be doing anything if we don't get out of here," he told me, tugging the pillow away. And eyeing me, as if trying to decide if I'd recovered yet.

"No," I said, and wrestled it back.

But more things were starting to surface from the fog. Things like a burning Welsh countryside, a crap ton of Light Fey—because of course Pritkin had been in the middle of a crisis when we arrived; of *course* he had. And a had-it-up-to-here Pythia who had already followed us through time twice and was apparently sick of it, because this time she'd brought backup.

Rosier and I had been left dodging a whole troop of the girls in white while also dodging the fire and the fey and the other fey who had shown up to try to kill the first group and—

It hadn't gone well.

In the bedlam, Pritkin had gotten away, fading into the dark like the mirage I was really starting to believe he was. Of course, so had I, but I couldn't do the counter-spell and Gertie had Rosier! And then she and a few other Pythias she'd recruited into a damn posse had tried to nab me, too. And when that failed they'd sent me back to my own time via some kind of portal and Gertie had dragged Rosier back here and . . .

And then I guess I'd come after him, hadn't I?

It wasn't like I'd had much choice.

And now she had us both.

Goddamn it!

I abruptly sat up, headache be damned, and Rosier handed me a glass of water. Which he had to stretch to do, since he was cuffed to the foot of the bed. "Victorian prudery," he said dryly. "To keep me from ravishing you while you slept."

"Then why didn't they just put you in another room? In fact, why are you here at all? You're a *demon lord*—"

"And you're a powerful sorceress who placed me under your control, and have been sapping my power to fuel your jaunts through time."

I paused halfway through a swallow to stare at him.

"Leaving me currently drained and incapable of posing a threat to anyone." He saw my expression. "Well, I had to tell them *something*."

"No! No, you didn't!"

"Think about it, girl! If I hadn't, they might have given me back to the damn war mages," he said, referring to the closest thing the magical community had to a police force. "Have you forgotten what happened last time?"

Not likely. Not after everything I'd had to do to get him back before the mages killed him, or the demon council's guards showed up to do it for them. That's why I'd checked the local war mage HQ before coming here; I'd assumed I'd have to break him out again.

But no.

Gertie was handling things herself this go-round.

Gertie was going hard-core.

"The further back we go, the more of a concern we

are," Rosier said, confirming my thoughts. "I heard them talking when I was coming out of that time freeze they slapped me with. Just snatches of conversation, but enough to know that they've elevated us from annoying mystery to serious threat—"

"We weren't that already?" Could have fooled me.

"No. When we were in Amsterdam, there was a chance you were just an acolyte who had slipped her Pythia's leash. But bored acolytes don't have the power to make it back fifteen hundred years! By the time we reached Wales, they were betting on one of those . . . what are they called?" He flapped a hand. "Crazy men, run about trying to change time, usually get blown up for their trouble?"

"The Guild." I swallowed, remembering how much my predecessor had loved them.

But Rosier just nodded. "That's it. Guild of something or other—I forget. But the point is, they now think you're dangerous—"

"Yes, thanks to you!"

"That cherry-covered freak was already determined to catch you," he pointed out. "I merely ensured that she would think you needed me, and would be back to fetch me—"

"Which would have been great except that I *do* need you and I *did* come back!"

"—and now, thanks to my foresight, we're together and can work on getting out of here," he finished, ignoring the fact that he'd basically set me up. "Speaking of which, how long until you can shift?"

I picked up the glass and drained it, hoping it would help with the throbbing in my skull.

Nope.

"Well?" he prodded.

I wiped my lips on the back of my hand. "Long."

"And that means?"

"It means *long*. We need other options."

Rosier scowled.

"And we *have* one. Don't we?"

Nothing.

What a surprise.

But then he did surprise me, by leaning over the bed, close enough to mouth, *Two*.

I blinked, brain still foggy, and followed his gaze to the door.

All it showed me was a tousle-headed blonde in an oval mirror, with dark circles under dazed blue eyes, wearing a high-collared white nightie. I guessed the shorts and T-shirt I'd started out with had offended local sensibilities. My new attire offended mine, making me look about twelve. It also did not give me any answers.

My eyes found Rosier's again in confusion.

He sighed. *Guards, on the other side of the door.*

Yes?

They have the key. He held up his chained wrist.

I looked from it to the skinny, hairy legs poking out from under his tunic. And the arms that in no way resembled his son's. And the too-soft middle. Rosier looked like he'd never lifted anything heavier than a champagne glass in his life.

Which might explain why he kept getting beaten up . . . by little girls.

Yes?

He sprawled across the bed to glare at me. And to whisper: "I'm a lover, not a fighter, but I'm damn good with sleight of hand. Just help me get them in here!"

Fine.

"It wouldn't have to be for long," I said, going with the argument I'd planned to have anyway. Because I wasn't the only one who could shift. Of course, Rosier couldn't time-travel, and his spatial shifts only went one place. But right now I'd take it. "A short trip into the hells—"

"No."

"Really short. Like a couple of minutes—"

"Not a couple of seconds."

"—just long enough for us to move a block or two and get past whatever wards they've got on this place—"

"Going into a minefield to avoid a fence. Yes, that sounds safe."

"You know what's not safe?" I asked, getting genuinely pissed. "Pritkin stuck in freaking Wales about to *die*, that's what's not safe."

"And if I could do something about it, don't you think I would?"

"Not if it meant risking your precious neck. You'll let your own son die when a small risk—"

"Small? *Small?*" Rosier was beginning to look a bit flushed himself. "I put so much as a toe in hell, any hell, and I might as well have a neon sign over my head reading FREE BUFFET! I wouldn't last two minutes—I doubt I would last one. And in case you forgot, this mission requires both of us, or I wouldn't be here talking to you!"

"Ditto! If I could do this alone, *believe* me—"

"Alone? You can't walk across a *room* alone—"

"I did pretty well when you abandoned me in freaking *medieval Wales*—"

"—without starting a war!"

"I didn't start it! I had nothing to do with it!"

"And yet there you were. There you *always*—"

"This isn't about me!" I yelled. "You have to be the most selfish, uncaring, infuriating man since—"

"Emrys?"

"Pritkin! It's *Pritkin*, you *prick*! And he's nothing like you!"

"He's *exactly* like me," Rosier said, scrambling across the bed to get in my face. "He doesn't want to admit it; he's never wanted to. You saw him, mooning over those damn fey. Ooooh, look, a Sky Lord! When they're nothing but insane murderous bastards, every single one—"

"No arguments here."

"—living in one measly, intensely creepy world—"

"Says the man from hell."

"—when he could have *thousands*. And the knowledge of millennia, time out of mind. But always, always that perverse boy was attracted to every damn thing besides his own birthright!"

"The fey are his birthright, too. You saw to that yourself—"

"A fact I've regretted every day since!"

"—and, in fact, pretty much every problem Pritkin has can be traced back to you, can't it?" I asked. "From leaving him to grow up with zero guidance, to taking him from earth before he was ready, to putting him in a terrible situation as your heir—"

"You understand nothing!"

"—to placing that damn prohibition on him—"

"To save his *life*, you wretched, wretched—"

"—to dragging him back to hell *again*, when you knew damn well—"

"That was your *mother's* fault!" Rosier moved like lightning, wrapping his free hand around my neck. "She took my sire, long before I was ready to fill his shoes! She left me and my people vulnerable. She forced me to have to find a way to increase my power, and now her daughter is trying to take him away! I hate you! I hate your whole damn family!"

The door burst open, a fact I was grateful for, since I wasn't entirely sure Rosier remembered that we were acting. Two war mages stood there, with their long leather coats and butt-kicking boots and annoyed expressions not looking all that different despite the era. But they didn't come any closer.

Maybe because one of them had a blowgun.

"Well, fuck," Rosier said as a dart caught him in the neck. He face-planted onto the bed. The door slammed.

I looked at it for a moment, then at my passed-out companion. And then I sighed and pulled the pillow back over my head.

Chapter Two

"There's always option two," Rosier said, sometime later.

At least, that was what I thought he'd said. But whatever knockout drug they'd given him was making his tongue loll, and it was kind of hard to tell. I looked up, but he just lay there and drooled at me. I waited for a minute, then went back to fiddling with the metal around my wrist.

It wasn't part of the handcuffs.

I'd given up on those. They were solid steel and probably overlaid with spells to make them extra hard to pick, given experience. Not that it mattered; I wasn't Houdini.

Of course, I wasn't a dark mage, either, but I didn't have a lot to work with here.

Tiny silver daggers, like links in an especially deadly chain, slid under my fingertips. I assumed Gertie had relieved me of my only weapon when I got here, but it didn't matter. I'd tried to get rid of the little bracelet a hundred times myself, after finding out that it had once belonged to a dark mage. But every time I took it off, it was back in place moments later, spit-shined and gleaming, to the point that I could swear it was smirking at me.

It kind of looked like that now, winking smugly in the light of a nearby lamp, like it knew what I was thinking. On a positive note, it could throw out little ghostly knives that looked about as substantial as mist but cut like well-oiled steel. On the negative, I didn't always control what they cut.

Or who.

"Did you hear me?" Rosier demanded.

I looked up again. I'd rolled him onto his back and

tucked the too-cheerful coverlet around him, because his
tunic kept riding up and I'd had enough trauma for one
day. As a result, he now resembled a colicky baby with
wild tufts of blond hair sticking out everywhere.

Huh. I guess part of it *was* genetic, I thought, and patted one down. "I heard you."

"Well?"

"Well what? You're the one who said no."

"What?" The colicky look intensified. "When did I say
that?"

I frowned at him. "A few minutes ago. You said no
shifting—"

"Shifting wasn't option two—"

"Of course it was. Mug the guards, option one. Shift
into the hells, option two—"

"That was your option two! I never—"

"That was my option one," I corrected. "This is option
two."

I held up my wrist, and his eyes focused on it. Or tried
to. But then I guess they managed, because they widened
alarmingly. "That's dark magic!" said the demon lord.

"Dark magic that just might get us out of here."

"Dark magic doesn't get people out of trouble," he
said, struggling with the blanket. "It gets them into it!"

"The mages who use it seem to do okay."

"Yes, until they get addicted to the magic they steal
from everyone they can get their hands on, and end up
little better than junkies! And start doing progressively
crazier things to get more of it—"

"I'm not talking about mainlining the stuff," I said—to
myself, because Rosier wasn't listening.

"—summoning my people, trying to trap them—think
of it," he said, green eyes blazing, "beings thousands of
years old enslaved to a group of idiots so hopped up on
their latest fix they can't see straight! Until we find a way
free and eat their *faces*!"

"Okay, I get that you don't like it—"

"I loathe it! All demons do. If you're smart, so will
you!" he added, panting a little because the blanket was
being stubborn. But he finally managed to get the arm
that wasn't chained to the bed free and flailed it around.

I moved back so he didn't accidentally clock me. "Then I assume you have a better idea?"

"Of course!" he said unhelpfully, and the flailing arm flailed some more. Until it landed on my leg. And then just stayed there, the hand clenching.

It took me a moment, because the other hand was clenched, too, on the edge of the bed, probably so he wouldn't fall off. And because he was still mostly wrapped in the quilt, like a cherry-covered burrito. And because he was scruffy and smelly and crazed-looking—

And pawing at my thigh.

"Eww!" I jumped back, all the way to the headboard.

"It's the only way," he insisted.

"Like hell it's the only way!"

"I'm an incubuth. I can lend you thome energy—" he said, around the foot I had smushed in his face.

"I *have* energy!"

"You have the Pythian power but can't access it. I can help—"

"Stop touching me!"

"—by increasing your personal strength—"

"I'm warning you!"

"—so you can shift uth out of here. Damn it, girl!" Rosier glared at me through a gap between my toes. "This isn't exthactly fun for me, either!"

"Then cut it out!"

"I'm not . . . going to die . . . because of you! Now *help* me—"

"Oh, I'll help you," I growled, and kicked him.

He reared back, holding his nose and looking outraged. "You bith!" he screamed. "You coldhearted bith!"

And then he grabbed me.

But he was still handcuffed to the bed, which limited his range, and wrapped in the blanket, which limited his motion, and apparently, he hadn't been trained in hand-to-hand combat by his son.

I had.

"Coldhearted? *Coldhearted*?" I got him in a headlock. "You're the most coldhearted, conniving, evil son of a bitch I have *ever*—"

"Get off me!"

"—known in my *life*—"

"If you kill me, who is going to help you get Emrys back?" he wheezed.

"I'm not going to kill you! I'm going to make you *wish* you were dead!"

"Trust me. Working with you, I already do!"

The door slammed open. We looked up. I expected more grumpy mages, probably pissed that we were making so much noise

That wasn't who I saw.

"Oh, fuck *that*!" Rosier screeched, and disappeared, just as a cadre of the demon council's personal guard flooded into the room.

And since he was still cuffed to the bed, it went with him.

But I didn't.

I hit the floor face-first, hard enough to see stars, not understanding how I'd been left behind. Until I saw the cut chain dangling off my wrist. And the ghostly knives gleefully zipping around the room, stabbing everything in sight. And the glass breaking, and the mages shielding, and the council's guards hunkering down in their armor—

And then the lights went out.

It took me a second to realize that Rosier was back. And that it was lucky I'd still been sprawled on the floor, because the bed was, too. I hit my head on the underside anyway, which was on casters, so it was just high enough to accommodate a pissed-off Pythia. And then another one was yelling: "Forget the demon! Get the girl!"

But the council's guards didn't take orders from anyone except the council. And a second later my chin hit the floor again, when half a dozen supernatural soldiers leapt onto the bed on top of me. And then went flying back off, because war mages do, in fact, follow the Pythia's orders.

Well, you know, most Pythias.

And then all hell broke loose.

There were suddenly bodies flying and hitting the floor and shaking the bed, and there went my chin again. And instead of stars I was starting to see more like whole galaxies. But not so much that I failed to notice the frantic, manacled hand waving at the end of the bed.

I grabbed it, and was jerked out and up. I had a split second to see Gertie herself blending in with the wallpaper, a bunch of war mages battling some faceless demon guards, and a confused, very young-looking version of my predecessor, Agnes. Oh, look, I thought fuzzily.

And then I was looking at something else. Something that looked a lot like the Shadowland, a minor demon realm with dark streets and shuttered buildings and absolutely nothing to recommend it, except that it happened to be close to earth. But I wasn't sure because I didn't get much more than a glimpse.

Because the bed had started rolling this way.

"Get up! Get up! Get up! Get up!" Rosier was yelling and pulling, and I was stumbling and scrambling, and he was heaving hard enough that I thought my arm would break.

Instead, I ended up on top of the bed, after having been dragged over the metal footboard less than ceremoniously. But that nonetheless would have been an improvement—except that the bed was still rolling. Rosier, damn him, had landed us at the top of an incline.

A big one.

"Help me stop it!" I yelled as our ride picked up speed, shaking down the hill on its little casters fast enough to throw up sparks from the pavement.

Or maybe they were from something else.

"Never mind," I said, and flattened out.

"What?" Rosier stared around. "Why?"

I jerked him down with me, just as a curved sword appeared, vibrating out of the footboard between us.

"That's why," I said.

Looked like some of the guys had tagged along.

Make that one guy, who must have been holding on to the bed when it flashed out, and was now running and then dragging behind us as we rattled down the street.

Fast.

But not fast enough to throw him off.

Because the council's guards don't get tired, or feel pain. They can't. They're spirits trapped inside golemlike bodies, only instead of clay, they're made of an almost impervious metal that takes a beating and keeps on killing. As this one demonstrated by launching himself from a prone position onto the bed—

And then lost a head, when a sword flashed and struck it clean off.

It went bouncing across the street and I looked up to see Rosier holding the blade he'd ripped out of the footboard. And then screaming, I thought to let off excess emotion. But I realized there might be another reason when, instead of collapsing, the headless body started whaling on him.

It wasn't doing a great job, not being able to see, but it was a small bed. And Rosier wasn't doing a great job of evading, either. Maybe because he was still handcuffed in place.

"Do something!" he shrieked, and I was trying, but pulling didn't work and shoving didn't work and when I grabbed for the sword that had gotten knocked out of his hand, a metal fist closed on it first. And the next second, Rosier was dodging rapid-fire sword blows that were raining down on the footboard, sending sparks flying and almost cutting through in places.

Cutting through.

"The cuffs!" I yelled at Rosier.

"What?"

"Hold out your cuffs!"

He looked like he didn't know what I was saying, but then I extended my arms and light dawned.

"Are you crazy?"

Then it didn't matter anyway, because the metal body went flying in a cloud of flames, sailing off toward a nearby building like a headless Tony Stark. I looked behind us to see half a dozen war mages booking it down the hill with enhanced speed, leather coats flying out behind them like action movie stars. And a great big grin of relief spread over my face.

Which was still there when the second fireball launched.

A mass of flames came boiling through the air, which is exactly as scary as it sounds when it's coming straight at you. I screamed, Rosier screamed, and the bed suddenly leapt up off the street and traveled maybe eight feet through the air before hitting down again. Because we'd just taken a turbo shot to the ass.

And then it burst into flames.

"What are they doing?" I screamed.

"Keeping us from escaping!"

Great.

Especially since we weren't escaping now, not on top of a merrily burning bed. And these weren't normal flames, and they were eating this way fast. And Rosier was still chained in place and the mages were still gaining and we were still tear-assing down the hill, until suddenly we weren't.

We were tear-assing through an open-air market.

An open-air market on earth.

A row of Victorian-looking buildings flashed by on either side, with tables set up in front piled with wares, and people diving for cover. At least most people. A vendor nimbly danced out of the way, but his cart didn't. And there was no way to avoid it with no steering and no brakes. And then it didn't matter when we hit it head-on and were inundated with a wave of hot water filled with . . . pigs' feet?

What had to be a couple dozen boiled pigs' feet slapped us in the face as we barreled through the man's big metal cauldron and kept right on going. Right at a bunch of kids who had been playing in the street, but who were now just standing there, mouths hanging open. Probably because they'd never seen a burning, speeding bed before.

I grabbed Rosier, who was trying to free himself by pulling the footboard apart, where it had been scored the deepest. "Shift! Shift!"

"Would you give me a minute?"

"No! Do it now!"

"We can't do it now! We're not clear yet!"

I didn't ask clear of what, because there wasn't time. I grabbed his head and forcibly jerked it up, pointing at the kids. "Now!"

Rosier's eyes got big, maybe because we were close enough to see the whites of theirs, and he gave a little screech—

And the next second, we were back in the Shadowland.

I breathed a sigh of relief.

I'd never been so glad to be in hell before.

Until a virtual hail of swords clanged off the bed frame
from in front, hard enough to dent it. And a bunch of
fireballs lit up the sky from behind. And the only question was, which group was going to kill us first?

The answer was neither, because we abruptly shifted
back to earth again, Rosier shrieking and the bed burning and now sword-riddled, and speeding more than ever
because it had just gotten renewed life from its brief stint
on the hill from hell.

A lot of life.

Like a Mach 2 amount of life, or maybe that was just the
impression conveyed by all the shrieking. And the *clackity,
clackity, clackity* of the cobblestones. And the neighing.

Neighing?

We burst out of the pedestrian-only street, which I
guess had been closed off for the market, into one filled
with horses and carriages and buses and—

And then our luck ran out. Or maybe it was the horse's
luck. I don't know. I just know that I saw a flash of rearing
horse belly and flailing hooves and the screaming white
face of a cabbie. And then we were careening off course
and heading straight for—

Well, crap, I thought, as the fetid stench of the Thames
hit my nose, right before we broke through a barrier and
took a flying leap—

Back into hell.

The bed hit down from maybe six feet up, hard enough
to bounce me back up to the point where we'd flashed in,
before I smacked down on top of Rosier.

Who dumped me onto the side of the street with a
breathless snarl.

I just sat there for a minute, clinging to the now sta-
tionary bed. We'd passed down the hill and almost made
it to the top of another, and the angle plus the bounce
seemed to have absorbed our momentum. We weren't
moving.

We weren't moving!

I stared around, half disbelieving. I was so dizzy that the street still felt like it was undulating beneath me. But it wasn't, and that was good. And the lack of swords and fire and mayhem was even better.

It looked like the crazies had dispersed while we were gone, either following us back to earth or spreading out around the area. Because all I saw were dark, vaguely modernish buildings, like a back alley in a normal city. Because the Shadowland pulled images from your own mind to cover up whatever the heck it actually looked like.

But the illusion only went so far, because a very unearthly wail suddenly rent the air.

My head jerked around. "What was that?"

Rosier didn't answer.

I looked up to see him frozen in place, dirty knees on the bed and the sword he'd pulled out of the footboard clutched in both hands. And staring in apparent dumbstruck horror at something down the street. I looked back around, but there was nothing there.

Except for another haunting, skin-ruffling howl that had me clambering back onto the bed really fast.

It came again, and our heads whipped around in unison, looking at nothing some more, because the top of the hill was in the way. And then it came from the left. Or maybe the right. Or maybe—

I couldn't tell. The buildings were closely packed and tall enough to act as an echo chamber. Which wasn't fun when the echoes were like these. The horrible sound came again, closer now, and I felt all my skin stand up, preparing to crawl off my body and go find somewhere to hide.

I seconded the motion and grabbed Rosier. "What *is* that?"

"Hellhounds."

"And those are?"

"Well, what does it sound like?" he snarled, and finally, finally, he was back with me. White and shaking, but back. Angry and scowling, but back. Chained to the bed, but back.

I shook him some more anyway. "So take us some-where else!"

"Like where?"

"Like anywhere!"

"I'm not you! Without a portal, I can only take us back to earth—"

"Okay!"

"—and I am chained to a bed, in case you didn't no-tice. An *iron* bed—"

"So?"

"—and we were headed for a river! I will *drown*."

Damn it!

"Then give me the sword!" I tried to grab it, but he jerked it away.

"It's our only weapon—"

"I know that—I just want to get the cuffs off you. Will you *listen*?"

But Rosier wasn't listening. Rosier was freaking out again. Maybe because those sounds were suddenly a lot closer, and there were more of them, and they were com-ing faster now, a baying pack of something that had picked up a scent it liked—

"Give me the damn sword!" I yelled.

"Get your own!"

And then a terrifying howl almost on top of us caused him to drop it.

We both went for it, but he grabbed it first, and I grabbed—

God, I thought, as something gelatinous and porky oozed up through my fingers.

And then it was too late.

A giant head appeared over the hill. And for a second, I thought it *was* the hill. Because it rose out of nothing, like all the darkness in the world had decided to congeal in one place. One great big slavering freakishly huge place. I'd seen *houses* smaller than that, only houses didn't have evil yellow eyes and an enormous drooling maw and weren't jumping for us—

And then stopping, halfway through the motion. And gulping and swallowing. Because I had reflexively thrown the pig foot I'd been holding, like that was going to *help* somehow.

Only it had.

The hound had stopped and was just standing there, steaming and black and blocking the view of everything with its enormous face.

Which was suddenly in mine.

The breath could have stopped traffic for a ninety-mile stretch. Drool was drip, drip, dripping onto the bed linens in slimy strings. Eyes bigger than my head were reflecting the still-burning fire, along with a vision of my body as I slowly, slowly, slowly bent down. And picked up another foot. And held it out—

And felt a wash of hot breath over my arm, which was somehow raising goose bumps anyway, maybe because my skin was still trying to get the hell out of there. And then a tongue, big and heavy as a rug, wrapped around my flesh. And withdrew, along with the tiny, tiny offering, but not with the arm itself, because I guess I didn't compare with good old pork.

And really, what does? I thought hysterically. If I had bacon, I could probably make him fetch—

Rosier grabbed my arm, his fingers like a vise. "Get. On. The. Bed."

"I . . . am on the bed." Well, I was pretty sure.

"Oh."

He snaked a leg off the side and gave a little push. I felt the hell wind start to ruffle my hair as we started down the hell road with the hellhound shaking the street behind us, while I lobbed pig foot after pig foot into its gaping maw. It didn't miss a one.

Until the darkness overhead suddenly congealed into a second hound, even larger than the first, which went for its throat. And then another crowded the street, which was almost too small to hold them despite being big enough for a couple city buses to pass each other with room to spare. But hellhounds are not buses and there was no room here, and that was before the council's guards decided to show back up, running up the hill toward us.

And abruptly turning and running back the other way

as we began picking up speed, the night boiling behind us, all black smoke and sleek, shifting fur and firelit eyes.

And sailing pig feet, because I was throwing them both-handed now.

"Put out your hands!" I told Rosier frantically.

"No."

"What do you mean, *no*?"

"I mean no," he said, grunting and straining, trying to break through the damn Victorian ironwork, which must have been forged in the same factory where they made tanks if they had tanks. I didn't know. I just knew it wasn't freaking *budging*.

"That isn't working!" I yelled the obvious.

"You can't throw those things and get these damn cuffs off me at the same time!"

"And when I run out? What then?"

"You're not going to run out. As soon as we get far enough to clear the river, I'm going to shift us back!"

I blinked. "Okay."

"Okay?"

"Okay! Sounds like a plan."

A slight bit of color came back to his face. "Yes, okay." He grinned at me suddenly, wide and relieved and startlingly like the younger version of his son for a second. "Okay! We'll do that!"

I nodded.

And then the street erupted in fire.

Chapter Three

"It was a good plan," Rosier said.

"It was." I ate pork.

"The Victorians weren't the most hygienic of sorts," he told me, eyeing my last trotter.

"They boiled it."

"And we carried it through hell."

"It was on a bed," I pointed out. "It didn't get anything on it." Except for a few fuzzies.

I picked one off and kept eating.

"I don't know how you can eat with that stench down there," he said, peering over the ledge we were sitting on, and glaring malevolently at the Thames.

It was shining under a full moon, which was glistening off the water. And off the streets, because it must have rained while we were gone. Time worked differently in the hells, so that might have been anything from a couple hours to a couple days. But whatever it was, it had left Victorian London looking almost pretty, with roiling gray clouds and shining streets and fresh air because the rain had washed the coal dust away.

We were sitting on the edge of what I called Big Ben and Rosier called the Clock Tower, overlooking the city. It wasn't a choice; I was feeling a little clearer-headed, but not enough to shift back yet, which was why I was eating. It seemed to help.

"I don't know how you can smell anything with no nose," I said.

"I *have* a nose."

"You don't even have a body."

It was true. The mages had shown up, unseen by us,

and collectively lobbed a spell we hadn't noticed until it nuked the air around us. Rosier had thrown himself over me and shifted us back to earth, all at the same time, and in doing so had saved my life.

And lost his.

Well, his body, anyway. Fortunately, a demon lord's spirit is a bit sturdier, meaning that he could generate a new one . . . eventually. In the meantime, I was used to hanging out with ghosts, so the fact that I could see the city through the shimmering veil of my companion's form didn't wig me out too much.

Unlike his sacrifice.

I knew he'd only done it because he needed me, but still. I couldn't figure Rosier out, and it bothered me. Half the time, he was oh, so easy to hate, a rotten, self-centered, narcissistic asshole I could have cheerfully pushed off the ledge if it would have done any good. But the rest . . .

The rest of the time I just didn't know.

But at least his current form was too dim for Gertie to sense, so we were enjoying the view unmolested, if not the noise. The huge mechanism was *tick, tick, ticking*, almost in sync with my heart. This close, it was uncomfortably loud, like it was yelling *hurry, hurry, hurry*.

"How much longer do you think we have to save Pritkin?" I asked Rosier, after a minute.

"A day. Maybe two. No more."

I didn't say anything, but he shot me a glance.

"There's time."

I laughed suddenly, and it hurt, because my throat was sore from screaming. One of these days, just once, I'd like to be the cool action figure type, like in all those movies. The one who casually walks away when a building is exploding right behind her, instead of shrieking and ducking for cover and possibly wetting her pants.

Of course, I'd always wondered how many of the people who made those movies had ever been in an explosion. Had felt the heat, smelled the smoke, and thought for a second their eardrums were going to rupture from the noise. And been sure that they were about to be burned alive any second now.

Like Rosier had been.

For me.

"What's so funny?" he asked, "sitting" on the ledge. Meaning his butt was hovering a couple inches over the top of it.

I glanced at him. "Time. I'm supposed to be master of it, but there never seems to be enough."

"Strange. I usually feel the opposite. But then, I've never been human."

"Try being Pythia. I'm expected to know . . . so much. Just so much. It's . . . overwhelming sometimes."

He tilted his head to the side. "Like what?"

I hesitated, because I hadn't expected him to ask. But it wasn't like it was a secret. It wasn't like the whole damn supernatural community didn't know anyway. "Like everything. Like how to use the Pythian power with no one to teach me. The stuff you've seen Gertie do? I can't do half that—"

"And yet where are you and where is she?"

I shook my head. "And even if I could, even if I ever get this stuff down, that doesn't scratch the surface. I'm supposed to know a couple thousand years of supernatural politics when I don't even know everybody's name yet. And to make up for a lifetime of magical training when I can't even do a proper protection spell. And to understand everything about the vamp world, including how to deal with the senate, when I grew up at the court of the vamp version of Tony Soprano! There's no *time*!"

"I know," Rosier said calmly.

"You *know*?" I adjusted my position so I could see his face again. "How do you know?"

A ghostly eyebrow rose, in an elegant arch. "How do you think it was for me? I went from carefree, bachelor prince to beleaguered ruler overnight, with damn little training myself. I think my father thought he'd have another son eventually—or a daughter. It's much the same with us. Someone, in any case, who would be more like him. I was never like him. I was more like my mother, he always said, but not fondly."

"They didn't get along?"

He smiled slightly. "They got along famously, for as long as it lasted—our kind rarely forms permanent bonds.

Her spirit, her joie de vivre, her vivaciousness, were all assets in a consort. But, like fathers for time out of mind, he assumed his son would take after him. Be strong, statesmanlike, astute. When I turned out to be . . . less than that . . . he didn't bother to hide his disappointment. Nor did he provide the training I was never supposed to need."

"And when you did need it—"

"You think you're lost? Try waking up one day to find that your father has been slaughtered, your court is in complete panic, and your enemies are taking the opportunity to invade. And that you, with your completely inadequate training and a power you've mainly been using to seduce sweet young things, are expected to save the day. *That* day. Right then."

There was an uncomfortable silence. Or maybe it was just uncomfortable on my part. Because my mother was the reason he'd been in that mess.

As hard as it might be to believe, looking at me, she'd been one of the creatures humans had once called gods. Not because of their morality, which they mostly seemed to find a foreign concept, or their justice, mercy, and wisdom, which they didn't have any of, either. But because what else do you call beings so powerful that they just mow down everything in their path?

Including Rosier's father, powerful demon lord though he had been, because even a mediocre god was on a whole different level.

And while my mother had been a lot of things, mediocre had never been one of them.

She'd been the goddess with a thousand names, who showed up in one form or another in virtually every culture on earth. But the one the world remembered best was Artemis, the Great Huntress. And guess what she'd best liked hunting?

And she wasn't the only one. The whole misbegotten pantheon had been thrilled when they discovered earth, while exploring a rift between our universe and theirs. Not because of humans, who they thought fit only for slaves. But because earth offered access to their real prey: the demons.

As I'd discovered on my search for Pritkin, the hells were composed of a vast array of worlds populated by a wide range of creatures, from the mostly innocuous incubi, to beings even the other demons called "ancient horrors" and did their best to lock away. But they all had one thing in common: they fed off other species—humans, other demons, even fey if they could get them. And they stored up much of that power for later.

Or, at least, they did until the gods showed up, to turn the tables and hunt them instead.

Most of the gods had stayed on their staging ground, earth, and waited for the demons to come to them. But my mother hadn't been content to just wait around. She'd gone into the hells themselves, searching out the fattest, juiciest prey, the ones with enough energy stored up to not need to hunt on earth. The ones who had ultimately made her more powerful than any of her kind. The ones who had allowed her to cast a spell throwing the other gods out of their new acquisition, and slamming the door behind them.

Leaving it all for her.

It would have been perfect, if her fellow gods hadn't fought back. But some did, and the battle drained her more than she'd expected. To the point that she was forced to hide among the human population, to avoid retaliation from the demon hordes who were now hunting her. She had become weaker and weaker over time, unable to hunt, to feed, at least enough to make a difference, for fear of betraying her whereabouts to those with memories as long as her own.

Most of the world didn't have that advantage, and they largely forgot great Artemis and her hunt. But the demons never did. Especially not Rosier, whose father had been one of my mother's last victims. Which made it both awkward and seriously ironic that we were having to work together now. But while the demons might not like me, they understood one thing.

We were all on the same side now.

It was why the demon council of my day, who wanted the thorn in their side named John Pritkin very, very dead, had nonetheless relented and given me the counter-spell. Not because they wanted to help the daughter of their greatest enemy, but because their paranoia was only eclipsed by their pragmatism. And they knew there was something worse out there.

Namely, the ancient beings that my mother had tossed out on their godly butts, who were currently pounding at the door, trying to get back in. And she was dead now and the spell she'd cast all those centuries ago to bar the way was starting to feel a little threadbare. And if it fell, it was going to be open season on all of us, whether weak and puny or old and powerful, because to the gods, we all pretty much looked the same.

And died as easily.

I glanced at Rosier, to find him staring out over the moon-flooded city, lost in his own thoughts.

"How did you do it?" I asked, because I really wanted to know.

"How did I do what?"

"Survive."

He shrugged. "The only way I knew how. I started bellowing orders in my best imitation of Father, acted like I knew what I was doing, cornered a few of his old advisers and stuck them to my side like burrs, and . . . made do. Mostly because of Father's excellent preparations, but people gave me the credit anyway. And afterward, I simply kept going. Listening to my own judgment sometimes, which I discovered wasn't so bad, after all; getting advice from people who might actually know what they were talking about when I could; and hoping for luck when nothing else worked."

I scowled. Great.

He saw my expression, and this time, he was the one who laughed.

"Did you think there was a trick to it? Cassie, do you think *anyone* is ever prepared for a job like yours? Do you think, had you been brought up at the Pythian Court, trained by the sainted Agnes herself, put through political instruction until it was coming out your ears—do you really think it would matter?"

"It wouldn't hurt!"

"And it wouldn't help. Not nearly as much as you seem

to think." He shook his head. "I came to be glad that I didn't know what I couldn't do. That I was too naive to read the signs, to realize how unlikely any of us were to survive. I remember pounding on the table in a war room—a leaky cave on some misbegotten world somewhere—with three armies outside and none of them ours, with half my forces thinking about changing sides and the other half so demoralized they couldn't be arsed to care, and yet I was still strategizing. Too stupid to know we'd already lost."

"And . . . did you?" I asked, because it had kind of felt like that for me lately, too. Like I'd already lost and just hadn't faced up to it yet. Because how did you fight a god?

It wasn't a question anybody could answer, since nobody had ever done it. Except for me and the guy I was currently chasing through time, but there had been some heavy caveats there. Like the fact that Apollo, the god in question, had already been crispy fried thanks to Mom's protection spell, and so was almost dead by the time he got here. And even then we hadn't fought him, because how the hell were we supposed to fight him? Instead, we'd led him into a trap where some hungry demons and a supernatural vortex had polished him off.

The only thing we'd contributed was to run away.

Fast.

Which frankly still sounded like a plan, because I'd mostly taken after my very human father, and the idea of facing down the god of war made me feel incontinent again.

But I couldn't run this time.

Not with a bunch of angry gods battering at the door, with a fractured supernatural community that it was my job to somehow bring together, and with a showdown coming that I had no idea—*no* idea—how to win.

The only clue I'd managed to find had been on the search for Pritkin, fifteen hundred years in the past, and I wasn't even sure I was right about that one. I was currently sitting on a ledge overlooking a big, open expanse, but it didn't feel that way. It felt like I was trapped in a cave, too, one with the walls closing in and the roof about to come down on my head. And me unable to avert the disaster I saw coming because the little less than four months between a life reading tarot cards in a bar and one supposedly leading the supernatural community wasn't enough, wasn't *close* to enough. It felt like I'd been *set up* to fail, and here I was, managing right on cue, and I couldn't—I just—I didn't—

Damn it!

I wiped an arm over my eyes and looked up to find Rosier watching me. Something passed over his face for a second, something I couldn't read. And then it was gone again, and he was making another of those elegant gestures he was so fond of.

"Well, obviously not," he said, answering my previous question. "I'm sitting here, aren't I? In this hideous thing." He looked down at his ghostly tunic in distaste.

I wondered why he didn't change it. Ghosts couldn't, but Rosier wasn't one. But maybe he was tired, too.

I leaned my head back against the wall. "So how did you get out of it?"

He shrugged. "I seduced the leader of one of the opposing forces, who thereafter switched sides halfway through the battle. He was behind our enemies and we were in front, and after a while of being sandwiched between the two of us, they broke and ran. And never lived down the ignominy of being beaten by a ragtag group of incubi. I made damn well sure they didn't."

"That was clever," I pointed out. "And what was it? Strong, statesmanlike . . ."

"And astute. And no, it wasn't. It was desperation, but it worked. And when desperate gambles work, they call them brilliance. Do it enough, and people start believing that you always can, that you always will. They follow people like that. They write legends about people like that."

"But . . . *you* still know the truth. You know you're faking it."

"Yes, but eventually you realize something: *the other side is, too.* At least as often as not. Learn what you can; do what you can; get others to do for you what you can't.

And fake it for all you're worth in the meantime." He shot me a look. "In other words, exactly what you've been doing."

I blinked at that. It wasn't exactly a compliment, but it was close. Somebody was basically telling me that I wasn't screwing things up as badly as I might be.

Hell, I'd take it.

Rosier just shook his head again. "Are you finished with that terrible thing?" he demanded, looking in distaste at the now stripped foot.

"You don't know what you missed," I told him, flashing a greasy smile.

"Come on," he said, extending a ghostly hand. "Let's go fake it some more."

Chapter Four

Half an hour later, Rosier was back in hell, doing whatever he did to recover from these things, and I was back in the casino I call home, trying to follow his advice. Namely, to get some advice, and from someone who might know what she was talking about. Assuming I could get her attention, that is. But she was behind a cash register, halfway across a shop in the casino's main drag, and I . . . was not.

And I wasn't about to get any closer.

"Mommy, Mommy, look! It's the corpse bride!"

I looked down to find a munchkin in a tutu tugging at my skirts. My singed, dirty, old-fashioned skirts, which were complementing my ash-covered body. And face. And hair. A quick glance in the shopwindow in front of me showed that they did, in fact, make me look kind of corpse bridey.

I sighed.

"I'm not, actually," I told the kid, still concentrating on the dark-haired beauty behind the counter.

Her name was Françoise, and normally, I'd have just walked in and said hi. We'd been friends for a while, even before she got her current job, prettying up the salon of the magical world's most famous fashion designer (according to him, anyway). But right now wasn't a good time to interrupt. Right now would be a good time to get lost, only time wasn't something I had a lot of. So I was skulking, trying to catch her eye through the hanging floral strands serving as a backdrop for a bunch of frolicking goddesses.

A bunch of curly-haired blond goddesses, I noticed, frowning.

And then frowned some more when I was tugged on again. "I want a picture! I want a picture!" the pixie demanded while trying to manhandle me into an appropriate pose, whatever that would be for a corpse.

I would have manhandled her back, but my hands were full. And Françoise took that moment to notice me. And to open her dark eyes wide and to shake her head, pointing at the disturbance I'd already seen, because how could you not?

I know, I mouthed. *But I need to talk to you.*

More headshaking, along with an attempt to mouth something back, only I couldn't tell what because the hand in my skirts had just become a fist, and I was being forcibly dragged away from the window.

"Darling, I think she's on her lunch break," a woman said, running up.

She looked a little odd, like maybe the airlines had lost her luggage and she'd had to cobble together an outfit from whatever she'd had in her carry-on. It had led to a mishmash of chic and street person: frizzy brown hair that looked like it hadn't seen a brush in a while, but which complemented sharp brown eyes behind expensive glasses. She had on a blue business suit that had cost money, but which was sadly rumpled. And which was being worn with a T-shirt instead of a blouse, one that proclaimed: "Once upon a time, I was sweet and innocent, then shit happened."

I need to get one of those, I thought enviously.

"I'm not on a break," I told her, which drew a skeptical look, probably because of the ICEE and the two food bags I was juggling. "I mean, I don't work here," I clarified—not at all, apparently.

Maybe because the ICEE was blue, and had stained my lips a deathly hue. And was in a coffin-shaped glass that was free with purchase because it cost all of ten cents when bought in bulk from across the border. But the kicker was where we were.

Dante's hotel and casino was a relic from the days when theme was big on the Vegas Strip. That was after the mob era, but before the short-lived family-friendly experiment, and definitely before the city's latest incarnation as a sleek adult playground for the well-heeled. Theme was out now, unless the theme was money, which was never out in Vegas, but Dante's didn't care because its theme served a purpose. Like, for example, hiding a bunch of real supernatural beings in plain sight, by advertising costumed actors prowling around the drag.

"I'm sorry," the woman said firmly, shoving a mass of fuzz out of her face. "But you're her favorite character. One picture . . ."

The sentence remained unfinished, but the idea was clear: I and my lunch, not to mention my mission, were to be held hostage to that pic.

Or not, I thought, as an outraged genius suddenly appeared in my face. *"You."*

I started for the door with my armful of stuff, since it didn't matter anymore. "That's not my fault," I told him, nodding at the disturbance.

"Not your fault?" Augustine barred the way into his establishment with a long, spindly arm. He always reminded me of a blond praying mantis, all arms and legs on a model-slim body, a fact heightened today by a jumpsuit in his favorite iridescent green. "You brought them here!"

"I brought them to the *hotel*," I said, trying to limbo myself under the obstruction without spilling anything. "I don't decide where they go—"

"Get them out!" he told me, shoving a knee in my way.

"From here?"

"Yes, from here! You're leaving—and so are they!"

"Tell them that," I said, looking past him. To where three cloth-covered mounds were roaming about, perusing the items on offer.

At least, I guessed that was what they were doing, but who could tell? They looked like animated mountains of laundry, to the point that I only knew who they were by the gnarled, yellowish toenails protruding like claws from under trailing silks, taffetas, and laces. A lot of silks, taffetas, and laces. Like half the store's worth.

I could understand why Augustine was upset—his inventory was getting ravaged—but it was his own fault. He was the one who had decided to put an antishoplifting spell on his wares, resulting in any sticky-fingered customers turning literally sticky. To the point that everything they touched ended up adhered to them like superglue.

It had caused grown men to return, blubbering in submission and missing some skin, after a wild ride on the outside of the taxi they'd become stuck to. But it didn't seem to be bothering the current group, judging by the dirty hand that had just emerged from one of the piles to finger a cashmere sweater. And to casually pull it off its hanger and to smack it on the growing heap over her left shoulder.

It did not stick to her hand.

I hadn't expected it to.

Minor-level spells weren't designed to ensnare ancient magical beings, who seemed to view this one as a useful alternative to a shopping basket.

"*You* tell them that!" Augustine said furiously. "You brought them here!"

"Oh, please," I said, looking up at him in annoyance, not half because I was still stuck between him and the door. "That was almost four months ago!"

It had been in the early days of this job, when I'd accidentally released the girls from the supernatural snare they were trapped in. Trapped for no good reason I could see, since the three old women known to mythology as the Graeae were usually fairly harmless. Of course, I didn't make a habit of pissing them off.

Unlike Augustine, who forgot about me when one of the mounds bent over to get a better look at a lower shelf, and bumped into an elegant display of hats. Which went flying when the table fell over, including a jaunty purple number that landed at a raffish angle on her long gray curls. And immediately transformed the wrinkled face beneath it.

The Graeae usually looked like baked-apple dolls, with a Shar-pei's worth of folds for a face and little else. That still held true. Only now the wrinkled visage peering out of the clothes pile also sported a full makeup job, including scarlet lipstick, rosy cheeks, and fake eyelashes, despite the fact that the latter had nothing to adhere to, since she was not currently in possession of the one eye the trio shared.

The lashes fluttered anyway as she turned her head this way and that, and then up, trying to figure out what had just happened. And finally realized that something was stuck to her face. Which she dealt with by feeling around with one clawed hand until she located the problem and pulled it off.

And ate it.

"What . . . did she just . . . how . . . *why*?" the girl's mother asked as Françoise all but flew over.

"Holograms," she told the woman firmly.

"Holograms?"

But Françoise had already pulled me inside and was hustling me away.

"Holograms?" I whispered.

"Eet is the standard reply. Most humans cannot see zee spells Augustine puts on zee clothes. But some of zem 'ave a leetle magic in zere blood, and for zem"—she shrugged—"zere are zees holograms."

"While in reality?"

She handed me a sign that had fallen off the display. IN A HURRY? CHAPEAU AND GO BY AUGUSTINE. YOUR MAKEUP AND HAIR DONE IN AN INSTANT. I blinked at it. You know, considering my schedule, I could really use—

"Can you take zem somwhaire?" Françoise asked, gesturing at the trio. "He ees only going to get worse zee longair zey stay here."

The he in question being Augustine, I presumed, who was now slapping at the Graeae with one of the fallen hats.

"I'm too pooped to pop right now," I admitted. "At least and carry anyone else."

In fact, I wasn't sure I could carry me. Spatial shifts were a heck of a lot easier than the time variety, but they still took energy. Which was why I planned on taking the elevator up to my suite, to rest and eat something more substantial than a few bites of pork.

But I had a question first.

"I have a question," I told Françoise, who was attempting to corral the hats.

She looked up, and the Grecian gown she was wearing slipped off one shoulder. It was the go-go version, with a too-short skirt and a plunging neckline, because Augustine knew how to get male customers into a woman's clothing store, yes, he did. But it looked good on her, like the elaborate updo her long, dark hair had been woven into, held in place by thin bands of silver.

She matched the shop, which I'd last seen dressed up like a circus tent. Now it was marble-floored and ionic-columned, with swags of diaphanous gauze draped here and there and pastoral murals covering the walls. Augustine was really going all out on this goddess thing, wasn't he?

"About zee chapeaux?" Françoise asked.

"No, about zee fey—I mean, about the fey," I said, bringing my attention back to her. "You lived with them for a while, didn't you?"

"Too long," she said grimly, probably because it hadn't been voluntary.

"But you know them pretty well, right? Better than most?"

I really hoped so, since my options were kind of limited. There weren't a lot of experts on the fey, especially the light variety. Their world had a habit of consuming any unwanted visitors and spitting out the bones. Not that Françoise had been unwanted. She was the kind of immigrant the fey welcomed with open arms.

Literally.

"Zey kidnapped me," she said bitterly. "I was a slave. What does a slave know?"

"More than I do. And I need to." And I guess something in my tone got through, because she looked at me from under a rack, where she was trying to reach a rogue hat.

"What ees wrong?"

I glanced around again, but the only people nearby were the mother and child, and they were busy watching the drama with open mouths. I squatted down beside her and lowered my voice. "I don't have that much time," I said quietly. "But I need to know everything you can tell me about their weapons."

"Zere weapons?"

"Not the everyday stuff. The special ones."

She frowned. "What special ones?"

I glanced around again. "It's only a theory, but I saw a weapon, a staff, that . . . Look, the gods fought all kinds of wars when they were here, right? With each other, with demonic monsters, even with humans. The legends all say so."

Her forehead wrinkled. *"Oui?"*

"Well, if you have a war, you have *weapons*. And if you read the old stories, they're mentioned pretty regularly: Artemis' bow, Thor's hammer, Zeus' thunderbolt—"

"But zee gods, zey are gone now." She looked over at the Graeae, who had just dealt with Augustine the same way they had with his clothing—by sticking him onto one of their backs. That left his long legs flailing around in the air, and his mouth yelling obscenities that, thankfully, were not in English. She sighed. "Most of zem."

"Yes, they're gone. But their weapons might not be."

"I don't undairstand."

I switched the ICEE to a new hand, so I could gesture around. "When the gods were kicked off earth, it happened fast. Like really fast. If it hadn't, they would have been able to throw off the spell banishing them, or kill the one who had cast it. Right?"

Françoise nodded. She knew as much about what my mother had done as I did, since she'd been there when I found out. *"Oui, c'est ça, mais—"*

"Françoise, they were banished *almost immediately*."

"Oui?"

"So maybe they didn't have time to *pack*."

She blinked at me, the hats suddenly forgotten. "Zen zere weapons . . . you sink zey 'ave left zem 'ere?"

"I think they might have left them in Faerie," I corrected. "It was a fey lord that I saw running around with one. And since we're facing the return of a god . . ."

"Eet would be nice to 'ave one of zere own weapons to fight heem with."

I nodded. "Look, I know it was a long time ago. But

time runs differently there, and the fey live a lot longer than we do. And if something *was* left . . . well, they would keep it, wouldn't they? Prize it, even? They always seem to be fighting—"

"Zey are always fighting zee Dark Fey," she corrected. "And zey do not need godly weapons for zat. Still . . ."

"Still?"

Her forehead wrinkled some more. "I did not know much of zere language when I first arrived, and I was just a slave. And zey do not tell stories to slaves. But zee man who bought me, he liked to claim zat he was descended from zee gods."

"Did you believe him?" Because it didn't look like it.

She scowled. "*Non,* I do not believe. I do not theenk he was descended from any god, unless eet was from Zeus' *cochon.*"

"*Cochon?*"

"Ees peeg."

It took me a second.

"His pig?"

"*Oui.*" Françoise nodded decisively. "As I say, peeg."

I smiled. "And what did Zeus' pig tell you?"

"Eet ees not what he say, but what he 'ave. A banner that his father carried into battle. A great battle, when zee fey say, zee gods fought beside zem. But zee gods, they whair already gone by zen. . . ."

"But maybe some of their power wasn't."

She nodded.

"Did you hear of any unusual weapons while you were there, even rumors? I need to know if any still exist, and if so where they are now. *And who has them.*"

She shook her head. "I was not looking for a way to fight, but to flee. But I could ask zee Dark Fey."

"The ones here at the hotel?"

"*Oui.* Zey do not like to talk about zee past, but eef I tell zem eet is for you . . ."

"Would that help?"

She looked surprised. "You treat zem with respect. And you helped zem—zey do not forget zat. Few 'ave ever bozered."

"Then ask them about the battle, and the staff. It was

called the Staff of the Winds. For a while, it was the personal weapon of the Blarestri king."

"Zee Sky Lords," Françoise said, her eyes widening slightly, the way everyone's seemed to when they talked about the leading group of Light Fey.

"That's what I was told. I don't know for certain that the staff was a leftover godly weapon, but if it wasn't, it should have been. And where there's one, there might be more. I need to know if they've heard—"

"I want a picture," a childish voice interrupted, and I looked up to see that the little ballerina had reappeared at my side.

"Not right now, sweetie."

"No. Now!"

I sighed. "I told you, I don't work here."

"But you're the corpse bride," she insisted, "and I wanna—"

"I'm not—"

"You're the corpse bride and I want a picture! Mommy, make her give me a picture!"

"It—it's just a picture," the mother said, walking over while still staring at the commotion. It had gotten worse, with the Graeae piling their newly purloined clothes on top of Augustine. I wasn't sure if that was because they were running out of room, or to shut him up, but if the latter, it wasn't working.

"Look, lady—"

"Just pose for a picture, would you?"

"No," I said, suddenly pissed. "I will not."

"Why? It would only take a minute."

"So does telling your child *no*."

And, okay, I'd finally been irritating enough to get her full attention. She turned around. "What does that mean?"

"It means that maybe giving your kid everything she wants—"

"Don't tell me how to raise my child."

"—isn't the best tactic for bringing up a well-adjusted—"

"Well-adjusted?" Her eyes took in my dusty, blue-lipped, shoeless form. "What would you know about well-adjusted?"

"More than you!"

"Just pose for the picture!"

"No! I am not the freaking corpse bride! My name is Cassie Palmer and I don't—"

But I didn't get a chance to say what I didn't do. Because a booming voice suddenly broke out, loud enough to shake the walls. *"CASSIE PALMER. CASSIE PALMER. CASSIE PALMER IS IN AUGUSTINE'S."*

What the *hell*?

Chapter Five

"What?" Augustine's perfectly coifed head poked up out of a pile of clothes. "What is *that*?"

"No!" The irate mother stared around, and then abruptly became a lot more irate. "Goddamn it, *no!*"

She bolted for the counter with the cash register, which also contained the gift-wrap station. And started throwing fancy cards, spools of ribbon, and luxurious wrapping paper around, looking for something that I guess she didn't find, because she kept doing it. And while that wouldn't have been a great idea anywhere, it was especially bad here, because Augustine didn't use normal paper.

Augustine didn't use normal anything.

As was demonstrated when a roll of shiny blue and silver foil rolled across the worktop and fell off the edge.

"You put that back!" Augustine demanded. "You put that back right now!"

But it was too late. The paper hit the floor, and immediately began folding itself into a long string of origami animals. Which tore off the roll and started sprinting through the maze of tasteful racks and tidy tables. Which suddenly weren't so tidy anymore, with paper tigers leaping on them, and paper elephants ramming them, and paper monkeys climbing them.

And gleefully throwing the perfectly folded wares at each other. And at us. And at the floor.

It looked like they were still stuck on last season's circus theme, which the formerly elegant shop was really starting to resemble.

And then a swarm of something flew in the open front doors.

"CASSIE PALMER."

"CASSIE PALMER."

"CASSIE PALMER IS IN AUGUSTINE'S."

The locator spell blared like a foghorn, screaming my name and confusing my brain. Which was already confused enough watching what looked like a couple dozen bats swoop in and start circling the room. I stared up at them, feeling like I'd been caught in a rogue game of Jumanji, while Augustine cursed and Françoise grabbed the crazy woman who was still trying to destroy the gift-wrap station.

Only to have her pull something out of her purse.

"Where is your *shield*?" the brunette screeched, brandishing what looked suspiciously like a wand.

"Get zat out of my face!" Françoise warned her.

"*Where is it?* You have to have one!"

"Get eet out right now, or I swear to you—"

"No, I swear to *you*—"

Françoise took the wand away from her and snapped it in two.

"What the . . . how did . . . you *bitch*!"

"Witch, actually."

"So am I!"

"But not a very good one," Françoise said smugly.

And then the circling cloud dove, in a black, shrieking, speeding mass.

I ducked, hands over my head, but it didn't help. The next second I was surrounded by a crowd of fluttering things that weren't bats, weren't birds, weren't anything I'd ever seen before, but were suddenly everywhere, including right in my face. And screeching something I couldn't understand because they were all talking at once.

"Don't answer them!" the woman—the witch—was yelling. "I was here first. *I was here first!*"

"CASSIE PALMER."

"CASSIE PALMER."

"CASSIE PALMER IS IN AUGUST—"

"Cassie! Zees way!" Françoise called, and I threw myself behind the counter. The not-bats followed in a streaming mass, only to go up in flames when Françoise, who is a very, very good witch, threw a fireball at them.

Of course, a mass of flapping, yelling, *on-fire* things is not exactly an improvement. But they didn't appear to be much more substantial than Augustine's origami. Because they disintegrated as I scurried out the other side of the counter, in puffs of ash that exploded in the air all around me.

At least the outfit couldn't get much worse, I thought, staring about.

And then jerking back when I found myself facing one that had been smart enough to head round the other way.

Up close, it looked less like a bat than an overlarge butterfly, since it had no body to speak of. Or even a head. Just a vertical slit of a mouth wedged in between two rapidly beating wings and yelling something.

Until it was plucked out of the air and eaten by Deino, the sweetest of the Graeae, who wasn't picky about her choice of snack.

But this one didn't go down so easily. In fact, this one didn't go down at all. It stayed in her mouth, thrashing about and making her look like she was chewing on a wad of black bubble gum. Or talking in a really exaggerated way, because her jaw kept going up and down, up and down, with words spilling out, only Deino didn't speak English.

But somebody did.

And now that there were only a few of the black things left, I could understand what they were saying.

"*Crystal Gazing* here," a woman's voice said, from somewhere over my head. "Lady Cassandra, can you comment on the state of your relationship with the vampire senator Lord Mircea? You're rumored to be lovers—"

"The *Oracle* here," a booming British voice interrupted, out of Deino's mouth. "Our readers would like to know what, exactly, was the nature of the creature you fought and killed at your coronation two weeks ago—"

"And why were you naked?" *Crystal Gazing* added eagerly. "Was it a ritual?"

"—they would also appreciate confirmation on the identity of the creatures you fought in the lobby of this hotel last week," the *Oracle* continued, speaking a little louder. "It has been speculated—"

"Or maybe some kind of sex magic? Our readers did a poll—"

"—that they were the personal guards of the demon high council—"

"—and you were voted sexiest Pythia by a margin of almost three to one!"

"But . . . but I'm the only Pythia," I said as the brunette witch dragged me back.

"*Witch's Companion* here," a tiny voice piped up, from somewhere behind me. "We were wondering if you could share a favorite recipe? Maybe a nice fall soup?"

"It has been noted," the *Oracle* thundered, "that they match the description of similar creatures glimpsed occasionally through time, and described by some of our most illustrious scholars—"

"Hang your illustrious scholars!" the brunette witch growled, getting in between me and what, at a guess, were a bunch of magical microphones. "I'm telling you, I was here first!"

"First to find her isn't first to press," *Crystal Gazing*'s avatar said condescendingly.

"The Pythia's first interview cannot be given to a rag like *Graphology*," the *Oracle* agreed, despite the fact that Deino was trying to root it out with her tongue.

"What?" The brunette bristled. "What did you just call—"

"Rag," *Crystal Gazing* repeated helpfully. "He called your paper a *rag*, dear."

"Or . . . or some decorating tips?" *Witch's Companion* said, fluttering around hopefully. "We're doing the fall cover on quilts—"

"No more than it can to *Crystal Gazing*," the *Oracle* continued pompously. "Which has no better quality of journalistic integrity than—"

"I *beg* your pardon?" His companion no longer sounded so amused.

"—the majority of American so-called newspapers—"

"Just what are you implying?"

"He's calling your paper a rag, *dear*," the brunette said acidly.

Crystal Gazing bristled. "May I remind you that my paper has been in press longer than either of—"

"Trash always sells. That does not make it any less trash."

"Bitch said *what*?" *Crystal Gazing* demanded. And then went up in flames when the brunette held a lighter under it.

"More than one way to start a fire," she told Françoise.

"CASSIE PALMER."

"CASSIE PALMER."

"CASSIE PALMER IS IN—"

"You're a reporter?" I asked the brunette, pretty unnecessarily at this point.

"What?" Augustine's profile appeared over Enyo's shoulder. The tallest and scariest of the sisters had slapped him on her back facing the other way so he couldn't look directly at us. But that didn't stop him from trying. "Are you here to cover the fall line?"

Everybody ignored him.

"Not a reporter," the brunette told me quickly. "Carla Torres—call me Carla—"

"I have a few other suggestions," *Crystal Gazing* muttered, from a burnt-up wad on the floor.

"—senior editor for *Graphology*," Carla said, smiling at me determinedly. And grinding the remains of the competition to powder underneath a stylish black heel. "A considerably better choice for you than that ridiculous tabloid *Crystal Gazing*, or that pompous British toady to the Circle—"

"If you mean the *Oracle*," Deino's captive commented, "you could at least have the courage to say so."

"I thought I just did!"

"And the girl?" I asked.

"My daughter." She shoved more frizzy hair out of her face. "You're rumored to like children. I thought you might find a kid charming—"

"*That* keed?" Françoise said, only to have the mother glare at her.

"You couldn't have just come up and introduced yourself?" I asked.

"Oh yes!" Carla threw out her hands. "Yes! *Why didn't I think of that?*"

"With respect, what do you think we have been attempting to do for weeks now?" the *Oracle* asked, a little indistinctly, since Deino had managed to push it over into one cheek.

"But you're never in," Carla said. "Or you're never up! Or those damn vampires you live with find some other reason that ensures no access—"

"And we were informed that you don't have an appointment secretary yet," the *Oracle* added, disapprovingly.

"—so when I spotted you in that ridiculous disguise—"

"It's not a disguise," I said.

"—which might have fooled the others, I don't know, but I've been doing little except staring at a picture of your face for weeks! I'd know you anywhere, and I've been camped out in this damn hotel for days. I barely sleep, I rarely see my family, and I strongly suspect I smell—"

"I wasn't going to mention eet," Françoise murmured.

"—but damn it! I will have that interview!"

"Or perhaps a pie?" *Witch's Companion* burbled. "We have our annual bake-off coming up, and we would love to feature an entry by—"

"Shut up!" everyone told her.

She shut up.

"Well, how about it?" Carla said, breathing a little hard. "You can't avoid us forever. And, frankly, I know some of my colleagues. If you don't tell your story, they'll tell it for you. And after the merry chase you've led us, believe me, it won't be a version you'll like!"

"That sounds a lot like blackmail," I pointed out.

"It isn't," the *Oracle* said. "It is—I am loath to admit—merely a cogent commentary on the state of our once great profession. Where will you find a Thomas Bowlby these days? Or a Sir Henry Stanley? 'Dr. Livingstone, I presume' has been replaced by celebrity gossip and sycophantic fawning, and I shudder to think what the future may hold for—"

"A 'she's right' would have sufficed," Carla said dryly.

"My dear woman, I was merely attempting to—"

"Prove that it's impossible for you Brits to say anything in a single sentence? I've often wondered if it actually pains you."

"Not nearly as much as working with the likes of—"

"Trust me, you would never *be* working with—"

"Who are all these people?" *Witch's Companion* suddenly asked.

"What?" the *Oracle* said huffily. "What people? My girl, we are trying to discuss important—"

"These people on the concourse. They're everywhere, and it's not even ten o'clock yet."

"The concourse? Where are— My God, she *is*!" he told someone, sounding outraged. "The little strumpet snuck down while we were distracted and is trying to steal a march on us!"

"I'm not a strumpet!" *Witch's Companion* said, her voice coming through clearly, but also hiccupy, as if the owner was being battered around outside. "At least, I don't think so; I don't know what that is. And I'm not trying to steal anything. I just want to show the Pythia our latest issue, but these men won't let me—"

"It's the damn paparazzi," Carla snarled, staring at the shop door. "We sit here for weeks and then someone tips them off—"

"Oh, that's rich, coming from you," the *Oracle* said. "Everyone knows you obtain half your stories through bribery, chicanery, and deceit—"

"At least we get stories that aren't a month old! When was the last time you had a scoop?"

"Hey!" *Witch's Companion* said. "*Hey!* Let me go! I don't want to—"

"We are not concerned with 'scoops,' " the *Oracle* said proudly. "We are concerned with the proper reporting of factual, well-researched, well-supported—"

"Can I yawn now?" Carla asked.

"Oh. Oh no," *Witch's Companion* said softly. "You're not paparazzi at all, are you? You're—"

The voice abruptly cut off, and her little black fluttery thing suddenly stopped moving and floated gently to the floor, like it was made out of tissue paper.

I bent down and picked it up.

And my bracelet started slamming into my pulse point hard enough to bruise.

"CASSIE PALMER."

"CASSIE PALMER."

"CASSIE PALMER IS IN AUGUST—"

My head jerked up, but I didn't see anything. The shop was designed to keep people's attention on the expensive wares inside, not on whatever was happening on the concourse, and it worked pretty well. All I could see were glimpses of the usual morning crowd, passing along the drag in colorful tees and unfortunate spandex.

I stood up and started walking cautiously toward the front.

"This is so typical," Augustine said bitterly, from behind me. "She's been the official Pythia for weeks now, but has she held a press conference? Given an interview? Made a single statement to *anyone*? I spend all my time trying to get press, and she spends hers avoiding it! It's no wonder we're inundated on a daily basis with nosy types, prowling around, hoping for a—"

"Cassie?" Françoise said, coming up behind me.

"—story, which wouldn't be so bad if they were planning to mention the shop or the brand—"

"Cassie?" Françoise said again, and then froze, her hand on my arm, as I pulled back a couple of the hanging floral strands in the window.

And no, I thought blankly, those weren't paparazzi.

"—but no. Couturier to the Pythia and do I rate so much as a mention?" Augustine asked, while on the concourse across from the shop, an army was assembling. They looked like tourists, but they weren't. And I didn't need the bracelet almost vibrating off my wrist to tell me that.

"Mon Dieu," Françoise whispered as a wave of power

washed over us like a hot breeze, causing the hair on my arms to stand on end. And the tacky T-shirts, too-tight shorts, and beer bellies of the crowd to ripple and change. And melt into what would have looked like black commando gear, if not for the long coats that commandos don't bother with, because they don't carry weapons that they mind everyone seeing.

War mages do.

Only I didn't think these were ours.

It looked like nobody else did, either, because Françoise suddenly turned and bolted for the counter, and the Graeae released Augustine, who hit the floor along with half his merchandise. Something slammed into place in front of the shop a second later, an almost transparent field wavering just beyond the pretty bow windows, which would have looked more at home on a Rue de Something in Paris than in the Wild, Wild West, because Augustine gave a crap about Dante's theming.

He obviously felt the same way about its wards, because that was a shield flickering out there, not that it mattered.

It wouldn't hold against that kind of firepower.

There wasn't a lot that would.

"CASSIE PALMER."

"CASSIE PALMER."

"CASSIE PALMER IS IN—"

I grabbed for my phone, before remembering that I didn't have it on me. And Françoise was already on the house one behind the counter, presumably calling security. But the casino's guys were used to dealing with drunks and shoplifters and people who won a little too regularly for chance. They couldn't handle this.

My guys could.

"Here." I looked up to find Carla holding out a phone. I took it and punched in the number I knew best while kiddo did a twirl on the tile, her pink tutu swirling out around her. I stared at it and tried to get my thoughts in order.

It didn't seem to be going so well.

My brain kept insisting that this wasn't supposed to happen. This happened *other places*, and then I came

back here to eat and sleep and banter with my bodyguards in safety. Unless I tripped over one of the cots that
were currently strewn around my suite, that is, because
the court I'd recently ended up with needed a place to
sleep.

And oh God.

My *court.*

"CASSIE PALMER."

"CASSIE PALMER."

"CAS—"

Pick up, pick up, pick up, I thought as the phone rang
and rang. It was midmorning, not a vampire's favorite
time of day, but normally my bodyguards worked around
the clock. But yesterday hadn't exactly been normal.

Not that I was sure what that was anymore. But I was
fairly certain it didn't include an almost-dead master
vampire, who happened to be the font of energy for the
extended family that ran this hotel. Including the group
of senior-level masters who formed my bodyguard, and
who were normally miniature armies all to themselves.
But who had been left limp as rag dolls after he was
forced to almost drain them to keep himself alive.

Which might explain why this attack was happening
now.

And why nobody was answering the goddamn phone.

"CASSIE PALMER."

"CASSIE PALMER."

"CA—"

"Get back! Get ba—" I yelled at the reporter, who
didn't need it because she'd felt the same massive energy
surge that I had. She grabbed her kid and threw herself to
the side, just as the burst hit.

And all but destroyed the front of the shop, ward and
all, splintering the windows and slinging a wash of glittering glass and burning wood through the air.

Straight at me.

And at Augustine, who I hadn't noticed come up behind me until we were both blown backward off our feet.
And through several racks of what had been expensive
clothes and were now burning tatters. And into a decorative column.

Which we bounced off and hit the floor, face-first, about the time that the shield he'd thrown around us failed.

I looked up through a haze of blood and saw him raising a similarly messy face with a snarl. The half-fey designer had always looked a little girlie to me. The perfect hair, the too-pale skin, the flamboyant clothes had just never registered as dangerous.

I was revising my opinion.

Until he suddenly turned tail and ran for the back, disappearing through a curtain.

And, okay, I thought. Maybe I'd been right the first time. But I didn't have time to worry about it.

Because someone else was calling my name.

And this time it wasn't a spell.

Chapter Six

"Cassie Palmer?" The new voice wasn't the harsh, almost metallic tones of the locator spell. Instead, it was quiet, calm, amused. "Is that really you?"

I got back to my feet, pushing shattered glass away from my bare soles. And picked my way across a mine-field to the burning hole that had once been the front of the shop. And looked out.

And saw a man in war mage gear standing on the other side of the concourse, holding a knife to the throat of the terrified girl he'd positioned in front of him.

She wasn't the unfortunate reporter from *Witch's Companion*.

I knew that because I knew her.

She was my acolyte, Rhea.

She stared at me and I stared back. Her long white gown was pristine and freshly pressed, and her waist-length dark hair was just a little mussed. She looked like she should have been attending a Victorian-era lawn party, not standing stiff and careful and slightly off balance because she was having to pull back from the knife to keep it from eating into her throat.

I'd been in that position myself recently. Only, unlike Rhea, I'd been pretty sure the guy in question wasn't going to kill me. Yet it had still been terrifying.

Rhea looked like she was about to throw up.

The war mage smiled.

The smile should have been attractive. He was, with blue eyes bright enough that I could see them from here, and dark brown hair worn stylishly long, just enough to touch the collar of a modern dress shirt. It looked a little odd under all the hardware.

Like the smile, which would have looked creepy on a corpse.

"Can I say," he said, looking me over as well, "you're not exactly what I expected?"

"I get that a lot."

"I apologize for the rudeness of our introduction, but some of my associates are a little . . . keyed up. We thought we'd have a fight to reach you, but instead—" He waved his free hand in the air, to indicate the now missing announcement.

"Must be your lucky day."

He smiled some more.

I turned my gaze back to Rhea, who was looking green, but also like she was starting to get it together. And she might, because she frequently surprised me. A member of Agnes' old court, Rhea had been the only one, other than the kids, not to take the bait the gods were offering and go power-mad.

In fact, she'd risked her life to come here and warn me about the imminent return of Ares, and the pleasure that seemed to give five of her colleagues. Then, in quick succession, she'd gotten scared by a coffee machine, yelled at a senior-level vamp, intimidated another into taking her shopping for the young girls who formed the rest of my court, and fed, comforted, and defended them fiercely until I got back. And then panicked and teared up when she thought I was going to kick her out for being useless.

And all that had been in the first couple days. Since then, she'd continued to show flashes of both timidity and excessive bravery, and I never knew which I was going to get. I thought the former might be the false front, acquired over a lifetime of being ignored and discounted at the court her mother had presided over, because a Pythian love child doesn't exactly have it easy in the world.

But frankly, a little timidity would stand her in good stead right now. Despite being a pretty formidable witch, she wasn't going to beat these odds. Excess bravery right now was going to get her killed.

"Don't look so concerned," the dark mage said, watching me. "I assure you, I don't mean any harm to Ms. Silvanus here. In fact, I fully intend to return her to you."

"In exchange for?"

"You have a piece of our property," he said gently. "We would like her back."

"Lizzie."

He inclined his head.

We were talking about Elizabeth Warrender, one of Agnes' old acolytes and my current rogues. Out of the original five, three were now dead, one—Jo Zirimis—was missing, and then there was Lizzie. Who had turned dark and started playing for the other team apparently without realizing that her team considered her expendable.

The other rogues had sent her here yesterday to take me out of commission while they raided a vamp stronghold in New York. One that contained a potion capable of boosting an acolyte's power enough to rival mine. And possibly enough to shift Ares past the barrier of my mother's spell.

Lizzie had succeeded—sort of. I still didn't understand how she'd known when I'd be back, stepping out of thin air at almost the second I returned, beat up and bleeding, from Wales. But she had, and, like Gertie today, she'd jammed a needle in my leg before I could stop her.

If it had contained poison, I wouldn't be here now. But it hadn't, because Lizzie was a little slow, and a lot fixated on becoming Pythia, while her savvier rivals had known the truth: once Ares returned, there wouldn't *be* a Pythia. There wouldn't be any magic workers, since he planned to kill us all.

I supposed that was one way to make sure no one ever challenged him again.

But they hadn't let Lizzie in on their insight, and she hadn't figured it out herself. Which meant she'd been under the impression that she couldn't kill me, since no one who kills a Pythia can ever be one herself. So she'd drugged me instead, and been captured in the process. And I had woken up in time to prevent the acolytes' plan in New York, mainly because they'd turned on each other while I was out, each wanting to end up as Ares' champion.

And to become the goddess he'd promised to make the victor.

I almost felt sorry for Lizzie. Everyone else had been going after godhood, and she'd just wanted to be Pythia. And still did, I assumed, since I'd left her alive and drugged upstairs, intending to deal with her later.

Only it looked like somebody else had decided to do the same thing.

"And if I refuse?" I asked.

The dark mage made a small moue of disappointment.

"Killing Rhea won't do you any good. You'll still have to battle your way through the wards on the upper floors to get to Lizzie, and they were created by some of the best wardsmiths the Silver Circle has," I told him, talking about the world's leading magical organization and the parent body of the War Mage Corps. "I doubt you'll find them as easy to fool as these."

"Oh no," he mused. "I shouldn't think so."

"And even if you survive—all two or three of you— you'll have my bodyguards to deal with—"

"Who I hear are not feeling well today."

"—and who are still master vampires of Mircea's family line! They'll drain you before you get in the door."

"Hmm." The mage nodded slowly. "You may have a point."

"And the Circle's men will be here soon, in force, and this whole thing is about to explode in your face. But if you give me Rhea now—"

"Oh, I couldn't do that."

"Why *not*?" I asked, trying to keep my voice steady. "If I won't trade for her, she's of no use to you. But if you give her to me now, unharmed, I promise—"

"No use?" the mage broke in, those blue eyes opening wide. "A Pythian acolyte is no use?"

Annnnnd the record scratched.

Time seemed to slow down as I stared at Rhea, who stared back, tearful, apologetic, terrified. Because she must have said something that let them know or guess her new status. I had elevated her rank as a reward for her warning, and because there never seemed to be enough of me to go around. I could really use an acolyte.

I just hadn't thought—so could somebody else.

"If you do not give us Elizabeth, we will have to see if this one can be . . . persuaded . . . to assist us," the mage said, running his free hand through her long, dark hair. "It may take some time, but there are ways. And she is so young. In the end, I think she'll do as we ask."

Looking at her face, I thought Rhea did, too.

Because she'd just gone white as a sheet.

My fingers wanted to curl, to clench, to eat into my thigh. It took a concentrated effort of will to leave them limp, to make my expression disinterested. To keep myself from using the last of my power to age his smile into *powder*.

I used to have better control than this.

Of course, I used to have fewer people I cared about, too.

"She was lying," I said flatly. "I barely know her. Why would I give her that kind of power?"

"Someone is lying," he agreed, with that same small smile.

I shrugged. "You don't have to believe me. You have the evidence already. If she was an acolyte, she could shift away from you." My gaze slid over to Rhea's. "Do you really think you could hold someone with the Pythian power if she didn't want to be held?"

Rhea gazed back at me, her eyes huge. *Take the hint,* I thought desperately. Because she could do this. Not fight her way out, no, but shift . . . all acolytes could do that, even untrained. I'd managed it for the first time with less knowledge than she had now—a lot less. Admittedly, my mother's blood had probably helped, but still. She *could* do it.

But it looked like Rhea didn't think so. Maybe she'd skipped those lessons, or never had them to begin with, since she'd just been an initiate until a couple days ago. Because she just stared at me.

"I think if she had that kind of skill," her captor said lightly, "she would have used it by now."

"Then she can't help you, can she?" I pointed out quickly. "She can't shift Ares here for you. But if you take my offer—"

"I also think," he said, his voice abruptly rising, "that you're lying—"

"About what? I don't—"

"—and stalling—"

"Listen to me—"

"—and that you should give me what I *want*—"

"I'm willing to discuss—"

"—before I get *impatient*," he screamed, the knife bearing down hard enough to dent his captive's throat, "and wreck this *whole goddamn hotel*!"

I stopped talking. The Black Circle weren't the so-called dark mages I'd grown up with, who'd been seminormal guys who got into trouble and couldn't get legit work anymore. The Black Circle were magic addicts and crazy men, and arguing with crazy doesn't work.

Not when the crazy is desperate.

And they were. Because Jo, the only acolyte left alive besides Lizzie, hadn't bet on the potion. Instead, she was off chasing the same weapon I was. And running her own game—without them—because if she found it, she wouldn't need any help. Supposedly, it was strong enough to punch through Mom's spell all by itself.

And I guessed Ares wouldn't have much use for the guys who had twiddled their thumbs while a girl brought him back, now would he?

So yeah, they needed Lizzie, and they needed her bad.

"I have to discuss this with my associates," I told him.

"No, we do this now!"

"No." I somehow kept my voice calm. "If you want the girl, I need a minute. And you will give it to me."

"You do not order me, *Pythia*. Perhaps what I'll give you is a corpse!"

"Kill her, then," I said, my voice harsh. "And I will shift upstairs and kill Lizzie before you can blink. And you will have *nothing*."

For maybe half the time I'd asked for, we just stared at each other. I didn't know what he was thinking, but I was wondering how I'd ever thought those eyes attractive. They were too bright, too wide, too wild. Like maybe he hadn't had his fix lately.

Or like maybe he'd had too much of it.

The whole crowd behind him was the same way, hopped up on magic and almost desperate for a chance to use it. It hovered over them like a fog, leapt from man to man like static electricity, welled up like a dam ready to burst. I couldn't negotiate with men like this. They *wanted* a fight.

I just had to hope they wanted something else more.

"A minute, then," he finally said. "No longer."

I turned and strode back across the shop.

It was mostly a blackened, charred mess, with heaps of ruined finery that I had to wend my way through. But at least the fires were out. And the people seemed okay, huddled behind the counter, which must have provided some protection. Because everything behind it looked pretty normal.

Except for the dead bodies sprawled on the floor, all of which looked like me.

It took me a second to realize that they were the mannequins from the shopwindow, and that Augustine had cut open their backs like a disturbed toddler with over-sized Barbies, and was stuffing something inside.

Something lethal, by the sound of it.

"Don'ttouchthatareyoucrazy?" the high-strung genius snapped at Carla, who was crouched on the floor assisting him. And who abruptly snatched her hand back.

"Sorry, but you said—"

"Chartreuse! Does that look chartreuse to you?" He pointed at a vial in a rack with a couple dozen others. They were all green.

Carla blinked at them. "Yes?"

"That's green apple!"

She reached for another vial.

"That's pear! That's pear!"

"You couldn't have made them different colors?"

"They *are* different colors!"

"Oh, for fuck's sake!" she said, shoving hair out of her face. "Just point!"

"I'll do it myself," he told her, and reached over to grab the rack.

And had me grab his wrist instead.

"What are you doing?" I demanded as Françoise hurried in from the back, carrying another rack of vials.

Outraged blue eyes glared up at me. "Getting us out of this—what does it *look* like?"

"I'm not sure what it looks like."

"I've been toying with a spell, to avoid the ridiculous fees models charge just to walk down a runway. I haven't perfected it yet, but it's good enough for our purposes—"

"Which are?"

"Consider them attractive grenades," he said, glaring in the direction of the mall.

"Grenades? But grenades are weapons—"

"Brilliant observation."

"What kind of weapons?"

"What do you mean, what kind? The lethal kind!"

He jerked on his arm, but I didn't let go. "Like the ones you've been working on for the Circle?"

He looked at me in exasperation. "What else do you think I have that could handle something like this?"

"Handle it how?"

"Would you let me go?"

"Handle it *how*?" I repeated, because I'd seen what one of those weapons could do.

The only way to end the war was to invade Faerie, where the leaders of the group trying to bring back the gods had holed up. But for all its skill, the Silver Circle balked at the idea of fighting a war in another world, partly because they didn't know enough about it, but mainly because their magic didn't work there. Augustine's did.

Being part fey and famously creative had put him on the list to make some of the weapons needed to fight a literal war of the worlds, and he had delivered. I knew this because one of my bodyguards had recently stumbled across a spell that hadn't made it to the finished stage. Yet it had still been almost enough to kill a master vampire.

And if it could kill one of those, it could kill anything.

"We're in a hotel full of people," I reminded him.

"Security has probably evacuated them by now—"

"In a couple of *minutes*?"

"The drag is clear," the *Oracle* guy said, from a chewed-up black wad on the floor, where I guessed Deino had spat it out. "The hotel employees scattered like rats off a sinking ship once they realized what was happening—"

"They've had plenty of practice," Augustine muttered.

"—and security dragged off the few tourists who were up this early. We think it will work, lady."

"And if any of that gets into the air-conditioning system?" I looked at Augustine, who didn't look back. "Can you absolutely guarantee me it won't kill everyone in the hotel?"

"*They're* going to kill everyone in the hotel!" he snarled, gesturing at the army outside. "Or hadn't you noticed?"

"The Circle will be here soon," Carla said, biting her lip. And looking at her child, who was crouched beside her, watching everything with bright eyes. I would have expected the girl to be sobbing in fear, but it looked like she had her mother's resiliency.

Which was ironic, considering that her mother appeared to have lost it.

Carla looked at me. "They will be here," she said again, as if waiting for me to confirm it. To tell her that I saw us all getting out of this, her and the child she suddenly clutched against her side. "They *will*!"

"Maybe, but not in a few minutes," Augustine said. "Twenty, and that's if we're lucky—"

"*Twenty?*"

"That's what they told Françoise. They have to get across town, and they have to assemble a force first," he said, glancing up. And noticing the desperate grip she had on the girl. "Although . . . although perhaps they can shave a few minutes off that," he finished weakly.

"But the Pythia is here! Half the *senate* is here—"

"Not at the moment. They're in New York," I told her, trying to think.

"But they're *supposed* to be here! Why is there no *security*?"

"There's plenty of security for a hotel," Augustine said. "Which is what this is supposed to be!"

He was right, and at the moment it was starting to look

like insanity that the vampire senate's West Coast headquarters was situated in a Vegas hotel. But after their old
HQ was destroyed in the war, they'd needed a stopgap
measure. And this place had been big enough, and the
guy who built it had been a paranoid nutjob who used
better-than-average wards, and it had recently been inherited by one of their own. . . .

None of which were sounding like such great reasons
at the moment.

"And nobody thought to maybe improve the wards?"
Carla demanded.

"They did—on the upper floors," I told her. "The
lower couldn't have the best wards because they're too
sensitive—some crazy tourist could have set them off."

"Why are we talking about wards?" Augustine demanded in a shrill whisper. "All we need to know is that
they're *down*. And without them, we're sitting ducks. Do
you have *any* idea what those people out there can do in
twenty minutes?"

"But we have the *Pythia*," the reporter repeated, looking between the two of us.

Augustine and I exchanged glances. "I assume you
can't shift back an hour or two and warn us?" he asked,
looking like he already knew the answer.

"If I could, I'd have already done it."

"Then can you shift us out of here?"

"No."

"Then it's as I said before—we have to get ourselves
out of this."

"Yes, but not this way."

"Then I hope you have a damn good idea," he snapped.
"I'm all out!"

I stared at the broken doll bodies of the mannequins.
And at my pulled pork sandwich trampled in the debris.
And at Deino, pulling on a scarf that was still stuck to
her, static cling–style.

"Yeah," I said. "I have an idea."

Chapter Seven

"Pythia!" The mage's spell-enhanced voice boomed through the lobby. "Stop stalling! Will you surrender the girl or not?"

"I will." I reappeared in the burnt-out hole of a front door. "How do we do this?"

"No!" Rhea shouted. "Lady, please—"

She cut off when the knife at her throat abruptly tightened.

"Have your people send Lizzie down," the mage told me, nodding at the bank of elevators across from Augustine's, near the lobby. "When she's in our hands, you'll get your acolyte back."

"Yes, in pieces!"

"You don't trust me?" He looked stricken. "And I thought we were having such a nice conversation."

The short break seemed to have improved his temper. He was back to the faux genial crap that was somehow more nerve-racking than the brief glimpse of crazy. He was also smiling again, and just the sight of that was enough to make my blood curdle.

"We'll meet in the middle," I said, trying to keep the revulsion out of my tone.

"We will not. Do you think me so foolish as to let you touch her? You'll shift her away, and as you said, I will have nothing."

"I won't shift her, because I won't be there. Some of my associates will meet you, and see to her safety. When she's in their hands—"

"*No!*" That was Rhea again, suddenly going from quiet

passivity to thrashing fury. "No, don't do it! Don't give them—"

"Rhea—"

"You *can't*," she pleaded. "You know what she'll do!"

"Rhea!"

"You can't let him come back! *Please*—"

"Who knew your acolyte was such a spitfire?" the mage said, holding on to the struggling girl with difficulty. "You know, I'll almost regret giving her back to you."

"Just bring her here!" I snapped. "My people will meet you halfway."

"Start the elevator, and I start walking."

I turned my head and nodded at Augustine, who was standing behind the counter with the phone to his ear. The elevator started moving a moment later. And then so did the mage, dragging a still-struggling Rhea this way. At the same time, Françoise walked out of the shop with a newly dignified Carla beside her, a buttoned-up suit coat hiding the irreverent T-shirt, and her hair and makeup freshly done, thanks to the stylish blue beret on her head.

And trailing the duo were three considerably less dignified types, covered in mounds of dusty couture.

"Not them," the mage said suddenly.

"They're harmless—"

"Bull*shit*. I know what they are, and I know who they're loyal to. They stay away or no deal."

I glared at him for a second, but the elevator was on its way, and there was no time to argue. I nodded at the two women in the lead, who had stopped to look back at me. And who caught the three lumbering mountains as they passed, fanning them out in a line behind them: one to the left, one at the center, and one to the right of the shop.

Leaving our side as ready as we'd ever be as the elevator hit the halfway mark.

"No," Rhea whispered, staring at it. "No."

"When it arrives, make sure it's her," the mage instructed his people. "No glamouries."

"This is my fault," Rhea said, her voice rising in panic. "I saw him return, and now I'm helping—"

"It's all right," I told her.

But she shook her head, violently enough that a thin line of red bloomed against the paleness of her throat. "It's not all right. It's my fault, and when he comes back—"

"Rhea—"

"—he'll kill us all! You, me." She looked up, toward the tower where my suite was, and her voice dropped to a whisper. "The *children*."

"Rhea!" I started toward her, suddenly afraid, but the mage jerked her back.

"Stick to the deal, *Pythia*."

"You don't understand—"

"*Stick to the deal!*"

"I'm sorry," Rhea whispered, her eyes finding mine. And in them was everything I needed to know, and nothing that I wanted. Because I'd seen those eyes before.

I'd seen them on her mother, right before—

"Rhea!" I screamed, making the mage jump and tighten his grip on the knife, because he didn't understand. She wasn't trying to get away. She was trying—

"No!" I shouted as a gout of blood stained pristine white cotton.

The mage jerked the knife back, but too late. Suddenly, blood was gushing everywhere, the mage was cursing, and the two women who had almost reached him were looking back at me, shock and horror on their faces. And then the elevator hit the lobby, and we were out of time.

"*Go!*" I yelled, and they didn't need to be told twice.

Françoise whirled and cursed the mage, who had let go of Rhea to stare at his bloody shirt in disbelief. He was blown onto his back and sent skidding across the highly polished floor while Carla's enhanced voice blared, "*Now! Now! Now!*" and someone cut the lights. Leaving only smears of neon staining the darkness as I ran for my acolyte.

And as three cloth-covered mounds began lurching toward the mages, with the uneven, staggering gait of a trio of couture-clad zombies.

Which somehow made them worse.

Which somehow made them terrifying.

And then the elevator dinged, and the doors opened. And what had to be a thousand black, screeching, flapping nightmares poured out, like every bat out of every hell. The magic microphones flew straight into the already confused crowd of mages, who proved that the Black Circle had something in common with its Silver counterpart, after all.

Because they immediately began cursing everything in sight.

That included the approaching fabric mountains, who were hit by what had to be a dozen spells each. They didn't fight back. They didn't even seem to notice. They just kept going, staggering toward the suddenly panicked group of men, who nonetheless got their shit together and flung a series of combined spells at them from all directions.

And, finally, that got a response.

I had reached Françoise, who was guarding the huddled girl with the expression of a woman who thought it was probably futile at this point. And it looked it. God, there was so much blood. I squatted beside Rhea, my heart in my throat—

And was knocked back on my ass by three explosions, at almost the same time, which shattered every window on the drag.

I looked up to see a glass avalanche pouring down the front of the Old West stores, bouncing off the wooden sidewalks and flying into the air. It looked like silver rain, like tiny fireworks reflecting the neon and sparkling against the dark, like a million years of bad luck I didn't need, since most of the windows had been mirrored. And it was earsplittingly loud, a jumbled cacophony that disoriented me and I was sitting down.

It was no wonder that, for a minute, nobody noticed the thin, watery substance spraying over the crowd, like the sprinkler system had suddenly been switched on.

It was peppering down along with shreds of couture, a few plastic body parts, and half of a blond wig. Because instead of ancient goddesses, the mounds that had just been blown to bits had been powered by Augustine's mobile mannequins. And had been stuffed with the potion that was now covering the crowd, most of whom hadn't gotten shields up in time because they were busy slaughtering harmless flying microphones.

The substance didn't hurt them.

It did confuse the hell out of them, though.

Including their leader, who struggled back to his feet, a dozen yards away, to stare around in confusion. And then down at his hand, where the fine mist was coagulating into a sticky, gluey mess. And then up at me.

"*This* is your idea of a fight?" he demanded.

"No," I rasped, my acolyte's blood on my hands. "*This is.*"

And suddenly, I couldn't see his hateful face anymore, because I was looking at something else: a darkened street, a shadowy hulk, a flash of recognition in firelit eyes. And a gut-wrenching power loss that, while not as bad as a time shift, had me screaming in pain.

Only nobody noticed.

Because something big and black and huge—and God, I'd forgotten how huge—had just joined the party.

For a second, everything stopped, the entire concourse staring at a hellhound the size of a house that stood steaming in the middle of the drag. And if it had been skin-rufflingly awful in its own milieu, it was utterly horrific here: claws that had to be three feet long, huge fangs dripping cascades of hot slime, skin knotty and bumpy and patchy with rank fur I could smell from across the room. And crisscrossed by the scars of a thousand battles with things worse than the Black Circle had ever seen.

And then it proved that Rosier had been right.

Demons really don't like black magic.

Or its users.

The hound gave a metallic shriek that had a number of mages ducking and covering their ears in pain. And then staying that way, their hands stuck to their heads, their thighs and shanks fused, their weapons useless unless they'd already been in their hands. Because Augustine's spell had started to solidify.

And, as a number of shoplifters could attest, it wasn't easy to shake.

Not that the mages had a chance to try.

The hellhound made a leap that covered half the drag, and tore into them, and I looked back down at Rhea, unsure of what to do. The idea had been to distract the mages, grab her, and run like hell. Down the length of the drag, through the emergency exit at the end, and up the back staircase, which would get the fight away from the populated sections of the hotel. And give us the aid of the much more lethal wards on the upper sections of Dante's.

Of course, this many dark mages might be able to overwhelm those, too, but it would take time. And they'd have a new set every level or so that we went up. And they'd have to banish the hound before they could even start. And by then, hopefully the Circle would have arrived to finish them off.

It had been a good plan.

I'd been proud of that plan.

It wasn't going to work.

Because the mages farther down the drag were not running to support their buddies, as expected. They also weren't running at us, because they hadn't been ordered to, or because they thought I might have another hound up my sleeve. They weren't doing anything, except standing there, eyes wide, watching the beast.

And blocking our path to the back stairs.

I stared at them blankly, knowing that I needed a new plan. I needed one now. But it was a little hard to think with my head reeling from the power loss, and with nothing left to work with: no weapons we dared use, no power, and no time.

And with Rhea on her knees, holding her throat, choking on her own blood.

I should have tried to shift her, I thought dizzily. But shifting two was exponentially harder than one—any one—and I'd been pretty sure I couldn't do it. And shifting only one of us would have left a Pythian magic worker in the Black Circle's hands, and was therefore useless.

But then, so was this.

Carla was kneeling on her other side, one hand on Rhea's head, the other on her gory throat, blood welling up between her fingers. And her lips were mumbling something that I really hoped was a healing spell. But whatever she was doing, it didn't look like it was working.

"Rhea . . ." I said pleadingly.

And then the hound gave another bellow, like every piece of metal tearing everywhere in the world, like a knife through the brain, like a physical pain. I jerked my head up to see the creature floundering, sliding on the slick surface of the drag. It took me a second to realize that the mages it had crushed under its claws had stuck there, forming screaming, bleeding pads that had bunched under its feet, causing it to slip whenever it tried to move.

And seriously hampering it.

Like the spells the outlying mages were starting to throw, which sizzled against its horny hide like the strokes of a lash. Or the potion bomb one tossed, which succeeded in blowing a chunk out of its shoulder. Or the mage that had become stuck to its slavering maw, sticking there like glue and blocking its main weapon.

Until it bit the struggling man in two.

And I guessed Augustine's potion hadn't gotten everywhere, after all. Because it managed to swallow the middle bit just fine. And to bellow at the room out of its trophy-lined mouth, making even some of the hardened dark mages stop and stare.

Which they were still doing when it crunched their partners under its feet, grinding them into the already gory floor, getting itself some traction. And then leaping for the main group, which was still holding formation, hurtling its massive body right through the middle. And sending a broad swath of men crashing into the far wall of the drag, like a freight train had just derailed and rolled over them.

I had a vague impression thereafter of screaming, panicked mages, some fused to the thing's hide, others crushed against the wall, including some that stuck there like macabre artwork, writhing in place or slowly sliding down toward the mass of bodies at the bottom.

But it didn't hold my attention.

Because the leader had grabbed the first of a group of fleeing men and started slinging them into another cluster nearby. "Form up! Form up!"

"We can't take that thing!" one of the men said. "Our best spells barely touch it!"

"You don't have to take it! Take *her*!" He flung an arm in my direction. "Who do you think is controlling it?"

And suddenly, our little group was facing a combined spell like the one that had almost destroyed Augustine's, and that should have incinerated us on the spot.

Except for one small thing.

Or make that three small things.

Because the real Graeae had just joined the party.

There was a loud, ululating cry, and the sister named Enyo somersaulted over our group, transforming in the process into a twelve-foot Amazon with four-inch talons, a mass of cascading gray hair and slitted yellow eyes. And a club, which she used like a baseball bat to send the spell boiling right back at the mages. Who threw themselves to the side, scattering like pins in a bowling alley, trying to get out of the way.

Some even managed it.

For a second, I was staring at the surreal sight of a massive hound, its hide now covered in a carpet of squirming mages, rampaging back and forth down the length of the drag. Of Enyo plowing into the fight with her club, sending more mages literally flying on all sides. Of a mass of magical microphones circling overhead, screaming abuse.

And of Rhea staring at the ceiling, the entire breast of her gown stained bright red, her eyes going glassy.

"I can't heal this," Carla told me, her hands red, her voice panicked. "It's too severe. The best I can do is slow it down, but it's not going to make a difference in a minute. We have to have a healer. . . ."

She trailed off, because yeah.

I didn't see any doctors in the room.

"Can you shift her?" she almost begged, for the life of a girl she'd just met. But it probably didn't feel that way.

Battle does that to you.

"No," I said, my voice barely recognizable. "I won't be able to shift again for . . . a long time."

"But there must be something you can do!" she insisted, staring at me with innocent faith. Which looked kind of weird on those hard-bitten features. "You're *Pythia*."

I stared back with nothing to say. A Pythia *was* supposed to be able to do something. A Pythia was supposed to be able to do anything. But it had never seemed to work that way for me.

I looked down at Rhea, lying on the floor in front of me, but I wasn't seeing her. I was seeing a man, old and withered, his salt-and-pepper hair leaning mostly to salt, holding one age-spotted hand over a terrible stomach wound. The other had clutched mine while he tried to tell me something before he bled out, while I'd worked desperately to save him.

While I'd failed.

Because being able to make someone younger or older doesn't mean you can heal their wounds. As I'd discovered the hard way, applying power to them merely gave you a younger corpse. I'd only managed to help one person—sort of—because his was a metaphysical disease, a curse, and making him younger had changed him enough that the curse no longer recognized him.

And even there I'd had help, help I didn't have now.

"But that man did not belong to you," a voice whispered in my ear, causing me to jump and look around.

The only thing I saw was Augustine, the reporter's little girl held fast against his chest, staring out at me from behind the distant counter. And the blackened, ruined storefront. And my own bedraggled reflection in smoke-clouded glass.

And a whisper in my other ear. "While this girl is yours, part of your coven."

I whipped my head back the other way, and stared at the reporter, who stared back at me, her eyes huge. "What is it?" she asked fearfully. "What's wrong?"

Take your pick, I didn't say, because she was weirded out enough.

And then so was I, when everything abruptly went dark.

Chapter Eight

I panicked, thinking I'd been hit with some kind of spell. It hadn't hurt, but it had been just that fast, just that debilitating. Like someone had thrown a switch, only there were no afterimages. There was no anything, just darkness, deep and velvety and absolute, except for a tiny pinpoint of light from somewhere up ahead.

Framing the body of the vampire walking toward me.

He was wearing only a pair of midnight blue sleep pants in a silky fabric that hung low on his hips. His chest and feet were bare and his dark, shoulder-length hair, usually caught back in a clip, was loose on his shoulders. He looked like he'd just gotten up, but the whiskey dark eyes were as sharp as ever.

"But the girl is yours," Mircea repeated softly, kneeling opposite me. "And you . . . are *mine*."

And abruptly, the scene shifted, giving me the weirdest split vision. Half the room remained dark, with the light barely limning Mircea's head and shoulders. But everything behind me burst into comparative brilliance—and sound and sensation: the spill of neon, the hound's unearthly bellow, the smell of gunpowder. . . .

"Which is real?" I whispered, confused, and put out a hand to where the dividing line between the two rooms boiled like steam. But when I tried to grasp it, I felt nothing, although the darkness receded faster now, like curtains closing—

Until a hand grasped my wrist. "They both are," Mircea said, and night bloomed around us.

He seemed to be controlling the division between our two spaces, working to get the distractions down to something I could handle. But it didn't help all that much. Because this place was plenty distracting all on its own.

I assumed I was seeing his court in Washington State, since that was where I'd left him. He'd been injured in an attack yesterday, and it must have been something to take down a man who, although he might look like a raffish thirty-year-old, hadn't seen double digits in five centuries. And who'd been storing up power for every single one of them.

Luckily, Lizzie had spilled the beans about her side's plans to finish the job, and I'd gotten to him before they had. I'd thought about bringing him here, but I didn't know anything about treating injured vampires, and doubted that my small human staff did, either. And anyway, they already had enough of those to worry about.

So I'd taken him home, where I guessed he still was.

Although it was hard to tell, when everything around him looked like I was trying to view it through somebody else's glasses. The warm wooden floor was just a smudge of brown, except for a small patch right around his knees. The tall windows, heavily draped against the day, were just darker smears. And the designs on the intricately carved wardrobe and the expensive carpets had all been smudged away.

I concentrated on a modernist painting on the opposite wall, and it slowly came into focus. It should have looked out of place, a bright splash of color in an old-world room, like it should have felt odd having a hand grip mine from across a continent. But it didn't.

He held my hand firmly but gently, careful not to let vampire strength bruise human flesh. He pulled it forward and the light came with it, like sunrise falling over a landscape. Leaving the room bisected between neon bright and dark, like the body of the girl lying on the floor between us.

"What do you want me to do?" I asked nervously, because I didn't know how to heal someone.

"You're already doing it," Mircea murmured, dark eyes sliding shut.

"I'm not doing anything," I said, trying to stamp down the panic clogging my throat. "I don't have the power to do anything!"

"Neither does a bridge, yet it serves."

I waited, but nothing else was forthcoming. I knew I should just shut up and let him concentrate. Healing was one of Mircea's gifts, and it worked equally well on humans as on vamps.

But it worked on humans who were *in front of him.* I didn't know how well it worked from a thousand miles away, but it had to be harder. And that was assuming he could do it at all, so shut up, shut up, shut *up*, and give him some time.

But I didn't seem to be able to. Because Rhea didn't have any time. And just sitting there while she bled out was—

I didn't seem to be able to.

"I don't understand," I blurted, and then bit my lip, practically vibrating with the need to do *something*, but not having a lot of options left.

"You have a metaphysical link to your acolyte," Mircea murmured, neon light from my part of the world flickering impossibly over his features. "And I have one to you. I am attempting to use you as a conduit to send her energy, as I would one of my masters who needed help."

"But I'm not one of your masters," I said, because I didn't feel like a conduit. I didn't feel anything, except for my fingers, blood slick and desperate, gripping his.

It was probably uncomfortable. If he was a human, I might have broken a bone by now. But he wasn't, and I didn't let go.

"No," he said softly. "Which is why I don't know that this will work. And she is very weak."

I gripped him tighter. "But you can try—"

"Someone already tried. I feel the spell . . . sluggish, slow, impeding the blood flow."

"A witch. She isn't a healer, but she wanted to help. . . ."

"She succeeded. Your servant would have faded by now, otherwise." But his expression didn't look happy. "What is her name?"

"Rhea."

"Rhea." He rolled it over his tongue. It sounded different in Mircea's voice, darker, sweeter, more exotic. And sent a shiver up my spine just from the power behind it.

Yet it had no obvious effect.

"Rhea." The second call was stronger, more compelling, but still sweet. Not a command, but an enticing murmur worthy of a siren. It would have had me running to him, fighting for him, struggling through an army to reach him.

The body between us didn't even appear to notice.

I swallowed, because Mircea wasn't just a vampire; he was a first-level master, one of only a few hundred in existence. They ruled the vampire world through the six senates, governing bodies of immense power. And Mircea wasn't just any old senator; he was second-in-command to the North American consul, and therefore one of the strongest vampires on earth.

And I felt every bit of that power when he tried again. *"Rhea!"*

It wasn't a request now; it was an order, fierce and demanding. I felt it like thunder in the air around me, like an earthquake in the floor underneath me, like an electric shock radiating through my body, making me gasp. And tighten my grip enough that I thought I might break my *own* fingers.

That damn call would have brought me out of the grave.

It didn't seem to be doing anything for her.

And we were running out of time—even I could see that. Rhea's usually pale skin was alabaster, her dark lashes closed, her chest barely rising. Only her blood moved, slow but determined, seeping out of the terrible wound to stain her neck, like someone's fingers had already done to her cheek.

She looked like a beautiful corpse.

"Maybe . . . maybe we need to try the other way," I said desperately.

Mircea didn't open his eyes. "What other way?"

"Seidr." It was a spell my mother had cast on me during a trip back in time, and which I'd inadvertently passed to him. I didn't fully understand it, which was why I hadn't been able to remove it. And it hadn't seemed like a priority, since it was just a communication spell.

But it was a powerful one.

More powerful than this, I thought, staring at the hazy dividing line still boiling between us.

But Mircea shook his head. "Cassie, this *is* Seidr. I tried reaching you the other way, the vampire way—"

"I'm sorry! I didn't hear—"

"Nor should you have. You are not vampire. It was an instinctive reaction when your distress woke me. But it didn't work, leaving me no choice but to try to access you through the Seidr link."

"But—" I stared around again. "It wasn't like this before."

Seidr wasn't like anything I'd ever experienced, other than for being somewhere in the flesh. In fact, it was almost impossible to tell that you weren't, except that people not in the link couldn't see you. It was clear and perfect, not like a vision at all, while the room behind Mircea had become even less distinct than before, like it might dissolve at any second.

"It might," Mircea said grimly, picking up on my thought. "Seidr is an expensive spell, powerwise—"

"But you *have* power," I interrupted. "I can feel it, just sitting here—"

And then he opened his eyes, and I saw it, too. They were amber bright, startlingly vivid against the washed-out room around him, and flooded with power. "But you do not," he said, "and you control the spell."

"But I told you—I'm not doing anything!"

"But the spell still originates with you, Cassie. My people do not know how to do a Seidr spell. And remember what we were told? It was designed by the gods to talk to each other between worlds. But we are not gods. Even you are not, although you carry the power of one."

"Power I can't access right now," I said, my lips turning cold as I finally understood. The Pythian power was virtually inexhaustible, but I wasn't. And when I was too tired, I couldn't channel it appropriately—if at all.

Mircea's dark head inclined. "Without a good connection, I cannot give Rhea the strength she needs. I have it, but I have no way to get it to her."

"Then send it to me! And I'll—"

"That still requires a better connection than we have,"

he said, patient with my panic. "Whether you or she is the intended recipient, I must have a stronger link. Otherwise, I can do little more than the witch already did, and slow down the process. But if you cannot strengthen the spell—"

"She'll die anyway."

"Yes."

He didn't qualify it, as a human might have, didn't tell me it would be all right when we both knew it wouldn't. He didn't say anything else, for which I was grateful. He just gripped me tighter, although it was getting hard to feel his fingers anymore, like they were dissolving under mine.

And they probably were, because I was nearing exhaustion. I'd given everything I had left to that last shift, pulling a creature from another world, something I'd only very recently learned that I could do at all. And now I was powering the Seidr link, or trying to, but I wasn't strong enough.

I never had been.

"You've done all you could," Mircea said softly. "You need what strength you have left."

He was right; I knew he was right. But it didn't help. I lost people; I always lost people. My whole life that had been the one constant, the one fucking thing I could depend on, and I couldn't—not *again*—

There was the ghost of a touch on my cheek, because he must have slipped out of my grip without me knowing. "You have to let *go*, Cassie."

Yeah, people had been telling me that all my life, too. To the point that I'd started to tell it to myself: don't care, don't love, let everyone and everything that matters slip away. Let life take them, let it have them, because it's going to anyway, because that's all it does: take and consume and destroy. It lets you feel happy so the pain hurts more, lets you have hope so it can crush it, lets you have love so it can rip it away. You can fight against it, but it's a trap, the whole damn thing.

Better get used to it.

But I wasn't used to it. I'd never gotten used to it. I was tired of it, sick to death of it, and furious, so furious I could barely see.

I bent over Rhea, my tears dropping onto her face, my lips almost as cold as her cheek. But somehow I wasn't kissing her good-bye. Somehow I was gripping her shoulders, shaking her, and then screaming at her like a madwoman. Or maybe it was the universe I was screaming at—I didn't know; I couldn't think. I just felt it, something hot and hard and furious welling up inside me, something I couldn't seem to control because *enough! You can't have this one, you can't take her—*

"Cassie!" Mircea had grabbed me, fingers biting into my flesh, but I didn't care.

"No, this one is *mine*! I've paid enough, I've lost *enough*!"

"Cassie!"

"*No!* This one is mine and you *can't have her*!"

And then I was being knocked aside, hard enough to hurt, and for a second I didn't understand what was happening. And I still didn't, when I saw Mircea, clear and bright and *there*, as solid as if he was right beside me. Like the room around him, which was suddenly vivid with color and sharp edges, like Rhea beneath him as he thrust her back onto the floor, straddling her with both hands around her neck, looking for all the world like he was trying to choke her to death.

But instead of killing her, he was doing something that brought faint color back to her cheeks, that caused a small movement of her chest, that caused her eyelashes to flutter and her fingers—because at some point I must have grabbed her hand—to move—

"What—" I began, because even now I couldn't keep my mouth shut. It seemed to be on a separate circuit from the rest of my brain, which was still screaming in denial even as I saw life flood back into Rhea.

"I should have realized," Mircea said, looking at me wildly, through strands of sweaty dark hair.

"Realized what? Mircea, how—"

"She's yours—you said it yourself!"

"But *how—*"

He suddenly threw his head back, laughing like a boy. And I just stared, wondering if I really was going mad. Or if he was.

"Mircea!"

"Your coven must work similarly to our houses," he said, eyes bright. "And, as you saw yesterday, when I all but drained the family, the power exchange works both ways. I can send power to subordinates, but they can also send it *to me*."

I blinked, suddenly remembering the small hits of power I'd gotten from my coven on a couple of occasions. I hadn't thought of it because I wasn't used to *having* a coven, which was what the Pythian Court actually was. And because the hits had always seemed so small.

But then, maybe I hadn't needed as much before.

I stared down at Rhea, who was still unconscious, but also very much alive. "She's powering the connection."

"The link between the two of you is," Mircea corrected. "And possibly your whole coven for all I know."

He grinned at me, the dignified master vampire suddenly giddy from the power loss, from dragging someone almost literally back from the dead, and from the same euphoria that was finally hitting me.

And then blurring like a bad radio signal when someone else called my name.

"Cassie!"

A wash of sound blasted over me, a raucous, out-of-tune blare that made me jump—and realize that the wedge of neon behind me had widened and brightened. And that hands were reaching through, shaking me, and pulling me back. Pulling me away from him.

"Help is coming," Mircea said, grabbing my hand, his voice strangely distorted. "Cassie—do you understand? Help is coming! *Hold on.*"

"I'm trying!" I told him, clutching his hand while feeling like a mass of taffy being stretched in two different directions.

And then my fingers slipped out of his, and like a door slamming shut, I was suddenly somewhere else.

I was suddenly somewhere horrible.

Chapter Nine

The quiet of Mircea's mountain retreat shattered, replaced by a mix of shouts and explosions and screams. And a weird *drub, drub, drub* that sounded like Dubstep and made me want to cover my ears, only my arms didn't seem to work. Or my eyes, I thought, staring around at a world gone red.

I blinked, but the view didn't change, except that Carla was suddenly in my face. "We've got to get out of here!" She was yelling at point-blank range, but I barely heard her. Because that weird sound kept getting louder.

I finally realized that it wasn't a drum, or crazy dance music. It was a series of powerful spells—the source of the red glow—exploding against something that bisected the drag a dozen yards away. Something wavy and indistinct, a barrier so flimsy that it looked like someone had stretched a piece of gold plastic wrap across the room.

"Thought the wards were down," I said thickly, trying to focus eyes that were still trying to see two places at once.

"They were," a different voice said, sounding satisfied. It took me a second to realize that it was bellowing from the little black thing scurrying across the floor like a spider, because it couldn't fly anymore.

"Grafton—the guy from the *Oracle*," Carla panted, trying to haul me up. "He used to be a war mage, like a thousand years ago."

"I heard that."

"You . . . got the shields back up?" I asked, attempting to help Carla, but just making things worse. My limbs were all mixed up, and nothing seemed to work right.

"Well, in truth there was nothing wrong with them," Grafton said.

"Nothing . . ."

"Other than the null the Black Circle had sitting on the controls," he added, talking about a mage capable of absorbing all magic within a certain radius. "We knocked him out, dragged him to another room, and—"

"Who is we?"

"A group of us—reporters, photographers, errand runners—something like forty people in all. We've been camped here all week."

"The second stories of these Wild West facades have actual rooms in them," said *Crystal Gazing,* who must have gotten a new avatar, because it was fluttering around my other side. "But nobody used them—until we realized that they offered a perfect vantage point."

"It's become rather like a shantytown," Grafton said. "With reporters from every major paper and most minor ones bringing in bedrolls and such, refusing to leave after your last escapade. We assumed something else might happen, and wanted to be on hand—"

"Be careful what you wish for," Carla muttered.

"—and fortunately so," he added. "Some of us know a thing or two about wards."

"Yeah, only now we have to hope the damn things hold together until the Circle gets here," Carla panted. "Which, in case you haven't noticed, isn't going so great!"

"That's the trouble with shielding common spaces," Grafton agreed. "You can't use the strongest wards, lest they mistake a guest for a threat. But the everyday variety, even expensive ones like these, will only hold so long against this sort of—"

"Will you shut *up*?" she demanded. "We have to move!"

She was right; one glance at the ward told me that. It was starting to look like a threadbare blanket, with obvious gaps in the golden weave. But I still couldn't seem to get my limbs to work.

And then Carla cursed and slung her purse over her head. And grabbed me under the arms. And started dragging me back toward Augustine's, like Françoise was already doing with Rhea.

"Augustine thinks he can get his ward back up," Grafton explained, spidering alongside us. "We're pulling back to the shop for an extra line of defense."

"Good idea," I said weakly, staring at several dozen spells that were exploding against the barrier and radiating outward, like acid dropped in water.

And at the pterodactyl-type monstrosities, physical wards from the lobby, that had swooped in and started picking up mages, only to hurl their mangled bodies at the wall. And at the taco cart and its flower-draped fake donkey, which was burning like it had been doused in gasoline. And at the Graeae, on the other side of the barrier near the lobby, who appeared to be hemming the mages in, keeping them on the drag as if waiting for the scary thing inside to slaughter them all.

Which would have been great, except that the scary thing appeared to have left the building.

I looked around—why, I didn't know; it wasn't like I could have missed it. But there was no giant hound anywhere. Some of the mages must have gotten their shit together and banished it. And without it, there wasn't much left to distract them.

As demonstrated when a mage taken by one of the pterodactyl wards managed a spell that set the thing on fire—and fell what had to be four stories when it released him. The dying ward then dive-bombed the group attacking the shield, exploding in fiery bits against their armor. But if it did any damage, I couldn't tell.

There were so many.

"How are there so many?" I asked, staring at what still looked like a couple hundred dark mages, maybe more, silhouetted against the brilliant golden sheen of the ward.

"That thing you conjured up ate ten or so," Carla huffed. "And stepped on another thirty or forty, I don't know. It was exorcised with at least fifteen still sticking to its damn hide! And those old women—and what the *fuck* are those old women—"

"The Graeae."

"—they killed maybe fifty more, before they ended up isolated over by the stairs—"

"Then why are there still so many?"

"Because they weren't all in here before! They must have been afraid you'd freeze time on them or something, and had backup spread around the hotel that came running when—"

A massive explosion cut her off, and magic prickled over my arms, so strong it was almost painful. The floor vibrated beneath us, enough to send Carla stumbling to the floor beside me. And a flash exploded across my vision, so bright it whited out the room.

For a second—a wonderful, heart-gripping second—I thought the cavalry had arrived.

Then I realized the truth.

"Fall back! Fall back!" someone yelled.

But there was no time to fall back. There was a rush of wind and a clap like thunder, and I looked up to see the middle of the ward billowing in like a tattered curtain, leaving a gap big enough to fit a truck through. But a truck wasn't using it.

An army of dark mages was.

And Armageddon arrived in an instant.

A spell hit the floor beside me, carving out a chunk of concrete the size of a wheelbarrow, and sending me rolling to the side. Another exploded just behind me, causing Carla to shriek and hit the floor again. More spells slammed through the air overhead, dug furrows out of the floor, and ricocheted off the building behind us, hitting a decorative light post and whipping it back at the break in the ward.

And at the mass of mages flooding through, right behind the barrage.

A few were tripped up by the post. More were lashed by billowing strands of the broken ward. But not enough, not close to enough. Because Françoise was trying to shield and also drag Rhea, and Carla was staring up in wordless horror, and I was on my hands and knees, trying to throw a spell I didn't have the power for and only retching and seeing the world swirl around me.

And then another spell was thrown, this one too close and too fast to dodge even if I'd been able to see straight. Only I couldn't. I couldn't do anything but sprawl there, watching the bright orange curse come boiling at me, knowing I had no way to stop it—

But someone else did.

A violently purple spell came out of nowhere, big as a beach ball, and slammed into the smaller one, sending it twisting off course and crashing against the ceiling. I was still staring at it, and at the brilliant trail of aftereffects, when a dozen more spells lit the air. Offensive red, orange, and yellow; defensive green, white, and blue; and more of those weird purple ones were suddenly blurring across my vision.

But that wasn't the weird thing.

The weird thing is that they were going the other way.

At least half of the spells suddenly shooting around were going *toward* our enemies, exploding against the advancing bombardment, or capturing the spells and sending them wildly off course. Some of the war mages ended up on their asses, because it didn't look like they'd expected much of a defense. But they were getting one.

I managed to get my head turned around, enough to see a tall, distinguished-looking old man with a paunch and a three-piece suit standing in front of Dante's, looking like a banker. And behind him was a crowd of people who didn't look like war mages, didn't look like a rescue squad, didn't look like anything except a random sample plucked off the street. There were student types with piercings, older men and women in suits, and a biker chick with pink hair.

And an elderly woman in a dress covered in cabbage roses, her bun of silver hair falling around her face and her teeth bared in hatred.

"That's for Celia," she choked, and sent a spell ripping through the air over my head, so hot I thought my hair was on fire.

And it finally clicked.

The reporters, down from their perch for a last stand.

But despite their courage, and despite the fact that they'd just stopped a dark mage advance cold, it was about to *be* their last.

Because they might know some wicked spells, but the point of war mages wasn't just what they knew, but what they *were*: magical freaks whose bodies produced many times the magic of a normal human's. So yeah, three or four dozen regular Joes might be able to hold a narrow pass for a minute or two. But the pass was about to get a whole lot wider, and they were about to get a whole lot weaker, and this wasn't going to work.

"Where are they?" Carla screamed. "Where's the god-damn *Circle*—"

"It's only been ten minutes," Françoise said, staring at me.

"Ten." The witch gaped at her like she was speaking another language. "What do you mean, *ten*?"

"I 'ave been timing eet."

"No. No, that's wrong. That's *impossible*!"

But it wasn't impossible. I'd spent two or three minutes talking to the mage, another minute or so in Augustine's, and maybe a couple more for the hound to run amok. And then Rhea . . .

No, it wasn't impossible at all.

I started fumbling around in my shirt.

Things got both faster and slower after that, like someone was playing around with time. But I didn't think it was me, since I couldn't even manage to get the high collar of the nightgown open. Maybe because of the shrapnel from that first blast.

Pieces of it were sticking out of the hands I'd thrown up to shield myself; out of my side, which was drenched with blood; out of one of my knees. And then another spell hit nearby and I gave up and tried to crawl. The pain was excruciating, because I think I was crawling *on* the shrapnel, but I did it anyway. Because it was that or die, make it to the shop or die, make it soon or die, making a rhythm that thrummed in my head, in my heart, in the blood in my ears.

But not so much that I didn't notice other things.

Like the violet spell, thrown by the girl with pink hair, which wrapped around a vicious red curse heading my way and stopped it cold, burying both of them in the floor. Or like the net spell that engulfed two mages who were running at me, and then constricted, throwing them off their feet. Or like the lasso that tripped up half a dozen more, because they hadn't seen the thin line snaking across the floor at ankle height until it was too late.

And none of it mattered.

Because the men behind the fallen were just stepping on their brothers in their eagerness to get at us. And the defensive spells from our side were already getting overwhelmed, having to try to pick up two curses at once, which didn't always work. And using offensive magic against well-warded dark mages was almost a waste of energy, most of it just glancing off to explode harmlessly against the floor.

We only had maybe half a dozen yards to the shop, but we weren't going to make it, were we? We were about to be overrun—

And then we were, when a stampede of impossible blue and silver creatures burst out of the shop, roaring and trumpeting and growling as they thundered past. And over, clearing us with the grace of leaping tigers. Which some of them were, I realized, blinking at the herd of Augustine's little origami animals sailing by overhead. Although they weren't so little anymore, being life-sized and savage-looking—

And utterly harmless, because they were still made out of freaking wrapping paper!

But the mages, who had just been decimated by the hound from hell, didn't know that. They abruptly shifted their target from us to the horde, which exploded in bursts of silver and blue confetti—also harmless. But there was a crap ton of it and it was everywhere and totally unexpected. And the reflective foil took on the colors of the offensive spells being lobbed around and—

And we had a couple seconds, didn't we? I realized.

"Pull back!" I yelled, trying to crawl and rip my collar open at the same time. "Pull back!"

I didn't know that anyone even heard. Panic had set in, and people were running everywhere, and plaster and glass were raining down, and the sprinkler system had come on and was further confusing the issue. Along with whatever Mircea was doing, because he was doing something. I could still see parts of that other room, along with a glimpse of glowing amber eyes—

Because he was trying to see through mine, I realized. And maybe he could, but I couldn't. Like I could barely move because two minds can't control one body.

"Cut the connection!" I yelled, choking on water and plaster dust. "Cut the connection. I can't *see*!"

And I guess he did, because the room suddenly snapped back into focus, and control of my body came with it. I stared around, still half-blind because of the plaster mask mixing on my face, my hands tearing at the damn collar. And finally grabbing the ugly necklace inside just as a blur of blue ran past.

It was Carla, freaking out like everyone else, but who stopped when I snagged her arm. "Do you have any microphones?"

"What?"

I slipped in the slush on the floor as I staggered back to my feet, only her hand on my arm keeping me standing. "The flying things—the microphones! *Do you have any more?*"

"What? Yes—I—yes." She stared at me like I was crazy. "Why?"

"Send one to the Graeae. Tell them to pull back to defend the shop—"

"But the tourists—"

"The mages aren't interested in tourists—they're interested in me." It wasn't a guess; fully half those spells had been aimed my way. Looked like the hound had made an impression. "Keep them that way. We only need ten minutes—"

"But, Lizzie, your court—"

"They can't reach Lizzie if they're busy trying to kill me! Pull everyone back behind Augustine's wards, have the Graeae defend you if they break, and make sure you keep my body in view—"

"Your *body*?"

"—and try to find a way out through the floor, the back, whatever. But do not take me out until you absolutely have to. They have to see me. They have to stay *focused on me*—"

But she wasn't focused, and who could blame her?

"What do you mean, your body?" She grabbed me. "Are you *hit*?"

"I'm all right!" I said, at the same time that a ghostly cowboy finally decided to join the party. "It's showtime," I told him.

Billy Joe, my ghostly companion for years now, yawned. "You know, I really hate it when you— *Holy shit!*"

The reporter was fumbling around in my clothes, looking for some terrible wound I didn't have instead of listening. But I saw Françoise staring at us from the shop opening, where she'd managed to drag Rhea. "Did you get all that?"

She nodded, handed Rhea off to a young man, and sent a huge fireball at a couple of mages who had just jumped back to their feet. It blew them backward, almost to the opening in the ward, where they crashed into some of their buddies on the way in. The flames hitting off multiple sets of shields all at once sent mad red flashes over the crowd.

And finally snapped the reporter out of her panic.

She snatched her purse off her back and started throwing things out of it, and I looked at Billy. "You've got babysitting duty."

"What?" He had been staring around, mouth open, hand holding on to the cowboy hat he'd been wearing for the last century and a half. But at that his head swiveled back to me. "Wait!"

But there was no time to wait.

"Get everyone back to the shop and get that ward up," I told the reporter as our desperate SOS took flight.

"And what are you going to do?"

"Buy ten minutes," I said, and closed my eyes.

Chapter Ten

Suddenly, everything was easier.

I gave a sigh of pure relief as the pain from a dozen wounds fell away, like my body behind me. Until Billy caught it, halfway to the floor. I felt him step inside my skin as I broke free, a warm, comforting presence who might not know what was going on, but who knew the routine.

Because we'd done this before.

When I first started shifting, I hadn't known what I was doing, but I *had* known that body – soul = corpse. So when I found out that Pythias often shifted in spirit form—easier and we didn't pick up any nasty plagues that way—I'd had some issues with it. Like possessing someone in another time, which I'd never learned to enjoy, and like returning to a dead body afterward.

I'd eventually realized that every other Pythia managed it by using time travel to return to their bodies at almost the same moment they left, making the interval away too short to do any damage. But in the beginning, I hadn't known that. So I'd handled it the only way I knew how: by leaving another soul behind in my place.

And since the only soul I trusted—more or less—was Billy Joe, he got the nod.

And to be fair, the only damage my body had encountered as a result was a hangover, because Billy took his pay in beer. I traveled mostly in the flesh now, but those early lessons hadn't been for nothing. Because I'd learned a thing or two about possession.

Like the fact that it didn't have to be voluntary.

And right now taking control of the dark mage leader,

even for a few moments, was the only way I saw us surviving this. But that required finding him. And after Enyo's initial assault, he'd pulled back behind his men and I hadn't seen him since.

And I wasn't going to this way, I realized.

The war mages' coats rose around me as I pressed through the ward, thick and black and suffocating. Worse, they had spells woven through them to provide an added layer of protection. And all those spells altogether left me feeling like I was sinking in a swamp of dark magic, one that had me choking and blind, with zero chance of finding anyone.

And I didn't have a lot of time.

Sooner or later, somebody was going to realize the obvious: that all they had to do to beat us was to organize themselves into a unit again. And stop trying to fit through the narrow opening that was restricting their numbers and allowing us to defend a small area. And just take out the rest of the ward—

And then somebody did.

I was still trying to see through the crowd when all of a sudden, I didn't need to. The leader jumped up on a barrel in front of the shops on the other side of the drag, putting him head and shoulders above everyone else. And grabbed a post so he could hang off the side, yelling and waving an arm.

"Form up! Form up! Damn you—form up!"

And *shit*.

I tried pushing forward, but nothing worked. There were so many bodies, and so much magic being slung around, I could barely tell where forward *was*. And then it got worse, as the gridlock around the "gate" started to pull back into formation. I ended up on the floor, getting trampled by boots that stomped right through me and coats that slung in my face and dark magic that weighed me down, like a heavy blanket—

Until the surreal moment when I pushed off from the floor, just desperate to get away, to get *up*—

And I did.

Way up.

It suddenly felt like I was a helium balloon some kid

had dropped, that was spiraling out of control, up and over the crowd and rushing toward the ceiling—

And then through it, into the conference room above, freaked out and flailing because I wasn't sure how to get back down again. Because I didn't *do* this. I stepped out of my body and into someone else's; I didn't go floating around like a female version of Billy Joe!

But at the moment, that's what I was. And I found that my thrashing did have an effect. I stopped just short of the ceiling, banked, and swooshed back around, like pushing off the side of a pool when swimming. Except the water was air and the air was in the wrong room and I needed to get back down there, get back down there *fast*—

Okay, little too fast, I thought, because the ceiling flew by in an instant, and then the crowd was rocketing toward me, and I was pulling up, flying out over their heads, banking and searching—

And finding.

The leader was still on his barrel, and a second later, so was I. And almost falling off the other side, because I didn't know how to stop properly yet. But I didn't need to. All I needed now—

Was to step inside.

I'd invaded the body of another dark mage once, one who'd shielded with wood. Or what had looked like wood, because we're talking magic here. But any element will work as long as it has meaning for you, since it's just a way to focus your power.

In his case, he'd chosen to visualize what looked like a wooden wall all around his body. Which had been lucky for me, since I ward with fire. My fire had burned through his wood, letting me in and putting me momentarily in charge. Until he figured out what was happening and kicked me out on my insubstantial ass, because the owner of a body always has an advantage.

I'd expected something similar this time.

I didn't get it.

There was no discernible wall, of wood or anything else, in my way, which should have worried me. But it didn't. Not until a horrible, shudder-inducing feeling hit as I breached the skin, which I didn't remember from before. Like I didn't remember the face that abruptly turned toward mine.

It was made out of fire—not good, not good, because I only knew how to shield with one element. And how was I supposed to burn through fire with more fire? But I didn't have time to worry about it.

Because, the next second, the eyes rose and locked with mine, and I realized that I had a much bigger problem.

Because they weren't eyes.

They weren't anything I'd ever seen before or wanted to see again. Just darkness, but not the normal kind. This was the limitless, unending black of a sky without stars. The emptiness an astronaut sees when his tether has just been cut, and his only way home destroyed. A void, horrible and deep and soul-destroying.

And pulling me in.

I screamed, and the fiery face laughed, laughed as I was drawn down, as I felt pieces of myself begin to disappear into that darkness, as my soul stretched and split and started to tear—

I screamed again, mindlessly, because right then I didn't have a mind. Right then I barely had anything. It had been just that fast, from shock to terror to terrible, mind-shattering loss, with no tether even in sight anymore as darkness boiled overhead, as it took my sight, as it poured down my throat, as I felt the world slip away. And like that astronaut, began to wheel in endless parabolas, still screaming—

Until someone grasped my fingers.

It wasn't a grip. It was barely a touch. But in the darkness of absolutely nothing, it felt like everything. I grasped it like a scared child caught in a nightmare, hugged it to me, tried to wrap myself around it, whimpering and sobbing and utterly, utterly terrified.

And that was before something hooked me on the other side, like a barb thrust into my side. Something that didn't want to lose its prize, something that was trying to drag me down into nothingness, something that was massive and strong and powerful, like no mage could ever be. Something—

That hadn't expected me to have help.

"Will you challenge me for her, vampire?" An amused voice shivered through the nothingness, as the fiery face looked upward.

And then around, as if it couldn't quite find its challenger.

"Looking for me?" Mircea's voice was a whisper, an echo that seemed to come from everywhere and nowhere. I was holding on to his fingers, but I couldn't have said for certain where he was. And it didn't look like my captor was having any better luck.

"You dare play games with me?" It almost sounded more surprised than angry.

"You'd be surprised what I dare," Mircea hissed. And this time, I was sure the voice had come from the left.

So was the face, which abruptly turned that way.

And as it did, a tiny bit of its grip on me loosened.

"No, no. As the humans say, you're getting colder," Mircea said, and this time, there was a definite thread of mockery in the tone.

It caused the face to flame up, so hot I could swear it burned me. And to twist to the right, where the voice had come from that time. But Mircea wasn't there, either.

Because a moment later, he was overhead whispering, "Surely, you can do better than that?" And then from the left again. "See, I was here all the time." And then from everywhere at once, forming an echo chamber that didn't make sense, because there was nothing for his voice to echo *from*—

Only there was.

I could see it suddenly, a hazy vision of the battle on the drag. Not clear, not even close. But like I was viewing it through some type of barrier, thick but transparent, and vaguely tinted. Something like . . .

Someone's skin.

Because I was out; I was almost out!

The power that gripped me had been so focused on finding Mircea that I had slipped away from it little by little. But it realized that at the same moment I did, and the fire that had been flaring in anger was suddenly burning everywhere. I saw it like an impenetrable wall, blazing all around me. Felt it like acid, etching into my soul. Heard it in my voice as I screamed and screamed and screamed—

And fell, as heavily as if I had a body again, slamming into something that I vaguely recognized as a floor.

For a moment, I just lay there, stunned and whimpering, barely conscious.

"Mircea?" I whispered, after a long moment.

But I couldn't hear him anymore. No more than I could that other voice, or feel its talons. I couldn't feel much of anything, except for aching loss, the memory of terror, and overwhelming confusion.

None of which I had the strength to do anything about.

So I just stayed there, feeling wet tile against my face, because the overhead sprinklers were still on. Eventually, I noticed that the water was pattering down on the rest of me, too, tiny drops hitting my body and face and rolling down my cheek. I lay there some more.

I didn't have a cheek.

I didn't have a hand, either, although there was one on the floor in front of me.

It was getting wet, too.

I swallowed, trying to focus, trying to think. But that was a mistake, since all my mind could focus on was that *thing* I'd just fought. On the feel of it eating my soul, tearing it away in great chunks, the darkness wolfing it down. Did you get it back? I wondered. Did you rebuild it like blood that was lost or skin that was shed? Or was part of you, a precious, irretrievable part, simply gone, gone for good, gone to feed the creature that had ripped you to shreds, that had raped your soul, that had—

Stop it! Just stop it!

After a moment, I did.

Okay.

Okay.

Okay.

Start with what you know.

I was on a floor.

A floor with boots. And mud. And men walking over me as if I weren't there, which made sense. Only, if I wasn't there, why were they avoiding me? Why weren't they stepping through me, like they'd done before? And why was one kicking me—

And yelling: "Get this bastard out of the way!"

I didn't see the speaker, but a second later, someone was dragging my legs to the side and cursing. And then kicking me again, when he dropped me with a thud. But it didn't hurt. It didn't hurt.

Of course it didn't; you're a spirit, some still slightly rational part of my mind said.

But if I was a spirit, how had he been able to move me? And why was my hand all bloody?

My eyes had adjusted slightly, allowing me to see it better. Or, rather, to stare at it, because it wasn't my hand. It was too big, too tan, too covered in clumps of dark hair on the knuckles when I didn't have any there at all.

I stared at it some more. And then at the arm connected to it. And then at the hole in the torso next to the arm, which was big and jagged and went all the way through, bisecting red meat and blackened ribs and—

And it looked like someone had thrown a fiery basketball through me.

No, I realized. Not a basketball. A spell.

And not through *me*.

Through the body—the very dead body—I was currently inhabiting.

For a moment, I didn't believe it. I watched the hand move and flex under my command, and I still didn't. I kept listening for a heartbeat I didn't have, for breaths I wasn't taking, for all the signs of a living body that weren't there because I hadn't ended up in one of those; no, no, I'd ended up inside a *corpse*.

So why was it *moving*?

Because it was. Slowly, sluggishly, my unshaven cheek scraping across the rough wooden boards of the sidewalk next to me, which should have hurt except dead, I was dead, so I couldn't be moving because it takes blood pressure for that, right? And . . . and air and . . . things. I didn't know much about magic, but I knew that, I *knew* that. The only creatures who could move around without those kinds of things were ghosts and vamps and—

Zombies.

I stared at the hand, and okay, yeah, it was looking a little zombiefied right now. Bloodless and dirty and blood-speckled, and if I saw that in a movie, I'd be like, yep, zombie. But it wasn't in a movie, or on TV. It was at the end of my *arm*, and I was in a *body*, somebody else's *dead*, disgusting, still slightly sizzling *body* and—

"Augghh!"

And, okay, I was definitely moving now.

"Augghh! Augghh!"

And people were noticing, and turning, and looking a little freaked out, maybe because I was screaming and thrashing around, or maybe because of the big hole in my chest, or maybe because of the gun in my other hand.

Because there was one.

A big one.

And the leader was right in front of me, his barrel just off the edge of the sidewalk I was spazzing out on, and he was turning along with everyone else within earshot, eyes widening, mouth opening, probably to tell someone to shoot the freaking zombie already—

But too late.

I was already dead.

And the next second, so was he, because he hadn't bothered with shields this far behind the lines. He fell off the barrel, blasted backward from the force of double barrels to the chest at almost point-blank range, and landed in the middle of the street, still twitching. I looked at him, everybody else looked at him, and then everybody looked at me.

And then I was staggering backward, riddled by bullets and spells and—

And zooming up out of the now useless body, scanning the crowd.

For my next one.

Because, okay, yes. This was a thing that was happening. Thanks to dear old Dad, who I knew less than nothing about because what I did know didn't make sense. But one thing almost everyone agreed on was that, before he hooked up with a goddess on the run, he'd been a necromancer—and a powerful one. And a weird one, because he hadn't dealt with bodies—he'd dealt with ghosts.

It was why, I strongly suspected, I'd been a ghost magnet all my life. I walked down the street, and ghosts came over to say hi and to tell me their life story—whether I wanted to hear it or not. I picked up a necklace in a junk shop and out popped a nineteenth-century cowboy. I went anywhere, did anything, and if there was a ghost around, it would probably come running.

Which was why the whole shifting-outside-your-body part of the Pythia job hadn't weirded me out too much. I'd dealt with ghosts all my life; being one had almost felt familiar. Zombies, on the other hand . . .

Zombies were new.

The closest I'd come was possessing a golem—one of the clay creatures rabbis used to make and war mages still did—only that hadn't gone so well. It almost hadn't gone at all until I discovered that Billy Joe's necklace, which contained a central stone that served as a talisman, also worked as a control gem for the golems. Shoved into their clay exterior, it had allowed me to ride an empty one around like it was a car—a huge, clay, robotlike car—and do some damage. But there had been a definite learning curve.

There wasn't one here.

Because unlike giant clay people, human bodies were *designed* to hold a soul. That wasn't a weird state for them—it was the default, and the trick necromancers used to control them. They placed a small amount of their soul in a dead body, using it like the control gem for the golems. To allow their magic to animate it.

And it looked like a whole soul worked even better. Now I just needed a body. And, thanks to the rampage from the hound from hell, there were plenty to choose from.

Of course, also thanks to the hound, they weren't all in great shape, or even in one piece, but beggars can't be choosers. Beggars have to take what they can get, even if that means taking a severed torso, which was nonetheless still clutching a machine gun. A machine gun that was soon spraying bullets in all directions, although not hitting all that much, since this body lacked serious motor control.

But it did the trick.

A bunch of dark mages had been headed this way, already looking panicked for some reason, a fact that was not helped by meeting a hail of bullets. The ones in front turned on the rest of the stampede, causing a tangled knot that had several so flustered they started attacking each other in an attempt to get away. And then running over me, trampling my bloody torso into the floor.

But hey, more where that came from, I thought, feeling a little giddy as I rose into the air again. Or a little crazed, because the next dead guy was laughing his head off as he sprayed bullets and threw potion bombs at his former buddies. And then kept it up even while getting stabbed by one guy who had shielded in time, with a vicious upward stroke that broke a few ribs before it bisected the heart—

And didn't hurt at all.

Because *Dead, motherfucker,* I thought, still laughing helplessly as I searched around on my new body's potion belt for something that would eat through a war mage's shields. He kept stabbing and stabbing, and cursing and cursing, and I kept walking and walking, because he was falling back and I didn't want to lose him.

And then I came up with something, a bilious green slime I'd seen on Pritkin's potion rack once, but hadn't known what it did.

I found out what it did.

The mage went up in green, phosphorescent-like flames, and then lost it as his shields buckled and failed. And then ran off through a thick section of mages, setting some of them on fire, too. And this time, there was no leader to re-form them into a controlled unit. They panicked and ran at another group, who started shooting at them to keep them away from their shields. For a moment, I had the satisfaction of watching two groups of dark mages try their best to kill each other, before I rose back out of my latest, all but minced, body.

And felt the room spin around me.

Chapter Eleven

I didn't know that you could stagger as a ghost, but I did it. I looked down at my torso, confused and fuzzy-brained, and realized that I could barely see it. A few minutes ago, my spirit had been reassuringly solid, almost bodylike except for the whole flying-around-the-room thing. Now it was virtually transparent, like Billy Joe's when he badly needed an energy draw.

Because spirits don't make their own energy, do they? Only bodies do that. *Living* bodies, which I hadn't been in. It was why even regular ghosts needed a talisman like Billy's to feed them power, or a donor like me to give it to them, or a graveyard to haunt to pick up the scraps of living energy that human visitors shed.

Because, otherwise, they would fade away to nothing when they ran out of power.

Like I was about to do.

I stared around, trying to come up with some options, but I couldn't see past the crowd. So I pushed off from the floor—easier this time, too easy, like I weighed about the same as a wisp of smoke. And quickly realized the truth.

I hadn't affected the fight much at all.

It was more disorganized now, with the leader gone, but something else was gone, too. The last gleaming strands of the great ward had dissolved, leaving Augustine's cobbled-together shield as the only barrier our side had. Which looked like it was going to last all of another second.

No, I thought blankly.

No!

But there was no denying it. After everything we'd

done, after holding out for so long, after putting up a defense that nobody could possibly have expected, it didn't matter. It wasn't going to be enough.

"Cass! Cass!" I jerked my head down, to see Billy's bright red shirt dodging through the sea of black.

"Up here!" I yelled, although it sounded more like a whisper. But Billy heard. And a second later, he was in my face.

"What are you—" he began, then got a good look at me and stopped. "Cass—you've got to get back to your body!"

"In a minute. I'm trying to—"

"You don't have a minute! And neither do they." He gestured at the shop, which had so many mages in front of it now that I almost couldn't see it anymore. "Everyone in there is about to get killed—and your body along with them!"

"Why haven't they left?" I asked, trying to clear my fuzzy brain. "I thought everyone was going to—"

"They tried. But Augustine—damn his eyes—was so worried about theft that he boxed himself in! There's nowhere to go."

"What do you mean, nowhere? There's plenty of—"

But Billy was shaking his head. "A slab of support for the parking garage is directly below him, and we don't have the firepower to blast through it. And even if we did, it's load-bearing!"

"Behind him, then—"

"Cass, the casino's *main vault* is behind him. It's solid and it's spelled. Nobody's getting through that thing! And moving side to side won't help when the other shops aren't in any better shape, and most don't even have shields! You've got to shift them out—"

"If I could shift, do you think I'd be *here*?" I asked, wishing I could think. But fatigue or panic or God knew what was clouding my head, making it impossible to do anything but stare at the battle. And at the shield, which was taking a hell of a beating.

I felt like that, too, like I could feel every blast myself. And if Billy was right, I was about to. But I didn't have anything left. I didn't have anything left.

"Cass, listen to me," Billy said, his voice tight. "The Graeae are supporting the shield, feeding it power, but they're looking pretty damn tired. And without them, it'll stand up to maybe a second of that kind of barrage. If you're gonna do something, it has to be *now*."

And yeah, it did, I thought, blood I didn't have pounding in my ears. Or maybe that was the spells, *thud, thud, thudding* against the shield, like the hands of that damn clock in London. Ticking down the seconds we had left.

London, I thought, as some thought scurried through my head, too fast for me to catch.

"Cass? I know this isn't what you want to hear, but there is a way out."

I looked up, to meet Billy's worried hazel eyes.

"I'm going to help you, okay?"

"How? How can you help us?"

"Not us. *You*. Look, I took a draw before I left. You couldn't really afford it, but I needed it to help you burn through one of these guys' shields—"

"What?"

"—and once I get him, once we're in charge, we're gonna push our way to the front of the line when they take the shop—"

"What? Billy, what are you—"

"*Listen to me*, okay? You and me, we're gonna get your body out of there. I'm not in it right now, so it looks like you're already dead. We say we want the corpse for a souvenir or—or that we got orders to take it to one of their leaders, or—"

"No!"

"—or *something*, anything, to get you out of this building—"

"I'm not leaving them!"

"Then you're gonna die with them!" He grabbed me. "Look at yourself! It's gonna be touch-and-go to see that you don't fade as it is! And there's nothing else I can do for you, okay? This isn't London—"

"London?"

"—there's no more tricks up my sleeve! We've got to move, and move *now*—"

"What about London?"

"Cassie—"

"Billy! What about London?"

"Damn it!" He stared at me, exasperated. "I just meant that you've won against some crazy odds, like when we were at Agnes' old court a couple days ago. I thought we were goners, but I took out those two mages, and then you pulled that stunt with the golem—"

"Golem." I stared at him.

"—but that won't help us now. Even if you possessed one, it's *one guy*—"

He cut off, probably because I was shaking him. "Have you seen one? Billy—*do they have one here*?"

"They got three, but what difference does it make? I told you— Oh, *shit*!"

That last was in response to my zooming off, up near the top of the ceiling. And desperately scanning the crowd. And spotting not one, not two, but three of the creatures, just like Billy had said, their bright orange clay standing out even in the gloom.

And even better, they were all together, clustered over in a clump at the edge of the fighting, along with their owners.

I tore off after them, with Billy on my heels.

A second later, I was hovering in front of a seven-foot colossus. Who should be able to see me, because it was a spirit, too. One of the incorporeal types of demons Rosier had talked about, who had been tricked and trapped by a mage.

And it looked like I was right. Because I'd no sooner landed than the huge head tilted slightly, and the clay eyes seemed to focus on mine. I swallowed, really hoping I was right on this.

"Billy," I said quietly, "possess a mage."

"Which one?"

"Any one."

"About time! I didn't think you were gonna come to your senses!"

He moved off and I looked up at the golem.

"Hello," I said nervously, and smiled. I don't know why.

It didn't smile back.

Of course, I wasn't sure it could; I'd never actually seen one of those faces move.

"Uh, look. I . . . kind of have a problem here," I said, trying not to sound as desperate as I felt. "And I was wondering—you're a demon, right? A powerful one? I was told that's the only kind the mages bother to, uh, to trap in one of these things, and—"

It just looked at me.

But it hadn't looked away, so I floundered on.

"Look, I kind of have an alliance with—" I stopped suddenly, because it occurred to me that maybe mentioning the demon high council wasn't a great idea. Some demons didn't seem to like them much, and what if this was one of those? It's not like I could tell. "I just meant that I, uh, respect your kind a lot, and I was wondering if maybe, if I release you—"

Nothing. Not even a nod. I started wondering if it spoke English.

"Look, if I release you, will you help me?" I asked in a rush. "These people, they're in trouble because of me, but I—I can't help them right now, and—" And that had probably been a mistake, too, because demons admire strength, and I'd just admitted that I didn't have any. But I thought that was pretty obvious anyway, and . . . and what had I been saying?

I stared at him, desperate and despairing, and tried to think up an argument that might work. But whatever connection I had to my brain wasn't functioning too well, or maybe it was my brain that wasn't. Because my body currently had no soul in residence, so it was in a state we call dying, and—

And—

And—

"Cass!" A stranger's voice shocked me enough that I jumped and whirled. And saw a dark mage standing behind me, grinning. "Got one!"

It took me a second, but the smile was the same.

Billy, I thought. Gun, I thought, because he had one in his hand. "Shoot," I said, because that one idea was still clear, clear like crystal.

Billy frowned. "Shoot what?"

"Him!" I pulled back out of the way, pointing not at the golem, but at the guy standing next to it.

"That guy?" Billy said.

"Yes!"

"That guy right there?" he repeated, now pointing with his gun—

In the face of a startled mage, who nonetheless got a hand on his weapon—

"Yes! Shoot him. *Shoot him!*"

And Billy did.

The blast echoed in my ears, the mage fell over, a look of surprise still on his features, and the man next to him shot Billy—or, rather, Billy's purloined body.

"Well, shit," Billy said, looking down at his chest.

I didn't say anything. Because I was too busy watching the golem. And the little energy crystal in its forehead, which had just cracked, turned gray, and started smoking.

The golem pulled it out and looked at it for a moment. And then dropped it on the floor, crushing it under a big orange heel. And turned those expressionless eyes on me.

"You are Cassandra Palmer?" a deep, gravelly voice asked.

"Yes."

"The one who killed Apollo?"

I swallowed, trying to decide if that was a trick question, but my brain wasn't up to it. I could only hope the truth was something he wanted to hear. "Yes?"

The shotgun slung across his back was suddenly in his hand, and ratcheting. "What can I do for you?"

I stared at him, so relieved I could barely speak. "Fuck shit up?"

He looked at me silently for a second, and then turned and shot the two mages nearest him, who were still firing at Billy. And who I guessed were the owners of the other golems. Because their control crystals shattered and burned as soon as the men hit the floor.

"One moment," the first golem said to them as their eyes began to glow. "We have a small job to do first."

"Oh yes. Oh yes, indeed," a sibilant voice whispered, from inside the nearest one.

The other just nodded.

The first golem looked at me. "Consider it fucked."

His body started to vibrate, and chunks of clay began cracking and falling off. But not as fast as the second guy, the one with the creepy voice. Who erupted from his shell in a glowing nimbus of power and then spread out across the space above us, like a massive, iridescent jellyfish.

I stared at it, mesmerized. It was beautiful. The silvery white strands glimmered, shot through with every color of the rainbow, riding on currents only it could see. . . .

It was *beautiful*.

"Fuck me," Billy whispered, back in ghostly form at my side.

"Get back to your body, small one," the first golem told me, still in its clay form. "And get your friends far from this place. Or the scouring may take them as well."

"What? No! Not them!" Billy said, because I was still staring stupidly upward. "And not the hotel! Just the bad guys!"

"We will contain it as well as may be," the golem told him. "But this space you call the drag is not safe. Get them out."

"But we can't get them out," Billy said furiously. "You don't understand! We need—"

But we didn't have a chance to say what we needed. Because one of the jellyfish tentacles reached out and brushed us—

And the next second, we were flying.

Billy caught me; I felt his arm go around me in a warm embrace, felt him pull me close, felt his anger when he said: "Demons! I really hope you know what you're doing, Cass. You just made a deal with the devil!"

Three of them, I thought, staring down at the drag as it blurred beneath us: dark and neon bright, spells flying, fires burning, artificial rain pelting down onto the black-coated half circle surging at Augustine's tiny shop. It was strangely beautiful, too.

I closed my eyes, just for a moment, so tired. . . .

"Cass! Don't you do this to me! Don't you fucking do this!"

I heard Billy's voice, but it was so far away, so far. And

this darkness wasn't like the other. It was warm, and welcoming, and peaceful. . . .

"Goddamn it, *I said no!*" Billy said, and the next moment, I felt him everywhere, all around me, all through me. He engulfed the rapidly dissipating strands of whatever part of me was still left, merging it with the more solid brilliance of his own spirit.

And then we *moved*, like we'd been shot out of a cannon. Rocketing back down to ground level, zooming past and then through the bodies of the jostling, straining men, sizzling along with the overstrained ward, while blast after blast of spell power buffeted us, strong enough collectively to be felt even in the spirit world. And then we were through, bursting into the middle of the ruined little shop—

And the next second, I was choking to death on the messy, bloody, trash-strewn floor of Augustine's.

Everything slammed into me at once: pain—God, so much pain—almost indescribable exhaustion, shock and the confusion of crashing into yet another body, and the fact that it was my own didn't seem to make that much difference.

Realizing that I couldn't *breathe*.

After a second it dawned on me that the sprinkler system was still going off, resulting in pools of stagnant water everywhere—including the one I was facedown in. It looked like I'd been propped up against the back wall of the shop, but I'd fallen over, probably after Billy left. And of course I'd fallen facedown.

I rolled over, gasping and choking, and finally heaving up a bunch of nasty-tasting water while trying to roll to my hands and knees—

And ended up retching and almost blacking out instead.

I lay there, pale and cold and trembling, taking heaving breaths while the room around me shook like an earthquake had hit it. Drifts of dust and plaster were raining down, along with what looked like half the ceiling; people were running everywhere. I didn't know why, because there was nowhere to go. And everyone was screaming, although I couldn't hear them even though my ears had just popped.

Because the barrage was deafening.

And then the screaming suddenly got louder, loud enough that I *could* hear it. And the ward started shivering, like it was caught in a high wind. And the latest raft of spells didn't stop at the surface, but stretched inward, heads forming as power piled up behind them, looking for all the world like the elongated blobs out of old lava lamps.

Until they broke through, the ward evaporating in an instant, with spells exploding and people screaming and diving for the floor, and the rest of the roof caving in.

A war mage jumped for me, his cape billowing out like a piece of the night, throwing some kind of spell I didn't know. But it was pretty strange, because suddenly, there were two of him. The original and a second like a shadow . . .

A red shadow.

I stared at the man's doppelganger as it hung in the air for an instant, only feet away from me, wondering what this new hell was, but unable to run or even move—

And then it collapsed, hitting the floor and splattering everywhere, like a bucket of warm red paint. Or a bucket of blood, I thought, blinking suddenly sticky eyelashes. Because that's what it was: all the blood in the man's body, which had been ripped out of him in a split second, leaving his exsanguinated corpse to tumble lifelessly to the floor.

And the torrent of blood to splash all over me.

I was still almost completely immobile, but I didn't need to turn around. I didn't need to see the next group of mages, who had been heading into the shop at a run, suddenly also preceded by leaping shadows. Didn't need to watch them tumble to the floor as their friends stumbled into and over them, as both living and dead hit down, sliding on a sea of red.

I didn't need any of it.

Because there was only one thing on earth that could do something like that.

"Shield!" one of the mages yelled. "Shield, you idiots! They've got—"

"Vampires," I whispered along with him, finally turning my head.

And saw a war mage jump for the six-foot-five-inch hulk of my chief bodyguard, Marco. He hadn't even made it all the way through the back wall yet, a fact that didn't stop him from plucking the guy out of the air halfway through the motion and *ripping him in two*. And then throwing the halves aside with a roar, all in one fluid movement so fast I could barely track it with my eyes.

And then he was through, bursting out of the wall that contained the impossible-to-break-into main safe of the casino.

Which I guess hadn't been so impossible after all, because he wasn't alone.

There was the redheaded southern charmer, Roy, who wasn't looking so charming as he leapt through the hole and plowed into a bunch of mages, who foolishly thought their shields would save them. And they did—for a couple seconds. But these guys had been at the front of the battle, and their shields were wrecked.

And a second later, so were they.

I saw portly Fred, who used to be an accountant and still looked like one, at least until he threw out his hands toward the latest wave of mages. And then pulled his fists apart in a savage motion, like someone tugging on both ends of a length of rope. It didn't exsanguinate the men, who were shielded, too. But it did cause all the blood in their bodies to suddenly relocate to one side or the other.

And I guess that wasn't healthy. Because I was left looking at a group of maybe ten guys, half of whom had dark flushed faces on the right side—and burst capillaries, and red-flooded eyes—and half of whom had the same thing on the left. And the next time I blinked, the group had parted down the middle, falling to either side like Moses had just shown up ready to party.

And then someone was grabbing me and jerking me off the floor and up to a furious, blood-drenched face. "Why the *fuck* didn't you call me?"

Blood was all over my face, too, and in my eyes, and dripping in my mouth when I tried to talk. And yet I felt my lips stretch into a smile. The last time I saw Marco, he'd been drained almost dry, that massive body too quiet, too still, so still that I'd wondered if I'd ever see it move again.

Guess so, I thought, head reeling.

"Cassie, I swear, if you don't answer me right this—"

"Tried," I said indistinctly. "Didn't have my phone. Had to use someone else's."

"Whose?"

"Hers," I said, looking at Carla, who was as blood-drenched as I was but seemed okay otherwise, except that she was screaming and screaming and—

"Who the hell is she?" Marco demanded.

"A reporter—"

"Damn it, Cassie! We blocked all their numbers weeks ago!"

I just stared at him for a second, and then I started laughing—why, I didn't know. But it felt good, it felt right, like Marco's bulk under my hands. Like the sight of Rico, the suave Italian, gently scooping up Rhea's unconscious form from behind the counter. Like seeing more people step through the mutilated wall, this time women with wands in their hands who I didn't know, but who Marco must have rounded up somewhere.

And who, along with the vamps, were fast clearing the shop. And in a few cases, heading beyond. And *no, no, no*.

"Pull them back," I croaked.

"What?"

"Pull them back! Pull everyone back!"

And to Marco's credit, he didn't waste time arguing. "To me!" he called, the deep bellow not needing any amplification.

And to him they came, blood-splattered vamps, the droplets already melting into their skin; the older lady in the floral dress, her face pale and pinched, cradling an obviously broken arm; Augustine, bloody and shaking, but also quietly enraged, his long white hands flexing and unflexing as he stared back at the mages; the chick with the pink hair, crazy-eyed and grinning, a wand in each bloody fist; and the rest of the group of sobbing, filthy, traumatized people.

All except one.

"Where's Grafton?" I looked around, but I didn't see him.

People were getting through the wall, scurrying on hands and knees through a tunnel of plaster and wood and warped steel. But I didn't see him in line. I didn't see him outside, either, where something was going on, something that sounded like a hurricane and looked like one, too, with chairs from one of the nearby cafés sailing by the missing windows, along with bits of paper and debris. And dark mages, running with their coats flying out behind them, and then flying themselves when they were suddenly ripped off their feet.

Carla, no longer screaming, but blood-drenched and pale, with her daughter's head buried in her neck, tugged on me. "Lady—we have to *go*."

"Where's Grafton?" I asked.

She didn't say anything.

"That's his name, isn't it? The older man—"

"That was his name," she said quietly, and handed me something.

It was small and black, and chewed and mangled. And now also wet and bloody. I looked back up at her.

"He died buying us the time to get back in here," the biker chick told me, from the line. "He went out like a goddamn war mage!"

Carla didn't say anything. She just hugged her child closer, looking at me with haunted eyes. And then handed the girl off to one of the witches for the trip through the wall, before heading through herself.

"Your turn!" Marco said, taking us toward the ruined wall.

I looked back at the drag, at what definitely looked like a hurricane now, at the glass and wood and bloody, burnt couture that was beginning to get sucked out of the shop. And my fist clenched over the small item in my palm. And then, with the shop starting to disintegrate around us, I laid my head on Marco's shoulder.

And we were gone.

Chapter Twelve

I woke up. That was sort of a surprise, since I couldn't remember falling asleep. Or going to bed, although I was in mine. And clean and bandaged and wearing an oversized tee, although I only knew that by feel because the room was dark.

Pitch-dark.

I sat up, heart hammering, although I didn't know why. And then I remembered why and slightly freaked out, despite the fact that I was safe; I was home. I *knew* I was.

But something was wrong.

I clutched Billy's necklace in a confused half panic. The faint light it gave off was usually too dim to see, but the darkness was so profound that it shone like a beacon, illuminating my palm and shining through my fingers. He was in there—I could feel him—although he wasn't coming out. Probably too exhausted. Ghosts don't recharge by sleep; they need life energy, and he'd used up most of his saving me.

I gripped the necklace tighter, until the gaudy setting bit into my palm, remembering how close we'd come. How very, very close. But he was *in there*. He was safe. And so was I, although it still didn't feel like it.

Something was wrong.

It wasn't a sound; all I could hear was the whoosh of the air-conditioning and my own too-loud breathing. It wasn't a smell; the only scent was the fabric softener the hotel used, and an antiseptic tang from the bandages. And it certainly wasn't a sight, since I could still barely see my own hand in front of my face. It looked like I'd slept through the day, because I could see a few faint stars gleaming through a crack in the curtains. . . .

I could see stars.

I pushed back the covers and rolled out of bed, and immediately regretted it. Everything hurt, a thousand little and not-so-little pains all suddenly vying for attention. For a moment, I just stood there, swaying slightly on my feet, wondering if this was what it felt like to get old. And what was wrong with my life, that I was asking that question at twenty-four.

Then I sucked it up and limped over to the bank of windows that I almost never looked out of, because the vamps kept the blackout curtains closed most of the time.

There wasn't much to see anyway. The neon glow from the big Dante's sign on the roof tinted everything a reddish hue and washed out the stars. Except for tonight, when a few, faint glimmers of light were just visible above the city's raucous glow, little diamond flecks against the deep midnight of the sky.

Because there was currently nothing to overshadow them.

The great sign had gone dark.

I had to fumble with the balcony doors, my fingers stiff and clumsy on the latches, to slide them open. And to step outside, staring upward as the warm desert wind hit me in the face and threw my hair around. And yet I still saw nothing, because the deep red glow had simply vanished.

"End of an era," someone said behind me, and I whirled to find Marco standing there, cigar tip flaring in the darkness. And then burning brighter when a gust of wind caught it, sending flakes of ash spinning off into the night. "Damn." He scowled. "That's one of my Behikes. Come back in before the breeze puts this thing out."

I came back in, shivering a little despite the heat, and he put a comfortingly large arm around me. I looked up at him in disbelief. "They closed the casino."

"They closed everything. No choice—there's not enough of the drag to put in a baggie, and the lobby's not much better."

"Then . . ." I swallowed. "Then all that . . . actually happened."

"Oh, it happened," Marco said, letting go of me so he could shut the door and stop the curtains from billowing in. He locked the balcony back securely, and then shrugged when he saw me noticing. "Habit. They've had wardsmiths crawling over this place all day. I doubt a fly could get in unauthorized."

"It should have been done a long time ago," I said, hugging myself. "We were vulnerable in the public spaces—we were even attacked there before. Why did no one think—"

" 'Cause the senate isn't used to feeling vulnerable. You know how long it's been since anyone challenged them?"

"The Circle challenged them," I said, thinking of the coup that Jonas, the current head of the Silver Circle, had pulled on Saunders, its corrupt old leader. The battle had played out here, with the two sides fighting each other in a miniature civil war. It had been terrifying.

At least I'd thought so at the time; I had a new definition now.

"Yeah, but that was played off as a fluke," Marco said. "Rivalry within the Circle that could have taken place anywhere. Saunders just happened to be here."

"And now?"

"Now the senate got hit two times in twenty-four hours, here and at the consul's own home last night."

"So they're taking action."

"Oh, I think you can safely assume that," Marco said dryly. "The other side just gave 'em two black eyes in a row. They just made the senate—the goddamn *senate*—look bad. Worse, they made 'em look—"

"Weak."

He nodded. There was no sign of humor on that big, handsome face, because there was no bigger insult in the vampire world, where everything was based on power. *Everything.*

Life revolved around the power you possessed, to protect your family, your wealth, and your position; the power of your alliances, which allowed you to collectively influence a larger segment of vamp society than you could have done alone; and the power of the senate, the pinnacle of vamp hierarchy, under which you and your whole society functioned.

And you respected that hierarchy, even when you didn't like it. Even when you chafed under the restrictions it put on you and your business and your personal desires. Even when you hated the senate itself, you stayed firmly in line.

Because you feared them more.

Because they had power almost beyond your comprehension. Because they made anyone who forgot that very, very sorry or very, very dead. Because ruling with an iron fist wasn't the exception; it was the rule, and you knew the rule and feared the rule and *kept* the rule, their rule, their law, because anything else was unthinkable.

At least it had been, until today.

I didn't know exactly what the senate would do now; I'd never seen them challenged like this. No one had. But I knew what a master vampire would do with his back against the wall, his power and authority in question, and his enemies gunning for him and everything he held dear.

And the senate had many, many more resources than any single vamp. So whatever form it took, their response would be big, it would be swift, and it would be vicious. I stared at the darkened Dante's sign, what little I could see of it, and a shudder went through me.

Marco hugged my shoulders again. "Come on, there's been enough of that for one day. You need to eat—"

"I'm not hungry."

"Well, I am," he lied, "and I'm going to order the biggest steak I can find. If you're nice, I might give you a bite."

I smiled slightly.

"And in the meantime, I thought you might like to see someone."

"Someone?"

Marco looked at me mockingly. "No, you don't need to eat at all."

"What?" I blinked at him. And then I remembered. "Rhea!"

He grinned at me, the cigar clamped firmly between big white teeth.

"Yes," I said. "Yes, I'd like to see her."

"Thought so."

He pulled me out the door.

The hallway outside felt odd, too, although this time, I knew exactly why. "Where are all the cots?"

It should have been full of them, or else they should have been scattered in my bedroom, tripping me up on the way to the balcony. I had a couple dozen initiates who all needed a place to sleep, which was why this place had been lousy with cots lately—in the bedrooms, living room, and lounge. Or, when the girls were up, stacked in the corners of the hallway so we had room to walk.

But now there was nothing.

"We made other arrangements," Marco said, lips twitching.

"What other arrangements?"

"You know, that can probably wait."

"Marco." I grabbed a forearm the size of my leg. Or maybe a little bigger, 'cause skinny legs have always been a bane of my existence. *"Where is my court?"*

"They're fine," he told me, reassuringly. "And they're close," he added, when I still looked alarmed, because my court managed to get in almost as much trouble as I did.

Then he shushed me, having just cracked open the door to the guest bedroom down the hall.

It was dark, too, but the drapes were open on a wall of windows, showing glimmers of the golden city beyond. It was also empty, except for a lump under the bedspread and a vamp in a chair. The vamp was reading a book, because to his eyes the room was perfectly well lit. But he looked up when we peered inside.

I couldn't tell what the book was, but the vamp was Rico, dark good looks showing to advantage in jeans and a tight white tee, and raising a finger to his lips before we said anything.

"How is she?" I whispered, to either of them, because they could both hear me just fine.

"Better," Marco said, after a pause, probably to ask Rico mentally. "Doc was here earlier, said she's gonna be out of it for a few days, and easily winded for a week after that, while her body replaces the blood she lost. That bastard of a mage did a number on her."

"He didn't," I said, my eyes on Rhea.

"What?"

"The mage. He wanted—that is, he was trying to trade her for Lizzie—"

"We know. We got that much from those reporters before they ran off, to file who knows what kind of stories. And the rest from the witches—"

"Witches?" I looked up. "What witches?"

"That's how they got her," Rico said softly, putting his book down and coming over.

"That is not how they got her," Marco said, quietly vicious. "That's how they *tried*. They got her because of the damn Circle—"

"You can't trust a mage," Rico agreed.

"Would someone please tell me what you're talking about?" I whispered.

Rico glanced at me. "We were out of it this morning, until the master woke us up and sent us the power to go after you. But, apparently, there were some of the Circle's men here last night—"

"Jonas brought them."

"Of course he did," Marco said, in a savage undertone. "He's been trying to get you, and your court, under Circle control ever since he got back into power. Figures that the first time we're vulnerable—"

I shook my head. "It wasn't like that. He came to see me alone, and only called them in later, after he found everybody unconscious. Except for Rhea and Tami, who were freaking out—"

"She's good at that," Rico said, rubbing his jaw.

"Rhea?"

"Tami. I thought she was supposed to be your housekeeper, but I'm thinking you should recruit her as a bodyguard instead. She has a mean right cross."

"She's not my housekeeper. She's my . . . organizer." 'Cause God knew I could use one. "And why did she slug you?"

"My fault." The dark eyes smiled. "When the master

woke us up, it was a little . . . abrupt. I think I startled her."

"He jumped up swinging, and she swung back, knocking him on his ass," Marco translated, making me bite my lip. Because Rico was the most obviously badass of my bodyguards, the leather-wearing, tat-sporting, gun-carrying one, when most of the others wore Armani like their master and debated things like plain or tassel-front loafers.

I doubted Rico had a pair of loafers, or if he did, I'd never seen them.

I also doubted that he'd ever been decked by a slim, pretty woman before. But then, Tami was pretty badass herself. And she didn't need leather to prove it.

She had a belt in jujitsu, the same color as her weave, that did that for her.

"I'm sure she's sorry," I told Rico, who was openly grinning now.

"She promised me some cookies," he agreed.

"I've had her cookies. I'd take a belt for them any day," Marco said, but he was still looking at me. Because he had the patience of Job, and the stubbornness, too, and I doubted he was going to let this go. He took his job as chief bodyguard seriously, and was not a fan of the Circle.

At all.

"Jonas said he called for backup so my court wouldn't be without protection while he figured out what was going on," I explained.

"And you believe that?" An eyebrow the size of a caterpillar went north.

I clasped my arms around me again, and told myself it was because I was chilly. The vamps had adjusted the temperature to compensate for all the extra body heat we'd had lately, and without it, it was verging on cold in here. "I don't *dis*believe him. He said he wants to work with us—"

"He wants to work with *you*. I think he could do without us just fine."

I sighed. "Look, I know his attitude could use an overhaul—"

"It's not just his attitude," Rico said. "He took the girl, didn't he?"

I frowned. "What girl?"

"The one who drugged you yesterday."

"What?"

"He took Lizzie," Marco confirmed.

"What?"

He nodded. "Turns out, you couldn't have traded her if you'd wanted to. The Circle's guys took her before we were awake to stop them—"

"Took her *where*?"

"Nobody knows," Rico said. "Jonas called a few hours ago, to check on Rhea—who is his daughter, I understand?"

I nodded, frowning.

"But it was a short call and the only information we gained is that he's back in Britain. Where the girl is . . ." Rico shook his head.

"She's probably with him," Marco said. "You know damn well that's why he left his men here last night. And why they didn't object to Rhea going out this morning. They probably saw it as a golden opportunity to make off with Lizzie before Cassie got back."

I didn't say anything to that. How could I? It was probably the truth.

I'd helped to put Jonas back in power, foolishly thinking we'd be allies. So far, his definition of that term seemed a little different from mine. And now he had Lizzie, and I didn't know where, but I needed to.

Because I wasn't the only one looking for her.

"Why did Rhea go out?" I asked, trying to get this straight in a head that was still half-asleep. "And what witches?"

"They were with us in Augustine's," Rico said. "Don't you remember?"

"Sort of." I vaguely recalled some women pouring into the ruined shop along with the vamps.

"You were pretty out of it, so no wonder," Marco said. "But if they hadn't shown up, we wouldn't have had a way past the wards on that safe, since the guys supposedly manning the front desk had supposedly fled. . . ." His jaw tightened. "It could have been bad."

"But what were they doing here?"

"They were worried about Rhea," Rico said.

"That's how the dark mage fuckwads got her," Marco added. "She gets a call—while we're still out of it, mind—and the damn Circle just lets her leave! They didn't even volunteer to go with her. They sent an untrained nineteen-year-old acolyte off *on her own*—"

"To go *where*?" I asked. "Why would she go anywhere?"

"Oh, that's the best part," Marco said. "That's the part I'm going to bring up the next time Jonas, or any of those Circle bastards, says a goddamn *thing* about us guarding the Pythia—"

"She received a phone call from someone claiming to be with one of the covens," Rico explained, glancing at his friend. "Saying they were upset that there weren't any coven girls in your court other than her, and they felt slighted."

I frowned. "But that's their choice. The covens don't usually send—"

"They didn't send 'em this time!" Marco said, loudly enough that Rhea stirred uneasily.

"Careful," Rico said, glancing back at her.

"Sorry." Marco looked at him sardonically. "Didn't mean to step on any toes."

"Just as long as you don't step on hers."

Marco's smile grew. "Wouldn't dream of touching your little charge—"

"She isn't my charge, but I will defend her," Rico said, watching to see that Rhea settled back down again. And then he glanced at me. "As I would any of your court."

"That's . . . good," I said, looking between the two of them, wondering what I'd missed. And then deciding I had enough to worry about already. "So one of the covens called Rhea?"

"No, one of the covens did not," Marco said flatly. "Some woman working with the Black Circle did, and the damn Silver let Rhea walk right out of here, on her own, to meet with them and take charge of the handful of little girls they were supposedly sending."

"And they grabbed her," I said, my jaw tightening.

"And they grabbed her," Marco agreed. "But luckily, she'd realized that she was going to be a little late—a couple of the kids have a cold, and she wanted to stop and get some medicine—and she called a friend of hers to tell her that."

"A friend?"

"In the same coven," Rico explained. "The one that had supposedly called her."

"The original call went through the hotel switchboard," Marco added. "So she didn't have a number to use to call 'em back. But she thinks, no problem, I'll just call my friend and she can let 'em know."

"But her friend didn't know anything about it," I guessed.

"Her friend wasn't even awake," Rico said. "But when she did get up a short time later, and received the message, she realized that Rhea might be in trouble."

Marco nodded. "She hadn't heard anything about any coven girls joining the court, and she made a few calls. Found out that nobody else knew anything about it, either. So she called Rhea back, but nobody answered, so she tried to call us, but the switchboard wouldn't let her through—"

"Then how did the Black Circle get through?"

The two vamps exchanged a look.

"How did they get through?" I asked again, a little more forcefully.

"We had the switchboard put a pass code on all your calls," Marco told me.

"And?"

"And only a couple people had it," Rico said softly. "They found one of them in his car this afternoon."

"In his . . ." I trailed off, but Rico didn't elaborate.

"Don't soft-pedal it," Marco said. "She's not one of the kids."

"I know that."

"Do you? Then tell her what happened." He looked at me. "They found him in his trunk. He'd been tortured, presumably until he gave them the code, and then locked in his car and left to bake to death in the heat."

"That was unnecessary," Rico said, frowning.

"No, it wasn't. This is war; Cassie needs to know the truth."

"And when she wakes up, will you tell *her* the truth?" Rico asked, glancing at Rhea.

"She already knows," I said, looking at the small lump in the bed. And then up to meet Rico's dark eyes. "That mage didn't slit Rhea's throat. She did it herself, so he would have nothing left to trade. She knows, Rico." I turned and went back to my room.

Chapter Thirteen

I ended up in the bathroom because I needed to be alone and it was the one place the vamps wouldn't follow me. I loved them like family—hell, they *were* my family, or as much of one as I'd ever had—but they weren't human. Not anymore. And sometimes they showed that in odd ways, like failing to understand the need for solitude.

Vamps didn't have solitude. From the moment they were Changed, they never had it again. I often wondered why they didn't go insane—more of them, that is. The constant buzzing in their heads, all those voices, all those thoughts, *all the time*—

I shuddered.

I could hardly stand being in my own head these days, which was getting cluttered with voices, too. Voices of all the people I hadn't been able to help, because I hadn't acted fast enough, hadn't planned well enough, wasn't strong enough. It was getting to be a long list. So many voices . . .

Except for the one I really needed to hear.

I sat against the side of the tub, pulled my legs up, and concentrated.

It didn't help that I didn't know how to do this. That, until a few days ago, I hadn't even known that I *could* do this. I'd thought of the Pythian power as, well, power, some bit of Apollo's strength that he'd given to the priestesses he'd claimed as his own.

And that was where it had started. But during all those thousands of years out of touch with its former master, it had become something more: an independent entity that guarded the timeline with the help of the Pythias it chose.

Like it had chosen me, but was probably regretting it, because I hadn't understood that we were supposed to be a team.

Until recently, when Rhea had given me a little Pythia 101, and I'd started listening for what my power was trying to say.

"Can I go back?" I whispered, into the silence. "Can I . . . *fix this*?"

Because I could. I hadn't had the strength for a time shift this morning, but now . . . I could go back, I could call the Circle, I could have them waiting when the dark mages showed up. I could talk to Rhea, tell her to ignore that phone call. I could visit the desk clerk, warn him that his job was about to get him killed.

And I could do it all in five minutes. Hell, less than that, if I was lucky. And then the deaths, the pain, the suffering—all of it would be gone, erased like it had never happened.

Because for them, it never would have.

But my power didn't seem to like that idea. Every time I thought about hitting rewind, all I got was a rising tide of black panic. My power wasn't human and didn't speak to me in English, or at all as far as I could tell. But I didn't think that was a yes.

"If we're partners, *talk to me*," I whispered. *"Why can't I do this?"*

Nothing.

It had been the same at the consul's last night, but at least then I'd thought I understood. The supernatural community was fractured, with the Circle, the senate, the demons, the covens—basically, every single group I knew of—off doing their own thing. Some of them had alliances, yes, but they were more on paper than anything else. Old hatreds ran deep, and old distrusts deeper. No one wanted to work together, not even now.

Until last night, when the bad guys gate-crashed a party at the senate leader's house, attended by the top dogs of most of the different groups. All of whom suddenly found themselves fighting side by side. I'd thought maybe that was what the power was trying to tell me: that they'd needed the lesson. It might have been costly, but in the end it might be far costlier if they never learned to work together.

That had made sense.

This didn't.

"They died because of me; they trusted me. *Please . . .*"

Nothing. Not even the faint, glimmering strands that had shown up briefly in my mental landscape last night, much less the sparkling ocean of power I sometimes glimpsed when I concentrated hard enough. Instead, the ocean I saw tonight was dark and heavy, with storm-tossed crests above deep blue depths that seemed to go down forever.

It didn't want me going back.

It really, really didn't.

I knew that in my gut, felt it in every fiber of my being, just like I felt the almost overwhelming urge to do it anyway.

Because I could override it. Somehow I *knew* that. What I didn't know was why it thought I shouldn't.

And that was a problem, since according to Rhea, the Pythian power used my clairvoyance to assess risks and outcomes. It was why I hadn't been plagued with the terrifying visions I'd had most of my life since becoming Pythia. My power had co-opted much of my clairvoyance, using it to poke around in time and see what was going on.

And for some reason, it had determined that today's disaster had been necessary.

But I couldn't see it.

"Show me, then. Show me *something.*"

But all I got back was more of that deep, dark ocean, mysterious, infinite, infuriating. And alien. Maybe too alien to see a handful of human lives as important. To something able to see the whole span of time, the whole extent of human civilization, maybe they hadn't been anything but specks on a map: just some old guy, just some front-desk flunky, just some pie-obsessed girl.

But to me they'd been brave and resourceful and innocent, and they'd deserved better. They'd deserved a lot better, and I should have been able to give it to them. But I couldn't and I didn't even know why, might never know why, and I *hated* this job, hated having so much responsibility—for people's *lives*—and never enough power or strength to go with it.

"*Show me*! You can't just say no and that's *it*. I'm not your slave!"

The words echoed off the tile box of a bathroom, because I hadn't bothered to whisper that time. But it didn't matter. The answer was the same.

"*Goddamn it!*" I yelled, and threw a slipper at the door, because it was the only thing I could reach.

And had it caught by a hand the size of a catcher's mitt.

I couldn't see anything but the hand and part of an arm, because the rest of the body was still outside. But I didn't need to. It looked like Lou Ferrigno and Arnold Schwarzenegger had had a baby—a baby that liked tacky golf shirts—so I was pretty sure I knew who it was.

I supposed I should have felt privileged that Marco had left me alone this long to wallow in stupid human angst. Because that was how the vamps tended to view stuff like this, as some weird human habit. They didn't angst. If something bothered them, they ripped its limbs off until it stopped.

And they were right—okay, not about limb thing, but about the part where this was a stupid waste of time that wouldn't help.

I just wished I knew what would.

"Is it safe to come in?" Marco asked, sounding muffled because he was still talking through the door.

"Are you really worried?" I asked dryly.

"Well, you have another slipper." The big head poked into the room and eyed me. And the bone-dry tub. And the fact that I was still dressed in the rumpled T-shirt I'd slept in.

Then he came in and sat down by the tub, too. "You okay?"

"Yeah."

"You sure?"

I didn't look at him. I didn't want to do this. I didn't want a heart-to-heart or cheering up or whatever this was supposed to be.

I didn't need comforting; I needed answers. "I survived."

"That's not what I asked."

"Marco, I'm fine. All right?"

"All right."

We sat there awhile, the girl in the crumpled tee with naked toes peeking out from underneath, and the giant of a guy in Ferragamos, staring at our feet in silence.

Marco *was* the loafer kind. Today's had tassels, to match the golf theme. I hadn't known they made them in size eighty-nine or whatever, but I supposed so. Of course, if you were having them made to order, I guessed they made them any damn way you told them to.

"It's just not every day that the Black Circle comes to call," he said idly, looking at the ceiling.

I closed my eyes.

I debated getting up, but it wouldn't do any good. He'd just follow me from room to room, like a puppy. A well-meaning, truck-sized, relentless puppy who was going to lick my face and make me feel better, whether I liked it or not.

"The Black Circle didn't do this," I said.

There was silence for another moment. "You *sure* you're okay?"

I turned to look at him. "Do you know why they're called the Black Circle, Marco?"

"A jab at the Silver, I always thought. Or maybe they're not that creative."

"Maybe. But it fits. They work in darkness, in shadows; nobody knows who they are; nobody sees their faces. Tony's mages—the ones I grew up with?" He nodded. "They used to talk about them all the time. One joked that he'd like to join up, but didn't know where to put in an application."

"Rumor is, they find you," Marco said, sounding amused.

I waited.

Because Marco wasn't stupid, especially about war. He'd started out as a kid in ancient Rome, where it had literally been deified, then been a soldier for a while, and finally a gladiator. And as a vamp he'd mostly been a bodyguard for his various masters for the last two thousand years, fighting their stupid squabbles until he'd been adopted into Mircea's crazy clan.

And ended up with me.

So yeah, Marco knew war. In all its guises and permutations. Which was why I wasn't surprised to hear him continue after a moment. "Yet they attack us in broad daylight, when they had to know they'd be photographed a couple hundred times before they left the casino."

"The power of modern surveillance."

He shot me a look. "Did they start out wearing glamouries?"

"Yeah, but they dropped them before the battle started. Not wanting the power drain, I guess."

"Better that than having every Circle roughneck in town on your tail an hour later! Unless they planned to level this place, and thought it didn't matter."

"Or unless it wasn't their idea."

Sharp, dark eyes narrowed on my face. "They looked pretty enthusiastic to me. We tried to get to you through the lobby before safecracking the hard way, but it wasn't happening. They were everywhere. And throwing spells that forced the witches to waste most of their energy shielding, or we'd have all been puddles of flesh on the floor. Those weren't flunkies, Cassie. They had some power behind them."

"They were Black Circle, yes, but they were foot soldiers. They weren't leading this."

Marco studied me for a moment, frowning. "I know I'm gonna regret asking this—"

"Ares."

The frown tipped over into a scowl. "I know you got him on the brain. After everything that's happened lately, I don't blame you. But Ares *isn't here*—"

"Not in the flesh."

"As opposed to?"

I hesitated, because Marco didn't like hearing about some of my . . . weirder . . . abilities. None of the vamps did. They liked thinking of me as the master's little human girlfriend who just had *really* bad luck sometimes, rather than facing what was actually going on.

Couldn't say I blamed them.

But I also couldn't explain this without getting a little spooky. Luckily, Marco dealt with that sort of thing better than most of the guys. Marco dealt with everything better than most of the guys.

"I tried to possess a dark mage," I told him. "The one in charge."

"You *what*?"

"I was out of power and we were about to be overrun. I thought, if I could take control of the leader, I could make him order the attack to stop—"

"And you thought they'd listen? A bunch of overpowered nutjobs hopped up on dark magic who were about to *win*?"

"And who were about to be overrun by the Circle." I saw his expression. "I know, but that's what I planned to tell them. That the Circle had gotten here faster than expected, and they had about a minute before they showed up in force. I hoped they'd scatter—some of them, maybe all of them—and by the time they realized it was a lie, maybe it wouldn't be."

Marco just looked at me.

"It wasn't like I had a lot of options!"

He looked like he was going to say something, but changed his mind at the last minute. "But you didn't get in."

"No, I got in. But it didn't help, because someone had beaten me to it."

The big head tilted. "Meaning?"

"Meaning it's hard to possess someone when they're already being possessed by someone else. There was another spirit in there."

"And you think it was Ares."

"I *know* it was. He was possessing that mage. Or doing something to that mage, I don't know. But he was *in there*. The way he felt, what he did—it had to be him. Which explains the attack, why it was his style, not theirs. His impatience, his arrogance, not theirs!"

"And now they're dead, and he's still out there smelling like a rose," Marco summed up. "Is that it?"

I nodded.

"And doing what? Looking for a new body?"

I hugged my knees. "I don't know. I don't know how much he can do, from the other side of the barrier. I don't even know if it was a real possession. He seemed to have . . . limitations."

"Like what?"

"Like it took him a second to see me, when I first moved inside. Not a long delay, hardly anything really, but—"

"But more than you'd expect from a god."

"Yeah. And then he attacked, but Mircea confused him enough for me to get away—"

"Wait. Mircea took on a *god*?"

"He didn't tell you?"

Marco stared at me for a second, and then burst out laughing. "No."

"What's funny?"

"I called him earlier—our way, you know?" He tapped the side of his head. "And he told me to switch to a phone *'cause he had a headache.* I thought he was joking!"

"He wasn't joking."

"Damn." Marco shook his head, still grinning.

And yeah, I supposed it would sound funny.

If you hadn't been there.

Eating, he was eating you. He was—

My hands started to shake and I shoved them under my armpits. "It, uh, it also took him longer to react to some of the things . . . that happened in the fight . . . than I'd expect from the god of war."

"Maybe he's not so good at this possession thing," Marco said, eyeing me. "You know it squicks out us normal types, right?"

"I'm being serious!"

"I know. That's what scares me."

"Nothing scares you," I said as one of his arms went around me, pulling me close.

And damn, it was *huge*. I didn't understand how some guys got so big. It was almost like they were another species.

Of course, Marco sort of was, but it didn't matter. He

felt solid, strong, reassuring. I might have even leaned on him a little. Maybe I needed a bit more of that comfort stuff than I'd thought.

"A lot scares me," Marco said. "Anybody says they're never scared is an idiot. But I've learned a few things over the years."

"Like what?"

"Like, if you don't want to burn out, you can't live here."

I frowned. "In Vegas?"

"No, not in Vegas! Although that probably doesn't help," he added wryly. "No, *here*. In this bathroom, huddled against this tub. Here with your hair falling in your face and your body shaking in memory—"

"That's not what I'm doing."

"—and from hunger, 'cause you're punishing yourself for not saving everything—"

"That's not what I'm doing!"

"—when you saved *some*thing. You saved a whole lot of something that wouldn't be here if you hadn't practically wrecked yourself!"

I got up. I suddenly wasn't feeling so comforted anymore. "So you're saying what? Be happy I survived and just forget everything else?"

"Not forget. Lessons won that hard you hold on to. But there's a difference between remembering shit when you need to and living in it. You do the job when you got the job; then it's done. Ever wonder why soldiers just back from the field are laughing and talking and playing cards instead of sitting in a corner reliving it all?"

"Because they're *crazy*?"

"No, because that's how you avoid the crazy. You do the job when you got the job; the rest of the time, you live."

I sat on the edge of the tub. Yeah, like I'd ever done that. Like I knew *how* to do that.

I grew up at a vampire's court, one of the ones where you didn't live; you survived. And even after I fled Tony's little house of horrors, it hadn't been much better. I'd thought I was getting out of a cage, only to learn that I'd just exchanged it for a different one, one of my own making, one where I hunkered down every night and hoped I didn't wake up to his boys busting down the door.

And then one day they did, but thanks to a warning, I wasn't there. And after that came the senate, "protecting" me as long as I did what it wanted. And the Circle, which was pretty much offering the same deal. And here I was, caught in the middle, still just trying to survive and to help everyone else survive, because that's what I knew; that's what I did.

That *was* what I called living.

"Cassie?"

"I'm . . ." I looked up, and met somber dark eyes. And for some reason, found myself telling the truth. "I'm not sure I know how to do that."

"Then maybe you need to be reminded. Get some clothes on and come upstairs."

"Upstairs?" I looked at the ceiling in confusion. "Marco . . . we don't *have* an upstairs."

He stuck his cigar back between his teeth. "We do now."

Chapter Fourteen

Marco left and I eased into shorts and a T-shirt, checking out the real estate in the process. Which wasn't looking so good. Which was kind of looking like I'd taken up roller derby, and sucked at it. But the parts were all there and they worked, more or less.

The less was an inch-long gash in my side, which was missing the concrete scalpel that had caused it, but had gained some stitches. It was not happy. And neither was I, when I inadvertently pressed too hard when rebandaging it and saw the room swim before my eyes.

I grabbed the dresser and hung on for a minute, dizzy and more than a little nauseated. It wasn't just the pain. It was the constant stress, the I-just-got-up-and-want-to-crawl-back-into-bed exhaustion, the utter insanity of the last few weeks but especially this morning. It was *everything*, and it hit all at once.

Great.

Perfect, even.

"Armored warrior . . . canopy of stars . . . must unify . . ."

The words would have been too faint to hear, except that my head had come to rest on the dresser, right in front of the source. I pushed around some clothes and found what I'd expected: a ratty pack of tarot cards. The girls must have been playing with them, before Tami found out and put them in here, because I never left them open.

For exactly this reason, I thought, as one shot out of the pack and hit me in the face.

It was still muttering to itself, as they all did unless the flap was closed. My old governess had a witch enchant them for a long-ago birthday present to me. I hadn't needed the explanations in years, but the charm was still going strong. Meaning that they enthusiastically informed me of their interpretation every time I pulled one out, even talking over each other when necessary.

Every time until tonight.

Tarot cards can be read two ways—okay, more than that, depending on which cards are drawn in a reading along with them. But mostly, there are two: upright and reversed. Good or bad, yin or yang, a positive spin on upcoming events . . . or a warning.

Or, in this case, neither of the above. Because the little guy in the fancy chariot had hit my nose and bounced off. Landing neither upright nor reversed, but on his side.

It lay there, vibrating slightly as it wrestled with itself, its grimy surface almost managing to obscure a bunch of symbols I'd seen before, and seen recently. There was the moon, my mother's icon, on his shoulder armor. There was the sun, Apollo's emblem, emblazoned on his chest. There were stars on the canopy fluttering over his head, like the ones on the card I'd drawn at the beginning of the odyssey to find Pritkin, and which had promised a long, tough road ahead.

I'd had no idea.

And finally, there was the little warrior himself, mostly silent at the moment because of the conflicting meanings of his two natures.

There are a lot of ways to interpret the chariot, and the card usually burbles on happily about all of them. But at its heart, it's a simple contrast: victory or defeat. Or, as it was now, a battle undecided, hovering on a knife's edge, able to tip either way.

I flicked it with a finger, pushing it upright. And heard what almost sounded like a sigh of relief from the little dude before he started telling me all about victory. Yeah, I thought, staring at him. But was it mine, or was it Ares'?

But on that, the card was silent.

I never made it upstairs. By the time I'd gotten myself presentable, I'd also received a text from the guy with my ticket to ride. Or, at least, my ticket to sixth-century Wales.

That was a good thing, because I obviously wasn't going anywhere without it. I barely made it to an apartment on the other end of the Strip, less than a mile away. And even then, I didn't stick the landing.

"Cassie!" Something clattered into what sounded like a sink, but I couldn't tell because I'd hit my knee and it was *that* knee, the I-crawled-on-shrapnel-across-a-blood-streaked-floor knee, and the pain was enough to momentarily blind me.

"You okay?" a familiar voice asked, closer now, and sounding concerned. Probably because I'd just screamed like a banshee.

That's another thing the movies get wrong. Why is the hero always so damn manly? Why is it not okay to scream a little when it feels like you just shattered a kneecap? Why are you supposed to suck it up and soldier on, without even a curse or two? Is that *reasonable?*

I must have said part of that out loud, because my companion sighed. "No, it's not reasonable," he agreed. And the next thing I knew, I was being hauled over to a black leather sofa that all but screamed bachelor pad.

That was fair, since the guy who owned it was a confirmed old bachelor.

Well, okay, not exactly old. When he had hair—which wasn't often—it was still dark, and the chocolate skin was mostly unlined. The handsome features looked fortyish, although it was hard to say. The war mage profession aged a person almost as much as being Pritkin's friend, and Caleb was both.

Lately he'd been mine, too, although he'd probably prefer not to be, considering the stuff I got him into. But there weren't a lot of war mages I could trust, especially senior ones who might know a thing or two. And who might be willing to keep said things from his boss.

"Do you have it?" I slurred. I'd planned on a few pleasantries first—hi, how are you, did your day suck as hard as mine—but right now I just really wanted—

"Thank God." I grabbed the little triangular bottle

Caleb pulled out of his jeans and downed a third of its contents. It tasted utterly, utterly vile, the kind that makes you shiver and shake and have to choke it down through sheer force of will.

But oh, it was sweet once you did.

I collapsed back against the sofa, gasping.

The Tears of Apollo was a potion designed to help the Pythias access their power. It worked by increasing our stamina—always a problem, since the power was virtually endless, but our ability to channel it wasn't. And channeling stuff meant for a god when you weren't one was a real bitch.

But with the Tears, we could not only hold out for longer; we could use more of the power at a time, allowing our spells to have more oomph behind them. That was why I needed it, in order to shift an impossible-sounding fifteen hundred years into the past after Pritkin. It was also why the competition had been after it last night, when they sicced Lizzie on me.

Agnes' old acolytes had only been given a narrow stream of the power for training, but access was access. They'd hoped that the Tears would widen the flow enough to rival a Pythia's power, allowing them to shift Ares past my mother's barrier. And it might have, except for one small problem.

They didn't have any.

The Tears was only used by one person, so potion stores didn't carry it and potion brewers didn't know it. The only people who did were the Circle, who traditionally brewed it for the Pythias, and the Pythias themselves. And the vampire senate, who weren't supposed to have it or even know about it, but since when had that ever stopped them?

The senate had three bottles originally, which seemed to be what a batch made. They'd acquired it back when I first got this job, because they'd had a little time errand they wanted me to do and assumed I'd need the help. That had left two bottles up for grabs, and Amelie—the strongest of the rogues—had grabbed them last night.

And had promptly gotten power drunk as all hell, not being used to that much access all at once. Partly as a result, she'd gone on a tear at the consul's house, instead of just shifting Ares over immediately. That had allowed me time to catch up with her, and to take the last bottle after our duel.

And this was it. The last bottle the senate had, and quite possibly the last bottle anywhere. Which was why I'd dropped it off with Caleb before I went after Rosier, hoping that one of his contacts could reproduce it.

Really hoping.

"You okay?" Caleb asked. I realized I'd closed my eyes at some point, and opened them to see the patented war mage scowl.

"Was your friend able to help?" I asked thickly.

The scowl ramped up a notch, and he sat back on his heels. "Yes and no. The good news is, he can make a pretty good guess at the contents. The bad news, like I warned you last night, is that an ingredient list is useless without the recipe."

"But if he knows what's in it—"

"It's not just about what's in it. It's about brewing time, temperature, method of combining ingredients—a hundred variables. Combine them one way, you get magic. Combine them another . . . a really expensive sludge."

"So he can't duplicate it?" I asked, to be sure.

"No."

"So how do I get more?"

"You ask the old man. It's your potion, Cassie. You're the Pythia—"

He broke off when I sat up and put my head in my hands, not sure if I wanted to laugh or cry. I was Pythia when other people wanted something or found it convenient, but when the shoe was on the other foot? Not so much.

"Do you have any coffee?" I asked, after a minute. "Tea? Something with caffeine?"

Caleb snorted. "Not what you'd consider coffee. Not if you've been drinking that nuclear waste John mainlines all day."

"I don't drink Pritkin's coffee and he doesn't eat my doughnuts. We have a deal."

"I'd hate to see the doughnut John would eat," Caleb

said, standing up. And circling around the little half wall that separated the open-plan kitchen from the open-plan living room.

He brewed stuff while I watched the Strip through the semicircle of windows to the left of the couch. And slowly began to feel stronger and more clearheaded. And lighter, like my limbs no longer weighed half a ton each. Even the pain from all those little, and not so little, wounds didn't seem to matter so much anymore. They still hurt, but I could ignore them.

For the moment. But experience had proven that one bottle of the Circle's special brew wasn't going to last me for long. And without it, in my current state, I wasn't going to be much use to anybody.

In a minute, Caleb was back with something that smelled good—genuinely good.

"You look surprised," he said.

I stuck my nose in the mug. "What's in this?"

"Amaretto."

I looked up hopefully. "Like those little cookies?"

Caleb sighed and got back to his feet.

"And maybe a sandwich?" I turned around and put my good knee on the couch so I could see him. The smell of that coffee had me suddenly starving. "Do you have sandwich stuff?"

"I don't cook."

"Making a sandwich isn't cooking. And what do you eat?"

Caleb looked at me over a muscular shoulder. "Take-out. This is Vegas."

"But you live here. Doesn't takeout get old?"

"No." He rooted around in the fridge. "Fish tacos?"

"Sounds good."

He stuck a nose in the container and made a face. "It wouldn't if you smelled them."

They hit the garbage can.

"Don't you have anyone to cook for you? A girl-friend?"

"War mage," he reminded me, sniffing a take-out bag. And rearing back, his eyes watering. "I gotta clean out this fridge."

"So war mages don't get the women?" I asked, only half joking. Because Caleb was a damn good catch. Handsome, brave, a world traveler—more than one world now—and judging by the apartment, he wasn't broke. But if there were any feminine touches around here, I didn't see them.

Even the artwork on the walls were line drawings, black on white and black-framed, more architectural than strictly beautiful. Sort of like the man himself: solid, straightforward, but more interesting than you'd expect when you got to know him.

"Women like security," he told me. "Safety—"

"What's safer than being married to a war mage?"

"—for their man, as well as for themselves. They don't like going to bed not knowing if he's gonna be there when they wake up, or if he's ever gonna be there again."

"Cops have wives," I pointed out. "And soldiers—"

"And they face some of the same kind of thing. But it's worse for us. Some of the stuff we work on . . . they can't be told what happened to us, when we don't come back. They may never be told. It's . . . difficult."

"So war mages don't settle down?"

"Some do. Some marry other war mages. Some get divorced and drink too much." He shrugged.

"Makes me wonder why anybody does the job at all."

"I've often thought the same thing about Pythias."

I made a face.

And then made a different one when a plate was handed over the counter.

It was a retrospective of Caleb's weekly intake. But since he wasn't as much of a health nut as Pritkin, there was actual *food* on there: broccoli beef still in its little carton, potato salad, dim sum balls stuffed with barbecued pork, chicken shawarma . . . and some of the requested amaretto cookies.

I dug in and Caleb watched me over the counter while sipping his own mug of coffee.

"So why can't you just ask the old man for the potion?" he finally said.

I swallowed. "Because I've tried trusting Jonas lately, and it hasn't gone well. I thought we had an understanding, but then he snuck Lizzie away this morning, before I got back, so now I don't know."

"You could ask him. See what he says."

"Yeah, I could," I agreed, around a mouthful of chicken. "Only I already did that a couple days ago, and didn't get anywhere. He claimed he didn't have any more, and maybe he doesn't. Or maybe he does, and he doesn't want to give it to me. He's afraid I'm going to go off somewhere and get myself killed, like I can't do that here!"

There was silence for another minute while I shoveled food into my face. It finally stretched long enough that I looked up and found Caleb regarding me moodily. "What?"

"You won't like it."

"Well, there's a switch."

He sighed and ran a hand over his head. It was the cue ball look today, so the recessed lights were shining on a slick dome that looked like it had too much to think about. At least if the wrinkles on the forehead were anything to go by.

"You look like a good gust of wind would blow you away," he finally said.

"Caleb—"

"And I've seen that look, all right? I've seen it a lot. I know war mages who would have broken from some of the stuff you've been up to, and I strongly suspect I don't know the half of it. Maybe Jonas sees the same thing, that you need a rest—"

"Yeah, I'll take a few days off, hang by the pool."

"I'm serious—"

"So am I," I said, a little sharper than necessary. Because how did he not get this? "I take a vacation, and Pritkin will be dead and Ares will be back, because I have two rogues still alive and I don't know where either of them is!"

"Two? I thought Lizzie—"

"Two. Jo Zirimis is the other, and she isn't even in custody. My power is ignoring her, acting like she doesn't exist, but she *does*—"

"Then why is the Black Circle targeting Lizzie?"

"Because they don't know where Jo is, either! Nobody

knows where she is—or when," I added darkly, because one of my now deceased rogues had claimed that she was going after the same godly weapon that I was.

But if Jo was trying to shift back fifteen hundred years, she was going to be trying awhile. I was assuming that was why my power was ignoring her, that she was shifting in baby steps, ten or fifteen years at a time, whatever an acolyte's thin stream of access would allow. And not getting anywhere. That or she was dead, too, because time travel was damn dangerous, as I ought to know. But that still left me with Lizzie to worry about, and I *was* worried.

"I need to know where Lizzie is, Caleb. I need to know what Jonas did with her, if she's secure—"

"I'm sure she is—"

"Are you?" I swallowed pork. "Because I'm not. Jonas took her away, and didn't even bother to tell me where—"

"You just said you weren't there."

"—or to tell anyone else! Or to wait for me to come back—"

"And do what with her? You don't have the facilities—"

"And he does?"

"He has more than you. And maybe he thought that's what you'd want—"

"So he asks me!"

I glared up at him, and for a minute he glared back. War mages—some war mages—tended to be fanatically loyal, especially to a guy they'd followed for decades. It was why Jonas' crazy coup of the Silver Circle had worked; a lot of mages had chosen to follow him or to just putz around on the sidelines rather than support his corrupt successor. At the time I'd been grateful for that, since coups tended to be a lot bloodier than ours had been. But now . . .

It could be really inconvenient now.

"Jonas is in Britain," I told him steadily. "That's all I know. I need to know more than that."

Caleb didn't say anything.

"Caleb—"

"We're getting perilously close to me crossing a line here," he said quietly.

"You didn't cross it when you helped me break Pritkin out of *hell*?"

"That was different. I'm supposed to help the Pythia. It's part of the oath." He winced slightly. "And the old man never specifically said not to break into a hell zone. . . ."

"So when I asked you said yes. Okay, I'm asking now."

"Yeah, but what you're asking now is that I give you classified information, which I don't have, by the way. I don't know where your acolyte is—"

"She isn't my acolyte. She's Agnes' acolyte, and she's about to be the dark mages' acolyte if I don't find her!"

"That's a leap—"

"I don't think so." I put the plate down, both because I'd finished inhaling the contents and because Caleb was too far away. I wanted to see his eyes. I climbed onto the sofa again and leaned over the counter. He shied back slightly. I inched forward, and his back hit the fridge. It should have been funny, the big, bad war mage running from the skinny little blonde, only neither of us was laughing.

"This morning, if I hadn't had help, I would have died," I said quietly. "I wouldn't have Ramboed my way out of it; I would have *died*. And if Rambo had been there, so would he. I can't fight this war alone."

"No one's asking you to."

"Aren't they?"

Caleb crossed his arms and shifted position slightly, putting his eyes in shadow again. "Jonas has to work with you. You're the Pythia. He doesn't have a choice."

"Well, he's been acting a lot lately like a guy who thinks he does. He's been acting like a guy who thinks he can run things on his own, can run this war on his own, and that isn't going to work. Not for any of us," I added when he opened his mouth to object. "We work together or we die together, Caleb. This morning showed that if anything ever did. But Jonas can't or won't see it, so I'm asking you—"

"Cassie—"

"—*I'm asking you*, as Pythia, for two things: Lizzie's location and the recipe. Can you get them?"

"You're not going to make this easy for me, are you?"

"I can't afford to. *Can you get them?*"

He closed his eyes and rubbed the bridge of his nose. It didn't seem to help. "Honestly? I don't know. I don't know where your potion is any more than I know where they have the girl."

"But you can find out?"

Dark eyes finally met mine, lit up by a stray beam when he raised his head, but I couldn't read them. Caleb was usually more emotional than some of his war mage buddies, more human, more willing to think for himself instead of blindly following orders. But tonight he was as stoical as I'd ever seen him. And as closed off.

"I suppose you're planning to shift back six months if I do, and find a maker? It takes that long to brew."

"I know. That's not a problem."

"But something else might be."

He stopped with just that, so I knew this wasn't going to be good. "Such as?"

"That potion. I know you think you need it, and I know it doesn't actually feed you any magic itself."

"But?"

"But it allows you to access an almost unlimited stream, doesn't it? The Pythian power is about the most potent source of magical power around, and the Tears let you basically mainline the stuff—"

I blinked at him. "You're afraid I'll get *addicted*?"

"I've seen how fast it gets someone. Half those guys you fought today probably didn't start out thinking, when I grow up, I want to be a dark mage—"

"Caleb."

"Some of them started with illegal skills from birth, and didn't like the restrictions we put on them. Some made bad choices when they were young, and just kept falling further and further behind. And some—"

"Caleb."

"—started out thinking they'd just take a hit or two, no big deal, just a little to help them heal faster, or study better, or impress a girl—"

"Caleb! I'm not a junkie!"

"No. But you are Pythia."

"Meaning?"

"Meaning nobody talks about it, okay? But I've seen how fast it burns them up. How fast we go through Pythias. Just normal use shortens their lives considerably, and what you've been using isn't normal."

I laughed, a short, ugly burst that escaped before I could bite it back. "So you're worried about my longevity?"

"Shouldn't I be?" He ran a hand over his head. "Look, I want John back, too. I think I've proven that. But you're the only Pythia we've got and we're at *war*. You need to stay safe. He'd say the same if he was here. You know he would."

I just stared at him for a moment. It was times like these that I felt the gulf between us, the widening gulf between me and everybody around me. Maybe because I'd been at the center of this thing for too long, maybe because I hadn't had enough rest—or any—lately, maybe because I was crazy. Or they were, which was what it was really starting to feel like.

"Tell me something, Caleb. Were you in the group dispatched to Dante's this morning?"

"Of course. I think every war mage in Vegas was."

"How long did it take you to get there?"

"From the time we got the call? Twenty-two minutes. It's something of a record: that many people over that distance—"

"I'm glad to hear it. We lasted nineteen," I said, and shifted.

Chapter Fifteen

"Get off the road." Rosier gripped my arm.

"Don't touch me!" I snarled.

"Then get off the damn road!"

"All right, all right, just don't—no, don't touch—don't touch!" I ran off the sheep trail pretending to be a road, sloshed through a ditch half-filled with water, and scrambled up the other side. There were old-growth trees hedging the path on both sides, the kind you don't see anymore because they went for fuel or something centuries ago. And bushes and undergrowth everywhere else, because this was Wales and Wales had some kind of law that required every inch to be covered in green. But for once, I was grateful for it.

I dodged behind a tree, completely and utterly skeeved out, and clung to the bark, panting.

"It's just a hand," Rosier said, in his teeny tiny squeaky voice.

"Don't talk, either," I said, trying not to hyperventilate.

"We have to—"

"I said, don't talk!"

He shut up. The army we'd spotted barely in time marched closer, still eerily silent. And I did my best to get my breathing under control before I passed out.

It didn't work.

"God!" I shrugged out of the backpack and ran off a little way, biting back a scream. I managed it—just—because the soldiers headed this way were fey, and those ears had to be good for something.

I finally got a grip and turned around to see Rosier sitting on top of the pack, legs crossed, smoking a cigarette. Which would have been fine, if they'd had cigarettes in medieval Wales. And if he hadn't been naked. And if he'd looked remotely human.

But he was in his disgusting white slug phase, which was apparently how demons recreated bodies, but which looked nothing like a human child.

Nothing.

I'd been carrying the icky thing around in the medieval equivalent of a backpack—a sack with ropes that fit over my shoulders. It had left him closer to me than I'd like, but at least I hadn't had to look at him. Now I did, and it was just as bad as before, and maybe a little worse. Because the suite had been dark, but now the moon was out. And the light filtering through the trees was glistening off the mucous membrane that covered him from bald head to webbed toes, and off the tracery of tiny purple veins spidering all over the stark white "skin." And pulsing.

I shuddered again and looked away.

The-thing-that-would-be-Rosier smoked.

The latest batch of troops started passing, but didn't see us because of the weeds. Good old Wales, I thought, as I edged as close as I dared to a bunch of bushes, which wasn't all that close. But even so, I could see flashes of moonlight through the foliage, gleaming off weapons and helmets, and feel the earth shake under my feet. Which, considering how light-footed the fey were, meant there were a lot of them.

A whole lot.

These were dressed in cloaks that seemed to blend in with the night, trying to fool my vision into believing that there was no one there. It didn't work, because there were too many of them, but it didn't help, either. I'd recently learned that the fey were handily color-coded, which made it easy to keep them straight—when you could see them.

The Alorestri wore a lot of green, because they lived in forests and marshes and I guess it was good camouflage. They were known on earth as the Green Fey, since that was what Alorestri meant in their language, and why bother coming up with anything better when the fey didn't? It wasn't their real name, which we paltry humans weren't good enough to have, but it worked for trade, which was what they were mainly interested in. They came to earth the most, but I'd gotten the impression that it was usually in small trading parties, not in however many were currently hogging the road.

Yet I didn't think these were the black-armored, human-hating Svarestri, either, but not because they almost never came to earth. But because we'd already encountered them on a parallel road, which was why we'd switched to this one and thought we were safe. Only it didn't look like it.

I tried to pick out a flash of blue or gold, the livery of the last great fey house, the Blarestri, or Blue Fey, but couldn't see one. Of course, with the moonlight bleaching almost everything shades of gray, who could tell? Anyway, I didn't know why I cared. The Blarestri might have a better rep in my day, when they and the senate seemed to have some kind of understanding, but this was sixth-century Wales. The last time I'd encountered them here, they almost roasted me alive.

I finally gave up and looked back at my traveling companion.

God, it just didn't get any easier.

"Why are there so many soldiers?" I demanded softly.

Rosier's small shoulders moved up and down. "I don't know. I anticipated some problems getting into court, but nothing like this."

"It looks like we landed in a war zone!"

It shouldn't have surprised me; things hadn't been much friendlier the last time we popped in. The Svarestri had stolen a prized fey weapon—the same staff I was after—and run off to earth with it. Only to be pursued by the Blarestri, the staff's owners, who intended to retrieve it and then feed it to them.

The result when they met up had been a battle for the ages, with me and Rosier in the middle, just trying to survive. And to grab Pritkin, who was being difficult because when was he not? And then that Victorian Pythia Gertie showed up, drawn by all the magic being slung around, and sent me back to my time, and the fey . . .

Well, it looked like their little quarrel was ongoing, didn't it? Which was not cool, since the staff they wanted just happened to be with the guy *I* wanted. Because Pritkin had snatched it before he left.

Rosier regarded me through a cloud of smoke. "There was always a war in this era. But things were supposed to be in a bit of a lull right now. The Pax Arthuriana, if you like—"

"Then why—"

"I just said I don't know. You're supposed to be the psychic."

"Clairvoyant! I don't read minds."

"Just as well." He blew a smoke ring at me.

It looked like our brief truce in London was over, which was fine by me. But something else wasn't. "So how are we supposed to get to court? They're *everywhere*—"

"Not everywhere," he argued. "Just on the roads. Which there aren't many of in this era, leading to bottle-necks."

"We didn't meet a soul last time!"

"We weren't that close to court last time. But this is the main road, and it gets more traffic. Although it's less bad than it will be. We're still miles out."

Yeah, thanks to Gertie, I thought viciously. She could home in on magic—especially the Pythian variety—so shifting straight into town hadn't been a good idea. We'd shifted into the middle of a burnt-out mill instead, a remnant of our last trip, hoping to confuse her about our real destination. And then booked it before she showed up. But it was hard to make time when you had to hack your way across what amounted to a jungle, or stop to dodge people every five minutes on the road, and ten to one, she was on our trail.

"If the fey are slowing us down, the same is true for her," Rosier reminded me.

"Yeah, except she has permission to be here. She can use all the magic she wants!"

Not to mention that last time she'd been with two other Pythias: her own mentor, some doddering old woman named Lydia, and what had looked like a Byzantine princess, all ornate golden robes and elaborate lacquered curls. They'd been an odd-looking group, but powerful. More powerful than me.

I started tugging at the backpack.

"What do you want?" Rosier demanded.

"The canteen— Oh God!" I'd worked it out of the side, but abruptly dropped it.

"What?"

"You oozed on it!"

I sat back against the tree trunk, closed my eyes, and just breathed for a minute. It could be worse, I told myself. We were *here*. Once these guys passed by, we'd get back on the road and should be at court by morning. I'd find out what Pritkin had learned about the staff, and where it might be in my time. And then, as soon as the cursed soul showed up, we'd be out of here. Out and back and everything would be just . . . well, not perfect, all things considered, but much better.

God, so much!

After a moment, I felt my spine relax and find a space for itself against the tree's rough bark. The ground was wet from the perpetual Wales weather, and the air was chilly enough that I could see my breath when I could see anything. But it was also weirdly soothing. The *tramp, tramp, tramp* of all those feet, the sigh of the wind, the peaceful darkness.

The clap of a slimy hand over my mouth.

My eyes flew open to see Rosier's horrible proto face staring into mine, the usually green eyes milky, the noseless nostrils flaring—

"Mmphh!"

"Shut. Up," he hissed, and a second later, I understood why.

Because a hooded fey was standing there, a dozen yards off, holding out some kind of glowing sphere. It was slightly bigger than a softball, and sloshed like liquid when he moved. Which he did when a twig cracked behind him, and he spun to meet another fey, whose spill of dark hair gleamed in the moonlight.

Which was what the light was, I realized, as the second fey crouched down to the ditch and came up with his own handful of water. It stuck together in the same way it might have in space, forming a wobbly orb that seemed to glow from within, catching and enhancing the beams filtering through the trees. Enhancing them into a good approximation of a flashlight, I realized, mentally cursing as the twin orbs threw shadows our way.

"See something?" the second fey asked. The spell I'd picked up on my previous visit to this era was still translating for me, but it looked weird, seeing his lips move out of sync with the words. Like a video gone wrong.

"Smell," the first fey said. "An odd scent. I don't know it."

They paused to breathe for a moment, looking oddly like a pair of vamps scenting the air. And my eyes focused on Rosier's still-lit cigarette, lying on the ground where he must have dropped it. Until his webbed toes crushed it into the mud.

"Your nose is better than mine," the other fey said, swinging his orb around. And causing Rosier and me to try to climb inside the tree trunk. Luckily, the nevertrimmed foliage hung low, casting a dark shadow. And we didn't move, didn't breathe; I think my heart might even have stopped.

Until the first fey smiled, a brief glint of white in the darkness.

"Always was," he said, and the two melted away like part of the night.

I contemplated throwing up, not least because Rosier hadn't released me.

"Wait," he whispered, so low that it might have been the sigh of the wind.

But it wasn't. Like it wasn't another shadow that moved just beyond the tree limbs, visible only because the misting rain was suddenly missing. In a man-shaped void.

I wasn't going to throw up, I decided calmly. I was going to pass out. From lack of air and from a general sense from my nervous system that it had had enough. It couldn't do this shit anymore.

But then the bastard moved off, too, as silently as he'd come, and I fell softly into the muck.

And just stayed there, trying to breathe quietly, while the rest of the troop trouped on by.

It was getting to me, I decided. All of this. It just was.

Not just shifting a ridiculous-sounding fifteen centuries, but everything. I thought maybe Caleb had been right: I needed a vacation. Somewhere sunny. Somewhere with a beach. And warm sand instead of perpetual mud, and a soft chaise instead of more freaking tree roots, and a hot guy—

"Which one?" somebody asked.

"What?"

"I didn't say anything," Rosier informed me.

I vaguely realized that I was on my back, and that he was wiping my face with what looked like a moist towelette.

Maybe because it was a moist towelette.

"Where did you get that?" I asked blearily.

"Out of the pack. Lie still," he added when I started struggling to sit up.

"Why? They're gone." Even the sound of footsteps had vanished while I was busy graying out.

"Humor me."

I humored him. I didn't feel so good.

"We need to get going," I pointed out, after a moment.

"In a while. Let them get well away first."

That . . . sounded like a plan, actually. I lay in the mud, staring up at the swirl of stars visible through the dark, wet canopy above. And waited while my hideous companion cleaned me up. Or made me as clean as anyone ever got in Wales, which wasn't very. Even the fey's hair had been dripping. . . .

"Is there a reason Pritkin's element is water?" I asked, after the wind tossed some in my face.

"Is it physically impossible for you to lie quiet?" Rosier asked.

"Humor me."

He opened his mouth to say something but then closed it again abruptly. "Well, obviously."

"And that would be?"

"I already told you, he's part fey—"

"What part?"

"An eighth, if you must know."

"An *eighth*?"

"Yes. His mother was a quarter, his grandmother half, and his great-grandmother—"

"Does he know?" Pritkin had always acted like his fey blood was minimal.

"I've no idea."

"You didn't talk about her? His mother, I mean?"

"No. She was dead. What was the point?"

"That she was his *mother*?"

Rosier scowled at me, like I was the one acting weird. "She was also part fey, and he was infatuated enough with the creatures as it was. Just like her, always talking about them—"

"His mother was always talking about them?" I tried to get up on one elbow, but Rosier pushed me back down with an irritated *tchaa* sound. "Then she didn't live there. In Faerie."

"Well, of course she didn't live there! How would I have met her in that case?"

"Then where did she live? Who was she?"

He scowled some more, but to my surprise he answered. "You already know that."

"I don't. Pritkin doesn't talk about it."

"But surely you've read the stories."

"The stories?"

"*Le Morte d'Arthur, Historia Regum Britanniae*, Chrétien de Troyes, and all that. Got half of it wrong, with writers more interested in a good tale than the truth. Camelot." He snorted. "When that name didn't even exist until the thirteen hundreds—"

"Rosier."

"—which is when they wrote all that twaddle about the Round Table. Ha! It was a table of *land* where the Romans had a theater. Arthur used it for 'discussions' with his nobles, which usually degenerated into great shouting matches, so I suppose the acoustics came in handy, after all—"

"Rosier."

"—and don't even get me started on the grail, what a load of horse—"

"Rosier!" He looked at me. "What part did they get *right*?"

He blinked. "A surprising amount, actually, considering the tales were passed down orally for hundreds of—" He saw my expression and stopped. "Arthur, for one. More or less."

"His name wasn't really Arthur," I said, thinking about something Pritkin had said.

"Of course it was. Well, one of them. People had all sorts of names back then. Roman names, Celtic names, titles, nicknames . . . but most people called him Arthur. And why not? Great bear of a man he turned out to be."

"Golden bear," I said, remembering the name's translation.

Rosier nodded. "And they weren't talking about a cuddly teddy. I saw that ridiculous *Camelot* on Broadway, and the mincing wuss they made out of Arthur—absurd! The only damn thing they got right was the hair color! The real man was a leader: decisive, ruthless, sharp as a tack—not an idiot led around by the nose by his adulterous wife! Why remember him at all if that's the hash you're going to make of—"

"And Pritkin? Did the legends get him right, too?" Because they didn't seem to fit the man I knew.

Well, okay, some of them did. The over-the-top magic, the endless curiosity, and the put-upon grumpiness were all familiar enough. Plus the whole half-incubus-wizard-born-in-medieval-Wales-serving-a-king-named-Arthur thing. But other things . . . sometimes it had felt like I was reading about another person entirely.

Like the Merlin of legend hadn't just switched names, but personalities over the years.

"Stop interrupting," Rosier told me.

"Well, if you'd get to the point—"

"Which I would do, and faster, if you weren't constantly intruding to pepper me with questions. Did no one ever tell you that's rude?"

I sat back.

"All right," Rosier said. "It's story time."

Chapter Sixteen

"There once was a king," Rosier said. "His name was Uther."

"Uther?" That sounded vaguely familiar.

"Well, not really. His name was Ambrosius Aurelianus, a Roman name for a Romanized Celt, but nobody called him that. It was Arthur's given name, too, by the way; he was named after the old man. They were both descended from yet another Ambrosius, who was a cavalry officer under the Romans before they left Britain. Caused historians no end of trouble, it has, all those Ambrosiuses—"

"Rosier."

"But Uther was the name his men gave him on the battlefield, meaning terrible or fearsome, and it stuck. And it fit. More so than the title he invented for himself: Riothamus, 'king of all the Britons.' " Rosier rolled his eyes. "War chief is more like it, of a ragtag group trying to hold Britain together after the legions pulled out. Half his 'subjects' were at war with him at any given time, and the other half certainly didn't consider him—" He stopped, seeing my face.

"There once was a king," he said dryly. "His name was Uther."

"Okay."

"Like his son, he was a great warrior. But unlike Arthur, he lacked an appreciation for the subtler virtues, not to mention any and all social graces. The dogs used to congregate under the table, right where he sat. They knew he dropped enough for a dozen men. Ate like a wild savage, spraying it about."

"And this is relevant?"

"Yes, in fact. Uther was a giant of a man, battle-scarred and weather-worn. His teeth were crooked and cracked from one too many fists to the face. He could barely see out of one eye, from the great scar running a hairbreadth away, which pulled it up as badly as the other lid drooped. It allowed him to leer and look perpetually surprised, all at the same time, which you have to admit is fairly impressive. And then there was that great cauli-flower of a nose—"

"I get the picture."

"I doubt it," he said dryly. "Men don't live that way anymore, don't fight like it, either. Even soldiers don't. Years of hand-to-hand with swords and knives, of hard battles and harder winters, of constant stress and a great group of savages who followed you only due to your being the greatest savage of them all . . . it leaves a mark."

"So Uther was unattractive."

Rosier laughed. "Yes, in the same way that a skeleton is svelte! He was one of the ugliest men I've ever seen, even after all these years. Which didn't matter to his men, of course, who were hardly the courtly knights of the storybooks. The local ladies were happy if they washed the dirt off once a month and remembered to only spit in the corners. But Uther didn't want a local girl, did he?"

"Didn't he?"

"Well, of course not! Or we wouldn't have a story, would we?"

"I don't know. You're telling this."

"I'm trying to," he said pointedly.

I shut up.

"Of course, there were plenty of girls who would have taken him, scars and teeth and warts and all," Rosier said. "And thought themselves lucky in the bargain. He was powerful and wealthy, by the standards of the day. Which meant you probably wouldn't be raped by one of the Germanic invaders if you married him, and might have more than one dress to wear. But Uther didn't want one of those girls. He might have, under different circum-stances, the way you might want hamburger if you've never had filet—"

"Thank you for comparing women to beef. I assume you mean he met someone else."

"Not some*one*, some *fey*. Igraine, daughter of Nimue, queen of what you humans call the Green Fey and the legends call the Lady of the Lake."

"What? Wait."

Rosier nodded. "That's what *I* said. Wait. Let's discuss this. But no, Uther didn't want to discuss anything. Uther wanted the wife of Gorlois, Prince of Cornwall—or so he called himself. Everyone was a prince or king in those days, and who was to tell them no? Rome had gone and Britain was up for grabs, and it was winner take all, with the winner looking like it might be the Saxons until the local Britons got some help. But not from Rome. They'd written telling their old masters that they were being overrun, and Rome had written back telling them to join the club. Rome was dealing with Attila at the time—yes, *that* Attila—and couldn't help, so the Britons turned to someone who could."

"The fey."

He nodded. "The Green, to be precise, who were more than happy to assist in return for some of those tolerant British women we were talking about. Always had a problem with their population, did the fey, and that went double for the Green living so close to the Dark and being at war with them half the time. People get killed in wars and have to be replaced, and human women made excellent . . . companions."

"Spoken like a true incubus. You mean they were enslaved in a foreign land."

"Spoken like a true modern woman, who hasn't had to deal with living in a perpetual war zone. What you consider enslavement, many of them viewed as escape—from famine, violence, disease, death. . . . In any case, it wasn't that foreign. People came and went much more freely then, living on both sides of the barrier. Like the beauteous Igraine."

"Beauteous?"

"Oh yes." Rosier leaned back against the tree, his eyes going distant with memory. "Hair a river of ebony, skin like alabaster, eyes as blue as a winter's day—and twice as cold. She inherited her mother's looks, but little of her magic and therefore decided to live on earth. Yes, war-ridden, diseased, and what have you." He waved a hand. "Amazing what people will do when they're smitten."

"Smitten. You mean . . . with Uther?"

He burst out laughing. "No, not with Uther! With her Cornish prince! Or so she liked everyone to believe."

"Then why are you telling me all this stuff about Uther?"

"I'm getting there."

"Oh God."

"Uther wasn't a man to let a little thing like a happy marriage stand in his way. Not when the lady in question wasn't just beautiful, but so well connected. Uther was trying to unite the Britons to fight the invaders, but petty princes like Cornwall were causing him no end of trouble. They saw no reason why he should lead the fight instead of one of them, despite the fact that he could crush the lot of them if he felt like it. But he couldn't crush them and the Saxons, too, so something had to give."

"And that something was Gorlois."

Rosier nodded again. "He was the leader. Kill him, marry his wife to keep the fey alliance, unite the 'king-doms,' and defeat the invaders. That was the plan."

"And end up as high king in the process."

"Well, why shouldn't he have? He might have been an ugly, uncouth boor, but he was a smart, ugly, uncouth boor, and damn good on the battlefield. He knew how to concentrate on what was important, and how to keep his people safe."

"It sounds like you liked him."

"I did. Well enough to help him, in any case."

"Help him . . . how?"

Rosier shrugged. "Gorlois wasn't the problem, not really. He'd just gotten delusions of grandeur after his marriage, and saw no reason why he should bow to some wild man from Wales. But he couldn't back it up where it counted; he couldn't defeat Uther in battle, which would normally have made dealing with him easy enough."

"Except for his wife."

"Yes. Igraine was the problem. She may or may not have really loved Gorlois; I was never sure. But she definitely loved how easy he was to manipulate. And therefore how easy it was to lay down terms advantageous to the fey but not so much for the Britons. Gorlois essentially did whatever she wanted, and insisted on equally harsh terms for everybody else or he would take his toys and go home, and they could fight the damn Saxons on their own. Yes, she liked her marriage just fine."

"But Uther didn't."

"No, Uther didn't. So he made war on Gorlois, and when the man sent his wife to Tintagel on the coast, for safekeeping, Uther asked for a favor—"

"Wait. Wait. I know this." A half-forgotten memory rattled around in my head, something I'd heard once, or maybe read. Something shocking enough to be remembered . . .

I abruptly sat up. "That was *you*! You helped him—"

"I said so, didn't I?"

"You helped him sneak into the castle—"

"It wasn't a castle then, and we didn't sneak. There was no reason to sneak."

"—and pretend to be Gorlois!"

"Emrys gets his ability at illusion from me," Rosier agreed.

"You helped him . . . you helped him . . . *rape Igraine*."

And despite everything, despite Rosier's demon lord status, I was still shocked. And appalled. And it must have come through in my voice, because he frowned at me.

"Yes, everything is so simple, isn't it? So cut-and-dried when you aren't fighting for your life every day, and the lives of your people—"

"Uther wasn't fighting for his life! He was fighting for a better position—"

"He was fighting for his *life*!"

Rosier tried to get to his feet, but they were still in process. So he ended up on his proto butt in the mud, glaring at me. It might have been funny another time, but right now I had to struggle not to punch him.

"Do you think the fey gave a damn about the humans they guarded?" he demanded. "They did the absolute minimum they could get away with—enough to hold the borders, but not to drive out the invaders, which would have removed the reason for their aid, wouldn't it? They were perfectly content to have the country in a state of never-ending warfare, but Uther—he might have been a man of war, but he wanted peace, lusted after it, much more than he ever did that cold fey—"

"Don't say it. Don't you dare say it—"

"—bitch who I doubt ever loved anyone. I didn't approve of what he was doing—"

"I'm sure! An incubus disapproves!"

"She says with such disdain! Knowing nothing about us—"

"I know enough!"

"You know *nothing*! My people do not rape!"

"No, they just use tricks, like incubus powers—"

"To *enhance*, not to *overcome*. We pride ourselves on our wit, our beauty, our goddamn charm! We do not need tricks!"

"Yet you helped Uther."

For the first time, Rosier looked slightly uncomfortable, but his voice was defiant. "It seemed the only way. The battle was raging that night, and Uther had instructed his men to take out Gorlois, regardless of the cost. He knew the prince's supporters would break and run as soon as they heard their leader was dead. But that meant he had to get to Igraine that evening, before she heard it, too. Otherwise, she might run off and marry some other, easy-to-manipulate type, and Uther would be right back where he started. He came to me and begged for help."

"And you gave it to him."

Rosier looked at me angrily. "If I hadn't, many more women would have suffered the same fate as Igraine. There's no black or white, girl, not in this story. Stop looking for it!"

"Meaning what?"

"Meaning that ever since Gorlois' marriage, the fey had been demanding more and more tribute for their aid. The old quota had been relatively easy to fill; as I said, there were always those who viewed Faerie as an escape from violence, want, and uncertainty. They might be slaves, but they'd be slaves with full bellies who slept in safety, and to many in those days, that seemed like paradise. But afterward . . ."

"Afterward?"

"It worsened every year. By the time the war broke out, mothers were hiding baby girls, swearing they'd been stillborn. Kidnappings were rampant, with girls forced to move about under armed guard. Battles were constantly breaking out among neighboring clans, just to take prisoners who could be given to the fey instead of the dwindling supply of local girls—"

"God."

He nodded. "And people were starting to ask why they should fight for Uther when the Saxons might at least let them keep some of their women. Something had to give."

"But . . . but why did the fey need *so many women*?"

"They claimed it was for their border war with the Dark, but I suspect that tension with the Svarestri was more worrisome. And then there was the lucrative trade their slavers had established with the Blue Fey, who might claim noninvolvement in our day, but who bought plenty of fertile human slaves in the past."

"But they had to know they couldn't keep it up forever," I protested. "Sooner or later, they'd end up more human than fey!"

Rosier shook his head. "The common practice was to have a wife of pure fey heritage to bear your true children, the ones meant to carry on your name and bloodline. And human concubines to bear your half-breeds, as many as you could manage. The stronger of those, the ones who inherited much of their father's magic, were kept in Faerie, where they were used as border guards and cannon fodder in the wars. Their lives tended to be brutal and short, although there were exceptions. Igraine, for instance."

"But she went to earth."

"Yes, as her mother's emissary. Running the slave trade was her way of proving her value. I assume there was some sort of agreement: manage the humans effectively, and when Gorlois dies, return to take your place at my side. . . ." He shrugged.

"And did she?"

"No. I doubt Nimue planned to give her half-human daughter a damn thing; set too many precedents. But in the end it didn't matter. Igraine had inherited her mother's beauty, but not her life span. She died a year shy of seventy."

"And the rest?" I asked. "The children who didn't get the magic?

Rosier lifted a brow. "Where do you think the Changeling myths come from? It wasn't substituting a fey child for a human one so much as dumping the rejects back on earth, to live out their lives as best they could. The more human of them probably did that well enough, but the rest . . ."

"The local people treated them like monsters," I said, remembering a story Pritkin had told.

He nodded. "And in so doing, provided another headache for Uther, who was constantly being pressed to stop the influx of these 'monstrosities,' some of whom lashed out at their persecutors in deadly ways."

"Can you blame them?"

"Perhaps not. But they weren't always selective in who they killed. In short, the whole thing was a giant mess, and as long as Gorlois remained in power, it wasn't likely to change. Uther therefore challenged him for his throne, trial by single combat. He sprang it on him in open court, knowing he was too proud to back down in public. But not to slip out of the fortress the night before the duel, and when Uther gave chase, to ambush him. And once blood had been shed, there was no way to avoid war."

"And Uther didn't try very hard," I guessed.

"On the contrary. A civil war is the last thing he wanted. That's why he challenged the damn man in the first place. He wanted Gorlois' forces intact, to help him take on the Saxons. Every death in that war was a loss to him, even the ones on the other side, and he was desperate to cut the fighting short before he destroyed his own army."

"So you helped him find a workaround."

"Igraine was the key to the fey alliance. Without her, the treaty would have to be renegotiated, probably on even worse terms than before. Thousands would suffer. But once she married Uther, well, he was not Gorlois. And not easily manipulated."

"But why would she marry her *rapist*?"

Rosier shrugged. "To avoid dishonor. To maintain the alliance that was as useful to her people as it was to Uther's. And to make his life a living hell, which, I may add, she did in spades thereafter."

Good, I thought. And then I thought maybe. And then I decided that I didn't know what to think. Igraine was a victim, but she'd also been an oppressor, running a trade that had destroyed thousands of lives. But Uther hadn't been blameless, either. He'd been put in a terrible position, but he'd also done a terrible thing.

I was beginning to think that Rosier was right. The stories made it easy: here were the good guys, here were the bad guys. Root for this group, hate that one. But the truth . . . was a lot more complicated.

"And what did you get out of all this?" I asked. Because I knew Rosier. He might have genuinely sympathized with Uther, but there was no way he didn't find a way to profit from it, too.

He didn't even try to deny it. "I longed for peace and stability in my lands as much as Uther did in his, but it was impossible on my own. I expended power as soon as I received it, defending my people, keeping the nobles in line, quarreling with the damn high council—a thousand things. My father had no such concerns, because there were two of us, working together to stockpile power to keep the family strong. With another incubus of the royal line, I could do the same. Instead of a house constantly on the verge of disintegration, we could be powerful again, respected, even feared. I told Uther that we could help each other—"

"How?" I interrupted, because Rosier could talk on his favorite subject for hours.

"My attempts to have a child among my own kind had been futile. Our birth rate is so low it might have taken millennia to sire a child—if I ever did. I came to earth looking for a human mother, because their fertility is legendary. But my children were too strong; they overwhelmed the women before they could give birth. So I tried the fey, hoping their strength would do the trick. But they damn well never get pregnant! I finally realized that a cross between the two, part human to aid with fertility, and part fey for resilience, might be the perfect combination—"

"So you came here looking for a broodmare."

"And I found one. I found the perfect one."

I narrowed my eyes. "Igraine?"

"No, not Igraine! Do you read at *all*?"

"Who, then?"

"Who do all the legends say was Merlin's great love?"

"Merlin? But you're not— Wait. *Wait.* Merlin helped Uther at Tintagel Castle. Merlin was the one who cast that illusion. The stories all say so, but Pritkin wasn't even born then—"

"No, but Myrddin was the name I was going by at the time, which was later Latinized to—"

"That's why all the legends say he aged backward!" I stared at him. "There were *two* of you!"

"Well, of course there were." Rosier sounded like that should have been obvious. "The stories became confused because I named him after me. I was too angry with his mother at the time to use the name she'd chosen, and—"

"And you look alike," I said as things finally fell into place.

"He received his good looks from me," Rosier agreed smugly. "Although I was hiding them somewhat at the time, to look less like a lusty rival and more like a valued counselor—"

"Rival for *who*? Rosier, who the hell did Uther promise you?"

He looked at me sardonically. "Who do you think? Who in the Arthurian legends is the only person to have the name *le fey*?"

Chapter Seventeen

"Morgana?"

"Igraine's daughter with Gorlois," Rosier agreed. "They had three, but she was the only one to inherit her mother's abilities, hence the sobriquet."

"But . . . *Morgana?*"

"Morgaine, in fact. Her name was also Latinized in the later—"

"But she was . . . she was some kind of evil sorceress! Or did the legends get that wrong, too?"

"No, they were pretty spot-on there."

"But you . . . but she . . . and *Pritkin*—"

"Considering who your mother is, I don't think throwing stones—"

"Morgana?"

"Stop saying it like that. It made sense at the time."

"How? How on earth does marrying an evil fey sorceress—"

"Quarter fey. And we never actually got around to marriage—"

"I don't want to hear this."

"She was lovely, like her mother," he said, ignoring me. "Only less cold, less distant. At least with everyone else. She didn't seem too fond of me—"

"Imagine!"

"Which was a problem, since I was not Uther, and do not rape—"

"Of course not."

"If I did, why spend all that time getting to know her?" he demanded. "Why teach her magic?"

"You taught her?"

"Who else? Genetics is an odd thing, and she'd ended up quite a bit more powerful than her mother. Naturally, it made her curious about her other relations—and their magic—but Igraine would never allow her to be taught. Afraid her daughter would run off to Faerie if she had the skill, and she wanted her on earth."

"But Morgaine had other ideas."

He nodded. "It was how I won her over in the end. I agreed to teach her magic as a seduction technique. It worked . . . in a manner of speaking."

"What manner? It either works or it doesn't."

"Ah, to be young. No. It either works or she imprisons you in a tree using one of your own spells, then goes off to explore Faerie. Fortunately, by that time she was already pregnant with Emrys and, once she realized this, she returned to give birth on earth and give the child to me."

"And you put him with a couple of guardians who thought he was some kind of freak!"

"Who told you— Oh, never mind." Rosier scowled. "Well, what did you expect me to do? I couldn't take him back with me, now, could I? What if he hadn't received my power? How would he have fit in on earth after growing up in the demon realms? Not that he *would* have grown up there. That damn court—they attacked him when I finally brought him back with me, did you know? Almost killed him, and that was after he was an adult and able to defend himself. Can you imagine what they would have done to a child?"

"So you left him on earth."

"It seemed the best way. I put him with a farmer's family for a while, then arranged for him to go off with Taliesin when he was older to get a bit of experience. The bard, part fey, little teched." Rosier tapped the side of his head. "But a good sort overall. Roamed about all over the place. Thought it would help with the transition to my realm if Emrys had seen more than a pigsty in this one."

"Arranged? Then you didn't visit him." It wasn't a question. The Pritkin of this time period and I had had a conversation about his childhood recently, and he'd never once mentioned his father.

He'd never mentioned him.

"It seemed the best way," Rosier repeated.

"Why?" I could feel my face flushing. "Because if he didn't get your abilities, he'd be useless to you? And you'd abandon him, like all those fey fathers did their unwanted children—"

"Don't be absurd! I would have provided for him—"

"Physically. But he would never have known who he was, *what* he was—"

Rosier looked confused. "If he didn't inherit my power, what would he have been?"

"Your son!"

Damn it, just when I began to think Rosier might have some redeeming qualities, he pulled something like this. And he wasn't lying; it was all over his face. He would have left a powerless child on earth, alone, with no explanation for his existence or further contact. He'd have written him off and moved on to the next experiment, and God knew Pritkin might have been better off if he had! But I knew what it was like to grow up questioning. To search out any clues to who you were and where you came from. To always wonder—what had they been like? Had they loved you at all? Had they—

Damn it!

"Did you even take him to see her grave?" I asked, after a moment.

"Whose?"

"Morgana's. Morgaine's."

"What?"

"His mother's *grave*. When you came back to claim him, did you—" I cut off. Because Rosier was suddenly looking . . . blank. Extremely blank. The kind of blank used by Vegas cardsharps and secretive vamps, which was a little odd on the face of someone whose coin in trade was emotion. "You didn't, did you?"

"I couldn't."

"Why not?"

"Her grave isn't on earth."

"Where is it, then?"

"I assume it's in Faerie."

"You *assume*? You didn't bury her?"

Rosier found an expression. It was crabby. "No."

"Who did?"

"I have no idea."

"You have no *idea*? She gave you this wonderful gift, the son you'd been wanting for centuries, and when she died, you didn't even—"

I cut off.

"She . . . *did* die . . . right?" I asked slowly.

"Of course."

"You saw the body?"

"Not . . . exactly."

"What do you mean, not exactly? You told Pritkin his mother was dead."

"She is."

"How do you know that if you didn't see her?"

"I was told she would almost certainly—"

"You were told? By who?"

"By Nimue, if you must know. Showed up with a whole cadre of fey. Wouldn't even let me speak to her. Said they had to rush her off to die in Faerie, where her spirit could be absorbed and reborn—or whatever their bizarre religion is, I don't know."

"No, you *don't*," I said, quietly furious. "But you told him she was *dead*."

"Because she is."

"Because you wanted him with you! You made him think there was nothing for him in Faerie!"

"There isn't!"

"His mother—"

"Is *dead*. And if she isn't, she never came back to see her darling boy, did she?" Rosier asked spitefully. "He's better off—"

"That's not for you to decide! I don't see—"

Anything, because everything abruptly went dark.

"Got her!" a strange voice said, just as strong arms went around me from behind. I stared around, processing the fact that somebody had just dropped a bag over my head.

"And look what I've got," another voice said, laughter threading through it. "Oh, ho, *yes*. We are about to be *paid*."

"Hang on. Let's get a look at her first." The bag, or

whatever it was, was abruptly pulled up, and a grinning fey peered in at me. One blue and one black eye surveyed my face for a moment, and the grin widened. "Oh yes, she'll do. She'll do quite well." He looked up at his companion. "Told you I smelled something."

And then the world winked out.

I woke up to the cadence of a man's long strides, the ache of a sore stomach pressed against someone's shoulder, and the light of a flickering torch as seen through wool. And the eerie *tramp, tramp, tramp* of what it took my brain a moment to recognize as the army I'd seen earlier. The one that sounded like it was all around us now.

"What's this?" someone asked, and my ride stopped abruptly.

"Runaway. From the earlier attack."

The bag was pulled up, and another fey peered in. A soldier, judging by the helmet, and by the lack of emotion on the coldly handsome face. At least what I could see of it before a torch was thrust into my eyes.

But I guess I didn't look like much of a threat, because the perusal didn't take long. "All right. Let this one through."

We started moving again, but the fey had neglected to pull the wool back over my eyes, giving me a view of a bunch of equally impassive faces in tight formation, closing up behind us. And what appeared to be some kind of checkpoint, composed of hastily felled trees, which we'd just passed through. And of my captor, who put me down a little distance away, for a rest.

It gave me my first good look at him, and what a sight it was. Bifurcated hair, ebony dark on one side and silver bright on the other, fell around a face with a noticeable pigmentation change right down the middle: half swarthy, and half pale as milk. It fit the mismatched eyes, leaving him looking like two people had been stitched together to make one. And they were both staring at me in annoyance.

"You're heavier than you look!"

"Then don't . . . carry me," I gasped. "I can walk—"

"And have you break for the tree line at the first opportunity? No."

"I promise . . . I won't do that—"

"Not to mention that if I set you down for too long, you're anyone's prize." He glanced suspiciously around at the surrounding troops, then reached for me again.

I held out a hand. "Wait."

"Cargo doesn't talk," he informed me. "Much less give orders."

"I'm not cargo!"

"One more word and I put you back to sleep."

"But—"

"And that's the word."

I woke a second time to noise—a lot of it. The bag was over my face again, but my hands were bound in front of me, allowing me to flip it up. From my vantage point, I mostly saw the fey's ass, which was thick with muscle and shapelier than I'd have expected for one of them. And a clanging peddler's cart behind us, laden with pots and pans and swinging chains, that was responsible for some of the racket.

The rest was coming from a crowd of people schlepping along the road or camped on the side. Dogs were barking, goats were bleating, a group of men were clustered around a fire, belting out a drinking song, and a crowd of fey and humans were yelling bets around a makeshift ring. Where two black-haired fey were wrestling, their shirts off, their bodies covered only in muddy loincloths.

At least they were until they got too close to a group of raucous women, who appeared to have had too much to drink. And who snatched one poor guy's butt covering, laughing uproariously as the fey looked around in confusion, his two pale moons shining in the firelight. For a second—until his opponent took the opportunity to toss him in the mud.

"Cheating! What do you call that? It's cheating!" a man started yelling as the crowd laughed and jeered and threw money at the victor, who started parading around with arms held high, like a boxer who'd just won a bout.

At least, he did until his opponent jumped up and smashed him in the face. And then lunged after the woman who'd cost him the match, who scrambled up, still laughing. And took off at a run, purloined loincloth held high over her head and waving like a banner.

I just stared.

The Light Fey I'd encountered so far had been . . . different. Violent and deadly, but unlike all the other people who kept trying to kill me, they hadn't seemed to get too worked up about it. As in, a Vulcan would have shown more emotion, a robot more personality.

Of course, my experience had been brief, and composed of disciplined soldier types, which I was guessing these weren't. In fact, I wasn't even sure that they were fey, not entirely. And that went for most of the spectators, too.

We waded through the crowd around the ring while I stared at slightly pointy ears on human heads, at a red-haired boy with dimples and freckles and bright silver eyes, at perfectly formed fey but of human height, and at a sweet-faced girl with needle-sharp teeth, more pointed than vamp fangs, and a mouth that was midnight blue inside. The only ones who appeared to be purebred were some of the merchants, who seemed to be human, and the guards scattered here and there, in dull pewter armor, who looked to be fey. But the rest were clearly mixed.

Like the guy I was plopped down in front of a moment later, near a large tent in the middle of camp.

He was dressed in a brown velvet tunic and leggings and was seated at a small table, scratching on a tablet with a stylus. Which was more impressive than it sounds, considering that his hands were even more webbed than Rosier's. He looked up. "What's this?"

"Payment."

The man's large, rather florid face got a little redder. "You lose ten slaves and you bring me one in return?"

"Ah, but this one's special."

"That's what you always say!"

"But this time, it's true." My captor tossed my backpack on the ground, spilling Rosier out into the dirt.

The merchant did not look impressed. "What in Odin's name is *that*?"

"He's mine." I grabbed Rosier, jerking him over to me.

He was slimy and muddy, and now also straw-covered, and the heart visible between his semitransparent ribs was almost beating out of his chest. I wasn't sure why, maybe adrenaline, or maybe dying again when you haven't fully formed yet was a very bad thing.

He didn't appear to be in favor of it, especially when the merchant pulled out a knife.

"He's mine," I repeated. "I need him!"

"For what?" The man looked revolted, which was pretty rich for a guy with gills in his neck.

"He's her familiar," my captor said, causing both me and the merchant to look at him in surprise.

"Her what?"

The fey grinned, rocking back on his heels. "She's a witch."

The merchant scowled. "I have too many of those already."

"But witches are worth more—"

"And human women are less trouble! She escapes before my buyer arrives, and I don't get paid at all, do I?"

"But he'll be here tomorrow. And to point out the obvious: pretty face, blond hair, magic." The fey rubbed his fingers together. "Coin."

The merchant did not look convinced.

"And big tits," the fey added, jerking up my tee. And looking smug, like he'd just made the sale.

The merchant looked sourly at my sports bra, which tended to flatten things out somewhat.

The fey's eyes followed, and he frowned, like he'd expected something different. "Be that as it may, she's worth at least . . . six of the ones I lost."

"Six of the ones you let those bitches steal, you mean, and not by half. Two."

"Five. None of the others were magical—"

"As far as I can tell, neither is she!"

"What do you call that thing?" The fey pointed at Rosier.

"I don't know what you call that thing, but I don't deal in that thing. I deal in women, and it ain't one!"

"Four, then. My final offer, or I go elsewhere. I could even try to sell her myself—"

"Good luck wi' that. There's such a glut tonight, you won't make half the price of the three I'll give ye—"

"Then it's true. Half the slaves in Britain are here tonight."

"Aye, Lady's orders. Wanted 'em all in one place."

"For what?"

"Why don't you go ask her?" the merchant said, exasperated. "Now, do we have a deal or not?"

The fey sighed. "Three it is." He leaned over to cut my bonds. "Don't worry, lovely one. You're going to a better place."

"Is that what you tell everyone you enslave?" I asked bitterly.

Only the special ones, he mouthed, his back to the merchant, causing me to stare up into that unique face in confusion.

Which only increased when it suddenly morphed, the features sliding from aquiline perfection to something else. Something with a too-narrow mouth, a too-large nose, and a pair of piercing green eyes. A very familiar pair.

"No. But in your case, it's probably true," the fey that wasn't a fey told me. "You're just the kind the nobles prefer, although they'd never admit it. You're going to spend the rest of your life eating sweets and having fat babies for your master. You'll be fine."

Just stay out of trouble, he told me silently while I gaped at him. And tried to process the fact that Pritkin had just sold me into sex slavery to the fey.

And then he was gone.

Chapter Eighteen

"All right, move out! We're clearing this area, all of you—get ready to move out!"

I stuck my head out of a tent flap a few minutes later, in time to see the merchant confront several dark-haired fey on horseback. "What's this?" he demanded.

The nearest rider looked down at the rotund figure with annoyance. "What did I just say? Move out!"

"But I have special permission—"

"Not anymore. New orders, all camp followers are to pull back to the stronghold."

"But I'm not a damn servant! I'm—"

"Doesn't matter what you are. If you're not fighting, you're not staying. Now move out!"

There was a sudden uptick in activity on the road as people rushed to obey, throwing saddles on donkeys and baskets on wagons and dousing campfires with practiced ease. Except for the merchant, who was still shaking his head. "You don't understand. I have a buyer—a very important buyer—coming in the morning—"

"Then he can see you at camp!" The soldier was starting to look annoyed.

"I'm not putting my stock in that cesspit! You can't expect—"

The merchant suddenly found himself airborne, when the fey reached down and jerked him up, as easily as I might have a kitten. "I expect you to follow orders, *hundr*, or you may find yourself on the auction block, instead of your cargo!"

A gloved fist opened, and the merchant's fine clothes ended up in the mud.

And ten minutes later, Rosier and I were in a cart, with what looked like a cage built onto the back of it, jolting along a wreck of a road.

We weren't alone. There were a dozen women crammed in with us, all of whom looked as cold and miserable as I was. My clothes had been replaced a rough linen shift with a halter tie at the neck—slave wear, judging by the fact that everyone else was dressed the same. It was thin and backless to the waist, and I was barefoot, since they'd also taken my shoes. But other than being robbed, I hadn't been harmed.

Unlike Rosier. He'd acquired teeth marks in his arm and a boot print on his face, courtesy of a dog, its owner, and his current resemblance to a chew toy. The damage was minimal, but he was looking a little spooked. I'd put him behind me, in a corner of the cage, but not before everyone saw. Which probably explained why our companions were huddled on the opposite side, staring at us with wide eyes.

I glanced behind me. Rosier had curled into a little ball, looking like he was cold, too. I put a fold of my skirt over him, and he looked up gratefully.

He really wasn't that bad, once you got used to him, I decided.

"He isn't so bad, once you get used to him," I told everyone.

It did not appear to help.

I shut up and stared through the bars at the passing countryside, which didn't tell me much, since it was the same close-packed tree line I'd been seeing for miles. Only not close enough. A thin rain had begun to fall, just as we were setting out, and while the top of the cage was covered, gusts of wind kept wetting us through the sides, making me shiver.

And curse Pritkin even harder. Last time I showed up in beautiful, sunny Wales, I'd expected to find him mending a tunic or cooking dinner or some other mundane stuff. But what had he been doing? Running from the fey he'd just ripped off to the tune of a priceless staff. And since they'd just stolen it from someone else, someone who was going to require a literal pound of flesh if he found out, they'd been *real* motivated to get it back.

We'd barely survived that little escapade, and now what was going on? Armies of fey on the road, Pritkin disguised as a slaver, and me . . . What the hell was he doing with me?

Had he wanted to get rid of me? I hated to believe it, but it was kind of looking that way. Maybe because I hadn't been in favor of the let's-steal-a-valuable-fey-relic quest he had going on.

I hadn't known what the staff was at first, not being an expert on fey weapons—or godly ones, either—and had only figured it out later. So, of course, I'd been all about returning it. And going back to whatever Pritkin called a home and hanging out until the cursed soul decided to make an appearance.

It had seemed like the best plan—it had *been* the best plan—but Pritkin hadn't approved. He'd wanted to know what the Svarestri were doing with the staff, why they'd been taking it to court, and whether it represented a threat to his king. And I was standing in the way.

So he sells me to a damn *slaver*?

"What?" Rosier demanded suddenly.

I looked down. "What's wrong?"

"That's what I'm asking you. You're looking . . . grim."

"Your son just sold me into slavery! How am I supposed to look?"

Rosier yawned. "He didn't."

"Oh, so I'm *imagining* this?"

"No, but there's something else going on."

"And you know that how?"

He shrugged. "Emrys hates slavery. I don't know what he's up to—I never know what he's up to—but he's planning something."

Yeah, something he couldn't let me in on. Something he couldn't talk to me about for *five seconds*. Something he didn't trust me enough to—*damn it!*

"Get some rest," Rosier advised, eyeing me. "You might need it later."

"You get some rest!"

"Good idea." He curled up under my skirts and went to sleep.

I jolted along in the cage, getting progressively more angry and miserable by the minute. And not just because of Pritkin. But because the rain was coming down harder now, drumming on the wooden roof and dripping off the sides. And making the dips and holes in the so-called road fill up with water, so that we got splashed every time a wheel hit down.

Not that it mattered. The wind was pretty much ensuring that we were all soaked to the skin anyway. Causing me to hug my knees, trying to preserve what body heat I had left. And making the thin shift I was wearing all but transparent. But it wasn't outraged modesty that caught my attention, and had me blinking down at my chest in confusion.

It was the necklace.

Specifically, Billy's necklace, which I wore so often that I tended to forget I had it on. But it was hard to ignore now, giving off a puddle of warmth against my icy skin, its central ruby glowing faintly through the halter's loose weave. And nestled heavily between my breasts as usual, despite the fact that it had absolutely no business being there.

The merchant had handed me over to a crabby old woman with black teeth and a harassed look. Who had dragged me into a tent, stripped me, and pawed through all my stuff. She'd taken everything, including my beat-up tennis shoes, my caked-with-mud T-shirt and shorts, even my underwear.

Yet she left me this?

It was even weirder when I realized that the necklace was heavy gold, set with a central ruby that acted as a talisman, along with several smaller ones on the sides. And while it was undoubtedly ugly as sin, with scrolls and flourishes and rococo doodads, it was also worth more than anything I'd seen in this entire country. Hell, for all I knew it might be worth more *than* the entire country, at least in this era, considering that most of what I'd seen of Wales consisted of mud and weeds.

Yet she hadn't taken it.

I clasped it through the damp material, wondering if I was imagining things. But I could feel the weight in my palm, and Billy's presence inside, just as I had in the suite. Too drained and exhausted to talk to me, or even to wake up from the stasis ghosts fell into when low on power, but undeniably there.

If I was imagining things, I was doing a good job.

My bracelet was sliding around my arm as well, but I'd half expected that. No one could remove that thing for long. But the necklace . . . I took it off all the time, since it was uncomfortable to sleep in. And if it had any special abilities to come find me again, they'd never shown up before.

I thought about it for a minute, and then I poked Rosier. "Do you see anything?"

He opened a heavy-lidded eye and looked at me blearily. "What?"

I showed him my front. "Do you *see* anything?"

He scowled. "Did you wake me up for this?"

"I'm serious!"

He sighed and muttered something that sounded like "women." "Yes, they're very nice. Can I go back to sleep now?"

I frowned. "What are very nice?"

"Oh, all right. They're better than nice, if you like that sort."

"What sort?"

"The big pillowy sort. I've always been more partial to the teacup variety myself."

I stared at him for a moment, and then I poked him again, hard. "We're not talking about my *breasts*."

"What, then?"

"The necklace!"

"What necklace?"

I stared. "You really can't see it?"

"See *what*? What are you blabbering about? Can't you see I'm *injured*?"

"He barely scratched you—"

"He almost put a boot through my brain after his mongrel tried to devour me! I'm in a delicate condition! I cannot have these sorts of things happening! And *you* are supposed to protect me. I would like you to know that I consider this a failure on your—"

I stopped listening, in favor of remembering that Gertie hadn't taken the necklace, either. At the time, I'd just assumed that was due to it not being a weapon. But a friendly ghost was a useful thing to have, as I would have expected a fellow clairvoyant to know. Yet she'd let me keep him.

I started looking around under my skirts and wrenching around, trying to see behind me. The knot of women crowded a little farther away, like they were afraid I was having a fit, while Rosier stopped his diatribe in order to scowl. "What are you doing?"

"Looking for something."

"For what?"

"For that," I said, stopping at the sight of a small green tail poking out from under my right knee.

I stayed very still, or as much as possible in a creaky old wagon with no shocks. And, for once, the tiny creature didn't scurry off. Instead, slowly, tentatively, a small snout poked out to match the tail. And, above it, bright black eyes gleamed in a stream of moonlight, looking at me timidly.

"It's okay," I told it softly. "You can come out."

It did, slowly, slowly, pausing every inch or so to look around, as if a hawk was going to swoop down out of the sky and snatch it up. But I thought that unlikely. Somehow I doubted even a hawk's eyes could see it.

Rosier's sure couldn't.

"Have you lost your mind?" he asked, staring from my face to my—as far as he was concerned—totally uninteresting knee.

I ignored him some more and held a finger down to the little green lizard. It hopped on board, the iridescent hide flowing smoothly from the skin of my knee to the back of my hand, then scurrying through my fingers and across my palm, before finally finding refuge under the ball of my thumb. And then disappearing altogether, when Rosier stuck his nose into the mix.

He thrust the stubby proto appendage to within an inch of my hand and then turned to look at me accusingly.

"What are you doing?"

"It's nothing—"

"Don't give me that! You tell me what you're doing right now! We are in *sixth-century Wales*—"

"I know where we are."

"Then you know this is not the time for you to have a mental—"

"I'm not having a mental anything."

"—breakdown, or to keep secrets from your partner!"

"Oh, we're partners now?"

"Just tell me!"

"I was going to, if you'd give me a second," I said, exasperated. "It's a ward."

"What?"

"A. Ward. One Mac made. He's a friend of Pritkin's," I added. "Or he was."

"Was?"

"He died," I said shortly. Because Mac was another of the people I'd lost on this journey. One who'd believed in me. One whose trust I had yet to validate, whose sacrifice I had yet to honor, because that could only be done one way—by winning this.

But it looked like he'd left me some help.

"Mac specialized in magical tattoos," I explained. "When he died, some of them transferred themselves to me. This is the last one left."

"What does it do?" Rosier demanded, squinting. Like that would help.

"I didn't think it did anything." Mac had been a war mage, before a debilitating injury led to an early retirement. He'd taken to making up wards in his spare time, to sell to the magical community. And, naturally, considering that his clientele mostly came from his old profession, the majority had been useful for battle in some way: improving senses, strengthening stamina, or acting as outright weapons. Like one in the form of a sleek black panther he'd named Sheba, which had attacked enemies with all the savagery of the real thing.

But garden lizards aren't known for their ferocity, and if this little guy had increased my abilities any, I'd failed to notice.

The bright black eyes reappeared, materializing on the skin of my knuckles, Cheshire Cat–style. The rest of it followed, somehow managing to seem solid and 3-D, despite being flat against my hand. Yet it could disappear again in an instant, fading away into nothingness.

Like the necklace.

I smiled, finally understanding. "Mac didn't make you to fight, did he?" I asked softly. "He made you to *conceal*."

Because what did a war mage need as much as his weapons?

A way to make sure that no one took them from him.

"What?" Rosier looked testy. "What are you talking about? What *is* it?"

"A chameleon," I said, wondering why I hadn't figured it out before. But then, I often forgot it was there, until its little claws pitter-pattered over my skin in the middle of the night, waking me up. Because mostly, I didn't even see it, a fact that I'd put down to shyness.

But no.

It was just doing its job.

It seemed uncomfortable out in the open, so I held it up to my shoulder and it hopped from there to my hairline, scurrying over the skin of my neck, making me shiver. Or maybe that was the cold. Because the rain had finally slacked off, leaving a star-studded sky peeking through gaps in the clouds. But the wind had picked up, causing me to pull closer to Rosier. Not that he seemed in the mood for a cuddle.

"I don't see how that helps us," he said testily. "Unless you're packing an AK-47 I failed to notice."

"It wouldn't help if I was. We can't go around shooting people—"

"According to you."

"According to common sense. It would change the timeline."

"Yes, and that would be a shame. The one we have being so successful," he said crabbily, and hunkered down under my damp skirts.

Rosier didn't seem to take roughing it well. But he had a point. As nice as it was to finally discover what my little companion did, I didn't see it helping us out of this. The same was true of Billy, who was too weak to materialize without a power boost I couldn't afford to give him. And my bracelet, which was too dangerous to use, since I couldn't predict what it would do. So, okay, I wasn't going to have to steal back my stuff from some peddler, but other than that . . . it looked like we were still screwed.

I sighed.

The rain dripped off the roofline.

We jolted around some huge boulders that were jutting out into the path, all mossy and green and running with rivulets.

And suddenly, a vista opened up before us.

Chapter Nineteen

I hadn't realized how high we were, since we hadn't seemed to be hiking uphill all that much. But we must have, or else we'd been higher than I'd thought when we came in. Because we were looking down into a vast, sprawling valley.

In the distance, the sloping sides of a mountain range receded in ranks, becoming darker and more indistinct until they were finally lost in mist. Below, the deep blue night was studded with flickering campfires, like a reflection of the heavens above. It caused an optical illusion, making it hard to tell where sky ended and earth began, and made me dizzy enough that it took me a minute to realize what I was seeing.

And even then I didn't believe it.

Because there were hundreds of them.

Hundreds and hundreds of campfires. Meaning that the army we'd passed on the road, which had now stopped for the night, had to be numbered in the thousands. Thousands of fey, more than I'd ever expected to see on earth—more than I'd ever expected to see period—and at their center, what looked like a whole city built out of tents.

The other women had gathered around, dirty hands clinging to the bars, pale faces staring out, momentarily forgetting their fear in the face of overwhelming awe. I doubted any of them had ever seen anything like it. I knew I hadn't—and that I hadn't read about it, either.

You'd think something like this would make the history books, I thought, as we creaked onto a narrow road, terrifyingly steep and rocky. I grabbed the bars, bracing

along with everyone else, and tried not to notice the sheer
drop-off on the other side. Or the pebbles rolling under
our wheels, which were plain wood and didn't have any
kind of traction. Or the fact that this wasn't the most well
balanced of vehicles.

All of which was still okay, more or less, until the merchant abruptly whipped up the horses.

Suddenly, instead of slowing down—which would
have been freaking *sensible*—we were all but flying down
the mountain, wheels rattling, cage swaying, women
screaming—and falling and tumbling because the crappy
wheels were only in contact with the road about half the
time.

"What's happening?" I yelled at Rosier, who had
wrapped himself around a cage bar, like a frightened
monkey. "What's he *doing*?"

"Trying to avoid that," he said, looking over my shoulder, his eyes huge. I turned in time to see a blast of spell-
fire tearing through the air and then through the cage,
shearing off the top right corner and sending us swaying
dangerously from side to side.

"What the *hell*?" I screamed as the horses whinnied
and bucked, the merchant shouted and swore, and we almost fell into the abyss.

As it was, I got thrown to the other side of the cage,
where for a second I was left staring down at a sea of
nothingness, just a blue-gray void of mist and vague
lumps that might be trees, and another cliff face rising
across the gulf, distant but near enough that I could see
shapes darting among the rocks.

And flinging spells, because three more were already
headed our way.

They streaked across the sky, red and orange and purple, strangely beautiful as they parted the mist, sending it
rolling up on either side. Like vertical fireworks or colorful torpedoes tearing through the sea. Which would have
been a lot more impressive if we weren't on the ship they
were about to sink.

"Get low!" I told the panicked women. *"Now, now,
now!"*

I pushed them down, the ones I could reach, but had

to break it off a moment later and dive for the floor myself. But it looked like the idea had been conveyed. We ended up clinging to the grimy planks, as flat as we could get, but thanks to the open bars of the cage, that still gave us a perfect view—

Of the rain.

Out of nowhere, the storm that had started slacking off turned violent, and in the clear night sky ahead clouds blew up. I watched as the mist in the valley congealed into boiling, purplish gray masses and rain began to fall, above us, below us, everywhere all at once. Drenching sheets that tore into the spells, shearing off their power, causing them to sputter and crackle and spit—

And die.

My heart hammered as I watched one dissipate right before it reached the bars. Another made it but had been blown off course, exploding in the air just above us, raining a cascade of bright red sparks down on all sides. But a third was still coming, lashed at by rain and storm, buffeted by wind, but somehow still on course. Like some magic heat-seeking missile that adjusted its path as we did, as we all but flew with no springs and no brakes, our eyes glued to the steadily approaching power ball that was getting smaller and smaller but was *still coming*—

And then it hit, like a massive hammerblow, sending us slamming into the horses, which screamed and grew wings, or so it seemed. Or maybe that was because the different parts of the storm had just become one massive torrent, the main core of its power driving down on us—and the road. Which went from dangerous, overgrown goat trail to something a whole lot worse.

I looked down at the flowing river of mud, at the trodden-down, slick-as-glass weeds, at a set of wheels no longer turning, because they were no longer in contact with the road, and thought, Oh.

And then we were over.

The next few seconds were a heart-stopping mass of confused images: the cage sliding and dipping and falling, and then flipping when we hit open air. All of us strangely silent as we tumbled around, because our hearts were in our throats. The rain, almost a solid sheet outside the bars. One of the horses, its mane streaming, its eyes wide and white-rimmed as it fell alongside us, pawing the air as it continued trying to run.

And the ground, speeding toward us like a green bullet, trees spearing up like daggers, huge boulders everywhere, death in a hundred forms waiting with open arms—

And continuing to wait as we froze midair, a huge rush of my power halting our fall midtumble.

Leaving me to yo-yo to a stop between the hard oak boards of the ceiling and floor, panting and shaking and screaming as I hadn't been able to before, the ones trapped behind my teeth by utter terror breaking loose with a vengeance.

"Ahh! Ahhh! Ahhhhhhhhhhh!"

And then something hit me in the face.

It took me a second to realize that it was Rosier, who I'd knocked loose from his death grip on the bar, sliming the side of my head before I managed to throw him off. And to scream some more. And to beat the ceiling of the cage, which was now the floor, not for any reason I could name, just because the massive surge of adrenaline had to come out somehow.

I collapsed back against the old boards, gasping and exhausted. Scatterings of rain sparkled in the moonlight above my face; women's shifts flowed out everywhere, like angels' wings; the slaver stayed suspended, caught halfway through a fall on the opposite side of the wagon from his horses, his eyes wide, his mouth gaping. Like the terrified faces that stared down into mine, all of them mirroring the way I felt, because I hadn't saved us yet.

I'd frozen us too soon.

There was no doubt about it. I lay there, staring past the merchant's motionless body, at what looked like the view from my penthouse in Vegas. Actually, the overgrown, windswept ground was the exact opposite of it, but the angle was similar. Because we were still dozens of stories high.

I reached over and pulled Rosier back into real time, and watched him flail around for a minute, screaming bloody murder.

And then clutching the ceiling-turned-floorboards,

webbed hands spread wide. "I . . . I think I wet myself," he whispered.

I didn't answer. I slowly got to my knees, wincing when I put weight on my sore one, and pushed a floating girl out of the way. And crawled over to the bars, squashing my face against the rusting metal until I grabbed hold of the merchant's tunic. And jerked him over.

I found the key for the lock on his belt, and got it open after a minute of frustrated swearing. And swung the cage door wide, allowing me to look down. And then just stayed there, as still as everyone else.

Except for Rosier, who crawled up alongside. "What is it? Are we too high up for . . . for it to be survivable?"

"Yep."

"Then . . . can you do it again?" He swallowed. "Can you let us fall for another few seconds, and catch us when we're about to . . . hit down?"

"No."

"No?" He looked at me, a little of the new, scared-shitless Rosier giving way to the old full-of-it variety. "Don't you think we need a little more than 'no' in this instance?"

"No."

"And why not?"

I pointed down. "That's why."

Rosier finally, very carefully, peered over the edge and into the void. And saw what I just had—namely, a glittering golden web, like from the butt of the world's biggest spider, billowing out below us. Or no, I guessed, not exactly a web.

"Is that . . . is that . . . is that a *net*?" he demanded.

"Looks like it."

"Why is it there?" He turned to me, looking almost indignant. And then he scowled some more, because yeah. The old Rosier was definitely back in charge now. "What are you doing?"

"Biting my nails."

"Why?"

"I don't have a clipper."

"You—" He stopped, and the scowl became a glare. "Stop. It."

"Why?"

"Because we have to get out of here, that's why!" Only it was more like "Becausewehavetogetoutofherethat's why," and now he was shaking me.

"Why?"

"Stop saying that!"

I sighed and left my hangnail alone. Mainly because I needed the finger to make a point. "One: a time stoppage doesn't last long. In a few minutes, we're going to finish that plunge anyway. Two: the only way for me to hurry that up is to use more power, which I don't have because I just did *a time stoppage*. Three: The only way for me to override *that* would be to take more potion, and do I have to explain why I don't want to take more potion?"

He sat there for a moment, vibrating, then leaned back over for another look.

It didn't appear to improve his mood.

"How much do you have left?" he asked abruptly.

"Two-thirds of a bottle."

"I don't suppose you could . . . just a sip?"

"A time stoppage is a major spell," I told him. "I'm usually wiped for as much as a day after. And that's assuming I start from somewhere good, not already bottomed out. Getting me back to the point that I could do anything would probably take as much extra stamina as shifting us here."

"Meaning we'd have only a third left."

"And considering how wildly successful we've been so far—"

"We'll trust the net," Rosier said sourly.

We just sat there after that, staring at the rain, waiting. I didn't know what Rosier was thinking, but I wasn't contemplating the view. I didn't know what threshold of power use Gertie needed to home in on us, but it didn't really matter. Whatever it was, I'd just blown the hell out of it.

She was going to be on top of us in—well, probably seconds after we landed. Maybe a minute or two if I was lucky. Which meant I needed a plan—and a good one—already in place before that happened.

But how was I supposed to get one here, suspended in the air, like a damn bird in a cage? I needed information. I needed the lay of the land. I needed *alternatives*—

And suddenly, I had them, a cascade of five—no, six— different options falling in front of my eyes, like a spliced-together video on fast forward.

"Slow down!" I said, because I was a little freaked out, and because I could barely see anything.

"What?" Rosier asked.

"Nothing." Because they'd listened. Or my power had, because this looked like the series of images I'd seen in my head the first time I tried to shift. But instead of a fall of centuries, I was looking at one made of minutes that had now slowed to a crawl.

And which, with a little concentration, I managed to rewind back to the beginning.

The first sequence showed a group of women sneaking through tall grass. Staying low, staying in the shadow of a cliff, staying almost invisible. Until they were forced out into the open in order to approach our web-encased cart, which did appear to have survived the fall. It was still intact, anyway, and framed by two screaming horses and a white-faced slaver, who was floundering around in the web and screaming, too.

Something that only increased when he spied the women. He began babbling almost incoherently, and then pleading, and then screaming again. All of which was abruptly cut off by an arrow through his throat.

The man fell back, caught by the web, until the women did something that made it dissolve. The wagon fell another story or so, a final jolt that had screams coming from inside again. While the web became a heavy fog that billowed up on all sides, spreading out over the valley, helping to hide us.

But not well enough.

The women ran forward, some killing the horses, to shut them up, I assumed. Others grabbing the merchant, checking him for a key he didn't have. Several others jerked on the door, found it open, pushed their way inside. And began to reassure the traumatized slaves.

Which might have worked better if not for the deluge of arrows suddenly coming our way.

I watched as if from a distance as the women outside the cage were skewered, dead before they fell, while the ones inside cursed and started slinging spells. The fog dissipated to show an advancing party of fey, dozens strong, emerging from behind what looked like every damn tree. And then—

I looked away, switching abruptly to the next scenario, trying to ignore the blood-soaked carnage that flipped quickly past my gaze.

But the next one wasn't any better. I saw myself, Rosier in my arms, running for the tree line as soon as we stopped bouncing in the net. Saw me get maybe a quarter of a mile before being nabbed by a large party of men. Saw me back at their camp, tied up beside a fire, while a circle of them gambled with some dice. Saw one win, heard him shout, felt him grab me—

And then I was fast-forwarding again, past scenes of my shift being ripped in two, of my naked body splashed with firelight, of me being forced to my hands and knees while the victor came up behind me—

I looked away, only to come back to a different group, this one with a pack of dogs, chasing me through the trees.

And then another, grabbing me as I splashed across a river, in the last direction possible from this starting point.

And, finally, of me staying put while the battle raged outside the cage, while blood dripped off the roofline in front of my eyes, while a fey ducked inside, eyes cold and assessing, and while a woman beside me with a bone sticking out of her leg was put down like a dog. I screamed, and someone grabbed me, holding me down as I twisted and fought. And broke away, panting and sniveling, my nose running, my eyes wild—

And finally managed to focus on Rosier, his own eyes huge and worried, watching me from across the still-suspended cage.

"Are . . . are you all right?"

I swallowed, staring around. At the glittering curtains

of rain. At the floating bodies of the women, still caught in free fall. And at the path I'd just carved through them, scrambling to get away from things that hadn't happened yet.

I let out a very shaky, very relieved breath.

"I—I don't think—" I began, only to be cut off by several loud thumps from overhead, and the sensation of the cage suddenly dipping.

Rosier's head jerked up. "What was *that*?"

I didn't answer. I just sat there, remembering that there had been six possible futures, not five. But I'd freaked out before I made it to the last one. Not that it mattered, I thought, looking up. I'd even thought that she'd be right on top of us.

I just hadn't meant it literally.

"What is happening?" Rosier yelled, as the solid wood overhead crumbled away in a large patch, hundreds of years of decay taking place in seconds. It was on his side, near the door, probably because Gertie didn't want to risk aging one of the women, and was big enough for a head and shoulders to fit through. Maybe a whole body if she didn't try it herself.

And she didn't, although why she didn't, I wasn't sure.

It wasn't like I had any options left.

Well, except for one.

"Tell your demon to stand down," she told me. "Or I will kill it."

Rosier looked upward, his face bewildered, and then at me. *Stand down?* he mouthed.

"And if I do, what then?" I called up, fumbling with my bracelet.

"Then the both of you live to answer for your crimes. Although considering the punishment, you might prefer not to."

"Unheard?" I asked, jerking a small vial off the dagger-filled chain, which I'd put there like a weird sort of charm, because it was the safest place I knew. "You would kill me without a trial?"

"Your actions have been your trial! How many chances have you been given? How many times have I had to bring you in? If you wanted to talk, you should have done it before—"

"I don't recall being given a chance," I said, trying to keep my voice steady as I shuddered through a taste like every vile thing on earth condensed.

"I don't recall you staying put long enough to use one!"

"If I do this time, will you listen?"

"*If* you do?" She barked out a laugh. "As if you have a choice!"

"Wrong answer," I said, and shifted.

Chapter Twenty

A moment later, I was in the same crouch, but no longer in the same place. For a second, I stayed put, disoriented from a shift I wasn't supposed to be able to make, and from the view. Which looked like I'd just stepped into the heavens.

The waterfall off the wagon had blocked much of the outlook from inside, but there was no such problem here. I could see the vast valley spread out below, the moon riding a wall of purple-black storm clouds above, and the huge arcs of lightning flashing between the two, because the storm still raged beyond the bubble of my spell. And us caught in the middle, rain beating violently against the small time stoppage as if it knew we shouldn't be here, as if it resented the tiny well of peace in the midst of its fury.

For a split second, despite everything, I just stared.

Like the girl on my left was doing. Her long, dark hair was undisturbed by the gale-force winds that couldn't touch her, yet her face was shock-pale, her blue eyes staring outward with the same awe that was probably in mine. Because she was young, so very, very young, that this just might be her first time at the rodeo.

It wouldn't be her last.

Agnes, I thought, my stomach clenching as I looked from her to Gertie, who was bent over, her ample rear in the air as she reached down into the hole on my opposite side.

Leaving me stuck between a Pythia and her heir, with no way to freeze them both.

Especially not when some movement of mine caught Agnes' attention, and she looked down—

And was tackled by a frantic blonde, coming up from the roof in a fluid motion entirely unlike my usual awkwardness, because desperation does wonders for hand-eye coordination. Or hand-knee, because I got a leg around one of Agnes', at the same time that my left hand grabbed her left arm and my right arm went around her throat, leaving her plastered against the front of me as she cried out, as Gertie spun, as Rosier screamed, because he was somehow dangling from the hand of a snarling Pythia.

And then everything froze, like another time stoppage, only it wasn't. The lightning still flashed; the girl in front of me still breathed in quick, shallow motions. Gertie's sharp brown eyes still glistened as she coldly assessed the new situation. And Rosier continued to thrash around and scream bloody murder.

Nobody had ever accused him of reckless bravery, I thought, wondering what came next. Because the idea of dueling Gertie was not . . . attractive. But we couldn't stay like this forever. My spell would unravel soon, and the only thing I liked less than the thought of dueling an experienced Pythia was dueling her while plunging through the air.

But I didn't have to worry about it, because Gertie decided things for me, stretching out her arm, and thrusting Rosier's small body over the abyss.

"I. Will. Drop. It," she told me, voice low and venomous.

"My spell will catch him," I replied, trying to keep my own voice steady, even while wondering if it would. And if I could shove Agnes at her and freeze them both before Gertie did something to Rosier or to me. Or before Agnes did. Or before I fell off the roof, because the damn thing was slippery as ice.

But my power didn't seem to have an opinion this time, maybe because it didn't work so well on fellow Pythias. Or maybe I was just having trouble concentrating. Which wasn't helped when Gertie made a sudden, savage gesture and half my spell collapsed.

The wagon tilted sharply toward me, one side abruptly reentering real time. And I started to fall, my feet slipping dangerously on the wet roof, with no hope of traction. Until my back hit a wheel and I managed to grab on. And to tighten my grip on Agnes' throat, because she was struggling now, and struggling hard. "Cut it out!"

"Let her go!" Gertie thundered.

"It's not my fault she's here!" I yelled as a wash of rain and wind slapped me in the face, and the wheel turned perilously behind me. "This is between you and me—"

"Let her go or I *drop it*! *Now*!"

"Let her go!" Rosier screeched, now dangling over open, active air. "Let her go!"

"There's a *net*!" I pointed out, furiously. "The witches—"

"Hate demons, and are savage in this era, girl!" Gertie said, looking pretty damn savage herself, even with purple-tinged curls whipping around her face. "And the wind down there would likely blow him off course in any case! Now let my acolyte go if you want to live!"

"Give me my partner, and we'll trade!"

"You're in no position to make demands!"

"Neither are you!"

Although I could be wrong about that, I thought, when a tunnel of quick time boiled through the remains of my spell, hitting me with a burst of wind as strong as a fist. I staggered back, ten minutes or more of storm all slamming into me at once, although that might not have been so bad: I had a damn death grip on that wheel. At least, I did until Agnes took that moment to slam her foot down on mine, to wrench away, to lunge for her mistress—

And to fall, because slanted, rain-slick boards are not forgiving.

I had a split second to see Gertie drop Rosier, reaching desperately for her heir; to see him plummet over the side, still screaming; to see Agnes sliding backward, unable to find purchase—

And then we were both falling, the force of her impact sending us over the side and into thin air.

I grabbed her, wrapped my arms around her, and tried to concentrate enough to shift. But I didn't get the chance. Because what looked like a mini cyclone blew up out of nowhere, right below us, the maw swallowing the world in darkness. And then swallowing us, the swirling bands of black closing over my head, the force of the disturbance wrenching Agnes away and pulling at me even as I struggled and tried desperately to shift.

Tried and failed, because I'd felt something like this before, and it wasn't a cyclone. I stared at the tiny scrap of sky still visible far above me, knowing that I was in the maw of a portal. Specifically, a time portal that Gertie had used on me a couple of times now, a return to sender that plopped me back whenever and wherever I'd started out.

It meant that Agnes was probably back in Victorian London right now, wondering, What the hell? And that I was about to be back in Vegas, in my damn apartment sans Rosier, sans Pritkin, sans anything to show for two-thirds of a bottle of potion. A bottle I couldn't replace at the moment, and wasn't sure I'd ever be able to. And *fuck* that, fuck everything *about* that, I thought, gritting my teeth and fighting.

And God, it sucked—literally. I felt like I was about to be wrenched in two, the forces inside the portal far worse than the storm outside. It felt like my flesh was being torn from my bones, like I was about to be turned inside out, like I was coming apart at the seams.

Felt like freedom, I thought, gasping and sobbing as my power flowed around me, as the storm bands of the spell dissipated, as I shot out of the great maw and realized one absolute, inescapable fact.

I was still falling.

Shit!

I shifted—somehow—with no real destination in mind except *down*. Which my power interpreted as several feet above the ground and on an incline. One I promptly smashed into with my face.

And then rolled down, hitting every rock and stick along the way, before finally coming to rest inside a small copse of oaks.

For a moment, I just lay there, staring at the wildly thrashing treetops. Lightning flashed, rain poured, presumably thunder crashed, but I couldn't hear it—my ears were seriously screwed up. Something to do with the awful pressure in that portal, which had left me looking at a scene out of a silent horror flick. All it needed was a guy in a cape.

Or a monster in a tree.

My ears popped after a moment, allowing me to hear the vulgar cussing going on somewhere nearby. Which broke off abruptly—I guessed because I'd just been spotted. "Well?" a furious voice squeaked. "Are you just going to leave me up here?"

I looked around and saw Rosier wedged in between two tree branches, glaring down at me. It looked like demon lords were sturdier than I'd thought. And then he started cussing again, fluidly, impressively, in a multitude of tongues, at Gertie, at the world, at me—

"Why . . . are you mad . . . at me?" I finally asked, when I could speak.

"You didn't let her go!"

"What?" I stared up at him.

"The *girl*! I told you to let her go!"

"And then what? Gertie would have—"

"Transferred her attention to you!"

"Her attention . . . was already . . . on me," I said, wondering what I was missing. "Did you hit your head?"

"Her attention was half on you and half on me. I needed her distracted—"

"For what?"

"For this!" And he held something out in his tiny fist.

Something that dropped at my side a second later, small and shiny and looking a lot like—

"A dart?" I picked it up.

"She wasn't planning to kill you," he told me, heatedly. "She was planning—"

"To drug me." My fist closed over the small thing, and my head jerked up.

"I managed to lift it off her in the chaos," he continued while I got shakily to my feet. "But I wasn't close enough to use it and she had me by the back of the neck, like a misbehaving kitten! If you had *listened*—"

"I thought you were panicking."

"I don't panic."

I looked back at him.

"I rarely panic. You need to learn some trust—"

"It wasn't about the trust—it was about the crazy."

"Sometimes you have to get a little crazy!"

"I'll keep it in mind," I said, locating a break in the treetops. And staring upward at a sky boiling with clouds, at a rainstorm pelting down, at a smothered moon hiding the insanity until a burst of lightning flashed, just outside the range of my spell. And illuminated an upturned wagon suspended impossibly in the air above us.

With its rider still in residence, because, like me, she'd just performed a major spell.

And she was *tired.*

"Wait here," I told Rosier.

"What? Why?"

"I have to get closer."

"Closer? What do you mean, clos—" He looked up. And then back at me, his eyes going huge. "Are you *insane*?"

"You're the one who told me to get crazy," I reminded him, trying to gauge the distance.

"I take it back!"

"Just stay out of sight," I said, a little harsher than necessary because the wagon was even higher than I'd thought. Gertie looked like a tiny doll, the horses like children's toys, the floating contents of the cage hidden by curtains of rain and almost indistinct.

But shifting her to me—definitely my first choice—wasn't going to work. Unlike shifting myself, that sort of thing wasn't instantaneous. It had taken me several seconds to latch on to the hound; if it took me that long with Gertie, and she felt it—

I'd lose the element of surprise, and it was the only advantage I had.

I took a breath and shifted.

Spatial shifts are usually easy compared to time travel. Like walking up a few steps instead of thirty flights—or a couple hundred in the case of Wales. But they also aren't usually done in almost pitch-darkness. Or aimed at a target that looked smaller than my palm. Or was wet and slippery and not entirely level.

Make that not level at all, I thought, rematerializing

along with a burst of lightning on the rain-slick wagon top. The flash was all but blinding, and close enough to lift strands of my hair and make me jump. And to explain why Gertie didn't immediately notice me.

Until I lost my footing and slid straight into her.

She fell, hitting down hard and sliding herself—into the hole she'd made in the roof to try to dart me. And it looked like I'd been right; she didn't totally fit. But halfway was good enough, because she got stuck, which would have been perfect if the wagon hadn't tipped and careened around from the shift in weight. And if I hadn't been forced to grab an axle to hold on to. And if she hadn't started slinging spells everywhere.

And if we hadn't started to fall.

"Son of a *bitch*!" I yelled, feeling my time spell start to unravel.

Lightning flashed, this time close enough for a small branch to get stuck in the bubble of slow time. It spread weird, neon light around as we began to tumble head over heels—or wheels over cage. And the fact that we were moving at only a fraction of regular speed didn't help, because that wouldn't be true for long.

And then the axle I was clinging to burst into dust.

The spell Gertie had flung missed my head, but left me with nothing to hold on to, and we were about to go over again. So I threw myself at her, grabbing her around the neck, trying to keep her from cursing me out of existence. And because she was the only thing I could reach.

But she didn't seem to like that, and a fist immediately started hitting the side of my head. "Get off me! Get off!"

But I couldn't get off, frizzy purple hair in my mouth or not, budding concussion or not, cursing bitch or not. Because I still had to get the dart into her. And because we were Ferris-wheeling around again. And because Gertie's butt wasn't as big as I'd thought and was about to come out of the hole.

"Damn it!"

I grabbed her hair, pulled her head to the side, and slammed the dart into her neck less than gently—

And the next moment we were in free fall.

But not because my spell had completely unraveled,

but because we'd fallen off the side that was in real time. And a few dozen stories go by really freaking fast in real time. I had a couple seconds to feel the wind, to smell the ozone, to see myself enveloped in glittering golden strands—

And then we were hitting down, Gertie cussing as the force of the drop sent my elbow into her stomach before wrenching us apart. I didn't know where she went, but the bounce sent me flipping back into the air, like a kid on the world's biggest trampoline. And left me staring around at a world gone mad, at a wildly skewing landscape, at streams of lighting and lashes of rain—

And at a hint of purple off to the left.

I didn't even wait to land. I threw the last spell I had energy for, giving it everything I had, praying it connected. And, for once, the universe decided to throw me a bone. Because the next second I was coming down alone, tumbling into darkness more gently this time, the majority of the momentum having been used up by that first massive jump. But it was enough to send me through several smaller bounces, bounces of victory, I thought, grinning like an idiot in sheer relief.

Until I looked up.

And saw the huge wooden thing now speeding down at me.

"Shit!" I somehow shifted to Rosier, barely managing the tiny spatial move, because my power was flat-lined.

And found him surrounded by girls in white.

Chapter Twenty-one

For a second, I stared at them and they stared at me, all of us looking surprised and vaguely horrified. And then they shifted out, all at once, before I could say anything. Leaving leaping afterimages in front of my eyes, the result of lighting flashing off their bright white dresses a second before they fled.

I went to my knees on wet leaves, half-blind and breathing hard, and wondering if I'd actually managed to intimidate somebody.

Or if, more likely, they'd gone to rescue the boss. Who my power obligingly showed me floundering around in a bog, miles from here, cursing as she realized what I'd shoved into her neck. And that her power wasn't going to get her out.

But her acolytes would.

We needed to get gone.

But my body didn't seem to agree. My body had had it. I grabbed Rosier, who the girls had helpfully fished out of the tree, hoping against hope to eke out one more shift. Only to end up sliding down onto my ass instead. While the heavy wooden wagon bounced around on the other side of the tree line, like a piñata caught between two candy-hungry kids.

I watched it blankly for a minute.

That wasn't something you saw every day.

But there were no witches this time, no rush to release the contents, no movement at all, except for the screaming, flailing horses. For some reason, the rescue party, or whatever they were, was hanging back, staying low, hiding in the shadows. Probably because of the next-level crap they'd just seen, I thought, grimacing.

And that was . . . that was bad, right? Not that I wanted them butchered by the damn fey, but . . . they were supposed to be, weren't they? Like the slaver was supposed to be shot through the throat and left to choke on his own blood, only he wasn't, either. Because the witches weren't there. So, instead, he was scrambling out of the net; he was staring around wildly; he was looking straight at me.

Or no, I realized, as somebody jerked me up.

He was looking at the fey behind me.

The next few minutes were a blur. Just the vague impression of being dragged here and there, of being loaded onto something—maybe another wagon—of rain soaking me and wind beating me, and Rosier whispering things I couldn't concentrate enough to understand. Maybe because I was already concentrating on something else.

Something I'd learned recently about people who were alive and weren't supposed to be. Something about when my power didn't seem to care about that. Something about the implications . . .

None of which I had time to focus on before we stopped abruptly and I tumbled out into a patch of mud.

I wasn't the only one. At some point, the other women had been pulled out of the destroyed wagon and loaded up alongside me. And whatever new conveyance we were on had been going pretty fast, and didn't have bars, so there was nothing left to catch us anymore.

But there were plenty of armored fey surrounding us, and a forest of spears in our faces.

I lay there, blinking back to awareness, watching firelight gleam on a circle of broad, flat blades. They were so shiny I could see my too-wide eyes reflected in the nearest, along with a few scattered raindrops and the frightened faces of the women behind me. And the merchant climbing down off a wagon and coming around.

And starting to curse.

"Put those damn things away," he told the ring of fey. "I've lost enough tonight!"

"You don't give us orders, old man—"

"No, but your Lady does! And she likes the work I do. So take it up with her!"

He snatched Rosier off the dirt beside me and started striding toward the entrance to a palisade. Like the checkpoint earlier, it looked recently erected from stripped, sharpened logs, some of them massive. Like the two that a couple of wooden gates were swinging from, currently closed against the night.

And which were hedged by two equally massive bonfires, which had somehow survived the deluge, and which the merchant was heading for with obvious intent.

Oh, *crap*.

I scrambled to my feet, wobbly-legged and dizzy. And stumbled after the man, catching up and grabbing on to his right arm for support, because I was about to fall over. And because it was the one holding Rosier.

"No," I said, breathlessly. "No, please. I told you; I need him."

He frowned down at me. "Why are you using a translation spell? Where are you from?"

"Somewhere else. And *I need him*," I repeated, because he hadn't let go.

The frowning intensified. "Your new master is never going to let you keep this thing! Best throw it on the fire now and be done with it."

"That's for him to decide, though, isn't it?"

"It's for him to decide *after he buys you*—"

"And my magic doesn't work without him," I added quickly. "You won't be able to prove I'm worth the extra money."

The meaty fist loosened slightly.

"He's harmless," I added, and we both looked at Rosier. Who did a pretty good job of looking harmless, all things considered.

The merchant made a sound that went with the disgust on his face. "Just keep it out of sight! If it bites anyone—"

"He doesn't have any teeth. See?" I started to pull up Rosier's gums, but the man stopped me with a retching sound.

"I don't want to see! Get it—no, put it in the bag!" He

threw my pack at me. "And keep it there!" He looked up. "Boy!"

I stuffed Rosier into the pack and stowed it under my arm as a kid came running out of the makeshift fort.

"Make sure she's put with the magic workers—under guard!" the merchant called after him as the boy started towing me toward the gate. "And get me an ale!"

And then the great gates were opening, and we were inside.

The cheery irreverence of the road camp was nowhere to be seen. Instead, hundreds, maybe thousands of women were milling around corrals, like cattle. Most of them were dirtier than the ones in the cage outside, the rain having mostly missed this place, and a good number looked haunted, like they'd been there too long. Which would have been five minutes for me, because the place stank like a sewer.

I gasped, eyes watering, as I was towed forward. Past pens of bleating sheep and screaming goats, past a mass of camp followers around tables and cauldrons, trying to turn the animals into dinner, past a bunch of servants scurrying around with armloads of firewood, past wagons piled high with barrels or vegetables, past a tent filled with gray-clad fey doing something I couldn't see because I was pulled by too fast. Past a hundred other sights, smells, and sounds that slapped me in the face, like the billowing smoke from a passing cook fire.

And into a corridor made up of two long rows of tables, one on either side, where new arrivals were being processed.

At least, it looked like that was the idea. But there was only a narrow space in the middle, which was completely filled with screaming, crying, desperate women. And struggling guards, who were attempting to organize the new arrivals, strip them of their possessions, and get them into outfits similar to mine.

It might have been going better, except the women's possessions apparently included their children. Who were being separated from their mothers and passed over the backs of the tables, to waiting carts. I doubted they were going to be hurt, considering how much the fey prized kids.

But the women obviously didn't know that.

One screamed as her daughter was ripped from her arms, and then leapt after her, scrambling frantically onto one of the tables. And sending baskets of runes and amulets, wands and rings, scattering everywhere in the process. And kicking and screaming, and calling the girl's name over and over, when one of the guards grabbed her and tried dragging her back.

Until she clawed his face with her nails, drawing long lines of blood, and he took out a batonlike club and punched her in the temple. Causing her to collapse like a dropped rag doll, her flame red hair brilliant in the torchlight. Almost as much as the blood seeping onto the ground around her probably fractured skull.

"What are you doing?" Rosier whispered as I realized that I'd unconsciously started toward the woman.

The boy was tugging at my hand. "Come on! Come on!"

But I didn't come on. I just stood there, my fist clenched on the pack rope, as several guards converged on the fallen woman. Only someone else reached her first.

There was a sudden commotion, loud enough to be heard over the din, and a small form shot out from under the table. "Mama! Mama!"

I didn't have to ask whose child it was; the hair was bright as flame. As bright as her mother's when she threw herself on the body, sobbing and repeating that same word over and over, while the two spills blended together. Impossible to tell the difference.

"Listen to me," Rosier said, his voice low and urgent. "There's nothing you can do. If she's dead, she died *fifteen centuries ago*—do you understand? You can't help her. You can only hurt us!"

"I understand."

"Then why are you still moving?"

I wasn't sure. A male fey in gray had just knelt beside the fallen woman, holding off the guard with a raised hand. Another fey, female this time, ducked under the table and put the child to sleep with a touch to her cheek. She carried her away while the slaver's boy practically pulled my arm off, yelling, "You come! You come!" loud enough to draw the attention of two nearby guards.

There was suddenly nothing left for me to do.

Except the obvious.

I knelt and picked a bundle off the ground and then got to my feet, just as the guards reached us.

They seemed more interested in the ongoing scene beyond me, where the fey in gray was saying something the spell couldn't translate to the red-faced guard, who didn't seem to like it. His hand tightened on his weapon, causing an audible gasp to run through the nearby crowd. But he hadn't raised it before what looked like an officer caught his arm, his grip as fierce as his expression. And all but threw him at the two guards in front of me.

One of them grabbed him while the other reached for me. "What did you pick up?"

"What?"

He grabbed my wrist. "Show me what's in your hand!"

I spread my hands open, both of them, palms up. "I stumbled," I said. "No shoes."

He looked down at my feet, and then back up at me, eyes narrowed. But the impatience—and fearlessness—of an eight-year-old saved me. "She been checked already," the boy told him, tugging on me. "She Budic's girl!"

And to my surprise, we were waved on through.

It wasn't much calmer on the other side as we fought our way through the crowd outside the pens. Fey were wandering about, sizing up the merchandise on offer, while a small army of humans rushed around, putting smears of paint on the women's tunics in various colors. Both groups ignored the weeping, traumatized chattel desperately asking after missing family members, insisting they shouldn't be here, or begging for help. Or, in more than one case, rocking mindlessly in the mud, with vacant looks on their faces.

"What's going on?" I asked Rosier, my lips numb.

He had climbed partway out of the pack and onto my shoulder and was staring around with big eyes. "This can't be happening—"

"Well, it looks like it's happening to me!"

"You don't understand. There's a *treaty*. It governs how many women the fey can take at one time. There are strict limits—"

"This is limited?"

"No." He stared around some more. "No."

And then we were dragged up to a harassed-looking man in the middle of the concourse, who pointed the boy toward a tent. One like all the others crowded into the back half of the enclosure, except that this one had a cluster of guards standing in front. And was pitch-dark inside.

At least to me. The torches burning outside the entrance had blinded me as we passed through, but I guess that wasn't true for everyone. Because I'd no sooner come through the door than somebody swore.

"What the hell is *that*?"

"The hell indeed," someone else said as the boy dropped my hand.

"You stay here," he told me as I looked around blindly. "You go out, the guards kill you. You understand? They kill you dead!"

"I understand," I said, my eyes straining to identify some gray blotches scattered here and there, in between pulsing afterimages.

"They kill you dead!" he repeated, just to be sure we were clear. Then he left me alone with the blotches. A few of which were starting to drift closer.

Judging by the sounds they were making, they weren't happy to see me. Maybe because I still had Rosier on my shoulder, like the world's ugliest parrot. I opened my mouth to tell them he was harmless, and then shut it again. Because I wasn't sure that they were.

"That's demonkind," one of the blotches hissed, from closer than I'd like. Almost close enough to touch.

"My demon," I said, skipping back. "Mine."

"And who are you?"

I swallowed. "Someone who's wondering why a bunch of witches—you are witches, right?" I asked as the blotches started to resolve into a semicircle of halter-clad women.

"Aye, we're witches. But not the kind that consort wi' demons!"

The speaker was an older woman, who frankly looked a lot like a witch. Or the common perception of one. She was missing the pointy hat and broom, but the hooknose, the wild black and gray hair, and the eye patch were perfect. Which made me wonder what the heck she was doing here.

I wasn't trying to be unkind, but "sex slave" was not the first description that came to mind.

Of course, that went for the rest of them, too. There didn't look to be one of childbearing age. Although I might be misjudging, since there also wasn't one without what looked like battle scars: a missing eye, a chipped front tooth, a literal scar bisecting a cheek, deep enough that it must have hit bone—twenty years ago.

"Well, maybe that's why you're still locked up," I said, continuing to evade the advancing throng. There were seven, maybe eight of them—it was still hard to see, especially in the corners—and I didn't like those odds. Not when the kindest-looking one also looked like she could take on a pro wrestler—and win.

"You watch your tongue, girl!" That was from a large woman with faded red hair and a belligerent expression.

"That might be prudent," Rosier said softly, into my ear.

"There's a time and place for prudence," I said. "I don't think this is it."

"Listen to your creature, girl," the redhead advised.

"Or what? You'll hurt me? Maybe kill me? And then what?"

"Then ye'll be dead! And your creature wi' ye!"

"And you'll still be stuck here, half-naked and defense-less—"

Someone hissed.

"—about to be auctioned off like cattle—"

"Have a care!"

"—or no, not like cattle," I amended. "Like *sheep*. Cattle at least try to escape—"

"And if we don't kill you, how does that change?" someone asked quietly, from behind me.

I whirled, because I hadn't noticed anyone there.

My vision was a little clearer now, probably as much as it was going to get, considering that the only light came from small rips in the tent fabric. They sent tiny fingers of dust-filled firelight stabbing across the space, one of which bisected the face of the first young woman I'd seen. And the first who didn't look like a witch.

She was pretty, with delicate features and a cascade of pale blond hair that almost reached her knees. And what might have been dark gray eyes that were leveled calmly on me. She didn't look like someone who was about to be auction fodder. She also didn't look like she was planning to stab me in the back the first chance she got, especially since she'd just had it.

"Give me a moment," I said to her, and closed my eyes.

I only had one question, since there was only one option I could see. But before I did anything, it would be nice to know if I was about to screw up the timeline.

You know, again.

But my power was doing the metaphysical equivalent of humming absently, with no apparent opinion one way or another. There was no sense of doom and gloom, but also no enthusiasm. If I had to use a word to describe the overall response, it would have been "meh."

We're going to have to work on our communication, I told it grimly.

"I have an idea," I said to them, opening my eyes. And found the witches looking at each other, like they thought I might be nuts. "But it depends."

"On what?" the blonde asked warily.

I pulled the items I'd picked up off the ground, and that my little chameleon had hidden for me, out of a fold in my skirts. "On whether these wands belong to you."

Chapter Twenty-two

A minute later, I found out what was behind the tent: more tents. Along with a surprised guard who was cursed through the fabric before he even realized he was a target. And then ended up a lump hidden behind the little movie the witches provided for anybody checking in.

It was supposed to be us, huddled in a circle, talking softly. And for an on-the-fly illusion, it wasn't bad, although it wasn't likely to fool anyone for long. But then, we didn't have long.

The auction was about to start.

From what I could see past a couple of barrels, it looked like the marking up had finished and the sorting had commenced. Sobbing young women were being pulled away from their older relations, who I guessed were being sold as generic slaves. And then further divided based on age or looks. Groups were being assembled by dealers who frequently changed their minds, unifying and then jerking apart families as they tried to form the best lots.

My hand clenched as I watched two sisters, judging by their identical long auburn hair, be stripped and examined by a grizzled man with the impersonal touch of a horse trader. The girl with the prettiest face was kept; the other was dragged off, sobbing, to another group, without even being allowed to get dressed first. Her shift was knocked from her hand by a passing servant and trampled in the mud, leaving her to try to cover herself with only her hair as she waited, alone and terrified, to be sold with a group of strangers.

I told myself that Rosier had been right. I couldn't stop

what was happening, what had already happened. However this had played out, it was over, long ago. But my job wasn't.

I *had* to get out of here.

But that was easier said than done. The camp was crawling with guards, both the official ones and the flashier, shiny-armor-and-etched-weapon type some of the slavers had brought. And even if we somehow got through all that, and through the warded palisade wall, an army was camped on the other side.

I bit my lip. I could use the potion, try to shift away. But even if I succeeded, that might make things worse instead of better. Because Gertie was still out there. And although she was currently unable to kick my ass, her acolytes had almost certainly rescued her by now. I doubted they were powerful enough to get her home, but they could definitely get her to her present-day counterpart, the Byzantine Pythia I'd seen with her last time.

And then *she* could kick my ass.

I was going to have to find another way.

"They're auctioning the people in lots?" I asked the blonde, who had crouched down beside me.

She nodded. "Human traders aren't allowed in Faerie. They sell the women in quantity to the fey, who take them back, clean them up, and auction them off individually."

"So each fey slaver will be leaving with a fairly big group?" I asked, to be sure I understood. "A group he doesn't know too well?"

"Not tonight," the redhead said, before the blonde could answer. She crouched down beside us. "Not wi' our people using the darkness to make them pay for every life they steal!"

"Your people?" I frowned at her. "You mean the crazy women who almost killed us coming in?"

She shot me a sardonic look. "They weren't tryin' t' kill ye, girl, else ye'd be dead. They were tryin' to save ye."

"Aye," Hooknose agreed, joining the party. "Let's see how much Nimue profits from her crimes!"

"Nimue? Then the Green Fey are behind this?" I

asked, suddenly noticing a few green tabards in the crowd. Most of the guards hadn't bothered with them, probably because of the weather. But the waterworks coming in should have been enough of a clue. Water was the Green Fey's element and they could do amazing things with it. If I hadn't been preoccupied—

I suddenly noticed that everyone had turned to stare at me, in various degrees of incredulity. "I'm . . . not from around here," I added weakly.

"Your home must be far if you don't know that Nimue considers this her personal fiefdom," the blonde said. "She thinks she can do whatever she likes with it."

"And what she likes is to renegotiate the treaty," the redhead commented heatedly. "And it was bad enough already!"

"A recent war with the Dark Fey depleted her numbers," the blonde explained. "She's insisting on doubling the levy."

"But the king refused, and damn right, too!" Hooknose muttered. "But now she's come in force, rounding up not only what she asked for, but every woman she can find!"

"They're even taking the children," a thin brunette despaired, her eyes on the camp.

"She's just trying to put pressure on the king," the blonde told her. "Nimue has a hard enough time feeding her own children—she can't want to feed ours, too."

"So she'll take them and the food!" the redhead said. "Leaving us just enough to raise a new generation. So they can come and pick them over, taking who they like, raping and plundering—no! This ends now!"

"How?" the thin brunette asked bitterly. "She has the leaders, and also the princess. And without them—"

"That's why we're here," the blonde said, seeing my confusion. "Nimue called the coven leaders to a conference, only to take them captive. We came on a rescue mission." Her lips twisted. "And soon thereafter needed rescuing ourselves."

"Would these coven leaders be able to help us get out?" I asked.

"Aye," the redhead said. "If we could find them!"

"We have to stick to the plan," the blonde said, looking around at the circle of women, who glanced at each other uneasily. "We have to try!"

"We don't even know that there *is* a plan," Hooknose argued. "If our boy's lying dead in the woods, the covens aren't comin'."

"And even if they are," the thin brunette put in, "we can't get the walls down without the leaders. The wards—"

"Wait," I said, trying to keep up. "What plan? And what boy?"

"A man, actually. Part fey. He's helping us coordinate an attack on the camp."

"The idea is to have the covens assault this place from the outside," the blonde told me. "Keeping the fey busy while we free the leaders. Each of whom can harness the power of an entire coven, hopefully enough to destroy the palisade walls—"

"Then everyone scatters," the redhead interrupted, hazel eyes flashing. "All the women in all directions while the covens fight off the fey. They may recapture some, but they'll never catch us all!"

"Not at night. Not in our own lands," Hooknose agreed.

"—but we were caught before we could find the leaders, much less free them," the blonde finished.

"And now our only hope is dead," the thin brunette said dolefully.

"You don't know that. He had to find the other covens, get them to approve the plan, then make it all the way back here—"

"And that was one of the best illusions I've ever seen," the redhead added enviously.

"Illusion?" I said, feeling my temperature start to rise. "What illusion?"

"Disguised himself as a slaver," Hooknose said. "One who was killed trying to sneak back some of the girls we'd rescued from the fey. Our boy volunteered to pass through their lines and communicate the plan to the rest of the covens—"

"And he made it," the blonde said firmly. "He must have. The illusion was perfect."

Hooknose disagreed. "Too flashy. I told him to tone down that hair."

"What does it matter?" the thin brunette wailed. "Knowing the fey, he's dead by now—"

"You know, I seriously doubt that," I said, watching a devil with two-tone hair run into the tent behind us and start thrashing around in the middle of the illusion. And then run out of the new back door and stare around like a madman.

Until he saw us. "Oh, good," he told me, and visibly relaxed. "You're here—"

And then I slapped him.

"Stop acting like you're hurt," I said, a few minutes later. "You're not hurt."

Pritkin felt his jaw for the third time. "It's mostly my feelings—"

"*Your* feelings? You *kidnapped* me—"

"I explained that. I was coming back—"

"I thought you were going to *court*."

"I am—I was," he amended as we plastered ourselves to the side of a tent, halfway across the camp. "This . . . came up."

"And you couldn't have told me? You couldn't have said *anything*?"

He shushed me, which didn't do much for my temper. And then plucked a guard I hadn't seen from around the side of the tent and handed him off to the witches. Before turning back to me, looking exasperated.

"There were too many ears around, and my disguise was wearing thin. The Green Fey are generally tolerant toward half-breeds, but with tensions this high—"

"So you left me with a *slaver*—"

"For a short time. So I would know where you were. So you wouldn't be taken as plunder, or end up in one of those damn pens—"

"I can take care of myself!"

"Yes," he said, suddenly intent. "*But so can the fey*, and there were a good many more of them than you, plus every slaver in the damn country scouring the hills for any woman they could find!"

"So you kidnapped me to keep me from being kidnapped?"

He started to say something, then thought about it for a second. "Essentially."

"That would only make sense to you," I said sourly.

"You two are . . . friends?" the blonde asked, looking up, as the limp fey was dumped into a barrel.

"Friends," Pritkin agreed.

"It's complicated," I said, at the same time.

He frowned.

I sighed.

"Friends," I agreed.

"It's complicated," he said, simultaneously.

She blinked.

The redhead laughed. "I used to have one of those sorts of 'friends.' "

"It's not like that," I said.

"I'm working on it," Pritkin told her.

I frowned. "Working on what?"

"What?"

"Which question were you answering?"

"There was a question?"

I blinked. The redhead laughed. The blonde looked like she was wondering how she'd ended up on a rescue mission with the Three Stooges.

"Is it much farther?" she asked. "To where they're keeping the leaders?"

"No, just there." Pritkin nodded toward a nearby pavilion.

And that was the only word for it. The tents in the back half of the camp had started out fairly basic, with a central pole and a dark weave. But they kept getting fancier the farther we got from the cattle pens. The air was cleaner back here, and the stars sparkled above white, multiroom mansions with gold designs on the canvas and bright pennants flying overhead. And this one was the biggest I'd seen, truly a home fit for a queen.

Only apparently, it wasn't.

"Not the tent," Pritkin said, and pointed to something past it.

Something that was a serious letdown.

I hadn't been able to get much of a feel for the layout of this place, because the fey's living quarters were scattered haphazardly, in a jumbled mass. But we'd almost worked our way through them, to the very back of the camp, where an open space lay near the palisade wall. In front of which was . . .

Well, it looked like a roof someone had forgotten to put a house under. And since it was a thatched roof, and since the mostly missing building was a big one, it was fairly comical-looking. Like a toupee a passing giant had dropped.

But, pathetic as it was, that's what the fey were using as a command post, probably because enchantments don't work so well on insubstantial, fluttering "walls."

If they did, we'd still be stuck back in our own tent.

"So, this is good, right?" I whispered. "It's *thatch*. One good fireball—"

"Would never touch it," Hooknose said, extending a veined hand.

The blonde nodded. "It's warded."

"No," Pritkin disagreed. "It's *warded*. We might get through with a week to hammer away at it, but we don't have a week."

He rotated his wrist, showing a crude hourglass etched into the skin of his forearm. Mages used magical tattoos for all sorts of things, but this didn't look like one, maybe because he hadn't had time. It did look painful—red and jagged-edged, like it had been done quickly and without a totally sharp knife.

But it was working.

Tiny red dots were flowing from the top of the "glass" to the bottom, and while I didn't know how long it took to empty, I did know there weren't many left. The covens were coming, and they were coming soon. And they were going to get butchered if we didn't manage to rescue the leaders before then.

"Then let's see what all of us can do!" the redhead said, starting up.

Only to have the blonde and the skinny brunette pull her back.

"There's also the small matter of the queen's personal

guard," Pritkin added dryly. "There's dozens in there, and they're staying put. From what I hear, no one's been in or out all day."

"You got inside?" I asked.

He shook his head. "I impersonated a camp follower assigned to deliver food, but the guards took it from me. After the attempt to free the coven leaders, they're not taking chances."

"Then how d'ye know the leaders are even in there?" the redhead demanded.

"The camp follower I told you about. He was allowed in earlier. He also saw another set of wards on an inner chamber, and six guards outside it—"

"It's the princess," the blonde said excitedly. "It has to be!"

"Princess?" I repeated.

"A fey princess," she told me. "She helped us organize the covens. She's been fighting alongside us."

"It would be easier to just get the coven leaders," Pritkin argued. "If she's fey—"

"We're not leaving her!"

"If she's fey," he repeated stubbornly, "she'll have to come to terms with her people over this, sooner or later, or be exiled. Do you think she wants that?"

"It's for her to say what she wants," the redhead said hotly. "It's for us t' get her out so she can say it!"

There was a chorus of agreement.

Pritkin sighed. "Then we're going to need the key."

"What key?" I asked.

He sighed again. "The one hanging around Nimue's neck."

Chapter Twenty-three

"Around her *neck*?" I asked, as Pritkin and I waited for the witches to get into position.

They were heading for the palisade wall, to start an enchantment to try and bring it down in case we failed. He and I were watching, ready to cause a distraction if it looked like anybody noticed. But so far, nobody had.

Maybe because everybody was at the auction. Other than a human chopping wood and a fey trying to reshoe a horse, there wasn't a soul in sight. It was too good to be true, and it was making my palms itch.

"That's what one of the guards told my source, when he offered to take a tray in," he confirmed. "She's the only one with a key."

"How are we supposed to get it, then?"

"*We* aren't going to get it. I am—if possible." He didn't sound like he was exactly in love with the idea. "I don't want you anywhere near the sea witch."

"Is that what they call her?"

"That's one of the things they call her."

Pritkin was looking grim, maybe because his plan to stow me with the slaver hadn't panned out. Although I thought he should have been pleased about that, since it solved a problem for him. A big one.

Instead of trying to figure out how to break the witches *out*, we were now trying to smuggle some wands *in*, and let them do it for themselves. Basically the same idea I'd had when I first swiped the things, back in the courtyard. The question was how to get them past the guards.

Which was where I came in.

As head of the Pythian Court, I was technically a coven leader. Meaning that I should be put in with the others, solving one problem. And my bracelet would solve the rest.

Because even if the fey found it, it would always come back. Including the new little charms that ringed it, the odd, ugly, sticklike charms that Pritkin had shrunk, and that the witches could unshrink and run amok with. Distracting the guards while he infiltrated Nimue's chambers for the key.

That was his job, because of his ability at glamourie. Mine was just magical munitions mule: get the stuff past the guards. So why was I sweating?

Maybe because my power remained uninterested in this whole affair, despite the fact that I was actively interfering in the timeline now, the very thing I wasn't supposed to do. The very thing I was supposed to prevent *other people* from doing. And now that my head was clear, I was remembering things, like what it had meant before when my power wasn't worried about changes in the timeline.

Something was about to go down, something bad, something that was going to make all of this irrelevant. Because that was what happened last time: a fey had died who wasn't supposed to, but my power hadn't cared. Because it knew that a battle was coming, one in which he *was* supposed to die, and the few hours' difference weren't enough to matter.

I was assuming the reverse worked as well. Like if those people who were supposed to die earlier today did so shortly from something else, they'd never have a chance to mess with the timeline. So my power wouldn't care, but I *did*, because I was here and Pritkin was here and we needed to get gone before the shit hit the—

"It's time," Pritkin said, abruptly enough to make me jump. He looked at me. "You all right?"

"Yeah," I said, a little breathlessly. "Yeah, I'm good."

I stopped fingering my bracelet and followed him.

The toupee turned out to be a nobleman's house, because apparently noblemen had different standards back in the day. But it was bigger inside than I'd thought, with a high ceiling under the conical roof, like looking up into a big straw hat. Just how big I wasn't sure, because a wattle-and-daub wall rose a dozen yards away with a door in it, blocking off the inner areas from what looked like a reception room.

Well, okay, it looked like the medieval version of a hunting lodge, with a fire, a table, and a few chairs covered with animal hides spread around. But no people, just like there hadn't been any guards on the door outside. It should have made me feel better.

It didn't.

"Wait."

Pritkin had already started for the door, but he turned to look at me. "We don't have much time."

"I know. But this . . . I need to know something first."

He raised an eyebrow.

"The staff."

"Yes?"

"Do you have it?"

"It's . . . safe."

"Safe where?"

He didn't say anything.

I bit my lip. "You don't trust me?"

"It's not me. . . ."

"Then who?"

"The king. He said—"

"What king?"

Pritkin stared at me. "The one we met yesterday?"

I just looked at him. "Yesterday" was a difficult concept when you jackrabbited around the timeline as much as I did. Like, really difficult.

"The one who tried to *kill us*?"

Not narrowing things down much.

"The one you somehow *froze in place*?"

And then I remembered: the face of an angel, if you didn't count the expression. Reflexes faster than those of anyone I'd ever seen, including other fey—almost including me, and I'd been *shifting*. And a shiny mailed boot stabbing down, not on me, but on the roof all around me, which had been thatch, too.

And which had broken, sending me falling straight into the hands of the Pythian posse.

I frowned. "You mean the blond—"

"Yes."

"—was the *Sky King*?"

"Yes. Caedmon. He told me—"

"Caedmon. You're on a first-name basis now?"

Pritkin's eyes narrowed. "After you disappeared—again—he agreed to let me take the staff back to court, to use as bait to try to find out what's going on. Or don't you want to know why all three of the leading houses of Faerie are currently on earth, at the same time, in the same place, with *armies*?"

I shook my head. "We already know that. The Svarestri stole the staff, and the Blarestri came chasing it. And now Nimue—"

"But that's just it. Why did they come? The Svarestri barely know this world. Why bring the staff here, where they are at a serious disadvantage even among other fey, who have at least some familiarity with it? And where their power doesn't work nearly as well as in Faerie? They steal a staff that could easily cause a war, and they bring it *here*. Why?"

"I don't know. But we're not going to find out if you lose it—"

"I told you, it's safe."

"But you won't tell me where."

Pritkin scowled. It was strange. The face was different—the face was a stranger—but that expression was hauntingly familiar. Except for one thing.

"I hate your eyes," I said suddenly, before I thought.

"What?"

"Not—I mean those," I said, gesturing at the blue-black combo he had going on. "Do you have to keep them?"

He looked a little surprised but shook his head. "No. The guard was about to change while I was here, and I wasn't using this face then, in any case. They won't know me any more than they will you."

"Is that why you think this will work? They don't know me?"

Pritkin looked at me for a moment, and then walked back over. He had that expression, the I'm-going-to-figure-her-out expression, which yeah, probably wasn't much of a challenge right now. It felt like I was stalling, even to me.

But I couldn't seem to help it. I didn't want to go in there. It had been okay from the outside, just a silly little hat of a house, but now . . .

I didn't like it now.

It felt like standing at the entrance to a cave where you've been told there's a monster, but you didn't believe it until you got there and, oh, look, a monster. Or like being in one of those old movies where you're at the top of the basement stairs, leading down into darkness, and the light switch doesn't work. And, worse, you're a blonde. Everyone is yelling at their TV, "Don't go in there, *don't go in there*," but you do because you're the *blonde*, which is Hollywood code for criminally stupid.

Only I wasn't, and I didn't want to go in there.

Pritkin's head tilted, as if some of my inner dialog was showing on my face. "That and the fact that the fey can sense power."

"And that matters?"

He held a hand just above my arm, and goose bumps rose to meet him. "You have power. Anyone who concentrates, anyone with the ability, should be able to feel it. If I'm to convince them that you're someone who needs to be put in a highly secured area, you have to be powerful."

I looked up at him. "Is that why this Caedmon doesn't trust me?"

"He didn't say."

"But you believe him."

"He said I should avoid you. He told me that you're dangerous."

"And *you believe him*?"

It felt important for some reason—some stupid reason, since this Pritkin didn't know me. We'd spent all of maybe a day together as far as he was concerned. Of course, it had been a hell of a day, and it was a day longer than he'd known the damn fey king, but still—

He stepped closer, until our bodies were almost touching. A finger tilted my chin up, and I looked into eyes that were finally familiar, vivid green shining through whatever spell he'd used before. "I'm with you now. I'm trust-ing you with this. And when this is over, I'll take you to court. We'll find out what the Svarestri want with the staff together."

I swallowed and nodded. "Okay."

We walked through the door.

I'd expected another big room on the other side, mak-ing up the other half of the circle. But instead, there was just a hallway, relatively narrow, with a low ceiling. It was almost claustrophobic, especially coming from the previ-ous room, and there were no windows. Instead, lanterns hung on the walls at intervals, throwing flickering shad-ows everywhere and ramping up the creep factor.

There was also a door, just one, at the far end, flanked by two guards.

They didn't look like the others I'd seen, in the camp and on the road, most of whom could have been knights out of some medieval flick from the sixties. The kind where they were too clean and had chiseled jaws and per-fect teeth, and looked like they smelled good despite rid-ing around in armor all day. But, I realized now, they'd also looked like something else.

They'd also looked *human*.

These two didn't. The differences were subtle, unlike with the Svarestri, who appeared almost alien, with skin so white it was practically ashen, and a weird springiness to their movements that human anatomy just didn't allow. These two had skin that looked like it saw the sun occa-sionally, and hair that was long and dark, instead of silver bright. But they still had the same too-tall, too-lithe builds, and faces that would never have made it onto a mannequin, no matter how handsome the features.

Because the cold haughtiness would have scared off all the customers.

After a brief glance, I concentrated on keeping my eyes on the ground at some indeterminate place in be-tween the guards' legs, trying not to notice the way the firelight streamed on burnished armor and in strange, foreign eyes. I also didn't glance at Pritkin, who had just put a hand on the back of my neck, because he was a slaver and I didn't think I'd look at a slaver for reassurance. But God, I wanted to!

And then a pike was thrust in my face.

It was shiny. Knife edged and deadly, but also really, really shiny. Like the ones outside the gate, there wasn't a speck of rust anywhere.

The fey took good care of their weapons; you had to give them that.

"What?" That was Pritkin, responding to something one of the fey had said, which I'd missed because I was entranced by the pike.

"I said, she goes in naked."

My head came up, and Pritkin's grip on my neck tightened. "Why?"

The fey exchanged a look. The question seemed to surprise them, like most half-breeds simply obeyed orders without question. And maybe they did, considering the aura these two were giving off. If they could bottle this stuff, they'd make a fortune from CEOs and drill sergeants everywhere.

But the macho vibe didn't seem to be having the same effect on Pritkin, and after a moment the fey who had spoken answered, I guessed because of the novelty value. "Witch smuggled in a wand. Killed a guard. Thus: new rule."

He reached for me.

Pritkin pulled me back. "She's already been searched."

And oh, shit, I thought, still staring at the nice boring bit of ground, which wasn't helping suddenly, because the room had just added a couple extra atmospheres.

"Strip her or we will." The voice was as cold as a mountain stream.

Looked like the novelty had already worn off.

For both parties. I glanced at Pritkin's arm, to check the hourglass, and saw a clenched fist and bunched muscles instead. The fey noticed, too, which would have been funny under different circumstances. Because they were worried about me, or about whether he was going to be dumb enough to throw a punch, but had totally ignored the pack he was carrying with the monster inside.

I'd brought Rosier along because it was that or leave him with the witches, who hadn't seemed like fans. And because I couldn't risk Pritkin's soul showing up with his father halfway across camp. And because nobody had seemed to give a damn about him so far, other than trying to feed him to the fire, so I was hoping he wouldn't be viewed as a threat.

It looked like I'd been right.

But this wasn't something Rosier could help me with.

I pulled out of Pritkin's grip and undid the halter. Nobody had bothered giving me a belt, so that should have been all it took. But the shift was still damp, and it bunched on my hips, forcing me to have to push it down before I could step out of it.

I stood back up, a hand awkwardly covering my sex and an arm across my breasts, my face flaming, and hoped that would be it.

But apparently not.

"That's better," the guard murmured, taking his time as he circled me. "That's much better."

"As you can see, she's not hiding anything!" Pritkin rasped.

"Oh, but I can't see that. Not yet."

He circled back to the front and stood there, waiting.

I flashed back to that girl out front, having to stand there for who knew how long, freezing, naked, and miserable. Getting pawed over by any passing fey, having any flaws pointed out and exaggerated to bring the price down, because they didn't care about us. They didn't care about anyone who wasn't them.

And that was exactly the problem with the gods, and the creatures who followed them. Maybe that was why my mother had gotten rid of all of them, because even the so-called benevolent types had often acted like humans didn't matter. Not their dignity, not their sense of self, not their sanity. Not even their lives. Human beings weren't real to them, weren't people; they were resources or servants or playthings or worshippers.

Or victims.

I was getting tired of being a victim. I was getting tired

of going through life hoping that someone didn't notice me. I was getting tired of hiding.

I dropped my arm and stared up at him defiantly.

The fey laughed. "She has spirit, this one. I like that. I might even bid on her myself."

"And what are your other three going to say?" the second guard asked, relaxing slightly and leaning against the wall.

"Nothing, if they know what's good for them," the first one said, swiping a thumb across a nipple, watching it peak. "That's your problem—you never learned that you can't let them talk."

"If you don't they sulk around for days. And you have to bring them something pretty."

The first guard shot him a look of disgust. "They're not your wives—they're your *slaves*. You bring presents to slaves?"

"Sometimes. It makes things easier."

"No wonder you have trouble. You don't know how to treat them."

"And you do?"

"Oh yes." He let go of my breast to trail a finger down my stomach.

Unlike the other, his eyes weren't black but blue, clear and bright and amused enough that I wondered if I'd been wrong, if there was some human in there, after all. Or maybe some things were just universal. The unwanted touch slid past my navel and continued to drop, down to where my hand still rested. Down to the last bit of me that was still concealed.

And playfully pulled up one of my fingers.

"Oh yes," he repeated. "But I like to try before I buy—"

Pritkin knocked his hand away. "She's not for sale!"

The fey looked up, and again, he seemed more surprised than anything else. "She's human. They're all for sale."

"Not this one. She's to go in with the others—"

"She goes in when I say, half-breed—"

"Then say it!" It was not a request.

But to my surprise, the fey merely smiled. Maybe because his friend had just joined the action. From leaning on the wall to hands on Pritkin's biceps, in the time it took to blink. Pritkin jerked his arms, which went exactly nowhere, and the first fey resumed his former occupation.

And lifted another finger.

"What are you concealing, lovely one?" he asked, watching Pritkin's reddening face. "And so carefully?"

A third finger was raised, and his eyes slid back to me. "Is it dangerous?"

A fourth.

"Or is it . . . sweet?"

He pulled my hand away, leaving me bare to his gaze. And to his touch, which immediately slipped between my legs. I choked back a sound of revulsion, but I guessed not well enough. Because a scuffling fight suddenly broke out between the other fey and Pritkin.

The first one barely glanced at them. "Oh yes," he said as he began to explore, "I think it's sweet."

He found the small nub hidden inside my folds and rolled it between his fingers, grinning when I recoiled. He did it again, and his eyes darkened when I cried out. "Let's find out if you think I'm sweet, too," he said, and pushed me to my knees.

But a second later, Pritkin was out of the second guard's grasp and between me and my tormentor, shoving him back with one hand, the other pulling me behind him. Which might have worked better if there hadn't been two of them. "Knife!" I yelled as the second guard lunged up from the floor, weapon in hand.

But the first one raised a hand, pausing the action, his eyes suddenly sharp and thoughtful. He glanced at me, and at the fist I'd curled into the back of Pritkin's shirt, in case I had to shift us out. And then back at Pritkin.

The eyes narrowed.

But he only said one word. "Why?"

Pritkin licked his lips, as if he'd just realized that yeah, that might not have been a normal response for a hardened slaver. "She's . . . a virgin."

The fey barked out a laugh. "I doubt it. But even so, our people don't care about such things, merely that they're good breeders. Where's the harm?"

"I said no—"

"And I say yes. And since she's just a slave—"

"She's *my* slave."

"Your slave."

"Yes. *I* found her. *I* brought her in. By our laws—"

"They're not your laws, mutt. Don't pretend otherwise."

"By your laws, then! That makes her mine. Taking her is theft—"

"You'll quote the law to us?" the second fey said, sounding almost more incredulous than angry, although the knife hadn't been sheathed. "I'll teach you some—"

The first fey held up a hand again, but that was definitely suspicion on his face now. "All right," he agreed. "Your slave."

"You can't be serious," the other fey began while I felt the muscles in Pritkin's back relax slightly.

And then tense right back up when the first guard spoke again. "You take her, then."

Chapter Twenty-four

I could shift, I thought, as Pritkin stared at the fey. My power didn't feel encouraging, but I didn't have to move us far. Just outside, just far enough to run—

But even assuming I managed it, Gertie and company would be on us like a pack of bloodhounds, and I *had* him. I had him. I had Rosier. I had everything I needed. Except for the cursed soul, which could show up any moment.

Pritkin was arguing, telling the fey a bunch of stuff they didn't care about, because they didn't believe us. He hadn't been any more convincing as a callous slave owner than I had as a cowed slave. We needed acting lessons, but we weren't going to get them. We were going to get something a lot more painful or I was going to shift us out of here, and neither of those outcomes was acceptable.

I slowly went back to my knees.

Pritkin glanced at me, and then did a double take.

I guess he hadn't expected that.

"With your permission?" I said unsteadily.

Pritkin didn't say anything, but he looked more than a little off balance. The fey seemed surprised, too, like they'd already decided we were not as advertised, and were just waiting for him to give them the excuse for a different sort of entertainment. But it looked like they'd settle for this one.

The second fey let him go, although he stayed close this time, rather than propping up the wall. The first raised an eyebrow, but it appeared the jury was still out. Because he moved back a little and crossed his arms, instead of attacking or dragging us off somewhere.

I looked up at Pritkin again.

And immediately had a sinking feeling. Because he wasn't on board with this. His hand was reflexively clenching and unclenching at his side, as if he was still planning to take on two of the queen's guard single-handedly.

And that . . . wasn't good. Even if he won, it wouldn't get us past the wards, or help defeat the dozens of soldiers inside that could quickly be outside. That was the whole point of this—to get weapons to people who could channel the power of entire covens. They might be able to deal with the fey; we couldn't.

So they had to let us in.

"With your *permission*?" I repeated, a little more forcefully, nails digging into his thigh.

He still didn't say anything, but the answer was clearly no. Or, judging from his steadily darkening expression, hell no. And that didn't make sense.

We'd faced a similar scenario with the Svarestri the last time I was here, and he'd shown no such shyness then. In fact, it had been his idea to use a PDA to distract a guard and get away, and it had worked, more or less. And the less hadn't had to do with the distraction, but with the fact that Gertie showed up shortly thereafter.

Yet this time, he was furious. I didn't know why, but I knew *him*. And hotheadedness had always been a problem for him even in my era, when he'd had centuries to learn to master his temper. He hadn't had them now, and this Pritkin had always seemed less controlled to me, his emotions closer to the surface, both good and bad.

And bad right now was going to get him killed.

"Please."

I stared up at him, desperate, pleading, but not able to say the words that might convince him with the fey standing right there. But something seemed to get through. Or maybe he just didn't see an alternative that didn't involve razor-sharp implements and our jugulars. He finally nodded tersely, a single up-and-down motion of his chin, and I scooted closer.

And was faced with having to actually live up to my bravado.

"The, uh . . . the tunic?" I gestured at it. "Could you, um . . ."

He jerked it off, along with the layers underneath—another tunic and a long, linen shirt—because of the cold outside. It was cold in here, too. To the point that I could see my breath, that my body was covered in goose bumps, that my knees would probably be knocking if they weren't all but frozen to the flagstone. The fire from the outer room was too far away to do any good, and if the lanterns gave off any heat, I couldn't tell.

Yeah, this is sexy, I thought, and tried not to shiver.

Pritkin paused when he was down to loose trousers and some strips of cloth that had been wound around his calves, like some sort of makeshift socks. Then he started removing those as well. I wondered why until I realized: they could bunch his trousers around his ankles if he needed to move quickly, trapping him. And he *was* planning to move. I could see it in the tension in his body, in the hard, angry set of his jaw, in the tight muscles of his calves when the strips were finally off and he stood there in just a loose pair of pants.

And looked at me.

I didn't know what his plan was. Maybe to pretend to play along, and move when the fey were distracted? Because I didn't see how that helped. Maybe to actually play along, and hope it convinced them? Because he wasn't looking like a guy who was ready to put on a show. Maybe something else entirely that I hadn't thought of, because right now I was having a hard time thinking about anything.

Except the obvious.

I licked my lips and slid my hands up his legs, feeling hard muscle and coarse wool, with little pieces that caught on my palms. I needed to lotion more, I thought irrelevantly. My hands were rough. They were also trying to shake, making me grateful that the trousers were held on by a simple drawstring.

I looked up again, and saw that unfamiliar face staring down at me, and the shaking got worse. I suddenly didn't know if I could do this, with two strangers watching me and Pritkin looking like someone else. I didn't know if I could do this . . . like this.

Not like this.

My breath started coming faster, but not out of excitement. I knew the signs; I'd had a panic attack or two in my time, and why not? With *my* life? Which had somehow led to me kneeling naked on freezing flagstones, about to fellate a friend I had way too much attraction to already, while two bored, voyeuristic fey used me as their substitute for a porno. And while the people depending on us got slaughtered because we were almost out of time.

Yet I just stayed there, gripping his legs so I wouldn't start trembling, so I wouldn't freak out because I *had to do this*. I had to do this or shift us out, and I couldn't shift us out, so I *had to do this*. But my body didn't appear to be listening, maybe because the strange sense of dread I'd experienced in the room outside was back, and adding to the panic. To the point that the roof seemed to be collapsing on top of me, the walls closing in, a scream building in my throat as my fight-or-flight instincts kicked in, and kicked in big-time. I had to get out of here, *I had to—*

And then it hit, so hard and so tangible that it knocked me out of my budding hysteria and left me looking around for the source. It felt like a gust of wind, only there was no wind in here. There couldn't be with no windows, and two closed doors. And even if there had been, it would have been cold and damp, like the night outside. While this felt like a breeze straight off a desert.

But not one of ours.

I glanced at Rosier, but all I saw was a lump in my discarded pack. But maybe I'd been wrong about him not being able to help. Because I'd felt something like this before, on another night, in another desperate situation. One in which Rosier had used his incubus powers to overwhelm my fear and panic, and . . . what had he called it? *Enhance?*

I felt like laughing suddenly.

What a completely inadequate word.

I sank back down, but this time, the hard stones beneath me were as comfortable as a pillow, the cold-eyed fey were simply gone, as if they'd never existed, and the frigid, dusty hallway was filled with a languid heat, heavy and fragrant, like warm honey.

And suddenly, this was just the easiest thing in the world.

My hands unclenched and smoothed up the tautness of Pritkin's stomach, feeling hard lines and soft hair, and muscles that jumped delightfully under my touch. I leaned in, pressing my lips to the clean, warm skin below his navel, and felt his heartbeat. I stayed there, mouthing that delicious piece of flesh for a moment, feeling it catch and give under my teeth, feeling him jerk. And then laved the little wound I'd made with my tongue, because there was no hurry, none at all. There was just this, just tasting the salt of him, feeling the warmth, enjoying the soft musk that perfectly complemented the perfume in the air.

And that suddenly intensified, along with my hunger.

I looked up. "Tell me if I do something you don't like," I whispered.

He just looked back at me, almost bewildered, as if that had made no sense. And to an incubus, maybe it hadn't. I held his eyes as I loosened the ties at his waist that parted at a touch, the fabric falling to the floor, to pool around his ankles.

For a moment, I just knelt there, pausing in admiration of the sweet curve, the soft blush of the skin, the thick upward slant. I kissed the side, and felt him leap. Slid my lips along his length and watched him swell behind my touch. Let my tongue glide over the silken head and reveled in the sound he made.

"Spread your legs," I instructed softly, because he hadn't moved, just kept looking at me with that same incredulous expression. But then the hard thighs moved apart, allowing me better access. And I took it, hands smoothing up tense legs to the taut muscles above, embracing him as I took him in.

And he felt good, God, so good. And warm, and solid and *alive*. I let my lips go where they wanted, giving to him freely what the fey would have taken by force. But

I must have done something wrong, because he made a sound like pain when my mouth finally closed over him.

I looked up to see his head thrown back, his throat working convulsively. And yes, that looked like pain on his face. Or maybe not exactly pain, I thought, as he suddenly looked down, green eyes blazing into mine with an expression that made my stomach twist and my hands clench on his thighs.

His body was silently urging me to hurry, but I didn't listen. Instead, I let my hands cup the velvety skin farther back, discovering globes so soft, so warm, almost hot, and so heavy, that it was impossible not to roll them between my palms. So I did, and felt him tremble.

I was, too, but I didn't care this time. It was unimportant next to massaging the velvet of his body, gently at first, and then harder and rougher, feeling it tighten under my touch. Next to letting my tongue glide over the silken head, teasing the tender slit. Next to hearing him swear when I started to pull.

And there was something about that sound that drove me the rest of the way into madness. That had me grabbing the taut, sleek mounds behind him, pulling him hungrily against me. That had me suddenly trying to take in all of him, every silken inch.

It wasn't remotely possible, but I found consolation when I pulled back, tasting the fullness of him, feeling him slide forever over my tongue. Until only the smooth head was still between my lips, allowing me to tease it, bathe it, suck it, suck it, *suck it*, until he was gripping my hair, was thrashing around, was staring down at me, wild-eyed and desperate, and very, very confused. As if he still had no idea what was happening.

Isn't it obvious? I wondered, and swallowed him back down.

Electricity prickled over my skin, and the warm wind I'd been feeling abruptly increased, howling in my ears as something built in the background of my desire, something unexpected, something huge—

That didn't matter, because nothing mattered, except

the power to make him shiver and shake and cry out, except the desperate sounds he made as I pushed a little farther each time, taking more of him than I ever had, taking everything, eagerly, hungrily, *so hungrily.*

Until, finally, finally, I somehow held all of him, his complete length buried inside my warmth, my lips closing on the root of his body—

And God, the sound he made!

I looked up, meeting his eyes, and that electric tingle became a lightning burst, flashing across my vision. Something lifted my hair, tightened my body, sent goose bumps flooding over my skin. Something that was screaming toward us now, like a runaway train, or a tidal wave tearing toward a beach—

"She's calling power!" someone said, just as Pritkin cried out, just as the wave broke over our heads, just as it came thundering and roaring and crashing—

And missing, because someone was dragging me away.

"No!" I screamed, kicking and fighting. "*No!* Let me go. Let me *finish*—"

But instead, the warm illusion shattered, disintegrating into a cold, cramped hallway, a guard's arm around my waist, a snarling face in mine—

And an explosion that took out the door the fey had been guarding, wards and all. And sent it hurtling down the corridor, like it was made of flimsy plastic. Until it slammed into two more guards coming this way and threw them off their feet.

"You were right . . . about the fireball," Pritkin said to me breathlessly. "Duck."

"What?"

He pushed my head down and put a fist through the fey's face behind me. At least, that was what it sounded like. I didn't turn around to see, because I was being hauled through the door, but the restraining arm around my waist had gone limp and fallen away, so I assumed we wouldn't be followed. That and the fact that I got a glimpse of the second guard, slumped against the wall as we ran over him.

Of course it wasn't what was behind us that was really the problem.

A bunch more fey appeared at the end of the hall, and these were smarter. And quicker, because they dodged the fireball—the huge, corridor-filling fireball—that Pritkin flung at them like it was nothing. But the wall behind them didn't.

They threw themselves out of the way, just in time, diving back behind the perpendicular hall ahead. And the wall they'd just been standing in front of simply . . . disappeared. Which would have been great—if the barracks weren't behind it.

"Shit!" Pritkin said as a couple dozen fey looked up from cots and dice games, along with a guy with a towel wrapped around his waist, like he'd just come from a bath, his hair still dripping—

And then flying, when he dove for a weapon.

"Shit!" Pritkin said again, and shoved me through a wall.

I was confused until I realized that there had been a doorway to our right, one I hadn't seen because my eyes had about a thousand other things to look at. And then another thousand as we ran through a series of dim, connected rooms, with soft draperies and pierced screens and low couches and delicate glassware. But no exits, which was a problem, considering the army of little cat feet pounding behind us.

"Shit!" Pritkin said, a bit more frantically.

"I didn't think you knew that word," I gasped, because that hadn't been a translation. And because he'd confused it for my name, the last time we were here.

"Figured it out," he said, and slammed us back against a wall.

This one didn't have a door, or if it did, we missed it. It did have a tapestry, a rich, vibrant thing in mostly greens, a hunting scene. I knew that without turning to look, because an enchanted deer had just scampered up my arm. And then another and another, a whole herd flowing across my body, fleeing a hunter. Symbolism that was not lost on me when a mob of fey suddenly appeared in the door, weapons out and eyes flashing.

Or no, I realized, it wasn't their eyes. It was the overhead lamp we must have hit on the way in, which was swaying, swaying, swaying on its little chain, telling them we were here or just had been. But they didn't know which, so they spread out, beginning a search of this room and the ones around it.

They didn't see us, because Pritkin's camouflage was that good. Hell, it was better than good, to the point that I could barely make out my own limbs unless I moved. And even then it wasn't easy, since the tapestry was already doing that. But the rooms weren't that big, and there were too many fey, and we had to be out of time.

All of which was suddenly less of a problem than the return of that dragging warmth.

It hit me like a blow, as strong as if it had never left, and maybe it hadn't. All I knew was that I wanted—needed—his hands on me. Not his arms, which were already around me, but his *hands*, rough and callused and—I picked them up and guided them where I wanted them to go.

God, I thought, as that grip took me, clenching unconsciously, making me moan. And then press back against him as the callused grip turned into caresses, which turned to strokes, which turned to kneads, and then back into clenches again. Before one hand pushed down my front and clasped something lower. And then he was stroking there, too, in a way that had me spreading my legs, had me writhing back against him, had me biting my lip so the groans in my throat stayed behind my teeth.

"What. Are. You. Doing?" Pritkin asked, which seemed a little strange, all things considered. But his voice was a hiss in my ear, and, oh God, that didn't help.

"What?"

"Did you cast a spell?"

"No. I—no." I was pretty sure. Like I was pretty sure we'd left Rosier back in the hall, so this couldn't be him. Could it? I didn't know. I didn't know anything right now, not with him pressing against me from behind, still hard, still eager, still—

God!

A fey came closer, checking behind a curtain, but I barely noticed, because something had just slipped between my legs from behind. Not inside, not yet, but he was warm, so warm, and he was *right there*. And moving now, stutteringly, haltingly, as if he was trying to stop, as if he realized how crazy this was.

And yet, like me, he didn't seem to be able to.

"We can't do this," Pritkin whispered urgently.

"Okay."

"We *can't*. I can't . . . maintain the illusion . . . if I'm . . . *distracted*."

"Okay," I agreed. And then bit my bottom lip when the strokes suddenly became longer and sweeter, rubbing along the full length of me from behind, like his fingers were still doing in front. And the twin torture was more than I could stand, ripping a soft moan from my lips before his head came down, silencing me with his mouth.

This . . . was not a huge help, I thought wildly. Because now there were three things stroking me, as his tongue joined the other two sources of madness, curling around mine, caressing the inside of my mouth and eating the sounds I was making, because I couldn't seem to stop. Not with shivers and shudders and then all-out quakes causing me to buck hard back against him, causing him to slip, not inside but *against* me, against the full length of me, and God, that was almost as good!

"Your name," he gasped as I shook violently.

"What?"

"Your name!" It was urgent. "Your real one!"

I tried to concentrate, but the question seemed irrelevant and anyway, my brain was busy: tightening my thighs, clenching down, making him work for it. I began to ride him on the outside of my body, and felt him shiver. Arched back against him, like a cat, and heard him groan. And then I was the one shivering, and shuddering, and losing all control as he started hitting that spot, that oh, so sensitive spot, with every stroke, his hands tightening on my body as the friction between us built and built and—

And now his groans were flooding my mouth, spilling over along with my own, and that was bad, but I couldn't remember why, and didn't care, didn't care, and then someone was yelling and someone was grabbing my arm and—

"Your name!"

And then nothing.

Chapter Twenty-five

I woke up dry-mouthed and fuzzy-brained. With no idea where I was, or why I was lying facedown on cold stone, in a small puddle of drool. Not that this was exactly a first.

What was a first, at least lately, was that I didn't feel like crap.

I waited for the usual pain/exhaustion/nausea combo to kick in, only it didn't appear interested. Instead, I felt like I had at Caleb's, after taking the Circle's special joy juice: distant acknowledgment of the body's dissatisfaction, but nothing screaming at me. Nothing at all.

Well, except that I was freezing.

Something was over my face. I pulled it off to discover that my slave outfit had been tossed on top of me. It was thin and fairly useless against the cold, but I put it on anyway while checking out the latest version of hell I'd ended up in.

Only to discover that it was just a cell.

I waited, crouched on cold stone, for the punch line. For the vicious ward about to fry me or the pack of slavering dogs about to attack me or the insane prisoner about to decide that I was a threat. But nada.

Just a cold stone block of a room, some straw on the floor, a couple buckets—one filled with water—and a pallet that nobody had bothered to ensure that I landed on.

I stared at it.

It even had a little pillow.

For a minute, I just stayed there, processing that, along with the fact that I wasn't even tied up. Then I got to my feet and walked to the door. There was a small, high win-

dow in it, like it had been made for someone a lot taller
than me. But by pulling myself up by the bars, I could just
make out a narrow hall with more flickering lanterns.

And the fact that nobody had even bothered to post a
guard.

I was starting to feel strangely . . . neglected.

However, they *had* searched me, and they'd done a
thorough job. Because everything was gone: Billy's necklace, Rosier and his pack, even my bright-eyed chameleon. I guessed the fey had seen something like it before.

But not something like my evil dark-magic bracelet.

The chain of interlocking knives around my wrist
made a soft *chink, chink* when I jumped back down. The
fey must have taken it, too, but, as always, it had returned.
Meaning that at least one part of the plan had worked. I
just didn't know where the witches were, or where Pritkin
was, or what had happened to Rosier, or what was happening in general.

But other than that, everything was fine.

I rolled my eyes at myself and decided to go find out.

"Do you think, just for once, we could not have a hissy
fit?" I whispered to my knives. "I need you to stab the
lock. Not the nearest guard, not another prisoner's butt.
Just the lock."

I got a definite spoilsport vibe back, which I ignored.

And then I remembered something else from the de-
bacle at Gertie's.

"And do it *quietly*."

To my surprise, they did. Well, more or less. The lock
was stabbed a dozen times in a few seconds by a couple of
ghostly knives doing a jackhammer impression. And
while it wasn't exactly quiet, it also wasn't loud enough to
bring anybody running.

Assuming anybody was there, since I'd yet to see a
soul.

I creaked the door open—carefully, because this was
too easy. Maybe the fey were testing me? Maybe this
was some sort of trap?

Or maybe, I decided, as I walked unmolested down
the hall, peering into other, empty cells, they just didn't
worry about you if you weren't at least part fey. So far, it

was the only thing I liked about them. Arrogance like
that had saved my ass more than once.

And it was about to save Rosier's.

I peeked around a wall from about knee height, then
abruptly jerked back. But a glimpse had been enough:
Rosier, in a cage, surrounded by fey, being poked at with
sticks. And with the haunted look of a puppy in the middle of a bunch of unsupervised toddlers.

Or, more accurately, like a specimen in a very strange
zoo, because he wasn't the only thing locked up. Cats,
birds, even an extra-large rat were in similar cages, arrayed
along one wall, making me realize why Pritkin had made
that comment about my familiar. Apparently, witches in
this era actually used them.

Who knew?

"Kill it and be done," one of the guards said. "It's disgusting."

"That would be a grave mistake," Rosier said quickly,
and then yelped when he was poked again.

"I told you to shut up," a different fey ordered.

"But you *want* me to talk. I've told you, she's almost
powerless without me—"

"An even better reason to end your miserable life."

"No! No, no, no!" Rosier said, making me tense up.

And peer around the corner again. The room they
were in was just the space where a couple corridors inter-
sected. It had been dressed up with a few cabinets and the
table Rosier's cage was sitting on, allowing it to serve as
both checkpoint and break room. But the fey were the
real deal, three of them and bristling with weapons, not
that they looked like they expected to use them.

Except for the one who had just pulled a knife.

"And forfeit that amount of coin?" Rosier asked, his
eyes on the blade. "She's powerful, as long as she has me
as a focus. You stand to make—"

"Nothing, cur. She doesn't belong to me!"

"But you could claim her—"

"Not until they chop off that lying bastard's head! And
even then she'll be the queen's prize, to do with as she
likes!"

"They're not going to kill him," another fey said. He was sitting, with his feet on the table, peeling an apple.

"How do you know?" the first one demanded.

Apple Boy looked up sardonically. "Don't you know who that is?"

"Who?" the second fey asked. "The *veslingr*?"

"A wretch," the other agreed, "but not so powerless. That's Nimue's grandson."

"What?" The other two stopped torturing Rosier long enough to stare at him.

He nodded, obviously enjoying the attention. "I was there when they caught him. He was trying to recover some of the magic he spent on the wards by using his slut, when he lost control and dropped his glamourie. I got a good look at his face before they hauled him off."

"Grandson?" The second fey was still looking confused. "You mean one of the princes—"

Apple Boy laughed.

The first fey looked like he'd just figured something out. And from the disgust on his face, it wasn't something he liked. "You mean great-grandson."

The fey at the table nodded. "Now you've got it."

"Got what?" the second fey demanded. "What are you talking about?"

"The polluted one. That half-demon thing Nimue should have killed at birth."

"Gods," the second fey said. If he'd been Catholic, he would have crossed himself.

"Why didn't she?" the first fey demanded. "Anyone else—"

"But she's not anyone else, is she?" Apple Boy asked, eating a piece of fruit off his knife. "The law is for peasants like you and me. The great ones do as they like."

The first fey bristled. "I'm no peasant. My grandfather—"

"And who was your grandmother, again?"

"Leave her out of this!"

"Why? She's the reason you're here, isn't she? And not only you. It's getting difficult to find a trueborn anywhere these days."

"*I'm* trueborn! I—"

"If you were trueborn, you'd be sitting in the ducal palace, instead of guarding a bunch of *kerlingar.*"

"But to let such a thing live," the second fey interrupted, obviously still appalled. "What was she thinking?"

Apple Boy shrugged. "Probably whatever she's thinking now."

"What?"

"He's in with her. Him and those witches."

"Maybe she's about to rectify a mistake," the first fey said, viciously.

"Rectify?" Rosier suddenly piped up. "What do you mean, rectify?"

"I told you to shut up—"

But Rosier wasn't shutting up. Rosier was grabbing the bars of his cage, looking a little crazed. "What do you mean, *rectify?*"

The fey smiled, and jerked him out. "Here. I'll show you."

Shit.

"The lanterns, down the hall," I told my knives quickly. "All of them. Go!"

They leapt up, always ready for some mayhem, and a second later the fey were leaping, too—and in the case of boots-on-the-table, almost falling on the floor—as the corridor behind them practically exploded.

They ran out, swords drawn, and I scrambled forward to grab Rosier. "Where's Pritkin?"

"About time!" he said shrilly. "I could have been—"

"Where's Pritkin?"

"—killed, where the *fuck*—"

I shook him. *"Pritkin!"*

"They took him to see Nimue," he said breathlessly. "That's all I know."

"And she's where?" Because the bizarro house was starting to feel like it should have filled half the damn valley.

"What part of 'that's all I know' did you not understand?"

I let go of him and started rifling through the cabinets,

looking for a handy diagram I didn't find. But I did find my stuff, jumbled in a basket. I threw Billy's necklace over my head, grabbed my ward, tossed the pack on my back—and jerked my head up at the sound of the guards thundering back this way.

"Well?" Rosier shrieked.

"There's nothing—"

"There has to be!"

"There isn't!" I slammed the last door, and he looked around frantically.

"The cages!"

"What?"

"Let them out!"

And then we were scrambling to release the familiars, all of which took off down the hallway. I took off after them, Rosier on my shoulder, because hopefully they knew where their mistresses were. But even if not, I liked this corridor better, since it was going in the opposite direction from the guards.

Who sounded *pissed*.

Damn, I wondered what my knives had been up to.

I didn't worry long, because it took everything I had to not get lost in the mazelike layout of the place. We thundered down the hall and through a door at the end at a dead run. Then turned into another, slamming into the wall on the curve, before immediately diving into a third. After that, I didn't even try to keep up with the twists and turns, because what was the point? It wasn't like I knew where I'd been to start off with.

But I knew where I'd ended up. Because if anything had ever said "queen's private chambers," that was it. I braked and jerked back behind a wall.

But the herd didn't.

They went barreling through an elaborate antechamber, full of rich fabrics, beautiful woods, thick carpets, and elaborate mosaics, yowling and barking and knocking things over. And a moment after that, the two guards who had been bookending an arched doorway were cursing and running after them. Rosier and I followed, through the door and into another line of small, interlocking rooms.

It wasn't the same one Pritkin and I had been in. That

had been done up in greens and browns, while this one was water hues, every tone of blue and white and green imaginable. But it had a lot in common with the other, like the fact that it was full of places to hide.

I dove behind a pierced screen as the two guards came back, carrying a pack of very unhappy runaways.

They passed by, the birds cawing and flapping, the dog snarling, the cats hissing and scratching the hell out of one guy's ear. And I picked up a blanket to cover Rosier and walked quickly in the other direction. Nobody looked at me twice, not even the duo of guards near the end of the line of rooms, because of course they didn't.

I was just a slave.

And then we were in.

"I asked the same question." It was a man's voice, but I couldn't see him. I couldn't see much of anything; there were too many butts in the way. "They say their population is growing and they need more food. They also hinted that they enjoyed the idea of weakening you. They worry about a possible alliance of you with the Dark Fey."

"The *Dark*!"

That was a woman—or a female, anyway. The voice was too lyrical to be human, although the scorn took the edge off slightly.

"You have common cause," the man argued. "The Svarestri's expansion is squeezing both of you. If you were to ally, they fear their ability to hold against such a union, one bolstered by the army of half humans you've built for yourself."

"They say." The scorn was dripping now. "And you believe them."

"What I believe is that they are willing to hold the borders for a regular shipment of food. No slaves. They don't use them, Nimue; they never have. And if they're as strong as you—"

"Are they? Are you sure about that? You had best be, Arthur. Betray us and you'll have more than the Saxons to worry about!"

Arthur?

My head came up.

The butts belonged to guards, who ringed the room ahead. I was in a small antechamber, dim because their bodies cut off most of the light, and unable to do anything to improve the view because of two more guards on the door behind me. They were facing the other direction, but might notice if I started climbing around on the furniture. Like the ones in front, standing in front of two pierced screens on either side of a small opening, could decide to turn.

And then someone did, but only to shift slightly, giving me a narrow view of the room through the gap. And of Pritkin, kneeling in the center, naked except for his trousers, with those powerful arms bound behind him. And balancing on the balls of his feet as he watched a dark-haired woman argue with a mirror.

Okay, I guessed she was actually talking to the man in the mirror, big and blond and red-faced, and rapidly getting redder.

"I'm not betraying anyone," the man—the king—said as I stared at him. "I have given you options; you choose not to take them. What do you expect?"

He did look like Arthur, I thought. Or the myth, at least: golden hair held in place by a shining circlet, close-trimmed blond beard, the weathered skin of a warrior, but with jovial crow's-feet at the eyes. But there was fey in him, too, if you knew where to look: eyes too blue to be human, movements too liquid, a voice that was almost an independent entity, with power behind it, rebuking, cajoling, entrancing . . .

Well, except to Nimue, who didn't appear impressed.

"I expect you to be sensible!" she snapped. "You are my blood, yet you ally with my enemies?"

"You sound like I'm joining them in making war on you—"

"You may as well be!"

The man's blue eyes flashed. "You say that to me? To *me?* When it is my people's blood that has made you strong? How many would you have in your army if not for our women? How would you feed them if not for our grain? Yet you demand *more*?"

"A temporary measure, owing to the recent war—"

"There's always a *war*, Nimue! It's one thing my father taught me! You'll never be free of it, he said—but he tried. For his people, he tried, and made that damn treaty with you—"

"Which you repudiate!"

It was thunderous, and the tension, already thick enough to be tangible, kicked up another few notches. I glanced over my shoulder, and, sure enough, the two guards behind me had twisted around this way. Luckily, they were still ignoring me, but I didn't know how long that would last.

I started working off my bracelet.

"What are you *doing*?" Rosier hissed.

"The plan," I said softly, and nodded to the row of women on their knees behind Pritkin—the coven leaders, I assumed. And our only possible allies.

"The plan failed spectacularly," he hissed. "And now the witches are in *there*. We are out *here*. What exactly—"

I held up my chameleon, which as usual when off the body was a small gold trinket. "You can get in there."

It took him a second. "I can't!"

"You can. It'll hide you—"

"It isn't designed to hide a *person*. It's designed to hide *things*. Small things—"

"You're a small thing!"

"But I'm not a *crazy* thing! What am I supposed to do? Crawl over and give the witches the wands—"

"Yes!"

"And then what?"

"And then they cause a distraction. And . . . and we get Pritkin out. . . ."

"You can't even convince yourself!"

"You have a better idea?"

"*Anything is a better idea*! Do you think the fey are just going to stand there while the witches cast a spell to un-shrink their weapons, and another to untie their hands, and another to—finally—do some damage?"

"Again—you don't like the plan, come up with a better one. I'm open to suggestions!"

"—that's the point of the tournament," Arthur was saying as Rosier glared up at me. "Come to court, Nimue.

If you are as strong as you say, you will defeat the Svar-estri and gain all that you wish. But if you're too afraid—"

"Too smart, you mean, to wager an advantage I al-ready have. Renew the treaty, Arthur. Increase the trib-ute to the amount I have asked for, and you will have the peace you seek."

"Or?"

"Or I will take your women, *all* your women, and leave you to see how long your men follow you without them!"

Arthur drew himself up, blue eyes burning, all hint of joviality gone. "Do not threaten me, Nimue. You won't like the outcome if you do."

"Neither will you," she said, turning around for the first time.

And for a moment, I forgot everything, even why I was there. Because she was beautiful. No, I thought, in stunned amazement, she was *beautiful*, achingly, heart-breakingly, unbelievably so. Raven-dark hair, flowing like a river almost to the floor, eyes like a sea storm, blue and gray and glinting in anger, a face so perfect it hurt, like a force of nature carved in flesh. Blue robes that flowed about her like waves when she moved and grabbed one of the witches.

And slit her throat.

Chapter Twenty-six

I stared at the dying woman, thrashing in Nimue's arms, and a horrible sense of déjà vu slammed into me. Her hair was long and half gray, and I couldn't see her face. But, for a second, it was Rhea all over again. A fact only heightened when Nimue looked up.

And the beautiful blue eyes flooded black.

Black like the endless night sky, without any stars. Black like the pitiless depths of the sea. Black like the eyes of a monster, a monster I'd seen before, a monster that—

Eating you, he's eating you. He's—

The room seemed to telescope, and that horrible feeling I'd kept having broke over me, freezing my limbs, tightening my throat, keeping the scream that was building trapped inside.

Until Nimue grabbed another victim.

And I made a sound that the fey didn't seem to notice, but that had Pritkin's head jerking around. Our eyes met, and suddenly, everything was happening at once: Arthur bellowing, women screaming, Pritkin out of his bonds and lunging, the room dissolving into chaos as a mob of fey jumped for him and he jumped for Nimue—

And wrenched something off her neck.

"Ohshit!"

I started, because all that had taken a couple seconds, and suddenly something was streaming at me over the heads of the crowd. Something on a fine gold chain, something that gleamed in the lamplight, something I would never catch in a million years, because I had the coordination of a clumsy two-year-old. Something that my hands plucked out of the air anyway, at the same moment that Nimue looked up.

And our eyes met.

"Volva," she spat.

"Sybil," the spell dutifully translated.

"Fuck," I whispered.

And then I turned and fled.

"Get the girl!" someone yelled as the room exploded in spells, and the two guards on the door sprang at me.

"Protect!" I gasped, and my knives all but leapt off my wrist, with no restrictions this time, because I didn't have time for any. I didn't have time for anything, except running like a madwoman, my weapons sending the guards staggering back as I pelted down the connecting chain of rooms, with no idea what I was doing.

Until I looked down.

And saw a bright silver key resting in the palm of my hand.

Okay, I knew what I was doing.

I just didn't know where—

"Secure the princess' chamber!" someone yelled.

Yeah, but where was it?

"No, you dolt. To the left!"

Thanks, I thought wildly as my knives caught up in time to send two more guards diving out of the way. I ran out of the queen's chambers and took a hard left. And kept on going, my weapons weaving a deadly web across the corridor behind me, while what sounded like every guard in the world thundered after me.

There were no little cat feet here. It was boots on stone, loud, echoing, deadly. Like the arrow that passed on either side of my head, cleaved in half by one of my weapons. Like the energy bolt that sizzled through the air, dissipating one little knife like steam. Like the bola that wrapped around my legs, sending me hurtling painfully onto stone, and then staring behind me at the crowd that was launching weapons—

That went over my head, since they were aimed at the space where I'd just been, and hit a group of guards coming from the other direction.

Six of them fell around me as my remaining knife

sliced through the strings on my ankles, before throwing itself, kamikaze-style, at the warriors behind me. Six of them, I thought, scrambling to my feet, nose running, terror pounding in my ears. Six of them, as I scampered down the hall, blood splattering the wall beside me, as someone reached for me and lost a limb. Six of them, like the number supposed to be around the princess' cell, so that meant—

"Princess! *Princess*!" I was screaming, because there were doors, doors, so many doors, and I had no idea—

A heavy hand grabbed me, my knife cleaved it to the wall, I tore away, and someone yelled, "Here!"

But I was already slamming the key home, hands steady—and how the hell were they steady? And turning the lock and falling in, a wall of fey at my back, my last knife going up in smoke deflecting a vicious curse. But it bought a second for strong hands to grab me, for them to jerk me inside, for the door to slam in the fey's faces—

And for a woman's voice to say: "I hope you brought a better weapon than that" as I thrust my wrist in her general direction.

My hair was in my face, my breath was coming hard, the massive oak door was *thud, thud, thudding* behind me, to the point that I could barely think. Certainly not well enough to explain the situation, to introduce myself, to do anything but gasp: "There's . . . a wand—"

"That's no wand," she said, her voice awed, before something was plucked off my bracelet.

And then the door gave up the ghost, slamming open with a crack like thunder, causing me to shriek and fall back. Unlike the woman. Who just stood there, a slim, dark-haired figure in a man's tunic and leggings, facing an entire horde of furious fey warriors. Holding what looked suspiciously like—

A staff, I thought, my eyes widening, along with the fey's.

Who were suddenly all trying to fit back through the door.

The woman helped them with that, laughing as she blew out the whole freaking wall. Huge boulders rained down, dust billowed everywhere, tiny shards of rock bit into my skin. And all the while, she laughed and laughed and laughed.

"Oh, *Grandmother*," she all but sang, and stepped out into the hallway.

Or what was left of it.

I tried to stand up. I don't know why. It wasn't like I could help. But my brain had given up at this point and I was pretty much going on instinct. And instinct said to get gone before the rest of the roof fell in. But something was—

Oh.

A big rock had fallen on my skirt, large enough to have bashed my head in had it been a foot to the left. I looked at it, dazed and breathless, as what sounded like the apocalypse started up outside. And then I started coughing and swearing and hacking and tugging, for what seemed like only a minute.

But it might have been longer, because suddenly someone else was there, kneeling in the dust. And pulling my hand away. And lifting me up into arms, strong ones, familiar ones, ones that went with the heartbeat pounding under my ear. And the voice cursing as we ran down corridor after collapsing corridor, because this whole place was imploding.

Until we finally stepped through something that crackled painfully around us, and out—

Into something worse.

Rain slapped me in the face, cold and stinging, bringing me back to full awareness. And to the fact that the funny little house was all but gone, the roof having caved in. Or having been ripped off, because I didn't see it anywhere.

I did see a sky, boiling overhead, laced with lightning. I saw rain slashing down, so thick it felt like a dam had burst. I saw wind throwing heavy tents around like they were made out of tissue paper, one flying at us too fast to duck. But it became snared on the front wall of the house at the last minute, covering the door and spreading out like a tarp overhead, cutting off the view.

But not the noise. Above the howling winds and drumming rain, above the *flap, flap, flap* of the heavy canvas,

above the creaking sounds of a house about to come
down around our ears, were screams. Hundreds of them,
maybe thousands.

"What's happening?" I yelled, practically in Pritkin's
ear, but he didn't hear.

He did put me down, into ice-cold water that reached
above my ankles. And I realized that I'd been so busy
staring upward that I'd failed to notice the water pouring
over the threshold, coming from what looked like a flood
in the camp. A really big flood.

"Come on!" Pritkin yelled, and I could barely hear
him. But I grabbed his hand, sloshing through the flooded
house, while bits of the remaining roof and walls rained
down around us, and the already waterlogged tent tried to
collapse on our heads.

A moment later my question was answered, when we
reached the door and he pushed the tent fabric up.

Revealing the burning hellscape beyond.

It looked like something out of a medieval vision of
the underworld, with screaming people and leaping
flames everywhere. The torches outside many of the tents
must have been blown onto the canvas by the wind, or at
least their sparks had, because a good number of the tents
were ablaze. Like the blankets on a crazy-eyed horse that
ran by, knocking over a man who slipped and then completely disappeared.

Only to reemerge a second later, gasping and shaking
his head—his very wet head—because he'd just been
dunked underwater. And I finally realized why the whole
area looked like it was lit by flickering orange flames: the
fire was being mirrored in the waves. And waves they
were, already knee deep in the lowest areas of the camp
and rising, as all the water from the higher land surrounding us flooded in.

The camp was in danger of becoming a small lake.
And one that none of the increasingly frantic crowd had
a chance of escaping, no matter which way they ran. Because the walls were still up.

Pritkin started forward, but I hung on to his arm.
"Wait. I have to—"

"The palisade!" he yelled, gesturing at it.

"I know!" I bellowed, because anything less than a hundred decibels was inaudible out here. "But there's something I have to do!"

"What?"

"Your . . . The creature I was with. I have to go back for him—"

Pritkin shook his head violently. "You stay with me!"

"I'll be right behind you!"

"No!"

"I *have* to!"

He just looked at me, eyes wild.

"What?"

"I have the strangest feeling you're going to disappear, and I'll never see you again!"

"You'll see me."

He didn't look convinced.

"You'll see me!"

"Then meet me back here. Right here! I'll come for you!"

I nodded, but he just stood there, looking torn.

And then he kissed me, sweeping me up off the floor, body hot and hard against mine while Armageddon swirled all around us.

Leaving me breathless and staggering when he put me down. Although that was probably just . . . just the wind. I gave him a push. *"Go!"*

He went.

I turned and sloshed back across the room, to the entrance to what I now understood to be a portal. It was snapping and cracking, and stinging my skin when I ducked inside. And found the whole place deserted and silent, except for rumblings from the still-shaking walls. Huge boulders were on the floor, and heavy oak beams were slanted across the hall, turning it into an obstacle course. One carpeted in dust that slid underfoot, adhering to my wet feet and ankles, and hanging suspended in the air.

I grabbed a lantern off the wall and held it out. "Rosier!"

Nothing. And the farther I went, the worse things got, as the dim light from the portal faded. Leaving my one, flickering flame as the only thing to illuminate whole corridors impassable from rockfalls, and a darkness so heavy I almost felt it on my skin.

Even worse was the thought that maybe there was nothing to find. That Rosier was so small and so vulnerable, and the fey had been so angry with me. And that maybe Pritkin would have thought to bring my "familiar" if there had been anything left to bring.

"Rosier!"

Nothing.

I picked my way through the rubble, cutting my hands and bruising my heels, and wishing that, just once, I'd go on one of these stupid things with a decent pair of shoes. But I didn't have shoes, and more importantly, I didn't have a map. Because, whatever freaky place this was, I guessed the fey knew it by heart, but I didn't.

I leaned against a wall for a minute, facing the inevitable. I was never going to reach Rosier like this. I was just going to have to hope that Gertie couldn't read through whatever magic the fey had on this place, and that I wasn't going to fall over from the strain, because this was *really* going to suck.

And it did, oh God, it did, I thought, feeling like somebody had punched me in the gut, just from shifting the short distance back to the queen's chambers.

Where the roof was currently falling in.

The fall from above knocked me back against a wall, and half buried me in dirt and weeds. But it didn't kill me, because none of the giant beams came down. Maybe because most of them already had, explaining why, after I finally dug my way out, it was so damn hard to walk.

The floor was a minefield of debris I couldn't see, since the lantern had gotten buried along with me, leaving the room pitch-black. And me coughing and gasping, because it was like trying to breathe through a sandstorm in here. Or like being buried alive, I thought savagely, floundering around, trying to get enough breath back in my lungs to call out.

"Rosi—" I stopped, coughing so hard I got dizzy, and tripped over one of the damn beams, sprawling in the wreckage and cutting my hands on some glass.

Glass I could see, I realized a moment later, glittering like diamonds against the dark soil. I looked around, and saw something glimmering through a crack in the rubbish. It was barely a gleam, but bright as a searchlight in the darkness. I brushed away dirt and sticks and someone's forgotten shoe, and discovered—

Part of a mirror.

It was just a shard, barely bigger than my palm, but it was enough to leave me blinking. Only not at my reflection. But at a flickering fire, part of a wooden floor, and a rough plastered wall with a bit of mural on it. It looked like the mural I'd seen behind Arthur when he was talking to Nimue. And that looked like part of his chair.

The man himself had gone, probably after everything went dark on our end.

But it looked like he'd left the lights on.

I scrambled up, cupping the small piece of glass in my palm. And a moment later, I was navigating the long, tumbled rooms of the queen's chambers, a flickering sliver of firelight illuminating my path. Well, sort of illuminating, since the place was pretty much trembling constantly now, with little siftings of dirt coming down like dry rain, making visibility lousy. But it wasn't sight that got my attention.

It was sound.

A pitter-patter of footfalls, light and fast, was the only warning before something crashed into me. And knocked me backward, into a pile of sharp-edged wreckage. And then slammed down, scattering rubble and crushing glass, but not my skull. Because I'd moved as soon as I landed, rolling to the floor and then scrambling back into the darkness.

The blow had knocked the mirror from my hand, leaving it wedged in the pile of debris, and me cloaked in gloom and billowing dust. I crouched against one of the half walls that separated the rooms, breathing hard and staring at whirling particles that glittered gold in the firelight. And which highlighted basically nothing at this distance.

Nothing except a slim, dark shadow, rushing out of the void and coming straight at me.

"Cassie!" someone yelled, and I jerked. And so did the figure, who hesitated and looked around. Allowing me to grab a large vase and throw it hard enough to wrench my shoulder.

I gasped in pain, the sound lost in the shattering of porcelain when the figure whirled and brought up a large stick, hitting the vase like a batter trying for the outfield. Shards went everywhere, causing me to cry out again as what felt like a dozen tiny knives pierced me. And then to choke it back and dart away, breathless and silent this time, because my assailant seemed to be working on sound, too.

For a moment, there was nothing but two shadows circling the dim beam of light, each looking for an advantage. And my assailant must have found one. Because the next thing I knew, I was hitting the wall and then the floor, barely understanding what had happened.

Until I saw someone looming over me, cudgel in hand, splashed by distant firelight—

And then eclipsed by it, when the weak beam from the shard suddenly became a blaze. A searing white glare, like staring into the sun, spilled out of the tiny thing, filling the room. It was so bright and so strong that it blinded me, despite the fact that I had landed underneath and wasn't even getting the full effect.

But someone was.

I heard a voice curse—a woman, although not Nimue. This voice was higher, lighter, and in pain. Probably from having her retinas burned out of her head, I thought, shielding my own eyes with both arms. It left me defenseless, but I didn't think it mattered. I heard flailing around, groaning, and then footsteps growing distant. Then nothing at all, as the room fell silent again and that awful light blazed on and on.

It finally cut out, as abruptly as it had come, leaving me panting on the floor, confused and afraid and seriously disoriented. And still blind—my eyes seeing only a leaping sheet of afterimages. But I wasn't deaf, and once more, I heard a voice.

I rolled to my hands and knees, trying to hold on to the floor, which didn't seem quite steady. Or maybe that was me. I didn't know; I just crawled in the direction of that thin sound, like a mother trying to find her lost infant.

Or something almost as small, I realized, as my searching hands finally found a tiny body trapped under the debris, in the next room.

I hadn't remembered to bring the shard, but it didn't matter, since I couldn't see anyway. But I didn't need to. Because the voice had resolved itself into the most profane curses ever devised, which managed to sound vicious even in a teeny, tiny, squeaky voice and—

"Rosier!" A huge grin broke out over my face.

The curses stopped. "Cassie?"

"Yes!"

"You get me out! *You get me out right now!*"

I sat back on my heels, grinning.

And then I got him out.

The good news, we discovered, was that the main corridors had a few lanterns still flickering here and there, which my slowly returning vision found helpful. The bad news was they weren't corridors anymore. Beams, and in some cases whole walls, had come down in our path, some of which I could climb over, but some of which were as tall as what remained of the ceiling, forcing me to backtrack. Or, in the cases where I could see past them, to shift.

Only that wasn't going so great.

"All right," Rosier said, sometime later. "Once more. It was just around here."

I shook my head, staring at the latest blockage and holding on to the wall for support. "I can't."

"You have to." The place shuddered again, the walls trembling harder now, like they'd been doing for the last couple of minutes. Because this wasn't a pass through to Faerie as I'd halfway expected. It wasn't a pass through to anything. According to Rosier, it was the magical equivalent of a Winnebago, a portable palace fey nobles took with them when they traveled so they didn't have to live like peasants.

It was carved out of a portal, something about looping it back in on itself to make a stable pocket—or whatever. I didn't get all of it. But I did get that said portal had been damaged when Pritkin blasted through it. And then again when the wacked-out princess started ripping the fey a new one. And now it was trying to collapse on us, and apparently bad things happened to you when you were inside a portal that collapsed.

But I still couldn't. I'd been reduced to doing line-of-sight minishifts, the very easiest kind, but I was out. I was out of those, I was out of everything, I wasn't going to be doing a damn thing without drinking the last of my joy juice, and I *wasn't* doing that. I wasn't, even if the rest of the ceiling came down on my head!

"What are you *doing*?" Rosier demanded.

"You said it's just through here, right?"

"Yes, but—I didn't mean *through* through!" he said, as I started digging my way forward, as dirt and debris tumbled down on our heads, as I struggled to breathe with lungs that were already caked with dust, as Rosier cursed and rocks fell and my hands kept digging and then clawing at the earth, which just went on and on.

Until another tremor shook us.

And this one was about a seven on the Richter scale, causing dust to billow and walls to crack and the floor to start bucking wildly under our feet. And the wall of earth in front of me, a previously impenetrable mass, to cascade away, like an avalanche down a mountainside. One that took us with it.

Rosier and I half stumbled, half slid out the other side, and then I grabbed him and ran for the portal, wishing the damn dirt hadn't mostly blinded me again.

And then really wishing it when we splashed down into a freezing lake of water, almost over my head.

Chapter Twenty-seven

I went under, just from the sheer shock, and came up gasping. And then gasped some more when we were almost run down. I'd been inside ten, maybe fifteen minutes, but everything had changed.

People were wading and swimming through what had to be a five-foot surf. And there was nothing to impede them now, since the only thing left of the little house was the wall holding the portal. And then not even that when it flared out behind us, causing me to duck as fiery bits flew over my head and the wall crumbled to dust.

Like the palisade, which was now just a few smoking piles of logs, crackling with whatever remained of the ward. Which probably explained why the once orderly camp was a working anthill of people, running, splashing, and scampering through the burning remains, making for the hills. And the fey weren't doing much to stop them; they barely even seemed to notice.

For good reason, I thought, staring upward.

Holy shit.

"What the hell is *that*?" Rosier screeched, sounding outraged.

I didn't answer. Like the fey, I was kind of busy. Watching the battle of the ages take place in the air above us.

Or, to be more accurate, a battle *of* the air—and water, and lightning, and fire, all of which were getting tossed around like . . . like things that get tossed around, I thought, my brain pretty much fried at this point. But it didn't matter, because how did you describe *that*?

At its simplest, it was two women, standing on opposite

hills in the open land behind the camp. Two dark-haired women with long raven tresses whipping around their heads as they faced off, although that kind of missed the point. The point being what was happening all *around* them.

I watched as what looked like a hurricane filled the skies, and as tornadoes snaked down, a dozen at a time, snatching men off their feet and sending them flying. As others ignited, turning the burning cinders of campfires into roaring maelstroms of heat and light, which tore through the army on the hillsides and cleaved red veins across the countryside. And as still more filled with water, one of which encapsulated three fey who had almost snuck up behind the princess, dragging them off the hill and threatening to drown them midair.

But they weren't dragging off Nimue.

A mighty rush of wind boiled around her, an impossible-to-defy act of nature that was nonetheless being defied.

By a shield.

There was a normal one on her arm, a small circle of bronze, barely visible at this distance. But out of it spiraled something huge, and almost the same color as the rain, making it hard to see against the night. Just a shimmering, gleaming disk, like the ones I'd seen Pritkin throw out at times, but far bigger and thicker. A magical shield large enough to cast a glowing nimbus over her and a few hundred of her people, gathered on the hilltop around her.

But it wasn't doing a damn thing for the rest of us.

The only things shielding us from howling winds and sleeting rain were the surrounding hills, which was kind of a two-edged sword, since they were also trying to drown us. Water was gushing down them in full-on rivers, crashing through the rifts and gullies between the high-lands, and pouring into what remained of the camp. To the point that people were actually *swimming* in the deeper areas now, while the few elevated ones were sticking up like islands in the sea.

It finally dawned on me why the fey would build a camp in a valley instead of on a hilltop like everyone else.

Because everyone else couldn't drown you if you pissed them off.

Not that drowning was really needed.

"What the fu—?" Rosier screeched, and then gurgled as I ducked us underwater. And watched through the waves as a brightly colored spell streaked through the air where we'd just been standing.

And then more and more, lighting up the night as I surfaced, to see multicolored spells flying everywhere, turning the water in the air behind them into long lines of steam. And causing me to duck down to my neck again and look for cover. But everywhere around us, a battle was raging.

It looked like the covens had arrived.

"What are they *doing*?" Rosier shrieked.

"Trying to get the women out!" I yelled as a nearby patch of water was vaporized by a spell hitting down.

"They're going to get them killed! And us along with them!"

He had a point.

I sloshed through the freezing water toward the only part of the house still standing—the tumbled group of rocks that had formed the chimney. It wasn't much, but at least we were protected on one side. And the rain wasn't slapping me directly in the face anymore.

Not that it seemed to help.

"We need to find Emrys," Rosier yelled, straight into my ear. "We need to find him *now*!"

"No shit!" But I still didn't see him.

But not from lack of light. Fires were burning everywhere, including underwater in spots, because magical flames aren't easily doused. But they do follow most other physical laws, like sending bright shadows flashing off bits of palisade and floating islands of tents, and reflecting off the waves, making the whole camp look like it was moving.

Which wasn't helped by the fact that it was.

Because there were still people in here—a lot of them. Some were huddled together like us, under whatever shelter they could find. Others were in groups, circled by slavers and their private armies, unable to run. Still others were crouched behind the remaining bits of wall, waiting for their chance to make a break for it. Or running around, shouting names in spite of it all, trying to find family members in the chaos.

I didn't give much for their chances. Not with flocks of bleating animals swimming through the surf, clusters of Nimue's guards battling witches, and knots of half-human camp followers sitting among floating piles of cookware, looking unsure whether to stay or run. But most had made the latter choice, which meant that there was movement, movement everywhere, and no way to tell in the dark which running form was Pritkin's.

"We need to stay here," I told Rosier.

"What?"

"Here! He said he'd come back for us!"

"And if he *doesn't*?" Rosier demanded. "If he's hurt?"

I shook my head. "He isn't!"

"How do you know?"

"My power would tell me!" It was the one bit of comfort I had. If something I'd done was causing a problem for the timeline, I should get a warning. More than that, I should be jerked to the source of the trouble in order to fix it, much as I had once been with Myra, Agnes' heir. Who had gone rogue before it was cool.

But my power was quiet, the golden cord that connected us at rest. Instead of thrumming like a harp string the way it should have been if I'd set Pritkin up for harm. And if I hadn't, he should be okay, because he'd survived all this before.

Right?

"Then where *is* he?" Rosier demanded.

"I don't know—"

"That's not good enough!"

"What do you want me to do, Rosier?" I asked, turning to look at him.

"Get down!" he screeched, full in my face, making me jump.

And to wonder how he expected that to help with three tornadoes suddenly twisting together in the skies above us.

The only saving grace was that they were high, very high. Giving us a perfect view as three savage coils of destruction braided together, becoming a single strand of hell. A boiling mass of fury that ripped through the air a moment later, stabbing down like a great spear, straight at Nimue—

And was absorbed.

I blinked water out of my eyes, thinking maybe I was seeing things. But that was undoubtedly what was happening. The almost colorless shield over her turned black and brooding, taking on the hue and pattern of the violently swirling maelstrom feeding into it. The one it finished swallowing a moment later, the surface of the shield bloating to maybe twice its already considerable size.

And then throwing it all back.

The princess took a flying leap to another hill as the storm's rage sheared off the crest where she'd been standing, sending a mighty blast of mud and dirt skyward. She also threw a whirlwind behind her, to counter the larger storm, I guessed, and try to slow it down. And it worked— sort of. A dozen small funnels peeled off the larger one, spiraling crazily out over the surrounding hills, ripping apart tents, chasing down groups of guards, and causing a hundred little shields to bloom against the night.

But it wasn't enough.

Because the main force of the storm hit a moment later, still more than capable of knocking her off her latest perch and sending her flying—

And me ducking, although I didn't need to. Her body spun through the air in our direction, but well above my head. And then splashed down in one of the lower parts of the camp, hard enough to cause a burst of water to fountain up at least a story high.

It splattered down on me like thick rain as I waded forward, trying to reach her before she drowned. While dodging the mass of people who were suddenly splashing through the water toward us. The previously disorganized crowd had just gotten their shit together in a big way, and were headed out of camp, battle be damned, and threatening to mow me down in the process.

"What the *hell*?" I asked Rosier as they passed us in a stream of hard elbows and churning water.

But he didn't answer. I glanced at my shoulder and found him with his mouth hanging open and his eyes wide, staring past me. At the dark-haired princess who was somehow back on her feet, throwing off the world-shattering blow with nothing more than a snarl.

I pushed a fall of soggy hair out of my face, and even through the pelting rain, I could see her better this time. A beautiful brunette with slanting blue eyes, ivory skin, and wicked red lips, who was doing a double take of her own. I thought that was a little odd, just at seeing me again.

Until I realized: she wasn't looking at me.

For a long second she and Rosier locked eyes, and the fierce expression she wore slowly changed into something else. Something I couldn't quite read, even when her face cracked and her lips curved, because it was just too bizarre. Until she burst out laughing, a sound of pure hilarity chiming over the chaotic scene like a peal of bells, and so incongruous in that setting that I could only stare.

And then stare some more when she leaned over and tweaked Rosier's little cheek.

"You should have stayed in the tree," she told him breathlessly.

Then she was gone, running back across camp as easily as if there was no flood, because for her there wasn't. Little patches of water solidified under her feet, like paving stones in a creek bed, catching her footfalls before she could make them. Like the wave that rose on cue, surging toward a remaining bit of palisade, up and over and carrying her with it, straight at—

"Oh," I said, staring stupidly.

And finally realized why everyone had been headed this way.

Because Nimue had caught another storm.

I had a moment to see lightning crackle off the surface of her shield, to see something catch fire inside it, to see an inferno spiral across the formerly colorless exterior, turning it into a raging disk of red flame—

Before it came pouring out, the twister exploding from the surface like a tongue of fire from a dragon's mouth, one that just kept coming, growing into a massive thread of fiery death that strained for the heavens—

But came hurtling back to earth when she suddenly released it.

The princess shielded, a speck of blue under the raging crimson torrent, but a group of Nimue's own guards weren't so lucky. The princess' shield deflected the fire onto them, exploding half of them into ash that scattered on the wind like confetti, while the rest—who had somehow managed to get shields up—went spiraling into the heavens. Just small black specks among the clouds as that destructive finger hit down, carving a divot the size of a swimming pool out of the hillside.

And then kept on going. Jumping from the hill down into camp, tearing a furrow through the waves, sending wafts of steam skyward, and ripping apart the few remaining tents before heading for a wagon. A wagon perched on one of the remaining bits of high ground. A wagon someone must have dragged up there because it seemed like the safest spot in camp.

A wagon full of children.

Time seemed to slow, the deafening noise to fade, the only sound remaining the beat of my heart. The only thing I could see was terrified faces staring over the edge of the cart, the approaching firelight reflected in their eyes. Along with the dead certainty that nothing would deflect it, because nothing was in the way.

Until we were.

I hit the ground, along with the water that had been all around me, because I hadn't had time to select it out. Heard my power clanging in my ears, telling me what I'd already instinctively known: that they weren't supposed to die today. Stared at the swirling red column, fear roiling in my gut, like the last of my potion, burning its way down my throat.

And then I was throwing everything I had at the gleaming vortex, a glittering wave of Pythian power, the purest expression of godly force on earth—

And barely made it flinch.

I stared in disbelief at the swirling mass of red and black and gray. Until I remembered: Caedmon, the fey king I'd met last time, had slipped out of a time spell, not once but twice. Because fey magic didn't respond to mine the way that earth's did.

It barely seemed to respond at all.

Stop, I thought, my hand outstretched, my heart racing dangerously fast as the column glimmered and gleamed, like firelit rubies. *Stop,* I thought desperately, straining as it filled my vision, slowing enough to be mesmerizing, but not enough to matter. "Stop!" I heard myself shout, as I felt the heat, smelled the smoke, saw the wind of it lift my hair. . . .

And then lift me, too, ripping me off my feet in what I guessed was slow motion, since my power was having a visible effect now. But it didn't feel all that slow. I went whipping through clouds of steam and smoke, the burning camp swirling dizzyingly around me, as I desperately tried to rein it in. As the maelstrom and I whirled together in a deadly dance that was only going to end one way, because I wasn't strong enough.

I couldn't stop it.

But a second later, it hitched anyway, like a bucking horse suddenly draped with a second lasso. And then again, stalling now, losing speed. And again. I couldn't see why, but I knew I wasn't doing it; I was still being spun around the glowing column of death, turning with its energy even as it slowed, as it tried to suck me in, as it reached out to claim one . . . more . . . victim. . . . Before finally grinding to a halt, as still and quiet as if it really was carved out of a single, giant jewel, gleaming in the darkness.

Like the three strands of golden power—Pythian power, I realized—that were connected to it. Like the three women glimpsed through the smoke, their faces lit up with reflected firelight, who together had tamed it. Like the face of the woman who jerked me out of the sky a moment later, down to a large, heaving bosom.

And a pudgy hand that tightened painfully on the back of my neck as I stared into furious brown eyes. "Oh." I licked my lips, tasting ashes. "Shit."

"You have no *idea.*"

Chapter Twenty-eight

"Gertie!"

Nothing.

"Gertie!" I slammed my palms against the blank white wall in front of me.

"Would you please stop?" Rosier asked, sounding as weary as I felt.

"This is my fault. I should have just shifted the wagon. Stupid—stupid!"

"Yes, it was," he agreed.

I hung my head. "You're supposed to argue with me," I said, although he was right. I'd used up the last of our potion and hadn't even gotten anything for it, because of course the Pythia of the time would be drawn to something like that. Of course she would. And of course she'd bring her friendly neighborhood posse along for the ride. I could have stayed in hiding and let them take care of everything, but I hadn't stopped to think, even for a second, and now . . .

I looked around, again. At nothing, again. Because there was nothing to see.

Absolutely nothing, except for a blank white cell. No, not even a cell. A white, rectangular box with no door, no window, and no way in or out, because a Pythia didn't need one, did she?

But I did, because my power was gone.

Not exhausted, not blocked, *gone*. Like Gertie had somehow stripped it from me. But she couldn't do that . . . could she? I'd been told that it was mine, until I died or passed it to a successor. That no one had the ability to take it from me, not Gertie, not anyone! I tried to convince myself of that even as I felt an overwhelming sense of loss, a terrible hollowness where our connection ought to be. Something that had become as much a part of me over these past months as a limb was missing, like a chunk carved out of my soul.

Gertie, I thought, and slid down the wall.

"You had a split second to make a decision," Rosier said. "Exhausted, in the middle of battle, whilst freezing to death. You made the wrong one. It happens."

"It doesn't happen. It *can't* happen."

"You can't hold yourself to that kind of standard. No one—"

He broke off when I put my head in my hands, as if realizing that the last thing I needed was another lecture. For a while, we just sat there in silence, me trying to think and Rosier . . . not doing much of anything. Because what was there to do?

"I never thanked you," I finally said, "did I?"

His eyes were closed, and they didn't open. But his voice sounded alert enough when he spoke. "Thanked me?"

"For helping, back at Nimue's. I think I might have lost it, and gotten us all killed, if you hadn't . . . intervened. So thank you."

"What are you talking about?"

Rosier didn't have any eyebrows yet, but he wrinkled some skin at me. And yeah, I guessed some crazy stuff had happened since then, hadn't it? "In the corridor," I said. "You know, with the two fey?"

The wrinkling continued.

"In front of the *portal*?" I could feel myself blushing. Trust Rosier to make a simple thank-you awkward!

"I simply told you where the gate was," he said, opening his eyes. "Although I didn't expect you to plow through a cave-in headfirst! I still maintain—"

"I'm not talking about that," I said, wishing I'd never brought it up.

"What, then?"

"Never mind!"

"You can't thank me for something and not tell me what it is," he said testily. "And it's not as if we have anything else to—"

"The sex, okay?" I snapped, spelling it out. "Happy now? Thank you for help with the sex!"

He blinked. "What?"

I glared at him, too tired to be interested in games. "Drop the act. I know it was you. You did the same thing in the car—"

"What car?" He scowled. "When have we been near any—"

"A couple of weeks ago? Spartoi? Dragon's blood? Ring any bells?" I made every sentence a question because Rosier still looked clueless. Although why, I had no idea.

It had been memorable.

A few weeks ago, Pritkin had been injured in a fight with the Spartoi. In fact, he'd been about to die, but we hadn't been near any help, and it might not have mattered if we had. Regular old dragon's blood is bad, but the blood of a shape-shifting demigod son of Ares was on a whole different level, and he'd been covered with it. It had been eating him alive.

I'd had to sit there, watching him die, with no ability to do anything. Except for the obvious, because incubi only heal one way. But he hadn't been responding, hadn't even seemed to know I was there, and I'd been frantic because I was about to lose him—

Until Rosier showed up, in spirit form, and used his powers the same way he had at Nimue's tonight.

"You saved us tonight, like you did in the car," I said, slowly and distinctly. "I was panicking, and you helped, and I wanted you to know—"

"I didn't."

"What?"

Rosier looked crabby. "The council blocked my abilities, remember? Worried I'd try a power play back in time, and give some of them what they deserve. I told you this."

"But . . . that was about magic—"

"It was about everything except the countercurse. And in any case, what do you think my abilities are if not magic?"

I frowned. "But you *did* help—"

"I did not."

"Then what *was* that?" Because one minute, I'd been freaking out, and the next . . . I felt myself blush again. "That wasn't me."

"Well, of course it—" Rosier stopped abruptly, and the big eyes narrowed. And when his voice came again, it was different. "You're telling me you didn't *plan* that?"

"Plan what?"

Instead of an answer, I got an explosion. One that left me flinching back in surprise. "You can't be serious! I thought you were playing a dangerous game, but under the circumstances, I understood. But now you're telling me—" He broke off, glaring. "You didn't know!"

"Know *what*?"

"That you've been feeding off of my son!"

I didn't respond, because whatever I'd expected, it hadn't been that. But it didn't matter. Rosier didn't give me a chance to say anything anyway.

"Remember Amsterdam?" he demanded. "When that Gertie creature caught up with us the first time?"

"I—yes, but—"

"Don't tell me you didn't feed! I sent you into the back of that bar to seduce him, and when you came out, it damn well looked like you'd succeeded!"

"That . . . wasn't a seduction," I said, because I was confused. And because I kind of thought they involved less yelling. "I was just trying to keep him in sight until the soul turned up. Only Gertie did instead, and he donated some energy so we could get away—"

"He didn't just donate!" Rosier snapped. "If that were the case, he should have been tired afterward, even haggard. But instead he was invigorated!"

I paused, because I'd noticed that, too. But it hadn't seemed like a big deal at the time. And, frankly, it still didn't. "So?"

"So how does that work? He gives you power, yet has more at the end than he started out with? That doesn't sound like a donation to me!"

"Then what does it sound like?"

"I think you know."

I just looked at him.

"How quickly they forget," he said dryly. "I was under the impression that this whole odyssey began when Emrys was sent back to hell for having demon sex—defined as *an exchange of power*—with you."

I had been about to say something, but stopped. Not because I understood what he was getting at, but because a flood of memories suddenly swamped me: lying on a hillside, a huge moon riding the clouds overhead, the hulk of a dead dragon steaming in the distance, and my life force trickling away into the dirt. Cold; it had been so cold. . . .

Pritkin had recovered from his wounds, but we'd gotten separated. And I'd ended up battling the last Spartoi on my own. I'd won, if you count dying later than him as a win. But then Pritkin had shown up, barely in time, and returned the power I'd given him earlier, saving my life. And forfeiting his own—the only one he cared about, at least—because he'd thereby broken the terms of a parole he'd been laboring under for more than a century.

Breaking it had sent him straight back to hell, and me on this crazy journey.

Rosier was right; that was where everything had started. But I still didn't see his point. "What are you getting at?"

"That a feedback loop of power was set up between the two of you that night," he said, still weirdly intense. "You gave him power in the car—he gave it back to you on the hillside, triggering the loop. Admittedly, it was a very poor one, which never had a chance to really get started before he was snatched away. But it *existed*. And apparently still does!"

"You're basing that on what? One incident in Amsterdam?"

"I'm basing it on *tonight*. We were stuck in that corridor, having to put on that bloody pantomime for the fey, because he couldn't break through the wards. Yet after a few moments with you, he shreds them like tissue paper! Where do you think he acquired all that power?"

"I—"

"He was pulled away that night, before the loop could finish, and no one canceled the spell. Leaving it *open between you*."

I shook my head. "No. I think I'd—"

"Oh, forgive me," Rosier interrupted. "I'm merely the Prince of the Incubi. What could I possibly know about it?"

I glared at him some more. "I don't care who you are! If I was carrying a major spell around, I think I'd notice!"

I certainly had before. A *geis* had almost driven me and Mircea insane before I managed to get it lifted. And the Seidr spell my mother placed on me, while less intense, had had really obvious consequences. So yeah, I thought I'd have noticed another open spell, especially one like that!

"My people's magic is more subtle," Rosier said slyly. "Have an increase in erotic dreams recently? Find yourself wanting sex more than usual? Find yourself *initiating it*, trying to scratch an itch you can't quite reach—"

"That's enough!" I snapped, massaging my temples.

God, I hated this stuff. Pritkin was the one who dealt with the metaphysical crap that went with this job, and explained things in a way that didn't have me wanting to hit myself in the head. Rosier didn't even try. But that didn't make him wrong. Because I was suddenly remembering some things, some very weird things, that had been happening lately.

Shifting back in time to Pritkin—in my *sleep*—because I had no other way to reach him. Establishing the Seidr link with Mircea—by accident—because of a little personal shower time that got out of hand. All kinds of crazy dreams, most of which—yes—had been pretty damn erotic. And then there'd been a few instances with Mircea, which, yeah, I had sort of initiated—

I blushed again.

"So what?" I finally said. "Even if you're right, what difference does it make? It didn't hurt anything, and it may even have saved our butts at Nimue's. I don't understand why you're so concerned about this."

Rosier just looked at me some more, with his huge, freaky eyes. And uttered a single word: "Ruth."

Annnnnd the record scratched.

"Shit," I whispered, and put my head back in my hands. The demons called their feedback loop "sex" partly because it was how new little demons were made. That was rare—like really rare—but something new *was* created every time a loop was in existence, namely power. The spell magnified whatever was put into it, many times over, which was why demons were willing to give a lot for a roll in the hay with Rosier despite his winning personality.

It was also why Ruth, Pritkin's ex-wife, had married him.

Her own family was part demon, but were very low on the power totem pole. They'd lived on earth because they were seen as little more than fodder in hell, with no respect from anyone. She'd been determined to change that, to go back to what she viewed as her rightful home in triumph, and with power to burn.

And she'd decided that Pritkin was going to give it to her.

She must have been thrilled to find a prince of the incubi slumming on earth, even more so when she realized that he didn't look down on her like other demons of his rank. That he didn't care about status in a world he'd never regarded as his. And that he had a ton of power she could access if she played her cards right, because he'd never had demon sex before.

It wasn't by accident. Pritkin was experienced enough with human women, but he'd left demons strictly alone. Not out of prejudice, but because the feedback loop sometimes exchanged more than just power. It was a blending of energies, in which traits from one partner could be left behind in the other. And for a man who already hated the demon half of himself, adding any more hadn't been appealing.

But the gap in his knowledge had left him vulnerable to someone willing to play on his emotions. Someone who knew that, while most demons could only sex up their own kind, the incubi could establish the loop with anyone. And that they could magnify the power many more times than the average demon.

And that was especially true of the ruling family.

Unfortunately for Ruth—and Pritkin—she underesti-

mated that last point. By a lot. The loop she initiated on
their wedding night—without telling him—took her power
but didn't give any back. It never had the chance. Pritkin
was so powerful that he drained her dry in seconds. She'd
ended up a burnt-out husk in his arms, and he'd ended up
a basket case, blaming himself because he hadn't known
how to stop it.

"I thought you were being clever," Rosier said quietly.
"That you'd assessed the situation, and decided to re-
sume the loop as a desperate bid to boost your power.
And if you could control it, that would have been fine.
But if you can't—"

"I didn't even know it existed," I whispered.

"—then we have a *problem*."

I looked at him. "Pritkin would never hurt me."

"Do you think he wanted to hurt Ruth?"

"I'm not Ruth. And I have the Pythian power—"

"But would it draw from that? Or would it draw from
you? Most people have one source of power; you have
two. What if it decides to pull from the wrong one?"

"It hasn't so far—"

"So far, we haven't had a real test. The first time,
Emrys was pulled back into hell while he was still giving
you power. He never had a chance to take anything back.
The second was cut short by Gertie's arrival. And this
time, the fey pulled you away—"

"He won't hurt me!"

"And what about the opposite?"

I stared at him. "What?"

Fingers, tiny but surprisingly strong, latched on to my
arm. "Your mother was a goddess, was she not? And one
who *fed very much like we do*. She pulled life energy from
whole demon armies, drained my father right in front of
his throne! Yet you're convinced you couldn't manage it
from one demon, who isn't resisting, and who even has an
open feedback loop between you?"

"But I haven't—I *wouldn't*—!"

"You *did* in Amsterdam. You must have. The Emrys
of that day didn't know how the process worked! He
couldn't have done it."

"But he was trying to give me power—"

"Yes, to give a simple donation. You were the one who turned it into something else. As you did tonight."

I was about to argue, but then I remembered Pritkin's face at Nimue's, which had seemed pretty freaked out. Like something was happening that he didn't understand and hadn't expected. Like he'd thought to maybe get a boost to his power, enough to get us out of there, and instead had gotten a turbo shot that had taken out the wards along with the whole damn wall!

Rosier was watching me. "You understand now."

I scowled. "I understand nothing! You used power on us in the car. If there was *any* chance I could drain your son—"

"The feedback loop wasn't in place then. There was nothing happening there but a simple feeding, which incubi do all the time. And in any case, Emrys was already dying. There was no risk—"

"There was plenty of risk!" I remembered Pritkin's face, afterward. How traumatized he'd been, how terrified that he might have taken too much. That he was facing Ruth all over again, something that had almost destroyed him, and that had destroyed his life.

After Ruth's death, Pritkin had gone storming into the hells, looking for his father. Rosier had known what she intended to do, but hadn't stopped her, probably hoping she'd succeed and that her fascination with the demon world would rub off on his son. Instead, Pritkin had blamed Rosier for her death and intended to return the favor.

The intentions hadn't panned out, but attacking one of their own had been enough for the demon council, who were already worried about the power of this strange hybrid. They'd demanded Pritkin's head; Rosier had protested; a deal had been made. Pritkin could return to earth, but as soon as he violated his father's prohibition, he was to return to Rosier's realm and stay there.

Forever.

It had left him that strangest of strange creatures: a celibate incubus. It had also left him in a holding pattern that had dominated his life ever since. One in which he couldn't use his incubus powers, which gave him much of his strength, or make lasting plans for the future, because he could be jerked back to hell at any moment, or have a relationship, or kids, or much of anything else. It had made him a perpetual tourist on earth, watching other people's lives but never able to have one himself.

All because of a woman's scheming, and Rosier's inability to understand what that had done to his son.

Sometimes I wondered if he ever would.

"You weren't in danger," Rosier was saying, because he really didn't get it. "Incubi instinctively know when they're draining a partner too low. I trusted Emrys to stop before then."

"But you don't trust him now."

"A feedback loop is not a simple feeding. It combines two people's magic, and it's . . . heady. Wild. Sometimes it feels like it's riding *you*. It isn't nearly so easy to control, especially for a novice—which both of you are!"

Those tiny fingers dug into my flesh, hard enough to hurt. "If you drain him and he ends up like Ruth, or if he drains you and I have no way back to him, the result is the same! Your mother took my sire; you will *not* have my son!"

I was about to respond in kind when I saw his face. Rosier didn't look angry so much as genuinely afraid. It could just be for his plans, formulated over hundreds of years, to use Pritkin as a backup battery for the royal house, generating the energy he needed to keep his nobles in check.

But seeing the expression in his eyes, I thought it could have been more.

"What do you want from me?" I asked simply.

"Something I never thought I'd say to any woman. But from now on, whatever happens, keep your hands off my son!"

Chapter Twenty-nine

Sometime later—maybe an hour, maybe more, because who could tell in here?—the same story was repeating itself. And I was considering going mad. "Gertie! *Gertie!*"

"Do you have to yell?" Rosier asked sourly.

"Yes! Don't you *get it*?"

"Not really. Enlighten me."

"No."

"No?"

"No! I don't want— God!" I put my head in my hands, fisted my still-damp curls, smelled the smoke that clung to them. Smoke from another time and place, a place where I'd *had* him. All I'd had to do was hold on to him, and I couldn't even do that. And now I couldn't get back, and if I didn't . . .

"No," I said, because Rosier was just sitting there, looking at me out of those weird eyes. "No, I don't want another conversation. I don't want to be told to calm down. I don't need to calm down. I need to get out of here!"

"Yes, you do."

"How?"

"What do we know?" It was crisp. And despite the squeaky quality of the voice, it sounded vaguely like Pritkin when the shit hit the fan. It should have made me feel better, but for some reason it only made me miss him more.

"That's the problem," I snapped. "We don't know shit!"

"On the contrary, we know a great deal more than we

did. Although I'm not sure how much it helps us in here—"

"Then it doesn't help us!"

There was a sudden silence.

"I'm sorry," I said, after a moment. "I'm panicking, and I know I don't get to do that."

Rosier gave a laugh, and strangely enough, it sounded genuine. I guessed when you'd lived as long as he had, you developed a weird sense of humor. Except about giant hellhounds and twenty-story drops and murderous fey.

And crazy exes.

I wanted to ask about Morgaine but didn't think this was the time. "You've had a day, too, haven't you?" I asked, instead.

"I've had worse." He looked at me narrowly. "Have you?"

"I . . . don't know." The days were kind of running together lately. I got up, I chased Pritkin through time, crazy things happened, I fell into bed—or whatever passed for it wherever I was. The next day, I got up and did it all again. It had sort of become my job description.

But it wouldn't be for much longer.

It wouldn't be tomorrow.

"If anyone ever had reason to panic, I think we qualify," Rosier told me. "But there's no such thing as an impregnable prison. If there's a way in, there's a way out. And, as I was about to say, we do know two things that apply here."

I ran a hand over my eyes. "What?"

"I can't shift out, and neither can you."

"And that means?"

"I'm not sure," he admitted. "But I can tell you this: in four millennia, I have never been anywhere that did not permit me to shift back to my home. Therefore this is either somewhere I've never been, or it's some type of illusion."

I looked up at the ceiling, where a Cassie-shaped blob looked back at me. This place wasn't mirrored, but it was vaguely reflective. Meaning that I saw indistinct versions of me and Rosier everywhere.

This one looked disapproving.

I looked away. "You can't see through illusions?"

"With my power intact, certainly. Without it . . ." He looked around. "I would still expect to be able to."

"But you can't."

"No. If this is an illusion, it's a damn fine one."

"Then you're voting for real?"

"If it weren't for that one thing, yes. But it doesn't take power for me to shift home; it takes a certain amount of effort for me to *stay* in your realm, and resist the pull back to mine. Therefore the dam the council put on my power should make no difference."

"Then . . . maybe she's blocking you somehow. Gertie, I mean. Or the Circle—"

Rosier laughed. It was scornful. "The Circle. They rather overestimate their abilities, particularly in regard to my kind."

"They've trapped demons before—"

"Not a member of council," he said shortly. "And not in bodily form. In any case, this doesn't feel like a trap— not the magical variety."

And no, it didn't. It didn't look like one, either, and I should know, having spent time recently in one of the Circle's little snares. It had been featureless inside, too, but just black, to the point that I couldn't tell if my eyes were open or not. Like floating in a sea of nothingness, which had been damn disturbing.

But less so than this, because I could shift out of those. I couldn't shift out of this. I didn't even know what this was!

I felt my fingers try to dig into the surface of the floor beneath me. It was cool, and smooth as glass, showing me back a vague reflection of my palm. Like the Cassie-blob that resided in the opposite wall.

It looked defeated.

And I couldn't be that, not when there was still a chance.

I got up and began pacing, as far as the maybe eight-by-ten space would allow. I didn't usually suffer from claustrophobia, but this . . . was getting to me. I felt like a caged animal. To the point that I could see myself throwing my body at the walls before long, beating my hands against them until they were bloody, yelling myself hoarse. Until I eventually went crazy, because who wouldn't in a place like this?

Maybe that was what Gertie had meant, when she said I might prefer death to my fate otherwise. Stuck in some featureless void, abandoned and forgotten. Conscious but unable to do anything, to help anything, while Pritkin died and the world went to hell and I waited for the gods to return and rip it apart, freeing me right before they killed me!

Goddamn it!

A ghostly knife speared the opposite wall, flung there out of sheer frustration, but it didn't help. Any more than it had helped the last time I did it, more deliberately, shortly after waking up. It also didn't bounce around, making a hazard for the two of us, or even so much as crack the surface.

It just . . . disappeared.

"This can't be real," I told Rosier. "My knife would have dinged it if it was."

"Then you're voting for illusion."

"I don't know what I'm voting for. I just want out."

I let my forehead rest against the wall for a moment, staring at my reflection, trying to think.

This time, it looked surprised.

I frowned.

It didn't.

What the—

I sprang backward from the shiny surface, and the reflection I'd been looking at abruptly disappeared. But not before I saw differences I hadn't seen up close: like the fact that the curls were gray, not blond, and the face was lined, not youthful, and the eyes were blue, yes.

But they weren't mine.

So, not a reflection, then. Somebody was on the other side of the wall. Somebody who had been peering in at us curiously. Somebody who might know a lot more about this place than I did.

And there was only one way to reach her.

"Stay here," I told Rosier shortly.

"What?" He looked from me to the wall I was still staring at. "What are you talking about?"

"I'm going outside."

"I thought you couldn't shift?"

"I can't."

"Then how—" His eyes got wide. "No."

"I won't be long."

"No!"

"I'll come right back."

"And if you *don't*? I'll be left in here with a corpse, and we'll have no chance, *no* chance—"

"We have no chance now! You said two days *maximum* until Pritkin's soul arrives. It's already been most of one. We *have* to get out of here—"

"But that Gertie woman is coming to question us!" He grabbed me. "She has to wonder what we've been up to. It's human nature—"

"Unless you're a *Pythia*, who's been trained to be seriously uncurious about the future," I said, trying to pry his hand off my leg. "Agnes went so far as to stick her fingers in her ears once, so I couldn't tell her anything, just in case she did something to change it. Gertie isn't coming, Rosier."

"She has to!" His previous calm was showing cracks now, like that was what he'd been counting on. That she'd show up and we'd bash her over the head or something. "She has to!"

"She won't."

"But there's no food. Someone has to bring food—"

"Rosier. Let go and step back."

"—and no *toilet*! How can you have a prison cell with no bloody toilet?"

"The same way you can have one with no door. We're not in Kansas anymore," I said, and stepped through the wall.

I felt my body fall away, unable to follow, but the other part of me had no such trouble. The part that had gone zooming around the drag with Billy Joe. The part that had just stepped out into . . .

I had no freaking idea.

There was a lot of darkness, but not total. Vague outlines of things were visible, here and there, faint and grayish white, like lines on an X-ray. Including a distant horizon, with flashes that looked like lightning.

I looked up, but there were no stars. Down, but the ground beneath my feet was just the same noncolor and vaguely rocky. Behind me—and finally, something looked more or less the same. Only from the other side.

Because I could see through the walls now.

Which was how I saw a figure flitting away on the opposite side of the cell, toward a long line of them, stretching toward the horizon.

I ran after her.

This place had weird static in the air that burst on my vision here and there, like tiny, too-close fireworks. It kept making me jerk my head back, and should have made her hard to see. But people were clearer than the walls, more solid—like Rosier, when I glanced over my shoulder, huddled near my collapsed form. His features were blurry at this distance, but his body was a solid chunk of off-white.

Like the figure who had just darted behind another cell.

"Wait!" I yelled. "Please! I need to talk to you!"

Only to find her gone when I rounded the corner.

Because she was hiding on the other side of the cell.

"I can see you!" I pointed out, and heard what sounded suspiciously like a giggle. "I can hear you, too!"

A hand came up to cover her mouth. And then she was off again, flitting across the barren landscape like a tissue blown on the breeze, and faster than me because she was used to this. I was only a temporary ghost, while she'd been at it for years.

I knew that because I knew her.

I put on a burst of speed, following her zigzag course between several more cells. And then abruptly reversed it, going around the other way on the next one, watching her parallel me on the opposite side. And keep checking behind her, but never once glancing across at me.

Until she ran straight into me.

Her head was still turned around, looking behind her,

when we collided. And I got blown backward for my trouble, ten or twelve feet, because ghosts don't take sudden scares any better than humans. "Aughhhh!" she screamed, staring at me as I lay there, looking up at her in confusion. "Aughhhh!"

And then she turned and fled.

Straight into a cell up ahead.

I scrambled to my feet and followed.

"Would you relax?" a man's voice said as I stepped through the wall. "I told you they can't follow us in—*Shit!*" That last was in response to his turning and seeing me. For a moment, we just stared at each other.

Well, I stared. He glared. It didn't do his slightly horsey features any favors. And the rest of him wasn't much more impressive, being tall and lanky, with a too-prominent Adam's apple and a mane of blond hair that was getting dangerously close to a mullet.

But I stared anyway. Even though I'd half expected it, considering that I'd recognized the ghost. But it was still a surprise.

My father turned up in the weirdest of places.

And he never seemed happy to see me in any of them. "You!" he snarled.

"Me," I agreed. "Look—"

"Save it!" It was venomous. "I've nothing to say to you people!"

"I—there's no 'you people.' There's just me—"

"Your bitch friend take the day off?"

"What?" I said, confused. And not just because I was talking to my long-dead father while one of his pet ghosts made little hissing noises at me from near the ceiling. But because he looked like he had no idea who I was.

And then I noticed his clothes: singed-knee pants, dirty white hose, a puffy shirt, and a pair of neatly buckled shoes—Pilgrim-style. He looked like he'd just stepped out of the sixteen hundreds. And then I saw the hat sticking out of his pack, a wide, floppy-brimmed number with a distinct bullet hole in it, one Agnes had given him at our first meeting.

And by the look of things, that had been pretty damn recent.

Well, recent from his perspective.

"Agnes . . . just brought you back here, didn't she?" I asked slowly, remembering the first time I'd met my father as an adult.

It had been a few months ago, after I'd gotten the bright idea to seek out my predecessor for some much-needed training. Only to find out that that was a no-no. Agnes had not been happy to see me, partly because my very presence threatened the timeline, since I'd had to seek her out in the past. And partly because she'd been busy chasing down dear old Dad, to keep him from screwing up time before I got a chance to.

After a memorable series of events that included her shooting me in the butt, she'd left with him, something I hadn't bothered to protest, since she still had the gun. And because I hadn't yet known who he was. And because I'd had other things to occupy my mind than whatever kind of jail the Pythias were running.

It was occupying it now. Specifically, I was wondering how Roger and I both ended up in the same prison at the same time, despite being nabbed centuries apart. And by two different Pythias from two different eras.

This, I thought, was exactly why time travel gave me a headache.

Not that Roger seemed to care.

"*Just?* She left me here to rot while I 'soften up.' Only guess what, sweetheart. Not so soft! I'm not telling you shit, no matter how long you bitches leave me—"

"I'm not trying to leave you anywhere."

"—in here, so tell your gun-happy friend she can shove that pistol where the sun don't shine—"

"I'm trying to get out, too."

"—because Roger Palmer doesn't break!" He looked at me defiantly. And then what I'd said must have sunk in, because he frowned. "What?"

"I'm trying to get out, too."

His eyes narrowed. "Is this some kind of trick?"

"No." I sat down, or I tried to. His cell had a bed, a single bunk shoved up against one wall, but I was still new to this whole ghost thing, and I mostly just bobbed around.

His ghost giggled. He glared.

I sighed. "Look—"

"No, you look. If you think you can masquerade as a fellow prisoner and have me spill the beans, you can think again!"

I didn't bother to deny it some more, since he wouldn't have believed me anyway. I just gestured around. "So, what's your plan? Stay here and rot?"

"Plan? Who said I have a plan?" He looked swiftly up at his ghost—Daisy, if I remembered right.

"Don't worry. I didn't tell her about the things," Daisy said, in a stage whisper.

"What things?" I asked.

"The sparkly things. I've been—"

"Shut up, Daisy!" Dad said.

"—hunting them. Oh, and I caught another one," she told him.

"Shut *up*!"

"—so we just need one more big fat one and I think—"

"Daisy!"

"—we might have enough. Or two or three of the smaller ones, but they're faster and harder to—ummph."

He'd snatched her down and clapped a hand over her mouth—which I hadn't known we could do—but it was too late. "Sparkly ones?" I asked. "You mean those flashes of light outside?"

"I mean you'd better get back to your body," he said nastily. "Or you may get stuck in spirit form permanently."

"And you wouldn't like that here," Daisy said, through two of his fingers. "Then you'd sparkle, too—"

"Sparkle?"

"—and I might have to eat—ummph."

"She's eating ghosts?" I asked, looking up at Dad. Who shoved overlong blond bangs out of his eyes and glared at me some more, but the expression had an edge of panic to it.

"She doesn't know what she's saying! She's old and a little—" He tapped the side of his head. "Or she was. And she drank a lot—"

"Mmump, mummh!"

"—in life and it affected her. Terrible memory—"

"That's a lie!" Her lips pushed through the back of his hand, until they protruded out past his knuckles. "Sharp as a tack," they assured us.

"You are not!"

"Am, too."

"Then where did we meet?"

She thought about it.

"Under the Forty-fourth Street Bridge," I said, and they both turned to look at me.

"Oh no. That's not it," Daisy said.

"Yes, it is," Roger said slowly. He frowned. "How did you—"

"You told me," I said. "Or you will. You didn't mention the city, but I assume—"

"What do you mean, *will*?"

"We become friends. In the future. Where I'm from," I clarified, because he was looking confused. Which was a little odd, considering that he was a time traveler himself, if an illegal one. "Look, I know we got off to a bad start—"

"A bad *start*? You're the reason I'm in this mess!"

"The reason you're in this mess was your decision to try to blow up Parliament and save Guy Fawkes the trouble!"

Before he met my mother, Roger had been part of a guild of time-traveling utopians, trying to improve the world by tinkering with the past. Thankfully—since they screwed up more than they helped—they mostly sucked at it. Time travel, that is, because the spells they used tended to blow people up more frequently than not. But Roger had somehow managed to get back to 1605 anyway, intending to do some meddling for reasons I was still kind of hazy on, maybe because he hadn't bothered to explain them much.

That was just as well, since when Roger did explain anything, it mostly didn't make sense.

And, right now, I had bigger problems.

"Agnes caught you and brought you back here—"

"With your help!"

"—and you've been rotting in here ever since, and now

I'm in the same boat. And I *have* to get out of here. I need your help."

"Help yourself," he said spitefully. "If you got in trouble with that damn Pythia, that's your problem. Maybe now you know what it feels like!"

"You have to help me!"

"I don't have to do anything!"

"At least tell me where we are!"

He laughed. "You're exactly nowhere," he said, and stepped through the wall.

Chapter Thirty

I followed him, which was easy because I was in spirit form. But he wasn't. "How did you do that?" I demanded.

"What?"

"*That.* You just shifted through that wall—"

"I didn't shift." It was irritable. "I can't shift."

"I *saw* you!"

"You saw me *phase.* Some of us have had to learn how to get by without the bright, shiny Pythian power to fall back on—"

"You—what?"

"—which won't work here anyway, so don't bother trying."

He strode off.

I caught up. "Wait a minute!"

"Would you leave me alone?"

"Explain what's going on, and maybe I will!"

He made a noise, a harrumph of irritation, which made me stare. I'd never heard anyone actually do that before. But then he threw out his hands. "What?"

I honestly didn't know where to start. "What's phasing?"

"Going closer to or further away from the real world. The further away you get, the less anything holds you, including wards. You're just not there as far as they're concerned."

"The real world? Then . . . where *are* we?"

"I already told you."

"You just said nowhere."

"Exactly."

"That doesn't help!"

"It's not supposed to. This"—he gestured around at the nothingness—"is where they put misbehaving time travelers. It's nowhere because it's nowhen. You're outside time."

He took off again, and for a second I just stared after him. Then I ran to catch up. *"What?"*

He sighed and pinched the bridge of his longer-than-strictly-necessary nose. "You know that old story about time travel, the party analogy?"

"The—no, I—"

He sighed again. "Okay. Say you're invited to a party—"

"What did you mean about outside time?"

"That's what I'm explaining! You're invited to a party, all right?"

"Okay."

"The invitation tells you three things, longitude, latitude, and height, only it puts it more like 'corner of Eighth and Elm, fifth floor,' right?"

"Okay."

"Could you get to that party?"

"I . . . guess so."

"Really? Then you should have no problem getting out of here. Most people would need a fourth direction. Or to be more precise, a fourth dimension. Most people would need to know when the damn party was!"

He took off again, and I followed, getting pissed now. I grabbed his arm. "That doesn't tell me anything!"

"On the contrary; it tells you everything. That party only exists as a destination at those coordinates *and at that time*. Otherwise, it doesn't exist at all. We don't live in three dimensions; we live in four, the fourth being time. Only most people never think about it."

"Okay, fine. But what does that have to do with this place?"

"You asked where we were. I told you nowhere, because we're not at the party. We can't be when time doesn't exist here. That damn Pythia shifted me outside it. No time means no time spells to let me get away from her. And I assume she put you out here for the same reason." He raised a brow. "You must have really pissed her off."

He took off again, which I'd pretty much come to expect at this point. And it looked like he was coming to expect things, too, because he stopped before I even managed to grab him again. "What *now*?"

"If my power won't work, how do we get *back*?"

"That way." He nodded to where Daisy was bouncing along, following an erratically moving sparkle until *bip*. It was gone. She glowed a little more brightly in her housedress and galoshes for a moment, before turning to grin at us triumphantly. "Got it!"

"Great," Roger said sourly. "Now go get one with some damn oomph behind it!"

She made a face and flitted off. I just stood there, looking at him. "She's hunting ghosts because they help you get out of here?"

"It's more of a hobby," he said sarcastically. "And they're not ghosts."

"Then what are they?"

"What remains of ghosts after they fade. This is the Badlands."

"The what?"

He looked at me in exasperation. "How do you not know this? You have a ghost." He looked pointedly at Billy's necklace, which I guessed he could see because Rosier still had my chameleon. Or because if there was one thing Dad knew, it was ghosts. "Don't you talk?"

"Not about this!"

"You sure? It's not exactly . . . but then, I suppose he doesn't need it, does he?" He picked up the necklace as easily as if it were solid. "That's what I thought. Talisman, right?"

I just nodded.

"With this he can go, what? Forty, maybe fifty miles away? And still make it back to soak up all the energy it collects for him. And since you're wearing it, that radius constantly changes, doesn't it?"

"Yes, but—"

"So he gets fed and doesn't get bored. Unlike all those

poor souls stuck in some overgrown cemetery somewhere, the kind nobody visits anymore. Ever wonder
what happens when the weeds come but the visitors
don't? Ghosts live off shed human energy, but if there's
no humans—ever wonder what happens then?"

"I—"

"Well, I'll tell you." He sat on an insubstantial-looking
rock and watched Daisy stalk another victim. "First, the
ghosts begin to starve. But they're not all equal, are they?
So pretty soon, the newer, stronger ones start cannibal-
izing the older and weaker. Until, eventually, they either
eat them all or drive them off to the Badlands. That's
where we are now."

I looked around. No wonder this place was giving me
the creeps. "So this . . . is like a cemetery . . . for *ghosts*?"

"In a manner of speaking. Only there's no visitors.
The only way to feed—as those who arrive with any sort
of mind left quickly realize—is to consume the scattered
remains of the less fortunate. If they do it enough, they
might even mange to escape—"

"Escape?"

He smiled sardonically. "Now you're getting it. Ghosts
aren't bound by the same rules as you or me. They can
transition here and back again, if they have enough power.
And here's where it gets fun: *they can take us with them*."

"Us?" I grabbed him.

"Us in the generalized sense. Not us as in you," he
clarified, prying my spectral hand off.

"But I told you, I have to get out of here!"

"Then use your own ghost. What am I, a charity?"

"But he's weak. He almost faded saving me—"

"Then lend him some energy."

"I can't spare any! You *have* to help—"

"I told you: I don't have to do anything. But you have
to get back to your body."

"Why?" I shot back, pretty sure he was just trying to
scare me. "You said there's no time here. So I can't die,
can I?"

"Maybe not. But you're still outside—"

"So?"

"So spirits without the body's protection are what again? Oh, that's right. Big wads of energy, free for the taking."

"And who's going to take it?" I demanded. "Some old ghost remnants?"

"Um, excuse me," Daisy said.

"No, little girl," Roger said testily. "But they're not the only ones out here, are they?"

"Aren't they? You just said—"

"That ghosts who fade can lose their tether to time and end up here, but it's by *accident*. Others come *on purpose*."

"For what? Why would anyone—"

"To hunt. All those territory-less ghosts—or what's left of them—might not be much individually. But together they form a nice, big pool of energy, and one with no awareness left to fight back. No hungry ghost is going to turn that down—"

"No way," Daisy interjected. "I mean, just look at them all."

"—and as a living being, you're more tasty than a thousand faded spirits."

"A human is still more powerful than a ghost," I pointed out.

"Than *a* ghost, certainly," Roger agreed. "But you forget—there's no time here. So you're not dealing with one era's ghosts but with all of them!"

"Well, I don't know if it's all, but it sure is a lot," Daisy said as I wondered why the air had started shaking around us.

And then I knew why.

"*Fuck!*" Roger said, and dove for the side of my cell, which was currently the nearest.

I just stayed where I was, rooted in place by the sight of an army of ghosts, thundering at us across the horizon. Like the *entire* horizon, because there had to be . . . I didn't even know. Thousands. Maybe tens of thousands, centuries' worth of predatory ghosts, the strongest ones, the most successful ones . . .

The ones that were almost on top of me, I realized, and dove back inside my cell.

"What did you do?" Roger yelled in my face as some-thing crashed into the wall behind me. Followed by a couple hundred friends, rattling against the exterior like gunfire. "What did you *do*?"

"I didn't do anything!"

"*Bullshit!* They don't act like this—they never act like this!"

"Then maybe *you* did something!"

"I know the Badlands—hell, I used to *live* in the Bad-lands! And the ghosts don't act like this!"

"Well, apparently, they do!"

"Not even for a disembodied human who doesn't have the sense to—"

I caught sight of my body sitting up, with my tits in my hands.

"—listen when someone with more experience tells her—"

"Are you *feeling me up*?" I asked Rosier, because I knew it was him. Even before I spotted his own small form, lying limp and lifeless on the floor.

"I give up!" Roger said, throwing his hands out.

"*That's* what's concerning you?" Rosier shrieked, over the gunfire sound effects.

"It's not helping!" I glared at him. "What are you *do-ing* in there?"

"Trying to keep you alive!"

"We're outside time! I'm not dying!"

"And I'm supposed to know this *how*?" he demanded, still clasping my breasts, as if for comfort. Until I knocked his hands away, although that probably would have hap-pened anyway.

Because we'd just rolled over.

I fell from the floor to the new floor. Which had been the wall, until the number of ghosts hitting us all on one side sent us clunking over. And then over again, and again, until it felt like we were in a wacked-out dryer set on kill.

"What are they *doing*?" I yelled, falling into Roger. Who snarled and pushed me off. Only to get my body's foot in his face, because it wasn't like there was a ton of room in here.

"Trying to shake us loose," he yelled back. "The cell walls are wards, to protect the living from spiritual attacks. Ghosts don't have the power to break through!"

"Daisy did!"

"Daisy is bound to me, as your servant is to you. The wards see them as part of us, and let them in!"

"Oh, good," I said, relieved.

"No, not good!"

"Why?"

"Because we need to get to the barrier in order to shift!"

And then Billy woke up.

"The fuck?" he said, materializing beside me and staring around. At Rosier's discarded body tumbling like a sneaker in the aforementioned dryer. At Roger, trying to brace in a corner. At me, attempting to hold steady in the midst of it all, hovering near the center of the roll. Until I gave up and grabbed Billy around the neck, just as Daisy drifted over.

"Hello, I'm Daisy," she said, sticking out a hand.

"The *fuck*?"

"No, the Daisy." She smiled at him. "Like the flower, you know?"

"Cassie—"

"We're in the Badlands," I told him breathlessly, which made no sense because this version of me didn't need to breathe. But it was one of those moments. "And we need to get out—"

"We're *where*?" His head twisted around to try to see me, because I was clinging to his back.

"In the *Badlands*. And a bunch of predatory ghosts are on the other side of that wall. We have to get out!"

"I— we just— Don't you ever take a day *off*?"

"Will people stop *saying* that?"

"Maybe I would, if I ever woke up to find you making pancakes or something!"

"Pancakes," Daisy said longingly. "I used to love pancakes."

"Who the hell is she?"

"She's a package deal with D—with Roger Palmer," I said while the damn man glared at me from the corner.

"Roger who?"

"Palmer," Dad and I said together, and Billy's eyes got big.

"Palmer? *The* Roger Palmer, like Roger Palmer, your—"

I clapped my hand over his mouth, and look.

It did work.

"Can we just get out of here?" I asked. "Please?"

"I have no idea," Billy said as Rosier's body *thump, thumped* through him again. "Nobody goes to the Badlands. Nobody sane, anyway. I sure as hell have never—"

"I can help you," Daisy said brightly. "It's easy. Look, I'll show you—"

"No!" everybody screamed as she started for the wall.

"What?"

"There's thousands of ravenous ghosts out there!" I told her, incredulous.

"There are?" Her eyes got big. *"Why didn't anybody tell me?"*

"Okay, so let me get this straight," Rosier said, running my body like a hamster on a wheel, in order to keep up with the barrel rolls. "We can shift out of this, but only out there"—he nodded at the wall—"in the midst of a bunch of predatory ghosts who plan to eat us?"

"Yes."

"And our ride doesn't even know how this process works, because he's never been here before?"

"Yes."

"And the only one who has experience is her." He hiked my thumb at Daisy. "Who is quite possibly mad?"

"I'm not mad," she said. "But you could have said something. I might have been killed!"

I looked at Roger. "Is there an alternative?"

He shook his head. "As far as I know, there's only two ways out of the Badlands. One, have a Pythia open a portal from our world, where her power works, allowing her to bring people in and out."

"And the other is to piggyback off a ghost," I finished for him.

"As long as they have the energy. You're going to have to feed yours."

"I can't. There's something I have to do, and it takes power—a lot of it. I've been taking a potion to enhance my stamina—"

"So take more!"

"I don't *have* any more. And even if I did, you can't enhance what isn't there. If I drain myself too low, it won't work—"

"Then you're shit out of luck, aren't you?"

I looked at Billy, but he was already shaking his head. "No way, Cass. I don't even have to know what's going on. I got nothing."

"You could feed him," I said to Roger, even knowing what the answer was going to be.

"I need my strength to feed my own ghost. She's not quite there—thanks to you, I might add. Shining like a lighthouse and luring every damn spirit in the place!"

I stared at him. I'd never gotten much affection from my parents, who'd died when I was four. I'd spent my childhood dreaming about them, sneaking around, trying to find out any scrap of information I could. Which hadn't been much, since my old guardian had instructed people not to talk to me. But I'd always wondered. . . .

And then I'd become Pythia, and gone back in time, to seek help from my mother in dealing with the demon council. Help she'd given, sort of. But there'd been no affection with it, no tear-filled reunions, no anything. Just grudging assistance and a swift push out the door.

And now my father was refusing even that, basically telling me to stay here and die for all he cared. I didn't know why it hurt after so long, and after plenty of other indications of how he felt, but it did. It hurt so goddamn much, even though I hadn't been born yet from his perspective, even though he had no way to know who I was.

Because it hadn't made a difference when he did.

"That's not going to help," he said, looking uncomfortable. "I told you, I *can't*—"

"But I can," Rosier said, his voice harsh. I looked at him, and found him scowling at my father. "Get back in here," he told me. "And get ready!"

I saw my face go slack as he stepped out of my skin. A second later I was stepping in, feeling the weight of my body hit me, pulling me the rest of the way to the floor. And to the rocks underneath, which bruised my palms when I abruptly hit down.

Because the wards were almost gone.

I hadn't noticed, floating in the air, because the walls still looked the same. But they weren't the same, maybe because nobody had expected them to have to put up with this kind of abuse. "The wards—" I gasped, looking up.

And was almost blinded by Billy Joe, shining like a searchlight.

And then everything happened at once: Billy grabbing me and me grabbing Rosier; Daisy jerking a surprised-looking Roger off the floor, and all of us falling through the collapsing wards. Which left us behind on the ground the next time the cell rolled over, where we were metaphysically trampled by a crowd of ghosts. Who'd gotten so into the rush to destroy the cell that they didn't immediately notice we were gone.

I lay there for a second, watching the mighty throng surge ahead, the remains of the small cell being tossed in front of them like a bouncy ball. And then we were up and running, dodging through the crowd of stragglers, who stared at us in surprise. For about a second.

Until their faces started to melt.

"Daisy!" Roger shouted as the spirits turned into nightmare fuel.

"Trying!"

"Try harder!"

"They're too close," she panted. "I'll take some of them with us!"

"Then take them!" he yelled, sending spells and ghosts flying. But that wouldn't work in a second, when the main crowd realized that their prey was trying to flee. "Daisy! Do it *now*!"

And she did. Or she did something as pain lanced through me, as Billy Joe snarled and threw a couple of clinging spirits off my back, as we pelted forward. And while the X-ray landscape changed all around us. A river swelled and declined, trees grew and fell, armies marched and fires raged and walls rose around us, new ones, familiar ones, like the stairs being built under our feet, lifting us along with them—

"Daisy, now!" Roger screamed as something latched on to the back of his neck. "Now! Now! Now!"

"Now what?" she asked, looking confused.

Billy Joe cursed, and jerked, a mighty heave that had me feeling like I'd left some of my bones behind—

But a second later we were tumbling into the real world—literally, because we'd just crashed through the railing on the second floor of the Pythian Court.

"Well, shit," Rosier said, right before we hit the floor, the very hard, very marble floor of the foyer, which would have hurt more, but I'd fallen on someone.

Someone who I guessed was Roger, because he was cursing underneath me.

Of course, that might have had something to do with the half dozen hungry ghosts still clinging to him, like leeches, as he shoved me off. And staggered to his feet, slinging spells and stumbling into things, because some of the ghosts didn't seem interested in leaving. And with the energy they'd stolen from us, they could afford to press the point.

I blinked and Agnes was there, looking years older than when I'd seen her in Wales, with a few more pounds and some crow's-feet around her sharp blue eyes. But younger than when she and I went adventuring in the sixteenth century, and caught a time-traveling weirdo mucking about in a cellar. Because that hadn't happened yet.

Billy had pulled us out too soon.

Her eyes focused on me, but there was no spark of recognition in them. Maybe because she hadn't gotten a good look at me while on that damn wagon. Or because that whole thing had been decades ago from her perspective. Or because my hair was plastered to my skull and covered in dirt, like my face and my still-damp slave wear.

For once, looking like hell came in handy, I thought.

And then someone screamed.

"You!"

I looked up to find Roger back on his feet, and pointing a shaking finger at me. "Every time," he gasped. "*Every* time!"

"What?"

"Every time I meet you, you ruin my life. This is your fault. *This is all your fault!*"

"What exactly is going on here?" Agnes asked, voice cold. She looked at me.

"He's . . . a madman," I told her, swallowing, and feeling like I'd just been kicked in the gut. "A Guild member and a . . . a necromancer. He was in prison in the Badlands, but he escaped—"

"No thanks to you!" he yelled, and lunged for me.

Only to find himself suspended in midair, probably courtesy of the house wards. Which only seemed to make him madder. He thrashed around, cursing, as ghosts fled the scene and Billy disappeared into my necklace.

"She's a necromancer, too," Roger yelled as a bunch of Circle guards joined the party, rushing in from all directions. "And a sorceress! She's got a demon with her now!"

Agnes' eyes returned to me, but Rosier was nowhere to be seen. And that was despite the fact that something small and heavy was clinging to my leg, like a limpet. It looked like my chameleon could hide him, after all.

"He was just here!" Roger shouted, furious. "They were both locked up together!"

"It's a lie," I said quickly. "I'm a Pythian heir, training in the Badlands. I was leaving when this man attacked me, having somehow escaped his cell—"

"Liar!"

"—and threw my, uh, my spell off," I said, hoping there wasn't a specific name for the portal. "I'm sorry to have disturbed you."

"And the clothes?" Agnes asked, with a raised brow.

"I was sent on a mission immediately after returning from one," I said, smiling weakly. "You know how that is."

She didn't smile back.

She did turn around, however. "Elizabeth."

Someone came out from behind her, from among the white-robed acolytes. For a moment, I just stared upward, at a very young version of my mother, her dark copper hair in a loose chignon, her white gown pristine. And looking down demurely.

"You've heard them," Agnes said. "What would you do?"

"Me, Lady?" The voice was soft.

"What would you do with the girl? Lock her up, or set her free?"

Mother looked up, and for the first time, our eyes met. Her expression didn't change, not wavering from polite interest. But she never so much as glanced at anyone else.

"She possesses the Pythian power," she said, after a moment. "Therefore either she is telling the truth or she's a rogue. If the former, we should send her back to her own time, for she is too weak to continue her mission. If the latter, the same is true, so that her Pythia can deal with her."

"Very good," Agnes said, looking at her with pride. "So be it."

And the next thing I knew, I was bouncing on my bed in Vegas.

Chapter Thirty-one

I woke up to a soft bed, a spill of light from an open door, and a familiar, velvety darkness. But not a familiar room. I sat up abruptly.

And immediately regretted it.

Pain ripped through my body, radiating outward from a hundred points. Old pain, from strains and sprains and bruises weeks old. Newer pain, from my side, from my feet, from the battle on the drag. Brand-spanking-new pain, clear and bright and soul deep, from ghost bites, from channeling too much power, from everything, all at once, forcing a sound out of me.

It was surprise.

I guess nothing else fit, I thought, and put out a hand to steady myself.

And found warm flesh, not cool sheets.

"Easy," someone said, and fingers closed gently around mine.

I looked up, struggling to see anything with the light from the next room blazing in my eyes. Until a dark head blotted out most of it. A very familiar dark head.

Mircea.

For a minute, I wasn't sure if my brain had conjured him up or not, and the view didn't help. Because he looked just like always: fall of smooth mahogany hair just brushing his shoulders; dark blue suit, the rich wool glimmering slightly in the low light; lashes too long and thick for a man, like the lips that appeared wine reddened without any wine. He should have looked feminine, except the strong features and broad shoulders never could.

"If I conjured you up, I did a good job," I told him blearily.

"I'm real enough," he said, and held a glass to my lips.

I finished the whole thing. It was only water, but it seemed to help. I lay back against the pillows again, feeling stronger.

"You sure?" I asked, glancing around. I'd been right: I didn't recognize this room. Not that I could see much of it, but the furniture wasn't in the right place, and there was no broad sweep of windows. Or any at all.

"I'm sure." Mircea leaned over and smoothed back my hair. "I tried to contact you through Seidr earlier, but it didn't work."

"Why not?"

"I don't know."

"Lord Mircea," someone said, from the doorway. Mircea didn't even turn around, but I looked past his shoulder to see a tall, thin shadow blocking out some of the light. A shadow with a shock of unruly dark hair and glasses he shouldn't need, because he was a vampire.

"In a moment," Mircea said, his eyes still on mine. "It hasn't worked since that incident at Dante's this morning."

I frowned, trying to jump-start my brain. "You think Ares did something?"

"I don't know," he said again, fingers combing through my hair, causing the pain in my head to recede slightly. Until I caught his wrist, because he couldn't spare the energy right now. He just smiled and switched hands.

"I thought at first that you were simply asleep, something I verified with Marco," he told me. "But it didn't work later, either. Although, in fairness, the fault could be mine. After yesterday . . . ."

I nodded. Mircea had been the target of an assassin, a traitor in the vampire ranks working for the other side, who had attacked him mentally. The plot had failed, but he'd been badly injured, only not badly enough from their perspective. The idea had been to finish the job during the attack on the consul's home, but Lizzie had spilled the beans under questioning, and I'd pulled him out before they could reach him. And half a day later, he'd returned the favor, saving both my life and Rhea's.

But neither of us had exactly emerged unscathed.

"Stop." I captured his hands, which had moved to my temples. "You need your strength."

"When you lead a family as large as ours, you recover quickly," he told me. "Assassins would do well to remember that."

I grinned, in spite of everything. "When you come at the king, you'd best not miss?"

He laughed. "Isn't that what I just said?" He tapped my shoulder. "Turn over."

I did, because it was easier than arguing. And because Mircea wasn't stupid. He wouldn't drain himself too low at a time like this. And because it felt—

Oh God.

The tension of the last few weeks rolled out of me in waves, following the strokes of his hands. I lay there, groaning out loud after a while, because I couldn't seem to stop, as he erased pain and stiffness from my back and arms and thighs and legs. And then he reached my feet, and I almost wept.

"Oh *God*."

"What have you been doing?" he asked, sounding slightly horrified, probably at the collection of cuts and bruises I'd managed to amass on hard Welsh stones.

I didn't answer, but not just because of the pain. But because moments like this were rare. Moments when it was just us, just Mircea and Cassie, without the rest of the world intruding. Without something—usually our jobs—getting in the way, screwing up our time together, and causing trouble.

Well, that and the thousand things we couldn't say to each other.

Like about the woman I'd seen in his chambers, when I went to rescue him. He'd been sleeping, exhausted from the strain of fighting off the attack, but she'd been awake. And predatory, with nails that had dented the skin of his chest, and small fangs just visible over bloodred lips as she snarled at me. She'd looked exactly like a feral animal, guarding its prey.

If she hadn't been naked, I might have thought she was there to eat him.

As it was, it was pretty obvious what she was there to do, and it had given me great satisfaction to send her and the sheet she was wearing to a particularly odorous cow pasture on Long Island. Tony had lent me out to one of his associates for a week there once, who had needed my Sight, but it had been my nose that had suffered. I could only hope the place had retained its charm.

But other than for a few seconds' amusement, watching her and her sheet flounder around in the muck, it hadn't solved anything. Except for getting her out of a war zone. Because I'd had to go back a few hours in time to rescue Mircea, so she'd gotten a free pass out of the hellhole the consul's home was about to become.

In other words, I'd saved the life of my boyfriend's lover, and I couldn't even tell him about it.

Because I was afraid he'd ask me about mine.

Not that Pritkin and I *were* lovers in any normal sense of the word. Today was absolutely further than we'd ever gone, and it hadn't exactly been by choice. Not once, in all the times I'd known him, had we touched when it wasn't an emergency. But when your partner is a half-incubus war mage, who only heals from one thing, and you're in the middle of a war . . . emergencies happen.

But I hadn't talked to Mircea about them, because how could I? To explain how Pritkin healed was to explain what he was, and I couldn't explain what he was. There had only been one half human, half incubus in recorded history, and Mircea had already shown way too much interest in Pritkin's background as it was. It would take that lightning-fast brain maybe a second to put two and two together and end up with Merlin, and that was a name that could never be said.

Not when the magical community practically worshipped the guy, almost as much as Pritkin worshipped his privacy.

I couldn't get him back only to ruin his life, so I *couldn't* say anything. But that meant no absolution when anything happened, no chance to talk things out, no opportunity to explain. Or to ask about any of the women mentioned in connection with Mircea, who he said he had nothing to do with anymore, but then I find her in his *room*.

I watched my fingers clench in the sheets, and knew I had to say something this time. Had to find a way to talk about at least some of it, because I couldn't do this anymore. It felt like I'd explode sometimes, with all the evasions, and secrets, and half-truths. I wanted things on the table for once, before this silence killed us.

"Mircea—"

"My lord, I do apologize." That was the vamp who hadn't budged from the doorway. "But they're starting. We really must—"

The man cut off abruptly, with a slightly choked sound.

Because, yeah. You didn't make a master tell you something twice. He must be new.

"I have to go," Mircea murmured against my shoulder. "But I wanted to be the one to tell you, before you heard it from someone else."

I rolled over. "Heard what?"

"The Circle fought off a dark mage assault this afternoon, at their main headquarters in Stratford."

"Stratford?" I sat up, a little too abruptly.

Mircea steadied me. "There was a battle, but the Circle prevailed. Attacking the creators of the most vicious spells on earth at their home base is not the act of sane men."

"The Black Circle isn't sane."

"No, but they aren't usually this reckless, either. They wanted something—badly."

"Lizzie." It wasn't even a question. "That's why they attacked Dante's. And if she was at Stratford—"

"She was, from what I understand. But they didn't get her," he said, holding me as I started to get off the bed. "They *didn't get her*, Cassie. I was told that most definitely."

I swallowed and stopped struggling. "Can I use your phone? I have—I might have a friend there."

He handed me a sleek black rectangle, but the screen was dark. "The focal wards are up," he explained. "It may be a while before you get a signal."

I should have expected that, after everything. And after watching the light from the next room dance off the side of his face, because it wasn't coming from electricity.

The big boys were up, the kind of wards most places only brought online in emergencies because of the power drain, and because they really messed up any modern tech they came in contact with—phones included.

"I can try to find out about your friend," Mircea offered.

"Caleb. Caleb Carter."

He nodded, and started to get up. "Wait." I caught his arm. "You haven't told me . . . what's going on. How are they doing this?"

"Doing . . . ?"

"This! All of this." I gestured around at an amorphous enemy, because that's what the Black Circle and their allies were starting to feel like—something that was always around, an unseen menace crouched in the dark, ready to strike. "How do they stay one step ahead? We fight off one attack, and there's another, almost before we can draw a breath. They're almost constant anymore—"

"You already know that."

"I don't!" I shook my head, trying to clear it. I still felt half-asleep, but I didn't need much thought for this. "The whole reason for attacking Dante's was Lizzie being there. But she wasn't captured until the night before they showed up—"

"Cassie."

"—so overnight they got hundreds of men to Vegas, verified that my guards were down for the count, calculated exactly how much time they had before the Circle could react, located and brought down the wards, figured out a way to grab Rhea . . ." I looked at him in bewilderment. "It's *impossible*."

"Not if the people planning this are in Faerie." Mircea sat back down on the bed, the firelight making his eyes gleam. "The fey timeline runs differently than ours—you know that."

I nodded.

"But what you may not know is that the rate of the difference isn't constant. It is often explained as if our two timelines are two rivers that generally parallel each other. But sometimes one or the other will divert, bulging out in an arc before coming back into rough synchronicity.

When that happens, the difference between time here and time there can be . . . extreme. We appear to be in one of those cycles now."

"So time in Faerie is running differently than here?"

"Faster—much faster. It won't last—it never does. But for a short span, they are essentially on fast forward. And they *knew this was coming*. The fey have the ability to chart the difference in our time streams with far more accuracy than we do. They've learned to predict it."

"Yes, but—"

"Think about it, Cassie. They plan an attack on one of our strongholds. Perhaps it takes weeks from their perspective. But from ours, it has been mere days, possibly only hours. They have the leisure to debate, to decide, to rest. If something doesn't work, such as the attack on the casino, they have time to recalibrate. While we are constantly running, on the defensive, getting hit here, there, everywhere—with, as you say, scarce time to draw a breath in between."

"And now they have a god planning their attacks for them."

"So it would seem." It was grim.

The last time we discussed this, Mircea hadn't wanted to believe that Ares was back. He'd wanted to keep this as a fight between the kinds of things he might know how to kill. But it looked like this morning had convinced him.

Or convinced him that he'd been right all along, I thought, watching his face change.

"That is why we *must* take the war to them," he told me earnestly. "We cannot remain on the defensive forever. They will attack again, and soon, before their advantage fades, and there is no way to tell what they will hit next. We must give them something else to think about."

I didn't say anything. He was right—I *knew* he was. But the method the senate had selected was . . . less than optimal. Way less.

They wanted me to use the Pythian power to age up a vampire, while his master fed him power—a *lot* of it. More than he could possibly absorb all at once without my help. It was similar to something they'd done for years called the Push, when—usually in times of war—a new master was needed pronto. But all that power all at once was a big gamble, one that usually resulted in a dead vamp.

You know, permanently.

But with the years speeding by like seconds, the hope was that the power would simply be absorbed, as if he'd actually lived and fed through all those years, gaining strength with each one. And that out of the other side of my time bubble would leap a brand-new master vamp. Who would need to quickly move aside, to get out of the way, because another would be coming through right behind him.

And then another, and another, because the senate wanted me to make them an entire army of masters. With which they intended to rip the fey, and the enemies we had hiding with them, a new one. Mircea had come to me all happy and excited, almost giddy with his new plan.

And hadn't understood my less-than-enthusiastic response.

It wasn't just about what it would take out of me, because aging someone like that wasn't as easy as the senate seemed to think. Or about the fact that I'd be too exhausted afterward to do anything else, including fighting gods. But about a question that no one could answer: what was going to happen when that army came back? What were a bunch of new masters going to do, freshly back from war and with enough power to do anything they liked? Who, if anybody, was going to control them?

"We shouldn't be talking about this now," Mircea said, his eyes on my face. "You need to rest."

I shook my head. "I'm all right—"

An eyebrow rose. "Is that why you collapsed in the middle of the consul's great hall?"

"The consul's?" For a moment, my mind blanked. And then it came back to me. Shifting into Dante's—or being shifted, because I'd had no control over it. The wards blaring a warning about Rosier's presence, almost deafening. Marco bursting through the door, several vamps at his back—

And me shifting out again, before they could stop me. Because I'd wanted . . . something. . . . My eyes widened. "Mircea—"

"My lord—" The tousled-haired vamp, who was clearly crazy, was back. For about a second, until he made a strangled sound and fled.

"There is something you need?" Mircea asked me.

"The Tears of Apollo."

He frowned slightly. "But you have it. I was told you took it from your rogue, after your duel."

Trust the senate to know everything that happened, even when nobody had told them. "I need more. It's a long story—"

"And I want to hear it, but I have to do this."

"Do what?"

"That's a long story, too," he said ruefully. "We need to talk—"

That was the understatement of the century, I thought, gripping his hand. Because I knew what came next. "Mircea—"

"—afterward."

"Mircea—"

"I'm not going anywhere," he said, seeing my alarm. Because our talks never quite managed to happen, or if they did, they got off on a tangent and never got around to the point. But this one had to.

"Just tell me," I said, hanging on to his hand. "You must have had a source, right?"

"A source?"

"For the potion! I mean, you got it from someone—"

"Yes, we got it from someone."

"Who? Just tell me that—"

Knowing dark eyes met mine. "If I do, will you still be here when I return?"

I bit my lip. Because we both knew the answer to that.

"I thought not." He bent over and kissed my forehead. "This won't take long, and then we'll talk."

I blinked and he was gone.

Chapter Thirty-two

"Mircea!" But the door was already closing. "Damn it," I muttered, and threw back the covers, wondering why it felt like someone had sewn lead weights into them. And stood up.

And immediately collapsed, because I had no strength at all. My legs might as well have been nailed to the floor, they were so hard to move. So I didn't. I just sat there, on a very nice Persian carpet of a type Mircea could probably have identified but I couldn't, and leaned my head against the side of the bed.

So this was what happened when the potion wore off.

I sat there some more.

I finally decided to lie down, because even sitting up was too hard. I'd have tried to get back on the bed, but it was ridiculously high and far away. Might as well have been Everest. I settled for staring at the ceiling instead.

It probably wasn't a good sign that it kept pulsing in and out. Or that the rug felt like it was spinning, very slowly, underneath me. I decided that there was a tiniest chance Caleb had been right, not about the addiction part, because how did you become addicted to something you could never find? But about the side effects.

They reminded me of a time when I'd used a power word I knew. It gave you a ton of stamina, like a week's worth, all at once, to let you deal with an emergency. And you had better deal with it, because you weren't just tired when it wore off. You were exhausted, passed out, useless, like for *days*, and—

And—

And *shit*.

I sat up. Okay, it looked like I could move, after all. Because my sleep-fuzzed brain hadn't remembered to ask Mircea the most important question of all: *what time was it?*

The seat of his discarded chair was close enough for me to grab it and pull myself to my knees. And then somehow, and I wasn't entirely sure how, I made it to my feet. And immediately wished I hadn't.

I stood there, swaying slightly and clinging to the back of the chair, both exhausted and in serious pain, because my feet were a mess. Mircea had done something—the cuts were closed and the bruises had taken on the purplish hue of days-old wounds—but they did *not* want to hold me. And the door . . . the door looked like I was staring at it through a telescope, from the wrong way round. It was laughably far, to the point that there was no way, just no way—

And then the vamp was back.

It was the same one as before, with the glasses and the hair that could use a comb, and the generic, off-the-rack suit that needed pressing. I wondered vaguely how he'd gotten past the makeover squad. Most of Mircea's guys looked like they got tackled and dragged to Armani first thing. Of course, maybe this wasn't one, because I didn't recognize him. Maybe this was . . . was the consul's, I thought blearily, as we stared at each other.

And as he grabbed me, just before I hit the floor.

"Not the bed," I said, because if I lay down, I wasn't getting back up. "What time is it?"

He just stood there, holding me awkwardly, and didn't say anything.

"What time is it?" I repeated, wondering why he was acting like he was hard of hearing when he was a *vamp*, and saw his pupils blow huge. And then this weird sound started coming from his lips. It wasn't words—I didn't know what it was—but it was freaking me out even more than I already was. "What *time*? What *day*? Damn it, say *something*!"

But he didn't. He did almost drop me, however, and then his arms tightened, making me yelp in pain. The freaked-out look intensified, as did the sound, which had

become a weird mewling cry, right in my face. And that
sent me the rest of the way into a panic.

"Put me down! Put me *down*!" I yelled. But the vamp
wasn't putting me down. And he wasn't stopping that
horrible, high-pitched keening, either. However, he did
take off running, through the door of the bedroom and
down a hall, so fast that the rooms we passed were just a
blur.

Like the faces that turned to look at us, and the stairs
we all but flew down, and the rug that almost sent us
sprawling before the vamp recovered, because his reflexes were better than his sanity. And the man who
stepped out of nowhere in front of us, dodging back and
forth along with the vamp, refusing to let him pass. And
causing the keening to escalate to the point that I'd have
feared for his heart.

Except, you know.

And then I recognized the man. "Jules?"

The handsome blond playing tag with the vamp nodded.

"Tell him you didn't mean it," he told me. "Tell him
now!"

"That I didn't mean what?"

"Whatever it was you said! Just say the words!"

"I didn't mean it!" I yelled, because the vamp's distress had reached earsplitting decibels.

And, just as suddenly, cut out.

He collapsed to his knees, taking me with him, and
Jules knelt beside us. "What . . . ?" I breathed, after a
minute.

"Later," Jules said, looking around. "Let's just get out
of here."

I followed his gaze. We were in a wide hallway that
would have looked at home in old Rome. Not the terra-
cotta and picturesque stucco version, but pure empire:
gorgeous inlaid marble floors, nooks with priceless statu-
ary, tasteful ionic columns. And, for some reason, the utter devastation of the place—it was currently lacking
most of the once soaring ceiling—gave it an added charm,
like ancient ruins.

Well, it would have if not for the crowd. Moonlight

spilled through the giant hole above, splashing us like a floodlight. But not enough that I couldn't see the ring of curious faces staring at us from the stairs and out of rooms, or just standing around the shadows, because the place was packed. And because the vamp had covered his face with both hands now, and was *sobbing*.

"What is it?" I asked, beginning to be seriously concerned. I put a hand on his arm. "Are you all right?"

And, oh God, here we go again, I thought, as he looked up at me, brown eyes huge, mouth already opening in distress.

"I didn't mean it!" I said, quickly. *"I didn't mean it!"*

The mouth closed again, with a pop.

For a minute, we just sat there, both of us fairly freaked out.

And then Jules took charge.

"Get up and bring her this way," he told the vamp, clearly and distinctly. "Now."

The vamp got to his feet and bent to lift me.

No questions, Jules mouthed at me, over his back.

I shook my head. No questions.

The vamp picked me up, a swift, graceful motion that belied the turmoil on his face. And followed Jules down the hall, one teeming with people. People in burnooses and saris, suits and ties, sarongs and kimonos, turbans and kaffiyehs, who passed us on all sides. Until we ducked inside a door, which Jules kicked shut behind us.

I gave an audible sigh of relief, and he grinned sympathetically. "Yeah. It's been like that all day."

I looked around, grateful that we were somewhere pretty normal. Well, except for a dozen lit candles on the coffee table, which provided the only light. But otherwise, it could have been a posh room just about anywhere: a couch, a couple of chairs, some probably expensive paintings on the walls that seemed oddly focused on cows, but overall I liked it.

The vamp must have, too, because I felt him relax a little.

"Put her on the sofa," Jules ordered.

The vamp put me on the sofa.

He had a watch on his wrist, which I might have noticed

sooner if he hadn't been screaming at me. "Four a.m.?" I asked Jules—carefully, with one eye on the vamp. But there was no reaction this time.

Jules nodded. "Yes, why?"

"What day?"

He looked at me in amusement. "That would sound weird coming from anyone else."

"Just tell me—please."

He did. And I relaxed back against the cushions, feeling like my spine had just turned to water. I must have only slept for a few hours. The second day Rosier had promised was still young.

I opened my eyes after a moment, to notice that the vamp wasn't looking nearly so relieved. He was standing beside the sofa, hands wringing, Adam's apple working. And glancing nervously at Jules, like he had no idea who he was.

"Jules Fortescue," Jules told him, extending a hand, which was strange.

Even stranger, the vamp took it.

It caught me by surprise, because vamps didn't usually shake hands. It was one of those human affectations that slipped away after death, maybe because it didn't apply to all the cultures and eras they came from. Or maybe because touching another vampire could cause auras to spark, and be taken for a challenge. Most vamps would have looked at Jules—who ought to know better—with disdain for even offering, but this one seemed almost . . . relieved.

Jules smiled and released him. "All right, that's a lie," he confessed. "It's actually Jimmy Tucker. My agent just thought it sounded more dignified the other way."

The vamp blinked.

"Yeah, used to be an actor," Jules said, sitting down. "It's okay if you've never heard of me. It was a long time ago." He hooked another chair with his foot, dragging it a few feet closer. "Go ahead, sit down."

The vamp sat. His eyes were still flicking around—at me, at a painting of a rustic hillside, at a rodeo rider cast in bronze on a bucking bronco. "Mine," Jules said, seeing the direction of his gaze. "This is going to be my office if anybody ever brings me a desk."

"Office?" I said. "Then they finally let you out?"

The last time I'd seen Jules, he'd been a sort of prisoner of the senate, although not because he'd done anything wrong. But because he'd done something unique, something that no vampire had ever done, at least as far as anybody knew. He'd turned human.

Or, to be more precise, I'd turned him human, in an attempt to save his life. He'd blundered into a terrible curse, one of the ones Augustine had been working up for the senate, and it didn't have a cure yet. So I'd lobbed a Hail Mary and tried de-aging him, to turn the clock back to before he was cursed, hoping that would lift it. And, for once, something had actually worked out—sort of.

I still didn't fully understand it, considering that physical wounds weren't similarly affected. A stabbed human just became a younger stabbed human, for example, but in Jules' case he'd ended up curse free. And that included the curse of vampirism, which had been lifted right along with the other, when he aged back to before it was laid.

It was what had given the senate the idea for their army. Because, if I could de-age someone, why not the reverse? It had also put Jules in a bad position, in a big way. Before the change, he had been one of my bodyguards, a master of Mircea's family line, someone with power, money, and influence. Afterward, he was a self-professed lab rat, and one I'd promised to help spring from his cage.

Only it looked like he'd already done that.

"For the moment," he agreed. "I'm their liaison to all the new vamps they're bringing in."

"What new vamps?"

"Ones like this guy." Jules leaned forward, elbows on knees, his usually expressive hands hanging down, calm and quiet. Like the casual smile in his blue eyes as he looked at the twitchy vamp. "I'm not going to ask you any questions," he told him slowly. "Neither of us is. Right?" He looked at me.

"Right."

The vamp looked seriously relieved.

"I'm just going to talk to Cassie for a bit. That's Cassie." He nodded at me. The vamp looked my way, and his face reddened. I wasn't sure why. For once, I was properly attired in tan capris and a pink blouse. There had been little pink ballerina flats in the room, too, arranged on the carpet, but with my feet, I wasn't sorry I'd left them.

"Hi," I said, wondering if that was safe.

Guess so.

"Any questions we ask are not meant for you," Jules told him. "Just relax for a bit."

The vamp visibly relaxed.

"So," Jules asked me. "What happened?"

"I have no idea."

He nodded. "Let me guess. You were with a vamp—someone more than a few days old."

It took me a minute, before my eyes cut to Twitchy. "A few *days*?"

Jules glanced at the guy again, who seemed to be taking the relaxation thing seriously. He was slumped in his chair, staring at cows. "Okay, maybe a few weeks. Definitely not over a month."

"A few— What is he *doing* here?"

It was a fair question, because baby vamps were, well, pretty useless. They were mostly carried for the first few years in any family, being given easy, human-level tasks that didn't require thinking anywhere close to morning, when their brains got all fuzzy. And which utilized the few things they were good at: lifting heavy items, running fast, and, uh, that was about it.

They weren't even trained much at first, because it took time for their senses to sort themselves out. You can't just go from a human nose to one like a bloodhound's and not have it throw you. Or from human hearing to suddenly hearing *everything*, including conversations a mile off. Or from human sight to vision that could act like a camera's zoom lens at will—or randomly, if you didn't know how to control it.

Which was probably why Twitchy had just grabbed the arms of his chair and jumped back—

At a sudden attack of cow.

"Oh, for— I said *relax*," Jules snapped, and then sighed when the guy promptly went limp.

"Sorry," he said as Twitchy slid off the chair and onto the floor, almost like he was boneless.

"You're not even one of them anymore," I pointed out, as Jules grabbed him and stuffed him back in his chair. And turned it to face the nice, blank wall to his left, huffing a little with the effort. "Why is he following your commands?"

"Because he's traumatized," Jules said, watching Twitchy for a moment to see if he'd stay put. He did. Jules went over to the cabinet with the bronco, which swung outward to show a hidden bar. "There's a reason they usually separate babies for a while, even from other family members. You know, bunk them with a mentor to see that they don't walk out into the sun or something, and give them a chance to adjust."

I nodded. Tony had had a special room he called the nursery, set up behind one of his businesses. Any new vamps he made stayed there for at least the first six months, and sometimes longer depending on how well they were taking it. Because it could be pretty shocking: hearing the family talking in your head all day, the whole bloodlust thing, the new senses . . . Most of the time, babies were considered to be doing pretty well if they didn't lose their minds and run amok.

You know, too often.

Although I'd never seen one quite this bad.

"Traumatized by what, exactly?"

Jules handed me a glass and then sat on the edge of the cabinet with his own. He didn't offer the vamp any. It would have been a waste of good whiskey; at that age, everything just tasted gray.

"Like I was saying, he came into contact with someone with power, right?"

I nodded. "Mircea."

"Hoo boy. Yeah, that would do it."

"Do what?"

"That," Jules said dryly, pointing his glass at the vamp. "Let me guess. New guy here was bugging the shit out of Mircea, who told him to be quiet, right?"

"More or less. How did you—"

"Had it happen to me once, as a newbie. Always liked to talk too much. And there was this guy—Roberto. You met him?"

"No."

"You haven't missed anything. He loves to torment the new arrivals, or he did. Mircea lent him out to another master a few years ago, and we're all hoping it's permanent. Anyway, someone told him my last name was Fortescue, and he thought that was funny as hell. Told me to 'keep a stiff upper lip, old chap,' laughing the whole time. I didn't know why. Till I realized: I couldn't move the damn thing at all."

"Move what?"

"My *lip*. Spent two days sounding like I had a serious speech impediment until someone figured it out and countermanded the order."

"But it wasn't an order. It was a figure of speech—"

"Not with power behind it," Jules said sourly. "He meant for that to happen. Like I said: dick. Mircea, on the other hand, sometimes just forgets how powerful he is. He spends too much time around upper-level types, where he doesn't have to watch it. He'd probably apologize if he realized, but he's kind of stressed right now, so I hate to bother—"

"Kind of stressed?" I felt my own blood pressure start to rise. "Why? What's wrong?"

"What's *wrong*?" Jules blinked at me. "Seriously?"

"Yes, seriously!"

"Well, let's see. You almost died this morning. Then you disappear all day and nobody knows where you went. The consul's own home was attacked, and half of it's in ruins, which is making it hell for me trying to find space for all the newbies, by the way. The rooms that are intact have mostly been claimed by senators and their retinues. I've managed to pawn some of them off on Louis-Cesare— new senate member, has a house near here—but it's still in progress and—"

"Jules."

"Oh, right. Well, on top of all that, Dante's is *trashed*,

and currently closed for business, the consul's in a mood, and Mircea's just been named Enforcer—"

"Enforcer?" I frowned.

"The senate positon. You know?"

I shook my head. I knew that the senate had been devastated by a series of attacks early in the war—like before anybody knew we were in one. And what with everything happening fast and furious ever since, they'd only just gotten around to filling the vacant seats. I'd even heard that some shuffling of roles was taking place, since the newcomers didn't always slot cleanly into the old positions.

But Enforcer?

"Why *Mircea*?" I asked. "The Enforcer acts like a beat cop, dragging back misbehaving masters. Sure, he could do that, but what a waste—"

"It's not a waste."

"How? He's a senior diplomat—*the* senior diplomat. How is that not—"

"The Enforcer also has another role in wartime," Jules told me gently. "You probably haven't heard about it, since it's been centuries since anybody used it."

"What other role?" I asked, confused.

"General."

Chapter Thirty-three

We were on the move again, at my insistence. The mute vamp seemed pleased, however, despite carrying me, since I probably weighed the same as a feather to him. And since he'd finally figured out that we really weren't going to ask him questions he couldn't answer, or send him back to work, where he'd probably have someone else do the same thing.

That would be bad, since it would directly contradict his former instructions to accommodate guests in any reasonable way. And clashing orders apparently did bad things to baby vamps' minds. So we needed to get the mute command rescinded ASAP.

But that wasn't the only reason we were headed to the basement.

"That's all I know," Jules said, keeping pace with the vamp's long strides. "Mircea's been named Enforcer, not just of our senate, but of the combined forces of all six senates."

"What?"

"I know." He nodded. "I never thought I'd live to see the day that the senates do anything but claw at each other. But now that they have, it makes sense that they'd need a ruling body to govern the actions they do as a group. He won't have anything to do with the Enforcer's role in, say, India. That'll be up to the South Asian Senate, since it just involves their turf. But if the combined forces are doing something, then it's his baby."

"Then they're arguing about who's going to be . . . on the senates' senate?"

He nodded, and dodged a guy in a flowing djellaba,

surrounded by half a dozen flunkies. "That's the rumor. Our consul's the leader. That's already been decided, but the rest of the roles . . . Well, from what I hear, the conversation's getting pretty heated. But Mircea was an obvious choice, with his war experience—"

"His war experience is five hundred years out-of-date!" I snapped because I didn't like this. I didn't like this at all. Human generals, okay, they sat in nice, air-conditioned command centers, well out of the fighting. But vampires . . .

Why did I think that wouldn't apply to vampires?

Maybe because it wasn't that way when they fought—at any level. Even those who would be consul had to fight for the job, defeating whoever already had it. Or, if he was dead, competing with all the others who wanted to try for it. The whole culture was built around personal power. Leading from the rear just wasn't a thing.

Which meant that vamp general might just be the most dangerous job on the planet.

"He's led vamp forces, too," Jules said. "Didn't you know?"

"No."

"It happened a couple of times. Not everybody was thrilled when the current consul came to power, back in the fourteen hundreds, and there were rebellions off and on for a couple centuries. The big ones were dealt with pretty quick, but the smaller ones were harder to stomp out, or even to find. Groups kept getting together, and holing up in the mountains—including some in the master's old stomping grounds."

"Romania?"

"Well, it wasn't called that then. But yeah, the Carpathian Mountains are a bitch if you don't know them. Or the language. Or the customs. And these guys were locals, meaning they had every pass watched, every cave booby-trapped, every town filled with supporters—"

"Why not just leave them there, then? How much trouble could they make in the Carpathians?"

"Plenty, as it turned out. That was just their base, because it was hard to get to. But they sent people out all the time to hire assassins, buy mercenaries, even talk to other senates, offering to start up a rebellion if they'd invade and take out the new regime. Something had to be done."

"And that something was Mircea?"

Jules nodded. "He and the consul met back in Venice, when he was really young. I don't know all the details, but he must have made an impression. 'Cause when the whole thing in Wallachia started up again, she thought of him."

I frowned, wondering why I'd never heard about this. But then, there was a huge amount about Mircea I'd never heard. Part of that was down to the whole never-having-time-to-talk thing. And part was vampire reserve, which I swear he'd made into a fetish. Prying any information out of him was a serious challenge.

Especially when he was so very good at changing the subject.

And his vamps had mostly taken after their master. Those less skilled in diplomacy had perfected a wide-eyed innocence or a stony silence, neither of which did me any good. But Jules wasn't a vamp anymore, so . . .

Jules wasn't a vamp anymore.

"Tell me about it," I encouraged him, and he grinned delightedly.

Maybe because people usually spent their time trying to shut him up.

"Of course, he was a lot younger in those days, so he was mostly there as an adjunct to Anthony," he said, talking about the current European consul. "Did you know he and our Lady were co-consuls back then? They ruled Europe together."

I nodded.

"Well, her job mostly involved sorting out the political mess her predecessor had left, by basically not doing a damn thing for years. Except taking bribes to let his masters do whatever they wanted, while he almost never even visited his own territory. He liked to live out in the desert, somewhere in Africa, I heard. But the result was a government that basically didn't govern."

"Which is why everybody was rebelling."

"Not everybody." Jules shook his head. "A lot of people liked the idea of a little law and order for a change, but those who'd been profiting off the old system weren't so happy. Some masqueraded as supporters, waiting to slip in the knife at the first opportunity. Those were the Lady's problem. Anthony's job was to root out the ones in open rebellion, and for that he needed somebody who knew the area."

"But if Anthony commanded before, why not have him do the same thing now? Why does Mircea—"

"Because he did just as much of the fighting. He didn't get the praise, of course. You know Anthony—or maybe you don't," Jules said, seeing my face. "But trust me, it's not his style to let someone else steal the glory. But the master did get a senate seat out of it, later on, after the Lady found out that one of the knife-and-rib guys was her closest adviser, and personally eviscerated him."

He grinned suddenly.

"What?"

"They say she did it at dinner, gutting him and serving up his still-beating heart on a silver salver, right there at the table! What do you think goes best with a dish like that? Mustard, or a nice wine sauce? Or maybe mint—"

He stopped, because the baby had started making those noises again.

"What?" Jules asked, and then remembered. "I didn't mean it," he said quickly, although it didn't help this time. We'd stopped dead in the middle of the concourse, and were in danger of being run over.

"What's wrong with him?" Jules demanded, prodding the vamp.

"What's *wrong with him*? You just told me he died maybe a couple weeks ago! And now he should be somewhere quiet, where he can absorb everything and rest. But instead he's here"—I gestured around—"in the middle of crazy, scary vamps, one of whom is telling stories about beating hearts and salvers!"

"I'm not a vamp anymore—"

"Jules!"

"All right, all right. I'm sorry."

"Tell *him*."

"It's—that probably wasn't true," he said to the terri-

fied vamp. "It was just a story I heard. And I thought it
sounded unlikely—"

"See?" I asked the vamp.

"—cutting it out and sending it to his next of kin is
really much more her style—"

"Jules!"

"—but it doesn't hurt to advertise, just in case anybody
else has the same idea. So that was the story they put
around. See? Nothing to worry about." Jules clapped him
on the back.

The vamp looked tragically at both of us, like meeting
us had been the worst thing that had ever happened to
him, including death. But at least the noise had stopped.
And a moment later, we started to move again.

I turned my attention back to Jules. "That still doesn't
answer my question. Why was Anthony not named Enforcer instead? I know he's a consul—"

"Oh, that doesn't matter. Most of the choice seats in
the combined senate will go to consuls. You think they're
going to let their own subjects decide policy that they
have to follow?"

"So, what's the problem?"

Jules shrugged. "Everybody hates him? He's had two
thousand years to make enemies. From what I hear, he's
done a good job."

"And nobody hates Mircea?"

"I wouldn't say nobody; you know how vamps are,"
said the guy who had been one a week ago. "But he's got
more friends than the reverse, which is kind of unusual.
And even more people think he's sort of trustworthy."

"Trustworthy?" I didn't think vamps knew that term.

Jules smiled. "Meaning he's slightly less likely than
the next guy to screw their forces over, to give his senate
an advantage once the war ends."

"Trust vampires to think of that now," I muttered.

"You have to look ahead. Everyone else will."

"That still doesn't explain why he had to agree. He's
done enough for the alliance!"

Mircea was the consul's chief adviser and go-to ambassador. The one people had started calling a miracle

worker after he successfully achieved a union—if only for the war—of the six vampire senates. No other vamp alive would have even tried that, and he'd pulled it off. And this was the thanks he got?

"I'm not sure it was exactly a choice," Jules said dryly.

"Mircea isn't a baby vamp! He's a senator who has put his life on the line more than once. He could say no if he felt like it—"

"It's not that simple—"

"Simple or not, it's better than dying!"

"Turn in here," Jules said abruptly, pulling on my ride. And redirecting us into a small alcove with a phone.

"Silence spell," he said, gesturing around. "On the outside. Which doesn't mean the phone's not tapped, but we're not using it."

"So why are we in here?"

"So I can tell you to shut *up*?"

I scowled at him. Jules scowled back. "Step outside," he told the baby, who started to leave, taking me with him. "No, just you!"

The vamp put me down and did as he was told, and I sat on a marble ledge poking out from the wall, to spare my feet. Jules stood, arms crossed, until he noticed that the curtain was still open. And swished it closed.

That left us largely in the dark, since the alcove still had a roof. The main corridor, which mostly didn't, had been a lot brighter. As it was, I could barely make out Jules' perfect profile as he watched shadows passing outside through the fabric's thin weave.

"What?" I said.

"The walls have ears around here—along with who knows what else?"

"And? I didn't say anything I wouldn't say to his face— and will, as soon as I find him. This is *bullshit*."

"You're preaching to the choir."

"They wouldn't even have an alliance without him, so they're what? Repaying him by making him even more of a target? Someone tried to *murder* him *yesterday*—"

"And will again. And maybe that's the point."

"What?"

Jules ran a hand through thick, wavy blond hair. "Look, I don't know if I'm supposed to tell you this—"

"Oh, you're going to tell me."

"Yes, I am," he agreed. "But only because you forced it out of me. I'm only human now, and can't be expected to stand up to—"

"Jules!"

He grinned, a quick flash of teeth. "That's just in case you ever slip up and say where you heard it. It helps to have the defense prepared."

"You're paranoid."

"And then some. But I doubt you'll be asked; it's common knowledge that the consul's worried about Mircea."

"Worried?" I frowned. "What do you mean, worried?"

"I mean, people aren't taking bets on which one of them will survive yet, but it's only a matter of time."

I stared at him. *"What?"*

He sighed. "Look, this always happens when a servant gets really strong, okay? Consuls need allies, but as soon as someone gets a little too capable, they have to start worrying. Is he gunning for my job? Is he planning to make a move? Does he have the power to challenge me? And in Mircea's case, lately, the answer to that last question has been looking more and more like a yes."

"And the first two?"

"Are assumed."

I shook my head. "But . . . she can't really believe he wants to kill her!"

"Can't she? How do you think she got the job? Consuls don't *retire*, Cassie. She killed her own master for the top spot; why would she think he'd balk at taking out a mentor? Mircea was already more or less ready, if he'd wanted to make a challenge, but lately . . ."

"Lately?"

For the first time, he looked conflicted. "A lot of things have happened lately, not all of which I can go into—no, I *can't*," he said, seeing my face. "That's the master's story to tell, if he chooses. But you don't need all that. Let's just say that he was pretty damn powerful already, although he was keeping it under wraps fairly well—"

"Under wraps? But everybody knows—"

"But they don't know that they know," Jules said cryptically. "Vamps still have a lot of human prejudices, right? Have you ever noticed that the guards people choose always look the part? Take Marco. He has a good brain, better than most. But he looks like a tough guy, so he spent centuries doing muscle work, even though a ninety-pound weakling at the same level could do as much damage—"

"I know that."

"But you may not know that the master used a variation on the theme, to fly under the radar for years. Who looks twice at the too-smooth, Armani-clad diplomat, with a woman on his arm and a drink in his hand? Especially when he's smiling and flattering and telling you how powerful *you* are . . . somehow people never think to wonder the reverse. Or not enough people. Even otherwise very smart people—"

"Like the consul?"

He shook his head. "No, not like the consul. She hasn't lasted two millennia by being careless. And I told you, she knew him from way back. But she knew her own abilities, too, and thought she could handle him."

"So what changed?"

Jules just looked at me.

"I—no," I said, seeing the truth in his face. "*No*! I had nothing to do with—"

But Jules was already nodding. "It started when he went crazy with that spell and bit you."

"You mean the *geis*?" I asked, talking about the spell that Mircea had put on me as a kid, linking us together for my protection at Tony's. But which had gotten screwed up after I became an adult and ended up almost driving him mad. "But that was lifted."

"Yes, but before that, he *bit* you," Jules said, reaching over and turning my head slightly, to show the two small pinprick scars on my neck. "That put a claim on you in vamp terms that he wasn't authorized to make."

"He was all but crazy at the time!"

"So he says—and I believe him," Jules said, putting up his hands. "Choir, remember? But not everybody is as trusting as I am, and it made you a permanent part of the clan. And bound you—and your abilities—to him in a way that the consul didn't like."

"Mircea doesn't control my abilities."

"But you've used them on his behalf before, right? A lot of times? And no offense, but you're also kind of obviously, um . . . what's the term I'm looking for here?"

I just looked at him.

"Sweet on him," he settled for.

"So, what exactly are you telling me?"

"Just that it's not too hard to figure out that she might feel a little threatened. When all this started, you were just some kid who'd inherited more power than you knew what to do with, and were clueless enough that maybe the senate could manipulate you. And she liked that version. She *really* liked it. I heard she was going around almost jolly, creeping everyone the hell out—"

"Must have missed that part." Jolly plus the consul did not compute.

"—but then she finds out that your mother was *Artemis*—"

"That doesn't have any—"

"—and that you've been raiding hell because some demon lord took one of your servants and you got *pissed*—"

"How did you know about—"

"—and suddenly you're changing me back into a *human*, something nobody even knew the Pythias could do! I mean, do you have any idea how big a deal that is?"

"I— That was an accident. I didn't mean—"

"I know." Jules crouched down in front of me. "I know. And I'm grateful. However things turn out, I'm grateful, okay? I couldn't have lived like that, how that curse left me, just a ball of flesh—"

He shuddered.

"It's over," I said, because the clear blue eyes were suddenly haunted. "You don't have to think about it now."

He bowed his head, his curls soft on my hands. "I know. I just wanted—" He looked up. "I don't think I ever properly said thank you. And I *do* thank you. However things turn out, I have a choice now, something my kind—my old kind—never get a lot of."

I didn't know what to say, so I just nodded.

"But you can understand, can't you, that your accident threatens the whole system? Do you have any idea how many unhappy vamps are out there?"

I swallowed. "You think I can expect a stampede to my door?"

"With their masters in tow?" Jules asked archly, and then saw my face. "No. But only because most vamps have a serious superiority complex. There are plenty of unhappy vamps, but that doesn't mean they want to revert to what they view as an inferior species. It would be like a human hating his life and deciding to become a dog. Most want a better master, or more power and status than they already have."

I leaned my head against the cool marble behind me. I wasn't sure whether to be relieved or not, to be told I might not have to worry about a problem I hadn't known I had. Not when another one was staring me in the face.

"So this is my fault?" I asked. "The consul and Mircea?"

"No. As I said, it always goes this way. It's the way their world works, and one reason I'm pretty sure I'm better off out of it. But you may have . . . sped things up a little."

"A little?"

"Like a century or so," he admitted. "And that was just last night."

"Last night?" I looked at him, confused again.

"How quickly they forget." He smiled. "Did you or did you not fight some kind of crazy time duel right here last night?"

"You saw that?"

"No. But again, rumors. So somebody saw it. Probably Marlowe," he added, talking about the consul's chief spy. "You know they call him Argus, right? Like the old monster with the hundred eyes . . . Anyway, from what I hear, they got a good, up-close look at exactly what a Pythia can do in a duel. And you do know how consuls are chosen? In a *duel*?"

I stared at him, unable to even feel surprise anymore. "She thinks I'd help Mircea against her?"

"I told you, I don't know. But the fact is, you *could*.

You could stop time on her, and she'd never even know it. You could negate all her abilities, without breaking a sweat, and have her dead before she could blink—"

"I'm not going to do that!"

"And I'm sure hearing that from you would make her feel so much better," Jules said sarcastically.

I massaged my temples. It didn't feel nearly as good as when Mircea did it. "She saw me duel a Spartoi," I said, talking about the hideous half-dragon sons of Ares. "Why didn't she freak out then?"

"Maybe she did. I'm not privileged to her thoughts, just the grapevine. But I saw what happened, and with all the trees and hills in the way, nobody got a great view. Plus, it was all over so fast . . . it mostly looked like he underestimated you, and you got lucky."

"Which is pretty close to the truth."

"Yeah, but then you got lucky again last night, and again this morning. You see how it goes. How long until it's not looking so much like luck anymore, or no more than anyone needs in a duel? That Spartoi might have underestimated you; I'm not sure she does anymore."

"So she's taking this out on him?"

Jules shrugged. "She needs you."

"She needs him, too!"

"For now. But if he was to die tragically in battle, say near the end of the war, after doing most of what she wanted . . ."

My jaw clenched.

"I'm not saying that's what she has planned. Maybe she just wants an experienced commander, someone she can trust, in charge. After all, she had to appoint some-*one*. But I find it a little interesting that the day after she gets an eyeful of exactly what you can do in a duel, Mircea is suddenly looking at a new position."

Yeah. So did I.

Chapter Thirty-four

The crowd hadn't thinned when we emerged. Not surprising. Four a.m. is the equivalent of five o'clock rush hour for vamps, when they're hurrying to finish up business before dawn comes along and spoils the fun. We rejoined the throng on the main concourse.

"So, what's the senate doing in the basement?" I asked, because I figured that was a safe subject. And because I wanted to know.

"Beats me," Jules said. "They've been even more secretive than usual and I'm a mere mortal now."

"You seem to know a lot for a mere mortal."

He threw me a grin. "People always said that I like to gossip too much. But, you know, it's strange."

"What is?"

"Now that I'm not a vamp anymore, people tell me things. Like the human servants. They never used to gossip in front of me, but all of a sudden, I'm one of the club. And the vamps—even guys I know—talk like I'm not even there. You'd think I suddenly became invisible."

I didn't say anything. I didn't want to talk here, for obvious reasons. But the fact was, for a clairvoyant, I was tragically uninformed. I needed info to do my job, but I always seemed to be the last to know everything.

It hadn't seemed like such a big deal at first, when it felt like I already had too much to learn. But now what I'd said to Rosier kept coming back to haunt me. There was so much I needed to know, just so much, and not all of it was protocol. I needed help.

I needed my own Argus.

Or, at least, a guy who really, really liked to gossip.

"What?" Jules said, and I realized I was still looking at him.

"We'll talk later."

He seemed to accept that, probably because ducking into another alcove, assuming we could find one, might look a little weird. Or because we'd just turned off the impressive main corridor, where the marble floors and walls had reflected the moonlight into some semblance of ambient lighting, and entered a dark stairwell. Very dark.

The only relief came from massive standing candelabras, old and brassy and dripping with wax, which kept me from being completely blind. But they were spaced pretty far apart, just spreading a thin sheen over the gloom on either side, that didn't quite meet in the middle. Vampires probably didn't notice, but it left me straining to see anything but jumping shadows.

And babies, because, now that I was looking for them, they were everywhere.

Flinching as they passed through the power fields shed by higher-level vamps. Mouthing replies to mental communications, like they were talking on an invisible Bluetooth. Tripping on carpet and running into walls because they couldn't see any better than me. Staring in awe at nothing visible, but probably at the auras vamps were said to give off, which acted like a signboard telling you family affiliation, rank, past masters, and a cornucopia of other information.

All of which had to be kind of overpowering to the uninitiated.

They looked like what they essentially were, a bunch of toddlers roaming around in search of a clue.

So what were they doing here?

"Substituting," Jules said, when I asked.

"Substituting for what?"

"For whatever all the older guys are doing."

"You mean the masters?" We'd hit a back stairwell, where the crowd was thinner. But even up top, I'd seen fewer masters than I'd expected at what had suddenly become vamp central.

"No. Just older. Like no longer babies. The kind of

Joes—and Janes—that used to make appointments and supervise the cleaning crew and answer the phones."

"What?"

He nodded. "They have the *cook* down there, from what I hear. Well, the guy who orders the food, anyway. The chef and his boys are human—"

"What are they doing with the cook?"

"You tell me. I mean, seriously, if you find out, *you tell me*. I'm dying to know."

The stairs finally ended in a narrow corridor, five floors down. Unlike the swanky areas up top, this was completely Spartan. Just a metal handrail on the stairs, unadorned concrete block walls, and a few bare bulbs overhead, now dark. And a dinged-up metal door at the end of the hall, with two large vamps standing in front of it.

No one was trying to impress anyone down here, which was clearly a staff area. And that included the staff. Who didn't so much as blink when we approached.

"Put me down," I told my ride, who immediately did as he was told.

God, I could get used to baby vamps.

The others, of course, continued to ignore my existence. I was too tired to try and read the clues, and figure out how old they were, not that it mattered. Old enough to lift the hair on my arms from the power they were putting off. Old enough to not bother being polite to some human who'd gotten lost. Old enough to be a problem.

Until Jules piped up. "Does the Pythia fight alone?" he demanded—oddly.

Even more oddly, it got a reaction. One of the hulking mountains, bald and stacked and jeans clad—like he wasn't supposed to be seen by the kind of people who would have his attire as their chief worry—blinked once. And looked at me.

His eyes narrowed.

"No," he said. And that was it.

"No what?" Jules demanded, because despite being a member of Mircea's tribe, he'd never been great with diplomacy.

Or with remembering that he wasn't a vampire any-more, and could be squashed like a bug if he touched that door.

I pulled him back.

"No what?" he repeated. "No, she can't get in? Be-cause she can *get* in. She can get in any damn place she—"

"Jules!" I said, and he shut up.

The vamp didn't say anything, either. For a moment, we all just stood there, not talking. Which they were per-fectly capable of doing all day, but I didn't have the time.

"I could shift through the door, but I'm tired," I finally said to Mr. Clean. "I need my strength for other things."

This, of course, also got no response. I sometimes for-got, dealing mostly with Mircea's crew, that vamps didn't tend to waste effort talking to humans. It was one reason they and the mages didn't get on. Mages would talk; vamps would look at them like they were bugs, assuming they acknowledged them at all; mages would get pissed. Unfortunate things ensued.

But I wasn't up to unfortunate things, not with feet that were killing me and a headache that was starting to pound at my temples again and a day that might not qual-ify for worst ever, considering the competition, but sure as hell hadn't been good.

"Let me rephrase," I said grimly. "I am *tired*. So, if I have to use power, I'm not going to use it to shift through a door that you could just open for me. I am going to use it to shift *you*. You will not like where I shift you to."

Mr. Clean remained impassive, but his buddy didn't seem quite so sanguine. He looked at me thoughtfully for a moment, then reached into his back pocket—I would have thought for a gun except he didn't need a gun. And, sure enough, he came back with something else.

Something like a folded-up newspaper.

"Yeah, okay," Jules said. "See?" He tapped the paper.

The vamp, who was just as big as his partner, but who had varied the Hulk imitation to include a buzz cut, scowled.

Jules stopped tapping the paper.

The vamp unfolded it and took a look.

I would have asked him what he was doing, but I didn't

need to. Because the whole of the front page was taken up with a picture of my face, blood-streaked and snarling, hovering over Rhea as she lay sprawled on the drag.

Because somebody, in the middle of all that, had thought to take a picture.

Reporters.

They might just be the craziest group I'd met yet.

"Not her," the other vamp said, glancing at the paper.

Buzz Cut frowned, taking his time. Or maybe it just took that long for the elevator to make it all the way to the top floor. Finally, he looked up at me, squinted, and then looked back down at his paper again. "Dunno."

"Oh, for—it's her. It's obviously her!" Jules said, which got him another scowl.

Warning number two.

I pulled him behind me.

"I don't have a driver's license on me," I began. And then stopped. Because the top of the paper had fallen over, revealing the headline. The massive headline that bisected the entire front page, in roughly the same size letters that had been used to announce the end of World War II.

DOES THE PYTHIA FIGHT ALONE?

"What is that?" I asked, taking the paper before I thought about it.

Strangely, the vamp let me have it.

"*Graphology*," Jules told me, with relish. "With a Carla Torres byline."

"Which means?"

He blinked. "Carla *Torres*. *Graphology*. It's . . . a major paper, okay? Like our version of the *New York Times*. And she's a senior editor."

"I remember her from this morning," I said, thinking of frizzy hair and cute glasses. And more of what the older vamps at Tony's had called moxie than most vamps I knew had.

"She remembers you, too," Jules said dryly. "And she went *off*—on the senate, the Circle . . . Hell, she was even bitching at the Weres for a while—"

"Bitching about what?"

"Read the title." He was staring at it over my shoulder.

"I don't know what happened this morning, but according to her, you basically fought off the entire Black Circle on your own. Except for some probably exaggerated help from a valiant group of reporters," he added, mouth twisting.

"It wasn't."

"What?"

"Exaggerated."

"You haven't even read it yet."

"I don't have to read it for that. I'd have been dead without them. And without Marco and the others. Even the Circle showed up . . . eventually."

"Well, not soon enough for her," Jules said gleefully. "And she's *pissed*. That's the evening paper, so she must have spent all day writing it. You can read it for yourself, but her main line was that, prior to yesterday, she didn't know what to think about you. She vacillated between some kind of nut who'd gotten into a dangerous position of power, to a stuck-up vampire protégée, to a dangerous rebel intent on upending the system. Or possibly all three. But now . . . ."

"Now?" I looked back at him, because I couldn't read it for myself. The only light in here was what spilled down the stairs, and it had been dim at the source.

He laughed. "She put an ass-kicking on *everybody*, and from what I hear, her fellow reporters are backing her up. And these people *hate* each other. They don't agree on what direction the sun comes up, but they are universally dumping on anybody who hasn't been helping you. There'd be a crowd of them out front right now, yelling questions, if the guys at the checkpoint weren't keeping them out."

I winced. "How's it going over?" I asked, pretty sure I already knew.

"Like a very large, very lead-filled balloon. You know the senate."

Unfortunately.

"Sure you want to go in there?" he asked, nodding at the door. " 'Cause you can hang out in the office with me."

"Is Mircea in there?"

"Probably. From what I hear, the whole senate is."

"Then I'm going in. I have to see him, and it won't wait."

I transferred my look to the vamp who'd given me the paper, folded it, and handed it back. "Let me in." It came out as the deadpan delivery of a master in a bad mood, but I didn't care. I'd given them fair warning, and I'd meant every word.

That cow pasture should hold two more.

Buzz Cut took back his paper and looked at it for another minute. And then up at me. And finally did something that left me blinking in surprise: he grinned. "You really kill a couple hundred mages?"

"I had a lot of help. Now, if you wouldn't mind?"

"Don't do it," his buddy advised.

"But it's her, man. It's her!" The grin was out in full force now, showing a gold tooth.

"It is not. It's some reporter trying to sneak in, and I'm not getting my ass kicked over this," he said, and put a meaty hand on my shoulder.

I sighed. Damn, this was going to hurt. I started to reach for my power, which felt sluggish and very unenthusiastic.

And then stopped, because I didn't need it.

Buzz Cut knocked Mr. Clean's hand away. "Show some respect."

"You did not just touch me."

"Just call someone!" Jules said—why, I didn't know. He knew as well as I did how this was going to go down.

"Grab the baby," I said quickly, and Jules snatched the wide-eyed innocent out of the way before a vamp fist knocked a two-foot hole in the concrete.

And then another one caved in the side of my defender's mouth, a fact that did not keep him from getting his buddy in a headlock. He spat bloody teeth, although not the gold one luckily, and grinned at me some more. While the other vamp thrashed and snarled, and used his foot to shred a line in the concrete.

Ours used his to push the door open. "No problem," he said indistinctly. "I got this."

We walked through the door.

At first, I couldn't see much, thanks to the consul's version of emergency lighting. There were more of the standing candelabras around the edge of what felt like a big room, clustered together in threes and fours. But unlike in the hall, where the ceiling had been too low, there were also chandeliers overhead. Massive ones, dripping slippery puddles of wax onto the rough concrete floor, and almost blinding me after the darkness of the hallway. The closest one was especially dazzling, and so big that it blocked the view of most of the middle part of the ceiling—until I moved a little farther in.

And forgot to breathe.

"What the—?" Jules whispered, his hand gripping my arm. The baby had stopped, stock-still, on my other side, his mouth open, his gaze directed upward in disbelief. I didn't know what vamp eyes saw, but to me it looked like a big black cloud hanging over the center portion of the room, with flashes of colors here and there that strained the eyes and hurt the brain. Because they weren't supposed to exist on earth.

Like the creatures who made them.

Because the consul had herself a basement full of demons, oh yes, she did.

Chapter Thirty-five

For a moment, I froze, the tiny-mammal-when-a-hawk-flies-over response kicking in with a vengeance. Like the let's-get-the-hell-out-of-here response that hit a split second later, the two orders crisscrossing in my brain, and giving me a good idea of why people in emergencies fall down so much. It's not that they're clumsy; it's that their feet are trying to follow two different commands at the same time.

Only, this time, I didn't fall. Maybe because Jules was still stuck in stage one and had a death grip on my arm. Or maybe because it had just dawned on me that there had been no reaction to our appearance. The cloud acted as if it hadn't even noticed us come in—which I doubted—but if it had, it wasn't doing anything about it.

As far as I could tell, it wasn't doing anything at all, except hanging out.

At vampire prom.

I blinked, but I swear that was what it looked like, now that I could see it: a big concrete rectangle of a room, large enough to have held two basketball courts end to end with room to spare. Only the spare was taken up with sets of old wooden bleachers hugging the walls, to complete the high school gym vibe the place had going on. And it was crowded, with maybe three hundred elegantly dressed masters and clusters of their more plebeian-looking servants, some sitting with comical discomfort on the bleachers, others standing about with glasses in their hands.

All it needed was a lousy band and a photo line.

And maybe an exorcist, I thought, staring upward again.

"Cassie," Jules said, turning to me, blue eyes wide.

"It's okay," I told him.

"How is it *okay*?" he whispered while the baby suddenly broke out of his stupor and flailed around a little before managing to turn around and grab the door.

In time to see it indent with the impression of a vampire body, causing him to yelp and fall back.

Nope, not that way.

I scanned the rest of the room, more carefully this time, but I didn't see Mircea. I did see the guy in chef's whites, standing among a group of regular old run-of-the-mill vamps at the far end of the room. They were too far away to make out expressions, but they were clustered together, closer than vamps usually stood, in what looked like a bad case of rather-be-somewhere-else.

No shame, guys, I thought.

No shame at all.

But they weren't leaving, maybe because they didn't have anywhere to go, either. And Mircea was still coming, and I still needed to see him and nothing had changed. I swallowed and straightened my shoulders.

"Come on," I told my two babies. And started walking before they could argue, in the direction of the nearest set of bleachers.

And found someone I hadn't expected.

The whole section was vacant, maybe because it wasn't as close to the action. Or maybe because of Rosier, who was sitting four rows up, looking fairly hideous, although in a new way. His size was almost back to normal, maybe a few inches too short, but at least he wouldn't fit in a backpack anymore. But the pale, almost transparent coloring and pulsing purplish veins were still there, along with something else.

"Are those . . . What are those?" I asked, looking at two thin membranes growing out of the sides of his head and wafting around in the air currents.

He scowled at me. "What do they look like?"

I didn't say anything. Because, taken with everything else, including the still-in-progress features and fishy lips, they looked like those things the Creature from the Black Lagoon had been growing. Almost exactly like.

"Fins?" I guessed, and was shot a purely evil look.

"Ears! Anytime now!"

"Okay." I climbed up and sat down. After a moment, my two shadows did as well, crowding close on my opposite side. Like trying-to-hide-inside-my-skin close. Under other circumstances, I would have said something, but as it was I just sighed. And nodded at the cloud. "What's going on?"

"You'll see," Rosier said testily, obviously not in the mood for a chat. "Do you have it?"

I assumed he meant the potion. "Working on it."

"Work—" He cut off, the pale complexion darkening. *"Do you know what time it is?"*

"I'm going to talk to Mircea as soon as he arrives." The flush deepened. "I can't just summon him, Rosier!"

Rosier didn't say anything, probably because of our audience. But his scowl intensified. And then something hit my lap.

I looked down. "What is this?"

"Eat it! I packed a bag full of supplies, which I had to sit on to save them from that thieving woman, but do you eat anything?"

I regarded the offerings with a serious lack of appetite. And not just because it looked like he'd cleaned out the discount aisle at hell's jiffy store. "Sit on?"

"They're wrapped!"

I didn't comment. I kept a couple items and handed the rest to my companions, because it's almost impossible to eat and panic at the same time. It's one of the reasons for food at funerals: it's life-affirming.

And it seemed to help.

I ate crackers and watched the Joes and Janes being prodded into a long, ragged line in front of the bleachers. They were facing away from us, but the expressions I saw before they turned were not enthusiastic. "What's wrong with them?" I asked Rosier, who was watching them, too. "They don't look happy."

"What difference does it make if they're happy? Servants do as they're told."

"Do your servants do as they're told?"

He snorted. "If I watch them like a damn hawk. But mine aren't part of some bizarre hive mind. They have free will."

"Vampires have free will." He shot me a look. "Okay, it's limited, but it's still there."

"For masters, maybe," Jules piped up. "Everybody else is screwed."

"You know that's not true," I said.

"What I know is that this isn't cheese." He regarded a small package of crackers with distaste. "And why is it sticky?"

"There's some peanut butter ones—"

"I'll wait."

The baby was eating his uncomplainingly—why, I didn't know. It wasn't like it would nourish him. But maybe the familiar felt comforting. Something normal and human in the midst of a world that was anything but.

I decided he had a point and crinkled cellophane—somebody had to eat the peanut butter ones—while Rosier scowled some more.

"Would you stop talking about snacks and tell me what you meant?" he demanded.

I looked at him. "About what?"

"You said vampires have *free will*, even nonmasters."

"Because they do. Technically, a master can force his servants to do what he wants. But he has to expend energy for that, plus, well . . ."

"Well what?" He looked more interested than I'd have expected.

"Well, there's service and then there's service. It's better to have them want to help you, to view the family as all in it together. Otherwise, when you need them the most, they might be just a little too slow, you know?"

"A little too slow?"

I opened up a cracker to lick off the peanut butter inside. "Alphonse—he was second-in-command of the vamp family I grew up with—used to tell a story about a guy named Don who'd had an abusive master. The guy had mental problems in life, and those don't exactly get better after death, you know?"

Rosier nodded.

"So, anyway, Don got sick of being beat on all the time, and cursed at and generally made into a whipping boy for his master's issues—and his master had a lot of issues. Final straw came when his master traded Don's girlfriend to another family for a tough-guy type to help with security.

"It didn't help with security."

Jules snorted.

Rosier frowned. "Why not?"

"Alphonse knew Don because his master was in the same not-exactly-legal line of work. Guys like that have enemies. One night, not too long after the girlfriend incident, Don's master was caught in an alley by an ambush and was really getting hammered. Now, it takes a long time to kill a master with bullets, and the guys assaulting him weren't getting close enough for anything else for fear he might drain them. So there should have been time for a rescue."

"Should have been?"

"Oh, shit," Jules said.

"Don't spoil it," I said. "Anyway, the master put out a call for help, and Don dutifully loaded up a vanload of guys and took off—on the most circuitous damn route he could find, with the most traffic and the most stoplights. Think of those taxis in Vegas that take you via the tunnel—they'll get you to your hotel, but you'll have a hell of a bill, considering the airport is actually visible from the Strip."

"But the master had given him a direct order!" Rosier seemed upset. Which was strange, since he'd never struck me as a rules-loving kind of guy.

"And he obeyed. But the master had neglected to give step-by-step directions, being kind of busy at the time, so what route Don took was up to him. By the time he got there, there was nothing left but the mopping up."

Rosier looked really annoyed for some reason. "But didn't that endanger him, too? I was under the impression that vampires can draw energy through the bond no matter where they are. The master could have drained his whole family trying to save himself!"

"But then who would rescue him?" Jules pointed out.

I nodded. "Don kept telling him he was getting there, he was getting there . . . and he did. Just a little too late."

Rosier scowled. "This . . . complicates things."

"Complicates what?"

"The invasion, of course!"

I stopped chewing. "What invasion?"

"What do you mean, what invasion? We're going to have to invade, aren't we?"

"Invade . . . what?"

"Invade—" He looked at me incredulously. "Has no one discussed this with you?"

I felt my face flush. There was a chance someone had avoided discussing it with me. "No. What are we invading?"

"Where is the support base for those trying to bring back the gods?" he demanded. "That Antonio of yours and the other vampires he's allied with, the damn Black Circle, your rogue acolytes, and who knows who else? Where have they all been hiding?"

"Faerie."

Son of a bitch.

"The senate is still planning to invade," I said, because of course they were.

"Well, of course they are," Rosier said. "No one wins a war by staying on the defensive. We have to take the fight to them!"

I glanced at the line of vamps. "And you think vampires are going to be . . . helpful?"

"Not helpful—*key*." He suddenly became animated. "A demon or a mage suffers an immediate and significant power loss in Faerie, just as the fey do in ours. *But vampires don't.* An army of them could give the fey something to worry about!"

"Maybe," I said, having heard this argument before. "But even if you're right, there aren't that many masters. And anybody below that isn't going to do you a lot of good in Faerie. And speaking of masters, the other side has them, too."

"But the other side doesn't have demons."

"But demons can't go into Faerie."

"Who said we can't?"

"You just did—"

"I said our power is limited there, which it is, although we could still raise hell in sufficient numbers. But what if we could go into Faerie . . . *without* going into Faerie?"

Jules and I exchanged a look.

"Think about it," Rosier said. "Vampires are magical beings, but they don't use magic—they don't sling spells or what have you. They simply are, and what they are is supported by the life energy they absorb from others. Feed them enough, and they just keep going. Like Energizer Bunnies. Energizer Bunny *tanks*. Energizer Bunny tanks *full of demons*."

"Oh my God," Jules said.

"What?" I asked, pretty sure I'd heard wrong.

But Rosier was nodding enthusiastically. "The idea is to have your vampires serve as housing for some of our stronger demons. Load them up, send them in, and just plow the enemy down. And end this, once and for all!"

I looked at him. His face was flushed, his eyes were shining; he looked like a guy who'd just seen God. Or, since it was Rosier, like a guy who was really, really high. Which was also what he sounded like.

"What?"

Some of the glow faded. "It could work."

"No." I shook my head hard enough to flop my hair around. "No, it can't."

"And why not?"

"Why *not*? For one thing, if your power doesn't work in Faerie, then it *doesn't work*. Whether you go in alone or with some vamps doesn't change that!"

"But it won't be working in *Faerie*," he said impatiently. "It will be working *in the vampires*. And as vampires are immune to the effects of that terrible place, so should we be, as long as we remain inside them. That's what a possession is—a symbiotic merging with another. We receive their immunity—"

"And what do they get?" Jules interrupted.

"Depends on the type of demon they end up with," Rosier said, frowning at him. "But at the very least, we can make them stronger than they already are, faster, more resilient, more deadly—"

Jules rolled his eyes.

"But vampires feed off *blood*," I said. "And not the fey variety. And only masters can pull enough from family to sustain themselves in combat." It was one of the main reasons Mircea had wanted me to make him an army of masters. Regular old vamps, which the senate had plenty of, would starve in Faerie.

"Vampires feed off *life energy*," Rosier corrected. "They just obtain it through blood. That's their conduit, as lust is for my kind. The method isn't important—the energy is. And with my people feeding them directly, they won't need a conduit, now, will they?"

"But . . . but spirits manifest *with bodies* in Faerie," I said, because this was starting to sound weirdly possible. "I don't know if that works with spirits who are already inside one, but if it does—"

"It doesn't. Adra tested it, with the help of your senate, yesterday," he said, talking about the head of the demon high council. "It was a very short trip, but no one exploded."

"Exploded?" Jules said faintly.

"Yesterday?" I repeated.

"When we ally with someone, we don't waste time," Rosier said proudly. "Your lot have been . . . Well, frankly, I don't know what you've been doing. But in case you haven't noticed, we are under siege. And the people inside a castle's walls, facing a determined enemy, don't just sit around waiting for the enemy to find a way in! Walls buy you time; good ones buy you a great deal of time. And however much I may despise her, your mother built a damn good wall. But it won't hold forever."

"Exploded?" Jules said, again.

The baby vampire ate cookies with a vengeance.

I just sat there, realizing that I'd been had. "Casanova— that whole thing with him, it was a setup, wasn't it?"

I was talking about a contest two days ago, between the world's whiniest hotel manager, who also happened to be the world's only demon-possessed vamp, and a monster from literally the pits of hell. Adra had set it up, supposedly to punish Casanova for an infraction of demon law.

Or, you know, to find out if a hybrid warrior would really work.

"Call it a test," Rosier said, seeing my face.

"Casanova was almost *killed*."

"And what do you think we're going to be? We can't keep having to win every battle just to stay at stalemate! This is the best chance either of our people are going to have—"

"But there are ways to do things. You don't just sell out your own side!"

"Yeah, like sending a vamp through a portal, with a demon inside," Jules said, low and angry. "One that might just manifest a body and rip him to shreds!"

"He didn't die," Rosier said, casting an irritated look at Jules. "Neither of them died—"

"But they could have!" I said, because he still didn't get this.

"People die in war all the time," he told me, proving my point. "But far less of them will do so this way. And vampires aren't just useful as troops. Reconnaissance is easy when you don't have to breathe or have a heartbeat or show other signs of life unless you choose. And then there's transport, for those who prove capable—"

"Transport?"

"That's what Adra and I were discussing when you interrupted us a few days ago, or whenever it was. I can't tell anymore. But if a vampire can carry one passenger, so to speak, why not two? Or a hundred? Or a thousand?"

"A *thousand*?"

"All right, possibly not a thousand. Possessions of that type tend to turn . . . odd."

"Imagine," I said, my head reeling.

"But a hundred is certainly—"

"And just how are these 'passengers' going to help when they're trapped inside a body?" Jules asked, leaning forward.

"Why trapped?" Rosier said crossly. "Is any spirit

trapped? One vampire can transport a whole squadron of demons, with no one being the wiser. Like a fanged version of a Trojan horse. Get inside a fortress and hey, presto. Instant army."

"But how do they get back *out*? Once they're corporeal, they can't just climb back into the tank, can they?"

"No. Which gives them a damn good incentive to take the proposed target, doesn't it?" Rosier asked evilly. "They'll need its portal to return to earth. Plus, while they are in residence, so to speak, they can give the vampire thousands of years' worth of information, tactics, strategy, advice—"

And a splitting headache, I thought dizzily.

"—it's perfect."

"It's *not* perfect," I said.

"It's perfect if they do as they're told. What you just told me is troublesome, however. I'll have to let Adra know—"

"You can let him know something else while you're at it."

"Such as?"

"Such as vamps don't do possessions."

"They don't," Jules agreed. "They really, really don't."

"The senate seems to think otherwise!" Rosier snapped.

"The senate can think anything it wants," I said. "But remember Don? Vamps aren't robots. You can't just order a bunch of them to load up on *demons*, go into *Faerie*, and fuck shit up! Oh yeah, and if you fail, you're stranded there for good because there's no way to get you out!"

"Yes, we can."

I sat back. "Well, okay, you *can*. And maybe you could tape it for me—"

"Damn it!" Rosier turned on me. "Casanova—the whiny little bastard! He was possessed for centuries with no ill effects. If anything, Rian was the making of him!"

Rosier was talking about Casanova's girlfriend, or his succubus, anyway. When they met, Rian had just left her second host, the famous Italian playboy, and was looking for her third. And she'd been looking carefully.

The incubi on earth were limited to three hosts before they had to return home to make room for other hungry demons. The demon council had imposed the limits to avoid overfeeding, and there was no way around them. Three strikes, that was it, and she was on her last one. She'd needed to make it count.

And she did.

Casanova, who was known as Juan Carlos before he adopted her former host's name, had been the newly made vamp she'd propositioned. From her perspective, it made sense: he would likely outlive the average human, possibly by centuries. Centuries in which she could continue to stockpile power long after her compatriots went home. From his perspective, he was getting the company of a lovely lady, who taught him how to get even more lovely ladies, along with virtually anyone else who caught his fancy. He just hadn't known one thing.

"Vamps don't do possessions," I repeated. "Casanova was too young to know any better, but the vampires you're talking about aren't. They're not likely to open themselves up to the control of somebody—or something—even for a war. And if you think they are, you don't know them very well."

"I *don't* know them, other than Casanova, and I've frequently wished I didn't know him," Rosier said. "But the senate does. And they think it will work!"

"I'll have to see it."

"You're about to," he told me, and looked up.

At the cloud of demons, now diving for the line of horrified-looking vamps.

Chapter Thirty-six

"Shit!" Jules yelled while I ducked, Rosier grinned, and the baby just sat there, crumbs spilling from his suddenly slack lips.

But the other vamps weren't so paralyzed. The signs of nervousness I'd seen before had been kept in check, out of pride or fear of their masters. But that tore it.

They broke and ran, scrambling in all different directions. Until booming calls went out, ordering them back into line. And giving Rosier a really good look at Don's strategy in action.

Because nobody had remembered to say where this line should be.

The result was an incredibly organized group of rioters, who reformed only to tear by us in a nice, straight line, despite the fact that some were still yelling their heads off. And ripping apart the heavy metal door like it was tissue paper, before trampling the battling vampires outside. Until their masters ordered them back again, which resulted in a neat about-face, but no slowing down.

And vamps in a hurry can *move*. The master's section itself was plowed into a second later, almost fast enough to give me whiplash, bleachers collapsing, people cursing, demons back to hovering overhead. And if a cloud could look nonplussed, they were managing it.

It looked like they'd been led to believe this would be easier.

I turned to Rosier. "You said Rian was the making of him—"

"What?"

"*Casanova*. You said Rian was the making of him. What did you mean?"

He told me.

I stood up.

"Where are you going?" Jules said, gripping my arm.

Only he appeared to have grown two left hands.

I looked down to see that the baby had latched on, too. The big brown eyes, made even bigger by the glasses, were pleading. He still couldn't talk, but the idea was conveyed, all the same.

"I'm not going far," I told him.

"We'll go with you," Jules offered, even while eyeing the door. Which was wide open and hanging off its hinges.

"You can go if you want," I said. "Both of you—"

"Not if you're staying."

"You're not my bodyguard anymore, Jules," I reminded him, because I didn't need another repeat of the scene outside.

"I know that! But there's things you don't know about vamps—I know, you grew up with one. But Tony wasn't a senator. They could try to put something over on you. I can help."

The baby nodded enthusiastically—why, I had no idea. Maybe because he didn't want to be left behind with Rosier. I sighed. "Come on, then."

The senate had been standing on the far side of the gym, I guess to get the best view. It had been a little crowded over there when I came in, packed with senators and assorted flunkies. It was a lot less so now, since many of the latter were helping to retrieve their wayward children. It made it easier to find a familiar face.

Well, sort of familiar.

As usual, it had the nondescript pudding quality of bad glamouries everywhere: round, blond, and unassuming. Its owner kept doing the Mr. Potato Head thing, trying out different stuff—a cleft, a mustache, or for today's version, dimples—to dress it up. None of it helped. It still looked like what it was, a more or less human facade to cover the not-at-all human thing inside. The not-at-all human thing that, I strongly suspected, would tip me the rest of the way into madness if I saw it, so I was content with the pudding.

I smiled.

Adra, better known as Adramelech, smiled wider, and held out a couple of warm hands to take the one I offered. "Pythia, how fortunate. We were just talking about you."

"How nice," I said, smiling at Kit Marlowe, standing to the demon's left, who was definitely not smiling back.

The senate's chief spy was a little disheveled, which wasn't a bad look on him. Tousled brown curls, an in-need-of-a-trim goatee, a gold earring sparkling in one ear, and a rumpled, only mostly buttoned-up white dress shirt left him halfway between Renaissance bad boy and Captain Jack Sparrow. Only both of those versions were more fun.

"Perhaps we should postpone," he muttered, to his other, not so genially smiling companion. Or to be exact, his frowning-slightly-in-annoyance companion, which she still managed to make look good.

The consul of the North American Vampire Senate was a golden-skinned, sloe-eyed, dark-haired beauty with a fondness for completely over-the-top dress. She'd toned it down today, maybe in consideration of the state of her house, to an Indiana Jones cosplay consisting of a pair of skintight brown leather pants, matching boots, a white silk "blouse" that revealed more than it covered, and two huge diamond studs in her ears—as in, Hollywood starlets had smaller engagement rings. Because we couldn't take this peasant thing too far, could we?

"Is Mircea here?" I asked Marlowe, since I was slightly more likely to get a response from him.

"He was delayed. Family matter. He'll be here shortly."

"Thank you." I looked at Adra. "Could I have a word?"

"Certainly."

We moved off. "Can you do a silence spell?"

"I believe I can manage."

I felt it click shut behind us, but I kept my back to Marlowe just in case. I looked up, and found Adra totally expressionless. Enough to leave me blinking, and staring at something completely masklike, with no signs of life at all.

Which gave the nondescript, faintly pleasant features the quality of a doll in a horror film as it slowly turns to look at you.

"My apologies," he said as life flowed back into the mask. "That's the problem with glamouries, if you aren't human. You have to remember to animate them all the time. Else they just . . . sit there."

Yeah, because there were no human features underneath for it to latch on to, were there?

I licked my lips. "If I help you, will you help me?"

The blond head tilted. "Help me how?"

"Get the vampires to do what you want. To accept the possession."

"And in return?"

"I want Mircea protected. And you want it, too," I added quickly. "Vamps like nothing better than to argue. If he dies, they could spend weeks, even months, debating over a successor. It could derail the entire war."

"And why would he die?"

"People die in war from all sorts of things. Even their own allies."

"I can assure you, my demons won't—"

"No, your demons won't."

Two pale eyebrows arched. They didn't look like he'd put any thought into them, leaving them the plain half-moons of the glamourie, but they managed to convey surprise nonetheless. And a question.

"I want two of your strongest as his personal bodyguards," I said. "He doesn't have to know about it. It would probably be better if he didn't know about it. But they absolutely need to watch him *all the time*."

"Even when he's with friends?" The pale eyes lifted, to take in the knot of people behind us.

"Especially when he's with friends."

Adra smiled, a brief quirk of fake lips. "So be it."

We walked back over to the group. The vamps had been dug out of the collapsed stands, and were milling about, looking miserable. And likely getting mental tongue-lashings from the masters they'd just embarrassed, because, of course, that was the most important thing. Among the smaller, senatorial group, talk was ensuing.

It stopped when we walked up.

Adra beamed at them. "Cassie would like to address our subjects."

"Why?" Marlowe asked immediately.

"To help with our unfortunate enthusiasm gap."

"You're saying she can fix this?" a harassed-looking master demanded. He was tall, Asian and handsome, a Chow Yun-Fat clone, if Chow was younger and had a sleek tiger tat prowling around his face. Since it matched those on two of the vamps now being settled onto another section of bleachers, I assumed he had skin in the game. His boys were adjusting the cuffs of their finely tailored suits, trying to look cool and calm and more pulled together than the rest.

Which might have been easier if they hadn't just been fleeing in terror.

"I'm saying new vamps are new," I said, forcing him to have to actually address me. "I've been watching babies run into walls for the last hour because they're still trying to see the human way. They don't even know how their eyes work yet. These guys aren't that bad, but they're still a lot closer to what they were than what they will be."

"Which means what?" he demanded.

"That masters at your level haven't been human in so long, you've forgotten what it feels like. They haven't. You want them to overcome their fear and do what you want? Not grudgingly, but full out, with enthusiasm? Then treat them as you would a human."

"And?"

"Give them an incentive."

Nobody said anything else, so I took that as a yes and walked over to the vamps. They didn't appear happy to see me. Of course, right then I doubt they would have been happy about much.

It was why I'd have preferred to do this later, after they'd had a chance to calm down. Or to take them somewhere else, where their masters wouldn't be glaring daggers at them the whole time. But I didn't have a later, and not just because of my own schedule.

But because it was almost dawn.

And while older vamps might not get as fuzzy-headed and slow as the infant variety, it still affected them. I could already see it in some of the younger ones, in nervously tapping feet, jerky movements, and agitated glances—although that last could have had something to do with the hovering horde. They weren't right on top of us. In fact, it looked like they'd pulled back a bit, possibly at Adra's command. But they drew the eye.

Unlike me. Few of the vamps were even looking at me, and when they did, their eyes didn't linger. And why should they? They had bigger problems than some barefoot girl who was almost as nervous as they were.

But Adra would only keep his word if I kept mine. That was how the world worked; nothing was free, nothing was ever free. And I couldn't let Mircea go into Faerie without protection.

Not if I wanted to see him come out again.

I cleared my throat. "Hi," I said. "I'm Cassie."

It wasn't quite as bad as the vamps on the door; a few of them, especially the ones in the front row, were listening politely—or pretending to. Probably because anything was better than what they'd be doing otherwise. But the rest were talking quietly, or staring at their masters, or glancing surreptitiously at a nearby exit, as if they were still planning to bolt.

I knew the feeling.

But instead I focused on the door, one I hadn't seen before, hidden between two sets of bleachers. And the plain wooden chair that was propping it open. Which a second later was propping me up, because yeah. That felt better.

I looked up, and found a lot more eyes on me suddenly.

It took me a moment. And then I realized: most vamps weren't my long-suffering bodyguards, and weren't used to shifting. Or whatever they thought I'd just done to make a chair appear out of nowhere.

Lucky accident, but I'd take it.

"Hi," I said again, a little louder. "I'm Cassie. The new Pythia."

And, okay, it looked like some people had read the

paper. Others clearly hadn't, or else they'd missed today's edition, because they were looking a little confused. But at least I had their attention.

Now I had to keep it.

"First, I want to assure you that no one is going to force you to do anything. You can go if you like, with no repercussions."

There was an unhappy stirring from behind me while the vamps in front just looked at me blankly.

"It's true," I said. "I was just informed, by a reputable source, that forcible possessions are rarely successful, and often do more harm than good—to both parties. If you're not on board with this, you won't be of any use."

More of them were looking at each other, and at their masters, but nobody got up. Probably being told mentally to stay put. The senate always thought it could order anyone to do anything, and most of the time it was right. But not this time.

I looked over my shoulder. "Was I told wrong?" I asked Adra.

"Oh no," he said. "A perfect possession, I've always thought, is rather like a marriage. It requires commitment in order to work. From both parties."

"Then you see the situation," I said, turning back to the vamps. "No one can make you do this—not your masters, not even you. If you were to try, but not be able to fully commit, it still wouldn't work. So, yes. If you don't want to be here, you can go."

Some of the former guinea pigs were maintaining the proper blank face of a vamp talking to a human, but a lot more were showing serious signs of relief. Several were openly grinning, and the fat little chef in the back row was all but vibrating. A black girl at the end of the first row jumped to her feet, with a toss of her braids and a defiant look at somebody behind me.

She would almost certainly pay for that later, but she didn't look like she cared much.

"However, I'd like to ask you one question first, if I could," I said, and saw her scowl. But at least she didn't take off. "Do any of you know Casanova—Dante's general manager?"

Looks were exchanged, and several hands were raised.

"Those of you who don't can ask the others. I'd like those of you who've met him to let this sink in for a moment: Casanova is a third-level master."

Nobody said anything, but several of them blinked.

Yeah, they knew him.

"Let me repeat that," I said. "Third. Level. Casanova, the guy with the world's largest cuff link collection. Casanova, who has his cologne made especially for him in Italy, because he says American scents break him out. Casanova, who once took an entire afternoon off because he accidently drank cut-rate champagne. *Casanova*, who is almost sure that he dated Marilyn Monroe once, only it was actually a transvestite hooker named Carl and nobody has the heart to tell him. Casanova, who by all rights should never have even made master, but who made it faster than many who eventually go on to become first level. And do you know how?"

"He belongs to Lord Mircea," a dark-skinned vamp in the front row said, looking envious. I wondered who his master was. Somebody who wasn't a senator, probably.

"Now, yes," I agreed. "But it's recent. He had a guy named Fat Tony for a master originally. Mircea made Tony—it's true—but you know grandfathered power doesn't always trickle down. Anyone else?"

"He came from a large family." That was a woman with hair curlier than mine, almost a blond Afro.

"Good guess; the larger the better, more power circulating around for everyone to share—unless your master is known as Fat Tony partly because he doesn't like to share. And Casanova's own crew is about normal-sized. Most of them work security at Dante's."

An Asian vamp, one without the tiger tat, raised his hand. "He has a demon. No, it's true—" he said as several others made noises.

"Ding, ding, ding. We have a winner. He has a *demon*. Her name is Rian. Oh yes, they come in female versions," I said as several of the guys' eyes widened. "And she's quite something. She picked him up when he was so new, so green, so fresh-out-of-the-grave confused, that he didn't know that vampires don't do possessions. He had no idea. And she was hot, and she told him she could teach him things—"

"I bet," one of the guys said, until his neighbor elbowed him.

But I smiled. It was good to see a few of them not looking so traumatized anymore. I'd had enough traumatized vamps to last me all day. And it wasn't like they actually had anything to worry about. Adra wanted this to work; he wouldn't have brought anybody he wasn't sure of.

"She did," I told the guy, who was a Latin lover type himself. "She took a poor farm boy, with no relatives, no connections, not even a decent master, and made him a star. She also did something else, because—did they mention this? Did they tell you?"

"Tell us what?" the Casanova clone asked.

"That when a demon possesses a body, part of its power leaks to that body. I mean, that's the whole point, right? From your masters' perspective? That you suddenly become supervamp?

"Well, I saw it happen. Just a few days ago. Casanova got himself into the duel of all duels, and as he'll tell you himself, he's a lover, not a fighter. No way was he walking out of there. But then Rian possessed him, and all of a sudden, not only did he win, but he walked away with it. But because of her power, her knowledge, not his—"

"And when they leave?" the black girl who had been first to her feet asked. She was standing to the side of the bleachers, arms crossed, looking far from sold. "Then we're right back where we started!"

"Are you? Casanova wasn't. Now, it's true, nothing happened overnight; he's almost four hundred years old. But then, he didn't become a master yesterday, either. And his demon—well, I don't want to hurt any feelings, but incubi aren't known to be the strongest demons around, and Rian wasn't even the strongest incubus, or succubus, in her case."

The girl frowned, as if this was news to her. "So you're saying her power leaked . . . and stayed?"

"I'm saying that every time she got a hit, he did, too. They share a body—or they did; she's gotten powerful enough to make her own now. But while she was in-house, he picked up some of the power she was generating. And over time, it accumulates. Of course, if you have more demons involved, or if they're stronger, or if they're using a lot more power than it takes to seduce somebody . . . say, like in a war . . . well, the person in question might not have to wait so long."

"You're saying we could be masters," she said sharply, coming half a step toward me. "Is that it?"

"I'm not promising anything. I'm telling you how it works. Some people have the drive, the determination, the—" I stopped, because conversation had burst out everywhere. Most of the vamps didn't appear to be from the same families, and so couldn't communicate mentally with each other, at least not yet. That was another master's perk, one they had probably wondered if they'd ever see.

And which they were currently making up for with shouting.

"Shut up!" she told them, and for a wonder, they did. She looked back at me, expression fierce. But her voice was surprisingly polite when she said, "Please continue."

"Um, I was just saying that there's no guarantees. Part of what makes up a master is power, sure, but the rest?" I shrugged. "Your guess is as good as mine. Some can hold on to the power that comes their way; some can't. But what this gives you," I told her—and the rest of them, since most of them were staring at me now—"is the chance to find out."

"And what if we find out we're not?" a tall, thin guy asked, out of a face that was mostly nose. "Cut out for it, I mean?"

I shrugged. "Then you're not. Some enjoy a life of service—" There was a burst of derisive sounds from different parts of the crowd, but the thin guy wasn't one of them. "—and there's nothing wrong with that," I added. "Those who feel that way probably shouldn't go. And let's be clear: not everybody who goes will return a master. It took Casanova two hundred years to hit that mark, even with Rian's help—"

"But we could shave off time. We could shave off a lot of time!" That was Latin Lover again, looking a lot less loverlike and a lot more martial suddenly.

"You could," I agreed. "Some of you might even go all the way; others might speed up the process for themselves considerably. But some might get very little out of it, unable to hold on to the power that becomes available. And some . . . will die."

The crowd was suddenly quiet again. It looked like all this was new to them, like nobody had talked to them at all. And they probably hadn't. They'd been ordered here by their masters like so many guinea pigs, with no chance to say no, with no chance to say anything. Because who gave them a voice?

"I've seen something of what the fey can do in battle," I said. "The demons give us an advantage: the fey don't know them like they do us, can't predict them as well. But it's not going to be an easy fight. Whatever power you get, you'll earn. But . . ."

I stopped for a moment, trying to find the right words. I hadn't expected to do this, hadn't come prepared. But I wasn't sure it mattered. They didn't need a pretty speech; they needed the truth.

And they deserved it.

"We're not doing this for the usual reasons," I said. "We're not going in for power or wealth or . . . or any advantage at all. We're doing this because, if we don't, we're not going to have to worry about who's master and who's not. I've seen the creatures we're fighting, and they don't care if you're a baby or a master or a senator. It's all the same to them. They hate us equally and they will kill us equally, unless we find a way to fight them. That's what we're doing today. That's why we're here.

"And we could really use your help."

Chapter Thirty-seven

"Good speech," Jules said, when I rejoined him.

"But did it work?"

"I think you convinced some of them." He looked over my head at the vamps, who had burst into conversation as soon as I left. "You were doing better till you got on the whole death thing."

"If the gods return, it's not going to matter if we're here or in Faerie. They have to know that."

He looked down at me, blue eyes rueful. "Unfortunately, that's the thing about imminent demise. People tend not to take it seriously until it's, you know, imminent."

I nodded, because he was right, and then had to stop to stifle a huge yawn.

He eyed me. "You look like you could use some caffeine."

"Is there coffee?" I asked hopefully, trying to see what the tables being used as a bar had going on.

"No such luck. There's a Coke machine, though, at the end of the hall." He nodded at the door.

"The consul has a Coke machine?"

"We human types get thirsty."

"And she makes you pay for your own?"

He laughed. "You know it. Got a preference?"

I shook my head. "Anything's fine."

He left and I made my way back to Adra, who had found himself a perch in the stands to watch vamps and masters have it out. It seemed like the demons had bothered to give Possession 101, after all; it just hadn't been communicated. It was being communicated now, and the result was . . . really weird.

I'd never seen so many young vamps talking back to their masters before, both loudly and in public. And from the shocked look of some of the masters, neither had they. But the usual power dynamic wasn't at play here. The masters, even those at senate level, couldn't force this on their servants, putting them in the unusual position of having to persuade.

And they *sucked* at it.

Adra seemed to agree. "They appear to be having some trouble with their servants," he murmured.

"That's what comes from giving orders for hundreds of years. You forget how to do anything else."

He smiled slightly. "I think Lord Mircea might remember."

"Hopefully, he'll be here soon." The senate could really use his diplomatic skills right about now. I looked at Adra. "Keeping him around would seem like a good move, if you're going to need his persuasive ability."

The eyebrows crawled up the forehead again. "Is that a roundabout way of asking if we have a deal?"

"And if it is?"

"Let us see how this plays out," he said, amused gray eyes meeting mine. And then narrowing, as he caught my expression. "Is there something else?"

I nodded. "A question—about possession. I thought—" I stopped. But then I went on, because whether I sounded stupid or not was the least of my problems right now. "I thought I saw Ares on the drag this morning, in possession of a mage."

"A mage?"

"The leader. The one rallying the troops."

"The one you yourself possessed?"

I didn't bother to ask how he'd known that. Three of his creatures had been there. "Yes."

"And when you entered him—"

"I found someone else already there. He attacked me, and I barely escaped. And then I saw him again, this afternoon—"

"Again?" That was sharper. "I was told the mage was dead."

"Not in the mage. In—" I stopped again, because everyone in the room could hear me if they wanted.

Until a second silence spell snapped shut around us, one that felt different somehow. And looked it, too. Partly opaque, it browned out much of the room. I didn't know why. And then I realized: no lipreading.

Adra wasn't taking chances.

"Tell me."

"Nimue," I said simply. "Fifteen hundred years ago. It was the same as on the drag: a darkness, a . . . coldness." I gestured futilely. "I know I'm not explaining it very well, but I *knew* him. And he knew me—or at least he knew what I was. He called me *volva*—it means seer."

"I know," Adra murmured, his face going blank.

It didn't bother me so much this time, because I hoped the reason was that he was thinking too hard to bother keeping up the facade. But I still didn't like looking at it. I stared out at the room, wondering where the hell Mircea was, and why nobody seemed to be noticing anything unusual about us.

But they weren't. The crowd ebbed and flowed beneath us, the ones who weren't part of the ongoing argument taking the opportunity to refresh their drinks or to group up, talking quietly. Nobody seemed to notice us at all—well, almost nobody.

I sighed, catching sight of the baby vampire, blundering over in our general direction. He must have seen Adra and me talking a minute ago, and now he couldn't find me. And he was getting distressed again; I could see it on his face, although I didn't know why. The most dangerous thing happening at the moment was that they'd run out of vermouth.

Even worse, Marlowe was following him.

Not obviously, not unless you were looking for it, but when the baby moved, a few seconds later, so did the chief spy. He was hunting for us, hunting for us using that poor, scared baby vamp as bait, and that was just—

"I see two possibilities," Adra said abruptly.

I turned back to him.

"A true possession requires a spirit physically entering someone's body. And Ares isn't here."

"But I *saw*—"

He quieted me with a gesture. "However, there is an interesting story in the *Iliad*. Ares was badly wounded in the Trojan War by Athena, and forced to withdraw. But before he left, he infused part of himself into the armor Achilles was to wear, hoping to cause him to throw the battle. Achilles was a leader on the opposite side," he added, seeing my frown.

And misinterpreting it.

"Infused?"

He nodded. "It appears that, on rare occasions, the gods would shear off a small part of their power, as Apollo did when he gave some of his to the Pythian Court. In this case, it was Ares, but instead of leaving it free, to take on a life of its own, he bound it to an object."

"A suit of armor?"

"Not just any suit; one made by the god Hephaistos, to protect Achilles at the siege of Troy."

"You're saying Ares could possess Achilles through the armor?"

"I am saying that he tried. But Achilles was a demigod, son of the sea goddess Thetis, and remained unaffected. However, when he lent the armor to his human friend Patroclus, it promptly drove him mad. He fought to his death, in a crazed frenzy. And the victor of that fight, a man named Hector, who took the armor as spoils of war, later committed suicide."

"Then Ares can possess an *object*?" I didn't know why I'd never even thought of that, when I wore something similar around my neck.

"In a manner of speaking. But there appear to be limitations. It isn't as strong outside its element, in this case war. It isn't an independent ghost, but merely some of Ares' energy, which is bound to an object and cannot leave it. It can therefore only influence one person at a time."

"Whoever's using it."

He nodded, and I immediately thought of Nimue. Rosier had seemed shocked by her actions; even some of her people had been freaked out. Like the fey in gray. His expression, as he knelt beside that girl, had been angry, but there had been confusion, too. Like that hellscape was out of character for the woman he knew.

Maybe because she wasn't the one calling the shots.

"You said two possibilities?"

"The attack you suffered at Dante's is . . . puzzling. A spiritual assault of the kind you describe should have left you unconscious at best, in a coma or dead at worst. Yet you slept for an afternoon and were on your feet again. Hurt, yes, exhausted, yes, traumatized, most certainly. But *functional* . . ."

"You think it was a trick."

"I think that, if Ares had left part of his soul here, we would have heard about it long before this," he said grimly. "And trickery is as much a part of warfare as battle. If Ares could demoralize you, persuade you that you were too injured to fight, it would help him, would it not?"

"Yes, but—"

"You told me recently that the barrier protecting us from the gods had been weakened by Apollo's arrival, allowing Ares to contact supporters on this side—including your acolytes. If he was in mental communication with the mage when you attacked, he wouldn't have been able to hurt you. But he could attempt to make you think otherwise."

"But I *felt it*. And I *was* weakened afterward." I looked up at him in confusion. "Wasn't I?"

Adra looked grave. "I do not think he can reach you here. But there are many things about the gods and their powers that we do not know. Be careful, Cassie."

Yeah, that was the real trick, wasn't it? I thought, as I felt his spell lift. The room went back to normal, light and sound flooding in: people talking, glasses chiming, the baby making a relieved sound and starting toward us. And then Adra's eyes lifted, in the direction of the door on the far end of the room.

"Ah. It looks as if we may receive some help, after all."

I followed his gaze, expecting to see Mircea at last—and I might have.

But someone else was in the way.

"Dorina!" I heard Mircea's voice thunder, felt his power flow around me, saw a stake pause in midair, headed straight for my face. And then it was slashing down, and someone was shoving me, and someone was screaming—

And then I hit the floor, at the bottom of the stands, hard enough to stun.

Although not as much as looking up and seeing the baby vamp, standing where I had been a second ago, because he must have been the one to shove me out of the way. And had been rewarded for his courage with stakes bisecting both heart and throat. The latter was so long the bloody tip jutted completely out the other side.

Until it was ripped out of him a second later.

"No!" I screamed as he turned to look at me, blood-splattered glasses gleaming in the firelight, and stumbled against the bench behind him.

But there was nothing I could do, nothing anyone could do. That blow would have taken vampires far older than him. It was another reason babies were kept separate from the rest of the household: for their *protection*, because they were so vulnerable at that age.

"No," I said again, my eyes filling.

And then his assailant was jumping for me, bloody stakes in hand, moving like a blur, as someone yelled: "Slow her down!"

Mircea's voice came again. "I *am* slowing her!"

But it didn't look like it to me. I had a split second to see a pair of firelit eyes, to hear Adra's voice booming "Assist," and to take the last breath I was ever going to if I didn't do something right fucking now.

And then a stake was splintering to pieces on the concrete where I'd just been, as I shifted behind the bar.

And almost threw up.

The room swirled sickeningly around me as I grabbed the table for support. Because my spell had unraveled halfway through, depositing me here instead of in the main hall above as I'd intended. And I wasn't going to be trying again, not for a while, which was a problem because she was still coming.

And it *was* a she. A she with a gleaming cap of dark hair, who I got a glimpse of as she stared around, hunting for me. A beautiful, golden-eyed she who looked really familiar somehow and—

"You have got to be kidding," I whispered, realizing that I was about to be killed by my boyfriend's lover.

At least I was until I upended the table, just as she caught sight of me, too. Glasses crashed; bottles spilled and shattered; a river of booze ran everywhere. And the small candelabra that had been decorating one end of the table fell into the middle of it all, with a bonus I hadn't expected. I'd just been trying to give her some glass to have to run across, because for some reason she was as barefoot as me.

But this works, too, I thought, stumbling back as the whole center of the room went up in flames.

And immediately thereafter exploded in screams and panicked, scrambling vampires.

Who became even more panicked when they realized that somebody, probably after their last escape attempt, had raised the wards.

The two humans who had been tending bar ran straight out the door, disappearing down the hallway. But the vamps who tried to follow slammed into something invisible, like birds hitting a plate-glass window. And then hitting it again and again, pounding against it as their fellow vamps piled up behind them, able to see freedom but not to touch it.

Kind of like me. I was human, so the ward should have let me pass, but I couldn't reach it. Not with all the bodies in the way, and not after the fire spread from a tablecloth to the kindling the vamps had made out of a section of old, dry bleachers. They went up, and a full-on panic set in.

The vamps in front were clawing at the ward now, their fingers bloody, while the ones in back turned around and stampeded back this way, trampling me and then the senate in their desperation to avoid the flames.

And the woman calmly walking through the middle of them.

No, I thought, staring in spite of everything, because vampires didn't *do* that. Vampires had the flammability of *gasoline*. Even masters ran at the sight of uncontrolled flames.

Except for this one, apparently.

And then she was on me.

I had a split second to see eyes like gold coins, fangs denting carmine lips, a bloody stake being raised in slow motion, either Mircea's doing or because my freaked-out brain was playing tricks on me—

And then I blinked and she was gone.

I staggered back and abruptly sat down, hair in my face, staring around blindly. And trying to figure out what had just happened. Which would have been easier if the crowd hadn't surged all around me.

But not to help me back up.

They were trying to get away from the battle I could hear but couldn't see, the ring of steel on steel echoing clearly over screaming vamps and cursing masters, and the feet trampling me as I tried to get up—

And ended up crawling under the second table instead, out of self-preservation. Nobody else was down here, maybe because it fronted the fire. Giving me a view past the askew white tablecloth and running people and crackling flames, at a fight. One almost faster than my eyes could track, between the crazy, dark-haired woman—

And the *baby*.

I actually rubbed my eyes, I was so convinced I was seeing things. He was dead; he had to be. Even if she'd somehow missed the heart—and she *hadn't* missed the heart—there was still the stake she'd driven straight through his neck.

And damn it, I hadn't imagined it! I could *see* it: a dark red gash that had threatened to take off his head. Like the bloody stab wound in his chest, which had flooded the entire front of his light blue dress shirt with a dark purplish red.

But despite all that, he looked fine—no, better than

fine. Better than he had a few minutes ago, when he was stumbling around the bleachers with the coordination of a two-year-old. Because it had to be five a.m. by now, and five a.m. was far too late for baby vampires.

But you'd never know it.

Suddenly, he had the grace of a master or a ballet star. Suddenly, he was freaking Baryshnikov in his prime, ducking and whirling and dancing out of the way of a blistering attack, liquid in motion and blinding in savagery, from the woman. I just stared, having never seen anything like it, and not seeing all that much of it now, because it was so fast.

But I was seeing enough.

I was seeing her jump up, maybe twelve feet in the air, and grab one of the hanging chandeliers, sending it crashing down onto the vamp's head. I was seeing him throw it off, a huge cast-iron piece, and start it rolling down the length of the room, shedding sparks and candles everywhere and causing vamps to jump backward out of the way. I was seeing the two of them race up and down the bleachers, the sword sounds coming from sections of the metal supports for the same, which they had ripped off and repurposed.

Until the baby grabbed hers *out of her hand* and turned it against her, suddenly ending up with two "swords," which he would have used to break her legs except she jumped over them and back-flipped. And didn't miss a beat. The woman, who was apparently Teflon coated, landed in the fire, grabbed a piece of flaming wood, and slashed it at his head.

It was a good move—it was a damn good move—using the instinctive fear of fire to make him drop his guard and rear back, then searing his retinas. And that sort of thing doesn't heal so easily. It's yet another reason vamps hate fire: burns are a bitch to repair. That move would have left most, even most masters, blind for at least a few beats.

And as fast as she was, blind equaled dead.

Only not this time.

But not because she missed. A rash of blisters appeared across the baby's face, a swath running from ear to ear, cutting him right across the eyes. Ugly, red, and excruciating-looking, they bubbled up and then broke, leaving me biting my lip in sympathy.

For a second. Because the next time I blinked, the burns were gone. Not better, not improved, not scarred over. *Gone*, wiped clean as he healed virtually instantaneously.

And suddenly, the room was silent.

Suddenly, the only sounds were my labored breathing and the crackling of the flames.

Suddenly, even the senate, which had been cursing and throwing young vampires off themselves, froze, a few with the offending vamps still in hand, in order to stare.

At the impossible.

Because the baby was walking *through the flames now*, dual-wielding his makeshift swords, forcing the woman back. Until she repurposed my trick. Finding a still-intact bottle and throwing it at his feet, where it exploded against the hard concrete and splashed everywhere, wetting his trousers. Causing fire to run up his legs and spike toward his torso, and the crowd to gasp in horror.

But not the baby. Another involuntary jerk, and he was back in control. A wave of his hand, a murmured word, and the flames died down and went out. And this time, even the woman stared.

I didn't know what she might have pulled out of her bag of tricks next, other than the knife that was already in her hand. And I never got the chance to find out. Because a shadow had taken advantage of the distraction to slip up behind her, one whose arm went around her throat, and whose murmured words in her ear seemed to do what steel bars couldn't.

And caused her to drop the knife.

And suddenly, the vampires went crazy.

If I'd thought they were loud before, it was nothing compared to this. You'd have thought their team had just won the Super Bowl, it was so deafening. And this from creatures who usually prided themselves on how silent and reserved they could be.

But not this time. The baby found himself abruptly

jerked up and paraded around the room, like a pop star crowd-surfing a mass of loyal fans. The yells and cheers were like the roar of the ocean; even the senate was suddenly talking excitedly—and *smiling*.

And then Jules pulled me out from under the table, soda can in hand. "Are you all right?" he yelled, to be heard over the din.

I nodded. I thought so. Honestly, I had no idea.

Like I had no idea what had just happened.

"What's going on?" I yelled back.

"They just . . . dhampir!"

"What?"

"I said, they just saw a baby vamp defeat a dhampir!" he screamed at me, grinning like all the rest.

I turned my eyes to the woman, who was now struggling in Mircea's hold. She wasn't going anywhere, but her fangs were out, her eyes were gold, and her beautiful face was set on snarl. I blinked. That . . . was a dhampir?

I'd never seen one before, but I'd heard about them. I'd heard all about them. They were the bogeyman. They were the vampire equivalent of John Wick. They were the half-vamp, half-human deformed monsters who hunted vamps the way vamps used to hunt humans, only with even more savagery and ruthlessness. Tony's guys had loved telling stories about dhampirs.

And Mircea was . . . What the hell was Mircea doing with one?

"What is going on?" I yelled again, because nothing made any goddamn sense.

Until I caught sight of the baby vamp again, grinning from his throne of cheering supporters. So happy that he never even noticed the shadow pull apart from him and flit over to Adra. The head of the demon council met my eyes.

"I think we have our deal, Pythia," he called.

Yeah, I thought. And the senate had their army, or at least the beginnings of one. Because the fight had done what I couldn't, and whipped up some legitimate enthusiasm.

Which might have been why the consul was smiling as she stepped forward.

"Lord Mircea," she called, her voice carrying over the din. Mircea's head jerked up. For a moment, he just stared at her, dark eyes wide. And then they slowly slid over to me. "Would you please secure—"

"*No!*"

"—your *daughter*?"

I stared from Mircea to the struggling woman in his arms, uncomprehending.

And then it hit me.

"*Daughter?*"

Chapter Thirty-eight

"It was a cow pasture!" I whirled on Mircea as soon as we left the hallway. "I had to get you out of that room, and I couldn't afford another fight, and—damn it! It was a *cow pasture*. The only thing hurt was her pride!"

"I know." He closed the door behind him, and damn if he didn't sound exactly the same as always. The velvet voice calm, the motions unhurried, the handsome face composed. It was infuriating.

We were back in the bedroom suite where I'd woken up, which was the only place he would talk, I suppose because he'd made sure it wasn't bugged. But it meant that I'd had to come all the way back up here without saying a word, feeling like I was about to explode. While he'd had the trip back to prepare the defense, as Jules would say. So this was probably going to be another master class in—

No! Not this time! "Then what the *hell*—"

"She is dhampir," he told me, still standing by the door. We were in the outer room with all the candles, and they danced in his eyes, making it even harder to read his expression. "They do not think as we do. Most . . . do not think at all. They are famous for their madness, almost as much as for their savagery. Dorina is . . . less unstable . . . than most. But her vampire half has been coming to the forefront more and more lately, and it has its own way of thinking about things."

"Her vampire half? What, is she some kind of split personality?"

I'd said it scornfully, but he nodded. "In a manner of speaking, yes. She was whole once, but her vampire nature threatened to swamp her human child's mind. I suspect that is why most dhampirs go mad: their two sides grow at separate rates, and one destroys the other. Leaving them vulnerable to hunters of all descriptions."

"But that didn't happen to her." Because if she was Mircea's child, his *actual child*, she had to be . . . God, something like five hundred years old. Or more, since he was almost six hundred himself. A five-hundred-year-old dhampir.

It didn't compute.

Of course, none of this did.

"I managed to separate the two parts of her nature," Mircea explained, "and build a mental block between them—it was the only way to save her life. But now that block is crumbling, and I cannot repair it. She inherited my mental gifts, and she is too strong. Her vampire half wants out."

"And to kill me, apparently!"

He shook his head. "You must understand, her vampire nature has not had the experience with our society that her human mind has. She is . . . something unique, a master vampire who has grown up, not only without a master, but also in almost complete isolation. Dory—the human side of her—dominated for centuries—"

"Why? If Dorina has your mental gifts, shouldn't she have been the one in charge?"

"Yes," he said patiently, "but that is what was causing the problem in the first place. I locked Dorina down to give Dory time to mature. I thought I was doing the right thing; otherwise, I would have lost both of them. But I . . . overdid it. Once the block was in place, Dorina was able to emerge only when Dory was under extreme duress, and her mental control was ragged. As a result, Dorina knows a great deal about combat, but very little about interpreting other types of human interaction."

I tried to process that. It didn't help much. "So she decided to kill me because I *ticked her off*?"

"No. She decided to kill you because she mistook your rescue of me for an assault."

"How?" I spread my hands. "I was there to *help you*—"

"But she had no way of knowing that, Cassie. Her human half was in control at the time, and the block I put in place still exists in some areas, giving her only intermittent knowledge of what Dory sees. I am not sure how much Dorina understood of what happened that night."

"Enough to be severely pissed!"

"So it would seem." He met my eyes steadily. "My guess is that she was somewhat nearer to the surface than usual, owing to the recent collapse of my barrier. She knew that Dory was watching over me as I slept, knew I had been injured, knew that a powerful witch with a type of magic she had never seen suddenly appeared and removed her protection from me—"

"But she saw you later. She knew you were fine—"

"Which could have been due to fighting you off, could it not? Or from having someone else rescue me. She didn't know you helped me; she wasn't there to see. Only that you removed my protection and thus, in her eyes, left me vulnerable."

"Making me an enemy."

"Yes."

He finally left the door and approached, but wisely didn't attempt to touch me. Another man would have tried to hold me, to comfort or to control. Or to figuratively pat me on the head, telling me by his every action not to be such a drama queen.

Mircea was smarter than that.

He just stood there.

But it hurt nonetheless, staring up into that beautiful face, wondering if I knew what was going on behind those eyes at all. Sometimes it felt like there were two halves to Mircea's personality, too. The human, who I loved and laughed with and trusted, because he'd always been there for me, for almost as long as I could remember. And the vampire—cold, calculating, and assessing—who told me only what he wanted me to hear and, I strongly suspected, manipulated the ever-loving shit out of me.

And whose real feelings I didn't know at all.

If anybody had a split personality, it was Mircea.

"You're upset; I understand," he said, dark eyes grave. "But you can rest assured that Dorina is not a threat to you."

"I must have missed that part!"

"I meant to say that tonight was . . . atypical. For one thing, Dory was seriously injured in the attack, and it made Dorina uneasy—"

"Injured how? Mircea, I sent her to *Long Island*. She shouldn't even have been here."

"She has a way of turning up whenever there's trouble. You two share that ability." He smiled slightly.

I didn't.

"I went to see her after I left you," he added. "And put her to sleep. She should have been out for the duration of the evening—"

"So what happened?"

"Someone interfered. Someone who knew she was on edge, and might be . . . impulsive. Someone who has surveillance over almost everything that goes on in this house, and therefore knew she might have a grudge against you. Someone who has the power to override my suggestion—"

"Someone?"

"The consul," he admitted. "Dory isn't the point. She was merely a tool. The consul is trying to separate us, to drive a wedge—"

"I thought she was trying to kill you! That's the rumor. Did you know that? Have you heard? Jules thinks they'll be taking bets on it next! And don't take this out on him," I added, because Mircea's eyes had narrowed. "He was only repeating what everyone knows. Except for me, apparently!"

"She doesn't want me dead."

"Oh no. She just gave you the most dangerous job on the *planet* for kicks! And you took it and never said a word—"

"It was only decided today. When should I have told you?"

That had been a little sharper, and I was glad for it. I wanted to ruffle him, wanted to break that perfect control. That was the vampire part of him, when I wanted the other Mircea, the passionate man with the flashing eyes and the terrible sense of humor and the honest emotions, the man who sometimes emerged when he forgot to be the senator.

"So you were going to tell me about it?" I said evenly. "We were going to talk?"

"Yes, as I told you earlier."

"Like we talked about the consul? You've known about that for—I don't even know. But a long damn time! You must have. Why didn't you tell me?"

"What would have been the point?"

"The *point*?" I stared at him.

"This is politics, Cassie. The usual court intrigue. It isn't something the Pythian power can help with—"

"This isn't about the power! This is about—damn it, Mircea! One day you tell me I'm your wife, that that's what this means—" I jerked aside my collar, showing off his marks. "And the next, you tell me I don't deserve to know anything about your affairs unless it's something the power can help with!"

"That isn't what I meant—"

"Then what did you mean?"

He did touch me then, gripping my shoulders. Only to run his palms down my arms to take my hands. It soothed me, even though there was no power behind it—I didn't know what I'd have done if there had been. But Mircea didn't need it; his presence was usually enough to calm me. But tonight, that might have worked against him; anger made it hard to think, and suddenly, I was clear-headed.

"I told you the truth," he said. "She doesn't want me dead. But she has noted my increasing power base. You are part of that, Dorina is part of that, Louis-Cesare—I have been drawing people to me, powerful people, not intentionally, but it could be misconstrued that way. And the more antagonism she feels from any of that number, the more she worries."

"So you were afraid I'd do what?" I asked incredulously. "Tell her off?"

"No, of course not. But your emotions are closer to the surface than ours. You have a good poker face when you choose, but you can't be on guard all the time, nor would

I wish you to. You shouldn't have to live like that, constantly watching everything you say—"

"Not constantly. Just when I'm around her."

He shook his head. "But she has spies everywhere. And they notice more than expressions—heartbeat, breathing patterns, a thousand tells a human would never see. And in your case, I needed to be especially careful. She only moved against her own master when she obtained an ally. She didn't duel him alone; Anthony helped her—"

"So now she thinks we're planning to do the same?"

"Thinks, no. But she wonders. She fears. Her antagonism toward you is born of that fear, although I doubt she would call it such. It has been so long since she feared anything, I think she has forgotten the taste. She wanted me to control you for the senate, but feared I was growing too close to you, and began pulling me away. Giving me work on the other side of the country, keeping me busy. I was to charm but not to be charmed, to control but not to care."

I blinked, slightly taken aback. Because that was the most honesty I'd gotten from Mircea in . . . maybe ever. But it didn't change this.

"Then how can you ask me what's the point?" I said. "She's *dangerous*—"

"All consuls are dangerous."

"Forgive me if I think that someone *two thousand years old*, who I saw turn into a writhing bunch of *snakes* once, who I saw strip the flesh off a guy in about a second flat with a sandstorm she conjured out of freaking *nowhere* is a little more dangerous than most!"

But Mircea didn't seem moved. "She isn't. Her abilities are impressive—after such a time, of course they would be. But other consuls can do as much. It is her plotting that has kept her on top for so long—"

"And this is supposed to make me feel better?" I moved away because his touch was soothing and I didn't want to be soothed. I didn't want to be distracted. I wanted answers.

He sighed, and ran fingers through his thick, dark hair. "No. But the fact is that she needs me—"

"And when she *doesn't*?" I rounded on him. "When

you return from Faerie a victorious general with a loyal army behind you? What then?"

And I actually saw him blink.

Goddamn it!

I closed my eyes. Sometimes I honestly thought that every damn person around me believed I was an idiot. Maybe Jules was right; even vamps still tended to trust their eyes over anything else. And to the eyes, I was a skinny blonde with flyaway curls and freckles, who frequently fell over her own two feet. But that didn't make me a fool!

And even if I had been, how much brain power did it take to add two and two?

God, I just . . .

I sighed, feeling the anger drain out of me, but not because of anything Mircea had done. But because I was just too tired to do this now. The adrenaline of the fight was wearing off, and the power I'd been forced to exert, little though it had been, had negated the shot in the arm I'd gotten from Jules' whiskey and Rosier's snack packs. I felt almost as bad as I had when I first woke up, and on top of all that, my feet were *killing* me.

"I do not take you for a fool," Mircea said as I opened my eyes to look around for a chair. "I never have."

"Are you reading my mind?" I asked sharply.

"Your face. I doubt I could pick up on even surface thoughts tonight. After the last two days . . ."

"Was that why you couldn't stop her?"

"Possibly. But I know Dorina's mind. I all but constructed it myself. I should have been able to prevent her from even entering the room, just as I should have noticed her tracking me to the basement. But I failed, from fatigue or from being opposed—"

"Then the consul *wanted* her to kill me? She's decided that she needs you, so I'll do as a target?"

"No." He shook his head. "The demon alliance you forged is the foundation of all she hopes to accomplish. We cannot fight the fey on our own, just as the demons cannot on their own. But together, we have a chance."

"Unless she's decided that Adra doesn't have a choice,

and would ally with her anyway. She may have needed me to forge the alliance, but she doesn't need me to keep it."

"But she does need you as Pythia. You have no heir, and even were you to name one, there would be no time for her to be trained."

"Then why is she siccing a pissed-off dhampir on me?" I asked, dropping into a chair by the fireplace. It was hot, this close, but the flames did more than the candles to dispel the gloom. They splashed Mircea's face with light when he joined me on the opposite chair and sat forward, the handsome face earnest and open and tender and concerned.

And damn, he was good!

"My guess is that she didn't realize that you were exhausted," he said. "She assumed you would be able to deal with Dorina easily, by freezing time around her if nothing else. But a short fight would have cemented your distaste for her—and for the one who hid her from you."

"And are we going to talk about that?" I asked steadily. "Or is this going to be another bullshit session where you distract me and I let you and nothing gets accomplished?"

His lips quirked, and he ducked his head. Mircea had always found my tendency to call a spade a spade funny. Maybe all those years of having to choose his words so precisely made hearing something blunt amusing.

Or maybe it was something else entirely, because who the hell knew?

"I will tell you the truth," he said, looking up, suddenly somber. "About Dorina, and a great many other things. If you will listen?"

Chapter Thirty-nine

"Long ago, I made a mistake," Mircea told me. "You know part of it, how my naïveté and thoughtless words helped to get my family killed. But I never told you the rest."

"Why?"

"Fear. Unlike the consul, I know it only too well. I have tasted it every day, for centuries."

I shook my head. "I know that's a lie. You're not afraid of anything."

"I wish that were true."

He stared into the fire. "Shortly after I was cursed, I attacked a young woman. The bloodlust was new to me; I hadn't learned how to control it then. How to feed without harming, how to take enough to stave off the madness when I felt it growing and was not near a willing donor. It overtook me, and if we hadn't been interrupted, I would have killed her. As it was, I had taken enough to return to my senses a short while later, and when I did . . .

"It terrified me, what I had become. I didn't know what to do. I had no master to teach me, nothing to go on but legends that informed me that I was now a monster, doomed to live as an outcast or to risk hurting everyone I had ever loved. I believed that I had to get away, before the same thing happened again, this time to Elena."

"Elena?"

"Dorina's mother."

Her mother, I thought. Of course, she'd had a mother. "So you left her?"

He nodded. "I gave her some money, or had Horatiu do so," he said, talking about his longtime servant. "I couldn't face her. The fear was clawing at me, the certainty that, if I saw her eyes, I wouldn't go, and I *had* to go. I believed that, utterly and completely. If I didn't go, I would kill her, and I couldn't bear that.

"I fled. In time, I settled in Venice. It was an open city then, a refuge—of sorts—for masterless vampires. A place where we would not be hunted. Years passed. I learned to control myself, to navigate this new life, and decided to return. I didn't know about Dorina then; she was born after I left. But I wanted to do what I hadn't before, and give Elena the choice. To be with me as I was, or to make a new life for herself elsewhere."

"Did you?"

He shook his head. "I didn't have the chance. A war had broken out, the first of a string of rebellions against the senate after the death of the old consul. Some of the fiercest fighting was in my old homeland. I wasn't allowed to go there until it was resolved, and if I had been, young and powerless as I was, I would almost certainly have been killed.

"Finally, the rebellion was put down. I went home. And discovered that I had a child, one that must have been sired while I was undergoing the Change. I was cursed, as you know, not bitten, and it takes a few days to complete the transformation. It is only in that narrow window that a dhampir can be created, which is why there are so few of them."

"It must have been . . . a shock," I said. Sort of like all this. That Mircea had had a mistress wasn't surprising; he'd been a king's son, after all. But this didn't sound like a passing fling. He'd gone back for her, even before he knew about the child.

She must have been special, this girl.

"Yes, but not a happy one for Elena," he agreed. "The townspeople viewed dhampirs as monsters. Dorina was seen as an abomination, only slightly less so than the one who had sired her. While I was gone, Elena had been pressured by the local people to give the child up, or to face exile herself, and she had nowhere to go. She also didn't know what kind of life Dorina would have in such a place, among those who openly despised her. She therefore allowed herself to be persuaded to give her to a passing Romany band, who valued dhampirs for their protection on the road."

I blinked. "She gave away her *child*?"

"Briefly. She almost immediately regretted it, and tried to find the band again, to retrieve her. But they had already traveled on, and her efforts were fruitless. She needed someone with greater resources for a larger hunt, and as it happened, my brother was on the throne. . . ."

"Which brother?" I asked, getting a sinking feeling.

"Vlad," Mircea said, his eyes rising from the fire for the first time, full of grief and remembered fury. He didn't have to tell me what had happened; it was there on his face."

"He *killed* her? Just for that? For asking for help?"

"He believed her story to be a lie, that she was trying to fake a family connection to get money out of him. And that she was taking a jab at his own low birth—his mother had been a Gypsy. So yes, he killed her," Mircea said, his voice rough. "In the most horrific way possible, killed her while I was away, killed her and dumped the body, I didn't know where. And then tried to kill me after I returned and uncovered the truth."

"But you didn't kill him." It wasn't a question; I'd met Vlad myself once, many years later. Still as crazy as ever, but very much alive.

Well, in an undead sort of way.

"No. I fled, having found Dorina and needing to get her to safety. I was far too weak to challenge him and his army at the time. But before many years had passed, his fortunes changed, and I returned. And was about to take my revenge when he told me . . ."

"Told you what?" I asked, because he'd trailed off.

Mircea abruptly got up. If he was human, I'd have said he was nervous, and needed to move. But in his case . . . I didn't know what to think in his case.

"He didn't even try to run when I caught up with him, in the barn of a friendly noble. He had been waiting for me, he said, sitting there on a mass of hay bales, dressed in the clothes of a peasant, which he'd been forced to adopt to avoid the enemies who were searching for him every bit as hard as I was. But you'd have thought he was dressed in velvets, seated on a throne of gold. His arrogance was as strong as ever, his belief in himself and his destiny unshaken. He laughed when I told him why I'd come."

"He was always crazy," I pointed out.

Dark eyes met mine. "But not stupid. People often conflate the two. They shouldn't."

He went to the bar to get a drink, and tilted the decanter at me, but I just shook my head. I watched him pour, wondering what he wanted it for. Mircea rarely drank, and usually then only to keep me company. Again, it almost looked like he was nervous, and wanted to give his hands a job.

"I had grown stronger over the years, and wealthier, with powerful friends," he told me. "Vlad demanded money for a mercenary army, and a contingent of vampires to ensure that they overwhelmed his enemy's forces. In return for helping him to regain his throne, he offered a trade."

"A *trade*?" I said, in disbelief. "After all he'd done, what could he possibly think—"

"You owe me that much." The hate on Vlad's face was palpable.

"I *owe* you? You can say that after—"

"Yes, I can say that after. *After being thrown away as a boy, given as a guarantee of a treaty Father had no intention of keeping. After being beaten—and worse—once he broke it. After seeing my younger brother whore himself to get out of the Turks' dungeons, the same ones I lived in for years, until the screams of the damned no longer woke me at night—yes, I can say it* after!"

I snapped back to the present, stunned and breathless. It had been a long time since I'd had a vision, and I had forgotten how hard they hit. I'd just been reminded.

"A secret," Mircea was saying, unaware. "Something he'd learned as a young man while serving as a page in Constantinople. Something I . . . did not know."

He settled back into the chair, his eyes hooded and

unreadable. "Did you know the Pythian Court wasn't always in London?"

I cleared my throat. "Yes. It's wherever the Pythia wants it to be."

"When Vlad was a boy, it was in Constantinople. In a run-down house in an overgrown street that reflected the condition of the city. The second Rome had shrunk to almost nothing, its riches gone, its glory days long behind it. There was no reason for the Pythian Court to reside in such a place. But Berenice—the Pythia of the time—was stubborn, and no one could budge her.

"One day, the last emperor, Constantine XI, took his page on a clandestine late-night journey through the back alleys of the city—"

Starlight and moonlight and reflections off puddles in the broken street. Nothing else, nothing more, not even a lantern to light the way. At home there would have been torches accompanying such a procession, the common people lining the streets to see a great lord pass. But here, the lord might as well have been one of the beggars slumped in the doorways, reeking of alcohol and piss. This wasn't how a king traveled, much less—

"Vlad! Keep up!"

"Apologies, Majesty." He broke into an undignified jog. The emperor's legs were longer than his, and he was practically running himself. At home, they had servants to run for them. At home, they moved with dignity, and left the running to lesser men. At home—

"Don't apologize, just keep up! It's too easy to get lost on these backstreets, young Vladimir."

"It's Vlad."

"What?"

"My name. It is not Vladimir."

"Isn't it?" The emperor looked distracted, searching for the right run-down house on the run-down street. "What's it short for, then?"

"Nothing. It's just Vlad."

"Really? I've not heard that one before."

Someday you will, Vlad thought. Someday everyone will.

"—to see the doddering old woman in her decrepit house," Mircea said as I jerked back to the present again. "Berenice never cared about money, and received them in her kitchen, while feeding dozens of stray dogs she'd adopted out of the back door. Vlad was not impressed, but the emperor didn't seem to care.

"He was there to beg for aid against the Turks, who were encroaching closer every day, and swore to give her whatever she wanted in return. Berenice said that she had all she needed, and that he should keep what gold he had and leave the city. That it would fall soon, and him with it."

"And did he?"

Mircea nodded. "He died dressed as a common soldier, fighting on the ramparts. He refused to leave, despite her warning, just as he refused to leave that night, staying and arguing with her for some time. During which time Vlad picked up several useful bits of knowledge, which he offered in trade to me, more than thirty years later."

"What useful bits?"

Mircea glanced at me, and then away. "I'm coming to that.

"After speaking with Vlad, I traveled to see the Lady myself. She was still there, in the same house, on the same broken street, with a new group of dogs her acolytes fed, for she was quite elderly by then. The city was different: the Turks were polishing up their captured jewel, and there was building going on everywhere. Except for Berenice's street, where it felt like time had stood still."

"Back again?"

The dark-haired girl with the pretty, round face and cheap tinsel earrings looked up at him from an undignified crouch. She was surrounded by mangy, underfed curs, all of which were nonetheless patiently waiting for the big bowl of scraps she was turning out into broken dishes. They were hungry, some looked to be starving, yet still they waited.

Like him, Mircea thought, hiding his irritation behind a smile.

"Back again," he confirmed.

"I told you; it could be days," she warned, laughing when a small puppy jumped up and licked her face. "Even weeks."

"I have time," Mircea said, and bent to help her with her task.

And, okay, I was beginning to think these weren't visions. Partly because I didn't get many visions anymore, the power bogarting my abilities for its own use, and partly because they didn't feel right. They had more of the hazy quality of dreams, soft-edged and lacking in detail.

Or memories, I realized, suddenly understanding.

Mircea was right—he was tired, and his perfect control wasn't so perfect just now. The Seidr link between us might be gone, disrupted by whatever Ares had done, but he was still a powerful mentalist. And he was *projecting*. His own memories, and one he'd picked up from his brother.

But I didn't think he knew it.

He was lost in thought, staring at the fire, oblivious. I should tell him, I thought. I should let him know . . .

That his mind was leaking the truth all over the place, no matter what his lips said.

"Cassie?" Some movement of mine made him look up. "Is everything all right?"

"Yes, I . . . think I will have that drink now."

"Berenice was in bed with a fever when I finally talked my way into an audience," Mircea told me as I saw him walk across two rooms, one richly furnished, lit by our shared fire, and one dim and shuttered. Weak sunlight streamed in through the louvers of the second, to stripe meager furnishings and a threadbare rug. And the frail old woman underneath the bedsheets, eyes watery with age and sharp with intellect.

"You bother me now, and with this?"

"I've waited for weeks—"

"I've kept kings waiting for months! While I've seen beggars, fresh off the streets. I see who I like, and I answer what I will! And your answer, vampire, is no."

"You won't even hear me out?" Mircea couldn't keep
a thread of anger from his voice, and she caught it.

*"I have heard you! Haunting my halls, as you haunt
my dreams, and I will hear you no more. You have your
answer. Now begone. Or I'll sic the dogs on you!"*

"She was . . . not inclined to assist me," Mircea said,
handing me a glass.

I hadn't even noticed him return.

I took it, spilling a little, because my hand was un-
steady.

"But I met her chief acolyte during the week she kept
me waiting," he added, settling back into his chair. "A
pretty little thing, dimples, big dark eyes, always laughing. Eudoxia was her name. She seemed well-disposed
toward me, and I thought, a new Pythia will reign soon. I
can wait.

"And I did—another twenty years—until my friend
and well-wisher finally came into power. The court had
moved at last—to Paris—and I traveled to see her there. I
brought expensive gifts. I was so excited—"

"It doesn't look like the biggest city in Europe," Mircea
said sourly, looking out the side of the creaking carriage.
By God, this thing was slow!

"You're too hard to please," Bezio told him, frowning
as he tried to recall which trinket went in which box.

"You had to take them out," Mircea said. *"You put
them back."*

"We'll be there soon." Big dark eyes looked at him soul-
fully. If his old friend had been a girl, instead of a huge,
hairy man, he'd have batted his eyelashes. *"Help me?"*

*"It'll take an hour to get there in this thing, and that's
if we're lucky,"* Mircea snapped. *"I knew I should have
ridden ahead!"*

"But you didn't." Bezio looked at him knowingly.
They'd been friends ever since his first years in Venice, and
the man knew him like no other. Which could be damned
inconvenient at times. *"I think you want to be there, and
you don't want to be, and it's making you surly."*

"I bungled it," Mircea said tersely. "I should have visited her before this. Should have written more—"

"You wrote plenty. You did plenty. Any more and it would have been too obvious. Like this." He held something up. "Don't you think this is a bit much?"

"No!" Mircea snatched the necklace, of huge pearls set in gold, and looked around for its box. Which could have been any of them. "Put it back!"

"Well, I will if I can remember where it went," Bezio said amiably. Mircea wanted a fight, to get the unbearable tension out of his system before they arrived, but his friend wasn't obliging. "You're taking a king's ransom—none of which you need. People have been bribing Pythias for thousands of years—"

"I am not bribing her!"

"But if it helps at all, it's only to get you in, and you've already got an in. But once you're there, they say what they say—"

"And what would you know about it?"

Bezio rolled his eyes. "Like I said. Surly."

"Yes," Mircea said, his eyes distant, "I was . . . hopeful. Until I saw her face. Until the second no."

I frowned, because I wasn't getting this. Even with help, I wasn't. "But . . . what was so important that you needed to see—"

He wasn't listening. His eyes were back on the fire; I wasn't sure he even knew I'd spoken. It didn't sound like it when his voice came again, rough with remembered emotion. "I asked her why; she wouldn't tell me. I begged her; she commiserated, seeming sincere. I raged at her; she had me removed. And later sent me a note, in her own hand; I have it to this day. Telling me to give up. To move on. To waste no more time on this fool's errand.

"I decided the problem was me. My self-importance, my boldness. I was still in those days much as I had always been: outspoken, opinionated, even brash. I said things to her I should not have said. I penned a note of apology. And afterward, I worked to change."

I didn't say anything. The words were pouring out of

him suddenly, this man who was usually so stingy with facts that I could group everything I knew about him on a single sheet of paper. It looked like I'd need a few more after this.

"It wasn't easy," he said. "Biting my tongue did not come naturally, and took years of study. Watching those older than I, learning how to speak without saying too much, how to smile when I wanted to snarl and go for someone's throat. Learning something that felt inherently dishonest, but I did it—I forced myself to, until it came more naturally.

"Eudoxia aged; she died. A new Pythia took the throne. And I returned, my arguments polished, my words carefully—so carefully—chosen. Like my gifts, which were far more lavish this time. I was growing rich; my family was expanding. I could afford it.

"And I was listened to. Her name was Isabeau, an auburn-haired beauty. Rescued from the gutter, after her parents died in a plague. Intended for little more than a servant, yet she surpassed them all. I thought she would sympathize, would understand what it was to lose everything, and have to claw your way back, and so it seemed. We had many pleasant visits walking in her gardens, choosing flowers for her table. I made her laugh. . . ."

"I don't know." Isabeau leaned against a tree, her abundant auburn hair a contrast to the dark gray bark. She looked back up the impressive sweep of lawn toward the chateau. "It's better here, outside Paris, but I don't like the grounds. They're too formal. Everyone is copying the Italian style these days, and torturing the poor plants into all sorts of ridiculous shapes."

"It's your garden," Mircea said, smiling. And leaning an arm on the trunk above her head. "Do with it what you like."

"I'll tell you what I'd like," she said, gray eyes becoming animated. "An English garden, have you seen them? They just let everything run wild, all over the place."

"Then why don't you?"

She sighed. "You know why. The Circle. They're so concerned with appearances. Berenice—Lady Aristonice—

is said to have lived in a hovel, yet I can't have a messy garden!"

"I wouldn't call it a hovel," Mircea murmured, tucking the fat pink rose he'd plucked behind her ear. "A little run-down, perhaps . . ."

She looked up at him in amazement. "You knew her? That was so long ago!"

"We don't feel time the way you do," he murmured, leaning in. "But I'll tell you something about Lady Aristonice, if you like. Specifically what she would have said to the Circle."

"And what's that?"

He leaned all the way in and whispered something in her ear, something that made her blush and then burst out laughing. "I'd like to see their faces!"

"Try it. What are they going to do?"

"I shudder to think!"

He tilted her chin up and kissed her, long and slow and expertly. "You're Pythia," he whispered against her lips. "You can do whatever you want."

Chapter Forty

The transition was harsher this time, like being underwater too long. I felt the grip of his mind, or of the vision—I still wasn't sure which it was—clinging to me, even as I surfaced. I couldn't breathe.

"Yes, I made her laugh," Mircea was saying. "And the answer, when it came, was no. And the next time. And the next."

I couldn't complain about a lack of passion now. The dark eyes were flashing, the hands clenching on his chair arms, as if to keep him seated when he wanted to stride around the room, and maybe punch things. He did neither. But his face . . .

"No matter what words I used," he told me, "no matter how I approached them, the gifts and favors and influence I put at their feet, it was always the same. My star was rising, I was on the senate, I could help them in their power struggle with the Circle—yes, it existed even then. I could give them so much, and I would have, freely, gladly, anything they asked . . .

"But it never mattered. Year after year, century after century, they never wavered. And they never told me why."

"And then, one day, you got a phone call." Tears were streaming down my face. I didn't know why. Couldn't think. Buzzing in my ears.

Mircea saw, and looked away, swallowing. "Yes. From Raphael. One of my subordinates had a true seer at his court. A young girl, just a tiny thing, ten or eleven. A girl whose mother was Elizabeth O'Donnell, the powerful clairvoyant and former heir to the Pythian throne, now a deceased runaway.

"I don't know if I can describe to you how I felt after receiving that call. I sat there for a long time, unable to think, unable to move. The damn phone was beeping, wanting me to hang up, but I couldn't even seem to do that. They told me that I sat there for hours, motionless. To me, it seemed like minutes.

"And then you got up and went to Tony's."

"And found you," he agreed. "A delightful child, a breath of fresh air, and a chance . . . the first I had had in centuries . . . of a *yes*."

"Come on!" I said excitedly. "It's just up here."

"I'm not as small as you." Mircea, cobwebs in his hair from the wine cellar steps, nonetheless followed me into the supersecret place in the back, the one with the small door that creaked—oh, so loudly—when you opened it. But everything creaked here, the old farmhouse sounding like a grumpy old man, bones groaning and breath rasping, whenever the wind shook it.

The wind was shaking it a lot tonight—Eugenie had said a storm was coming. Good—no prying ears to figure out what we were doing, and ruin things. Not that anyone seemed to, when Mircea was around. It was funny, seeing them all bowing and scraping, and acting like he was as dangerous as Alphonse, with his huge muscles and scary face.

Not that I found Alphonse so scary anymore. I'd watched too many horror movies with him, seen him jump when the monster appeared, and laugh to cover it up. He loved being scared, though, so he always came back for more.

I didn't find the movies scary myself. When you live in a nest of vampires, Freddy and Jason and what's-his-name from The Shining *just don't seem like that big a deal. But Alphonse still jumped.*

"Are we almost there?" I looked back to see Mircea all hunched over, his nice suit getting wrinkled. That was too bad; I liked his suits, so elegant! And his gentle way of talking. And his laughter—I'd never seen a vampire who laughed so much!

Or anybody else around here, I thought grimly.

"Is it close?" I asked Laura, and she turned around to

look at me. She wasn't cramped; she was fine. Of course, she was littler than me now, although we'd once been the same size. But ghost kids don't grow up, so I was taller. But not so much as Mircea.

"Is your boyfriend getting tired?" she asked slyly, and then laughed before I could answer.

"He isn't my—" I began, and then bit my tongue before I said any more. Damn it, Laura!

She just laughed some more. "Yes, it's close," she said as the house shook from the wind and, finally, rain.

"It's a bad one tonight," Mircea said, looking around, although there was nothing to see. Nothing except dark, lightened by the greenish ghost light Laura shed. But he couldn't see that. But his vampire eyes could probably make out the tunnel anyway, cut under the house by someone, long ago, Alphonse said for bootlegging. All I knew is it was dank and dark, and I hoped Laura was right. I wanted out of here!

"Stop." She stuck her head clean through the wall, leaving me looking at the stump of her neck until she pulled back out. "Dig here."

"It's here," I said to Mircea, who crawled up behind me, garden shovel in hand.

It didn't take long. The box wasn't buried deep, although a tree root had wound around it. I was practically vibrating with excitement by the time he finished and finally pulled it free. And then opened the old hinges.

"Is anything in there?" I asked breathlessly, unwilling to hope.

"Of course there is. I said so, didn't I?" Laura demanded.

"I think so," Mircea murmured, pulling out a decaying velvet bag.

And spilling the contents onto his palm: tarnished silver and gleaming gold, and dark rubies flashing in the ghost light.

And then more brilliantly, under the light of a dozen candles, because the storm had knocked the power out. But they lit my room well enough, as Mircea piled my hair on top of my head and clasped the best of the jewels around my neck. "There. What do you think?"

*I just stared. I'd never thought of myself as pretty be-
fore, never once in my life. As far as I knew, no one had.
But now . . .*

*He dropped his hands to my shoulders and kissed my
cheek. "What a lovely woman you're going to make someday."*

*And in that moment, watching him stand tall and
strong and handsome behind me, I believed it.*

"I wanted to bring you to my court so badly," he told me,
as I surfaced from my own memory. "But I didn't dare.
The fear was . . . debilitating. The thought of the Circle
claiming you, of you going into the Pythian Court, of you
becoming another of those smiling girls who only knew
one word . . .

"I left you with Tony, whose court was not watched as
mine was, whose court was barely watched at all. I had
the *geis* put on you, to keep you safe, until the power
would pass . . . to someone.

"It seemed a long shot. Lady Phemonoe had an heir, a
capable girl, by all accounts. I had no reason to believe
she would not inherit. But hope is not reasonable—hope
is terrifying and exhilarating and devastating and,
frankly, sometimes stupid. But I clung to it anyway. I
lived in hope.

"Lady Phemonoe died. The power passed. And it
passed to you."

"Why not tell me all this then?" I rasped. "I've had it
for *months*—"

"And for months I've tried. I almost did, that night in
London—do you remember? When I told you about my
family?"

I did. He'd rambled on and on, about how his parents
had died, how he felt responsible, a hundred things. He'd
finally gotten to a point: that he worried over me, perhaps
excessively, because of others he had lost.

But he never told me who.

He never said her name.

"I wanted to a dozen times," he said now. "But I was
afraid. Even hope can die, and I had clung to mine for so
long it had become a comfort, a crutch, almost a friend. I

had become used to telling myself: someday. Someday you will find the words. Someday your moment will come. Yet, once it did, I found that the charming words choked me—the easy smiles died on my lips. I wanted to ask, but once I did . . ."

"Hope was gone." My voice was hoarse.

He nodded. "One way or another. And so I found excuses for saying nothing. And there were plenty of them, and none pretenses. The war, the consul's demands, family business—a thousand things."

"Then why now?"

"You know why. No one has ever waged a war like this, Cassie. No one ever thought to do so. But we have no choice, and so we will go. But before I do, I need an answer. Before I do, I need a *yes*."

"To what? What do you *want*, Mircea?" I already suspected—hell, I *knew*—but I needed to hear it. Needed to know I wasn't going mad.

"A simple thing. An easy thing. I caused the deaths of my family, but could not save them. Cannot, even with your help, for they were killed too publicly, in front of too many witnesses. I am not a fool; I know they are lost. And in fairness, my parents knew the risks when they took the throne. Someone else did not."

"You want me to save your mistress." It wasn't even a question. It was all over his face.

The woman had brown eyes and black hair that spread out over the pillow. He was looking down at her as they rocked together, moving inside her in a slow, smooth stroking, down, away, back, down, away, back. Her hands splayed across the small of his back, her dark eyes closed. Her lips parted as she rose to meet him, her throat and breasts glistening. He lowered his mouth to the hollow above her collarbone.

And she whispered a single, devastating word.

"Not your mistress," I said numbly. "Your wife."

"How did you—"

"Your *wife*?"

Mircea licked his lips, but he didn't deny it. "We married very young, and in a time of constant conflict, when I was frequently gone. All in all, I doubt we spent a whole year together. But she will always be the mother of my child. My only child, Cassie," he said, coming out of his chair, going to one knee in front of me. "The only one I will ever have, the one who has suffered so much, more than I can explain to you. The one who deserves to know the mother she lost—and she *can*."

"*Mircea—*"

"My wife did not change history; my wife was a peasant girl who died a terrible, unfair, undeserved death. Taking her out of the timeline, bringing her here—what will it hurt? Who will it harm? How is it any different from her dying as she did? It will change nothing—"

"You can't know that!"

"I can! We proved such a thing was possible, with Radu—"

"That . . ." I stopped, chills breaking out on my skin. "That . . . was a *dress rehearsal*?"

"No." Mircea's eyes widened. "My brother was . . . We were already going to the same place he was imprisoned, you and I, on that errand of the senate's. It was the perfect opportunity, a chance that might never come again—"

I got up. I couldn't sit there anymore.

Mircea caught my hands. "What would be the harm? Tell me! None of the others would say. They said no, no, no, but never a reason! How will the rescue of one woman, one innocent woman, make any difference? And I know how to find her now. Vlad wouldn't tell me. He told me about the Pythias, that they had the power to save her, but would only tell me where she died if I helped him. But I couldn't put that monster back in power, and he wouldn't help me until the crown was back on his head—"

"I understand."

"Yes, you do." Mircea nodded. "You saw how I kept him alive for so long, waiting him out, yet he was implacable. He knew I needed a day, a place, a time, and he wouldn't give it to me. Wanted to force me to kill him without it, a final victory. A way to punish me for refusing him the crown. But with your help—"

I pulled away and walked a few feet, dazed. I had nowhere to go, but I needed some space. And some air; the room was stifling.

I felt him come up behind me, but I didn't turn around. "You told me once that Radu was your only family," I said. "Yet you had a daughter—"

"A daughter who was not part of my life. Who was more than half-mad, who despised me, and saw me as little as possible. Perhaps once a decade, and only when I forced the issue—"

"But she existed."

"And still does. Don't make her pay for my mistake. I should have told you about her, but I was afraid that would bring up a conversation about her mother, and I—every time I would think I should tell her, I *have* to tell her, I would also think, this is my last chance. If a girl I helped to bring up, who knows me, who—"

He stopped, but not in time.

"Who loves you," I finished for him, turning around, my voice breaking. "And I do. Because you made sure I would. To get that yes."

"No." He shook his head. "No, my feelings changed—"

"And now I'm supposed to go get your *wife?*"

"She isn't my wife, Cassie! Till death do us part was quite literal in my case. But she is my only chance to atone for youthful stupidity that destroyed my entire family! She died a tragic death because of me. I can't save my parents, I can't put my family back together, but I *can save her.*"

"And if I do this," I said, my voice trembling with something I couldn't name, "if I give you your yes, you'll give me the potion?"

"Yes."

"Now? *Right* now?"

"I will get it for you. I swear it—"

"Then you don't have it."

"Our contact in the Circle was purged with Jonas' coup. And even had he not been, he said he would have no chance to get any more. But I will find—"

I shifted.

Chapter Forty-one

I landed in a corridor somewhere. I wasn't sure where. The pain of a shift I couldn't afford was debilitating, sending me stumbling into a wall and dropping to my knees. Or maybe that was something else.

I stayed there, in semidarkness, breathing hard. I felt stunned, sick, more than slightly nauseous. I'd heard that old saying, about words feeling like a strike to the gut, but had never really understood. How could emotion hit like a fist?

Like this, I thought, just like this, fighting to breathe while scenes and images and clues I'd ignored or pushed away crowded in from all sides.

Mircea visiting Tony's when I was a kid, and staying *for a year.* A man with worldwide business interests, a huge family, responsibilities to the senate, yet he takes off a year to sit in the wilds of Pennsylvania. Even Marlowe hadn't understood it.

I'd overheard them talking while on a trip to the past. Jonas had wanted to ransack Tony's office for something he hoped could help in the war. And while he was doing that, I'd overheard a conversation between Mircea and Marlowe, the latter having shown up after his friend had lingered at his disreputable child's house for months.

Marlowe hadn't been happy to discover that I was there, or that my mother had once been heir to the Pythian throne. It had sounded like he thought Mircea was holding out on him, and hiding me in the boonies to avoid sharing a potential Pythia with the rest of the senate. There'd also been something about all those Pythias

Mircea had visited, but I'd had to make a run for it before I heard the whole story.

Well, I had it now.

A pretty little thing, I thought, remembering what he'd said about Eudoxia. Like he'd called Isabeau an auburn-haired beauty. Had he charmed them, too? Had he spent time with them, talked to them, held them? Had he—

Of course he had. Like he'd spent a year at Tony's, charming a lonely little girl. God, it must have been so easy! Nobody had ever spent time with me before; most scarcely seemed to notice me. My friends were Rafe, one of Tony's vampires who was rarely there; my governess, Eugenie; and Laura, a little ghost girl I used to talk to when she showed herself; because there was no one else.

Until suddenly, there was. A handsome, charismatic stranger, with laughing dark eyes and a kind face, and—and I was panting again, holding on to the wall, fingers curling into my palms because I'd loved him, God, I had! From the start, from the first moment he'd smiled at me; he'd changed everything.

Anyone else would have been grooming me, with an eye on the future, but not Mircea. He wasn't stupid. It's a little hard to tell someone in love with you that you want her to go retrieve your *wife*.

No, he'd wanted me to think well of him, to remember him fondly, to be willing to do him a hell of a favor some-day. He'd never realized that the affection-starved child had fallen in love with him. If he had, he wouldn't have used the *geis*, which thrives on emotion, as a protection spell. Not when it can magnify, if something goes wrong, binding two people into a permanent master-and-slave arrangement, with the "master" being whoever had the most power.

Mircea had backed off quickly when he discovered that, years later, after I was an adult. Because, with the Pythian power on my side, who would be master and who slave? But that was after the spell had been doubled, and was close to driving him mad. He'd been glad to cooper-ate with me to get it lifted, to find a way out of the trap he'd inadvertently laid for himself. But by then the damage had been done, hadn't it?

By then I was wearing his mark.

My fingers found it again, the two little bumps. Just two tiny marks that, to a human, would barely even be visible, but to a vampire were as good as a wedding ring. But he hadn't meant to give them to me, had he? I didn't need to guess about that; I *knew*.

The Pythian Court had modernized in a lot of ways, but it had holdovers, too, sacred rituals, ancient magic. The Pythias were the brides of Apollo, and the ritual for the passing of the power included an avatar in the form of an acceptable man. One who stood in for the god at the wedding—and bedding—ceremony.

And Mircea had chosen someone else.

Of course he had. He was playing the part of the avuncular uncle, my childhood protector, my *friend*. So Tomas had been selected, a vampire I knew and liked, and Mircea had stepped gracefully aside. Until the *geis* kicked in, binding us in a marriage that he'd never worked for, never wanted, because he wanted someone else.

He wanted her.

I swallowed, trying to deny it, but how could I? I'd been so flattered, but I'd always wondered, even as a child: what did he see in me? Just a skinny thing with scraped knees and bruised elbows, because I couldn't walk across a room without falling down. A crazy thing, who talked to ghosts more than people, because people didn't seem to like me so much, did they? Except for Mircea . . .

I sobbed; I couldn't help it. My heart hurt—God, it *hurt*. I'd loved him, I loved him still, and he'd never cared about me. It had been an act, to get back some woman who'd been dead five centuries, while I was *here*, right now, and—

A phone rang. It took me a moment to realize that it was coming from me, since the ring tone was wrong. Because it wasn't mine.

It was Mircea's.

The one he'd lent me to call Caleb, but I couldn't call

Caleb, and then I couldn't call anyone, because it was shattering in a million pieces on the opposite wall. I looked at it for a moment, broken into shards, and then I crawled over and gathered up the pieces, cradling them to me, I didn't know why. I couldn't put them back together, any more than I could fix this. Any more than I could fix anything.

"Cassie."

I looked up, and only saw a blur. But it was a blur with a woman's voice—a familiar one. Rian.

For a moment, I couldn't understand what she was doing in New York. And then I realized: she wasn't. She was where she'd been for the last few days, ever since Caleb had had to go back to work: guarding Pritkin's body. I'd shifted back to Dante's but hadn't realized it because the corridor was so dark.

Trust Casanova to save on lighting, I thought, and laughed harshly.

"Are you all right?" Rian, who was in bodily form, crouched awkwardly beside me. She moved so gracefully in spirit, but she hadn't had a body for that long, and she wasn't so good with it yet. It was like a teenager trying to learn to drive and bumping into a curb, or in her case, the floor, when she abruptly sat down, taking the last foot or so all at once. And looking surprised.

But her soft, dark eyes and expressive face were the same as ever as she gazed at me.

I didn't have an answer. There wasn't one she wanted to hear.

She took the phone from my hand. There was a text frozen on the screen. I didn't know what it said, but I guessed it was enough.

"Oh, Cassie," she whispered.

"He intended to ask me to go back for her," I said dully. "Probably right after Radu. I didn't know what I was doing then, what being Pythia even meant. It would have been easy to talk me into it. But he didn't get the chance before the *geis* complicated things. And later, after everything we'd gone through, the pain and the triumph and . . . *everything*, how could he ask me then? How could he ask me to retrieve his *wife*?"

Rian didn't say anything. I was oddly grateful for that.

"Then the consul got involved, separating us, because of her paranoia, and giving him no chance to lock me down. And he needed that, didn't he? Had to be sure of me, sure I'd do anything for him, and he wasn't sure. That's why he was so upset over that army. Not just because the senate wanted it, but because it was the first time I'd ever said it. It was the first time I ever told him no."

There was more silence for a while, long enough for me to start to feel ashamed. I couldn't afford to just sit here. I had—God, so much to do. But I didn't know how to do any of it, and for the first time in all this, for the first time since the whole crazy journey began, I was starting to think the words. The ones I'd never allowed myself to say.

The ones that seemed more likely every minute.

"They get obsessed, the older ones," Rian said softly.

I lifted my head. "What?"

"I've seen it before. I've seen it in Carlos, although he won't admit it. But it's there, a burning need for the respect he never had in life. It's the root of almost all he does, even how he dresses. The nobles of his youth, the *caballeros* he grew up with—you could tell them by their dress. They were so flashy. . . ."

I wondered what the hell she was talking about.

"It's why he so wants this hotel to work," she continued. "Not for the money, but for what it *represents*. When he was young, you were only important if you were a landholder, someone of means. You were looked up to, almost worshipped by the small folk, and envied by the impoverished gentry, of which his family was a part. Now it's prosperous businessmen who hold that position, and he so wants to be one, Cassie! And needs to be, in truth."

"Needs to be?"

She nodded. "It's as I said: they get obsessed, the older ones. It's something different with each of them, each one I've known, at least: wealth, beauty, fame, power. . . . But it's always something that eluded them in life, something that caused them great pain, something they feel they *must* overcome."

"And if they don't?"

The beautiful head tilted. "Haven't you ever thought about it? How the great ones gain in power every year, with each new family member, every new master. Yet how many as old as the consul do you see? The younger ones die of all sorts of things, but the old ones, the powerful ones, the ones who rival some of our lords in strength—what could kill them?"

"Plenty of things." Vampires didn't die of old age, but there were lots of other ways. Most of which involved others of their kind. "Duels, wars, conflicts with other masters . . ."

"Some, yes," she agreed. "But all? Where are all those millennia-old masters? The ones as old as your consul could fit in a large room. Where are the rest who started out with her? They were numbered in the thousands once, yet now . . . where are they?"

"I told you," I said, wishing she would leave me alone. "They fight all the time—"

"Yes, but the older, the stronger—they should win, shouldn't they? But we know that isn't always true. It wasn't when your consul came to power, when she killed a being thousands of years older than herself, one of legendary strength."

"She had help," I said, remembering what Jules had said. "Anthony fought with her—"

"But he was the same age as she. And you know how it is. A sixth-level master is many times stronger than a seventh, each step you take being an exponential increase in power. So how much stronger was her master? He was said to have been five thousand years old. How could both of them, how could an *army*, have taken him down?"

I'd had enough. "Does it *matter*?" I asked, starting to get up.

Rian caught my arm. "It matters," she said urgently. "If you care for Mircea as I think you still do."

I stared at her, feeling my face turn ugly. "And did he pay you to say that?"

The dark eyes flashed. "I owe him no fealty; if anything, the debt I have is to *you*. You helped Carlos when you didn't have to, when almost no one else would have.

Even after I betrayed you, and gave my master information about your plans. I thought it was the right thing to do, the best way to help both my lords, but I was wrong. I am trying to make amends."

"By doing *what*?"

"By *explaining*. By telling you what they won't, what most of them refuse to even acknowledge to themselves. But I've lived long enough to see the truth of it. The ones who survive are those who find some peace with their fixation, either by obtaining it or by letting it go. Those who don't . . . they lose their duels because they lose their minds, or maybe their focus is a better way of putting it. Nothing seems real anymore—nothing matters, except for their obsession. It becomes their fatal flaw, and sooner or later, it *will* destroy them."

"So Mircea has to get his wife back in order to survive?" How convenient.

"He doesn't have to get her back," Rian said, shaking her head. "But he does have to resolve this tension, his guilt over what happened, his longing to repair the family he lost. At the very least, he has to come to terms with her death, and he hasn't done that."

"And I can't help him, Rian."

"You resent him that much, then?" The beautiful eyes were sorrowful.

"No, I mean I *can't* help him," I said, throwing off her hold and struggling to rise. "I can't help anyone!"

"That's not true—"

"Really?" I staggered against the wall and then got my back to it, wanting to curse myself for weakness that I couldn't afford. "What have you seen me do? I've been running around everywhere, but what have I *done*?"

It was her turn to look confused. "You saved your court—"

"I was the reason they were in danger in the first place! My acolytes blew up the court trying to kill *me*. If I never existed—"

"Apollo would be back and we would all be dead."

I shook my head. "That was more Pritkin than me. And now he's gone and I can't get him back, no matter how hard I try. I'm supposed to be . . ." I fluttered a hand, because I didn't have the words. "More than this. Artemis' daughter, demigoddess, Pythia, they sound so impressive, but they're *lies*. They're titles for someone else, someone powerful. I'm just Cassie." I slowly slid down the wall and finally said the words I'd been thinking for weeks. "And I can't save anyone."

Rian was silent for a moment. "You saved Marco."

"Marco was never in danger."

"On the contrary. Marco was traded from master to master, because he was showing signs of madness, and he was powerful enough to be dangerous. It was looking grim for him, until he found a master who was strong enough mentally to keep him in line. And until he found you. Being assigned as your bodyguard was the best thing that ever happened to him. I do not know what his obsession was; you will have to ask him. But he seems to have finally made peace with it."

I thought back to what Marco had told me about his daughter, the one he'd lost when she was young. And then I thought about my giant of a bodyguard, so huge he almost looked like another species, yet so gentle as he held a tiny initiate in his arms, as if she were spun glass. Jules was right; Marco looked like a bruiser, so that was how he'd been treated. But it wasn't what he was, and it wasn't what he'd needed.

He'd needed what my crazy court had given him: a chance to protect the youngest and most vulnerable.

The ones who reminded him of the girl he lost.

"My court did that," I said, after a minute. "Not me."

"And did your court fight that battle this morning?" she asked, smiling slightly. "Did your court defeat four out of five rogues, in something like a day?"

"But that's just *it*," I said, low and vicious, not understanding why she didn't get this. "One's still out there, I don't know where, and one is all it takes. And I'm no closer to finding her or defeating Ares or rescuing Pritkin than I was when I started! I go back to freaking Arthurian Britain, again and again, and what good does it do? I'm still treading water. Or running on some kind of treadmill, exhausting myself but not getting anywhere!"

"Maybe you just need some help."

My head jerked up at that, because that hadn't been Rian. It took me a second to focus in the darkness, because we weren't near a window, so almost the only light was a bloodred exit sign. It gleamed on an approaching bald spot under a wispy comb-over and off a horrible tie that even darkness couldn't help.

Fred.

My bodyguard. Looking more like the accountant he used to be and less like a blood-covered fiend, at the moment. "You got a phone call," he informed me.

My lips twisted. Of course I did. I knew Mircea. No way was it going to be that easy.

"I'm sure."

But Fred was shaking his head, a weird little grin breaking out over his face. "No, trust me. You *want* to take this call."

Chapter Forty-two

My suite was still mostly empty when we entered, and looked like a hurricane had hit it. The once-missing cots were jumbled up against the far wall, open packing boxes were scattered everywhere, and a lone drawing in crayon lay under the coffee table. But otherwise, it had been stripped bare of everything except the generic hotel furniture and deliberately tasteful knickknacks it had come with.

And the old pattern of bullet holes in the wall.

I glanced at them, but not for long, because my "phone call" was taking up the entire expanse of windows leading to the balcony. The glass sweep usually reflected distant neon, headlights, and the vague half darkness of the city at night. But now it was all burning roots and tumbled bricks and what looked like it had been an underground tunnel, until something happened.

Something bad.

But the man ducking under a fiery root looked to be okay, and a genuine smile of relief spread over my face when he stood back up.

"Caleb!"

"Still here." He grinned back, widely. It was a little weird to see that expression on the usually stoic face, almost as much as seeing the dark eyes shining and the usually deliberate movements fast and jerky. He looked like he was high on adrenaline and ready for a fight, although the only other people I saw in the corridor were white-suited figures trying to put out magical fires.

"And everyone else?" I asked.

"We took some hits." The smiled faded slightly. "But nothing like we might have. Thanks to you."

"To me? I wasn't even there."

"But your warning was. I got here just before everything went to hell."

"My warning about . . . ?"

"Lizzie?" He looked slightly incredulous, maybe because we'd talked less than a day ago. But to me, it felt like a week.

"And Jonas listened?"

He nodded. "I don't know if he believed me or not, but he tripled the guards and ordered the main wards put online. You should have been here! The wards went up and *bam*. We were hit almost the moment after, by everything the Black Circle had! I think they assumed our guard would be down, after they took on the vamps and then Dante's earlier. That we wouldn't expect another attack so soon. But they found out otherwise, once the new weapons deployed—"

"What new weapons?"

"Some stuff we've been developing, ever since that thing with Apollo—"

He looked over his shoulder, and then had to get out of the way as what appeared to be a whole platoon marched past. I almost did the same, because they looked so real, and like they were coming straight out of the wall at me. But the heavily armed men and a few women disappeared a second later, melting into the air like 3-D images in a movie theater.

And leaving me staring at Caleb again—or, more accurately, at his back.

"Caleb!"

"I'll tell the old man you're here," he said, turning around to walk backward, despite the fact that the tunnel appeared to be anything but level. But he never lost his footing. "He had to go put out some fires!"

"Literally?"

He laughed—actually *laughed*. "No, not literally—at least I don't think so. But, for once, stay put!"

He deftly dodged another fire unit, then disappeared

around a bend in the tunnel. And the people in the white hazmatlike suits ran straight out of the wall and through my middle, causing me to stumble back a step or two, because the illusion was a little too good. And then to move back even farther, because I didn't want to experience that again.

Which was when I heard cursing coming from the kitchen.

After the day I'd had, I fully expected to see an army at the gates, or a fire run out of control, or *something* for the adrenaline flooding my system to expend itself on. I did not expect what I saw, when Fred and I burst through a door off the lounge. I did not expect—

A dancing chicken.

I just stood there.

It *was* a chicken, and it was dancing, on the kitchen countertop.

There were a bunch of people standing around looking at it, too: a scattering of initiates, including a Cindy Lou Who clone clutching a beat-up doll; some war mages, looking grim; the pink-haired girl from the drag; three tough-looking women, glaring at the mages; and a smattering of vamps. Including Roy, in a brown-and-tan-checked suit that set off his red hair. But suddenly, no one was making a sound.

The chicken wasn't, either, but I guessed that was excusable, since it was dead. And raw, and wearing those little paper things on the end of its leg bones, like ruffled socks. It looked like it was ready to be put in the pan with the carrots, potatoes, and onions sitting nearby. But, instead, it was up on its legs, doing a jig.

"What is *that*?" one of the mages finally demanded, pointing at it.

"The cancan?" Fred guessed, causing the man's weather-beaten skin to flush with anger.

"I'm sorry!" A skinny boy was huddled against the cabinets, looking freaked. Maybe because a war mage had just drawn a weapon on him. Jiao; my brain supplied a name in the split second before the mage was disarmed, the gun ending up in the pink-haired girl's hand.

"Give it back!" the man warned her.

"Ask nicely."

"Give it back or spend the rest of the year in lockup!"

"For what?" I interrupted. "You were the one threatening a *child*."

The man started, like he hadn't noticed I was there. But even when he did, it didn't seem to matter. "The child is a necromancer—and a strong one!" he rasped. "Why is he here?"

"Why are you?"

The flush was back, darker this time. "We've been assigned here—"

"By who?"

"Who else? Who guards the Pythia?"

"The senate, at present."

"The *senate*?" That was another mage, older and grizzled, with the war mage scowl firmly in place. His eyes took in the motley crew in the kitchen, half of whom I didn't even know, with disdain. "This whole lot should be locked up."

"Uh." That was a third mage, a young blond with a severe military haircut that wasn't making him look any older. Or any better, considering the jug ears that stood out almost perpendicular to his head. They looked vaguely familiar.

"Uh, what?" his older companion demanded.

"Uh, please don't make her mad?"

And it clicked. The younger guy was one of the group of mages I'd sent for a bath in Lake Mead recently. And who was not looking like he wanted another trip.

"Do you know how to swim?" Roy asked him kindly. He and the other vamps were just standing around, observing but not interfering. If Pink Hair hadn't grabbed the gun, one of them would have. But now that Jiao wasn't being threatened, they had returned to the vague, slightly bored interest of people watching TV.

If the Circle and some witches wanted to kill each other, why should they care?

"Not that well," the young man admitted. "And all the weapons—"

"Act like small anchors, don't they?" Roy commiserated.

"They really do." He looked at me. "Please, lady, we have orders—"

"From Jonas?"

He nodded. "We're supposed to be here. And you need us—"

"Didn't need you this morning," Pink Hair said, her eyes still on the flushing mage.

"And you're here . . . because?" I asked, not wanting to offend, but also not being all that comfortable with a reporter hanging around the suite.

Not that there appeared to be too many people to report on, since most of my court was still missing.

She shot me a grin. "Presents."

"What?"

"All of us, from the covens." She gestured around at the three tough-looking women. "After this morning, they decided you needed some competent help."

"Competent!" the red-faced mage exploded. "As if the covens would know the meaning—"

"At least we get to a fight on time."

"Yes, suspiciously so! Almost as if you *knew*—"

"That's it," one of the other women said, pulling a wand just as the mage made a gesture. That was thankfully blocked by his own man.

"Have a care," the grizzled mage hissed. "Assault the bitch and you know damn well—"

"Call me bitch again, old man, and see what happens," the witch warned.

"All right, out!" I said. "All of you! Except you, Jiao," I added, because he was still looking freaked.

"This is not an issue for the Pythian Court. This is a Circle matter," Red Face protested, as if I hadn't spoken. "That boy was doing illegal magic—"

"Five."

"Five? Five what?"

"Four."

"Oh, shit," Jug Ears said, and started pushing for the door.

"Three."

"This is ridiculous!" Red Face spluttered. "You're harboring illegal children alongside Pythian initiates—"

"What is ridiculous is that we are in a *war*," I said, low and furious. "*The* war, because if we lose it there won't be another. And this"—I gestured at the goddamn chicken—"is what you *focus on*?"

The man started to say something, but his older companion cut him off. "Do what she says. Take it outside."

"Damn. And I wanted to see what happened when you reached one," Roy said.

I shot him a look and he disappeared, too, taking the wide-eyed initiates with him. Jiao stayed where he was, but the chicken suddenly keeled over, landing back against the pan, propped up on its wings like its little feet hurt. I knew the feeling.

I knelt in front of him. "You okay?"

He nodded.

And then he crumpled, and I caught him on the way to the floor, because he was just a kid, and a war mage had had him at gunpoint. "I'm sorry," he gasped. "I didn't mean—"

"I know. It's all right."

He shook his head. "It's not. I messed up. But I was just—the girls, they wanted to see—"

"The initiates asked you to show them what you could do."

He swallowed, and nodded. "They . . . some of them are just little, you know? And they aren't like us. They aren't used to . . . all this." He gestured around at an amorphous "this" composed of gods and wars, or more likely from his perspective, of fear and pain and constant anxiety, because that was what he'd known before he met Tami.

It was what almost all Tami's kids had known, including me, before she came into our lives and changed everything.

She only had one biological child, a son named Jesse, who had been born with an unauthorized ability. In his case, he was a fire starter, which had gotten him a fast trip to one of the Circle's schools for dangerously talented youth, as soon as his power manifested. This had not gone down well with Tami, who was not the sort you wanted to piss off. Not when she had somewhat unusual magic herself, being a null, a witch who could suck the magic out of anyone or anything she met.

Including the wards the Circle used on their schools.

Jesse had shortly thereafter been back home, and the Circle had had a new vigilante to worry about, someone who made it a habit to waltz past their wards, pick up children at risk of spending the rest of their lives locked away, and waltz back out with them. She'd also collected runaways like me, eventually ending up with quite a collection of jinxes, telekinetics, invokers, taunters, dream walkers, and yes, even necromancers. Jiao was one of the latter, and he had a favorite parlor trick.

Only, from the Circle's perspective, the unauthorized animation of a chicken was apparently on par with raising an undead army.

"You didn't do anything wrong," I told him.

"Then why do they say it is? Why do they—" He cut off, biting his lip, refusing to cry in front of me, because he wasn't a little boy anymore. But he wasn't a man yet, either, being all of twelve or thirteen, and hard-jawed stoicism was out of his range. So he just stood there, looking miserable, and making me want to send a certain war mage to the middle of the ocean.

"Because they're afraid."

"Afraid . . . of me?" He looked up. "But I can't do *anything*—"

"Not yet. They're not afraid of what you can do, but of what you might do. They don't understand magic like ours, and it scares them—"

"Like . . . ours?"

"My father was a necromancer. I have a little of his ability."

Jiao looked at the chicken, and I laughed. "No, I can't do that. I don't . . . It's not bodies with us, but ghosts. But it's still considered necromancy. And you know what?"

He shook his head.

"It saved me this morning. You know we had a battle?"

His eyes brightened. "Everyone knows. They won't let us watch it, though—"

"Watch it?"

"On the security replay. Some of the vamps said it

came through pretty good—until the cameras blew off. But Tami won't let us see—"

Good, I thought, making a mental note to thank her.

"—but maybe you could—"

"There's not much to see," I said. "I left my body behind, and . . . did some things . . . and the video won't show that."

"But if people saw—they always say what I can do is wrong, but if you used it—"

"It isn't wrong, Jiao. It's not the magic, but what you use it for, that counts. You understand?"

"I understand, but *they* don't. They want to lock us all away—"

"They're not going to do that."

"But they *have* done it," he insisted. "They're still doing it! There were lots of necromancers at school—"

"Lots? I was always told it was a rare gift."

He shook his head. "Not really. But those who aren't that strong, who don't have accidents that keep happening, they try to hide it. The Circle lets almost anyone out before us. They think we're evil—"

"But you're not," I said firmly.

"No, we're not," he said, looking at me. And then he hugged me, spontaneously, as the sound of arguing came from outside.

I hung my head. "Stay here," I told him.

"But—"

"Right. Here. Okay?"

He sighed. "Right here," he said, and slumped back against the cabinets.

And I went out to see what fresh hell had just descended on us, only to discover—it was the same old crap.

But it seemed there was a new twist this time.

Tami was standing in between a war mage in full battle kit, and a hard-nosed coven witch in . . . Well, I wasn't sure. Unlike the Circle, the covens didn't appear to have a dress code. Or if they did, it might be summed up as "Come at me, bro."

Two full sleeves of tats, some of them magical, crawled over arms almost as muscular as a man's. They were visible because of the sleeveless T-shirt she was wearing, over a pair of old jeans. More were visible on her neck, disappearing into her short, dark hair. And her piercings ran the gamut from eyebrow, to multiple earlobe, to nose, to a barbell through her bottom lip.

If I'd been trying to find someone less spit-and-polished than the Circle's crew, I couldn't have done any better. But looks didn't equate to power, and there was enough leaking off her that I was surprised it wasn't sparking off the fridge. Because she was *furious*.

I didn't know what the war mage had said, but the tension in the room was thick enough to cut with a knife. At least, it was for a second. Until they found out exactly what a pissed-off null could do.

Before I could say anything, the two combatants staggered and the mage went to one knee. The woman remained standing but looked like she'd just been hit by a Mack truck. Her face turned white, which was pretty impressive, considering her natural skin tone was a deep olive, and her wand fell from her hand.

Not that it mattered. She wouldn't have been able to use it anyway. I doubted either of them could have thrown a spell to save their lives, and might not for days. A null was to magic what a vamp was to blood.

And they'd just been exsanguinated.

"A little lesson, boys and girls," Tami said as they tried to breathe. "My house. My rules."

"I thought it was the Pythia's house," Pink Hair said, sidling closer to her friend.

"Who put it under my management, making it *my* house. And in my house, you pull a weapon—any weapon—and that's a paddlin'. Unless there's a Black Circle army busting down the door, your weapons stay secured. This is a suite full of children, something you're gonna know, something you're gonna *remember*, every time you get that urge. 'Cause if you don't—"

The two former combatants groaned, and the witch finally did go to her knees, mouth open, eyes wide.

"—I will drop you," Tami told them. "You *get* me?"

"I . . . think they get you," Pink Hair said, grabbing her friend, while Jug Ears pulled away the dazed-looking mage.

"Would someone explain what just happened?" I asked.

Tami opened her mouth, but the grizzled mage beat her to it. "The witch provoked him, but he was out of line," he admitted. "We're on edge—all of us. We missed the battle this morning—"

"Damn right, you did," Pink Hair muttered, until I looked at her.

"—and another this afternoon. We want to be there." He gestured back at the living room. "At HQ, where we're needed. Not here on babysitting duty—"

"Then go."

"We've orders," Red Face gasped.

"Which I'm overruling. Jonas needs you more than I do—and I'll clear it with him in a moment, when we talk. Go."

The two men looked at each other.

"Now. Or I'll send you myself."

It was an empty threat, but they didn't know that. And it didn't look like they cared. They went.

"Damn straight," Pink Hair said, and I rounded on her.

"I appreciate the covens sending you," I said, trying for diplomacy. "However—"

"However?"

"—Tami is right. There are some ground rules."

The tattooed witch had fought her way back to her feet and retrieved her wand, although I noticed she tucked it away. All while eyeing up Tami, as if she'd never before realized what a null could do, if you were dumb enough to let one actually touch you. Tami could pull magic from across a room, but it was harder, and she wouldn't get as much.

But skin on skin?

Yeah, you were fucked.

But the experience didn't seem to have softened the woman's attitude any. "She doesn't want us," she told the others. "I told you."

"She hasn't said that," Pink Hair replied, but her eyes were on me.

"I didn't say that because I didn't mean that," I said. "You helped this morning, in a big way. I appreciate it—"

"But now you'd like us to kindly fuck off," the tough chick interrupted.

"What I'd like you to do is stop finishing my sentences," I said, sharper than usual, because my nerves were shot.

She looked surprised, like she wasn't used to being challenged. And I didn't give her time to recover. "As I was saying, I appreciate the covens' help this morning, and welcome it now. But there are rules—"

"Like what?"

"Like everyone gets along," I said, watching her. Because I was pretty sure that had been deliberate.

The mages weren't the only ones who didn't like babysitting duty.

"If you don't want to be here, then don't be here," I said, my eyes taking in the whole group. "But if you stay, then you accept that this is a family. Not a job, not a burden—a *family*. If you can't handle joining one that's made up of people you don't approve of, then you know what to do."

Nobody moved.

"I'll fix it with the covens for you," I added. "I don't have as much pull with them as the Circle, but I'll do my best—"

"We're not leaving," Tough Chick said, crossing her arms.

It sounded final.

"Then you agree to the rules?"

There was a long, silent moment, and then more silence. But I finally got a nod. And not just from her. The other three witches followed her lead, and so did Jug Ears, who I was surprised to see still taking up space over by what had been a bar before somebody made off with it.

"And where the hell's my court?" I asked Tami, who rolled her eyes.

"It's a long story," she said. "Take your phone call. I'll be finishing up dinner if you want to talk."

I nodded. Roy sidled up beside me as we walked back to the living room. "Vetted?" I asked, almost silently, but his ears didn't need the help.

"They're clean. Well, clean enough." He slid me a glance. "Of course, you could just send them away."

"I've been preaching unity for a while now, and as soon as we get some, I send them packing?"

He grinned. "Be careful what you wish for."

I was trying to think up a suitable reply when Fred returned. "Your party's on the line."

I reentered the living room to see Jonas striding down the burning tunnel in full battle regalia, some sort of black shiny armor that made his white hair all the whiter by contrast. And on either side of him was a woman: one tall, thin, and dark-haired, maybe somewhere in her early forties, the other old and round and grandmotherly, with hair almost as white as his. I wondered what they were doing in an underground bunker that still looked to be on fire.

And still coming this way, despite the fact that they'd just left the wall of glass behind.

"Jonas," I said, preparing to ask him to step back a little, because the weird 3-D effect of the spell was confusing my brain.

Really confusing, I thought, as the three of them stepped down onto carpet, their shoes denting the plush pile.

And then kept right on coming.

Chapter Forty-three

A swarm of leather-coated war mages streamed around the figures, enveloping the trio in a flurry of activity for a second, before dissipating like mist—and leaving them behind. Because they weren't images. They'd just walked out of a freaking wall, crossing half the world in a millisecond, without so much as breaking stride.

And there was only one group in the world who could do that.

"The children," I whispered, stumbling back into Roy.

"What?"

"Get them out! Get them *now*!"

I heard raised voices, running feet, and felt Roy jerk me behind him, none of which would do any good against the two Pythian acolytes with Jonas—and how the *hell* were there more acolytes?

"Cassie—" Jonas said.

"Get down!" I told him, and threw everything I had, trying to shift the women far enough that we'd have time to get the kids out, at least.

But nothing happened, except for a power drain that dropped me to my knees and ripped a sound out of my throat. And did nothing else, because the women never even moved. Except toward me.

And toward the line of snarling vamps that were suddenly in the way, guns and fangs out, forming an impenetrable wall. That was just as suddenly gone—where, I didn't know—dismissed by a wave of a hand. And I was scrambling back, trying to reach the stairs, even as spells were going off and people were screaming and glass was shattering, including the whole line of windows.

But nothing touched the women—not the first damn thing.

Of course it didn't.

And then everything abruptly went quiet. Not frozen, but slowed way the hell down. Jonas raised a leisurely arm, to deflect a curse. The witches piled up in the doorway, their latest spells barely moving in front of them. Fred paused with a child under each arm, slowly reaching for another. And Roy, who had somehow avoided whatever had happened to the other vamps, was caught halfway through a lunge, body tensed and arm outstretched, like a pro football player diving for a ball.

Or a vamp diving for an acolyte who was no longer there.

Because she was standing in front of me.

I scrambled back, head swimming, nose running, elbow bruising on the iron railing of the stairs. Which I grasped, pulling myself up. If I could reach the door, if I could force them to chase me, if I could lead them away from the suite—

But the younger one shifted, appearing above me at the top of the stairs. And the older one grabbed me from behind, her grip surprisingly strong. Leaving me trapped between them, desperate and caged and helpless—

And clasped to a massive bosom while someone made shushing sounds, like to a traumatized child.

For a moment, we just stayed like that, in a weird tableau.

And then the younger woman bent, consternation on her face, and put out a hand—

Causing me to flinch back, breathing hard, because I didn't understand this—I didn't understand any of this!

"Lady," she murmured, and let the hand fall. And looked, in apparent loss, at the older woman.

"Told Jonas not to do it this way," White Hair said. "Damn man never listens!"

She released me and then just stood there, frowning. "I'd curtsy," she said surreally, "but my knees, you know. I get down and I might never get back up."

I stayed where I was, splayed against the railing, the blood pounding in my ears.

"Who are you?" I finally whispered.

"Your fail-safes, lady," the younger one said. She came down the stairs and curtsied, as elegantly as if she'd been in a fine drawing room. But when she looked up, her face was fierce. "The Pythia doesn't fight alone. The Pythia never fights alone!"

"I didn't know," Jonas said quietly, because we'd moved to Rhea's room. He'd wanted to see his daughter, and I'd wanted to get away from the scene in the lounge.

An extremely pissed-off Tami—and God, it had been glorious—had taken the children and the chicken "upstairs," whatever the hell that meant, while Roy and the vamps cleaned up. And attempted to calm down our new recruits. It hadn't sounded like they were having an easy time of it, the witches having been exposed to two forms of magic they'd never encountered in a span of minutes, which hadn't improved their mood.

But I, for one, was past caring.

"No one knew," Jonas added. "That was apparently the point. To have a senior acolyte from each generation who retains her skills, in case of a serious threat to the court. From what I understand, the idea originated as a way to guard against a Pythia and her heir being injured at the same time. An unconscious Pythia wouldn't be able to pass on the power, but also wouldn't be able to use it. Hence—"

"A fail-safe," I said, staring at the two women, who were standing by the bank of windows, talking softly.

"Yes."

"And you think we can trust them?"

"That, you'll have to determine yourself," Jonas said heavily. "I would have said we could trust Agnes' acolytes, had I been asked, and I knew them better."

"Then why did you bring them *here*?" I whispered. "If they're working for the other side—"

"In that case, why would the Black Circle need Lizzie? Why risk so much to gain her abilities if they already have two acolytes, and with more power than I've ever seen her use?"

I shook my head. "Maybe they want her for something else—"

"We questioned her all night and half the day. If there's anything of interest about that girl, I can't find it."

"But you took her anyway," I said accusingly. We'd recently had a clash over authority—namely, him ignoring mine—and I thought we'd sorted it out. And then he went and did the same thing again!

But Jonas wasn't looking apologetic. "You weren't here. I didn't know when you would be. And we are at *war*. If there was a chance—even a slight one—that she knew Ares' plans—"

"But she didn't."

"No." He sighed suddenly, and rubbed his eyes. It looked like Lizzie wasn't the only one who had been up all night. "As far as we can tell, she was a stooge, nothing more."

"And these women?"

"I know Abigail—the younger—from Agnes' court. She left to be married a year or so after your mother's arrival, and supposedly after giving up access to the power. She was competent, but as far as I knew, there was nothing remarkable about her."

"And the other?"

"Hildegarde von Brandt, a formidable member of Lady Herophile's court—"

"Gertie's?" I said sharply, and got a nod from him— and a warning look from Rico, who was back at Rhea's side after being shifted to the lobby with most of the other vamps. He didn't seem happy about having two more Pythian acolytes hanging around.

He wasn't the only one.

"Yes," Jonas said, softly. "Her abilities were always formidable. If a fail-safe system was in effect, I can see her being chosen."

"But why keep it a secret? How am I supposed to ask for help if I don't even know they *exist*?"

"Ask them," Jonas said dryly. "All I know is, that damn paper came out, and I shortly thereafter received two very unhappy visitors who demanded an audience with you. After what you'd been through, I think they were afraid that you wouldn't see them without an introduction. I made the call and you know the rest."

"No," I said, "I don't know anything," and walked over to the women.

"Lady," they murmured with Hildegarde nodding in lieu of the dreaded curtsy.

Like I gave a damn.

"Why are you here?" I asked abruptly.

They exchanged a glance.

"We're supposed to be here," Abigail said, after a moment. "If the court is in need. It is why we exist—well, why the position does—"

"The court's been in need for a while. The court was just *blown up*," I pointed out.

"The building was blown up. The court was rescued by you," Hildegarde corrected, with equanimity.

Unlike her younger counterpart, she seemed completely unfazed by all this. The bullet-ridden wall, which I'd caught Abigail staring at, had passed without so much as a raised eyebrow. The motley crew of punked-out witches and pissed-off vamps had been managed with a cheery "Well, hello there." And now a distrustful, beyond-annoyed Pythia was being regarded kindly, but with no discernible worry.

Maybe because she'd just seen me have trouble walking up a flight of stairs.

If they wanted to hurt me, they could have done it already. So that left the question of what they did want. "What do you want?" I asked.

"To help you," Abigail said, her thin face distressed. "When I read the paper—I knew I should have come sooner—"

"Why didn't you?"

"I did— Well, I tried. When Lady Phemonoe died and Myra was named a rogue by the Circle, I sent a letter to the Lord Protector—"

"To Saunders?" I asked, naming Jonas' predecessor. The one who had been corrupt as hell, and had wanted my head on a platter before I found out what he'd been up to.

He'd almost succeeded.

And damn, I could have used a couple of acolytes then!

"Yes," she confirmed. "He was . . . He made me uneasy. I felt his answer was just an attempt to gain information about me. I'd written anonymously, and he didn't like that. But we're not supposed to reveal ourselves unless absolutely necessary, and I didn't know him. I set up a meeting, but he had people there, and ambushed me. I got away, but it was a close thing, and before I could decide what to do next, Jonas had removed him and assumed his role. And you had been named Pythia."

Hildegarde nodded. "I had considered coming forward as well, but everything resolved itself quickly, and the court did not appear to be in danger. As far as I could tell, this was merely a disputed succession, with the Circle trying to retrieve both of you to see where the power would go—"

"They were trying to kill us and put their own candidate on the throne!" I said heatedly.

"But that wasn't the story the papers put out, was it?" she asked mildly. "And I have been away from court for some time. My old avenues for gossip have long since dried up"—her lips twisted—"and died off, in most cases."

"We're not supposed to reveal ourselves unless absolutely necessary," Abigail repeated. "If everyone knew who we were, and there was an assault on the court, they might target us, too."

"And then where would we be?" Hildegarde agreed.

"Where I've been for the last four months?" I snarled, and then leaned on the wall and put a hand on my head, because that wasn't helping. "Why are you *here*?"

"You know why. The paper made it clear that things were not as we'd assumed. And after my talk with Jonas, it appears they are even graver than I feared. You have not managed to retrieve your last rogue."

"No."

"Then forgive me, but why are *you* here?" she demanded. "A rogue is a priority. Your power should be pulling you wherever she is—"

"My power." I laughed suddenly, I didn't know why.

Probably because, lately, it didn't feel like I had any. "I don't think it knows," I finally said. "It's been ignoring her."

"That's impossible," Hildegarde said severely. "A rogue is a priority—*the* priority, until she's dealt with. A determined rogue could destroy everything!"

"And I had *five*," I said, suddenly savage. I had a headache, I had too many problems to keep track of, and I didn't have time for a critique from someone who hadn't even been here. "I only found out about them a couple days ago. Three are now dead and one is in custody—"

"That is admirable, lady," Abigail murmured.

"And useless without the last," Hildegarde said, echoing something I'd thought back in the corridor.

"What do you want me to do?" I demanded. "My power doesn't seem to know or care where she is, and I can't find her without it! I've been working on something else, and it hasn't so much as—"

"On what?"

"None of your business!"

For the first time, Hildegarde looked less than grandmotherly. "I am not asking for details," she said curtly. "My point was that if you have been going to the same place and time as your rogue, your power wouldn't have had to pull you anywhere."

I shook my head. "I haven't."

"You must have!"

"I *haven't*! An acolyte couldn't—" I cut off, suddenly remembering the attack in the fey version of a Winnebago. But that had been *Wales*, the place I'd almost wrenched my guts out to reach—and that was with a potion Johanna didn't have. No way had she managed it.

"You've remembered something," Hildegarde said.

"One of the other rogues told me that Johanna Zirimis—that's the one who's still out there—is after the same thing I am. A . . . sort of relic. One she thinks might be powerful enough to bring back a god—"

"Then how can you say she's not a threat?" Hildegarde demanded.

"Because she couldn't have managed it. She's an *acolyte*—"

"A determined acolyte can manage a good deal, I assure you," she snapped.

"Fifteen hundred years?" I snapped right back.

"Fifteen . . . *hundred*?" Abigail looked appalled.

I nodded. "That's why I'm exhausted. And if it almost killed me to shift back that far, do you honestly think an acolyte could manage it? *Any* acolyte?"

"No," Abigail said, glancing at her friend. "It isn't even a question."

Hildegarde pursed her lips, looking puzzled and vaguely annoyed.

"So like I said," I told them, "I don't know if Johanna died on her quest, or hasn't started it yet, or what, but—"

I broke off, because the door had just opened, and somebody was backing into the room: Jiao, carrying a tray for Rhea. It contained some sort of soup, and smelled good. He shot me a smile.

I smiled back.

And then I frowned.

"What is it?" Hildegarde asked sharply.

"Jonas," I called, because Rhea was awake now, so there was no more reason for silence.

He looked up.

"Do you have a photo of Johanna?"

He didn't answer, being busy putting another couple of pillows behind Rhea. But he made a gesture at the stretch of windows beside me, which abruptly changed, from night in Vegas to a photo of a girl. One with dark hair and beautiful green eyes, almost startlingly so against an olive complexion.

I took in the face, but it didn't help much. The damn Winnebago had been too dark, and too clogged with dust for me to be sure. It might have been her; it might have been anyone.

"Can I talk to Lizzie?" I asked, and that request seemed to be a bit more complicated. But by the time Rhea had polished off a third of the soup, a new face was in the window, one with dark circles under her eyes and matted blond hair, because it looked like Lizzie had gotten even less sleep than me.

And I'd just disturbed that. There was an unmade cot behind her, bolted to the floor, which she was attached to by what I assumed was a set of magical cuffs. A fact that reassured me not at all.

"She needs to stay drugged," I told Jonas. "Until she gives back the power."

"She is. We're monitoring her closely."

"Not closely enough! There should be an acolyte with her!" Hildegarde said.

"Are you volunteering?" I asked.

"You—" Her eyes widened. "You don't have *any* acolytes?"

Rhea waved slightly from the bed. Abigail's face went from worried to just slightly above horrified. Hildegarde cursed—rather inventively.

"Hilde—" Jonas began.

"Damn it, Jonas, what the *hell* have you been doing?"

"I didn't know that fail-safes existed—"

"But you did know there were other acolytes! Even former initiates would have been better than nothing. Why on earth—"

"He wanted to keep control of the court," Abigail said, softly. She looked stunned, almost hurt, like she couldn't believe it.

I couldn't believe that she was twenty years older than me.

It's not the age—it's the mileage, I told myself grimly, and walked over to the windows. "I want some answers, Lizzie."

"I've told them everything I know," she spat. "A hundred times! They keep asking the same stupid questions—"

"Maybe I can think of some new ones."

She looked at me resentfully.

"Johanna Zirimis," I said. "You knew her?"

"Of course I knew her. She was an acolyte!"

"But did you know her well?"

"Nobody knew her well. She was some kind of weirdo."

"What kind?"

Lizzie rolled her eyes. "Oh, there're kinds now?"

I nodded at the mage behind her, who allowed her to

sit back down on her cot. Her rather uncomfortable-looking cot, with a lumpy mattress and a paper-thin coverlet. Which didn't stop her from looking at it longingly.

"The sooner we do this, the sooner you go back to sleep," I pointed out.

She scowled. "She was a loner, all right? Nobody liked her. She always had her nose in a book. And she was a PA, which sucks if you had to actually earn your spot, like I did—"

"PA?"

"Political Appointment?" She looked at me like I was slow. "When the Circle needs a favor from one of the big houses, one that happens to have a daughter at court, they pull some strings and get her an acolyte's position. She's never going anywhere, of course—well, not Jo, anyway. She didn't even have a good grip on the power. But she made acolyte before I did, and my family is just as—"

"She wasn't good with the power?" I cut in. "How do you know?"

"She wouldn't duel us. The rest of us, we practiced all the time, but not her. Like I said, all she ever did was read—and talk to herself."

"Talk to herself?" A chill ran through me.

"Cassie," Rico said, and I turned to see Rhea sitting up in bed, waving at me.

"A pad of paper," Jonas told Rico, who shot him a look. Because he didn't take orders from mages, and because he'd already been reaching inside his coat, where he had one ready.

He handed it to Rhea, who scribbled something that Rico brought over to me.

She's lying. I saw her and Jo together often.

I looked up at Lizzie, who was suddenly less belligerent and more worried. "What did she say?" she demanded. "And why can't she talk?"

"Some of your friends paid us a little visit this morning," I said, turning the pad around so Lizzie could see it. "And I don't think she believes you."

"Who the hell cares? Who is she? Some coven nobody! My family—"

"Nobody?" I hadn't noticed Jonas coming up behind me, but he was suddenly there, his face white and scary. "My daughter with Lady Phemonoe is *nobody*?"

Lizzie stared. And then she swallowed, and looked at Rhea. And then she crumpled.

And talked—a lot.

When she was finished, I glanced at Jonas. "I'm going to need—"

He held up a hand—with something in it. "I know what you need," he said tersely. "But there's a price. I want to see your parents."

"Good. So do I."

Chapter Forty-four

"You're positive this is necessary?" Jonas whispered as we crouched in the darkness, under a bunch of dripping leaves.

"Yes, if you want to do this—"

"I don't *want* to. I *have* to," he said, sounding aggrieved. "Your mother was prophesied to help us against Ares!"

"She did," I reminded him. "She helped me kill four of the five Spartoi. I couldn't have taken them without her—"

"Those were his *sons*. The prophecy was about *him*. And in no way have we received any assistance with him!"

"You want to complain?" I nodded at the pale blue fairy-tale cottage that my parents had called home, almost twenty-four years ago. Or right now, because we were back in time. "Go complain."

Jonas muttered something.

"What?"

"I said, like this?" he repeated, looking down at himself with distaste.

"The price for my mother's help with the demon council was that I never return. If we want help, we have to make sure they think I'm not here *again*, but *still*."

"That explains the glamourie. But why am I wearing only a *blanket*?"

He had it wrapped around him toga-style, or maybe venerable senator–style, because the frat party vibe didn't go so well with the expression on his face. Or Pritkin's face, because that was who had been with me the first time I was here, and I couldn't very well show up with a new partner. Pritkin's features could handle anything from annoyance all the way up to incandescent rage, but pinched disapproval . . . not so much.

But my parents didn't know that.

"It's complicated," I said. "But this is the only way."

"And you think your mother is going to fall for this?" he asked, adjusting the blanket's folds over one shoulder.

"No. Which is why we're not talking to her."

A light winked out in an upstairs window, leaving the little courtyard dark and silent. Except for our footsteps, as we scurried for the kitchen door. It was unlocked, of course, because we were on the estate of a psychotic vampire with a bunch of trigger-happy family members. Locks were superfluous.

Not that there were any vamps in sight. No one was, except for Daisy, slumped over the table like a very odd drunk. Or, to be more precise, like the "body" my father had constructed for her was currently empty.

Dad had developed a takeoff of the golem spell, giving his ghosts a corporeal form so they could serve as bodyguards for him and Mom. Only instead of clay, Dad's golems appeared to have been made out of whatever junk he'd had lying around. And a bucket, which Daisy had made into a slightly lopsided head, because he hadn't thought to give her one.

I breathed a sigh of relief. I hadn't been sure I'd gotten the day right; fine-tuning exactly when I showed up in time had never been my strong suit. And the maybe quarter bottle of potion Jonas had found in his nightstand hadn't helped nearly as much as it should have.

"I'll go first, and check it out," I said, and for once, he didn't argue. Maybe because he was busy. Staring in consternation at the makeup Daisy had, somewhat inexpertly, applied to the bucket.

I crossed the kitchen to a door I hadn't been through last time, where an odd-looking glow was leaking in to splash the tiles.

And found a living room filled to the brim with . . . stuff.

It was on tables and shelves and stuck in corners. It

spilled out of boxes and was piled high in baskets. It had taken over the sofa and replaced the books that had once occupied built-ins on either side of the fireplace. It was everywhere. And it was glowing.

Liquid light splashed wood-paneled walls, most of which was somewhere along the blue spectrum. Which wasn't too surprising considering that, in magical terms, blue and green were the colors of milder spells—or in this case, spells with the equivalent of run-down batteries. Everywhere I looked were old wards, decaying amulets, dried-up potions, and shield charms that weren't shielding anything anymore.

It was a room full of magical junk.

Well, mostly. A few items looked like they might still have some oomph. A couple boxes were bobbing up and down, as the power levels in crumbling levitation charms ebbed and flowed. Half of a small end table was flickering in and out of sight, and an odd sort of duel was going on between an EverFlame and an extinguisher spell. But for the most part, they just gently glowed, splashing the walls with wavering, underwater light.

"Don't touch anything!" Roger's voice came from behind a bunch of boxes. "Some things are at the iffy stage right now."

Yeah, I thought, watching a bug zapper on a box near the window. It was painstakingly burning out all the pictures of bees on a kitschy set of floral curtains. It turned what looked like a tiny feeler on me as I edged around the pile, but I guess I didn't look sufficiently insectlike, so I sidled by unscathed.

And found Roger, sitting at a desk, working on something that required a magnifying glass on a stand to see. He looked up, the light glinting off glasses perched low on his nose. They were magnifying, too.

Either that or he had the world's biggest pimple on his left cheek.

His hair had flopped into his eyes, and he peered at me through the strands, like it was hard to see outside the circle of light. "Oh, good," he said, after a second. "I thought it was that officious mage."

"Not quite."

"Hmm." He sounded disapproving. "I've been told I'm not allowed to ask questions. But if I was, I'd wonder where that vampire you were tearing around London with is."

"Mircea," I said, my lips a little numb.

Roger nodded. "He may be dead, but he's still a better catch."

"It's not like that," I said, glancing at what he was making. It didn't look like much of anything, just a few scraps of metal. "Pritkin and I aren't . . . I mean, we don't—"

"Really?" He looked surprised. And then relieved. "Oh, good. It's just, well, Pythias always end up with war mages, don't they?"

"Do they?"

"Oh yes. Makes sense when you think about it. Who else do they meet? And if they do go on a date, who is there, glowering at the poor chap the whole time? Makes a man feel intimidated."

"It didn't intimidate you."

"Yes, well, wasn't the same sort of thing, was it?" He looked at me over his glasses. "By the time your mother and I officially met, we'd known each other for over a decade."

"After I showed up?" I asked, because no way hadn't they connected the dots by now.

"I suppose you could say you introduced us," he said dryly. "Although we'd have likely met in any case. She used to hunt out there."

"In the Badlands?"

He nodded.

"Why?"

"Same reason as the rest of them. She was hungry."

The little creation he was working on started smoking, and he let out an abortive curse and slapped a shield spell over it. Just before something smattered against the inside and oozed its way down the sides, pinkish gray and viscous. Roger sighed and grabbed a towel.

"Why not go back to hunting demons?" I asked as he mopped up. "That's how she got powerful before, right?"

"That's how she became *more* powerful," he corrected. "Enough to build that barrier of hers. But she was already more so than her prey when she started, or they would have turned the tables fast enough!"

"Like the gods did in that battle, after the wall went up?" I said, remembering something I'd been told.

He shook his head. "While it was *going up*. Her fellow gods realized what was happening at the last moment, and almost overwhelmed her. She triumphed, but was brought so low in the process that, afterward, any demon powerful enough to be useful was also powerful enough to be dangerous."

"So she hunted ghosts instead?"

He shrugged and threw the smoking rag into a shielded trash can. "Life energy is life energy, wherever it comes from: demons, ghosts, or the Pythian power itself—which was part of Apollo's life force once, if you recall. It's what drew her to the court, but as an acolyte she had very limited access. Hunting augmented that slightly, and in the process we kept . . . meeting up."

"Meeting up?"

"When she was dragging me back to my cell," he admitted, and I grinned.

"How many times did that happen?"

"More than I care to admit." He rooted around in a basket for what turned out to be burn ointment, for a few red patches on his hand. "But we finally got around to talking, and discovered that we had . . . mutual interests."

"Like what?"

"A lot of things," he said, not looking at me. "But in time, she agreed to help me escape from that damn court, and . . . well, we kept in touch."

"While you were bilking the Black Circle out of their power?"

Last time I was here, Roger had told me how he'd joined up with the dark mages after Mom sprang him from jail, supposedly to construct them a ghost army. The Black Circle hierarchy had been receptive to the idea, which had promised invisible spies on the Silver Circle, and possibly even foot soldiers in the coming war, if Dad's weird ghost golems worked out. In reality, he'd never given them a damn thing, instead using the opportunity

to gain access to their magic, which he'd plundered merci-
lessly. I still didn't know why.

"Trying," he agreed. "And running. And hiding . . . It
was an eventful decade."

"I know the feeling."

"But it's different for you, isn't it?"

"What is?"

"Dating." He blinked at me, eyes looking as large as
an owl's behind the glasses. "Vampires don't intimidate
easily, especially not that one. And they must find you
fascinating."

"Why must they?"

"Your position for one. They love power better than
any creatures I ever met. Even demons . . . well, all right,
maybe not more than demons. But on average, you know.
And then there's your necromancy—"

"I'm not much of a necromancer," I said, trying to
steer the conversation to the reason I'd come.

"Of course you are," Roger said. "I told you, necromancers don't just deal with dead bodies. We're like any
group—we specialize. And my specialty was always
ghosts. You get that from me."

"I don't have to be a necromancer to talk to ghosts," I
pointed out. "Clairvoyants do that all the time."

"But they don't carry one around with them, do they?
They don't donate energy to make said ghost more mobile. They don't essentially make a servant out of him,
have him run their errands and spy on their enemies and
do a little mental snooping, if they think it's warranted."

"Are you sure?" I asked, because this was kind of relevant right now. "I haven't spent a lot of time around true
clairvoyants—"

"Well, if you had, you might have noticed that they
weren't being followed around by a wad of ghosts."

I smiled suddenly, because he sounded so serious. And
with those glasses . . . "Is that the proper term?"

"What?"

"A murder of crows, a gaggle of geese, a wad of
ghosts . . ."

He put down his instruments in order to look at me

disapprovingly. "You can joke all you like, but it's true. Clairvoyants *talk* to ghosts. What you do goes far beyond that. But, of course, that couldn't possibly be necromancy, which only deals with rotten flesh and oozing bodies and . . . well, whatever else the Circle can dream up to keep the public so scared of us that they lock us away."

"You're locked away because so many of you go bad," Jonas said, from the doorway.

Roger sighed. "You again. I thought you'd gone out to play in the rain."

Jonas opened his mouth, but I got there first. "You have to admit, a lot of necromancers do end up working for the dark."

"Well, of course they do." Roger looked surprised. "What else is open to them?"

"You found work with Tony—"

"Yes, and it's been such fun."

"And there are plenty of freelance necromancers—"

"Patching up vampire boo-boos, what more could a man ask for?"

"—and you *have* magic. You could—"

"*You* have magic. You wouldn't be able to do much in our world without it. But where does it go, hmm?"

"Go?"

"What is it used for?" he asked. "Magic isn't just this lump of power, is it? A reserve to be employed any way you wish. That would be like saying that any human could play the piano beautifully just because he has fingers!"

"Well, of course people have different talents—"

"Yes, and what they can do is largely limited by those gifts. Look at me. When I was a boy, I wanted to be a war mage—"

Jonas made a strangled sound and Roger shot him a glance. "Oh yes, laugh all you like, but the fact remains that I *had the power to do it*. I was strong enough." He turned his attention back to me. "They make you do these tests, you know, when you come in, to measure your magic. To see if you've got what it takes. If you don't generate enough, there's no need to go any further, because you won't be able to cast the kind of spells you'd have to learn anyway."

I nodded.

"Well, I passed. I passed all of them," Roger told me proudly. "There were three of us, from my old neighborhood, and we all tried out at the same time. We'd played war mages growing up, and the idea that it could become a reality . . . it seemed like a dream. But only one of us made it, and it wasn't me."

"But you just said—"

"That I was strong enough. My body generates enough magic. But the path my magic chose to take was one of the unauthorized ones. In other words, I had the potential to be a great necromancer, but not much of anything else. And there's no academy of necromancy, is there? I had all this power, but nowhere to use it."

"So you became a dark mage," Jonas said, crossing his arms.

Roger glanced at him. "No, although that's how the dark gets plenty of its followers, let me tell you. The Circle practically slaps a bow on their heads as they shove them out the door!"

Jonas started to say something, but I cut him off. "So what did you do?"

Roger waved a hand at his collection. "What you see. I became the magical version of a garbage man, someone to defuse old charms before they blow up in someone's face. The same sort of job a scrim gets," he added, talking about magical humans who produce very little magic. They were considered handicapped, although some of the ones I'd met seemed to be doing okay.

"It's an honorable profession," Jonas said stiffly.

"Says the man who never had to do it," Roger returned acidly. "It pays well, yes, because of the danger, so most scrims don't care. But I *did*—yet had no chance of ever moving on to anything better. Do you have any idea how that rankles? How disgusted it makes you with the whole system, which seems designed specifically to ruin your life?"

I thought of Johanna, and wondered if that was how she'd felt. Because, according to Lizzie, the Pythian Court had had its very own necromancer, long before I showed up. And one who specialized in ghosts, at that.

I didn't know why it had surprised me. I knew there were other necromancers around, even those with the much less common specialty of ghost-whispering—my own father was proof of that. Yet it had, just as it had surprised Lizzie, who had slowly put the pieces together.

Along with a plan to profit from them.

At first she'd intended to rat out Johanna, hoping to get her spot as acolyte. But that was before Jo offered to show her the Badlands, and how, if you stayed close enough to the time barrier, you could spy on people without actually being at the party yourself. It was how Lizzie had waylaid me, the second I returned from an earlier trip to Wales. I'd wondered how she'd stepped out of nowhere at just the right moment; I hadn't realized, it was more like no*when*.

Thanks to Lizzie, I'd figured out a few other things, too. Like how an acolyte could travel fifteen hundred years into the past without needing the Tears of Apollo. Because, when you step out of time, it loses its hold on you, doesn't it?

Like it loses the ability to determine when you'll step back in.

Lizzie hadn't told me that; Lizzie didn't know. But I knew what I'd seen, on that brief trip with Billy Joe. How, when we got close to the time barrier, the location had stayed the same, but centuries had passed in seconds. And I was betting that a ghost whisperer with a good mind and a tenuous grip on the Pythian power might also figure out another way to travel through time.

And to bring back a god, when acolytes with more traditional magic had failed.

"So you decided to join the Guild," Jonas was saying. "To wipe out history, erase countless lives, and remake it in your favor. But no, that isn't dark!"

"It also isn't true, and I wasn't talking to you!"

"You weren't a member of the Guild?" I asked.

Roger looked uncomfortable. "It's . . . not in the way you think. Something happened and . . . afterward, there wasn't much choice anymore."

"There are always choices," Jonas said. "You made the wrong ones. Don't try to excuse them now."

"I wouldn't waste my time trying to excuse anything to you!"

"J— Pritkin, can you give us a minute?" I asked. Because I wasn't going to get anywhere this way.

I expected an argument, but didn't get one. "Come outside when you're through," was all he said, and he slammed out.

"Typical of the breed," Roger said, looking after him. "Well, except for the demon part."

"He's not so typical, once you get to know him."

"I don't want to get to know him," Roger said, and then he looked down, at the hand I'd put on his sleeve. "But then, I don't suppose I will . . . will I?"

I met his eyes, and he looked . . . well, he looked like a man who was truly seeing his child for the first time. And the last. "It was the price," I said. "She wouldn't help me unless I promised not to come back."

He shook his head. "She would have, you know. That is, I'm almost sure. She was quite . . . It hurt her, that we didn't get more time with you in London. She said, of all the things life had stolen from her, that was the worst. I didn't understand what she meant, not until . . ."

He looked up, at the second story, where baby me was sleeping. "I suppose that's why I'm not supposed to ask the obvious. Why you're here. Why you couldn't just ask us whatever you wanted in your own time."

I swallowed. Because yeah. It was kind of obvious, wasn't it?

"It's all right," he said softly, his hand tightening on mine. "Considering what we're up against . . . well. We knew how things might have to go."

"But it doesn't have to," I said tentatively. "I could help. . . ."

A blond eyebrow went north. "And did you ask her about that?"

"No."

He smirked. "What would this be, then? Mother is sure to refuse, so you ask Dad?"

"This isn't funny. You don't know what's coming—"

"And I don't want to."

"Why?" I demanded. "You were involved in a group whose whole purpose was to change time!"

"Yes. And I've learned a few things since then."

"Such as?"

He leaned back against the desk, the wavering light sending ripples over the surface of his glasses. He must have seen that it was bothering me, because he took them off and wearily rubbed his eyes. They were the same color as mine, I realized. Mother had blue, too, but hers were a rich almost-violet. But his were the same plain shade as mine.

Human blue.

"It seems like it should be the answer to all our dreams, doesn't it?" he asked, smiling. "If you control time, you control everything. When I was your age, I believed that with absolute certainty. I could do it; I could change the world." He looked heavenward, or maybe just upstairs. "But I think it ended up more the other way around."

I didn't say anything for a moment. I was struggling with whether or not to tell him what was coming. It was the last thing I was supposed to do, but how else could I make him understand? And we *needed* their help.

"Roger—"

"No."

"You won't even listen to what I have to say?" I demanded, confusion, fear, and anger mixing into a familiar acid burn in my stomach. "I could help—"

"Cassie—"

"I could!"

"No. Not even the Pythia has power over death."

It was quiet, but it stopped me cold. "What?"

"Your mother is dying," he told me gently. "Whether by the Spartoi's hand or not, nothing can stop that now."

"But . . . she's immortal—"

"Which does not guard against illness or injury."

"She's been hurt?"

"She's been *starved*. For more than three thousand years. And as with humans who go without sustenance long enough, it takes a toll."

"But . . . I have the Pythian power. If it's energy she needs—"

"It's gone beyond that. She discovered that when she went to court. She could still manipulate the power, still use it, but it didn't repair the damage. I am afraid there is nothing on earth that can."

"But there has to be a way—"

He shook his head. "Do you think she didn't look?"

"There *has* to be!"

"Listen to me." He dropped his tools so he could take me by the shoulders. "You have your mother's gifts, as well as mine. There's no knowing what you'll someday be able to do—what you can do now, if you only knew. No Pythia has ever held that diversity of talents—"

"Then let me use them to help you!"

"You would try, but you would fail. No," he said, shushing me. "Not for lack of ability. But for lack of understanding."

"Understanding *what*?"

The blond head tilted. "That, sometimes, the only way to win is to lose."

Chapter Forty-five

I found Jonas around the side of the house, standing by what looked like a Dumpster. Well, sort of. A few random sparks flew up as I approached, and made pinging noises against the lid, which was half up and reflecting a bunch of moving colors beneath.

"Stay back," Jonas said grimly.

I started to ask why, but then another spark flew out and landed on a paver. Which shimmied and shook—and disappeared. Or so I thought, until I ran into it a second later.

"What?" I asked, standing like a stork so I could examine my possibly broken toe.

Jonas shielded his hand and plucked something disgusting from inside the Dumpster. It was iridescent purple and quivering, like a large piece of fresh liver. It didn't smell like one, though.

"That doesn't help," I said, now torn between holding my nose and my foot.

"Concealment charm. Or it was. You press into it things you wish to hide—jewelry, keys—and it conceals them from detection spells." He glanced at my foot. "And most people's vision."

Great. Like I needed help killing myself. I edged around the sparks. "What else is in there?"

"Junk," he said, dropping the lid with a clatter. "The magical variety: old wards, potions, and amulets. They're at the dangerous stage, with too little magic to properly hold the spell, but too much to be thrown away. The lot needs to be disenchanted, to release the remaining magic, but instead . . ."

"Somebody threw them in a Dumpster."

"Your father." Jonas glowered at the house. "He enchanted the inside of the receptacle, but it remains a serious risk. Collectively, there's a good deal of magic in there, most of it unstable. I can't imagine what he wanted with it."

"The same thing he wanted from the Black Circle," I said, sitting on a nearby bench.

"He told you?"

"Enough."

Jonas sat down beside me.

"It's a long story," I said, "but I'll try to condense it. The Spartoi weren't affected by my mother's eviction spell, because they were demigods. That gave them a tether to this world, allowing them to hunt her. Her spirit is an essential part of the barrier spell, so they hoped killing her would bring it down and reunite them with their father."

"I know that," Jonas said, sounding impatient.

I ignored him.

"Mother stayed ahead of them for a long time, but they finally caught up with her at the Pythian Court. She got away, with my father's help, but they had money and connections, and there were five of them. It was only a matter of time before they found her again."

"So your parents took refuge here." Jonas looked around at the dense forest, the wet ground, and the silvery moon, riding high above the trees. "There are worse places, I suppose."

"A lot worse. Most of the supernatural community ignores vampires. They're seen as weird and dangerous, and they're very distrustful of outsiders, especially mages. They aren't the first place—or the second or third—where anyone would expect a human to go for help, especially not when the vamp in question is a vicious, two-bit hood like Tony."

"Then how did your parents manage it? As you say, vampires rarely trust a mage."

"A mage, no. But a necromancer . . ."

"Ah." He sat back against the bench. It was wet, but I guess when you're dressed in a blanket, it doesn't matter so much. "The one time being on the wrong side of the law is helpful."

"Yes. Tony always liked working with criminals, or at least those under suspicion. Gave them fewer options, and more reason to stay on his good side. Plus, Roger was a decent mage, and the vamps don't get a lot of those."

Jonas nodded. Most of the mages the vamps were able to acquire—except for people like Mircea, who could afford the best—were pretty down-market. Tony had lost a lot of business through the years from spells that went wrong, because somebody hadn't known what he was doing.

"But getting close to Tony didn't solve their problem, did it?" Jonas asked.

"No. It bought them time, but the Spartoi were going to find them sooner or later, and without the Pythian power, my mother wouldn't be able to fight them off."

"And she had a child to think about," Jonas said, watching me.

I stared at the moon, flirting with the branches of the trees. "She knew if they found out about me, I was dead. She also knew that she was dying, because of the starvation that had been dogging her for years. It had driven her to the Pythian Court, but even the Pythian power wasn't enough anymore. It had sustained her, but it hadn't repaired the damage. Nothing on earth could."

"Nothing . . . on earth?" Jonas said, and damn, he was quick. Quicker than I'd been.

"My parents had a plan," I confirmed. "But for it to work, they needed the Spartoi out of the equation. But they had no way to kill them. So they did the next best thing."

"Which was?"

"They killed themselves—at a time when they knew the Spartoi would see it."

"I . . . beg your pardon." Jonas stared at me.

"Tony had ordered a hit on them," I explained, "for refusing to turn me over as commanded. Roger knew the assassin he planned to use—they'd worked with each other before. And while Jimmy wouldn't have been willing to walk away, he was perfectly happy to take a bribe to set up the hit at a time and place of my father's choosing."

"I wasn't referring to logistics!" Jonas stared at me. "You're saying they *wanted* to die?"

"Not wanted to, no. But it was happening anyway. Mother was dying and Roger wouldn't leave her, so—"

"I still don't see how death was a solution to anything!"

I shook my head. "You wouldn't—no one would unless they were an expert on ghosts. It's like my father told me the last time I was here—there's no limit to how much power a ghost can consume. In bodily form, Mother would be easy prey. But as a hungry spirit?"

Jonas just looked at me.

"She knew her fellow gods," I explained. "She knew they would likely try to come back separately, each of them wanting to rule it all. Which gave her a chance. She'd been able to drain powerful demon lords in seconds once. Why not a god, if he was distracted by battle?"

Like, for example, with the very demon lords she'd helped me get on my side.

I'd wondered why she'd been so insistent on talking to the council on Pritkin's behalf, to the point of putting the Seidr spell on me so she could use my time-travel abilities to speak to them from beyond the grave. Yet she'd then spent most of that speech ignoring him, in favor of getting me powerful allies. It made more sense when I realized: she'd also been getting herself a powerful distraction.

"But surely he would notice," Jonas insisted. "And turn on her!"

I smiled slightly. "Yes, he would turn on her. On a newly reinvigorated Artemis, full of stolen godly power, the same power that had weakened him. On the great huntress, the goddess who had torn swaths across whole demon armies; who had followed demon lords back to their home worlds and struck them dead before their thrones; who had single-handedly evicted the entire pantheon from earth and slammed the door behind them. And who knew she was literally facing the fight of her life."

Jonas blinked, absorbing that. "So your mother had to die . . . in order to live."

I nodded. "The gods aren't like us. They don't die so much as . . . fade, when they run out of power. And as damaged as Mother was, only absorbing the full power of another great god would be enough to bring her back. She could drain him dry and return to her old self, but not in the body she was in. It couldn't absorb that much power fast enough. But a ghost could."

"And if you're prepared to die anyway, why not let that death serve double duty and protect your child?"

I nodded.

Jonas frowned. "They were lucky, then, that Tony decided to kill them!"

"Luck had nothing to do with it," I said, and watched his eyes widen.

He had no idea.

"True seers are rare," I reminded him. "And my parents had stressed my abilities enough that Tony's desire for one was at a fever pitch. He didn't really understand how visions worked then; I think he was under the impression that I could just turn it on whenever he wanted, making him big bucks."

"And giving him reason to kill your parents?"

"Not at first. But vamps don't see things the way we do. My father worked for him; my mother and I lived on his estate; we were all under his protection. As far as Tony was concerned, I was already his. But when he commanded that I be brought to court, my parents refused." I shrugged. "The outcome was predictable."

"It doesn't sound predictable to me. To just *assume*—"

I shook my head. "They didn't assume anything. Tony had bugged the cottage—he was always paranoid—forcing my father to have to come up with a spell to control what he heard. But, for some reason, Tony had never considered that the reverse might be true. After all, who would be crazy enough to bug the office of a psychotic master vamp?"

"Your father," Jonas said dryly.

"Yep. And Tony's second-rate mages never found it. That's the problem with cheaping out—you get what you pay for."

"But that left their child in the hands of a *murderer*,"

Jonas said, sitting forward. And then cursing and drawing his blanket back around him, after it slid off one
shoulder.

"You sound so appalled."

"But . . . their *child*. In the hands of one of those
things—"

"That's why it was perfect. Mages stick with mages.
Deliberately putting a child into a vampire's hands
wouldn't even occur to most people."

By Jonas' expression, it clearly wouldn't have occurred
to him.

"And they never intended for me to stay there," I
added. "The idea was for me to hide out at Tony's for a
few years, during which time he had every reason to keep
me healthy, and then to be discovered by Mircea. My father had visited him, supposedly as Tony's emissary, but
really because he wanted to get a look at him—and at his
security. He liked what he saw."

"But they couldn't have known that Mircea would
take you, or even find out about you!"

Sometimes I forgot that, while Jonas knew more about
magic than I probably ever would, he didn't know shit
about vamps. "Remember how I told you that Tony already considered me his, because a human who worked
for him had me?" I asked gently.

Jonas nodded.

"Well, that applies doubly to vamps and their masters.
Usually, someone like Mircea won't come swanning in
and just scoop up one of their children's toys—it's considered poor taste. But if that toy is a valuable asset—especially
a game-changing asset like a possible Pythia? Hell yes,
it's gone. And Tony knew that."

"Yet he managed to keep you a secret for years."

"Because I was only four when my parents died. Tony
essentially lost me at eleven, when one of his own people
ratted him out to Mircea. It actually went pretty much
like my parents had thought."

"Even with the Spartoi?"

"Yes. They knew my mother was all but drained, and
that seers rarely see anything true about themselves. As
hard as it might be to believe that a second-rate gangster

had managed to kill a goddess, if they *saw it happen*, and verified the reason—Tony said that Dad had been cheating him—well." I flipped a hand. "They thought it would work."

"And it did."

"For a while. The Spartoi didn't know of my existence, because Tony kept my identity a closely guarded secret. He was afraid that, if anyone ever found out who I was, they'd tell the Pythian Court and he'd lose his prize. And because I don't think they expected it. Even after I surfaced again as Pythia, it took the Spartoi time to accept that the goddess most famous for her virginity had actually had a child."

"Still, they could have sent you to us! We're the rightful guardians—"

"And gotten me killed? We found a Spartoi in your organization, remember?"

He scowled, but didn't argue, because he couldn't. One of the Spartoi, who could look human enough when they wanted, had infiltrated the Circle's public relations office, because it got all the scandal first. They'd expected my mother's spell to eventually unravel after her death, and when that didn't happen, they'd started looking for a reason.

But they'd never found me.

My parents had hidden me well.

"But surely, if the Spartoi saw your mother killed, it would have satisfied them," Jonas said. "Why did your father also have to die? He had a child—"

"Because he was the *necromancer*. His soul is what keeps them anchored here, just like it kept the spirits of his ghosts anchored in the crazy bodies he built for them. Just like the control crystal keeps a demon anchored inside a golem. Without him, my mother's soul would transition beyond the confines of the barrier—"

"Which would then fall."

"Yes."

Jonas looked faintly amazed. "They thought of everything."

"Except Tony taking the snare into another world. He'd been here for almost a century; there was no reason to think he would suddenly decide to leave. And if he did, that he would go into Faerie. It surprised even Mircea, who knew him better than anyone. No one expected him to suddenly join the other side in the war."

"Why did he?"

"No idea. Like I still don't know what my father was doing in that cellar in London, where Agnes nabbed him, if he wasn't a tried-and-true member of the Guild. He won't explain that, like he won't tell me what he and Mother talked about, that convinced her to release him. There's a lot I still don't understand."

"Such as who made the trap for your parents' souls?"

I glanced at him, slightly surprised. "No, I know that. So do you."

"I do not."

"Jonas," I said gently. "You just saw him working on it."

"That—" Jonas' eyes flew back to the house.

"When Dad said no, you can't have my baby daughter, no, I won't bring her to court, Tony freaked. Nobody told him no. Well, maybe Mircea, but no human. And certainly not one in his service. So he waited awhile, then told Roger he had a problem with an associate and wanted an unusual kind of revenge. He wanted a snare, one that was impossible to break out of, one like Dad had mentioned to him once, months before. He thought it would be amusing to have Roger create the trap for his own soul."

"So your *father* made the snare—"

"No, my father made the talisman." I pulled Billy's necklace out of my shirt. "Like this. Only much more powerful. One that could sustain my parents' souls while they waited for the gods to return. But a goddess' soul takes a lot of feeding, even as a ghost, so the talisman had to be able to draw many times the usual amount of life energy from the world."

Jonas finally looked like something had made sense. "That's why Roger joined the Black Circle—to pillage them."

I nodded. "He joined after Mother released him from jail. He needed a fantastic amount of power to create such a talisman, and didn't know where else to get it. It worked pretty well—he got most of what he wanted before they discovered what he was up to."

"And the rest he took from these . . . things?" Jonas gestured at the Dumpster.

I shrugged. "It's what he knew. And how he persuaded Tony to work with him. Magic can be sold, if you're willing to take the time and risk to extract it from what other people view as junk. And the more unstable it is, the more profit there is in it. It also gave him and Mom a reason to live separately from the main house, because of the risk of blowing it up. And since Tony knew shit about magic, Dad could siphon off a good deal of power from the stuff he was sent with no one being the wiser."

"But why give the talisman to *Tony*?" Jonas persisted. "Wouldn't it have been better to bury it somewhere? Put it in a safe-deposit box? Stick it in a *wall*? Why deliberately give it to that maniac?"

"It's a powerful magical object, and there are plenty of people who could sense it," I reminded him. "Bury it and it could be dug up. Put it in a safe-deposit box, and it could be stolen. Place it in a wall, and said wall might be knocked down. But Tony loves his trophies, and is well equipped to protect them. And with him, there wasn't any risk of the holder dying and the talisman passing to someone who might want to disenchant it. Vampires are the closest things the world has to immortals anymore. Especially paranoid ones like Tony."

We sat in silence for a moment. I don't know what Jonas was thinking, but I wasn't thinking much of anything. The successive shocks of the last few days had left me almost numb. Which was better than the alternative, better than going over all the might-have-beens, all the ways in which everything could have gone so differently. If the gods hadn't fought back quite so hard, if Tony had just stayed put, if Apollo had returned, full of rage and vengeance, and been met, not by a bunch of demons, but by one very hungry, very determined, goddess . . .

But he hadn't.

My parents had had a good plan, but it had failed. And now we were left picking up the pieces. Which would have been a lot easier if they would *listen* to me. But Roger had made it clear that that wasn't happening, just like Mother had the last time I was here.

They'd seen me now; they knew that part of their plan had worked.

They just didn't understand—it wasn't the *right* part.

I realized that Jonas was looking at me. "We're not going to get any help, are we?"

"Not from my parents. What help they could give us, they already have. This is our fight, Jonas."

We listened to sparks ping off the inside of the Dumpster for a while. "I wanted to thank you," he finally said.

"For what?"

"Your warning. About the Black Circle. Caleb arrived with it just before they hit. If we hadn't been prepared . . ."

"I didn't send him with a warning."

"I beg your pardon?"

I took a breath. "I sent him to steal from you. The potion, if he could get it, or the recipe if he couldn't. I guess he decided to talk to you instead."

He bowed his head. "How did we get here?"

"I don't know."

"You were right. I haven't been treating you as a Pythia. It's difficult to see anyone in that role . . . besides her."

"I know."

"But you *are* Pythia." He shot me a glance. "And you're going back."

I nodded. "To find a weapon of the gods, and a man who knows how to wield it."

"And the potion . . . the bottle I found, is it enough?"

"No. But a full one wouldn't be, either. I'm too tired. I barely got us here."

"Then how?"

I looked at the house. "There's another way."

Chapter Forty-six

The woods were lovely, dark and deep.

And then we shifted in.

I hit the ground with Hildegarde on top of me, and then Abigail slammed into her. And finally Rosier appeared out of nowhere and collapsed on top of us, and I started seeing stars. Only no: the silvery trails through the trees were something else.

"Grab her!" I wheezed, and another ghostly presence shot off through the branches, but it wasn't Billy Joe.

He was too busy bitching at me.

"I told you . . . this was a bad . . . idea!"

"Why are you . . . breathless?" I gasped, because I was the one with six hundred pounds on top of me.

"Because that . . . was the most insane thing . . . I've ever done!" he screeched, spectral hat tipped back on his head, hazel eyes huge. "What the *hell*?"

He was talking about our trip through the Badlands, which we'd reentered in order to take a shortcut to the past. Dad had lent me his two ghosts, and with Billy Joe hopped up on Rosier's power, we'd been able to carry four: me, Rosier, and my two new acolytes, who were looking like they very much regretted the trip.

But we'd managed it, although we'd had to exit a few years early in self-defense. And then immediately shift away from the tide of hungry spirits that had poured out after us. It had been like somebody rang a dinner bell—thanks to Daisy, who had wandered too far out and brought something back with her.

Something huge.

I hadn't gotten a good look at it before we were enveloped by a horde of panicked ghosts, all trying to get away from whatever it was and to snack on us in the bargain.

Which was probably what had Daisy so spooked, I thought, as she was dragged back through the trees, protesting.

"I was just stretching my legs," she said haughtily.

"Damn it, woman! You don't have any legs!" the colonel said, his muttonchops vibrating in indignation.

"Do, too," she said, and then peered down worriedly as I struggled to get up.

"And this is no time for a stroll!"

I couldn't agree more.

The idea had been to arrive incognito, because phasing didn't use the Pythian power. Or any magic at all, at least none that a normal magic worker was likely to detect. I assumed that was how Johanna had been evading me: my power could only find her if she used it, or messed up the time stream, and so far, she'd done neither. We, on the other hand, had just made a big damn entrance.

"Think they noticed?" I asked Hildegarde, who was lying on her side, panting.

"If they didn't, they're blind," she wheezed, and sat up.

"You okay?" I asked Abigail, who was still flat on the ground and not looking okay. Her once-nice updo was everywhere, and her brown eyes were like saucers.

"Fail-safe is usually more of an . . . honorary position," she whispered.

"Well, it's been upgraded," Hilde said. "Help me up!"

They struggled back to their feet while the colonel stepped in front of me. Dad's second ghost was an old gentleman wearing a blue uniform with massive epaulets whom I'd briefly met once before. He'd seemed pretty unfriendly then, but Roger vouching for me had worked wonders.

"There appear to be a number of hostiles in the area," he reported.

"Hostiles?" I repeated, and immediately, a series of images started cascading in front of my eyes, courtesy of the power's viewfinder to the future. I hadn't asked for them, but I guess it thought I should know that a forest full of Pythias were converging on our location.

Hilde was right: they knew we were here.

Like, *all* of them.

For a moment, I just stared as what looked like every Pythia in the last fifteen hundred years flipped in front of my eyes.

"They're not supposed to be doing this," Abigail said, apparently seeing the same shit I was. "They're not even supposed to meet!"

"Gertie has been breaking the rules," I told her as my power roamed outward, trying to find a path through the insanity.

And kept on looking.

"She always did," Hilde murmured while Abigail continued to stare into space, caught somewhere between horror and fascination. It didn't look like the Pythian power usually put on this kind of show for the acolytes. At least, I really hoped not, because some of them were out there, too.

Make that all of them. My power's field of vision suddenly widened, leaving me staring at what looked like an army in white. The forest was *crawling*; no way were we getting through all that.

"Change of plan," I told everyone hoarsely.

A moment later, Abigail took off, the colonel on her heels, and I looked at Hilde. "Are you sure you want to try this?"

She nodded. "If I can find Gertie alone, I can phase in and surprise her."

"Yeah, but will she listen?" It wasn't exactly her strong suit.

"She'll listen to me." It sounded certain.

"How do you know?"

She shot me a look. "She's my sister."

And then she and Daisy were gone, too.

"I knew she reminded me of someone," Billy said, but I barely heard him. I was too busy watching the forecast change.

My new helpers were tearing a swath through the trees, shifting here, there, and everywhere. Causing Pythias and acolytes to peel off after them—and the images flipping in front of my eyes to continually rewrite themselves. Until, finally, I saw a slender path opening up ahead.

But not for both of us. Not when Rosier was wearing bright crimson, I guess to celebrate being back to normal, and because God forbid he dress like a commoner. Or make any effort to blend in.

I grabbed him. "We're going to have to split up."

"Split up? We can't split up! Emrys doesn't even know me in this—"

"We have to!" I shook him a little, when he looked like he was going to protest again. "Get to the city. Find Pritkin. Stick to him like glue—"

"And what are you going to do?"

"Get you there," I breathed as someone shifted in, almost on top of us.

Rosier took off—no one ever had to tell him twice—and I shifted an acolyte into two others, who had just appeared through the trees. The trio went down, but there were more right behind them, their dainty dresses in marked contrast to their expressions. Like the first girl, who was already jumping back up, a snarl on her face.

I thought of the group I'd stumbled across last time, and wondered where all that useful timidity went. And then I threw a slow time bubble behind me, at a warning from Billy Joe. And caught a Pythia who had just shifted in, her power signature markedly stronger than the girls'.

Oh, I thought.

That's where.

And then I fled. A quick succession of jumps in the opposite direction from Rosier left my head reeling and my stomach queasy. And my hands shaking from effort, because yeah.

Not going to be doing this much longer.

"Options," I breathed, but that was the problem—my power was already showing them to me, and they all sucked. There were four Pythias zeroing in on the power of my last spell, and no way could I take four.

"Billy—"

"For the record, I think this is a *really* bad—"

"*Billy—*"

"Maybe we could talk to them, try to explain—"

"They don't want explanations. They want my head!"

"And a bunch of hungry ghosts don't? You don't want to go back there!"

"Well, I don't want to stay here!" I said shrilly as a tree exploded beside us.

"Shit!" Billy said, and shifted.

But the weird, formless vault of nontime was a lot less formless this go-round. "What did you do?" I asked, staring at the X-ray landscape around us.

The forest was still there, in chalky off-white sketches, like an architect's drawing. I put out a hand, and the exploding bits of wood from the tree passed right through it, twisting slowly in the air but weightless, like they weren't even there. Because they weren't—or, rather, I wasn't.

But I wasn't in the Badlands, either, at least not entirely.

"What did you *do*?" I asked again as a figure appeared through the trees.

"I . . . don't think I totally committed," Billy said, looking as spooked as I was.

"What does that mean?"

"I think it means we're sort of . . . on the fringes," he said. "Like what Lizzie did to you. You're not at the party, but you've got your nose pressed to a window."

I didn't answer. I was busy watching a familiar-looking Pythia stalk me through the brush. One with big dark eyes and long, dark curls and cheap little tinsel earrings— and a power signature that almost knocked me down, because she was unbelievably strong.

Or had a hell of a lot of acolytes with her, I thought grimly, as she walked right through me.

And paused.

Eudoxia, my brain supplied as she whirled, her usually pleasant face vicious.

"Billy—"

"We're skimming along the surface of time," he told me quickly. "She can't see us, but she can probably feel us—"

"Then take us farther out!"

"I can't take us farther out, or we're gonna be ghost

fodder! Plus, I only have so much power. Every time I transition, I get weaker, and that little demon bastard's not here to top me up!"

"So what would you suggest?"

"Athenais! Lydia! Gwenore!" the woman called.

"Run!" Billy said.

"Over here!"

We ran.

It was surreal, not bothering to dodge the trees, just pelting straight through them. And straight through the three hazy figures suddenly appearing out of nowhere, right in my path. One of them, Gertie's mentor, Lydia, stopped in her tracks and spun around as I passed, her black, witchy garments flowing about her.

And slashed her walking stick through my X-ray body.

I swear, for a second, I felt it—or felt something, like a rush of wind.

One that packed a punch great enough to send me staggering.

"Here!" she called. "She's phasing!"

"So much for that idea," Billy said as I recovered, which would have been easier if I hadn't tripped over a tree root.

A tree root that was suddenly normal colored, and solid. Like the patch of ground all around it. Like my foot—

For a second, until Billy jerked me back—physically and into nontime—just as Lydia's stick jabbed down where I'd been standing.

"Cass! Be careful! If they touch you—"

"Got it," I gasped, ducking as that damn stick slashed through the air again, just over my head.

And then I was tearing toward the tree line.

"Options!" I breathed, because the river was coming up. *"Good* options," I clarified, which didn't seem to help.

And then I saw—

"What are you *doing*?" Billy asked as I broke out of the trees onto a rocky beach—and kept on going.

Onto the water.

It was no less solid under my feet than the land, despite the fact that my brain kept telling me it should be. It was more than a little trippy, though; the skies were overcast, and the wind was surging, sending waves rolling all around me. Like the ones slapping the ghostly outline of ships along the opposite shore, making them bob at their anchors . . .

"Billy?" I said, looking down, because I'd just realized my feet were wet.

And then we were under.

"Sorry! Sorry!" he said, jerking my soggy form back into nontime. "It's a learning curve!" he yelled as I coughed out a lungful of water.

And then froze, a hand over my mouth, as two shadows splashed across my body.

I looked up to see two Pythias walking through the waves just overhead, as if on a glass ceiling above me. One had her face turned away, but the other . . . was Isabeau. She looked older now, with a few crow's-feet around the big gray eyes, and strands of gray in the abundant auburn hair. But it was definitely her.

And her companion, I saw a second later, was Eudoxia.

Bet they have a lot to talk about, I thought viciously, before Billy jerked me down.

They didn't notice, despite the fact that the water was no more opaque than anything else here. Because who looks beneath your feet? But I could see them perfectly, walking through nontime as if it was no big deal, as if strolling on the surface of a wavy sea just outside time's grip was an everyday occurrence. And maybe it was.

They had a word for it, after all.

"That's just so freaky," Billy said, and I turned to agree. Only to see him standing eyeball-to-eyeball with some type of shark. The waterway here was a tidal river, according to Rosier, letting out into the nearby sea, and deep enough for oceangoing vessels to make their way up it.

Or oceangoing fish.

"Death has been so much more interesting than life," he told me, staring at the creature in fascination. "Sure, you give up some stuff—some really important stuff—but then you get to do things like this." And he reached out, one finger just poking through the skin of time.

And booped the shark's nose.

"How close to the real world are we?" I asked, as the startled predator raced off.

"Close as I can get us. I am *not* comfortable with wacky ghost land. We need to get back where we belong—"

"Not with them chasing us."

Hazel eyes cut to me.

A couple minutes later, I was wading ashore, a long, wooden dock on one side, and the walls of Arthur's city on the other. While behind, sailors yelled and fell back as the sails they were struggling to furl suddenly went up in flames. Because a ghost tripping on demon power was ripping through the line of ships.

I crouched on the rocky soil near the dock and watched Billy go a little crazy. He almost never had energy to spare, especially lately when I'd been too tapped out to feed him. But that hadn't been true of Rosier, and he was taking full advantage. On half a dozen ships, barrels hit the ocean waves, lanterns went flying, sailors yelled.

And hot oil flew, causing fires to spring up everywhere.

Eudoxia started while still among the waves, her forehead wrinkling suspiciously. Isabeau looked around from the deck of one of the now merrily burning ships, where she'd just rematerialized. Maybe because searching something when your feet keep trying to float through the floor isn't so easy.

Or when the massive sails, which had been rolled tightly against the weather, abruptly unfurled, the wind billowing them out to full capacity, causing the ship to jerk hard against the anchor.

Until that line was cut, too.

The mighty vessel careened off toward the opposite shore, the startled Pythia still on board, and Billy swooped down beside me. "I'll keep 'em busy, do what I can to lead 'em off," he said, grinning like a maniac.

"Get back as soon as you can," I said, watching Eudoxia shift to her beleaguered former apprentice. "I'm going to need you. I can't use the power without bringing every Pythia in history down on my head."

He made a face, but then grinned again, having too much fun to argue. He pulled me back into real time, my feet suddenly encountering hard rocks and shifting sand, and I watched him zoom away. And then switched my gaze to the forest, scanning for movement among the trees.

I didn't see any, but they were out there, and Billy was right; this wouldn't fool them for long.

I turned and headed for Camelot.

Chapter Forty-seven

Despite everything, I took a moment to stare at the real Camelot. According to Rosier, it hadn't been called that until the thirteenth century, when some French poet decided he liked the name. In all the older texts, Arthur's main seat was Caerleon, the sprawling stone-built city of the Romans, originally designed to house the six thousand soldiers of the Second Legion Augusta.

And looked like it still did.

On my left was a bustling port town, where white stuccoed buildings with red terra-cotta roofs sat side by side with thatched Celtic structures. Straight ahead, peering over some rooftops, was the old Roman amphitheater, its multicolored pennants shining brilliantly even on an overcast day. To the right, above a rise of ground, were the turreted stone walls surrounding the old city, built by the Second Augusta to withstand tribes of warring Celts. And, finally, on a hill overlooking it all, were the tall gray towers of a castle.

I teared up unexpectedly, I didn't know why. Something about seeing a legend in the flesh, so to speak. Or maybe it had to do with the way the late-afternoon light hit the city, glinting redly off marble arches and sparkling fountains, and adding life to the gold paint someone had used to carefully pick out the scrollwork on centuries-old porticoes.

Of course, there were other things the light hit, too. Like the many-times-patched plaster that was crumbling yet again; the rusted, salt-encrusted ironwork meant for a drier clime; the wooden roof tiles that had been carefully shaped and painted to resemble the terra-cotta ones that nobody could get anymore; and the once proud Roman road cutting through it all, its surface now pitted and potholed. It looked like a city trying to recreate the splendors of the past, but not getting it quite right.

Yet that didn't seem to matter so much. In fact, to me, it just made it all the more impressive. Not Hollywood pretty and unbelievably clean, like the only Camelots I'd ever seen, but like people had lived and fought and loved and died here.

Maybe because they had.

According to Rosier, the cracks in the plaster weren't artistic license but mended bones, the rivers of rust below the old gutters tears of blood, the broken cobblestones fractured teeth. Rome might have built this place, but it hadn't defended it. It had up and left one day, with almost no warning. Leaving the local people, many of whom thought of themselves as Roman, too, after centuries of its rule, high and dry.

And prey to every invader with a boat and a sword, and every hill tribe looking for plunder.

Until Uther, with his uncouth swagger and keen mind, and a grandfather who'd served in the Roman cavalry. And a son, born in the city his father had bled for, and dedicated to the same goal: holding civilization together. And, for a while, they'd actually pulled it off.

Just like in the stories, the old fortress had become the base for cavalry units trained in the Roman style. And while not quite the knights in shining armor of the fables, they were devastatingly effective against the disorderly foot soldiers of the local chieftains. The revolts that followed Roman withdrawal were put down, the Saxons repulsed, and for one brief, shining moment, peace had reigned. An era that must have seemed truly magical to a people rent by war both before and after.

An era the world would remember as Camelot.

"Girl! Are you deaf? I said get out of the way!"

It took me a second to realize that the guard was talking to me. He was one of a group of soldiers who'd run up to help the beleaguered sailors. While I was just standing there, dripping, in the rough woolen dress and cloak Augustine had whipped up for me, to approximate female attire of the period.

But not female attire of the wealthy, I guessed, because I got a cuff to my ear when I took too long.

I got out of the way.

And scrambled up the hill to the shade of an oak tree, where a Medusa snarl of eels was lying in the dirt. They were waiting to have their skins stripped off by a curly-haired boy who did not appear enthusiastic about the work. But not because of the bloody eel carcasses, which he handled with the indifference of long experience.

But because he was missing what looked like the greatest medieval faire ever.

And so I stared some more. I'd heard the sound of a crowd from the pier—music playing, hawkers calling, people talking—but had thought it was coming from the city. And maybe some of it was. But the teeming mass in front of me was plenty big enough to account for it all on its own.

The walled city on the one side, and the port town on the other, had a grassy gap in between them. And that, plus the open land along the river, was clogged with people. I'd hoped to catch up with Rosier and help him locate Pritkin before Billy got back, but how was I supposed to find him in this?

How was I supposed to find *anyone*?

Everywhere I looked there were tents and performers and overly excited dogs. There were drunk adults and laughing kids and gap-toothed old women selling mead. Over by the city walls, an archery contest was going on, with regular roars of approval from the crowd. Closer in, a swarthy type with a hooknose and a wand was painting stories in the air with fire: battling knights and fierce dragons and a princess in a tower. And a little way off, a couple of enterprising guys had rigged up a clay oven on a cart, so they could sell fresh-baked pies to the crowd.

The pies smelled heavenly, to the point that my mouth started watering, but I had no money. So I pulled out a pouch I'd slung around my neck, because I couldn't afford to be hungry right now. Although cranberry nut bars seriously lost out compared with fresh-baked meat and bread.

Only somebody else didn't seem to think so.

I looked down to see Eel Boy staring longingly at my snack. For a kid who worked at a food stall, he wasn't exactly overfed. The arms and legs under the rough tunic were thin, and the cheeks, while not sunken, lacked the expected layer of baby fat. I glanced at the burly guy on the other side of the tree, stirring a pot of stew, who looked like he ate all the leftovers, and who wasn't paying us any attention.

Then I crouched beside the boy. "Want one?"

He looked from the peeled bar to me and back again. And licked his lips. But he didn't take it.

"It's yours," I said, and took out another, after putting his on the edge of my dress.

I got my wrapper off and started eating, and the next time I looked down, he had a mouth full of PowerBar and was chewing furiously. I grinned. I'd still rather have had a pie.

I ate my bar while scanning the crowd some more, but instead of Rosier I kept finding fey. Maybe because they were everywhere, making up at least a third of the revelers. And while I didn't know a lot about the Light Fey, I knew enough to find it creepy that members from the three major houses were standing around the same pie wagon, and not trying to kill each other.

Well, the Blue and Green were standing around the wagon, debating the virtues of venison versus lamb. The Svarestri, in their black-and-silver finery, were just nearby, watching everything with flat gray eyes, their expressions making even the drunker members of the crowd give them a wide berth.

The pie guys kept looking at them narrowly, like they were driving off business, and eventually picked up their mobile kitchen and moved a dozen yards away, over by some sausage sellers.

The Svarestri didn't even seem to notice. They stayed where they were, arms crossed, eyes fixed on the docks. Where people trying to bring up baskets of slippery fish were being dive-bombed by seagulls and blocked by the crowd that had stopped to gawk at the still-smoking ships.

Or at the new one just coming into view.

I hadn't noticed it before, because it was almost impossible to see at any distance. Or even closer up, because it looked like the whole thing was coated in the cloaks the fey wore, the kind that reflected whatever was around them. The result was a ship that looked like it was made out of the waves themselves, translucent and watery bright, with sails that caught and reflected the rays pouring through a gap in the clouds.

It was beautiful.

And suddenly, that traffic problem got a whole lot worse. A trumpet pealed, a distant, pure note that had heads turning and conversations falling silent. And the next thing I knew, I was being squashed against the tree, me and Eel Boy, who had grabbed his basket protectively when what looked like the whole damn city descended on us.

After the second elbow to the ribs, I climbed up the tree after the boy, who was scaling it like it was horizontal.

Of course, some of it was, the burls and knots on the old trunk making convenient hand- and footholds, allowing us to get above the crowd. We found a perch on a more or less level limb, where he plopped his basket down and continued shucking eels as the throng surged below. And as the ship came closer, gliding silently up the river while more soldiers joined the fray, shouting orders at each other to hold back the crowd.

"Clear a path! Clear a path!"

The locals had obviously dealt with the soldiers' short tempers before. Because there was a sudden surge away from the docks. Except for a couple of sailors, who were shoved unceremoniously aside, arguing loudly because their boat was still burning.

Nobody cared.

"Clear a path! Clear a path, damn you!" The dock *was* clear now, but the soldiers weren't satisfied, forging a wedge into the crowd, cutting a route from the pier to the grassy open area between the two towns. They'd just finished when the ship glided to a stop.

"Who is it?" I asked the boy, whose disbelieving dark eyes rolled up at me.

"Seriously?"

I blinked at him. Had that been sass?

He smirked.

That had definitely been sass.

"Who else would have a ship made out of *water*?" he asked.

"It's not actually made out of water," I said. "It just looks like it is."

"Oh, right." He didn't bother to hide a smile.

I looked back at the dock. And was just in time to see the hull, sails, and even the delicate rigging, which had all been gleaming translucent pale in the sunlight a second ago, suddenly disintegrate. And plunge back into the river, a fantastic mass of water all falling at once, with a splash big enough to drench the crowd almost as far as our tree.

But not the small knot of people who had appeared on the dock.

Most of them I didn't know, but that wasn't true of the two dark-haired women in the center. Nimue walked out of the tsunami as dry as if the water didn't dare touch her. She was wearing a sea green dress with layers of silk so fine they foamed up around her like the tide. And might as well have been made of it, when compared to the rough wool of most of the crowd.

They'd fallen largely silent, just staring. But not at the dress, or at the jewels scattered through her long, dark hair that could have been captured seawater, or at the dark-haired warriors surrounding her, tall and chiseled, with armor and shields that lacked the dull glint of metal in favor of the shifting, mercurial nature of her element. In fact, as amazing as it seemed, they weren't looking at her at all.

They were looking at her companion.

The princess was dressed more simply, her rich brown hair in a simple plait, her dark green dress devoid of adornment, maybe because of her status as prisoner. And there was no doubt that that was what she was. The guards weren't there to protect Nimue, who was basically an army all on her own. They were hedging her granddaughter, who must have been recaptured after the fight.

And who wasn't looking so good. The strong, vibrant woman I'd seen last time was gone. She looked pale, defeated, and more than a little ill. And that was before she suddenly collapsed.

The crowd reacted before the fey did, with a rumble of surprised distress and an unconscious surge forward. One that had the soldiers shouting again and pushing back. And people falling and getting trampled, and chaos threatening to break out.

Until another blast of trumpets shivered through the air, and a mass of horses and riders burst out of the walled town.

The soldiers on crowd control were dressed in rough woolen tunics, crude leather belts and leggings—in short, like everyone else, except for iron helmets. But the men galloping toward us wore finely wrought bronze armor that looked like fish scales and gleamed ruddily in the late-afternoon sun. And blazingly white tunics and crimson capes, embellished with a bright red dragon.

My companion suddenly surged to his feet, excited in a way he hadn't been over magic ships or fey queens. He stood on the branch to get a better view, his eyes gleaming. "The king!" he shouted. "It's the *king*!"

The cry was taken up by the crowd, loud enough to shake the leaves around us. And a second later, I saw him, too, the blond-haired king from the mirror at the head of the riders. Ones he didn't need, because the crowd parted before him like the tide.

He paused next to Nimue, but only to pull the unconscious woman—his half sister, I realized—onto his horse. Other horses had been brought for the queen and her entourage, but Arthur didn't wait for them to mount. As soon as the princess was secure, he turned and spurred back the way he'd come, the crowd surging and cheering, the soldiers shoving and fighting, and me just sitting there, silently.

Because, for once, fate had done me a favor.

I didn't know where to find Johanna, and if she continued to phase instead of using the Pythian power, that wasn't likely to change. But it didn't need to. Because I might not know where she was, but I knew what she *wanted*.

And the last time I'd seen it, it had been in the princess' hand.

I looked around one more time for Rosier, but there was virtually no chance to locate him in all this. I'd gotten him here; I was going to have to trust that his knowledge of the city would be enough to help him find his son. I had to talk to the princess, which meant that I had to get in that castle.

I started looking for a way to get down from the tree.

And then somebody grabbed me.

Chapter Forty-eight

I jerked my head around, hoping to see blond hair and green eyes—and I did. Just not the right ones. I found myself staring at a stunningly beautiful face: perfect masculine features, flashing emerald eyes, hair like captured sunlight. And sculpted lips that curved in a vicious little smile.

A fey, I thought in confusion.

A Blarestri fey, judging from the blue velvet jerkin.

A Blarestri fey king who wanted his staff back, and oh, *shit.*

The green eyes abruptly darkened, from emerald to jade, and the fingers on my arm dug into the flesh. "I know what you are," he hissed. "I know what you *did.*"

Well, that makes one of us, I thought, a little hysterically. Because the way I remembered it, he'd won our last encounter. He'd shoved me through a roof, into a group of Pythias, who had promptly sent me back home. Leaving him with the staff, which he'd decided to lend to Pritkin, and why was that on me?

But I didn't say that. I didn't say anything. Because a knife had just flashed into his hand, between one blink and the next, and the words died in my throat.

Which meant that my mouth was closed when a bucket of eel guts was dumped on his head.

"Go!" the boy told me, and jumped into the furious crowd, many of whom had just gotten splattered, too.

Good idea, I thought, and hit the ground on the other side of the limb, scrabbling away on hands and knees.

Thankfully, Nimue's group had just departed, spurring their horses toward the castle, and thus ending the crowd's interest in the docks. So everybody was swarming back this way. And I do mean *everybody*. I was almost trampled a dozen times, along with being knocked about, pushed, and yelled at, none of which mattered because I was back on my feet, I was darting through the crowd, I was—

Getting jerked back against the torso of an incredibly powerful, incredibly bloody, incredibly pissed-off ancient being.

And then someone tried to burn us to death.

The king let go, the crowd scattered, people yelled. And I stared up at a mass of fluttering flames, dancing overhead. Flames that resolved themselves into birds, small ones with fiery wings, molten eyes, and bodies that flung a cascade of sparks—

Mostly behind me, I realized, as they swarmed through the air in a vicious arc that never once touched me. But which threw the equivalent of a wall of fire between me and the king. I spun in time to see Caedmon enveloped by flapping flame, and looking like he hadn't expected that, either.

And then someone grabbed my hand.

It was the swarthy, hooked-nosed performer, who had been entertaining the crowd a second ago, and was now pulling on me. "Hurry! It won't hold him!"

"Who—" I began, just as the face morphed into another green-eyed blond, this one with stubbled cheeks, hair like a cow's breakfast, and a nose that wasn't much better than the glamouried version. But which was a lot more familiar. "Myrddin! What are you doing here?"

"Rescuing you!"

"No! You can't—don't get involved in this!"

"I'm already involved," he said, jerking me into the crowd.

"What? Why?"

He stared at me in amazement. "I lost the staff."

And then we were pelting ahead, down the riverbank and through an open-air market, with vendors and stalls and a tavern-in-a-tent, its benches spilling out into the middle of the road, and filled with fey.

Blarestri fey.

"Shit," Pritkin said fervently, although the fey barely seemed to notice us.

Until a furious command rang through the air: "Stop them!"

And suddenly, benches were being knocked over, a dozen blue-clad giants were on their feet, and twelve swords were glinting in the sun.

"Shit!" Pritkin said, on a slightly higher note, and split. Literally.

I'd seen him do something like it before, but I'd been a little distracted at the time. So it was a shock to see his body replicate itself in a long string, like an accordion of Pritkins, spilling out of his skin. And out of mine, I realized, as a couple dozen Cassies jumped away from my body, scattering in all directions.

Not that it helped. Unlike the Svarestri we'd fought last time, these fey weren't fooled. Maybe because they hadn't taken their eyes off us the whole time.

Until half the river suddenly slammed into them—and the tavern, and us—in a wave the size of a house.

I came up gasping, and swimming on what had been low but dry land a second ago, and was now a new inlet.

But I didn't think Pritkin had done it, because he'd just pulled a major spell out of his ass, and you didn't get two of those back-to-back. And because some Green Fey, two men and a woman, were sitting along a tree limb, mugs in hands, grinning down at the chaos. And especially at their floundering blue counterparts, who didn't seem to appreciate the dunking.

"I thought the Green were mad at us," I said, staring up at them, because the fey made no damn sense at all.

"Slightly . . . annoyed," Pritkin corrected breathlessly.

"They tried to *kill* us!"

"Those were the queen's personal guard, and they were under orders. These aren't. And I am Green Fey—partly."

"And this means?"

"That," he said as several furious Blue Fey staggered back to their waterlogged feet and headed our way.

And were bitch-slapped by another wave for their trouble.

"Better run, brother," one of the Greens called helpfully.

"Obliged!" Pritkin called back.

"Don't mention it. Wouldn't want to deprive Mother of the pleasure of dealing with you herself!"

And then I was jerked up, and we were running on top of the water, the way I'd seen the princess do the last time we were here. Not that we were as graceful. But then, she hadn't had so many waves to worry about, causing the "ground" to feel like a fun house floor. Or as much floating debris to jump over. Or as many fey acting like blond-haired sharks, and trying to grab her from below.

Although that was preferable to what looked like a giant fist made out of air, the outline formed from twigs and debris, which plunged into the water just behind us. It threw us off our feet and almost caused us to get jerked up when it reversed course. But one of my doubles went flying instead, like a blow-up doll caught in a hurricane.

And was ripped apart a second later, exploding far overhead, like a firework made out of steam.

I stared upward, caught between terror and more terror, and seriously considered shifting. But before I could, Green Fey flooded the scene, what had to be two or three dozen of them, running across the grass-turned-lake-turned-battlefield, not attacking the Blue Fey or helping us, but getting terribly, terribly *in the way*.

The wind stopped, I guessed because the king, while perfectly happy to make mincemeat out of us, was unwilling to do the same to a bunch of his fellow fey. Especially when their queen had a vicious temper and was in a murderous mood already. And, anyway, he didn't need to.

It wasn't like we had anywhere to go.

Except back under.

Another wave hit, and before I had a chance to take a breath, or even to close my mouth, we were underwater again. And swimming for all we were worth. And slogging through the grasses at the edge of the brand-new lake. And emerging, not as Cassie and Pritkin, but as two waterlogged Blue Fey, our gorgeous attire ruined, our blond hair straggling around our faces, just like the half dozen others also wading ashore.

Every single one of which was being met by another fey, like the one who stepped in front of us. He must have been a new arrival, because his uniform was dry—and fancy, with gold embroidery in a design I didn't understand but that Pritkin apparently did. Because he stopped abruptly.

The officer—at a guess—took a look at the arm Pritkin had slung around my waist, to help support me, and his eyes narrowed. He said something I couldn't hear, because I had water in my ears as well as my lungs. Until I went into a coughing fit, and they popped.

"—half-drowned," Pritkin was saying. "Getting him to a healer."

The officer looked at me some more, and I attempted to look half-drowned.

It wasn't difficult.

It also wasn't enough.

Wind blew up around us a second later, like a miniature cyclone that caused my hair to flutter and my heart to pound. But it wasn't like before; it wasn't an attack—at least not yet. More like being caught in an oversized hair dryer.

But whatever it was, Pritkin didn't like it. I heard him swear, and then saw him throw out a hand. And as quickly as it had blown in, the little gale died. Leaving me staring around, my nose running, my half-dried hair stuck to my face—and the officer looking far more relaxed.

"May I get him to a healer now?" Pritkin demanded, the words more polite than the tone.

But he wasn't rebuked. "We were told to check. Go."

We went, stumbling through the debris of the market, and up a path by the shore, trying to keep to the grassy edge to avoid leaving muddy footprints in our wake. Because we would be. The Green Fey's illusions, like much of the rest of their magic, seemed to involve water in some way, and we were losing ours.

Fast.

I looked down to see skinny, freckled arms and rough, wet wool, instead of muscles and velvet. Pritkin still had his illusion, complete with cape, which he threw around me to hide my very un-fey-like features. But it wouldn't last for long. Beads of water dotted the "cloak" and stuck to his "skin," like his whole body was sweating.

And then I saw a young bearded man gesturing furiously from inside a tent.

It was across a dirt path from the riverbank, where dozens of sheets and articles of clothing had been laid out in the sun to dry. And where a young woman was whacking the hell out of some more piled up on a rock with a wooden paddle. We headed for the tent, crossing the path and dripping in the dirt, leaving an obvious trail behind us.

Until the man turned over a tub of water, spilling it everywhere. "Mallt!" he called.

A woman in a neighboring tent, older, plumper, and surrounded by children, nodded. And sent the bevy of kids out into the path, churning up the mud, and adding dozens of footprints to our own. And then running up the street, laughing and playing, and hindering a group of fey coming this way.

The tent flap closed behind us, and what looked like a skin of water splashed the dirt at our feet. Pritkin, now back to normal, went to his haunches, head down, breathing hard. And looking like he might pass out.

But he didn't get a chance.

"Under here," the man told me. "Quickly!"

We crawled under a table strewn with dirty clothes, some hanging off the sides, waiting their turn for a wash. Baskets heaped with more were quickly shoved in front of us. And then the tent flap was pulled open again, leaving me peering out from between pieces of soiled laundry at the little bit of street I could see.

"Damn fey," the man muttered. "You'd think it was their town!"

"They think it *is* their town," the woman said, coming in. She was red-haired and red-faced from exertion, and picked a fussy carrot-topped baby out of a basket. "They say they protect it—"

"Rather protect it myself, and take my chances. They treat us like slaves, not men in our own land!"

"And what do y'think the Saxons would do?"

"The Saxons are *men*. You can outfight 'em, you can outlive 'em, or you can outbreed 'em." He smoothed a hand over the baby's fiery fuzz. "Or, worse comes to worse, you can mix w' them and make a new people. What can you do with bastards that never die? They don't belong here, and I'm not the only one sayin' it!"

"Well, don't say it so loud," his wife said. "You'll upset the babe."

The man looked at Pritkin for support, who nodded, still breathless. "The fey . . . will protect us, but keep us exactly as we are . . . while the world goes on without us."

The man looked at his wife. "Y'see? Bad times come, but sometimes they need to. Or you die anyway, of stagnation and rot. I know how I'd rather go out!"

"Would you stop that talk?" the woman hissed, hugging her child. "I want her protected!"

"And when they come for her? Who'll protect her then?"

The woman looked at him fiercely for a moment, then deliberately pinched her child, I didn't know why.

Until I saw two fey breaking off from the group to approach the tent.

I pulled back into the shadows.

"There!" the woman said, her voice annoyed. "What did I tell you?"

"What's wrong w' the child, anyway?" her husband's voice demanded. "Have you lied to me, woman? Are you part banshee?"

She snorted. "More like you. Snore loud enough to wake the dead, he does," she told someone.

"How would you know?" he demanded. "When do I get t'sleep? All night, it's the same thing—loud as thunder, she is!"

The man had a point. The kid's outrage was impressive. And I wasn't the only one to think so. One of the fey I could now see was wincing in pain, while the other looked vaguely horrified.

"Picking up, good sirs?" the man yelled.

"What?" The first fey looked at him while the other started trying to push inside, I guessed to start a search.

But the cauldron the couple was using to boil clothes was in the way, bubbling merrily. The man plunged in a paddle, and steam erupted everywhere, causing the fey to jerk back. And then the woman was blocking the small avenue that was left, along with the human foghorn.

"Let me by," the fey told her.

"What?"

"I said, let me by!"

"You'll have to speak up," she screamed, almost in his face. "She's teething."

"What?"

"Teething!"

The fey looked at the child in concern, as if it was some alien creature. A tiny, smelly, very loud alien creature. It suddenly occurred to me to wonder how often the fey dealt with babies, considering their birth rate.

Judging by his face, not a lot.

"Then what's that smell?" her husband asked, leaning over.

"You're right," the woman said to him, peering into some sort of proto diaper. And releasing a stench worse than anything the dirty clothes were giving off. "I guess she's not teething yet, after all."

The fey's look of horror intensified.

The man plunged another paddle into the water, giving off a cloud of steam like a dragon's breath. "Picking up or dropping off?" he asked again, in a cheerful bellow.

"Neither," the fey said, and fled.

The woman stayed outside the tent, to ward off any more interlopers with the terrifying child, while the man went around to the other side of the table, where Pritkin had already scrambled out. And pulled open the back flap of the tent, to look out over the open space between the towns.

"All right, then, Myrddin?" he asked.

Pritkin nodded. "Thanks to you."

"Glad t' help. But they'll be back, when they don't find anythin' elsewhere. Best be gone by then."

"Can you glamour?" I asked.

Pritkin shook his head. "Not now. Not for two."

"Not two. One." I pulled my hood up. "I'm going to the castle—"

"The castle?"

"I need to see Morgaine."

"Why?"

"To ask her about the staff. She was the last to have it—"

"And why do you want it?"

The question was as hard as the hand suddenly wrapped around my wrist. I looked down at it in confusion. "Does it matter right now?"

"Yes!" He looked at me, green eyes searching. "The king caught up with me, after you disappeared, at a camp in the forest. I think he would have killed me, if there hadn't been three or four covens' worth of witches around!"

"I'm sorry—"

He shook his head. "I got away. But he is convinced there was a conspiracy between us to steal the staff. Either that, or that you were using me to get your hands on it for some nefarious purpose he won't talk about—"

"And you believe him?"

"I don't know what I believe! I saw what you did. I saw you save those children, back at camp, and then I saw you get taken by those . . . those magic workers. And then the king said—" He stopped abruptly, his eyes on my face, searching. "I don't know what to believe," he repeated. "But you're not getting out of my sight until I get some answers!"

I licked my lips. I couldn't tell him—he knew too much already. But I couldn't *not* tell him, either, if it meant sitting here until the fey caught up with us. And he would—he was absolutely that stubborn.

"All right," I compromised. "I'll tell you what I can. But not here."

"Where, then?"

"I told you." I looked up, at the distant gray towers. "I need to get in there. Can you help?"

Pritkin thought for a moment, his eyes on the castle. And then they switched to something coming down the main road, next to the theater. The one leading to the walled city.

I couldn't tell what it was; too much dust was billowing around. But I guessed Pritkin could. "I have a way in," he told me. "But you may not like it."

"Trust me. If it gets me in, I'll like it."

Chapter Forty-nine

I didn't like it. "Are you sure there's no other way?" I asked, frowning.

One pale brow arched. "You'd prefer to fight your way in?"

"I'd prefer more than half a shirt!" I said, tugging at the handkerchief hem, trying to get it to meet the skirt. Which would have been easier if said skirt had started higher than my hips. And if the tugging wasn't threatening the shirt's already low neckline. And that was despite me picking out the most modest of the costumes.

"Isn't this going to get them looking at me more, not less?" I demanded.

"But not at your face," Pritkin replied, and ducked when I threw a pillow at him.

The little wagon we were in was full of them, probably because the thing didn't have springs. Just costumes, masks, rolls of canvas backdrops, and a large, stuffed dragon's head on a stick. We'd had no choice but to join the players, who had rumbled into town during the chaos, because there were anti-glamourie charms on the castle. Pritkin's abilities wouldn't help us there, even if he rested up. Which was why I'd slapped on a face full of makeup to go with the bright crimson outfit.

Of course, that wouldn't help, either, if somebody ratted us out.

"Are you sure you can trust them?" I asked as the wooden box we were in swayed and shook, partly because of the road, but also because the girls up top kept leaning over.

Tonight they played for the court, tomorrow for the townspeople, and they were busy drumming up business. Which meant that, instead of furtively sneaking in through a back door like I'd hoped, we were heading for the main city gate on the medieval version of a party bus. A bright red, blue, and green party bus, with a bunch of waving, shimmying, half-naked girls on top. One word to a guard . . .

But Pritkin didn't seem worried.

"I arranged the job for them," he told me. "They'll help us."

"There are other jobs."

"Not as many as you'd think." He was trying on different wigs, because he was better known at court than I was, and the current one did him no favors. Of course, that would have been true of anyone except Ronald McDonald.

I pulled it off, substituting a tasteful, forgettable brown.

"They started in Constantinople, playing to large audiences," he said as I tried to stuff his cowlick underneath the wig. "But once the emperor closed all the theaters, they had to take to the road. Their fortunes have been mixed ever since."

"He closed the theaters?"

Pritkin nodded, looking up at me with a grin. "Ironic, when you consider that his own wife was an actress before they met. Theodora was famous for dancing in nothing but a single ribbon. And then there was that business about Leda and the swan—"

"A swan?" I frowned.

"More like a goose and some strategically placed grain. They say she—"

"I don't want to know," I said quickly.

He grinned some more. "But he needed the church on his side, and they don't like the theater."

"Why?"

"We're all licentious fiends," he said, steadying me with hands on my hips as we hit a pothole.

Considering that it was something like the ninetieth one, that didn't seem strictly necessary. And then I looked down, to find that his eyes were especially green next to the new, dark hair. And open and clear . . . and inviting. No strings, no agenda. Just the promise of pleasure, shared and given.

I swallowed and picked up a comb. "I can't."

"Why not?"

I tackled the bird's nest on one side of the wig, where it had been crushed in a trunk. "So, so many reasons."

"Name one."

"You first."

"Ah, but I don't have any reasons," he said while the thumbs began to move in slow circles on my hip bones.

I shot him a look.

They stopped.

"I mean, you tell me something first," I clarified.

He looked a question.

"Back in Nimue's . . . thing," I said, because I doubted "Winnebago" would translate. "You wanted to know my name. My real one. Why?"

I immediately wished I hadn't asked, because a lot of the fun faded from his face.

"It's okay," I said quickly. "You don't have to answer."

"No, it's fair." He looked up at me, through a fall of brown hair. "You know the old couple I told you about? The ones who raised me?"

I nodded. After Morgaine's supposed death, Rosier had dumped him on a farmer's family, who'd thought he was basically Satan incarnate, and then fled. It made me angry all over again, just thinking about it. I knew he'd had a reason: that if Pritkin didn't end up with his power, he'd be better off growing up in this world, where he had at least a small chance of fitting in. I even agreed with it. That is, I agreed with the *idea*.

The execution, however, had left the fey knowing more about Pritkin's true heritage than he did.

"I spent most of my time with the old woman," he continued, "but one day the old man decided to go fishing, and agreed to let me tag along. I was quite excited. I was never allowed to go anywhere—officially."

"But you went anyway."

He grinned. "But I hadn't been caught in a while, so I suppose this was their way of rewarding me."

I rolled my eyes and started on the other side of what I was deciding was more dust mop than wig.

"In any case, we were halfway to the lake when we met one of the farmer's friends. They stopped to talk, and I wandered off, trying to catch frogs for bait. They must have thought I was out of earshot."

"And what did they say?" I asked, carefully. Because the smile was gone again, lost—not in the usual anger—but in sadness.

"The old man's friend asked about me, specifically why they would take me in when they didn't even know what I was. There were so many Changelings then, some who grew up to be dangerous, that it was a fair question."

I nodded.

"But the old man said he wasn't worried. My father had dropped me off, and my father was human. Making my mother the fey—or part fey, as he'd been told—in this instance."

"The opposite of the usual situation."

"Yes. The old man believed that she was some tavern wench or farmer's daughter, a descendant of one of the Returned that my father had lain with for a night or two. Then passed by the same way in a year and realized he had a son. One he was willing to support in case I turned out to have any magic."

I didn't say anything. That was uncomfortably close to the truth.

"He gave them money and a name—Myrddin. But he never gave them hers. The old man joked that he wasn't sure he even knew it—or that she knew his." Pritkin's tone was light, but his jaw was tight. He saw me notice, and relaxed it. "I would want any child of mine to know, that's all."

"So you make sure, if things are getting a little heated—"

"To ask. Although I have usually done so before that!"

I remembered that he'd introduced himself to me, the first time we met here, despite it being in a somewhat . . . compromising . . . situation. He hadn't gotten my real name then, but he'd been persistent. Because he'd want any child of his to know who he was, where he'd come from, *what he was*. Instead of growing up never knowing anything, like he had done.

And, okay, right then I genuinely *hated* Rosier.

"Hold on!" Pritkin said, a hand on his fake hair, and I realized that I'd been combing a little too hard. Like enough to pull out a small patch of fur, or whatever the matted thing was made of.

I frowned at the comb. Even when wearing a wig, Pritkin had terrible hair. It was like he was cursed.

"Your turn," he said, and for a moment, I didn't know what he meant.

"You said it would be difficult?" he prompted.

I winced.

But he'd just told me something uncomfortable, and very personal, so . . .

"It's hard to explain," I repeated. "You don't know him."

"Ah. A rival." He looked like he'd just figured something out. "Do you love him?"

"That's a strange question." I went back to work, trying to cover the bald spot.

"And an easy one. If you're together, of course you love him."

"I . . . yes. Of course."

"That doesn't sound very sure."

"I'm sure."

"It's just that you hesitated."

"I did not!"

"All right."

I combed fur for a moment. "It just . . . for a long time, there were so many things I didn't know about him. We didn't talk much, and when we did, it never seemed to be *about* anything. We'd have these conversations, but later, I couldn't remember us actually saying anything. And then, when he finally *did* . . ."

"When he did?"

I put the comb down and picked up a pot of something I'd noticed when I was doing my own makeup. "What is this?"

"Putty. They use it to make bruises and scars, and to

change the shape of facial features. Harder than wearing a mask, but it lets the audience see the eyes."

"Hold still," I told him, and slathered some on his most memorable feature.

"You have to move quickly, or it will set up," Pritkin said, sounding slightly worried. And slightly nasal.

"I know how to do makeup," I said, but sped up a little. I had a lot of ground to cover.

"This man, he is older than you?" he asked, after a minute.

I snorted. "You could say that."

"What's so funny? Is he . . . very old?" Pritkin frowned.

"Let's just say that, in age, experience, and knowledge, he pretty much outclasses me. Or maybe I just don't know what I'm doing. He's my first relationship, and I don't think I'm doing it right. Sometimes I wonder what he's even doing with me. And then . . ." I swallowed and looked away, putting the little pot back in place as an excuse.

"And then?"

"And then sometimes I think I know," I said shortly.

"That does sound complicated."

"It is."

"Too complicated, for a first relationship."

"What does that have to do with anything?"

"First relationships are supposed to be easy. Simple. Fun."

"Fun."

"Yes, fun." He tilted his head, which made his fake nose go all wonky. He waggled it back and forth, until it resembled a lying Pinocchio's. I sighed and pulled it off. "Don't you like to have fun?"

"Yes, but that's . . . Relationships are supposed to be serious."

"Why?"

"Why? Because you're talking about spending your life with someone!"

"Someone who's not any fun."

"He's fun!"

"You sound defensive."

"I'm not," I said, and grabbed a rag to remove the rest of the nose. "He's fun when he has time to be. It's just . . . he's busy. So am I."

Pritkin pursed his lips at me. "This relationship of yours sounds like a lot of work. I'm glad I'm not so busy. Or so complicated."

"You're plenty complicated!"

"Not at all. When I'm hungry, I eat. When I'm tired, I sleep. When I see a pretty girl, looking at me with eyes as dark as the ocean, with hunger in them, so much hunger . . . I oblige."

I stared down into burning green eyes for a moment, and then looked away again.

"That's because you're . . ." An incubus, I didn't say, because there was a possibility he didn't know yet. "Young."

"Yes. So are you."

Yeah, right. "I don't feel like it much lately."

"Then feel like it now." He saw my expression, and laughed. "Not like that. Well, unless you change your mind. But there's other ways to have fun, you know."

"Like what?"

"Like this." And he pushed open the back door with his foot.

I looked at him with alarm. "What are you doing?"

We were still moving, which didn't stop him from catching hold of the roof and somehow vaulting up on top. And then reaching down, when I peered out the back, and grasping my arms. "This," he said, grinning.

"Um," I said, because the ground was suddenly looking very hard.

And very far, when he pulled me up in one fell swoop, like flying. Depositing me beside a fat guy with a tambourine and maybe three teeth. All of which he bared at me in a lopsided grin. Pritkin rapid-fired some introductions, and then plopped a straw hat down on my head, probably because the gate was coming up.

There were people lining the road on both sides, and running to catch up, like it was Mardi Gras and we were the only float. The girls laughed and waved, some guy went to town on a lyre, and in a minute, the craziness had infected me, and I was laughing, too. And trying to hold on to my hat, before the wind sent it flying.

Pritkin snatched it out of the air and put it back in place, green eyes gleaming.

"If he gets you, I get this much," he said, and kissed me while the girls laughed and flashed the guards, and the tambourine shook, and the wagon trundled through the gate, unopposed.

And that was how we entered the city.

Chapter Fifty

The players were housed in tiny plain rooms off the kitchen, which seemed to make everybody happy.

"Used to sleeping under the stars, or with his foot in m'face," one of the girls told me, hiking a thumb at the tambourine guy. "This is luxury."

"Don't get too comfortable," the lyre player, a tall man with sharp cheekbones, said. "Dinner's at sundown. Then we're up." He looked at Pritkin. "Why don't you start taking everything to the main hall?"

I guessed that was for the benefit of the kitchen staff, despite the fact that none of them seemed to be paying us any attention. Until a frazzled girl came over, with sweat on her brow, and handed me a wooden tray. "Take this up if you're going."

"You take it," the cook said, bending over a pot on the fire. "Don't be giving your tasks to those who have their own."

"But she's going anyway—"

"And doubtless will be carrying her work with her."

"Not with those arms," the kitchen maid said, looking at me critically. "Don't they feed you where you're from?"

She grabbed my pathetic excuse for biceps, but before I could say anything, the cook had turned around. He was a kind-looking older man, but was clearly tired of repeating himself. "Why does everything have to be an argument with you?"

"I'm not arguing," she argued. "But my feet are killing me."

"You're arguing while the food's getting cold. Now take it up—"

"But I must have been up and down those stairs fifty times today."

"The fey take you, girl! If I have to tell you again—"

"Fey don't want her," a young man said, looking up from chopping something. "Too lazy, and whines too much."

"I'll show you lazy—" she said, and started for him.

" 'Pona!" The cook was looking genuinely angry now. "The princess isn't feeling well, and she's waiting for her food!"

"All right, all right, I'll take it," the girl said sullenly, and reached for the tray.

I pulled it back. "I'll take it," I said, giving the cook what I hoped was a winning smile. "Where is she, again?"

The stairs turned out to be every bit as much of a bitch as the girl had claimed, stone, steep, and slippery. And packed. I kept being buffeted to one side or the other, but Pritkin couldn't help much. He was carrying a pitcher of ale on one shoulder and a heavy roll of painted canvas on the other, where they could help to hide his face.

"We lost him . . . remember?" I panted. "You could probably ditch the disguise."

"You just want help carrying that tray."

"Which doesn't . . . make it any less true."

"You don't lose a fey lord that easily," he informed me. "He'll be back, and it would be well for both of us if we have the staff when he does. Speaking of which—"

"Later."

Pritkin glanced around at all the people, many of whom were shooting us annoyed looks for blocking half the stairs. "Soon."

The main hall was like the rest of the castle: utility combined with plundered beauty. There were numerous long tables and benches, simple, sturdy things, without adornment. Like the iron sconces on the walls, which a prop department would have sent back for being too plain. But the big gray blocks of the floor were intercut with areas of intricate tile work, some featuring vines, others with geometric shapes, none of them matching. Like someone had dug them out of other floors and brought them here, plunking them down like so many area rugs.

They gave a weird, funky vibe to the place, colorful and eclectic.

Likewise, the walls weren't bare stone, as the movies had taught me to expect. Red plaster with a green border circled three sides of the large room, decorated with banners embroidered with red dragons. The fourth wall was white, but not plain. A faded mural of a woman inside a silver circle looked down at us benevolently, metallic paint still glinting in spots, here and there.

"Arianrhod, Lady of the Silver Wheel," Pritkin told me. "The king's father had it brought here, block by block, from the old bathhouse. Said she had a kind face."

And a familiar one, I thought, staring upward.

"She's also known as the goddess of the moon," he added.

"I know."

We went through an archway and up a flight of curving stairs, to a wide hallway with a skinny guard. He was slumped against an arched door, looking bored. But he straightened up quickly enough when we approached.

"Dye your hair, then, Myrddin?" he asked while checking us for weapons.

Pritkin sighed. "I'd be obliged if you didn't mention to any fey that you saw me."

"In trouble again, are you?" the guard asked, amused, and peered under the cover of the tray Pritkin was carrying, since we'd switched loads after the hall.

"Roast pork with sage, lamb and nettle stew, blackberries and cream, ale," Pritkin told him.

The guard looked wistful. "When's our dinner, then?"

"I was told sundown," I said.

"Aye, but we won't eat then, will we? What with the hall packed with guests." He looked at the pork, which did smell heavenly. "Probably should check that for poison—"

I slapped his hand.

It was unthinking, and could have been a big mistake, but he just sighed. "Worth a try."

And with that, we swept in.

As the king's half sister, Morgaine was housed in the royal apartments, which looked like a fey had designed them, since they followed each other like cars on a train. And I guessed this was the station, where several trains met, what we'd have called a study. I walked slowly forward, trying not to stare like a fangirl, and probably failing spectacularly. Because it was exactly like I'd imagined. *Exactly.*

There were parts I recognized from the shard of mirror I'd found at Nimue's: the thick oak slab Arthur was using for a desk, the great stone fireplace, the mural I'd glimpsed a tiny piece of, which turned out to be a cavalry charge done in hasty sketches and vibrant with life. And something that had been out of view of the mirror, something over the mantel, something that looked like ...

I stopped dead in the middle of the room, my heart pounding. "Is . . . is that—"

"The king's great sword," Pritkin confirmed. "A gift from the Lady upon his accession."

"You mean . . . Excalibur?" I whispered.

Pritkin looked confused. And said something that the spell didn't translate, but which sounded like he was clearing his throat. I glanced at him. "What?"

He repeated the sound, which I guessed hadn't been a mistake, after all. "It means Hard Lightning in the old tongue," he told me. "You see the chimeras, on the hilt?"

I nodded. What looked like two lions, if lions had birds' wings and snakes for tails, twined together to form the grip. They were cast in bronze, and so finely wrought that I could see the individual scales on the serpents, the feathers on the wings, and the ripples in the lion's muscles. It was breathtaking.

"They're nothing compared to the blade," Pritkin said softly. "A wondrous thing, like no other, bright as flame."

I glanced around at the empty room. "Could . . ." I licked my lips. "Do you think we could see it?"

He chuckled. "Not according to legend."

"What?"

"It is said that the wielder is protected, but for everyone else, the blade is dreadful to look upon, a sword of fire that blinds an enemy—or a whole host—before it cuts them down."

"Blinds them," I repeated, and suddenly, that searing brightness I'd experienced in Nimue's rooms made more sense. Arthur must have returned during the attack and unsheathed the blade in front of the mirror. Half blinding me, and forcing Jo to run off because she could no longer see to fight.

I blinked, realizing that my life had been saved by King Arthur, wielding Excalibur. And Billy Joe's words came back to me. Yeah, you gave up a lot for this job, but sometimes . . . it was almost worth it.

Pritkin was looking at me. "Don't you think it's time you told me what this is all about?"

"I—" I began, and then stopped, at the sound of raised voices from somewhere nearby.

We left the tray on the desk and moved into the next room. It was a sitting type with a loom in a corner, which I assumed wasn't Arthur's. And another door, which was partially open.

But it was enough to show me the king, striding up and down, still in the armor he'd ridden out in. It was bronze, and shone redly in the setting sun through a bank of long, tiny windows. The reddish light glazed his blond hair as well, and flashed in his eyes when he suddenly turned—to face Morgaine, sitting on the edge of a divan.

I quickly retreated slightly.

"It's not a matter of what I want," he said harshly. "I cannot hold this country without help! The Saxons are too many, and their weapons are too good. And many of them also had family in service of the empire. They're not like the local chiefs; our tactics don't surprise them—"

"I understand—"

"Do you? Then why ask this of me? Why ask for what I cannot give?"

"I'm asking for time only," Morgaine said, her voice calming. "Grandmother *will* come around. She has no choice. Be patient—"

I felt Pritkin tug on my arm, and glanced up, to see him looking troubled. I guess he hadn't signed on to eavesdrop on his king. I had no such problem, but if Arthur unexpectedly stormed out, we were going to be in trouble. I looked around and then moved to the darker shadows behind the door, the only real choice. It meant I couldn't see inside anymore, but I could hear just fine.

What are you doing? Pritkin mouthed.

"Then you care for us so little?" Morgaine was saying. "That you would sell us to our enemies?"

"You chose the fey side of our heritage. I chose the human," Arthur replied. "But I am hardly so cruel. I care for both; I am working for both. You must trust me—"

Pritkin was still looking pointedly at me, waiting for an answer I couldn't give. So I gestured at the next room, where Arthur had just done it for me.

"How can I trust you when you will tell me nothing?" Morgaine demanded. "You ask me for trust, yet you will give none?"

It was Pritkin's turn to point.

Arthur and I sighed.

There was a lull in the conversation, accompanied by the sound of a stool being dragged across stone. When the king's voice came again, it was lower, both in tone and position. "I will tell you this. The Svarestri came to me, after Grandmother's latest demands, and offered to exchange her protection for theirs. They said they wanted food for their people—"

"That isn't *all* they want," Morgaine said, her voice sharpening. "They want to weaken us, to divide our family—"

"More than that." The king's voice dropped, to the point that I was straining to hear him, even this close. "They want to make a weapon, one with which to seize all Faerie. They want to steal from me, to make this weapon possible. But instead, I will steal from *them*—and make a protection for our people such as the world has never seen. A protection even the combined armies of Faerie could not undo. And let them make slaves of us then!"

"What?" Morgaine sounded as confused as I was. "Arthur . . . I don't understand."

"Neither did I," he said. "But their ambassador made a mistake. He slipped up and called the staff they stole from Caedmon a *spear.* He only did it once, and only because he was surprised I had heard of the theft. Worried, lest I realize they planned to follow up one with another. But I played it off. They think us so foolish, it was easy to make him believe—"

"Believe what? Arthur, what are you *talking* about?"

"A story, one I heard as a child. Of a great set of armor, made by a god and worn by a hero. It was damaged in battle, some pieces beyond repair, but four remained: a helm, a shield, a sword . . . and a *spear.*"

"Oh my God," I whispered, and then clapped a hand over my mouth.

But no one inside seemed to notice, maybe because Arthur's voice had risen again in excitement.

"The pieces were lost after a great battle, and scattered, until rescued by the gods and gifted to the great fey houses for their protection, for no human could wield them without going mad. It was said they had been imbued with the power of the *gods themselves*—"

"Arthur, what are you saying?"

"That I've finally found a way for both our people. Think of it, Morgan! Your name means Bright Sea, but how often are you there? Your people spend half their lives in the woods, constantly fighting. But if the Svarestri lost their helm, the one that gives their king so much of his power—what then? Would you still be fighting then? Or would the Dark Fey push him back to his own lands, to wither on those damn cold rocks? Would he not have to offer accommodation then, cede lands then, *make peace then*?"

Pritkin and I stared at each other. He looked as shocked as I was. It looked like Arthur had been playing his cards pretty close to his chest.

"Why shake your head at me?" his voice came again, after a brief moment. "Isn't this what you've wanted, too? Why you've trained the covens? There will be no need for slaves if there is not constant war! It brings surcease for all—"

"It brings *war* for all," Morgaine said, her voice trembling with some emotion I couldn't name, because I couldn't see her. "Arthur, do you really think Aeslinn will lie down and just allow you to take his helm from him? If you fail, he'll kill you. If you succeed, he'll come for you. And you will not be able to withstand him, for you cannot wield it! Recreate this armor if you like, but there is none to *wear it* anymore!"

"There doesn't need to be." Arthur didn't sound even slightly abashed. "The Svarestri plan to pour all the power of the different pieces into one, to combine their strength—*and so do I.* But instead of choosing a weapon, as they would, I will make another choice, Grandmother's choice—"

"Grandmother's? You mean—" Her voice broke off. And when it came again, there was wonder in it. "You plan to expand it, don't you? Her shield. To increase its size—"

"Until none may touch us!" he agreed eagerly. "Let the Saxons come, with all their men. Let the fey, let the gods themselves! We will be safe, Faerie pacified, and Aeslinn toothless. We can do this, Morgan. We can bring about all that my father wished, and more than he dared to dream. *Now* do you understand?"

Yeah, I thought, feeling dizzy. Yeah, I kind of thought I did.

Chapter Fifty-one

Pritkin gripped my arm, because apparently he'd decided it was time for that chat, like right freaking now. But my head was swimming too much to care. I let him pull me back into the outer room, unprotesting.

"Is that why you want the staff?" he asked softly. Well, the tone was soft. The hand on my arm was another matter. "To make a *weapon*?"

"No—"

"Who are you working for?" he whispered harshly. "It can't be the Svarestri—they tried to kill you. And the same is true for the Blue Fey—and the Green!"

"It's a gift," I said numbly, which didn't help.

"And it can't be the king. I saw your face just now—you didn't know all that. Some, but not all."

"No."

"Who, then? Who else is involved? *Who is it?*"

"I'm not working for anyone," I said, because he was starting to flush, and I was afraid he'd drag me in to Arthur, demanding an explanation. And that would be bad, that would be very bad, because Arthur—

I looked up at Excalibur, gleaming on the wall, the firelight glinting off the carved figures on the hilt, turning them from bronze into solid gold. It was beautiful, even with the blade hidden. Truly, a piece of art. Which if it had been forged by a god would make sense. But if that was true, then Ares was infused in the sword, just like all the other pieces of that cursed set of armor Adra had mentioned. Not all of him, no, but part of him, enough to drive a fey queen close to madness.

What had it done to Arthur?

He hadn't had the sword that long, not the millennia Nimue must have had her shield. But he wasn't Nimue. He was only a quarter fey, and while he wasn't mad, was he *influenced*?

I didn't know, but I knew one thing.

"They can't be allowed to get all the pieces," I told Pritkin urgently. "The Svarestri are planning to make a weapon with them, but not to use on the fey. They're trying—"

Shit!

The door opened, and I whirled, kneeling in front of the fire, hoping the desk would hide me. And throwing on some more wood in case it didn't, like an exotically dressed chambermaid. Beside me, Pritkin went into a deep bow, low enough to hide his face, because the billow of sea green skirts I'd glimpsed could only belong to one person.

Fortunately, queens rarely glance at the help, and Nimue continued through to the inner rooms without pausing, presumably to see her granddaughter. Along with four of her personal bodyguard, who I guessed were there for Morgaine, because none of them stayed in the outer room. And then they actually closed the door!

As soon as it snicked shut, I scrambled onto the desk, which didn't turn out to be close enough. So I scrambled down again and tried dragging Arthur's chair back a few feet, which was all I needed. But the damn thing was heavy English oak, and might as well have been made out of lead.

"Help me!" I told Pritkin, who wasn't helping.

Instead, he was standing there, arms crossed, eyes deadly serious. "If you want my help—or even my silence—you're going to tell me what you're doing. Right now."

"Trying to save our asses," I whispered while tugging and heaving. "The fey aren't trying to get some advantage in a war. They're trying to bring back a *god*—"

"What?" He blinked, like that wasn't the answer he'd expected.

"—*the* god of war—who's going to murder us all, except his devout Svarestri worshippers, no doubt. Which will bring peace, but not the kind I think you want!"

"What are you talking about? Stop that and answer me!"

I stopped, but not because he told me to. But because I needed his help to do this. No way was Excalibur just hanging on a wall with no protection. It was probably warded all to hell, and while I might eventually manage to reach it, I couldn't do shit about that.

I blew a strand of sweaty hair out of my face.

"Look, I can't tell you everything, but . . . I'm after a girl, someone working with the Svarestri. I was told that she wants the staff to punch through a . . . a sort of spell . . . that's protecting earth, and bring back the gods. But if one piece of the armor was enough for that, the Svarestri would have already done it. It looks like they need it all: Nimue's shield, Aeslinn's helm, Caedmon's staff, and . . ."

I looked up at Excalibur, hanging on the wall, and Pritkin's expression darkened.

"No."

"We have to take it!"

"No!"

"It's the only way—"

"You are not talking about stealing the king's sword!"

"We don't have a choice! We don't know where the staff is, or how to get it back. But the sword is *right there*—"

"We have to tell the king!" He started for the door.

I lunged over the desk and caught his arm. "We *can't* tell him! The armor was infused with the soul of a *god*—the same god they're trying to bring back! Anyone who's owned a piece is suspect!"

He stopped moving, I guessed because he'd have to drag me along to get any farther, but he still looked incredulous. "You can't seriously think—"

"Can't I? What do you think is wrong with Nimue? Was that *normal*, what we saw at camp? Was that what you'd have expected from her?"

Pritkin paused, forehead wrinkling. "No. She has the

reputation of a fierce foe with a . . . lively . . . temper. But she is not reputed to be cruel."

"Maybe she isn't. But the shield played on her fears, her desire to protect her people, her growing paranoia. She was probably a hard nut to crack, but she's had it a long time, and the Svarestri have made sure she had no choice but to use it. You told me so yourself, when we were in Faerie, remember? How they constantly attack the Dark Fey, taking their lands, forcing them into conflict with her—"

"But that's Nimue. Arthur—"

"Has the *sword*!" I gestured at it. "Achilles' freaking sword that I'll bet you anything Nimue took from the Dark Fey and gave to him!"

And finally, it looked like something got through. "She captured it after a battle," Pritkin said, sounding numb. "But she couldn't use it to full effect; fire isn't her element—"

"So some little voice told her to bring it *here*, where it's been whispering to Arthur ever since, promising things he's yearned for his whole life. Dreams of a peace he's never going to get because the Svarestri are going to reassemble that armor and kill us all!"

Pritkin stared at me, and then at the door, clearly torn. He'd heard most of the story from Arthur's own lips, and he'd seen the bloody mess at Nimue's camp. Yet, for a moment, he just stood there.

"She has the shield, and possibly the staff," I told him desperately. "And the Svarestri have the helm. That means the sword—"

"Is the only thing left."

I nodded. "They *can't* get their hands on it."

"And your role in all this?"

"To make sure they don't!"

Pritkin didn't answer, but he suddenly picked up the massive chair and deposited it by the wall. He climbed up, his hands running over the length of the blade from a good two feet away, scowling. "Understand this," he said grimly. "The sword stays with me. If you attempt to take it—"

"I won't."

"Good. It's not that I don't trust you—"

"Of course not."

He glanced down. "I *do*. But that's the problem. I've known you all of three days. And here I am, stealing the king's sword for you!"

"It isn't for me."

"And that . . . incident . . . yesterday. I've never—" He looked down at me again. "If you've spelled me, I promise you'll regret it!"

"I haven't! Can you hurry?"

He went back to work, muttering something, although whether at the sword or at me, I wasn't sure. But a moment later, it sprang off the wall. "What did I just say?" he asked, pulling it away when I reached for it.

"I was just going to hold it while you got down!"

He jumped down beside me. "I'll manage."

"You think I'm going to disappear with it, don't you?"

"If I thought that, I wouldn't have helped you. But you know what they say. There's no honor among thieves—"

"So it would appear."

My head jerked up, because that voice hadn't been Pritkin's.

Only to see a furious, damp, blood-splattered king of the fey breathing at me from the doorway.

Goddamn it.

Half an hour later, I was in a dank cell, stuffing my face. It wasn't my idea; Caedmon's fancy-dressed officer, who had shown up with him for some sort of parlay with Arthur, had gotten it into his head that we'd not only planned to steal from the king, but to poison him, too. So he was letting the punishment fit the crime.

The tasty, tasty punishment.

God, I hadn't realized how hungry I was!

"More bread?" I asked Pritkin, who was being forced to eat, too, only not looking so happy about it. He shook his head. "Then do you mind if I—?"

He passed me the bread.

The officer's eyes narrowed as I used it to sop up the last of the lamb and nettle stew, which hadn't sounded particularly appetizing, but tasted divine. But not as

much as the pork, with its crispy caramelized skin, like
meat candy. Or the blueberries, plump and sweet, and
swimming in warm cream. I made a desperate little sound
and saw some of the guards looking at the depleted tray
with envy.

They were missing dinner because of us, or more accurately, because Arthur had a problem with their boss
just killing us. Of course, he also had a problem with us
stealing his stuff, even though Pritkin had tried his best
to explain. But that was a little hard with Arthur yelling
and Morgaine staring and Caedmon demanding his staff
back—until I happened to mention that Nimue probably
had it. . . .

Which might have worked better if she hadn't been
standing right there.

But we weren't dead yet, and we'd even gotten dinner.
Most of it, I corrected, as the officer reached over and
snatched the tray away. I didn't know why; it was pretty
much empty at this point. But I supposed he thought it
could be used as a weapon or something.

Sure, I thought resentfully, one wooden tray and my
skinny arms against a roomful of fey, thick stone walls,
and nothing to cheat with.

Like nothing, because I'd been calling Billy for almost
the whole time, and where was he?

Of course, he might not know that. Sometimes I
thought we had a connection: I'd feel him before I saw
him, or he'd swear he heard me calling. But sometimes he
said that when I hadn't called, too, so who knew? But
damn, I wanted out of here!

Apparently, the fey felt the same, because one of them
cleared his throat.

"Sir, perhaps we could cycle out—"

"He's a triskelion," the officer snapped. "You're going
nowhere."

The fey blinked, and slid a surprised glance Pritkin's
way, but didn't say anything else. I, on the other hand,
had nothing else to do with my mouth, now that my dinner was gone. "Triskelion?" I asked.

"Someone who owns three elements," Pritkin murmured, before the officer yelled at him to shut up.

There was silence for a moment.

"Is that unusual?" I asked, because I'd kind of gotten the idea that the fey weren't allowed to hurt us, and I'd been yelled at before.

"Fairly," Pritkin said, hiding a smile.

It didn't look like he liked the officer, either.

"So, how many do most people have?" I asked, and found a fey in my face.

"Be. *Silent*," the officer told me, in what was the closest thing I'd ever heard to a genuine hiss.

"Or what? You'll throw me in a cell and take away my food? Oh, wait."

"Oh, shit," Pritkin murmured admonishingly.

And yes, he was right; antagonizing the fey was stupid. But right now not antagonizing them was just as stupid, since nothing was happening. And if nothing continued to happen, we lost.

"How many?" I asked again.

Pritkin looked at the guard, and a little smile escaped his lips. "One."

And, okay, something was happening now, I thought, as the fey jerked Pritkin up.

And was quickly surrounded by his own guards, looking concerned. One of whom even dared to put a hand on his arm. "Sir, the king said—"

"I don't take orders from a human king!"

It had been pretty savage, but the fey wasn't deterred. "But the lord was standing right there, and if he hadn't agreed . . ."

"We can't hurt them unless they try to escape," another fey recited.

The officer looked back at Pritkin. *"Try,"* he ordered.

But Pritkin just stood there, with that same little half smile.

Until the officer released him with a sound of contempt.

After a moment, everyone settled back down, and the room grew quiet again.

"So," I asked, "what do they call someone with four?"

I didn't get an answer, but coincidentally, that was the same number of fey who grabbed the officer, halfway through a lunge. And that included the guy who'd been standing by the door. Which probably explained how we came to be inundated by a flock of beauties bearing gifts.

The door slammed open, showing a bemused, human-looking guard. And a flood of dark-eyed, silk-clad, tassel-bedecked lovelies, each with a platter or basket or pitcher. Or, in the case of one girl with wildly improbable crimson hair, a basket of fresh-baked bread rolls that she started tossing to the famished fey.

"Did you think we forgot you? Poor darlings," she cooed, to the very surprised, very pleased-looking soldiers.

Well, apart from one.

"Stop that! Stop that immediately!" the officer told her, only to have her laugh and shake her tassels at him. Xanthippe had been a lion tamer's assistant back in the day, and not much fazed her.

"Who ordered this? *Who ordered this?*" he demanded, as his men began dividing up the bounty.

"The princess, handsome one," a dark-haired girl with some of the biggest tassels I'd ever seen said. And smacked a kiss on his outraged cheek. "She thought you might be lonely, all the way down here."

Several of the men sniggered, but the officer didn't seem amused. "I wasn't informed. And what is *that*?" he demanded, focusing on the two large pitchers a dark-skinned beauty in yellow fringe was carrying in.

"Relax, lover," Xanthippe said. "We know the rules. It's just wine."

"Wine! Do you have any idea what he can do with wine?" He gestured savagely back at Pritkin. "Get it out!"

"But what are they supposed to drink?" the dark-skinned girl asked. "The men look thirsty." She looked around. "Aren't you thirsty?"

There was a general murmur of agreement, which didn't seem to make the officer any happier. "I said no," he told the girl, pushing her toward the door. "Get out!"

"Watch the shoes," she said, which were cork-heeled wedges at least five inches high.

But he didn't listen. And the next thing I knew, a big

earthenware pot of wine was smashing onto the stones, fey were cursing, girls were yelling, and the other pot was pouring all over the officer, when the dancer wobbled and fell into him. And then . . .

And then . . .

I stared around, mouth full of roll, as the room suddenly got darker. And farther away, although that wasn't possible—was it? But it kind of seemed like it was. Maybe because the stones Pritkin and I had been sitting against were moving, opening up like they were swallowing us whole, pulling us back into our own little tunnel, one that hadn't been there a second ago. And then abruptly closing behind us.

The yells, shrieks, and girlish laughter abruptly cut off, leaving us entombed in a womb of stone. One that was moving a whole lot slower than it had been a moment ago. And then barely moving at all, stones that had been almost liquid suddenly solidifying again, gritting against each other, groaning in my ears. And pressing against me to the point that I could . . . barely . . . breathe—

Pritkin, I thought, because I didn't have enough air in my lungs to scream.

And then we were out, popping like a cork out of a champagne bottle, hitting open air and falling what had to be six feet, onto a hard patch of dirt.

Chapter Fifty-two

I lay there, stunned and half-choked, because I had been trying to breathe through bread. But the fall seemed to have jarred it loose, and I spat it out, all the while staring at the wall above us. Which was still moving in a very unrocklike way, as if it couldn't remember where all the stones went.

"Myrddin?" I said nervously, and didn't get an answer. I looked over to find Pritkin on his back, appearing unconscious—or worse. "Myrddin!"

"I'm all right." It was faint.

"Are you sure?" I scrambled over.

He opened his eyes to look at me, and they were almost completely red from popped blood vessels. "I . . . hate . . . earth magic."

It didn't look like it liked him too much, either.

But it obeyed.

"So," I asked, after a moment, "what *do* they call someone with four?"

He huffed out what might have been a laugh, and shook his head at me.

And continued to shake it when the earth suddenly moved underneath us. Enough to blast a bunch of birds out of a nearby tree, like they'd been shot from a cannon. And to throw me on my butt when I tried to get up.

I looked at Pritkin. "Did you—"

"No."

He rolled to his knees, staring at the lightning scribbling warnings across the sky. And illuminating blue-black clouds stacked high above skirts of rain. That wasn't so weird; we'd been inside the castle for more than an hour. They'd had plenty of time to form up.

Except that they were everywhere, on all sides, at least the ones I could see. Just huge gray sheets rushing toward us, illuminated here and there by neon flashes. One of which hit a lone tree, far in the distance on a hill, exploding it into burning pieces that were almost immediately doused by the incoming tide.

And that was exactly what it looked like, I realized: a tide rolling over land, drowning everything in its wake.

Then another tremor hit, as if the earth itself was angry.

"The kitchens," Pritkin said, pulling me up. "They're not far."

We ran.

The hill on which the castle sat had no trees, probably for defense. But down below, a small orchard ringed the base, the dense foliage swaying in the rising wind. Beyond it, I could see the walled town, its cook fires glittering in the night and sending thin threads of smoke skyward, which were being pulled off center by the winds. And which looked so small and insignificant next to the power of nature.

Everyone else must have thought so, too. Because there was frantic activity around the festival tents, as vendors and partygoers alike scrambled for cover. While out in the harbor, the boats dipped and rolled, the water beneath them cresting gray and white, like clutching hands, cold and angry.

"Come on!" Pritkin told me, pulling on my hand, because I'd unconsciously stopped to stare.

"Sorry."

We'd just rounded the side of the castle when a thin, cold rain began to fall, the first outriders of what looked to be an onslaught. It hit a moment later, drenching us as we pelted across a garden clinging precariously to the slope of the hill, tripping on cabbages and mushing beans. And then through a door, our muddy feet messing up the clean-swept hall next to the kitchen.

Cheerful golden light splashed the stones in front of us. While behind, the moonlight was eclipsed by cluster-

ing clouds, cutting off as suddenly as if someone had
flipped a switch. I turned around to stare at it, a weird
feeling coming over me, while Pritkin wrestled with the
heavy slab of the door, trying to swing it shut with rain
lashing at it in gusts like hammerblows.

But he got it done, just as the cook poked his head out
of the kitchen, a spoon in one hand and a bowl in the
other. And a frown on his face. "What's this, then?" he
asked as some kind of sauce seeped onto the stones.
"What's happening?"

"Storm blew up," Pritkin said dryly.

The man sighed. "And here I was, hoping to sneak off
down t' the faire later. Just my—"

He broke off when a shudder ran through the stones
under our feet, hard enough to send us stumbling against
the wall. That would have been worrying enough in a
modern structure, but this wasn't one. This was basically
a mountain made out of stone.

Which had just shaken noticeably.

"All right, what *is* this?" the cook demanded, about
the time we were mobbed by a mass of people coming
from inside the castle. One that quickly filled the tiny
corridor.

"What is this? *What is this?*" the outraged cook was
yelling, barring the way into his precious kitchen while
we hugged the wall on the other side to avoid being trampled.

And then some genius opened the door.

The hall immediately became a maelstrom of flashing
light, screaming people and lashing rain. "Close the door!
Close the door!" everyone at this end yelled.

But the ones getting drenched weren't listening. Or
maybe they couldn't hear over the booming thunder, because the whole place sounded like we'd been caught in a
giant kettledrum. It was deafening to the point of being
painful, and I guessed they thought so, too. Because they
were turning around, they were rushing back this way,
they were—

"Myrddin!" I yelled.

"Stay with me!" He pushed me ahead of him as the
stampede hit, sweeping us and everyone around us along

with it. We burst into the area with the stairs, which was considerably larger than the hall, but no less packed. And was getting worse, because more people were flooding in all the time.

Along with something else.

I stared for a moment, nonplussed. Because a frothing mass of water was churning around the fleeing crowd, gushing down the stairs like an indoor waterfall. And causing them to trip and fall and others to pile up behind them. We fought our way to the side and watched them sort themselves out, panicked lords and ladies in their finery, wide-eyed servants in their livery, and several furious-looking actors, each carrying half of a wooden horse.

Pritkin grabbed one of them by the arm. "What's going on?"

"What does it look like?" The tall man with the sharp cheeks was livid. "Had to ruin everything, didn't they? *The fucking fey!* First decent-paying job we've had in months—"

"Ruin what?"

"My purse, for one thing! Who's going to pay to see us now? With that for entertainment!" He gestured savagely back at the stairs.

"Entertainment?" I said worriedly. "What entertainment?"

"They're fighting," the big tambourinist said, his voice slow and thick.

The tall man nodded angrily. "Dinner hadn't even started before that damn cold-eyed fey—"

"Which one?"

"The Winter King, they call him. I know what I'd like to call him!"

"Aeslinn?" Pritkin's grip tightened. "What did he—"

"I'm trying to tell you, aren't I? Son of a bitch picked a fight, with that crazy-eyed sea witch—"

Someone fell into us, and he broke off, cursing.

"What happened?" Pritkin demanded.

"She got mad," the tambourinist said.

"What do you think happened?" the tall man yelled. "Now let me go. I'm getting out of here!"

Which, yeah, would be a good plan, I thought, as they swept around us.

Except that we needed the sword, and the sword was up *there*.

"Is there another way?" I asked Pritkin, who was staring at the stairs-turned-waterfall.

"Not from here. Not without—" He broke off when a slender opening appeared in the throng. "There!"

"Not without what?" I asked, one hand in his, the other protecting my head as we plowed into the fray.

"Not without going back outside," he yelled to be heard above the din.

And okay, that wasn't appealing. I could hear the thunder from here, sounding like the whole castle was under siege. And feeling like it, too. The room shook again, people screamed, and the crowd got even crazier. A panicked guy ran into me, and then kept on going like I wasn't even there, threatening to trample me.

But Pritkin pulled him off and shoved him on his way, and somehow forged us a path up the middle of the stairs. There was less water there, people's bodies dispersing it to either side, although that changed as we climbed. The people grew fewer, yet the tide seemed to be growing weaker.

No, not weaker, I realized.

Just changed.

I lost my footing and staggered against a wall, my fingers brushing through something hard and cold and crumbly. Which threatened to freeze them in place before I snatched them back. As it was, the pads had wrinkled up and turned faintly white, like frostbite was imminent, even after such a brief contact.

"Pritkin—" I said nervously, forgetting to use the right name, but it didn't matter.

Because a booming voice overrode mine, magnified by the stairwell. "Not in my house! *Not in my hall!*"

"Where, then?" a man's voice demanded. "For I will have recompense—"

"Oh, and in *full*!" That was a voice I knew: Nimue's. And sounding furious.

Okay, the waterfall was starting to make more sense now.

Pritkin had crawled up the remaining stairs, to peer out the top. I tried to join him, but the strange frost covered everything. It glittered in the spill of light from above like diamond dust, turning our surroundings into a beautiful, glistening ice cave. But it burned on the slightest contact, like cold fire.

"Here." Pritkin pulled off his outer tunic and tossed it down to me, and I gratefully put it on. It was damp, but not as much as my own clothes. And better still, it provided a barrier to the frost. I let the sleeves hang over my hands, like makeshift gloves, and crawled up the remaining stairs.

Despite the crowd down below, there were still people in the great hall—a lot of them. And from what I could see, they were all fey. Including someone in the middle of the room, who I saw in glimpses through a forest of legs. Someone wearing elaborate black and silver robes that glittered like starlight. Someone with long silver-white hair, a gleaming circlet on his brow, and eyes like storm clouds.

Someone I'd seen before.

"Their *king* was the one chasing us through Faerie?" I whispered, but Pritkin didn't reply. Maybe he didn't dare, since we were within earshot of the fey. Or maybe he was too busy staring at the woman facing off with Aeslinn.

Nimue had found time to change, because she was now all in blue: a long, dark velvet robe with white and green embroidery, so subtle and so fine that, even without enchantment, it flowed like the sea whenever she moved. It was a hell of an outfit, but she didn't need it. Her long hair drifted out about her, as if floating on invisible ocean currents, and her eyes were lightning. I'd thought she looked scary facing off with Morgaine, but apparently that had been, in Tami's terms, merely a paddlin'.

I didn't think that was what she had planned for Aeslinn.

Yet this was the guy who had brought down a mountain—hell, almost a whole mountain *range*—trying to bury us. I felt another shiver run through me. This . . . wasn't going to go well, was it?

As if in answer, a deafening *crack* caused the staircase to shudder, hard enough to send a cascade of ice down the stairs. And to send us tobogganing down with it, maybe a quarter of the way, before Pritkin managed to catch us. He braced on the now ice-free rock at a turn of the stairs while I held on to his arm and Aeslinn's voice boomed like we were in an echo chamber.

"Careful, Sea Witch! You come perilously close to naming me coward!"

"Indeed?" Nimue's tones rang out, clear as a bell. "That was not my intent in the slightest."

"That is fortunate, for your—"

"I meant to state it outright."

The room above exploded in loud voices, along with what sounded like actual explosions. Another *crack* caused the rest of the ice from above to suddenly cascade down the steps. Onto us.

"You *dare*—" Aeslinn thundered while Pritkin thrust me at the wall, shielding me with his body. And somehow holding his position while flakes of the stuff burst around us, hitting the curve and going everywhere. And burning whatever they touched, like sparks from a too-close bonfire.

"Yes, I dare!" Nimue's furious tones shivered across my skin like a physical thing. "As you have dared, for centuries, making war with me by proxy, not willing to face me yourself! Too long have you squeezed us, forcing the creatures of the dark onto our lands, allowing the abominations—*whom you armed*—to burn our towns, kill and ravage our people—"

"Abominations?" The contempt dripped. "I should think you would welcome them. Everyone knows your people are nothing but mongrels, intermarrying with vermin, destroying—"

"Have a care!"

"Oh, I will. I *do*. And when my armies march into Avalon, I will put your half-breeds to the sword, along with any polluted blood I find—"

"Your armies march only in your dreams, Dirt King." There was a savage form of mirth in the words now. "You will never have the numbers. The only way to take my throne is if I offer it to you—"

"As if anyone would want that collection of bogs and marshes—"

"—and I do!"

The room above suddenly went deadly quiet.

"Face me in combat," Nimue challenged. "Now, tonight, according to the ancient rules you're so fond of. And we will *settle this*. The winner becomes ruler of both kingdoms; the loser . . . receives the appropriate funeral rites. Duel me, King of the Wastelands. Or, once and for all, declare yourself coward before all Faerie!"

There was no sound for a long moment; even straining, all I could hear was my own frantic heartbeat.

"The only thing I will declare is your line extinct, once I finish with you."

The room detonated, in shouts and curses and more of those strange crashes. And then Arthur's voice cut through the din, loud as a foghorn. *"If you want to kill each other, do it outside!"*

The fey must have agreed, because the next noises echoing down the stairs were bootheels on stone, and a lot more shouting.

Pritkin crawled back up the stairs again, to peer out the top. "They're leaving," he said. "Everyone's heading for the Table—"

"Even Arthur?"

He nodded. "And he's not wearing his sword."

"So what are we doing here?" I asked, jumping up. "We can get it in the confusion. Come on!"

And then somebody kicked me in the chest.

It was just that fast, and wholly unexpected because there was no one there. And just that painful, since it felt more like someone had just driven a boot *through* my body, the shock alone overwhelming. I fell backward, clutching for purchase I couldn't find on the slippery stairs and couldn't see.

Because everything had just gone black.

Chapter Fifty-three

I crashed down into a freezing flood. The shock left me gasping, the water I breathed in left me choking, and the confusion left me reeling. I just lay there for a moment, stunned and drowning, staring at the surface.

And then I started thrashing my way back up.

It was hard—way more than it should have been, since judging by the bruises on my backside, the water wasn't that deep. But it didn't seem to matter. It felt like all my energy had just been sucked out of me. And the thing was, I *knew* that feeling. I'd felt it before. But, like everything else, my brain wasn't cooperating.

Maybe because it was running out of oxygen.

And then somebody jerked me up.

I stared in confusion at a man's unfamiliar face. It was too dark to see much, but faint traces of firelight from somewhere gleamed off the beads of water in his beard and the crazy in his eyes. Which quickly went from hopeful crazy to crazy pissed.

"You're not Dyfrig!" he said accusingly.

I tried to answer, but all that came out was a flood of water, all over the man's clothes. Not that it mattered; they were already soaked. But he didn't seem to appreciate it, nonetheless.

"Where is Dyfrig?"

"I . . . don't know," I choked, which didn't seem to be the right answer. Because he threw me against a stone wall, yelling the same thing, over and over. "Where is he? What did you do with him? *Where is Dyfrig?*"

"I don't know, I don't know!" I said, and then cut off with a pained cry when he started shaking me, and my head hit the wall. And then did it another time or two, because the man clearly didn't care if he bashed my brains out.

"Oh, *Dyfrig*," I gasped, and grabbed his arms. "I . . . thought you said something else. I saw him . . . over there!"

I didn't even know where I pointed—it was dark, and my head felt like it had been cracked open. But amazingly enough, it worked. Crazy Man splashed off, and I fell back against the wall, dazed and panting.

And very confused, because I wasn't on the stairs.

I was in a low-ceilinged, stone-built tunnel flooded with water and people unhappy about it. Maybe because more was pouring in every second, spilling through grates, trickling down walls, and gushing off another staircase-turned-waterfall at the far end of what I now recognized as the dungeons. The same ones Pritkin and I had just escaped from.

And now that my brain was getting back to work, I had a pretty good idea why.

And that was before someone chuckled in my ear.

Someone I didn't see, even when I whipped my head around.

"That was clever," a woman's voice said as I stared at more darkness. "For a minute, I thought you were a goner."

"J-Johanna?"

Genuine mirth echoed off the walls, free and easy and sincerely amused. "Of course. How many ghosts do you know?"

"You're not a ghost!"

"Close enough," she whispered as something detached itself from the ceiling, dropping down at me like a huge bat.

I ducked down into the almost-waist-deep water, but it didn't help. A spectral talon reached out for me and I slapped it away, causing my hand to feel like it had been flayed to the bone. And my attacker to give off a high-pitched screech and tumble through the wall, in a thrash of black smoke.

"So it *was* true." Johanna's voice came again, sounding amazed. "You *are* a necro!"

"So are you!" I snapped, trying to spot her in the darkness.

"Ah, but I'm not Pythia." The hateful voice echoed strangely in the confined space. "I wouldn't even have been an acolyte if they'd known. Yet what do we have here? A filthy necromancer as one of the chosen! I had to see that for myself.

"And now I have."

Her tone should have warned me, a second before something erupted from the water, clawing at me. I felt searing pain and the sting of lost power, before I managed to throw it off my shoulder. And to stumble backward, hitting the wall again. And staring around wildly, because I hadn't seen where it went.

"You should be more careful," Johanna chided. "One more accident and you're finished."

"That makes two of us!" I said, furious and afraid. Because that hadn't been an acolyte. That had been a ghost. Like the one that had attacked me upstairs, not kicking me in the chest so much as diving right through it, mugging me of power in the way that only one thing could.

And shifting me here in the process.

Or no, not shifting, I thought. *Phasing.* Because she couldn't afford—

My thoughts broke off when two more shadows dove for me. And they were coming from both directions this time, too fast to dodge and too deadly to survive. I screamed, a sound lost among all the others, and started to shift—

And stopped halfway through the spell, magic stuttering around me, when the shadows froze at a word from their mistress.

"How am I finished?" Jo asked, after a beat. "From where I stand, I'd say I'm well ahead."

I didn't answer, too busy struggling to breathe, because an aborted spell is a *bitch*. And because that wasn't what she'd meant. She'd meant "You just traveled fifteen hundred years into the past and were mugged by a ghost. How can you shift?"

Didn't expect that, did you? I thought savagely. She'd known I was a necromancer, probably tipped off by something one of her ghosts saw. But not that I'd figured out her special way of slipping through the centuries, by just avoiding them altogether. But I had, and as a result, I wasn't as exhausted as I should have been after a jump I'd never had to make.

I eyed the spirits warily. They just hung there, barely a haze on the darkness, just one shade of black among many. And bigger than before, because they'd wised up. They were dispersing themselves, so I'd have a harder time grabbing them next time.

And there'd be a next time, just as soon as Johanna figured out how to kill me before I brought the Pythian posse down on our heads. The posse that was mainly looking for me, but who might catch her in their net, too. And that would be inconvenient, wouldn't it?

Like it would be for me if they missed her.

"Cat got your tongue?" she demanded, while I tried to watch both shadows at once.

And therefore wasn't watching the fey, who were going cell by cell now, doing a systematic search and pushing people this way. One of whom elbowed me as he passed, panicked and terrified. And caused me to stumble back into a cell.

I recovered almost immediately, but it didn't help.

The ghosts were in the doorway now.

"Give it up, Johanna!" I said, furious at myself. "When you thought you only needed the staff, you stood a chance. Grab it and run, before anyone knew you'd changed anything. But now—"

"And what about now?"

The voice came from somewhere in front of me—I thought. I couldn't be sure because I still couldn't see her. Because she was phased, and therefore just out of reach. Or was she?

I had a flash of Lydia, the witchy-looking Pythia, slashing through the air and almost gutting me. Instead, she pulled me partly back into real time, because Billy's paranoia had ensured that I was almost there anyway. And so was Jo; she had to be, or else how could she talk to me?

And if she was close enough to talk, maybe she was close enough to make a mistake, too.

I resisted the urge to finger my bracelet, and concentrated on locating that voice.

"Now you need the whole suit of armor, or what's left of it," I said to her, my ears straining. "And every Pythia for the last fifteen hundred years is out there, just waiting for one of us to screw up. You'll never get all four pieces before they grab you!"

"Who says I'm trying to get any of them?"

I kept searching for her in the darkness, but that threw me. Not just the words, but the tone. It said that one of us was delusional—and she didn't think it was her.

"You've been chasing the staff—"

"Oh yes, all over the damn countryside, thanks to you." The amusement was mixed with annoyance now. "The idiot fey. They had it *in their hands*, until they allowed some half-breed to steal it back. And the fey of our time couldn't even tell me where it happened, since the idiots in question got themselves killed shortly thereafter! But my ghosts and I tracked it down nonetheless, painstakingly, over *weeks*. Just in time to see the half-breed taking it off to Faerie with you."

I had a sudden image of that night, the unnatural explosions, the fiery forest, the trees toppling in crashes that shook the earth and sent waves of sparks skyward. And Pritkin tear-assing down a river like it was a highway, with a bunch of murderous Svarestri on his heels. He'd picked me up along the way and we dove through a portal, because we hadn't had a lot of choice. I'd had no idea that Jo was even there, but I really wished she'd come along for the ride.

There was a good chance she wouldn't have made it back.

"You should have joined us," I said, and heard her snort.

"I preferred to take my chances at Nimue's, where I knew the staff would show up eventually. The fey had told me that much, at least. But heading into that hellhole hadn't been my idea of fun, either, until you forced it on me—"

"And you failed again."

"I didn't fail." It was sharp. "I blended in perfectly, just another human slave. I might as well have been furniture! All I had to do was wait for the half-breed to bring the staff to me."

"Because that's what was supposed to happen," I guessed. "Before you and I got involved. He freed Morgaine."

I was trying to keep her talking, in order to pinpoint that voice. But it fluctuated in and out, one second a shout, the next a whisper. And sometimes sped up or down, like a kid playing with an old-fashioned turntable.

Or like an acolyte having trouble straddling the barrier.

"Who went on a tear," Jo agreed. "And despite showing up a day late, when attacks from the covens had heightened security to a ludicrous degree, he somehow got in anyway. Both of you did. But you didn't have the staff. I watched them search you, and later looked through your possessions, but it wasn't there. How did you manage it?"

"Trade secret," I said, wondering if there was a reason the ghosts were framing the doorway, instead of standing in front of it. But if I sent my knives and I was wrong . . .

I didn't think it would be good if I was wrong.

"Don't tell me, then," she said spitefully. "It doesn't matter. I already won!"

"You—" I stopped, halfway through a thought. "You don't have the staff."

"I don't *need* the staff. Do you still not get it? Something I did—or you did—caused it to end up in Nimue's greedy little hands after the battle, instead of disappearing like last time. Morgaine was supposed to die valiantly, and her grieving grandma to forget to look for the staff until it was too late. By the time she did, somebody else had already snatched it, and it disappeared from history, seriously screwing up Aeslinn's plans."

"His plans? Then . . . all this happened before."

"Of course! What do you think I'm doing here?" It was scornful. "They tried with three last time, which was all they had, but it didn't work. They realized they had to have four, but although they searched for the missing staff, they never found it."

"But this time, Morgaine survived—"

"And the staff went to Nimue," Jo agreed, "who brought it here. That's why she wants to fight Aeslinn tonight, before Caedmon figures it out and forces her to return it. It's also why she insisted on the ancient rules, which allow almost anything—including using two godly weapons to your opponent's one!"

"But . . . the staff isn't her element—"

"Which means it won't work for her as well as for Caedmon, but it *will work*. Enough to give her the edge. Or it would—if Aeslinn hadn't spelled the arena! As soon as the duel starts, so does the breach. And from what he told me, it won't take long."

"If he had all four pieces," I said, feeling seriously off-kilter. Like my brain had noticed something, something important, but had too much to watch to figure it out. "And he doesn't—"

"Doesn't he?"

"That's why you pulled me out! So we couldn't get the sword—"

"Is that what you think?" She laughed. "I pulled you out because you're a menace! At the mill, at Nimue's—both times it should have been easy. Just pop out and grab the thing. But then you showed up, no idea what you're doing but shedding chaos anyway! But not this time. Everything is set up perfectly, and I'm not about to let you ruin it."

"It's already ruined!" I stared around. "Missing the sword or the staff—it doesn't matter! They're still one piece short!"

"Oh, but they're not. Nimue is taking them the staff and shield as we speak, and Aeslinn already has the helm. And as for the sword . . ." She laughed again. "Arthur, the stupid prick, *buried it*. Under the sands of the arena—"

"No." I shook my head. "No, I *saw*—"

"You saw a pommel and a sheath. That's all anybody ever sees. Otherwise, it sears your damn retinas out, like it almost did to me. That's when he did it, you know? Last night, when we were wrestling in Nimue's caravan, he was here, drawing the sword to replace the blade with another. The real one is now under the arena, where he

plans to use it to fool Aeslinn. As if a being thousands of
years old was likely to be taken in by any trick a human
could devise!"

"It's already there?" I asked numbly, feeling hope
erode. At the back of my mind, I'd assumed that Pritkin
had it, that he'd hidden it somewhere, glamouried so the
fey couldn't find it. And maybe he had.

But if so, he'd hidden the decoy.

The real one wasn't there.

"So yes, he has them all," Johanna said, sounding ex-
ultant. "Now all we have to do is sit back and wait."

"Sit back. . . ." I stopped, because suddenly, nothing
made sense.

And then everything did, and my heart froze in my
chest.

"You . . . you're not trying to take the staff out of the
timeline, are you?" I asked. "You're trying to bring Ares
back now. You're trying to bring him back *here*."

It seemed impossible. Didn't she get the implications?
She was a time traveler. She had to!

But it didn't sound like it. "Why not?" The voice was
amused. "In our time, the Circle is perfecting all kinds of
nasty new weapons, and the demons are gathering in
force. But here . . . who is waiting here?"

"But this Ares *doesn't know you*. He doesn't know
anything about you! If you bring him back now—"

"Ah, still thinking like everybody else." Johanna clicked
her tongue in disappointment.

"Then how should I be thinking?"

"Like a Pythia! Or, better yet, like a *necromancer*."

"A necro—" I stopped.

"Now you're getting it." She sounded like a teacher with
a particularly dim-witted pupil. "If you're outside time,
you're outside time. It has no hold over you. And right now
Ares is outside time in his own universe, waiting for a door
to open into this one. *Any* door. And it will be here, where
the other gods are conveniently banished, where the magical community is small and divided, and where no one, no
one at all, is expecting it."

I put a hand to my head. It was reeling so hard that I
literally thought I might be going insane. "But . . . but

even if you bring through the Ares from our time, he's still planning to kill magic workers! All of them—or didn't you get that?"

"Oh yes, I got that." And suddenly, there was something besides amusement in her tone. "He's planning to kill all the magic workers . . . like those who marginalized me, belittled me, humiliated me my whole life, because my magic was different from theirs? *Those* magic workers?"

"But this is the *past*. Johanna, if the magical community ceases to exist, so do you! So do both of us!"

"Do you think I care? Do you have *any* idea—no, of course you don't." It was acid. "You don't know what it's like to grow up smarter than everyone else, more talented, more powerful—just not in an accepted way. So they shun you, or if you manage to successfully hide what you can do, they condescend—God, how they did! To *me*, who was a thousand times better than any of them!"

I didn't say anything. My heart was pounding. I had planned for a lot of things, but not this. To fight the battle where I had almost no allies and a thousand enemies—no. Not *here*.

"I wanted to kill myself so many times," Jo was saying. "Dreamed about it, lusted for it. But something always stopped me. Some rage at the unfairness of it all, the knowledge that I could die, but they would still be there, that they would *win*. Even if I took some with me, what was that? A handful out of a whole society? When it was the whole damn thing that had cursed me! Some passed the laws, others agreed with them, others just couldn't be bothered to change anything, despite knowing they were wrong. When Ares was making his little pitch, trying to get us on his side, I was thinking the whole time—this is it. *This is how I do it*."

I tried to force myself to think, but this time, my brain wasn't cooperating. Part of it was concentrating on the sound of the search growing closer: cell doors banging, people shouting, fists hitting skin. Another was watching the ghosts, who would be on me in a second if I didn't. And a third just kept repeating: Not here, not now. Not here, not now. *Not here, not now.*

"The others wanted prestige, power, fame," Jo said scornfully. "Imagining themselves some conqueror's queen, or listening to his empty promises of godhood. Or freaking out because he showed them visions of the destruction of his enemies. He planned to use us and then cast us aside, but me? I was sitting there the whole time, thinking about how I could use *him*."

"Use him . . . how?" I asked numbly, watching Caedmon's officer slosh furiously past the cell.

"How do you think? I'm not bringing back a god. I'm bringing back a *weapon*, a weapon against the world that hated me from birth. Let them die—let them all die! And I will laugh in the flames!"

"You're crazy," I said as the officer appeared in the door again, walking backward, his face incredulous. "You're completely insane."

"If I am, it's because they made me that way. But soon, it won't matter. In a few minutes, the duel starts and everything changes. And unfortunately for you, I want to be there to see it," she said. And then three things happened at once: her ghosts dove for me, my power flooded around me, and the officer tore through the door—

And fell into a barely phased woman, who was too angry to straddle nontime properly, and was knocked out by his passing.

And into my arms.

"So do I," I breathed, and shifted.

Chapter Fifty-four

"Are you *mad*? Let me go. Let me *go*!" Jo thrashed in my arms, but her ghosts weren't around to help her this time. They'd been excluded, along with the mad-eyed officer and a crap ton of freezing water. Leaving just the two of us to rematerialize in the middle of the great hall.

And almost fall through the floor.

I stared around in shock while struggling to hold on to the writhing girl. Because this place . . . What had happened to this place?

The great hall had been cleaved down the middle, like from the stroke of a giant ax. Far above our heads, a dome of ice had formed over the gap, which would otherwise have been open to the skies. Moonlight or starlight or some kind of light was flooding in, eerily blue and enough to allow me to see rain lashing at the top of the dome. But the ice held, holding it back, making it look like we were standing inside the world's biggest snow globe.

The rain scattered the rays, strobing the room like a disco ball, and glistening off the snow that had covered everything. Including the sides of a huge scar in the floor, the other half of the ax stroke, which we'd almost fallen into. It was six feet wide in places, tearing a swath across the stones, ruining the mosaics, and clawing through the delicate mural of a smiling goddess on the wall.

I stared at the ruined portrait, and a cold shiver ran through me.

And then one of a different kind, when Jo stamped on my insole, elbowed me in the stomach, and broke away. Only to whirl back around and punch me in the face. It was hard enough that I tasted blood, and the next blow was worse, throwing me back on my ass, and scattering burning snow everywhere.

No one had bothered to mention that the bookworm was built like a jock.

I rolled when she tried to stamp my head into the stones, and felt that strange snow start to sear the side of my face.

"You bloody idiot!" she growled, and came for me.

Only to stumble when I jumped back to my feet and shifted behind her, getting her in a choke hold.

"Don't you understand?" She fought and thrashed. "They'll kill us both!"

"Thought you wanted to die," I breathed as reality wavered and shook, as the air tightened around us, as magic swirled and hissed and arced across the room like lightning, prickling on my skin and sparking off the walls.

"Not before I *finish this*!" Jo snarled. "Now let me *go*!"

"Too late," I whispered, because it was—for both of us.

And suddenly, the big, empty room wasn't empty anymore.

Instead, we were facing a crowd of Pythias and their acolytes, arrayed like the audience at a play in the round. Splashed with falling rain-shadows, backlit by glittering ice, they were everywhere: Grecian robes and antique gowns and outfits I didn't know and couldn't place. Like the leopard skin draped across the shoulders of an African Pythia, her black braids swinging. Or the wild red curls of a girl in homespun and furs, like something out of *Beowulf*. Or the cold-eyed stare of a woman dressed like a pagan priestess, her elaborate dark chignon and elegant pleated gown looking like she'd just stepped off an ancient frieze.

Exactly how far back did they go for help? I wondered, staring around, while the women looked back, silently. They didn't move, didn't talk, didn't even seem to breathe, or maybe I just couldn't hear them over the sound of my own labored gasps. I was suddenly seriously impressed with my new acolytes, who had somehow managed to keep this many Pythias confused and off my ass.

As if she'd heard, a furious woman with a head of pale purple curls pushed through the crowd, dragging my two helpers by the arms, before throwing them into the open space between us.

"What have you *done*?" It thundered like the fey's voices had earlier, like we were in a concert hall or a great cathedral. But she didn't need the acoustical help. I was already plenty intimidated, thank you, Gertie.

I licked my lips and tried to figure out where to start, only to have Jo beat me to it. "A great deal," she said quickly. "I'm so grateful to see all of you! My name is Jo Zirimis and I'm a Pythia, too—"

"Liar!" Hildegarde snarled, from off the floor, silver curls in her face, blue eyes flashing.

"—with a rogue acolyte!" Jo said, raising her voice to talk over her. "One who has been eluding me for months—"

"It's not true—you know it's not true!" Abigail said tearfully. She looked rough. Her smooth brown bun was down in a tangled mess, her nicely made-up face was pale and tear-streaked, and her carefully pressed homespun was muddy and wrinkled and sprinkled with leaves and hay.

I sent her a sympathetic look, but there wasn't much more I could do. Except to release Jo, because the Pythias weren't going to let her leave, any more than they were me. Not until we finished this.

Which would have been fine if I'd had any idea how to do that.

My hopes had been pinned on Hildegarde, but it didn't look like the ties that bind had been used for anything but securing her wrists behind her. And I didn't think she'd made much headway before that, because Gertie was giving me a look that might best be described as incandescent rage. But, for once, she was asking for an explanation, which was something.

"I'm the Pythia. She's my rogue." I gestured at Jo, who gave a scornful laugh.

"You know better than that," she told them. "You've seen what she's done—and so has Caedmon. Ask him if you doubt me. I warned him about her days ago!"

"She did." I hadn't seen the supermodel of the fey world until that moment, because I'd been concentrating on Gertie. But he was there, among the crowd, and he didn't look any happier with me than she did. Dark green eyes surveyed me without pleasure, the beautiful face cold, the expression unreadable. "She and a man of our time stole a valuable relic from me. I also caught them attempting to steal the king's sword, earlier this evening."

"To keep it away from Jo!" I said, a little frantically, because his words had caused a murmur to go around the room. "Myrddin explained that—or he would have, if you'd given him a chance—"

"He had his chance." The gaze was glacial. "His king was two rooms away. If he had a warning to give, he could have done it."

"There wasn't time, and Arthur—" I broke off, because explaining that the king had planned to defraud the fey—including Caedmon—wasn't likely to help my case. Arthur was never going to admit that. "There wasn't time," I repeated. "And there's less now. The duel is about to start, and when it does—"

"You see? She has no excuse," Jo said, talking over me. "I apologize for allowing her to cause such upheaval, but if you will help me—"

"You're not a Pythia!" I snapped.

"It's true, Gertie," Hildegarde said. "For once in your life, stop being so stubborn and *listen*."

"I've listened enough."

"You haven't listened at all—you never did!" She appealed to Lydia, whose black robes stood out in stark contrast to the more colorful garb around her. "You know how she is—"

The little white-haired woman nodded. "Aye, I do. And I know how ye were, too, always so softhearted. That's why I trained her. This job takes a thick skin—"

"And a clear head," Gertie added, her eyes still fixed on me.

"Damn it all! I haven't been influenced!" Hildegarde thundered.

"And if ye had, what would ye say?" Lydia asked her, not unkindly.

"And what about me?" Abigail demanded. "Have I been influenced, too? You can't believe—"

"I believe what I've seen!" Gertie said, throwing out a hand in my direction. "Five times she's escaped me! Five times I've had to hunt her down—"

"And who else besides a Pythia could do that?" Hildegarde demanded.

"A rogue heir," Jo said quickly. "I misspoke before. She was an acolyte, until I recently promoted her, something I can assure you—"

"You lie!" I said, feeling my hands clench and blood flood my face. God, how I wanted to—

"Don't do it, Cass," Billy said, suddenly zooming in.

I stared upward in surprise, and no little anger. "You took your time!"

"We got held up. First with the posse and then—"

"And then *what*?"

"—with some rogue spirits headed this way."

"Somebody had given them a power boost," the colonel said, zooming in behind him, his mustache twitching. "And we'd expended most of our extra. Otherwise, three on two is hardly sporting—"

"But delicious," Daisy said, burping.

"You see?" Jo asked. "To my horror, I discovered that she's a necromancer, using illegal skills in unprecedented ways—"

"You're the necromancer!" I said, furious.

"Then whose ghosts are those?" she asked sweetly.

"We'll show you," the colonel snarled, diving for Jo before I could stop him. Forcing me to snatch him out of the air, to keep this from descending into chaos.

And then pausing, when I noticed everyone staring at me.

"That . . . probably wasn't your best move," Billy murmured as Johanna practically crowed.

"See?" Her eyes flashed. "Did you see? *I told you*—"

"Aye, we saw," Lydia said as the murmuring got louder.

"Cassie—" Abigail said, looking appalled.

And yeah, I screwed up. "I—I am a necromancer," I told them, because obviously. "But I'm Pythia, too—"

"They would never make such a creature Pythia," the leopard-draped woman said. She wasn't speaking English, but the spell translated her voice just fine. And it looked like everyone else was using something similar, because there was a lot of nodding suddenly.

"Please!" I said, trying to think of something that would convince them, something that wasn't "the fey are about to bring back a god," because that wasn't likely to help. But what else did I have? "The fey are about to bring back a god," I said, with a sinking feeling. "If you don't help me—"

"I already heard that story," Gertie said, walking toward me. "Do better."

"How?" I spread out my hands. "How do I prove I'm Pythia? How does any—"

"She's not a Pythia," Jo spat. "She's a filthy necromancer who infiltrated the court, and I formally request that you help me—"

"One more word," Hildegarde told her, "and I swear—"

"Be silent! Both of you!"

Gertie must have done something to enhance her voice, because it echoed everywhere, enough to bring down a filtering of powder from the rafters. I looked at her through the veil of snow, and knew this was my last chance. Come up with something now, something she'd believe, or she'd take me back. Or, considering her expression, kill me where I stood.

"Well?" she demanded.

I flashed on an image of Pritkin, somewhere fighting alone. But he couldn't do this alone. None of us could. It had been the same ever since I started this job, clinging on by my fingernails, always feeling off balance, like I was barely treading water, and then only because of the people holding me up: Jonas and Pritkin, Tami and Rhea, Marco and Caleb, Billy and Casanova, and even the consul at times—

And one I'd known long before all of them.

My eyes widened.

Gertie frowned. "What?"

"There is something that unites us," I said. "All of us for the last six hundred years, at least. One shared experience that she doesn't know about, but I do!"

"Don't listen to her!" Jo said, grabbing my arm. "She's a liar! She was always—"

I jerked away, scanning the crowd. And spied a dark, curly head and an elegant gown, but the same pair of cheap tinsel earrings. "Eudoxia!"

The head came up.

"Mircea visited court, when you were still living with Berenice—do you remember?"

She nodded.

"He helped you feed the dogs," I said, concentrating on that fleeting memory. "He wanted to see the Lady—"

"But she was sick," Eudoxia said, and then flushed when everyone suddenly turned to look at her. "She was sick a lot."

"Yet he got in eventually. He always does. And then he came to see you, after you moved to Paris." I searched my mind, trying to remember. "He brought you a—a necklace." I tapped my throat, seeing again the lustrous chain. "Big pearls set in gold—"

"Yes." She looked surprised. "I don't wear it much. It's . . . not really my style."

"—and he asked for something, didn't he?"

She nodded. "Yes, he wanted—"

"Don't say it!"

She paused, her mouth still open, while I looked for—"Isabeau!"

"Yes," she said, before I could ask. "He came to see me, too. And stayed . . . for a while."

"Because he wanted something, the same thing he always wants. The same thing he's asked of every Pythia for *six hundred years*." I whirled on Gertie. "The same thing he asked of you. I can tell you what that was. Can *she*?"

I gestured at Jo, who backed up slightly to keep from getting hit, while everyone looked at her.

"Well?" Gertie demanded. "What of it?"

"I—this is ridiculous," Jo said, still smiling. "I . . . receive so many petitioners. We all do. You can't expect me to recall one man out of thousands—"

"Not a man," I said, advancing on her. "And Lord Mircea is *memorable*."

"Can't argue with that," someone said.

"Every Pythia for six hundred years has received the same *vampire* with the same request, soon after their accession if not before. And not for a fleeting visit. He comes to charm, to entice, to bribe if necessary, anything to get what he wants. *What does he want?*"

"How would I know?" Jo snarled. "He didn't come to see me yet—"

"No, he didn't, did he? He might butter up another acolyte, but you—you were just a political appointment, there to round out the court and buy the Circle a favor. He wouldn't waste time with you—"

"You lie! She lies!" Johanna looked around at the sea of faces, but didn't seem to find it helpful this time. "I—I just took the throne. That's why I'm having so much trouble with—"

"Just took the throne, yet ye already have an heir?" Lydia asked, black eyes steady.

"It's true, I swear. We do things differently in my time—"

"But Lord Mircea *doesn't*," I said, driving home the point. "He does the same thing he's always done, the same thing he's done for centuries, and visits each Pythia in turn to beg for one thing. The return of his *wife*. I know that because he came to me, too. Because I am *Pythia*, you are a *rogue*, and this is *over*. You are *beaten*, Johanna!"

"Nobody beats me!" she snarled, and lunged.

The next thing I knew, I was skidding on my back, but not across burning ice. The ice cave of a room had disappeared, flashing out in a wink. To be replaced by a vast, echoing field of—

Nothing.

I skidded to a stop, which took longer than normal, because there was no friction and nothing to grab on to. Just blackness, stretching to infinity. Deep and dark and with no discernible horizon. Just a few, faint, almost invisible to the eye—

Sparks of light.

I tried to scramble to my feet, staring at what looked like distant fireflies, but weren't. And almost fell over, because I didn't have feet. I didn't have anything. I looked down to see a ghostly outline of my body shining in the darkness, but brighter, because I wasn't a ghost.

But I was close.

"Johanna!" I screamed, but she was nowhere to be seen. Nothing was, except the vague illumination I was throwing on the ground, the light of my spirit etching the darkness. Because she hadn't just knocked me out of time—she'd knocked me out of my *body*, sending me into the Badlands as a disembodied spirit. I didn't know how.

Even worse, I didn't know why.

And then I figured it out.

I heard a roar, deep in the distance, but loud enough to make me jump. And something pale as milk appeared on the horizon, shining like a beacon. Something huge—a giant figure, even at a distance—and rapidly getting bigger. Something man-shaped that was striding and then running this way, only it wasn't a man. It wasn't anything like a man, and it never had been.

Even before I killed it.

And then it was on top of me.

I looked up, up, up, to what a second ago had been an empty void, but which was now filled with—

A foot.

Specifically, the sandal-clad foot of a golden god, shining like his symbol in the night. Light like from a pale sun spilled out impossibly around us, impossible because he couldn't be here, he couldn't be anywhere, because he was dead. Dead, which meant ghost, which meant he could be here even though I'd killed him, killed him and flushed him down the metaphysical equivalent of a toilet—

Straight into the Badlands.

A fact that he seemed to recall quite vividly.

"Pythia," he hissed.

And then that foot was coming down on me.

Chapter Fifty-five

Somebody screamed, but I didn't think it was me. Because I was experiencing the sensation of being squashed flat as a pancake. And I *was* experiencing it, since spirits don't have the same issues as humans with broken bones and rent flesh.

They do have other problems, though.

I felt the power loss, immediate and deadly. And realized that Apollo was trying to do to me what Daisy had done to all those faded ghosts, and steal whatever remained of my energy. But I wasn't a remnant, and it hadn't worked entirely.

But it had come close.

By the time he lifted up his foot, I was too weak to fight, or even to peel myself off the ground. I just lay there, watching Billy circle around, trying to reach me. But he was being given no opportunity. I'd killed Apollo, and he was determined to return the favor.

But he was going to tell me about it first.

"A lifetime," he hissed, bending down. "That's what it has felt like. Subsisting off these tattered dregs, watching the world I couldn't enter, watching *you*, and waiting. And now you're here."

It was a hand this time, smashing down on whatever was left of me, pulling my remaining energy away. And worse than anything, even worse than dying, was knowing what he was going to do with it. "You're going back," I whispered.

"Ironic, isn't it?" he asked, in faux sympathy. "Draining you will give me life again, and the Pythian power will do the rest. Who knew that the small piece of myself I carved out all those centuries ago would be my salvation? But with it, I can hunt. With it, I can *feed*. Before long, I'll be as strong as I ever was. My only regret is that you won't be here to see what I'm going to do to your friends, to your *world*, in your name. But I assure you, it will be—"

He cut off, I didn't know why. I could hardly breathe, barely think. Everything was a panic of pain, horror, and hopelessness.

But I could still see.

Enough to make out the light that had just appeared in the distance, shining so brightly it hurt. If I could have moved, I'd have shaded my eyes. Instead, I just lay there, looking at what appeared to be a small star fallen to earth. Or an angel. Or . . .

A god.

A real one, a living one.

Because Caedmon suddenly didn't look like himself at all. I'd thought him beautiful before, with features so perfect they didn't seem real. But I could barely see them now, so eclipsed were they by the radiance of his power. Did you miss one, Mother? I wondered vaguely. Did you miss . . . ?

But she couldn't have; the spell couldn't have. But it could have missed a demigod. One not half human but half *fey*.

And I guessed that made all the difference.

Next to Caedmon's brilliance, I was dim, powerless, uninteresting. Next to him, I was barely visible, just a shadow on the darkness. Next to him, I almost didn't exist at all.

And Apollo must have thought so, too. Because he suddenly took off, drawn, like every other ghost I'd ever met, to the biggest source of power around. Leaving me to die in the darkness alone.

Or with Billy, who was doing something.

Instead of enveloping me as he had done on the drag, he was pushing and pulling and heaving and yanking. I didn't understand why until I noticed that the number of sparkles in the air had increased. And that the pitch-blackness had lightened. And that there were ghosts zooming around now, zooming around everywhere, like hunters circling wounded prey.

Billy couldn't carry me and fight them at the same time, so he was taking turns. But the closer to the barrier we came, the thicker they became, until they felt like a smothering cloud. Until I could barely see the darkness anymore. Until Billy was forced to drop me, standing over me with his usual pleasant, round face contorted into something unrecognizable, and a dreadful screech emanating from his lips: the tearing-metal sound of a ghostly challenge.

Many of the smaller spirits fled, not willing to take the risk. But the larger ones stuck around, deciding that a feast was worth a fight. And that was bad—that was very bad—because there were a lot of them and only one of Billy, and he couldn't fight them all.

"Billy," I whispered.

"We're going to make it!"

"Billy—"

"Shut up, Cass!"

"I won't shut up." Because we weren't going to make it; there were too many. And while none of them wanted to be first, as soon as one attacked, they'd all be on us. I knew that because I knew ghosts—and so did he. "If you stay, you'll just die, too. But if you run—"

"Shut up!" He turned that horrifying visage on me, but it didn't work. Because it didn't look terrible to me. It looked like a friend. One I was suddenly desperately afraid for.

"—they'll let you go," I sobbed. "Please, Billy, they don't want you—"

"Too bad, because they're going to get me!" he snarled. "Next one who tries it never tries anything again. How bad you want it, huh?" He stared around at the all-enveloping cloud. *"How bad?"*

That last was a scream, echoing through the air. It was pretty intimidating, even to me, and it might have worked—on humans. But these weren't. And while some had enough sanity left to understand the threat, plenty didn't. They didn't understand anything anymore—except hunger.

"Billy!" I screamed, glimpsing something coming this way. But it was too late, because it was too fast and too strong and—

And ours.

I stared as the colonel swooped down, colliding with two ghosts that had been sneaking up behind us. The trio turned into a whirlwind of flashing lights and screeching voices, while another ghost, this one huge, shot past them and jumped Billy Joe. The two immediately became embroiled in a fight so furious it was impossible to tell where one started and the other stopped.

But the dam had burst now, the attack giving the hovering spirits a chance to descend in force. Hard nips, painful gashes, and biting wounds seeped what remained of my power out into the air of this place, like a haze of blood. I screamed and fought, even knowing it wouldn't do any good, because they were literally eating me alive.

And then a ghostly screech, louder than any I'd heard so far, louder than any I'd ever heard, shivered through the space around me. It was deafening, a piercing din that cut through my head like a stake to the brain, making me cry out. And momentarily stopped the attack when the ghosts, most of which were too nebulous to have faces, nonetheless gave the impression of looking up—

Just in time to be swallowed whole, like a school of fish by a diving whale. Only the whale was an old woman in a neon-lit housecoat, so bright she seared the eyes, and so solid she might as well have been human. Daisy roared, I stared, and she took off, chasing after the remains of the fleeing mob.

I looked around but couldn't see the colonel. But I caught a glimpse of Billy off to my left. And it looked like he was winning, too, the smear of his red ruffled shirt slowly eclipsing the blue of his assailant's. Unfortunately, the ghost had drawn him off, leaving me open to be savaged by the smaller spirits Billy had frightened away, who flew back at the first sign of an advantage.

What felt like a dozen wasps stung me all at once. And each tiny bite, each bit of stolen power, left me more vulnerable the next time. From within my body, they wouldn't have been able to hurt me much, but without it—

I wasn't going to last long without it.

But Billy had gotten me close enough to the barrier that it spilled a haze of light all around me. I could see it. I could even see through it a little, although what I could see didn't make sense. Just an empty room, swirling with snow light, with not even my acolytes remaining.

But I didn't care about that now; I only cared about getting back—into time, into my body, into some kind of protection—for all of us.

My friends wouldn't leave without me, so I *had* to get out.

I had to.

I started crawling, the ghosts coming with me, still feeding. I lashed out when I had the strength, ignored them when I didn't, and crawled as fast as I could. Until the light got stronger, flooding the area around me, while the screams and screeches and muffled roars from behind grew fainter.

But not the ones that had come with me.

They even sounded like insects, I thought, a constant buzzing in my ears. But increasingly, they didn't feel like them. The spirits weren't biting now so much as leeching on to me, a dozen, maybe two, hanging off my sides, my back, my thighs, while more circulated, trying to find an open spot. I could feel my remaining strength going into them—not as fast as in Apollo's attack, but fast enough.

They were bleeding me dry.

My hands finally found the skin of time, and scraped across it, desperate, shaking. No, I thought, watching the ceiling slide by in fits and starts, as someone dragged my body across the floor. No, I'm not dead yet; no, please help! But they couldn't hear; they didn't come.

And I was running out of time.

I got to my knees, pounding against the barrier with my fists, but there was no way in. And then a spirit darted in from the crowd, bigger than the others, brighter, stronger, and latched on to my throat. It felt exactly like an animal bite, fangs sinking deep, causing me to scream in agony. And to rip it off, blind with pain and with the shimmering energy that the move released.

The discharge of power caused something like a feeding frenzy, the cloud of spirits suddenly so big and bright that I couldn't even see the barrier anymore. I couldn't see anything, except for pulsing brilliance. And, increasingly, I couldn't feel, my body becoming lighter and fainter, and dimmer, as my own light began to fade.

"Immortals don't know how to die, do they?"

It was Roger, back in the cottage, talking to me while Jonas waited outside. The place was so pretty, a doll's house of a home. And cozy. Made even more so by the faint rain falling past the windows. It was a strange counterpoint to his words.

I looked back at him. "Don't they?"

"No, I don't think so. Just as most humans would not do very well as immortals, the gods do not handle it well when confronted by death. They don't have our peace with it."

"I don't have any peace with it," I said bitterly.

"Compared to them? Yes, you do. We humans have an instinctive knowledge of death. We are born, knowing that, one day, we will die. It gives us certain advantages."

"I don't see any."

"Don't you? Each day is more precious when you know you don't have an infinite number of them. Each experience more savored, each friend more valued. We may live shorter lives, but in a way, we live fuller ones."

"Is that what Mother wanted? To live fuller?"

He paused and pushed the ridiculous glasses up his long nose. They reflected the light of the weakened spells, making them run with rainbows, like some novelty item out of a souvenir store. They should have made him look ridiculous.

They didn't.

"She told me recently that she felt like she'd only really begun to understand life as she reached the end of it. I've thought about it a lot, and I think, at the root of it all, that was the problem with the gods. Always fighting, always striving to outdo each other, to leave a mark, because, ultimately, nothing they did seemed to matter. They knew the centuries would wash it all away. And they were right, weren't they?"

"The same is true for us," I pointed out. *"Someday no one will remember us, either."*

"Ah, but that's not really the point for us, is it?" The rainbow lenses tilted, the changed position allowing me to see the thoughtful eyes behind them. *"Whether someone remembers us or not? We're not gods, waiting in their temples to be worshipped. We're part of a dynamic, ongoing world, and we have our own immortality through what we achieve, or through the children we leave behind. She will continue through you, as I will.*

"Never forget that, Cassie. You're my child, too."

His child, I thought, fuzzily.

A necromancer's child.

A necromancer.

Slowly, as if in a dream, I reached out. And grabbed one of the swarming pulses of light. And squeezed.

And watched my hand slowly brighten. It looked like I was wearing a brilliantly colored glove for a moment, next to the dimness of the rest of me. Until another small spirit darted in and began to feed, leeching the light . . .

No, I thought dizzily.

Not the light.

The power.

I closed my hand on it, too, crushing the gnawing thing inside my fist. Like the other, it felt tangible, real. And soft and spongy, like it was oozing up through my fingers for a second.

Before suddenly sinking inside.

My hand brightened again, and I stared at it, mesmerized even with the continued attack. Because it wasn't only brighter. It was stronger.

I grabbed a small ghost leeching off my breast, and crushed it like the last one. And yes, I felt it, and yes, it was good, and potent, and . . . *more.* Quickly, before I became too weak to fight back.

Already, it wasn't easy. The smaller ones were mindless, little more than freed energy, the kind that would turn into sparkles in the air when they degraded a bit more. They hurt in small ways, and gave back in small ways, when I grabbed fistfuls, ripping them off me.

Many of that kind skittered off when I started fighting back, some instinct telling them to flee. But others stayed. Too mindless to know what was happening or too drunk on power to care.

Or too strong to think they'd lose.

And they might be right. Because the ones who didn't belong here, the hunters, had increased their drain. Trying to finish me off when they realized they had a fight on their hands.

I ripped a huge leech off my side, gasping in pain. It was amorphous, too busy feeding to manifest features, and plump and bright with stolen energy. *My* energy. I felt it rake me with claws, snarling and thrashing like a wild animal as I fought it, with my back against the wall.

A wall that was suddenly feeling more porous.

A moment ago, it had been hard as glass; now it was more like rubber, giving behind me, but not enough.

The creature in my arms clawed and squirmed, but I was a *living* spirit, and I was stronger. I hung on, hugged it to me, felt its power begin to seep into mine. Felt life flood back, felt pain, a thousand weeping wounds, felt the barrier give some more, stretching like taffy. But still holding.

I needed more power to break through, but it was a double-edged sword. The more I fed, the brighter I became, attracting attention from the larger fight. A lot of attention.

I stared as a mass of spirits broke away from the main cloud and headed my way. I fought and twisted, knowing it was now or never, and sent a swarm of the smaller things tumbling into the void. A number of the larger ones left of their own accord, sensing that we were about to be overrun. Except for the creature in my arms, which was noticeably dimmer now, having given back much of its stolen energy.

But not so much that it couldn't grab the fabric of time and rip it open, in a desperate bid to get away.

But not as desperate as I was. I held on, even as it scattered itself, knowing this was my last chance. I felt myself falling, felt my senses return, felt freezing cold. And then

I was slamming back into a body writhing in pain, Jonas' last dose of Tears having been completely stripped away.

The aches and pains of the past, plus a flood of new ones, hit me all at once. I screamed, a sound that echoed in the vastness of the great hall, almost causing the woman holding me by the arms to drop me. Johanna, I realized. And a second later, I realized something else: one of the reasons my body felt like it was on fire was that it was being dragged across burning ice, straight toward—

I rolled and somehow broke her hold, right on the edge of the great gash running the length of the room. The one she was trying her best to shove me into. I stared over the edge as she got behind me, and I saw our reflections for a second in a flood of cold, dark water.

I didn't know why she thought it would hurt me; the drop only looked to be a couple stories.

But if she wanted me in there, I didn't want to go.

"What does it take to kill you?" she snarled, struggling for purchase on the ice-covered floor.

Until I suddenly twisted, flinging her off her feet using one of the moves Pritkin had taught me. And then over my shoulder, grasping and fighting to the last, still trying to take me with her. She might have succeeded—except one of my hands had just frozen to the stones. I hung there, half in the gash and half out, clinging on with deadened flesh—

And realized why she'd wanted me down there.

Because the water wasn't cold; it was supercooled. Some strange alchemy had kept it in a liquid form, right up until she crashed into it. And instantly turned the water into a field of ice, one that crept over her stunned face, freezing the skin, whitening the hair, and icing over the eyes that were still staring up at me in shock and hatred.

"More than you," I whispered, and rolled onto my back.

Chapter Fifty-six

I just lay there for a long moment, panting and dizzy, staring upward. The room was strangely beautiful from this angle. I couldn't see the ruin all around me, the broken mosaics and slashed mural, the overturned tables and muddy boot prints. Just snow, clear and white and dazzling, and highlighted every now and again by lightning flashing beyond the ice dome, sending little spots of light spinning crazily across my body.

It was beautiful.

It also wasn't helping with the dizziness, or maybe that was me. I didn't know; I only knew I had to get up, to find out where my acolytes had gone, to warn them about what was about to go down in the arena. And to hope they still had the power to do something about it, because I didn't.

I didn't have the power to do anything except lie there, trying to will myself back onto my feet. But my feet weren't listening, and neither was anything else. I was alive; I was breathing; my eyes were focusing, more or less. But that was as good as it got.

And that wasn't enough.

I thought I'd become thoroughly familiar with exhaustion these past few weeks, thought I knew every desperate description and pooped permutation. But I'd been wrong. So, so wrong. I was bone tired, wearier than I'd ever been in my life, to the point I honestly thought I could go to sleep, right now, right here, with no trouble at all. And for a split second, I wondered if it mattered. What good could I be to anybody like this? I was half-dead, my power utterly spent, and the battle hadn't even started yet.

Which meant there was still time to stop it, if I could get my lazy butt off the floor.

I tried rolling over, to use my hands as leverage, and was quickly reminded that one was still stuck to the ice. So I rolled back the other way, toward the chasm this time, tugging and yanking on a hand that felt less like it was trapped by the skin than by the flesh underneath. I started prying it up anyway, feeling like cursing—

And then felt like it a lot more when I looked down.

At Johanna's body still frozen in place. At the clawed hand still raised, the fingers stiff and pale as marble. At the frost-covered face now a ghostly oval, framed by hair like a spectral halo. And at the eyes—

Which weren't nearly as dead as I'd thought.

I hung there, panting and exhausted, trapped by my own abused flesh, watching something boil behind Johanna's dead eyes. Something black and terrible. Something that burst free of the ice a second later, hurtling through the air like a striking fist.

And then it was on me.

I didn't have time to move. I barely had time to acknowledge what was happening before she hit like a ton of bricks, and then kept on coming. Because death to a necromancer is a malleable concept, and Johanna wasn't ready to go.

But she was very ready to make sure that I did.

In seconds, I felt the tethers to my body thin and slip and start to falter. Because she was trying to tear me loose, like she'd done when she knocked me into the Badlands. She'd lost her body, so now she was trying to take mine.

And I didn't think she planned on giving it back.

But she'd already pulled this trick once, and it didn't have the element of surprise. And she was a ghost, fresh and filled with power, but a *ghost*, and this was *my* body, and that carried certain privileges. Like exorcising . . . stubborn spirits . . . who needed . . . to *die* already!

I hurled Johanna out with a gasp, using up power I

couldn't afford—but then, neither could she. Without a body, ghosts run out fast, and there was only one way for her to replace hers. If I drained her enough, it would force her into the Badlands to hunt.

Where, if I was lucky, something might just finish the job for me.

And a second later, she did take off, an amorphous black cloud streaming across the wide expanse of the room. But she wasn't headed for the Badlands. She was headed for—

Shit, I thought, watching as she dove straight into a fey who'd just run in the door. And not just any fey. A Svarestri warrior armed to the teeth who began shaking and convulsing as she fought him for control.

I stared at them for a second, and then started frantically trying to pry my hand off the ice again. It hurt like hell, the pain white-hot and startling. I ignored it. I'd have more than torn flesh to worry about if she managed to—

And then she did.

The Svarestri's head suddenly shot up and turned my way. And the next time I blinked, he was coming at a dead run. So I left my hand alone and finished the job Johanna had started, bursting out of my skin and into his, just before the sword in his hand could slice through my throat.

The sword stopped midair, quivering; my soulless body collapsed behind me; and my spirit and Johanna's fought a last-ditch battle for control. And she was fighting hard. But here's the thing, Jo, I thought, gritting teeth I no longer had. Everything is harder when you're a ghost. Everything. To the point that even beat-up clairvoyants can be a real problem.

Especially if they happen to be necromancers, too.

Slowly, slowly, the sword began to waver. Slowly, slowly, I moved more toward complete control of this body. Slowly, slowly, I started to force her out—

And then everything happened at once: Jo fled, her power all but gone; the sword clattered harmlessly to the floor, barely missing my head; and I breathed a small, cautious, please-let-this-be-the-end sigh of relief.

But of course not.

* * *

A screaming bolt of red tore through the air, exploding in a mass of sparks that set the stones above my head on fire. "Damn witches," someone cursed as I jerked back out of the way.

And wondered why the very male voice had sounded like it was coming from me.

"That wasn't a witch," someone else said as I looked up at a high-arched doorway, at a tunnel splashed with fire and spell-light, at two huge torches flaming on either side illuminating a small area of well-trodden dirt. And at the stadium wall rising high above that, with bright pennants flapping in the wind, despite the rain that was still pissing down.

Because I wasn't in the great hall anymore.

There were a thousand questions crowding my mind, because I'd never possessed a fey before, and trust them to make it freaky. But only one really mattered. I tried turning my head, to look down the tunnel at the duel, but it didn't want to go. It was looking outward instead, at dark figures highlighted by flickers of spell-fire in the distance. And searching for the one that had just gotten a whole lot closer.

"Who is it, then?" I heard myself ask. "We were told there were witches—"

"Oh, they're out there, some of Morgaine's creatures. But there's a mage with them, too. He's the one you've got to—" My companion cut off, and I glanced around to see a Svarestri warrior staring at me curiously.

Probably because my hair was on fire.

"Here!" My companion shoved me around. And did something that resulted in my head feeling lighter and a great length of burning silver hair landing on the dirt at my feet. "It's spelled," he hissed.

I felt myself lick my lips. "Right."

"And watch out for the mage," he added. "He's said to be good with glamourie, so don't trust anyone."

"Including you?" I heard myself joke.

My companion smiled slightly.

And then both our heads jerked up as a barrage of spells exploded against the wall behind us and the dirt in front of us, throwing the latter up like a curtain. One that a group of Svarestri burst through a second later, in a less-than-orderly fashion, yelling orders to pull back, pull back. Which was kind of unnecessary, since my companion and I were already double-timing it into the tunnel along with everyone else.

"We're outnumbered!" one of the fey yelled—an officer, judging by his fancier outfit. "Open the gate!"

"Tell him," my companion said, nodding at me. "I don't have the password."

Everyone looked at me.

"I— We have orders," I heard myself say. "The reinforcements—"

A spell crashed against the top of the archway, sending a gust of fire through the opening, like a bellow out of hell. Shields bloomed, my companion's covering both of us, just in time. Yet I could still feel the flames, hot and bright—and wrong. Unnatural, like the creatures who cast them.

"By the time they show up, we'll be dead!" the officer thundered. "Open it now!"

"You should do what he says," my companion advised.

"I can't open it now! You know what—"

My voice cut off when another spell hit the archway, a glancing blow this time. And then rattled around inside the tunnel before smashing against our shields. My eyes lifted to see that the night outside the arch had turned smoky bright with spell-fire and loud with curses and screams.

And busy with what looked like hundreds of dark figures dashing through the smoke, headed this way.

"Open it!" the officer yelled—needlessly. Because my hands had already started fumbling at my belt for a set of keys. They were clumsy with panic and slick with sweat, and for a second, I didn't think—

There!

The lock turned; a muttered phrase dropped the shield. And a second later, we were surging through the opening. Only instead of a troop of Svarestri warriors, I was suddenly surrounded by a flood of dirty, ragged, wild-haired—

"Witches," I hissed, right before what felt like a red-hot poker bisected my ribs.

"To answer your previous question," my companion said, his silver eyes flooding green. "Especially me."

And then the world exploded in fire.

I scrambled back, panting and clawing desperately at my side—

For a big-ass knife . . . that wasn't there.

For a moment, I just sat there in flickering darkness, shaking and disoriented, which was starting to feel like my default. Only this time, it was worse, because at least I'd known where I was before. Now . . .

I had no freaking clue.

I should have been looking out through the fey's eyes, at my body sprawled on the ice. Instead, I was seeing something that looked like the view from many eyes, hundreds of them, spotting the darkness. All showing me different scenes and angles of Arthur's city.

It reminded me of a surveillance setup in a high-rise or a jail, with cameras on multiple locations being projected onto rows of TV monitors. Only instead of TV, these were free-floating images that drifted in the air all around me. And showed a city descending into chaos.

I saw people sloshing through swamped roads, heading for the woods, bags of their possessions thrown over their backs. I saw others huddled in their homes, looking fearfully out of gaps in the shutters. I saw still more fighting alongside the covens, which had arrived in force, with hundreds of witches flooding into the city.

All of whom seemed to have decided that Arthur didn't really need an amphitheater, after all, because they were trying to burn it down.

The wooden lattice of seats above the great stone base caught fire as I watched. And a moment later, half the arena was engulfed in a roaring blaze that defied the rain. The wind was blowing strongly to the left, and banners of flame three or four stories high started blowing with it, scattering sparks onto the fleeing crowd.

And onto the phalanx of Svarestri reinforcements

double-timing it from the direction of the wharf, looking a thousand strong, maybe more. It was hard to tell because of the darkness, and because the scenes weren't like movies shot with a steady cam. They were rolling and shaking and running, crisscrossed with spell-fire and lightning, and slashed at by rain.

And then I was moving, too, as the space around me suddenly convulsed, sending me rolling across the floor.

And straight into—

"Round them up! Don't let them scatter!"

My borrowed neck twisted, but I couldn't tell who had spoken. A gust of wind had just slapped me in the face, carrying enough rain to blind me. All I could see were a bunch of running, panicked faces, scrambling around the rocky ground near the docks.

"Who?" my current avatar asked, his voice sounding as confused as I was. "The humans?"

"No! Not the damn humans! Our own!"

I turned to the side, pulling up a hood to shield my eyes, while I searched the crowd. Their frightened faces were highlighted by the inferno in the distance, by the spells exploding here and there, and by the lightning gathering in force over the arena. While rain continued to bucket down, not as hard as before, but hard enough to cause the torch I was carrying to sputter and hiss.

And then this body spied a fellow fey on the ground, a little distance off. He had a local girl beneath him, her skirts up around her waist, her face set in horror. Until I ran over and pulled him off. "Get back in formation!"

He shrugged off my hold. "For what? We'll never get through that." He gestured at the open plain before us, where what looked like an army of witches were battling to protect the fleeing humans, and to bar our approach to the arena.

It had turned the open ground between the cities into a hell pit of smoke and blood and fire, and drifting clouds of steam that formed whenever a spell hit one of the many puddles of water. The women's shadows darted among the clouds, concealed one minute, and splashed grotesquely large onto the side of the haze the next, like the field was

*full of misshapen giants. They looked like the shadow
puppets I'd laughed at as a child, only no one was laughing
now.*

Including the fey on the ground, who had grabbed the
frightened girl as she tried to flee, jerking her back. "We
may as well amuse ourselves until reinforcements arrive,"
he said as I stared down at him. And felt a wash of borrowed anger spread through me.

Borrowed because it wasn't mine. It wasn't in response
to the girl's terrified screams as the fey fell on her again.
Wasn't at seeing him rip open her clothes, spreading her
naked in the mud. Wasn't in sympathy as her hands
grasped the dirt beneath her, desperately seeking some
grounding as her body shook from his renewed thrusts.

No, it was anger that he'd soil himself with such a creature, fury that he'd neglect his duty to do it, and cold determination to stop him.

My right hand jerked him up a second time, throwing
him to the side, while my left—

"No!" I yelled as a spear flashed into my hand. One
pointed not at the fey, who had scrambled back out of the
way, but at his prize. I had a split second to hear the girl
scream, to see the spear light reflected in her widened
eyes, to feel my borrowed muscles bunch.

And then I threw us to the side—stupidly, because I
wasn't in charge here. I was just an observer, using someone else's eyes to see. But it didn't matter; I couldn't do
this. Couldn't just watch through a murderer's eyes as he—

And I wasn't. The ground exploded in front of me, cutting off the view, while the blast from the spear sent me
stumbling back into the soldier behind me. We went
down, but through the rain of flying earth I glimpsed the
girl, snatching up her tattered clothes and staggering to
her feet, before abruptly bolting off into the night.

Because the fey's attack . . .

Had missed.

Chapter Fifty-seven

A moment later, I was back in flickering darkness, thrown there by what felt like an earthquake. And forced to grab for what my mind seemed to have decided was the floor, although it felt more like a bucking bronco. Because the quakes kept coming.

I didn't know why, and couldn't even seem to concentrate on the question. I couldn't seem to concentrate on anything, probably because I'd been away from my body too long and was getting fuzzy-brained. I needed to get back—soon—but there was something telling me not to. Something I'd just seen, but couldn't currently remember. Something . . . damn it!

I looked away, over to one side where the images were fewer, trying to clear my head.

And got caught up instead with what some witches were doing.

It looked like they were trying to cast a ward around the arena, to protect their sisters inside. But they hadn't finished, and they were too close, way too close. Because I only saw through Svarestri eyes, and that meant—

"No!" I yelled, stretching out a hand as a dozen women were blasted with a line of those energy spears, so hard that they were launched into the air still burning. The rest of the Svarestri reinforcements appeared on the plain a moment later, dropping the glamourie they'd been using so quickly and so uniformly that it looked like they'd stepped out of thin air. And I'd been right.

There were thousands.

"Say again."

My head came up as someone's voice echoed in the space around me.

"Say again. We didn't hear that, sir."

Sir?

For a moment, I just lay there, uncomprehending. Before noticing that a few of my outstretched fingers had slipped inside the image. Like dipping my hands into a pool. Only it wasn't a pool, was it?

Like these weren't TVs.

They were *minds*.

Svarestri minds, linked through some kind of spell. A communications spell, because they had to coordinate the attack someway, didn't they? And their king was kind of busy right now.

Unlike their captain, I thought, staring around.

"Sir? Can you hear me?"

"Yes," I rasped. "Yes, I can hear you. Pull back."

"Sir?"

"Pull back! The king—the king has another plan."

"Sir . . ." It was the voice's turn to sound confused. *"We're under attack. Can you confirm—"*

"It's confirmed! Pull back!"

Something rocked the image, leaving me unsure whether the convulsion was on my end or theirs. Or both, I thought, as I was jolted around at almost the same time that the ground erupted under the fey, enough to throw them and the remaining witches off their feet. And causing the Svarestri to look to their leader for instructions.

"Damn you, pull *back*!" I yelled. *"Now, now, now—"*

"Pull back," the fey in charge started yelling. *"Pull back! Pull back! Pull—"*

The voice cut out and I was snatched violently out of the image, and up to a face I couldn't see, because it was made out of shadow. But I didn't need to see it. There was only one spirit in here besides me, the one whose body I'd hijacked. And it looked like he'd figured out that he still had company.

Probably about the time I started yelling orders.

And then agony tore through me.

I staggered and went down, my vision blurring, my

hearing fading in and out. And wondered if the fey had just made a killing blow. And maybe he had, but the severity of the attack was also my salvation. A glittering cloud of my power flooded the air, blazingly bright in the darkness, causing the fey to stumble back in surprise.

And giving me a chance to tear away.

I scuttled under some nearby images, power still gushing out of me because I didn't know how to stop it. I was panting in pain and fear, ducking and dodging, trying to find a path through the constantly moving images, to see a pattern in their movement. But if there was one, I couldn't tell.

Until I focused a little too long on one off to the left, where I thought I saw a familiar face. Only to have it suddenly speed toward me, like a freight train. No, I thought desperately. Not now—

And then it grabbed me.

"What happened?"

It was Rosier's voice, harsher than I'd ever heard it.

I opened my eyes, and got an odd glimpse of a room, like I was lying on the floor with people's feet scurrying in front of me.

Maybe because I was lying on the floor with people's feet scurrying in front of me. My hair was in my face, and this time it was brown. This body was annoyed by that. It wished it had enough strength to remove the glamourie. It didn't want to die with brown hair.

Or in a female guise. What if the glamourie was too good? What if no one came back for him? What if they left his essence to be absorbed by such a place, always alone, always searching, always trying to connect to what he could never hope to see—

Someone kicked me.

"This one." It was the older, redheaded witch I'd met at Nimue's. She looked like she'd like to kill me again, only I was already pretty close. She must have thought so, too, because she didn't waste the energy.

"One of your own?" Rosier asked, looking confused.

"No. Svarestri." In her mouth, the name sounded like a curse. "His kind gutted him and slapped a glamourie on

him, so we'd think one of ours had been wounded. We had this place locked down while we tried to break Nimue's spell and get the princess out. But you know how she is. A healer won't refuse help to the injured."

"And now that she is the one injured?"

The redhead's lips all but disappeared, and she didn't answer. But she shook her head. For a moment, no one spoke.

"And Emrys?" Rosier rasped.

"He showed up just after everything went to hell. Got caught up in the fighting one floor down, or he might have seen it. Glad he didn't."

"Where is he now?"

The redhead looked defensive. "We told him. We had to. The damn Svarestri came after her as soon as Aeslinn sprang his trap. They knew she was a threat, but they don't know about him. Don't even know he's her son. She hid him well."

"Hid?"

The redhead opened her mouth, but someone else made a sound. And Rosier turned away. To where Morgaine was resting by the fire.

I thought that was odd. Why was she on the floor? Sure, she had blankets around her and a pillow between her and the wall, but still . . .

And then I noticed the blood-soaked breast of her gown, and understood.

"I always wanted to be fey," she said softly as Rosier knelt beside her. "My mother's dream, passed on to me. She sent me to court, when I was young. But I—" She broke off, gasping.

"You don't have to speak." Rosier's voice was gentle, unlike any I'd ever heard from him, but Morgaine shook her head.

"No. I want to. I must."

He didn't try to dissuade her again.

"My sisters stayed behind. Their magic was weak, and they didn't seem drawn to it as I was. But I jumped at the chance. It was so lovely there, so unlike anything I'd ever seen. I thought my father's stronghold fearsome once, a great craggy fortress on the coast, the waves smashing

into the rocks below like thunder whenever there was a storm. But hers . . . the throne room sits in a huge cavern, under a river. Did I ever tell you?"

He shook his head.

"It glides along suspended overhead, like a great jeweled snake. It casts the most beautiful light everywhere, emerald rays streaming down and moving across the floor. It makes the whole cave gleam like a gemstone. . . . It's beautiful. Like so much about their world. . . ."

She trailed off, and for a moment, I thought that would be it. She looked pale, her face almost waxen. The only color came from the soft glow of the fire.

But she rallied. "It was my mother's dream, but it was mine, too. Fey magic was so much stronger, its pull so much sweeter. Earth magic came hard, and grudgingly, to my hand. But theirs . . . tasted like honey."

"Temptation usually does," Rosier said softly.

She nodded. "But I couldn't see that then. I couldn't see anything, except that I was a quarter fey with no chance of being more. Just some little charity case, tolerated for my connection to the throne. And then only because my mother was showing signs of age. She would not live long, they whispered. Someone else would have to take her place, and manage the trade in the humans they keep as we do draft horses. When I refused, I was sent back to earth in disgrace. Where I met you, and your clumsy attempts at seduction . . ."

"They weren't clumsy." Rosier smiled slightly.

"For an incubus, they were clumsy," Morgaine said, laughter in her voice. And then a hitch. Rosier's fingers tightened, but she shook her head at him, swallowing. "But the approach didn't matter once I realized . . . all those women you'd been with, all those fey. They gave you more than you knew. Not a son, but talents, skills, elemental magic . . ."

"I had no idea."

"How could you? You didn't use it. But I did." There was wonder on Morgaine's face now, despite the pain. "You can't imagine how it felt, after that first time, to discover that I could control the winds. Baseborn, they'd

called me, and lack magic, and unclean—yet suddenly I owned two elements. And owning the second made the first so much stronger! Tasks that I'd had to strain to accomplish became almost effortless. I didn't know what to think, until you happened to mention something about abilities passing over. . . ."

"I wondered why you stayed," Rosier said. "I'd taught you the basics; you could have learned the rest on your own. I began to think you cared."

And maybe she had, a little. Because there was sorrow in the beautiful voice the next time she spoke. Fey voices were so expressive; it sounded like spoken tears.

"I didn't care for anyone in those days, or anything but my own ambition. My long-held dream was within my grasp, and it was all I could see. I thought, if I acquire them all, if I do what no one else has ever done—then. They must accept me."

"And acquire them you did."

She nodded weakly. "Some of those women, fey of every type and clan, had gifted you with their power when you joined with them, and I took it from you the same way. And it happened so quickly. I already had water and wind, and soon after came fire. So easy to manipulate, almost like a liquid, too. The final was earth, small and stubborn, and so hard to coax forth—"

"I never bedded a Svarestri," Rosier said. "But someone must have carried a thread of their blood, weak and dilute, but enough. One of the Returned, perhaps . . ." He trailed off.

"Perhaps. But it came. Finally, it came to me, and I had them all! But by then, you had something, too. . . ."

"A son."

"Yes." The expressive voice rang hollow now. "I should have stayed."

"You had no choice. Nimue took you."

"There are always choices." Her beautiful eyes grew distant. "You would have found it amusing, I think, to see me return to court. Expecting triumph, expecting praise, expecting . . . I'm not sure. All those new powers . . . Can you imagine my horror, when I realized they only made *things worse? Three-quarters human, yet able to outshine them all. Three-quarters human, yet owning four elements. And having acquired them in such a way!"*

She had to rest for a moment before continuing, and the room was strangely quiet. The only sounds were the crackle of the flames, and the hiss of rain from outside the windows. I didn't even hear anyone breathing.

Even the tears streaming down the blond witch's face were silent.

"Grandmother wouldn't let me tell anyone," Morgaine said. "She silenced those who knew, or thought she did. Wouldn't let me use my powers, wouldn't let me go back. And by the time I finally escaped, and fled here . . ."

"Yes?"

She laughed suddenly, and the sound was bitter. "I had gained a small amount of wisdom at last, enough to know he'd be better off without them, without me. A half demon possessing four elements? They would have killed him. At least your people look at power, not bloodlines, and I knew he'd be strong—"

"They're not his people. He never—" Rosier broke off.

"No." The sorrow in the voice was almost overwhelming now, a tangible thing. "We didn't give him one of those, did we? You wanted a son, to help you hold your kingdom; I wanted power, to give me access to mine. Neither of us thought about what he might want. Or where he might fit in, if he didn't share our ambitions."

"Yet you sent him tonight," Rosier said, a question in his voice. And then his head tilted. "The gods used elemental magic, didn't they?"

"A different one for each piece of armor," Morgaine confirmed. "And once they are fused together, only one who commands them all can—" She broke off, choking.

"Let her be," the redhead said harshly, coming forward.

"No," Morgaine said. "Please."

"What would you have of me?" Rosier asked, bending close to hear her, because her voice was fading.

The lovely eyes rose to his. "You named him Myrddin. . . ."

"Sea Fortress. It seemed . . . appropriate."

"But I named him Emrys." She clutched his hand. *"Immortal. Don't let it be a lie!"*

"I don't have my power here—"

"You are Prince of the Incubi! And you are his father. Rosier! Bring back—" The voice hitched and went silent, and the lovely eyes fixed, unseeing. And just that fast, she was gone.

"Our son," Rosier finished for her.

"Cass! Cass!"

I looked up, tears streaming down my face, to see a hazy version of Billy's red shirt dodging through the images. I stared around, suddenly afraid, but there were no murderous fey in sight. Just Billy, looking frantic and furious. And then vastly relieved when he spotted me.

"You're in *here*?" He zoomed over and started shaking me. "Why are you *in here*?"

"I— It's hard to explain—"

"Never mind. Just get out! Get back inside you!"

"I can't. I think I ended up in one of the leaders, and he—he has some kind of communication spell on him." I stared up at Billy's freaked-out face, and the pieces finally came together. "Billy, I think it might be Seidr!"

"So?"

"So Seidr doesn't just let you see what's happening." I looked around at all those images, all those minds. And remembered Mircea saving Rhea's life from a few thousand miles away. "It lets you *influence* it."

"Cass!"

"Just listen! I've been stepping into minds that are linked by the spell. I possessed this guy, kind of by mistake, and now I can leap into any of them! I don't have to fight the fey for dominance. I don't have to burn through shields with power I don't have. I don't have to do anything—"

"And I say again—*so*?"

"So I think that's why Ares cut Mircea's Seidr connection to me on the drag. I'd blundered into the spell he was using to communicate with the leader, and it made him vulnerable. He was afraid Mircea would use it to hurt him—"

Billy shook me some more. "Ares isn't here!"

"But someone else is. If I can find the right mind, I may be able to help—"

"Help yourself! You—" He broke off, staring around wildly. And then pointed at a nearby image. "There!"

It took me a second to realize that he'd found this body's eyes. Which were showing me another battle between witches and Svarestri, only this time, they were in the great hall. And they were fighting over me.

Literally.

A bunch of Svarestri were near the door to the right of the hall, maybe trying to rescue their beleaguered captain. Only instead, they'd run into some witches coming through the door to the left, from the stairs leading down from the royal suite. The predictable had resulted, with the battle taking place over my and the fey's prone bodies. And knocking us about every time the floor shook from a deflected spell, which was pretty much all the time now.

Something that was not great news to a person hanging precariously over a massive gap in the floor.

"Come on!" Billy yelled, to be heard over the sounds filtering into the fey's ears from outside.

I shook my head. "Not yet! There's something I have to do first!"

"Yeah! Not die!" Billy screamed, and then screamed again as the body we were in was hit by a spell, causing it to flop around all over.

I guessed that was what had distracted the fey from searching for me—a greater threat. Only it had just become great enough to convince him that he couldn't deal with the problem outside until he solved the one within. Because a second later, he appeared out of nowhere, standing over me, sword in hand. It was a shadow, too, but that didn't matter. It was made from his own energy, which meant—

It was deadly, I thought, looking at one just like it suddenly sticking out of his stomach.

The fey looked down at it, too, for half a second, before toppling over and smashing into smoke against the floor. It wouldn't last; he wasn't dead. This whole thing would have disappeared if that were the case. But he was hurt, and that meant—

"Whatever you're trying to do," Billy yelled, sword in hand, "do it now!"

I stared around, knowing I didn't have long. But it wouldn't take long. If I could only find the right image, the right *mind*—

And then I did. It was small and far away, but when I concentrated, it zoomed toward me. Like a wide-screen TV and then a theater screen and then an IMAX, filling my view.

And this time, I let it come.

Chapter Fifty-eight

The sky was blue again. It arced overhead, like an upside-down bowl, clear and strong and perfect. I could see glimpses of the fight that raged beyond: the shadow of a body, as if thrown against the sky, magnified to giant-sized before disappearing again. Streaks of light, like deadly rainbows, flashing overhead. Flames dancing in the distance, like trees glimpsed through fog.

But all of it strangely peaceful.

Because all of it was outside the watery protection of Nimue's shield.

Under the dome, the Svarestri I was possessing dodged a stinging arc of sand and then threw it back, laughing. Because earth was his element, and wasn't likely to work against him. And because Nimue was at a serious disadvantage.

Aeslinn's brain obligingly informed me that the fire the witches had started had been aimed at the shield. Being attacked by a wave of Svarestri early in the duel had forced her to encase the combat area in her protection, ensuring no further interference. And putting Aeslinn's device completely out of reach.

I could see it now, glowing under the sands of the arena: Arthur's sword was pulling power from the other pieces of that cursed armor, and becoming stronger by the second. But one look at Nimue's face showed that she was too lost in an Ares-inspired frenzy to notice. And no one else could reach it until the duel ended.

But it didn't look like that was going to be anytime soon. A tornado exploded through the small area under the dome, sweeping the body I was using off its feet and into a maelstrom of fury. But not for long. As soon as Aeslinn hit earth, it flowed over him, cradling him, pulling him in. Building a bulwark around him that the pounding winds couldn't penetrate, and allowing his opponent to exhaust herself for nothing.

Yet he didn't go on the offensive when the winds abruptly stopped, raining sand down everywhere. He didn't do anything. Because he wasn't trying to win; he was trying to run out the clock.

And he was succeeding.

Pritkin and the witches were turning the stadium into an inferno to try to evaporate that shield, and let them in. But it was like trying to burn through the sea; all their spells barely touched it. And deploying it had limited Nimue to a single weapon in an element that was not her own.

The result: she was losing, but not fast enough. And I couldn't help her; the immense amount of effort needed to throw that other fey's spear offside had been nothing to this. No matter what I did, Aeslinn's efforts remained undisturbed, elegant and lightning fast. I wasn't the one holding him back—he was.

He was teasing her, egging her on, keeping the fight going and them entrapped in their own little world. But not hurting her—not really. Because then . . .

What would she do then?

I stared at Nimue, at the beauty hidden behind a mask of blood, at the eyes gone wild, at the face set on snarl. It was easier to see the woman within now, to glimpse the iron usually covered by velvet, the warrior instead of the queen. And the vicious pride that matched anything Aeslinn could boast.

I thought I had my answer.

Which was why, the next time Aeslinn sent a blast back at her, laden with cutting sand and smothering earth, I didn't oppose him. Instead, I helped, adding whatever small effect I had to the strength of his assault. And maybe I was more powerful than I'd thought, or maybe he was just overcompensating for my previous efforts. But for whatever reason, the blow landed.

And it landed hard.

I heard Nimue scream, saw the shock register, saw her personal shields dissolve in tatters. And saw her look up at the only other protection available to her, which was also the only thing keeping out the inferno. It was barely a flicker of her eyes, but it was enough to tell me that I'd been right.

Because if she was going down, she was taking Aeslinn with her.

He realized it the same moment I did, but he was half-way across the arena and the shield's source was on her arm. He dove for it anyway, and with his speed, he might have made it. I'll never know if throwing everything I had left at him was enough to slow him down, or if Nimue was just that fast.

I only know he missed.

And suddenly, the world was fire.

It burned through the towering stands that rose around us on every side. It blew through the air in flaming bits scattered through choking clouds of smoke. It roared in the howl of the winds that were released when our protection dropped. And it sizzled in the avalanche of spells that threatened to melt the very sand underneath my feet.

Instead, they knocked me backward, throwing me the length of the arena, like a blow from a giant's club. The body I was using hit the stands, felt the searing heat, saw a mass of flaming wood towering precariously overhead. And then saw it come crashing down in a cascade of fire, like a flaming waterfall, as I screamed and screamed and—

The world shifted and slurred, with the fire running together in long blurred lines across my vision. Ones that swiftly changed from orange-red to blue-black, and from intense heat to freezing rain. I realized that I was tearing through the sky, my body racked with pain, like it was still on fire even with a torrent bucketing down around me.

I had a second to understand that I was back inside my own skin, and that the rain felt like a massive deluge because I was speeding through it, my thighs clamped around something that looked a lot like a broom. And that there was a witch behind me, throwing curses at the fey running below, a wand in either hand, and *laughing* despite the speed of the ground rushing by underneath. And then something hit us, blowing us out of the sky and sending us crashing into the ground.

The impact was enough to stun me and possibly more. For a moment, I couldn't see, couldn't hear, couldn't move. There was a roaring in my ears, a numbness in my limbs, and a feeling like my chest might just explode.

Because I also couldn't breathe.

And then my body convulsed and flipped to the side, allowing me to gasp in air like a beached fish. And to realize that we'd landed in the great field in front of the arena, which was now mostly churned-up mud. And charred grass from the world's biggest bonfire raging a few dozen yards away.

It wasn't nearly far enough.

The heat was scorching, hitting my face and then my palm when I raised it to shield my eyes from the sparks flying everywhere. Including upward, where I watched in disbelief as what looked like a fiery gash opened up in the heavens. Red and livid against the haze of firelight and vast blue blackness, it looked like a great wound towering above us, one that my mother's spell was trying hard to close.

Trying, and failing.

Because Aeslinn's device was still intact.

We'd tried to slam the door, but we hadn't been fast enough, and now Ares had a foot in it. Or a hand, because that was what my mind insisted I was seeing. A giant hand, ripping through the fabric of space and time, forcing his way into our world.

"Options," I whispered, but this time, my power didn't respond. Maybe because of the lead weight that seemed to be dragging on me, as Ares' power tamped down whatever remained of mine. Or maybe because there was nothing to show.

Billy Joe emerged from my skin, where I guessed he'd possessed my body while I was away. I hadn't noticed, since for once he'd been silent. And still was, staring upward in disbelief for a moment, before looking at me, his eyes huge. "He's coming through."

I didn't say anything.

"Cassie! What the *hell*?"

"We lost."

"What? You can't just— *Do something!*"

He was staring at me, like a child expecting Mommy to fix this. And suddenly, I was angry. Suddenly, I was furious. "I *did*. It wasn't enough."

"Then do something else! Don't just lie there and say we lost. You're Pythia!"

"So are they!" I gestured outward. I didn't see the others; my eyes were too bleary with rain and blowing ash, and I doubted they were stupid enough to be out in the open anyway. But their power was here, slow and sluggish, spreading across the ground like fog.

And useless, just like mine.

Because of course it was. Ares might not know he had half the Pythias who ever lived here, but he knew he had at least one. And one is all it takes.

So he wasn't taking any chances, wasn't risking having one of us flit back in time and get more, wasn't going to let us do anything. And God, he was powerful! He wasn't even here, was still struggling to push open a door that was trying its best to close on top of him, was still battling my mother's spell. Yet my power was all but useless.

I suddenly remembered something she'd said once, to the demon council. Reminding them how she'd fought whole demon armies to a standstill in her day, and how Ares was every bit as powerful now as she had been then. And about how, if he came back, we would have no way to stand against him.

And here I was, seeing the truth of it.

I stared upward, the tears on my face mixing with the rain, and despaired. How had we ever thought we could do anything? Small and puny, weak and frightened. How had we ever thought—

And then someone grabbed me.

I was jerked up out of the mud, not by the Svarestri soldier I'd been expecting, maybe because most of them had stopped fighting and were also just standing there, looking upward in awe. But by someone else. Someone familiar. Someone with burning green eyes staring at me out of a blackened face.

Someone I'd never thought I'd see again.

"Pritkin?"

He grabbed my shoulders, but instead of hugging me, he pushed me backward. "Go!"

"What?"

"You've got to get out of here! Now!"

"Why?" I looked around, and realized that we were about to be trampled. Not by Svarestri, but by witches, a great mass of them tearing out of the fiery arena and headed this way. Some were on foot, their shields gone, their bodies blackened by smoke and ash. Some were on brooms, laden with two or three passengers each, some with the ends on fire. Still more had enchanted whatever they could find, like the burnt remains of the stadium benches, to carry their wounded, because they wouldn't leave them behind.

And I realized that while I'd been lying in the mud feeling sorry for myself, they'd been rescuing their sisters from an inferno.

One Pritkin was heading back into.

"Wait!" I grabbed his arm.

It was hot to the touch—too hot. But not as much as it was about to be. Ares' arrival had caused the arena to flame up, like gas poured onto a fire. It was almost incandescent from this close, a searing ball of heat and light, like a small sun. Too bright to even look at head-on—and impossible to survive.

Especially with water shields that would evaporate in seconds.

"Let go!" Pritkin was trying to pry my hands off, but it didn't go as planned.

"Why?" I challenged him. "So you can die for nothing? We failed—"

"We didn't fail!"

"What are you talking about?" I yelled. "How is that not—" I cut off, choking on a blast of smoke and flying ash. But still hanging on.

"We didn't fail!" Strong hands gripped my biceps,

shaking me. "The shield is down, Aeslinn and his creatures have fled, the witches are clear or getting clear—"

"But the device is still in there!"

"Yes, and unprotected! His men pulled Aeslinn out before he could reengage the shield. The device is vulnerable, if I go now!"

He tried to push me off, but it didn't work. "So why not take it out before? Why wait to evacuate everyone?"

Nothing.

"Pritkin!"

He tried to pry off my hands, and he wasn't kidding this time, but I'd let my fingers break before I let go. He stared at me, hair and face almost black, eyes reflecting the flames that burned behind him. And thought about lying.

But he sucked at it; he always had, at least with me. And then I was shaking him, shouting, "Tell me!"

"It's absorbed too much power," he admitted. "Destroying it will release all that, all at once. The explosion . . . could level half the city. Now do you understand? You have to get away, to the river or beyond, to be safe."

I stared at him. Everything was coming too hard and too fast. I couldn't keep up anymore, couldn't think. Couldn't process what he was telling me, except I guessed part of me had. Because my nails sank into his skin, hurting him, but I didn't care. I was suddenly screaming and thrashing, and actually pulling him backward, this man who had sixty pounds on me and most of it muscle.

Until he did something that ended up with him behind me, too fast for me to counter even if I'd been thinking straight, and got an arm around my throat. I could feel his chest against my back as I fought, could feel his too-rapid breathing, could hear his voice in my ear, telling me things I didn't care about because I only cared about one thing.

And he wasn't coming with me.

"Listen to me—"

"No!"

"You must! I have to—"

"No. *Please.*" It was a mewling cry, raw and humiliating any other time. But not now.

"*Listen to me*. If I can return to you, I will. I swear it. Nothing else—" He cut off, abruptly, and the arms tightened. "But I have to do this. There's no time to explain, but there's no one else who can. I have to go. You have to let me go."

I just shook my head, my hands gripping his forearms, feeling like the world was shattering around me. I didn't care. He was going to have to pry me off. He was going to have to—

"Listen." It was gentler this time, and he somehow turned me around, made me look up at him. I was crying now, great ugly sobs that racked my body and tore at my mind, but I didn't even try to hide them.

"I can't," I said brokenly. "Please don't . . . I *can't*. . . ."

A filthy hand pushed the muddy hair out of my face. "I don't believe that. I don't believe there's anything you can't do." He finally did something other than fight me, and the kiss tasted of smoke and ash and spent magic. "I think you might be the strongest person I know."

I shook my head. I wanted to tell him that I wasn't, that he was wrong, that he'd always been wrong about me. But I couldn't. I couldn't seem to say anything, even when he pulled away. And I felt something inside break and shatter and splinter. I collapsed, falling to my knees, staring at the ground because I couldn't watch him walk away.

And then stagger and fall, hitting the ground unconscious a few yards in front of me.

I looked up, shocked and horrified, expecting to see a Svarestri looming over us. But instead—

"Rosier," I breathed.

"Damn boy." The demon was holding his hand. "Jaw like a rock."

And then he shoved something into my hand.

I looked down to see a scrap of parchment. It looked like it had been torn out of a book, with careful, cramped medieval writing in the center, and a manic scrawl along the edges. I stared at it, utterly confused. "What is this?"

"The spell."

I looked up. "What?"

"The countercurse. I rewrote it in the common tongue.

Emrys can put it on himself. When the soul arrives, have him read it."

He actually started to stride away, before I got my shit together and grabbed his leg. "What? Why? Rosier—"

"I have the same abilities he does," he told me testily. "I'm the one who passed them on to him! And whatever else they did to me, the demon council can't block fey magic."

"That doesn't explain this." I held up the paper. "What's going on?"

Unlike his son, he didn't try to lie to me. "I don't have enough strength to come back."

"What?"

"I came on this journey to benefit me," he said abruptly as I stared at him. "I told myself it was for the good of my people, but that's a lie. I wanted to prove everyone wrong, to show them I was my father's son, after all. Not bothering to think that *I* was someone's father, too.

"I never acted like it. I never had a father; I had a taskmaster who was never satisfied with anything I did or was. I hated him, but I've treated Emrys . . ." His jaw clenched. "Pritkin. I've treated Pritkin just the same. All his life. I can't change that, but I can do this."

"Rosier . . ."

"Immortal she named him. Let me be!"

He jerked away, and strode into the fire before I could stop him.

Chapter Fifty-nine

I just stayed there, on my knees, staring into the fire until it seared my retinas, I didn't know why. And then a passing witch jostled me, and slowly, sluggishly, I came back to life. In the middle of a scene of carnage and chaos, unsure where to go or how to get there.

"Here!" A witch, a dishwater blonde all of three feet high, poked me. "Get him on here!"

I looked around to see that she was pulling a wonky contraption behind her, consisting of a broom on one side and a bunch of blackened sticks on the other, with a few bench seats in between. It formed a slightly lopsided, floating gurney already piled high with moaning bodies. It didn't look likely to take another, but Pritkin was out cold, and I couldn't carry him.

"Help me," I said breathlessly, and together we somehow maneuvered a hundred and eighty pounds of muscle onto the pile. It left the crazy contraption barely a couple of inches off the ground, but it was still mobile. More than me.

"Think you ought to get on, too," the witch said, eyeing me as I stumbled along behind.

"If I do, it'll drag the ground."

"Won't matter as fast as we'll be going," she said, hazel eyes flashing. "Now get on!"

I nodded, and started looking for a free spot, only to stop abruptly.

Not because of the *crack* that suddenly resounded across the battlefield, like a hundred cannons going off. And not because of the wound in the sky, which abruptly widened, drowning the plain in crimson light. Not even because of the ground underneath us, which had begun to undulate constantly now, rippling outward from the arena like water after someone tossed in a stone.

But because of something I couldn't see, flowing over my skin like a cold wind, raising goose pimples despite the heat. It was like nothing I'd ever felt. Like twining fingers with twenty different hands all at once. Like being pulled into a woven tapestry, where every person was a thread, a color, a knot wound into the others.

I looked up, to where Ares' head and shoulders had just appeared in the sky. It was an impossible sight, one that should have had me staring in awe or shivering in fear. But instead, I was shivering in something else.

Something that was part of me but not me, and not the other Pythias I could feel as if they were clustered all around me. But something that joined us because it shared us. The creature Apollo had unwittingly created all those centuries ago, when he shaved off some of his power, had become something else, something more. Something that threaded through all of us, combining our strength into one last stand, with everything it had and everything we had, its partners and its lovers.

And in that moment, I knew Agnes had been wrong when she told Rhea it didn't feel as we did, that it wasn't human as we were. And maybe it didn't and maybe it wasn't, but it felt something. A genuine, overflowing love and compassion for the world it had adopted, and for the people it had worked through.

All of them.

And suddenly, the sky bloomed with Pythias.

Portals opened everywhere, like the one Gertie had shown me once: blue skies, gray skies, sea and stone and forest, against red. Strands of power reached out, like the lassos the Pythias had put on a boiling column of light to save me. Because one strand couldn't stop a force of pure energy, but three could.

Or, I thought, staring upward, *dozens*.

Something tore through the cacophony all around us, through the crash of lightning and the din of battle, through the crackle and hiss of fire meeting rain, through the yells and curses and the rumble of the ground beneath us. Something that sounded very much like a scream. It boomed across the landscape like thunder, shuddered the ground under my feet, sent shivers up my spine.

And then had me ducking back down into the mud, in terror and awe, as great Ares roared, tearing at the leashes that had ensnared him, snapping some, but unable to escape others, looking for all the world like an animal being held down by ropes.

Or no, I realized suddenly. Not held down. Held *back*. Because the new arrivals were trying to force him back into the gash. While the other Pythias, the ones who had followed me here, the ones who were borrowing what little power I had left, were doing something, too. And then the power shivering through me, through all of us, roared *back* at the crazed god.

And opened up a massive tornado behind him.

It tore into existence like a great beast, clawing at the sky. It screamed across the horizon, engulfing half the world. It was so powerful that I could feel it, even from here, churning up the metaphysical currents like a hurricane, sending waves of power shuddering through me, over me, around me. Like nothing I'd ever felt before.

"What . . . what . . . *is that*?" the tiny witch demanded, her eyes huge.

"Return to sender," I yelled, remembering the storms Gertie had conjured up against me. "They're trying to send him home!"

And they were trying hard.

Power lashed at him from the portals in the sky. An epic storm pulled at him from behind. Ares roared again, a shudder-inducing sound, and one that was more than that. It was *pained*.

They're hurting him, I thought, a tiny flame of hope igniting inside me.

They're hurting him!

And then the field flooded with fey.

The Svarestri reinforcements I had sent away were back, charging and yelling, like a furious wall descending on us. For a moment, I didn't understand—what did it matter anymore? What did anything here on the ground matter?

But then I realized: they thought the witches were doing this. They thought they had conjured up the battle in the skies that was hurting their god. And they had decided to do something about it.

The little witch looked at me and I looked at her, but neither of us moved. We were ridiculously outnumbered, with most of the covens having fled the field, and those who remained already busy with battles of their own. We were out of power and out of time, and about to be slaughtered.

And then someone yelled on our other side, from the direction of town. A lot of someones. And before I could turn my head to see who, they were everywhere, surging all around us—another wall of fey. Only these . . .

Were in blue.

And green, I realized, as a passing Alorestri flung a puddle of water on a charging fey, enveloping him in a skin he couldn't shake, despite tearing at it with both hands. A watery skin that covered his body, his head, and finally his face. And drowned him on dry land.

A second later, a mass of men and horses thundered by our little cart on both sides, shaking the ground and almost running us down. And I looked up to see Arthur leading a charge that pushed like a spear into the middle of the Svarestri forces, tearing them in two. And cleaving a clear path behind them.

"There!" I yelled at the witch. "We have to get to the river!"

She nodded and threw me one end of the rope, and snatched up the other. We took off as fast as we could, which wasn't that fast. But not because of the weight of the cart, which the charm made almost negligible, or the straggling horses we had to dodge, or the fighting going on everywhere.

But because the ripples the arena had been putting out had just turned into all-out waves.

Earth fey, I thought grimly, as horses whinnied and fell, as Arthur's charge broke, as the nearest section of the burning town shuddered and shook and collapsed into a sea of rubble. And as we plowed determinedly ahead, despite the sledge being so low that it hit the back of our legs with every stride. Until a piece of earth like a tidal wave came speeding *toward* us and tilted it over, throwing us to the ground and scattering the wounded everywhere.

That wave was followed by another and then still more, the smaller ones from behind suddenly nothing compared to the ones from in front. And a glance showed that it wasn't targeting us. It was happening everywhere, in a huge circle around the battlefield. The Svarestri were encircling us, not with more soldiers but with their element, refusing to allow us to escape.

Because they didn't know who was behind this, so they planned to just kill everyone they could find.

"I'm sorry! I'm sorry!" the little witch said as I turned back around. And noticed that the broom was no longer attached to the sledge.

Because she and the witches who could still move were climbing on board.

"No!" I said, trying to reach her past the rolling waves of earth. "No, take us, too! Take us with you!"

"Too heavy. I'm sorry!"

"No, please—"

"I'm sorry! I'm sorry!" And then they were gone, flying up into the air as I clutched Pritkin and watched our last lifeline spiral away—

And be hit by two Svarestri spears, one from either side, and be blown out of the sky.

Suddenly, everything got louder, or maybe it was just my heartbeat speeding up, pumping blood to my ears as I watched the burning bodies rain down. Or watched part of it, because I couldn't even make out where they'd landed. The battle raging above was easy enough to see, but lower down smoke and steam and spell-fire were everywhere, confusing my eyes; screams and crashes were doing the same to my ears; and waves of earth were destroying my sense of direction, throwing me off my feet and freaking me out every time I tried to stand.

So I crawled instead, using the rope to grab the last

piece of charmed wood, which was now floating fairly high with nothing on it. Until I pulled it down and strapped Pritkin to it and started dragging him along with me. Because the witch was dead, so this spell was going to unravel pretty damn fast and I couldn't renew it.

I couldn't do much, including crawl effectively, although that was partly because of the dirt constantly hitting me in the face. I finally gave up and climbed on board with Pritkin, draping myself protectively over him. And pushing us along with my feet, ridiculous though that was, because it was all I could do.

And to my surprise, it worked.

Like really worked, like body-surfing on dry land, which was so insane I decided not to think about it, and just go with it. And suddenly, we were *moving*, coasting across the ground under the protective haze, pushing off from each crest and zooming down and then up the next, like a crazy toboggan. We're getting away, I thought, an insane grin spreading across my cheeks. We're getting away!

And then a barrage of fey energy spears flew past, barely missing us. And took out a group of witches running just ahead. Who were hit so hard and so fast that they were dead before they plowed into the ground.

I stared at them, my mouth dry, my heartbeat hard enough to actually hurt. And that was before one of the dead decided to abruptly roll over and sit up, a large chunk of her torso gone, her hair on fire. And her slack features becoming animated once more as a spirit in search of a body suddenly acquired one.

And this time, it didn't fight back.

You have got to be kidding me, I thought, as the dead eyes met mine.

And then Jo was coming.

But this wasn't my first time at the rodeo. Which was why one of the corpses behind her caught her ankle, tripping her up just before she could reach me, leaving her splayed on the ground. And slamming her filthy, shoeless heel into my borrowed face as I hung on, trying to keep her away from the two bodies now slumped over the gently revolving sledge.

Jo turned around, snarling, and I snarled back out of a half-missing mouth. A fey who had been bearing down on us both turned a whiter shade of pale and backed away, only to get taken out by a witch's curse. But not before dropping his spear, which didn't go out. It lay there, eating its shape into the dirt, while Jo and I stared at it.

I didn't know what she was thinking, but I had always assumed that those things were a spell given form, since the fey just materialized them when needed. And maybe they were, but they must have run on different rules from human magic. Because this one spluttered and hissed but continued to burn, despite the very obvious death of its caster.

And then we both went for it.

We grabbed it at the same time, adding more cooked-meat smell to the smoke and blood and ozone-laced tinge of expended magic already in the air. I had the pointy end, but it didn't matter, even when she shoved it through my already damaged middle. In fact, it made this easier, my new rib cage working to help trap it as we scrambled to our feet and started doing a strange sort of waltz through the battle, using the spear to throw each other around as rain pattered down and people stared and Jo finally realized why I was willing to dance with her.

And then her face burst into flames.

The blaze in her hair had become a conflagration, like the one the blunt end of the energy weapon had created in her chest. She was literally cooking in front of my eyes, and that was before her body went up like a Roman candle when the fat ignited. I staggered back, shocked despite my alarming new threshold, and grabbed a fey for balance. Who screamed and tried to get away, but my hands had fused to his shirt. And I belatedly realized: I was melting in the middle of my own personal inferno.

The fey screamed again, a strange, high-pitched note of pure terror, and pulled out a knife. A moment later, my spirit was slamming back into my own body as my borrowed one all but exploded against the ground—except for the severed arms. They were still clutching the sleeves of the now terrified fey.

He tore off through a cloud of smoke and I looked around, trying to spot the next threat, but there didn't seem to be one. I didn't wait for one to show up. I grabbed the sledge and took off, pushing Pritkin toward the relative safety of the river.

It was quieter here, most of the fleeing people having gone to the docks. I could see them in the distance, a huge, squirming mass illuminated here and there by flickering torchlight. I didn't follow them. There weren't going to be enough boats, and anyway, I had no way to get there. The sledge was already starting to drag the ground; in a minute, I wouldn't be able to move it at all.

So I headed for the little tent belonging to the launderer. It was somehow still standing, maybe because it was sheltered by a couple of spreading oaks. The dirt road in front had turned into a river, rushing like a torrent. But the tent was on higher ground and still dry inside when I pulled open the back flap. And shoved the sledge inside.

I looked around, panting slightly. The young couple must have had to leave in a hurry, because their freshly dried wares were still in place. Including a pile of them on a woven mat just inside the back that looked incredibly comfortable.

For a second, I just stood there, feeling bad about messing them up. It had started to rain harder on the way here, and we were both soaked. And then I wondered what the hell was wrong with me, worrying about laundry in the apocalypse.

I tipped Pritkin off the board and into the middle of the pile, and sat beside him, because there was nothing else to do. Except wonder if that last battle had finally drained Jo, or if she'd be back. And why she cared.

If it had been anyone else, I'd have understood the attack as a personal vendetta. But Jo had been planning death-by-god anyway, allowing Ares' return to wipe her out of existence along with the rest of us. So, at best, I'd pushed up her timetable a little, which hardly seemed worth this kind of risk.

And if she was still afraid I'd manage to interrupt her plans . . . how? I was exhausted, out of power, and dragging around a guy with a possible concussion. As far as fighting went, I was done. And possession drained ghosts faster than anything else. She was risking missing the big finale, and for what? Killing someone likely to die anyway? It didn't make sense.

Especially considering what was happening in the skies above us.

Because Ares was winning.

I pushed the tent flap out of the way and stared as a torso the size of a skyscraper shoved its way into the world. The sonic boom of ripping space and time came again, but it seemed distant this time, dull. Like the rain blowing in to wet my feet, like the burning sensation in my throat, like everything. Grayed out, unimportant. Lost in shock and pain and grief so great it didn't matter anymore.

And then came a light so bright that for a moment it seemed like day. And an explosion so huge it rocked the ground underneath me, and rained dirt and debris and a small piece of bright red wool down in front of me. Rosier's color.

I watched the burning piece of cloth be doused by the rain, and felt my face crumple.

I guessed I could feel something after all.

Like the arms, coming around me from behind. Not an attack this time, but an attempt at comfort. From someone who deserved it more than me.

"It didn't work," I said unsteadily, before he could ask. "The device was destroyed, but Ares . . . he's too far in."

He was having to struggle for it, to fight. But he didn't just have his foot in the door now, but half his body. Rosier's sacrifice had been brave, and ultimately successful. But it didn't matter.

You can't close a door if someone's standing in the middle of it.

"Your name," Pritkin said suddenly, his voice hoarse.

"What?"

"Your name."

I huffed out something that sounded strangely like a laugh. And maybe it was. What else was there to do at the end of the world? "Does it matter now?"

His arms tightened, and when his voice came again, it was desperate. "Your name . . ."

I twisted, trying to look at him, but his arms held me fast. "If it really means that much to—"

". . . is Cassie."

I just sat there for a second, unmoving. And then I did turn, having to fight his hold. And when I did—

His eyes were emerald. Not green, not jade, but pure emerald, shining in the darkness like a light was behind them. Because one was.

Soul light.

I felt like crying and laughing all at once. He was finally here, the person I'd chased through centuries of time. Only to arrive too late.

"Tell me! That is your name?"

Pritkin looked like my answer was important. Like it was the most important thing in the world. Like it was something he'd clung to, through whatever personal storm he'd been living all this time.

I got up on my knees and took his head between my hands. "My name is Cassie Palmer," I told him steadily. "And I love you."

Chapter Sixty

I kissed him, and he tasted the same as before: like ash and smoke and spent magic. Like I probably did, but I didn't care. I didn't care about anything but the warmth of his mouth and the strength of his arms, and having someone with me at the end. And not just someone. The person I wanted more than anyone else, that I'd searched for, loved for, God, so long.

As I'd have admitted a long time ago, only I was really good at ignoring the impossible.

But it wasn't impossible now. Nothing was. And I guessed he thought so, too, because the next moment he was pushing me back into the mountain of clean laundry and pulling my dress over my head.

Outside, things were deteriorating rapidly. The sounds of battle came in gusts, blown on an increasingly violent wind. Burning sparks cascaded past the tent, adding the scent of fire to the smell of linen and mud and ozone. The sky was burning, with boiling mountains of clouds streaked with the light of that terrible wound.

I barely noticed.

The unnatural light haloed Pritkin's head as he finished stripping off his tunic, reflected in his eyes, made him look more like his father's side for a second. And then more like his mother's, when sparks like fireflies danced in his hair. But when he bent over me, he was once again the man I knew, finding my lips, pulling me into an embrace that blocked out everything else.

And then fire took us.

But not with devastation and fury, as I'd half expected. Not with the wrath of an angry god. But with something else, something that had been waiting a very long time. Something that was rushing at us like a massive wave toward a beach. And this time, there was no one to stop it.

It broke over us a moment later, in a storm of mouths and hands and hearts beating together. It swept away clothes, quieted inhibitions, masked pain. Pritkin's hand smoothed carefully over my side, because a ragged bandage hid an injury that was nowhere near healed, but I didn't feel it.

I didn't feel anything but hunger.

And power. I could sense it puddling on my skin wherever his hands rested. Could track the prints of fingers and lips as they explored me. Could feel it scintillating off that terrible hair as it swept across my body, brushing breasts and stomach and thighs as he kissed his way down. Could feel it flood inside me when he found my center, when his lips closed over me, when he—

God!

I arched up, and it felt like time slowed. The floating embers in the air became a stream of rubies. The drag of Pritkin's stubble over my thighs was like the scrape of velvet. The sheen of water on his bare skin a shining coat, like the armor I'd seen on the fey, like the cascade of watery diamonds tumbling in through the tent flap as the wind shifted.

I felt every one. I felt *everything*, arching under the heavy droplets hitting my breasts, and then under Pritkin's lips as he chased them down, as his fingers replaced his tongue elsewhere, as I felt the tent rock, like from another earthquake, except nothing was moving but me. I tried to stay grounded, to think, before sensation tore me off this earth and sent me spinning into madness. But it was impossible. The tide had me now, and I was helpless to do anything except squirm and shudder and make soft little sounds at the back of my throat that I couldn't seem to stop or control.

Pritkin groaned, and that sound in that voice had my back arching until I thought it would break, my fingers tightening into fists in his hair, needing something, anything to ground me. But nothing helped. It was too much sensation, far too much, and I couldn't even think clearly enough to ask what was happening.

And then I didn't need to. Because something looked up at me, but it wasn't Pritkin. At least, not in the form I knew. An incubus stared at me out of his eyes, thin and starved and desperate. He didn't say anything, but I could feel his emotions battering me. He hungered, he *hurt*, but if he fed, he hurt others. So he had starved, for so long, so long . . .

"It's all right," I said unevenly. "You . . . won't hurt me."

But he didn't believe it, was already backing down, was sinking away from me. And I realized why as Pritkin's head dipped again, his lips drawing runes whose meanings I'd never known on my skin. I'd always thought those symbols were to enhance sensation, but I'd been wrong. Goose pimples retreated as he painted my skin in magic, heat cooled, the light bled back to simply light. And I cried out at the loss.

"No! I don't want you to—"

But he wasn't listening. He'd become afraid to feed, to take what he needed so badly. Afraid to be who and what he was. Rosier might have been wrong about some things, but he'd been right about at least one. Pritkin wasn't human. And trying to be so was killing him.

"You can't hurt me," I said, my hand in his hair. And there was enough of that other still there that he rubbed up against the touch, like a cat. Thoughtlessly sensual in a way that Pritkin never was.

"I could. I *did*—" His fear bled through the words, raw and anguished, and my conviction answered it.

"No. Not now."

I had been afraid my whole life, but there was nothing left to fear. Nothing for either of us. And I'd rather die by his hand than Ares'.

"Take what you want," I said steadily. "Take everything."

And the power roared back.

I could see it when he finally entered me, in sunburst flares of pleasure exploding across my vision. Could hear it in the blood roaring in my ears as I writhed under him, struggling to accommodate his size. Could feel it with every movement, slow and stuttering at first, as if he was as overwhelmed as I was, and then with longer, surer strokes that made me squirm and cry out. And then lock my legs behind his back, pulling him farther into me, pulling him as far as he would go.

Until his heart beat, strong and sure, at my core. Until we moved together as one. Until, instead of riding the power, we were swept up by it, carried off with it, into a maelstrom of light and force and sensation.

I cried out, and heard it echo in his throat. Saw our shadows splashed on the ceiling of the tent, as if there was a fire burning inside instead of out. Saw it grow brighter and brighter, until the light burst into a thousand fractured rainbows, whiting out the shadows and spilling out the door.

And then I saw, not with my eyes anymore, but with my mind: power sweeping around in a huge arc, like a glittering wave. Or an ocean, I realized, watching the enormous span of the Pythian power shimmering and dancing as if under a distant sun. I saw it all, just for a moment—

Before it came crashing down—on Pritkin.

I screamed, afraid that it would hurt him, would rip him apart. And maybe it would have, except that all those years, all that lonely starvation, had done something, hadn't it? The incubus part of his soul had withered and shrunk, barely clinging to life. It was hollowed out now, empty, a vast, echoing cavern full of exactly nothing. Waiting—

For a tsunami.

Like the one that was pouring into Pritkin. It would have killed another incubus; it should have killed him. But the great void at the heart of his being took it gladly, more perhaps than any other incubus had ever taken, because no other of his kind could fast for so long. And instead of killing him, it reanimated a part that he'd almost forgotten, one that suddenly remembered how to feed, how to love, and how . . . to magnify.

A second later, I found out exactly what a starved incubus of the royal line can do when presented with a banquet. Because all that power, doubled or tripled or whatever it was now, came roaring back. I cried out, in agony and ecstasy—and disbelief, because I'd never felt anything like it. And because I'd assumed it would rejoin the Pythian power, where it came from. But it didn't.

It came back to me.

Suddenly, I could see the light shining out of my pores, feel it screaming through my veins, taste it in my throat as it bubbled over into laughter, insane, impossible laughter because it was good, so good, so *much*. Too much, overwhelming my body, mind and spirit, the feel of him surging into me, the strength of him under my hands, the emotions I'd denied for too long, all of it.

So I sent it rushing back into Pritkin, who magnified it again and sent it back to me, beginning a thrumming, heart-stopping, explosive cycle that went on and on until I thought I would die from it, die and not care.

And then climax ripped through me, and the world exploded.

I vaguely understood that the tent had just been torn away, blown off by the hot desert wind flooding all around us. Dimly saw the trees above thrashing as if in a hurricane, every leaf shining like a floodlight was beneath them. Distantly knew that this was dangerous, so dangerous, because I was human; I couldn't hold this much power. It was why the Pythian power was separate from its hosts. We borrowed it when needed; we didn't inhabit it, or it us. We wouldn't have lasted a day if we had, before it burned us up.

Like this was about to do to me.

Because Pritkin had just given it back, everything he could, one last time. And then rolled off, gasping and stunned, his body shaking from his own climax, and from the strain of holding that much power. Because he wasn't meant for it, either.

We couldn't handle it, neither of us, not even both of us. I had to get rid of it. I had to get rid of it *now*.

And there was one obvious target.

I looked up at Ares, so huge, so strong, so powerful, towering in the skies above us. And knew I couldn't take him, not even now. I had power, yes, enough to fight him, enough to hurt him, but not enough to *win*. I needed a god to fight a god, but I wasn't one. I was just Cassie Palmer.

And yet Johanna had come back for me. . . .

Which was why I reached out, not with my human hand, but with a much more ephemeral one. And grabbed not the air, but something beyond it. Because Jo had seen what I couldn't, that there might be one more trick up my sleeve. Not the Pythian way, and not from my mother's blood. But something far more human.

Because I had a father, too.

So I reached out a spectral hand and ripped open the fabric of time. Not in the small, barely there way, like when I tagged along with a ghost. But in a great gash that tore across the entire length of the battlefield, like a jagged arc of green lightning.

It spilled a long line of illumination onto the bloody scene, a cascade of ghost light, pale and gleaming. And swarming. Not with dozens or hundreds, but with thousands of ghosts, all of them fleeing ahead of another god, a dead god, one who emerged back into the world, his mind set on revenge, his eyes searching for me.

Until he saw what towered above me.

And just like before, Apollo forgot the snack I represented, in the face of the banquet on the horizon. I blinked, and the next time I looked, the real battle was raging, this time between two gods. One who had thought he was about to win, and one who knew he was about to die, unless he drained his foe quick enough to make it a fair contest.

Neither of them thought about us.

Neither of them cared about us.

Just as they never had.

But oh, we cared about them. As demonstrated when, far in the distance, there appeared a shimmer of blue. And was answered, on the other side of the battlefield, by a brief, blinding flash of light. And then, closer in, close enough to flash me a smile, a shining demigod held out a hand.

And a black, burnt, pathetic-looking stick came tumbling through the smoke and fire, straight into it.

No, I corrected myself.

Not a stick.

A staff.

I huddled over Pritkin, looking at the reflection of the battle in a nearby puddle, as three beams of pure elemental magic hit the thrashing duo in the sky. Apollo never even seemed to notice, too focused on draining Ares to pay attention to anything else. And maybe still too ghostly to feel all that much.

But someone else did.

It wasn't a roar this time, but a scream: of pain, of outrage, but mostly, of incredulity. That such paltry creatures could hurt him, that they would think to turn his own gifts against him, that they would *dare*. And that they were winning.

Because Ares was powerful, yes, almost beyond belief. But he was also currently besieged on all sides: by the ropes and snares of Pythian power, by the great maw of the storm behind him, by Apollo's hungry ghost. And now by three god-forged weapons, wielded by masters of the elements.

But underestimating the god of war was never a good idea. A second later, the blue dot of the shield winked out, going dark and dim. I didn't know why until a beam of pure energy boiled through the air and hit the staff in Caedmon's hand, shattering it into a hundred pieces. He staggered back and went down, hurt, but I wasn't sure how badly. But that was two prongs of the attack gone, and only one remained.

And as luck would have it, it was another of us paltry humans who stood alone.

And maybe that was what did it, made Ares look away before his next blast landed. Made him turn toward his other tormentor. Made him careless.

I only know what I saw. In the middle of a great battlefield, a tiny figure on a spotted gray horse faced a towering god. And lifted his miniscule sword high, straight into the line of fire. Where the reflection of his blade, god-wrought and mirror bright, sent Ares' own power hurtling back at him, completely overwhelming and utterly unexpected.

And tore the battling gods to shreds.

Chapter Sixty-one

I awoke dry-mouthed and disoriented, and with a vague sense of panic. So, just like normal. Until I started to get up.

And felt something brush against my arm.

My nerves were so raw I would have screamed, but my teeth were still firmly clamped on my bottom lip. So I jumped instead, and rolled off the bed, and whirled and saw—

Absolutely nothing.

For a moment, I just stared about in confusion at the empty, darkened room, pulse pounding madly. And then I felt it again. A soft, barely there touch against my hand, like the brush of a feather.

Or like the brush of silken curls on a little girl's head, I realized, finally looking down. At the two- or maybe three-year-old child standing in the spill of light from the bathroom. And wearing a little white nightgown that made her look like an escaped cherub.

I sat back on the bed, weak-kneed and shaking, and she crawled into my lap.

And promptly fell asleep.

"I'm sorry," Tami said from the doorway, her gaze on my face. "But she said you needed her, and she wouldn't take no for an answer."

"She's *three*," I said unsteadily, hugging the warm little body. Which snuggled closer and muttered something indistinct.

"And I thought she might have a point," Tami added dryly. "Those vamps always say the same thing: she's fine. She's good. She's strong. You could be bleeding out and I think they'd still say that."

"Weakness is the worst insult in their culture. They'd feel like they were betraying me to admit—" I broke off, because I didn't want to admit anything, either.

Tami didn't call me on it, but her expression was eloquent. "But it makes it a little tough to determine if you are, in fact, okay," she finished.

"Yeah," I said. "I'm okay."

She came over to take the child.

"She's fine," I said, holding on. I'd woken up to enough blood and death lately. Seeing her instead was . . . nice.

"Come on, then. You can put her to bed."

"Where?" I glanced around. "We don't have any cots."

"We don't use cots anymore."

"Then what do we use?"

She smiled.

"Oh, holy *shit*."

"That's what I said," Tami told me as we stepped off the elevator after a short—like *very* short—ride. "Nice, isn't it?"

"Nice," I repeated, my lips going numb.

"I know, but you've got to see past the decor. The woman has no taste at all. But we're in the process of dealing with that," she added, looking satisfied.

I turned around and tried to get back on the elevator. But Roy, the southern redhead, was blocking the way. "She's going to kill me," I told him, trying to sidle past.

"Naw, she needs you," Roy said, turning me around, and steering me into a much bigger, much more opulent atrium than I boasted. "If she liked you, she might still kill you. But if she needs you, you're golden."

"Until she doesn't need me anymore."

"Yeah, but the way things are going, that might be a long time," he said cynically. "May as well enjoy the perks while you've got 'em."

And the perks were . . . the perks were nice, I thought, staring around at the finest of marbles on floor and columns and walls. At a glorious star pattern expertly inlaid into the floor. At the softly chiming chandelier overhead, glittering brightly enough to almost blind me after the dimmer light of my suite. And at the impressive double doors to the casino's finest penthouse, guarded by two more vamps who were trying to appear casual, but whose lips were twitching worse than Roy's.

And then openly grinning, as one of them caught my eye. "About time we got some decent accommodations around here," he told me.

"Define decent," I said, feeling a palm leaf, from a potted plant that I was sure had to be fake.

But no. Just perfect. Like the view when Roy threw open the huge double doors.

"Decent," he said, and ushered me into a scene of majestic luxury and utter insanity.

Dante's finest penthouse had always been breathtaking, but it had definitely received an upgrade from the last time I saw it, going from Vegas glam to something approaching mansion status. Or maybe palace status, since after I was unceremoniously kicked out a few months ago, the resident in chief had been none other than the current consul and uncrowned queen of the vampire world. Who lived like the crown was already firmly perched on her beautiful brow.

"No, no—open *that* one next," Tami said. She strode ahead and was now standing in the middle of the living room, ordering around a couple of senior masters like she'd been born to it.

Her weave was up in a curly ponytail today, which didn't even reach the shoulder of the nearest mountain of vampire flesh. Not that it mattered. Vamps had long ago adjusted to the idea that size did not equate to power. And judging by the look the two guys exchanged over her curly updo, they'd already learned that it was easier to just go along with the tiny woman with the huge attitude. Because a second later, one of a number of square, flat wooden crates was pried open, and the front fell off to reveal—

"What is *that*?" I asked, staring in disbelief at the painting inside.

"What does it look like?" Tami asked, sounding satisfied.

I knew damn well what it looked like. "You have to take it back!"

"Like hell I'm taking it back," Roy said. "I almost ruptured something lugging all of them up here."

"Lugging them up from where? *Where did you get them?*"

"Oh, you know." He grinned. "They were just hanging around."

"So was this one," a cheeky fourteen-year-old named Jesse added, carrying in one of the hula girl posters from the tiki bar downstairs.

One of the very scantily clad hula girl posters.

"Nice try," Tami said, stopping her son with a hand on his chest.

"But you said we could decorate our rooms any way we want—"

"I also said I'm trying to cut down on the tacky."

"It'll be in my room. Nobody'll see it! Not like those things," he added, nodding at a bunch of statues being hauled in from the balcony.

Or what had been a balcony. But the expansive space had been enclosed since I last saw it, with curving windows arching overhead like a solarium, and plants, columns, and statues framing the pool. It looked like a Grecian grotto—or maybe an Olympian one, I thought, staring as a familiar visage was carted past.

"What is that?" I asked.

"Part of the tacky," Tami said, frowning at it. "We're fighting the gods and she's decorating her garden with them? And whoever heard of a painted statue?"

"Used to be all the rage, back in old Rome," Marco said, coming in from another room. "Painted clothes and skin, shells for eyes—so they'd glisten—and decked out in flowers for the festivals. Idea was to make them look like real people, not those creepy white things they fill the museums with."

"Then why'd they make so many of the other kind?" Jesse asked.

Marco shrugged. "They didn't. The paint just wore off."

"Tami," I said grimly. "Why. Are. We. Here?"

She blinked at me. "You told me to manage things; I'm managing them."

"Yes, but—"

"And first priority was more room. Two dozen people stuffed into a three-bedroom suite? And that was just the girls. I'm surprised the fire marshal wasn't out here—"

"Probably too scared," another vamp said, heading out the door with a statue tucked under each arm. And having to perform a balletic move to avoid the two guys in painters' whites coming in with cans and a ladder.

"Mural in the master. Get rid of it," Tami told them shortly.

"Wait. What's wrong with it?" I asked.

"You don't want to know."

"*I* want to know," Jesse said, starting to follow them.

Until Tami caught him by the collar. "Aren't you supposed to be entertaining the kids?"

"Jiao's got that covered."

"Do I want to know what that means?"

He pursed his lips. "Probably not."

"Go *help* him," Tami said, and pushed him toward the lounge.

"Tami," I said ominously.

"And finding somewhere with enough room wasn't exactly easy," she added, like nothing had happened. Tami had a lot of practice with chaos. "Not one safe enough, that wouldn't absolutely embarrass you to live in—"

"I don't embarrass easy."

"—and that wouldn't embarrass the office of Pythia, when you had people in—"

"Nobody comes here!"

"Nobody comes here 'cause a certain group wouldn't let them in," Tami said, eyeing the nearby vamps. "But they can't hide you away forever. I know, I know," she said, holding up a hand. "People were trying to kill you. But you still have to function."

"She has a point," the girl with the pink hair said, from a nearby sofa, with a baby on her lap.

"So, let's review, shall we?" Tami persisted, holding up a finger. "One, you needed a safe place to come back to. And if a whole army of dark mages couldn't get in here the other day, I think this is about as safe as it gets. Unless you wanna live in a bunker—"

"There's an idea," Marco said, crossing massive arms

and scowling at us. Probably because he was going to have to sell this idea to the boss. "About the only thing we haven't tried—"

"Didn't work out in the desert, did it?" Tami asked, referring to the old supernatural UN, which had, in fact, been a lot like a bunker. One that was now a glass slick in the sand.

Marco's mouth closed, and he scowled some more.

"Two, accessibility," Tami steamrollered on. "People have to be able to see you. To petition, ask advice, etc. This place is in the middle of Vegas. Doesn't get much more accessible than that."

"Nobody is asking me for advice, either," I pointed out.

"Well, they might be, if they could get to you!" Tami looked exasperated. "Look. I'm not saying let the whole world in. But there are people who need to see you and who you need to see. You're *Pythia*. That has responsibilities attached."

"Tell me about it."

"I'm trying," she said seriously. "You aren't a vamp possession, to be locked away in a safe until they call. You're an independent agent and you have a job to do. And everybody is just going to have to learn *to accept that*," she said, looking at Marco.

Who, to my surprise, didn't say anything.

"Three," Tami said. "Her Highness decided when she moved in here that it was too small and shabby, and that she couldn't possibly be expected to live in such squalor—"

"I doubt she put it quite like that," I murmured, still looking at Marco.

"She put it exactly like that—tell her." Tami grabbed Fred in passing, who had a phone stuck to his ear.

"Okay, yeah," he agreed. "But you know English isn't her first language—"

"She's lived here for a couple hundred years!"

"But she don't get out much."

Tami rolled her eyes. "My point," she said stubbornly, "is that her people spent most of the last two months gutting the whole floor and rebuilding it to make room for her most-needed servants. Who apparently number in the double digits and don't like sharing. It's perfect!"

"But it isn't *ours*," I pointed out. "We can't just move in—"

"Why not? The consul's in New York—"

"Where her house was just destroyed! She'll probably be back any day now—"

"—and isn't that what she did to you? Just came in, kicked you out, and took it?"

I opened my mouth, and then closed it again.

Because sort of.

"And never even bothered to talk to you about it, right?" Tami persisted. "So, basically, you could say that you've been graciously allowing her to live here—"

One of the vamps choked back a laugh.

"—in recognition of the fact that she had a bigger household than you. But now that you have your court, you've decided to take it back."

I hesitated. It was damn tempting, especially after everything she'd pulled. But I kind of thought our relationship was bad enough.

"Listen to me." Tami took my hand, the one that wasn't curved under an increasingly heavy little girl butt. "It's like you said to Jonas' secretary the other day: you can move your court anywhere you choose. He wants you in London; the vamps want you here. Think she's going to kick you out only to see you run into the Circle's waiting embrace?"

Marco came over and took the sleeping child. "The kids have been running around the casino all day, laughing and looking for things to decorate their rooms," he said gruffly. "The place is closed, so Casanova doesn't care, just so long as they're returned when and if."

"Undamaged?" I said, looking at the expensive paintings worriedly. Because I was pretty sure I'd last seen them in the vault, part of an investment portfolio the old owner had put in place. And my decor tended to have a really short shelf life—

"Cassie?" I looked up, to see that Marco's dark eyes had gone soft, maybe because the little girl had snuggled into his huge neck.

"What?"

"They've been *laughing*."

I blinked at him, remembering the grubby, traumatized kids I'd helped to rescue from their burning, about-to-explode house, just a few days ago. Nobody had been laughing then. I'd wondered if they ever would again.

"I'll think about it," I said, spotting Rico, who had just come in. "Rhea?"

"Good. You want to see her?"

"Yes, but . . . there's someone else I need to see first."

There was a small party at Pritkin's bedside: Hilde, Abigail, and Rian, the latter sitting off to one side, along with Billy Joe. Who was looking green.

More so than usual.

"You all right?" I asked, putting an arm around him.

He looked up smiling. And then made a face. "Got a sour stomach."

"Billy. You're a ghost. You don't have a stomach."

"Well, I got a sour something." He gave what could only be described as a yack. I moved back a few feet.

Rian continued quietly reading a book. She looked the same as usual: calm, serene, beautiful. I wondered if anyone had told her. "Rian," I said. "I just . . . uh . . . I wanted to say—"

"We'll talk later," she said, smiling. "Your friends have been waiting for you."

I walked over to the bed. I hadn't been to visit Pritkin this whole time. He'd been at Caleb's for a while, because hell wasn't safe for him, even now. Then here at the hotel, after Caleb had to return to work. And neither of them was exactly hard to get to. But I hadn't been able to bear it.

And now it was exactly as bad as I'd feared.

The eyes that were usually hard and angry, or narrowed cynically, or wide in alarm—or occasionally, warm or playful or amused—were now closed, the too-light eyelashes almost invisible on the badly stubbled cheeks. Nobody had apparently thought to shave him, and he was halfway to a respectable beard.

I looked over my shoulder. "Has he remembered anything?" I asked Rian.

"He hasn't woken up yet." She saw my expression. "This isn't a spell anyone is supposed to survive. But once you applied the countercurse—"

"He applied it," I said, biting my lip. And looking back at him. "What if he pronounced it wrong? What if the rain smeared a word? What if—"

"Cassie. Give it time."

I didn't say anything. But I felt like I'd given it enough time. I felt like I'd given it a world of time. I wanted to shake him, to see those eyes open, to—

I sat down on the edge of the bed.

"Jonas was in here earlier," Hildegarde informed me, without preamble. "Someone ratted you out."

I looked up. "What did he want?"

"To know what happened to your war mage. To know what was going on. To ask us where we all went off to, and what we did, and what we knew—a thousand things!"

"We didn't tell him anything," Abigail said.

"Damn right." Hilde's silver curls bobbed angrily. "He knows better than to question an acolyte about a mission! That's for the Pythia to tell him—or not—as she chooses!" She looked at me severely. "You're going to have to rein him in."

"I could use some help with that," I said honestly.

Hilde looked pleased for a moment. And then she frowned. "It was quite exciting, I must admit. But this . . . frankly, it's usually seen as a job for the young."

"I met the young," I said dryly. "They almost killed me."

"Good point."

Abigail was glancing between the two of us, but not looking like she wanted to volunteer. At all. They both looked like they'd had a bath and a meal, but her eyes were still wider than when I first met her.

Yeah, I thought.

This life does that to you.

"You have a family," I remembered.

She nodded emphatically. "I really have to get back. But I could stay for a week or so, help you settle in?"

"You've done enough," I told her. "I'm very grateful."

She teared up suddenly. And then rose in order to drop the most perfect curtsy I've ever seen. "It is an honor to serve," she whispered. And glanced at Hilde, who was looking off into space. And gave her a little kick.

"What? Oh yes. An honor," Hilde said. "You know, the main problem with Jonas is that he's simply used to too much access. Got spoiled, what with his relationship with Lady Phemonoe. He needs a few more degrees of separation, to remember that access is a privilege, not a right. . . ."

Billy made another yacking sound, and then a hurk. Abigail looked at him in alarm, and took Hilde's hand. "Perhaps we could discuss this later?"

"Oh yes." Hilde squinted at me and then patted my hand. "I'll be upstairs, in case Jonas comes nosing about again, all right?"

I nodded. She appeared to be looking forward to it.

They left.

I looked back down at the bed, where Pritkin had yet to so much as stir. "The Pythias took his memories," I told Rian. "They said they had to, or it would have changed time. But he's supposed to get them back."

"I'm sure he will."

God, I envied her serenity! On a number of levels.

"I did have a question, if you feel like answering," she said, after a moment.

"What?" I looked back at her. "Sure."

I expected something about Rosier, because I knew they'd been close. But it wasn't what I got. "Your ghost told me what happened. Well, some of it. One thing, though, I didn't understand."

"One thing?" I didn't understand half of it, and I'd been there.

She nodded. "The killing blow, the one that destroyed Ares. It was made by Arthur, was it not?"

"Yes."

Her head tilted. "But that is what I find odd. As I understand it, he was part human and part water fey. Yet he wielded a fire weapon?"

"It was more like he boomeranged Ares' own power back at him."

"Yes, but how did he do that? For that matter, how did he wield Excalibur at all? I know it's a little point, but it bothered me. I wondered why Nimue would even give the sword to him in the first place."

I thought about it for a moment, and then laughed, suddenly remembering Rosier's description of the ugliest man he'd ever seen. Almost inhumanly so. "If I was going to guess," I told her, "I'd say Arthur had some fey on both sides. It also might explain why his symbol was a dragon."

Her eyebrows lifted.

Billy hurked and coughed and made a strange *hnnnz* sound in his throat that was just . . . really off-putting. I sighed. What the hell did you do for a sick ghost? I'd never even heard of such a thing.

But I wasn't taking him to any necromancers—that was for sure.

"I can give you a draw after breakfast," I said.

"I don't want a draw. I want this thing out of my throat!"

"What thing?" I asked warily.

And got some more hurking sounds in reply.

I wanted to ask him where he'd gone off to, on the battlefield. One minute he'd been there, right beside me, and the next he was gone. Not that he could have helped; we were both tapped out. But still . . .

I wondered what he'd been up to.

"Just remember," Rian told me. "Whatever else happened, Ares is dead."

"But Jo isn't. Not completely."

"But she's just a ghost. What can a ghost do?"

"You'd be surprised."

And then there was a slight stir on the bed.

I scrambled up and leaned over, to find green eyes open and staring back at me. Awake and aware. And alive.

For a moment, I just looked at him. I couldn't seem to say anything. And for once, neither did he.

"We were warned that it might be a while, before he gets his voice back," Rian told me. "In fact, all the senses are likely to be a bit . . . askew . . . for a few days. The spell is somewhat disorientating."

Yeah, I bet.

I sat down on the bed, and Pritkin managed to grab my arm, after several tries. He tugged me down to him, and for a moment I felt guilty, because I was kind of relieved that I'd have a few days to sort out what to say to him. After everything we'd been through, I honestly had no idea.

But apparently, I was the only one.

"I remember," he said, in a hoarse whisper.

I met his eyes, and from only a few inches away, they were . . . intense.

I swallowed. "Um. You remember . . . what, exactly?"

He smiled. And I swear, it was the evilest thing I've ever seen.

"Everything."

Oh boy.

But then Billy saved me.

Hurk, hnggg, hnggg, hnggg! Yak yak yak yak.

And then Billy coughed up Rosier.

Conclusion

Rian and I were heading downstairs, both because Caleb had shown up to relieve her, and because she had a demon lord to escort back to hell. A very wrung out, very tired, very subdued demon lord. Who was getting told.

"Your father kept everyone in line through power," she said severely. "Power you helped him acquire, but which he never thanked you for. You have done equally well through diplomacy, shrewd dealing, and sheer audacity. How are you not his equal when you did more with less?"

Rosier didn't say anything. I wasn't sure he could. But Rian didn't seem to care.

"For centuries, all I've heard was 'I need a son,' 'I have to have more power,' 'I need a son to help me.' But all that while, you were handling things perfectly well without one! And speaking as one of your subjects, may I say that I quite prefer the life we have now to the stories I've heard about your father's era?"

Rosier managed to look meek.

"And may I assume, after everything you've been through, that you've learned something? And that Pritkin is no longer to be required to live under the sword of Damocles? May I tell him that he is free and able to choose his own path from now on?"

Rosier appeared to stiffen slightly at that, and to grow a backbone—or whatever the wispy steam version was. Until those dark eyes flashed, and she shot him a look of utter scorn. And he gave what sounded like the faintest of sighs.

And folded.

"I'm going to pick up Casanova for lunch, and afterward take Lord Rosier home," Rian told me, shifting her pale blue Birkin bag to her other arm so she could punch the elevator button. "If you need me, Carlos can get you in touch."

She air-kissed me, and stepped onto the elevator.

"I think I am going to enjoy the next few weeks," she told Rosier. "There are any number of things I've intended to say to you."

Rosier somehow managed to give off the appearance of alarm, despite being basically a whiff of smoke. One Billy had enveloped as he had me once, before he utterly dissipated. And had sustained him with his own life force until Rosier could accumulate enough sticking power to keep from fading.

He was going to owe him big-time, after this. I briefly wondered what kind of gift you got a ghost. And then I thought of Billy and Rosier, and the sheer amount of mayhem the two of them could cause together, and decided I didn't want to know.

"Oh, I almost forgot," Rian said, placing a delicate Jimmy Choo in the elevator doors. And digging around in her purse. "Lord Mircea sent this for you." And she pulled out a flat, rectangular package. "But strangely, it was delivered to John's room."

"To . . . Pritkin's?" I asked, getting a bad feeling about this.

Rian nodded distractedly, wrestling with the air conditioner currents for her lord and master. "I was asked to pass it along."

"Thanks," I said, my mouth dry. And watched her leave.

The package was expensively wrapped, of course, in gold and white stripes. There was also a card. No salutation, just a single line in a beautiful, flowing script.

Perhaps the lady would like to reconsider?

I looked at it for a long moment. And then tore the paper off all at once. Like a Band-Aid, I thought grimly, wondering why Mircea had sent me a book.

Until I saw the title. I stood there in Dante's hallway,

holding a beautifully illustrated copy of *Le Morte d'Arthur.*
The most famous book ever written about King Arthur . . .
and his court.

Mircea, I thought furiously, looking back at Pritkin's
room and crumpling the note in my hand.

And then I shifted.

Ready to find
your next great read?

Let us help.

Visit prh.com/nextread

Penguin
Random
House